The Legend of Gold

and Other Stories

Photo: K. Kaneizaka, 1968

The Legend of Gold
and Other Stories

≈

Ishikawa Jun

*Translated from the Japanese with
an Introduction and Critical Essays by*
William J. Tyler

University of Hawai'i Press

HONOLULU

Publication of this book has been assisted by grants from the following organizations:
The Suntory Foundation
College of Humanities, Ohio State University

Library of Congress Cataloging-in-Publication Data
Ishikawa, Jun, 1899–
    [Selections. English. 1998]
    The legend of gold and other stories / Ishikawa Jun : translated
by William J. Tyler.
      p.   cm.
    Includes bibliographical references.
    Contents: Mars' song — Moon gems — The legend of gold — The
Jesus of the ruins — The raptor.
    ISBN 0-8248-1968-3 (cloth : alk. paper). — ISBN 0-8248-2070-3
(pbk. : alk. paper)
    I. Tyler, William Jefferson. II. Title.
PL830.S5A6   1998
895.6′344 — dc21
                                         98-16636
                                         CIP

Designed by inari

For Masao Shimozato

CONTENTS

PREFACE

I am gratified to be able to bring the breadth and depth of the works of the Japanese novelist Ishikawa Jun to a non-Japanese speaking public. Ishikawa is a seminal figure in Japanese letters: an important modernist, an early existentialist, a resistance writer, and a superb stylist. That he has not been more accessible can be attributed in part to the complexity of his prose and in part to fixed notions concerning the canon of modern Japanese literature.

Several years ago I published *The Bodhisattva, or Samantabhadra* (New York: Columbia University Press, 1990), a translation and critical study of *Fugen,* a novella that Ishikawa wrote in 1936. *Fugen* is representative of Ishikawa's earliest works, and it received the Akutagawa Prize, Japan's most distinguished literary award, in 1937. Here I present four stories and a novella, published from 1938 to 1953, that belong to what might be called the second phase of Ishikawa's long career, namely, his response to the tumultuous events of Japan's war, defeat, occupation, and return to peace. Meanwhile, Donald Keene's translation of *Shion monogatari,* a novella of 1956 (which appeared as *Asters* in *The Old Woman, the Wife, and the Archer* [New York: The Viking Press, 1961]), anticipates the long "fictional constructions" that Ishikawa wrote after the chaos of the early postwar period subsided. Alas, it has been out of print for many years and is difficult to obtain. Moreover, of the novels that Ishikawa wrote between 1956 and his death in 1987, none is available in translation. Given their considerable length, I suspect we shall have to wait yet awhile for them to appear in English. But that is another day's story.

I wish to express my appreciation to the late Ishikawa Iku, who granted permission to translate the works included here and who was generous with her time and hospitality whenever I traveled to Tokyo; to Ishikawa Maki, who now represents the estate of Ishikawa Jun; to Komai Yoshiko, for special permission to use the illustration by Komai Tetsurō that appears on the cover; and to Katō Yūya of Chikuma Shobō Publishing Company, for many kindnesses.

In addition, this project has been supported by a Translation Grant from the National Endowment for the Arts, Washington, D.C. Publication subvention was also received from The Suntory Foundation and the College of Humanities at Ohio State University.

Steve Rabson was instrumental in encouraging me to translate "Mars' Song," and this led to translation of the other works. Mildred Tahara, Doris G. Bargen, and the late E. Dale Saunders read and commented on early versions of the translations; and Doris Bargen as well as Alan Kennedy made a number of helpful comments when it came time to revise the penultimate draft of the critical essays. Ōmori Kyōko and Junko Ikezu Williams assisted with checking the translations against the original Japanese, as did Suzuki Akiyoshi with "Mars' Song." I am especially grateful for the care and alacrity with which Sharon F. Yamamoto, my editor, and Susan Stone and Ann Ludeman of the University of Hawai'i Press have seen this book into print.

Responsibility for translation strategies and interpretation of the works is mine and mine alone. Diction and tone are especially important concerns in conveying Ishikawa's style. Occasionally I have taken liberties (such as "Turn it off!" for *"Yamero"* in "Mars' Song") and given additional emphasis ("No more 'Mars'!"). I have introduced considerably more paragraphing than is found in the original texts in order to make Ishikawa's penchant for reversals in argumentation, or what the grammarian calls adversative correlations ("yes, but . . . no, but"), read smoothly in English. I have sought to retain the commingling of past and present tenses, especially in those passages where Ishikawa slides between chronological and psychological time. I have highlighted the storyteller's voice (*"Sate"*: "Now, where were we?"); and in the case of the stories in the garrulous style, I have used apposition and amplification to handle Ishikawa's use of compound verbs and thereby to make explicit what is doubly implied (for example, "even now, when times have changed and his intermediary here on earth has been *separated like chaff* from the grain and *driven out* as an impostor" for *"hatsuho wo . . . kamigakari ga* tatakidasareta *ato demo"*). I have also sought to make the cinematographic qualities of the original equally visual in English.

Early on, work on the manuscript would have been far more difficult had it not been for a summer at "The Field," thanks to Hank and Jean Dunbar, or access to word processing facilities through the kindness of Betty Romer, director, Academic Computing Center, Amherst College. Susan Todd of the Voter Computer Center, Middlebury College, was also helpful in getting the final draft into suitable computer format. I also appreciate the help of Frank Hsueh, Tom Kasulis, and Jim Unger, chairs, and Nikki Bado and Debbie Knicely, administrative assistants, Department of East Asian Languages and Literatures, The Ohio State University.

Masao "Shigeru" Shimozato has been unfailing in his support, and Robert Wallace provided a sanctuary in Vermont for final stretches of work. Xiaomei Chen, DB, Gene Fortunato, Marilyn Greenfield, Charles Klopp, Adelaide Miller, Thomas Randleman, Thomas Rimer, Hiroaki Sato, Tajima Takashi, Richard Torrance, and Warren Watanabe have all been enthusiastic supporters of this project.

Dale Saunders, Ishikawa Iku, Sumner Greenfield, Shimozato Maki, Ohki Kyūbei, and Mary Watanabe also gave it their benediction, but in two years that were oftimes dolorous, they passed away one after the other. Now there is no means, save this publication, to thank them.

To be vouchsafed a time and a place in which to write and translate is both a necessity and a luxury. Indeed, one can never predict when life will surprise us with its moments of serendipity. One afternoon late in a golden summer when my work was nearly done and I had put finishing touches to the translation of *The Raptor,* I stepped into the garden at Green Mountain Place. There had been reports of raptors in the area, and suddenly I caught sight overhead of what I knew only from books or the news. Mirabile dictu, a lone peregrine falcon swept down from a flawless sea of blue, and making a long, grand arc, it sailed serenely through the air. It seemed to hover, however briefly, and in that instant to tender a look of hawk-eyed approbation. Such are the epiphanies of life, and it is by the poetry of the wings of raptors that we are uplifted.

Can we not say that heretofore modernity has been an understudy in the drama of history, and it has been anxiously awaiting its chance to appear on the stage? Until now it has been made to stand in the wings, unheard and unseen, its potential cloaked in the heavy curtains of possibility. As of this moment, however, suddenly there has been an opening, and it has stepped into the limelight to take its place on center stage.

"The Legend of Gold" (1946)

. . . He could feel the beat as it was transmitted from one thick wall of the prison to the next and as it traveled along the floor. Surely it was the rhythm of all human beings who, extracting every ounce of energy that can be squeezed from the human frame, take to their feet in revolt even if they are repulsed time and again. It was the beat of the movement of all who continually hurl themselves against an undefined and inexplicable force.

The Raptor (1953)

INTRODUCTION

The four stories and one novella that appear in translation here represent the best and most frequently anthologized short fiction by the Japanese novelist Ishikawa Jun (1899–1987). Published between 1938 and 1953, they also span the most tumultuous years in twentieth-century Japanese history — from Japan's invasion of China in the summer of 1937 to prolonged war, defeat, and occupation in 1945, to final reinstatement in the community of nations in 1952. Thus, these works allow us to hear a rare Japanese voice raised in protest against the war, the popular interpretation of defeat, and the meaning of peace as it was to be defined early in the postwar era. As political documents, they are bold and outspoken: the Japanese wartime authorities banned "Mars' Song," and when the Allied Occupation censored "The Legend of Gold," Ishikawa deliberately withheld it from publication. As literary texts, they are equally avant-garde: written in the wake of Ishikawa's "dashing entrance" *(sassōtaru tōjō)* upon the literary scene in 1935 and his initial acclamation as winner of the Akutagawa Prize for Literature in 1937, they rank in the forefront of what one prize committee member identified as "the spirit of modern novelology" *(kindai shōsetsugaku no seishin),*[1] or what I shall call here the modernist movement in Japanese prose. As works with a simultaneously progressive political and literary bent, they also speak to two lacunae in the study of modern Japanese literature, namely, the neglected areas of political writing and literary experimentation.

The history of dissent during the war by a handful of Japanese writers has gone largely untold in English. In the mid-1960s, attention was directed to the general topic of Japanese writers and their involvement as patriotic zealots or collaborators in the promotion of imperialism at home or on the battlefield. Yet it is startling to realize how little was written then and how little since.[2] It is as though, once the issue was given a hearing, the heavy tome of history snapped shut, and we are left with only the dull echo of "case closed." Such is not the case with the literature on writers and the war in Germany, Italy, or even Vichy France. In pursuit of new revelations and insights, scholars revisit these topics with considerable regularity. Surely reexamination of the case of Japan is also important and long overdue.

It is hardly a whitewash of the past to recall, moreover, that there were voices in Japanese literary circles who not only refrained from joining the heated chorus of what Ishikawa calls "Mars' Song" but also were courageous in speaking against it. In fact, one might argue that as the events of the war recede by more than a half century — the coffin lid of history now closing over heroic and putrid alike — it is far more instructive in our global age to ask not who conformed to the old enmities but rather who chose to be different and to dissent. How was it that these uncommon voices managed to be independent and farsighted? To hear them again requires that we reopen the books and proceed with the time-consuming task of sifting through the evidence to provide scrupulous documentation. By revisiting Ishikawa Jun in translation and telling his story in the critical essays, this book hopes to provoke a larger discussion by presenting at least one part of the missing picture.

A similar predicament obtains in the case of modernist prose in Japanese: it too is a movement that has not been chronicled. Although modernism has been a key term in the discourse on twentieth-century Western literature since the appearance of Cyril Connelly's *The Modern Movement: One Hundred Key Books from England, France and America* (1965) and Irving Howe's *Literary Modernism* (1967), it has received scant attention in the case of Japanese. This fact is doubly perplexing given all the talk concerning Japan as the preeminently post-*modernist* culture. If so, whither its modernist phase?

The label *"modanizumu"* in Japanese literature has been confined largely to the futuristic experiments of minor poets and imitative Dadaists from the 1920s or, more recently, the beginnings but inanitions of Satō Haruo, Yokomitsu Riichi, Itō Sei, and Hori Tatsuo.[3] It has been treated as a foreign affair in which Japanese writers flirted with European avant-gardism before wedding themselves to traditional and domestic themes. Kawabata Yasunari, Tanizaki Jun'ichirō, and Mishima Yukio are the classic examples of this theory of writers' inevitable "return to Japan" *(Nihon e no kaiki),* and it has been applied even to authors provisionally identified as modernist. In short, modernism has been seen as a passing fancy.

Overlooked is the considerable body of experimental writing that began appearing in Japan in the 1920s and reached a high point of production in the 1930s. It can be argued that, following the dead-end passage of naturalism and the I-novel in the Taishō period and the collapse or suppression of left-wing ideological prose after 1928, Japanese writers began to experiment seriously with narrative construction (both under the influence of and independent of foreign stimuli), and it is these experiments that give real meaning to the "revival of the arts and letters" *(bungei fukkō)* that occurred in Japan in the early and mid-1930s.[4] One recalls, for instance, Tanizaki's playful deconstruction of narrative authority in *Shunkinshō* (1933; trans. *Portrait of Shunkin,* 1963) and Nagai Kafū's sauntering novel-within-the-novel *Bokutō kitan* (1937; trans. *Strange Tale from East of the River,* 1965) as examples of modernist experimentation that are available in English. But the works of other experimentalists such as Makino Shin'ichi, Kajii Motojirō, Yumeno Kyūsaku, Edogawa Rampo, Hisao Jūran, Inagaki Taruho, Okamoto Kanoko, Uno Chiyo, Tachibana Sotoō, Ryūtanji Yū, and Yoshiyuki Eisuke remain virtually unknown outside Japan owing to inattention and a very limited number of translations. Meanwhile in Japan, for a decade or more the critic and scholar Suzuki Sadami has taken the lead in calling attention to modernist writers, getting their works before the reading public once again, and rethinking their place within the historical schematization of modern Japanese literature.[5] Thus it is that writers who have been treated in the past under the overly broad rubric of "antinaturalists" *(han-shizenshugi-sha),* narrowly pigeonholed in unhelpful categories such as "the newly emergent aesthetes" *(shinkō geijutsu-ha)* and "actionists" *(kōdōshugi-sha),* or abandoned to the no-man's land of sui generis can now be better understood as belonging collectively to a major movement or Zeitgeist called Modernism. Their work has also paved the way for postwar writers such as Abe Kōbō and Ōe Kenzaburō, whose novels are more commonly identified as modernist.

ISHIKAWA JUN BEGAN early in his career to ask what was fundamentally modern about contemporary consciousness East and West. Translating novels by André Gide into Japanese (*L'immoraliste* as *Haitokusha* in 1924; *Les caves du Vatican* as *Hōōchō no nukeana* in 1928), and then drawing upon Henri Bergson's concept of élan vital in his study of the novel titled *Bungaku taigai* (All about Literature; 1942), he argued that a modernist orientation resided not in a fixed point of view or philosophy but in movement, energy, or spirit; and while he considered his concept of "the movement of the spirit" *(seishin no undō)* to be no more than a working hypothesis, he looked to it for whatever he found to be spontaneous, relativistic, pluralistic, and free in the history of art and ideas. The measure of the novel, he wrote, lay not in the traditional literary norms of characterization or emplotment, but in the quality of the energy that the novelist unleashes upon the blank page with which every writer begins.

In his maiden work, *Kajin* (The Beauty; 1935), he employed parody of the first-person narrator as his means of departure from the unmediated authorial voice of the naturalistic I-novel. "I, I, I . . . ," the story begins in a mocking, deprecatory tone. "It was as if the sluice gates of my pen had opened and the backwater that is myself surged forth in an endless torrent." In his first novella, *Fugen* (1936; trans. *The Bodhisattva, or Samantabhadra*, 1990), he took his metafictional approach a step further. In addition to the seriocomic treatment of the narrator, he introduced the concept of *mitate*, "doubles" or "look-alikes," to create a multilayed or palimpsest structure. In constructing his novel by having analogy call forth analogy (which, mirror-like, reflect previous parallels and allusions), he sought to liberate it from the traditional chronology of rising and falling action and thereby give the text a high degree of stylistic complexity. While analogies are not deployed as heavily in the works in this anthology, Ishikawa's layering technique is to be found in the multivalent play on the word "traces" in "The Jesus of the Ruins" or the brand name "Peace" in *The Raptor*.

The four short stories are conceived in the same seriocomic, first-person narration as "The Beauty" and *The Bodhisattva*. Likewise, they are written in the garrulous style in vogue worldwide in the 1930s and 1940s. By *The Raptor* Ishikawa had switched to writing in the third person, and his style, now characterized by shorter sentences and paragraphs, became noticeably streamlined. Yet in making his prose easier to read, he sacrificed none of the parodic tone, kinetic rhythm, use of "today" as a story's pivot in time, or long and close-up shots produced by the zoom-lens effect of his narratorial eye. Moreover, his works began to grow in length, the literary parodies and social satires of *Aratama* (The Bad Boy of the Gods; 1963), *Shifuku sennen* (On with the Millennium; 1965), *Kyōfūki* (Chronicle of a Mad Wind; 1980), and *Hebi no uta* (Song of the Snake; 1987) being analog constructions of four to nine hundred pages that are not only verbal tours de force but also call to mind the great solo marathons of linked-verse composition undertaken by the *yakazu* improvisationalists of the Edo period.

At the same time, Ishikawa remained outspoken on contemporary issues, whether as literary critic for the *Asahi* newspaper (1969–1971) or as essayist writing under his nom de plume, Isai. He joined forces with Abe, Mishima, and Kawabata at the time of China's Cultural Revolution in an "Appeal for the Protection of the Autonomy of the Arts and Sciences" (1967); and he appeared for the defense in the famous *"Shitabari* trial" (1975), in which the novelist Nosaka Akiyuki, in a deliberate challenge to Japanese censorship laws regulating erotic materials, was prosecuted for reprinting and distributing an allegedly pornographic novel by Nagai Kafū.[6]

Ishikawa was not one to boast of his posture of resistance during the war. To the contrary, in 1960 he took the initiative in unearthing and republishing three wartime fragments that he considered to be shameful lapses. And he often scoffed at the suggestion that his works had a political or social thrust. Calling them *uso* or "lies," he insisted on their worth as solely fictional constructions or fabrications. This attitude reflects in part his desire to be identified as a writer of the "pure novel" after the manner of the French Symbolists and André Gide. At the same time, it is a pose adopted from the literati writers of the Edo period, when an author feigned disengagement from politics to avoid censorship or, quite literally, being handcuffed by the Tokugawa authorities. But the fact that an author pronounces his works to be lies or fabrications alerts us to the possibility of a hidden or subversive agenda. Japanese scholars have been particularly attentive to the elements of indirection, camouflage, and false scents by which, in sending up a cloud of smoke *(kemu ni maku),* as the conventional saying goes, Ishikawa sought to protect himself from censure. Accordingly, one also needs to read for allegory:

indeed these stories are not simply tales of a man who loses his cousin to suicide or belatedly learns to ride a bike. Furthermore, it is necessary for the reader who is not conversant with Japanese history and customs to know that Ishikawa alludes to his times when he refers, for example, to the "Concept of Guilt" in "The Legend of Gold" or to "Peace" in *The Raptor*. As for the "Concept of Guilt," he has in mind the slogan of "The Repentance En Masse of the Hundred Million" *(ichioku sōzange)* that circulated in the postwar press as a popular expression of contrition for war guilt. Meanwhile, "Peace" refers to a brand of tobacco marketed in celebration of the end of hostilities in 1945 and upgraded and repackaged in 1952 to commemorate the end of the occupation. Since these allusions point to a deeper reading of the texts, they are discussed in further detail in the essays that follow the translations.

The artistic subtleties of indirection and allusion notwithstanding, one is struck by the sheer audacity and bold clarity with which Ishikawa enunciates his social or political positions. He is often outspoken at the same time that he uses allegory and metafiction to reiterate his overt or literal message in a thoroughly literary way. Moreover, seen in comparison with Japanese writers canonized in the West as aesthetic and apolitical — take the example of Kawabata (1899-1972), who is Ishikawa's exact contemporary in age — Ishikawa does seem atypically bold, political, and perhaps even "un-Japanese." But that semblance is due in part to efforts in the past to identify Japanese writers in terms of what makes them most orientalist or non-Western. Moreover, in the historical evolution of the introduction and reception of Japanese letters abroad, there has been a marked tendency to marginalize fiction concerned with politics, be it the political novels of the Meiji era, the proletarian literature written by left-wing writers in the 1920s, or the works of the so-called new aesthetes from the 1930s who attempted to address political concerns from a nonideological position. The recognition of Ōe Kenzaburō as Japan's second Nobel laureate in 1994 has done much to reveal the activist side to Japanese literature. As a matter of fact, the emergence of writers like Ōe in postwar Japan points to the debate that ensued after the war over writers' responsibilities in times of trouble and peace, and Ōe has spoken of Ishikawa as an important model in the formation of his own attitudes concerning the role of the novelist as social critic.[7]

Although we cannot assume a one-to-one correspondence between Ishikawa and his central characters, nonetheless the works presented here constitute a metafictional portrait of a writer who lived through war, defeat, censorship, and a fair amount of privation. They present a catalog of the wellsprings of his independence and good humor: the feisty and cosmopolitan disposition of a native son of Tokyo; the cool and unruffled sophistication of the comic versifiers and pun-book novelists of the city Edo, most notably Ōta Nanpo; the mentoring example of the anti-establishment novelist Nagai Kafū, who appears as the patrician Mr. Gūka in "Moon Gems"; as well as the raw courage and naked energy of a new postwar generation of Japanese as represented by the plebeian woman in red in "The Legend of Gold" and the wild child of "The Jesus of the Ruins." Moreover, an encyclopedic command of world literature and thought emerges in allusions to the New Testament, Jacobus de Voragine's thirteenth-century classic on the Lives of the Saints, *Legenda aurea,* and the poetry and erudition of the literati of China and Japan. It is an eclectic list: Mars, Jesus, *kyōka* comic verse, Pali, a Peace cigarette. Yet in taking world culture as his musée imaginaire, and combining and juxtaposing artifacts and icons East and West, Ishikawa sought to push language — especially Japanese — beyond its limits to create the language of tomorrow, "Futurese," or in Japanese, *ashita-go.* "In order for something to be so," as Einstein once remarked, "first we have to think it."

WHEN ONE CONSIDERS the furor pro and con that engulfed the mayor of Nagasaki, Motoshima Hitoshi, after speaking forthrightly of Hirohito's culpability in the war as the emperor lay dying in December 1988 — as well as, more recently, the brouhaha that canceled the Smithsonian Institute's retrospective on the atomic bomb or the row that ensued in Japan over an exhibit illustrating atrocities committed in the Nanjing Massacre — it appears there are words that are still unspeakable, and closure on the historical record and meaning of the war eludes us still.[8] It may be far more difficult than we realize to escape the rhetoric of the past and soar beyond the prisonhouse of the status quo.

Yet there is cause for optimism, because the language of the future appears already to be in the making with the emergence in Japan of late of a discourse on a new kind of cultural hero. One thinks of the recognition now being accorded to Sugihara Chiune, the "Japanese 'Schindler' or 'Wallenberg.' " It has become widely known in Japan that, by exercising discretionary powers as a diplomat and issuing transit visas while posted in war-torn Lithuania, Sugihara created a brief window of opportunity in the summer of 1940 for Jews to escape both pogrom and holocaust.[9] Or, one is reminded of the long and valiant battles fought in the courts of Japan by the historian Ienaga Saburō, who has endeavored to keep in check those forces who have glossed over the harsh realities of Japanese imperialism in the writing and authorizing of school textbooks.[10] Nor should we forget the example of Mayor Motoshima, who, breaking the funereal pall of "self-restraint" *(jishuku)* urged upon every citizen by the powers-that-be, courageously addressed issues of imperial, national, and personal responsibility for the war and stood by his beliefs even at the risk of his life. To this new and honorable list, I would add Ishikawa's name and his parables of war and peace.

How responsible is each of us for the oftimes crotchety world in which we live? And how far are we expected to go in setting it aright? These are difficult, even tortuous questions, as we are often caught by conflicting sets of loyalties and demands. One must approach a reexamination of social and intellectual accountability with the reluctance of trepidation, taking care to avoid an air of condescension. For, after all, to take up the tome of history that has been closed, to reopen the books both figuratively and literally, and to inquire again into the issue of writers and the war is not only to weigh the acts of others but also to bring ourselves before the bar and ask by what high standard we too shall be judged.

I

The Stories

MARS' SONG

≈ 1938 ≈

I

There it is again . . . that song. How shall I describe the feeling it evokes in me? It is twilight. I sit in my room alone. To my ear comes the clamorous sound of the popular refrain. It originates in the madness of the streets, its frenzied crescendo rising to a fever pitch to assault my window. It is "Mars' Song" of which I speak.

> *In this realm with gods somnolent,*
> *Where the voice of wisdom has fallen silent,*
> *utterly silent,*
> *What will ensue in the hour when you, Mars, rise and gird for battle?*
> *"How bold!" "How valiant!" they sing. . . .*

The voices become a chorus, which becomes a tempest that like a smoldering fire not yet bursting into flame spits forth an acrid smoke, the blackness of its soot blanketing every household, its grit penetrating into every corner, there to wither city arbors and asphyxiate backyard fowl and family pet. There, in the gaping mouths raised in song, one sees the malaise of our times, open and inflamed like a wound. . . .

. . . yet writing in this fashion will not bring me to the beginning of a novel. In point of fact, I have spent the last few days trying to apply myself to its composition, flailing about in my own small way on this rickety chair, thrashing out this idea or that, but making no progress whatsoever. All that I have garnered from my pen are these few lines of verse, the raspings of exclamations too puerile to bear repeating. Is this poor acrobatic act, this wretched display of prosody, the best I shall have to show for myself in this season that Mars' exhortations and his angry call to arms have rendered so oppressive? I fly into a rage at the sound of the voices and the derisive smiles I see floating on the faces of the crowd. But no sooner have I picked up my pen, my fingers itching to say something in protest, than I tear up each sheet of paper and toss it into the air. Frustrated, I trample underfoot these pages that, scattered now upon the floor in shreds and pieces, are not unlike the disorganized and unresolved state of my emotions.

But why do I allow myself to be upset by the mundane affairs of the world in the first place? After all, is it not an axiom of novel writing that an author puts pen to paper only after he has severed all ties to terrestrial sentiment and its attendant distractions?

I rise from my chair, and turning in the direction of the popular refrain as it echoes from a distant corner, I shout, "NO!" And gritting my teeth in an effort to suppress the wave of revulsion that wells inside me, I lift my pen once again. Dismissing all further thought, anything that might seek to intervene and impose itself upon me, like a madman, I begin to write. Come what may, right or wrong . . . so be it . . . novel . . .

THIS IS AS FAR as I had written last night. How shameful of me to have produced so little — why, not even a line that might be worthy of being called a sentence in the narrative of a novel. How could I bear to stay in this room a moment more?

I bolted the premises and went for a walk. I stopped at a bar and had a drink. Then I settled upon the idea of seeing a movie. Just the right place for a quick nap, I told myself.

Except for the flickering image on the screen, darkness embraced me. As I let myself be absorbed into the quasi-light, I sat back and slipped into the empty crack of unconsciousness in which we human beings allow ourselves to be packed together in a room yet decline to acknowledge our mutual existence. Presently I began to nod, my head bobbing ever so much like a doll whose eyes open and close as it is tilted. . . .

. . . when all of a sudden I was jolted awake by the sound of a frightful boom. I looked up at the screen to see a gigantic battleship projecting the long barrel of its guns over the clear, blue surface of the ocean. Doubtless a shell had just been fired, and a single puff of smoke played momentarily about the mouth of one of the guns as a pale, white thread wisped from the barrel and then disappeared in the air. Indeed it was all so innocent-looking, and the now silent muzzle appeared so cool and nonchalant that for a second I was reminded of a bucolic setting in which an old man, basking in the noonday sun, lights his pipe and lets a column of smoke rise from its bowl.

Yet let there be no mistake about what I perceived in that brief moment when I was jolted awake: behind a smokescreen of feigned nonchalance lay a powerful weapon. It took its careful aim and hit its target with uncanny accuracy.

I froze in my seat.

The picture on the screen shifted to a rural village where the riverbank was lined by willow trees. A group of young, able-bodied men had gathered in front of a half-destroyed farmhouse and were looking quite pleased with themselves. Seated in the center was their captain.

He is older; his beard, fuller. It flutters on the breeze as he smiles broadly and rests his hands on the heads of two small boys who stand in front of him. He is smiling. Nonetheless, the grip of his hand holds the boys firmly in place. . . .

The nationalities of the two boys and the man clearly differ. The scene is intended to be a vision of peace itself, a happy interaction between the peoples of different nations. Yet caught as the boys are — between, on the one hand, the foreigners' camaraderie and, on the other, the obvious plight of the rivers and mountains of their homeland — their faces are devoid of any expression whatsoever. No tears. No sadness. Not even nihilistic despair. Nor is there a smile feigned for the sake of the camera. A terrible necessity compels them to remain silent even as their very silence fairly shouts with the unequivocal cry of "NO!"

In the face of their "NO!" how small and feeble my own must sound. Whatever effect can it have? I have been unable to produce a single sentence for the novel that I have sought to create; what is more, I have chosen to cover my ineptitude by having a drink and taking a nap in a theater. . . . I am mired in shame and drenched in a pool of cold sweat. Getting up as inconspicuously as I can — my tail tucked between my legs (had I a tail!) — I slip from among the legs and feet of the people seated in my row and make my way out of the theater. . . .

Once again, I find myself in my solitary room in a modest apartment house located on a backstreet of the Ginza. The room is awash with the color of twilight as I sit at my desk, pen in hand and my ears abraded by the sound of "Mars' Song," its refrain having grown shriller with each passing day. Writing no more like a madman, let me collect my thoughts and put them down on paper. Let me pinpoint with my pen the locus of my sanity, even if my recalcitrant instrument hesitates and has yet to move. . . .

My back is to the door, but — click — I hear the knob turn. I look around and see the door fly open with a bang. In rushes a young girl, who throws herself across the bed along the wall. Her whole body shakes as though convulsed by a terrible cry that, struggle as she may to contain it, causes her to burst into tears. . . .

The atmosphere in the room has been altered irrevocably before I have had time to launch myself into the world of the novel. For the moment I shall have to compromise and, letting my pen deviate, begin this story with actual facts.

II

What was I to do? The girl was in tears, and as she sobbed the pleats of her yellow suit jacket quivered where the material was gathered in pleats about the shoulders. I could only ask,

"What's the matter, Obi?"

My cousins, Fuyuko and her younger sister Obiko, had lost their parents in recent years, the deaths of the mother and father coming in rapid succession. Fuyuko married, having already found a suitable mate in a newspaper photographer named Aioi Sanji, and the young couple set up house in Kamata, a suburb of Tokyo. Meanwhile, a brother, who became head of the family and who made a living running a fishing business in Kanagawa Prefecture, agreed to see Obiko through to the end of her studies at a girls' school in Surugadai in downtown Tokyo. Obiko had taken a room in the apartment house where I lived in the Ginza. It was her brother's idea to put her under my supervision, although no one could be more ill-suited to the task than I. Consequently, Obiko took advantage of my negligence, and she pursued all of the lively distractions typical of the Ginza, a highly unlikely neighborhood for a schoolgirl. She left the apartment building early in the morning and was gone until late at night. From time to time she invited over a group of her friends, who carried on in her apartment without the least regard for the neighbors who lived next door. I had little idea what Obiko did from day to day as she pranced about town. But here she was in my room all of a sudden. She had thrown herself on the bed and was crying her heart out.

The characters with which Obiko's name is written were meant to be pronounced "Tarashiko." It is an atypical reading of the characters, the unusual name having been chosen by her father, who had been a dabbler in classical poetry. Of late, however, "Tarashiko" preferred the more likely and popular pronunciation of her name as "Obiko." She went about introducing herself as "Obiko," or even "Obi" for short. Moreover, she insisted on writing her name in roman letters instead of characters. She claimed that "Obi" was not a Japanese word at all but derived from the name of a river in a foreign country. She had taken it as a nickname, and I found myself using it as I spoke to her.

"What's the matter, Obi? What are you crying about?"

I stood up and turned on the light. The room was starting to get dark. Obi's face was buried in the covers on the bed.

"How about if I buy you a bottle of eau de cologne?" I said, trying to coax her into talking with me.

But she was not the least bit interested in blandishments. To the contrary, she lifted her head from the bed and, with a look of utter seriousness on her face, seemed to dismiss my lightheartedness as inappropriate.

"Why would anybody go and drop dead if the person doesn't have a good reason? I mean, especially if the person didn't have any reason at all?"

There was an impassioned, even desperate tone to her voice, the white heat of her rhetorical question making the sobs within her breast suddenly roil and rush to her throat. She struggled to choke back the tears, stammering out at long last the words:

"Fuyuko is dead!"

I was stunned.

"Fuyuko is what?"

"She's . . ."

"How can she be dead? And why didn't you tell me right away?"

"I'm trying to believe it's not true. I keep telling myself she has to be alive. But I know it's too late. She's dead, and that's all there is to it."

The color had drained from Obiko's tear-stained cheeks, and her face was contorted in pain. She sat on the bed, her eyes staring off into space.

Without noticing it, I had crumpled in my hand the cigarette I had taken out and was about to smoke.

"You're not making sense. All right now, out with the whole story."

"But I'm afraid."

"Afraid of what?"

"To even say it. No, that's not it. I mean, there's simply no way to explain it . . . but I know I'm right."

Obiko bit her lip. It was as if a mental fog had enveloped her brain, and she was using each and every word to cut through it.

"Maybe I've been all wrong in the way I think about things. I always thought that people needed a reason to die. But once you're dead, what does it matter to you? It's the living who aren't satisfied until we have a reason. We're the ones who need reassuring. When I came face to face with the possibility that Fuyuko might not be alive, I didn't know what to do with myself. All I could worry about was, what if it's true? What would we say?"

"When was all of this supposed to have happened?"

"I dropped by the house in Kamata a little while ago. But the front door was locked, and even though it was time for Fuyuko to start dinner and she ought to have been home, when I went around to the back, the kitchen door was barred from the inside too. As I was standing there wondering where everyone was, I heard somebody come up behind me. It was the maid who works for Fuyuko.

"Did I know where her mistress had gone? It was getting dark, but I could see she was about to burst into tears. 'She sent me out on an errand, and when I got back the door was locked. I checked with the neighbors, but they hadn't seen her go out either. Of course, Mr. Aioi isn't home yet.' The girl was holding a package of meat from the butcher shop. She did not appear to know what to do next.

"I asked her how Fuyuko looked. 'No, ma'am,' said the maid, 'she wasn't dressed to go out. She's been in the best of health lately. She was even talking about a trip that she and Mr. Aioi were planning for this coming Saturday. . . .'

" 'She must have stepped out for a minute,' I said, trying to reassure the girl. 'I wonder what's keeping her. . . .'

"I walked back to the frosted-glass sliding door to the kitchen, and pressing my nose against the narrow crack along the doorjamb, I tried to peek inside. . . . That's when I noticed the smell. It was a terrible, disgusting odor. . . ."

According to Obiko, the dawning realization of what was happening at the house came as a complete surprise. She backed away from the door, inscribing an unsteady circle of steps on the ground. But then, she spun around and pressed her back squarely against the doorjamb.

It was gas all right. What she had smelled coming from the kitchen was gas. But she was determined to keep it a secret and not let the smell get outside.

"You needn't worry," she announced to the maid in an oddly excited and merry tone of voice. "Fuyuko will be home in no time. But I'm in a hurry so I have to say good-bye for now. Tell her I was here and said hello. I'll drop by again in a day or two." Abandoning the distraught maid, she raced down the street, oblivious to everything.

"But why did I run away like that?" Obiko asked herself out loud, as she struggled to understand the logic of her own reaction. Hadn't she been the first to sniff out trouble and detect the smell of death in the air? Didn't she know Fuyuko was trapped, unable to move, in the midst of something that reeked of poisonous gas? How could she leave her? They were flesh and blood sisters, weren't they? Or had the shadow of death, which had stolen up from behind and caught her off guard, been a sight so unexpected and so intimidating that, fearing for the safety of her own life, she had become thoroughly discombobulated?

But — "no, no" — this could not be happening. First of all, why would Fuyuko want to die? It made no sense at all. She led a happy, tranquil life as a result of having married the gentle and warm person that was Aioi Sanji, her husband. His parents had provided for him, even though he was not the eldest son, and he had brought to his marriage with Fuyuko the financial advantages that came from his share of the family fortunes. Nor was there any reason to believe the bond between Fuyuko and Sanji was troubled in any way — to believe, for example, that either party was engaged in some sort of clandestine romance outside the marriage. No, that was simply not possible.

Perhaps Fuyuko's daily routine had been too quiet, and the blandness of it had taken the life out of her. But that made no sense either. Never one to play the smart aleck, she was not the type who would resort to suicide simply to prove the point that she was bored. To the contrary, the absence of a child and a certain weakness in her lungs had been the "pepper," so to speak, of their married life. They had provided just the right pinch of seasoning to a relationship that might have been too dull and ordinary otherwise.

Nor was there reason to believe Fuyuko might have been overcome by some sort of grand and vainglorious notion that, by committing suicide, she could spice things up a bit more and thereby elevate the mundaneness of her life to the level of high tragedy. By nature she was simply not that extravagant or melodramatic. It is only in novels that people are happy enough that they can afford *not* to go on living.

But, why then, the foul smell? The question would not go away.

"Gas? Did someone say 'gas'?" Obiko was caught in the throes of a terrible dilemma.

Maybe, just maybe, it was not gas after all.

But if it wasn't gas, then what in the world was it that smelled so bad? What foul and rotten thing had taken hold of Obiko and, by driving her to wit's end, made her heart race and tear itself apart?

Suddenly she remembered the tops of the spring onions she had seen discarded on the ground by the kitchen door. The image virtually leapt out at her and made her eyes water and burn. She seized upon it and, clinging with all of her might to the bright green of the onion stalks, she sought to persuade herself.

"What gas? Why, it was the scallions I smelled."

Try as she might, there would be no denying the presence in the air of an odor—a gas—that clung all the more tenaciously to the inside of her nostrils. The certainty of its smell, the undeniable fact of its existence, pinned her down and held her to account. There would be no explaining it away, no matter how she tried to dodge the question or to parry its thrusting point. Obiko was thrown back by a fierce blast of wind, and a hulking black object rumbled before her eyes. It startled her from her reverie, and she found herself standing at the railroad crossing that gave access to Kamata Station. A freight train was barreling down the tracks.

"My head was spinning as I stumbled on board one of the cars on the city commuter line," she continued. Obiko alighted several stations later at Yuraku-chō, and collapsing across a bench on the train platform, she struggled to decide whether to turn around and go back to Fuyuko's house. She felt utterly weighed down and oppressed by her inability to make up her mind. It was only after much debate that she had managed to drag herself to this apartment. My throat had become parched as I listened to her. I swallowed hard to get rid of the bitter taste in my mouth.

"Hmm. . . ."

"What? . . ." said Obiko, responding nervously to my reaction.

"I guess you must be right. It's probably too late. The reason being . . . but, no, that's not what I mean to say. You said you could tell she was gone from the smell of the gas. And I can tell from the way you talk about it. No, it's not intuition or anything like that. It's just the simple truth of the matter, and that's the way things are. I'm sure she's dead."

At some point I had gotten up from my chair and crossed the room. Obiko and I were now sitting in a row on the bed. She was at one end; I, at the other. An insect crawled across the wall. Obiko's voice echoed with a low, hollow ring that seemed to pursue the insect as it inched its way up the wall.

"Why did Fuyuko need to die? Here I've spent all this time wondering why she ought to be living, yet I haven't once tried putting myself in her place and looked at things from her perspective. Maybe it was something she did in a fit of pique or anger. Or something forced her into a corner and drove her to despair. I haven't even thought about anything like that."

"That may be true, Obiko, but what I don't understand is why you didn't break the glass on the door and try to save her?"

Obiko threw herself across the bed. She clutched at the leg of my pants, digging her fingernails into my thigh. Her sobs came in great waves.

"What a bad girl, what a mean Obiko, I've been! If only I had acted right away, I could have gotten Fuyuko out in time. I might have saved her life. I should have been prepared to do anything to save my sister. But, no, not me. I didn't do a thing. . . ."

Her whole body shook as it convulsed with each sob and gasp for air. "I don't understand it either. I don't understand how I could have run off and abandoned her like that."

Obiko pulled herself away. Burying her face in her hands, she leaned over the edge of the bed, sitting motionlessly. The insect crawling along the wall had disappeared. Outside the room, night was falling, and the lights of the city looked like the heads of nails that had been hammered into the darkness. A shiver ran down my spine as I sat there in the cold, unheated room.

Obiko took a deep breath, and throwing back her head, she ran her fingers through her hair. And then, in a tone that sounded almost categorical, she announced, "Obiko isn't going to worry anymore." In addressing herself in the third person, she spoke as though she were a child and as if she were speaking of someone else.

"The truth is Obiko had used the last of her allowance for this month, and she went to her sister's house to borrow money. How is that for you? Obiko was going to borrow money from somebody who wasn't even alive. How petty can a person be? . . .

"When I think how she ran from the back door because she was feeling too ashamed . . . and abandoned Fuyuko for no other reason than her own embarrassment . . . it scares me to death, and my knees start to shake. . . .

"But Obiko is going to be all right now. Obiko has made up her mind that she will have nothing more to do with death and dying or with people who go about killing themselves, especially in times like these when too many people who don't want to die are dying every day in faraway places. That's why I can't understand how anybody could be so selfish as to kill herself without a reason. . . .

"No, I'm not blaming Fuyuko. How should I know why she did it or whether it was right or wrong. I just don't want to think about it, that's all. What's done is done, and that's it. . . . That's right, Obi, pull yourself together. Okay, here we go. . . . That'a girl, Obiko. Didn't I say we weren't going to think about these terrible things anymore?"

Obiko produced a compact from her purse and proceeded to powder her nose. And then, pulling out a Max Factor eyeliner, she penciled in two archly drawn brows.

A sound truck was moving along the street beneath the window. A great shout went up from the crowd. The flapping of innumerable little paper flags cut the night air.

What will ensue in the hour when you, Mars, rise and gird for battle?
"How bold!" "How valiant!" they sing. . . .

"There it is again," I said, heaving a sigh of consternation and collapsing across the bed. In the same instant, Obiko jumped up and, rushing across the room, threw open the sash. Turning to the crowd in the street, and filling her lungs with a great breath of fresh air, she raised her right arm and waved it back and forth in salute. In unison with the rising chorus of voices, she shouted,

"Banzai!"

I clamped my hands over my ears.

Whatever made me behave like this? Had the tympanum of my inner ear been pricked by a great and intense grief secreted within Obiko's shout to the crowd? Or was it that, in mourning Fuyuko, I would have no part of a rousing hurrah?

Or was it something far simpler? —a mere physical reaction that, via a prophylaxis of the mind, interrupted the sound and, for the sake of my mental health, kept from my ears the popular refrain that I found so difficult to commend?

III

"Doubtless you think it strange. Because it is. But I had ceased to consider it that way because I got used to it happening every day. . . .

"But, no, that's not quite what I meant to say. It is only now, in looking back, that I realize how odd it was. At the time I didn't think it very out-of-the-ordinary.

"Fuyuko had acquired a peculiar habit. Perhaps it was a game, or she meant it as a joke, but in the end it got completely out of control. I know it's all my fault. I should have been more vigilant. But saying that now won't make amends. It's all too sad. I failed her. In the presence of all of you who have come today, I wish to publicly express my apologies to Fuyuko for having failed her. It is something for which I feel great regret and am profoundly sorry."

The telegram that arrived the following morning informing us of Fuyuko's sudden death had come as no surprise. Obiko and I set out to Kamata to attend the wake to be held at the house.

Having formally addressed the group of thirteen or fourteen family members and friends who had gathered at the house, Sanji turned to the memorial altar and casket that had been set up at the front of the living room. He was kneeling before it, and placing both hands on the tatami mats, he bowed deeply to the deceased.

It had been late the previous night when Sanji returned home from a meeting with colleagues at work. He had been startled to find all of the doors locked, and by the time he broke in and discovered Fuyuko in the room at the back of the house, which was filled with gas, nothing could be done for her. She had died of asphyxiation.

Convinced her mistress went out on an errand, the maid had gone to a neighbor's house. Not knowing what more to do, she had borrowed space in the neighbor's kitchen and sat waiting for Sanji to return home. She was in a terribly confused state of mind; moreover, she was worn out from having sat so long with nothing to do. Meanwhile, because each house on the street was set off from the next by a garden, the gas had gone undetected. Besides, the neighbors said there was little reason why they might have suspected something amiss, because Fuyuko and Sanji were known to be happily married.

As to what Sanji had to say about the "strange tale" of Fuyuko's behavior, the story went as follows:

SANJI AND FUYUKO had married four years earlier. He was the third son of a well-to-do family from Tochigi Prefecture. He had gone to college, graduating from a private university in Tokyo; and as for his military obligation, he was fulfilling it by serving as second lieutenant in the Army Reserve.

Since his college days, photography was his hobby. He had pursued it with a passion, and in the process he had turned himself into a first-rate professional. Moreover, he had been recommended for and had accepted a job at a newspaper, where he was currently employed as a photographer. Money had never been of much concern; and so thoroughly did Sanji enjoy his work at the office, he decided to build a darkroom at home. As for other avocations, there was none of which to speak. He had tried his hand at billiards, but it never amounted to more than a passing interest. Other potential indulgences went no further either: he really could not drink, and being serious by nature, it never occurred to him, when introduced to a woman he did not know, to try to crack a joke, let alone pursue her. He devoted himself singlemindedly to Fuyuko, sticking close to their nest much like a bird protecting a chick.

And, in that nest smelling sweet and dry as a fresh bed of straw, Fuyuko spent her days reading, except for those hours when she bustled about happily preparing her husband's meals.

As for what Fuyuko read, her preferences ran almost exclusively to works for the theater and, among theatrical works, to translations from the European stage. She devoured translations of Western drama indiscriminately, showing no concern for their quality, good or bad. What's more, she often memorized plots or committed certain passages to memory. As a result, it always came as something of a surprise to realize, when engaging Fuyuko in a discussion on literature, that she knew virtually nothing about any other genre.

On holidays, she and Sanji took short trips, or they went to the cinema. In particular, they never failed to see performances of *shingeki,* or the "new theater" being created by contemporary Japanese dramatists in imitation of the Western stage. As time passed, Sanji also came to share Fuyuko's taste for modern theater. So it was that he added reading and seeing plays translated for the stage to his list of personal interests.

I T WAS ONE RAINY SUNDAY about a year ago. Fuyuko, who had been sitting in a rattan chair on the verandah reading a volume from the complete works of a famous foreign playwright, turned suddenly to Sanji, who was toying with a roll of film.

"Sanji, it says here, and I quote, *'Feigning deafness may be forgivable, but taken to extremes, it may cost your life.'* What do you think it means?"

"What's that?" he replied, as though taken by surprise.

"It says, *'Feigning deafness may be forgivable, but . . .'*"

Sanji was baffled. Fuyuko's question had come from out of the blue, and he had no knowledge of its context. "It means just what it says, doesn't it?"

"But . . ."

"But why not? If that's what's written there, that's what it means, doesn't it?"

"I guess you're right, if that's all there is to it. Still, I wonder what it's really supposed to mean."

"Search me. I'm no scholar."

Although Sanji claimed ignorance, Fuyuko's question — "What did it really mean?" — stuck in his mind, and he anticipated she would have something else to say.

But there was not a peep more out of her. Sanji finished working with the roll of film. When he happened to call her, and call her by name, he was greeted by silence. There she was, sitting motionless in her chair and not saying a word. She wouldn't even turn and look at him.

"Hey, Fuyuko! What's wrong?"

Sanji got up and walked over to her. He reached out and rested both hands on her shoulders.

"What's wrong?" he asked, repeating his question in a gentle tone of voice.

Fuyuko stuck a finger in each ear and, pursing her lips, made a sound like a person who had been gagged. At the same time, she looked up at Sanji and smiled at him with her eyes. Sanji was startled at how beautiful his wife's eyes could be.

"I get it. You're deaf and dumb, aren't you?"

He took Fuyuko's face in his hands and stroked her hair. He pressed a kiss against her tightly sealed lips.

On that day that was all that happened.

But there were other occasions when Fuyuko did the same thing, especially if she was in a good mood. One time she was mute; the next, she went blind. Each time Sanji had been only too eager to respond to her initiative, and he had played the supporting role in the little dramas she created.

One evening, when Sanji returned from work, he was startled to find Fuyuko hobbling about the house, dragging one foot like a cripple. He was convinced she had injured herself and was on the verge of going out to call the doctor. Yet, once again, Fuyuko was cured instantly when he played his part and acted the role of her miracle worker.

On another occasion, Sanji awakened one morning to find Fuyuko, who was lying next to him, holding her breath and making her arms and legs as rigid as possible.

"Fuyuko . . . is . . . dead," she said, stammering out the words.

"Stop it, will you, you silly fool."

"Maybe I'll try suicide next."

"And what happens if you end up killing yourself?"

"Now there's a silly question! Who wants to die? Not I. I'd never be so foolish as to use a gun or take poison. There'd be no way to call things off when they got dangerous, because the minute you think you've gone too far, it's probably already too late. Really committing suicide wouldn't be the least bit fun. I'd prefer to do what looks like the real thing but isn't. Something that's like a lie but sounds like the truth, but really isn't. I'd arrange it so I could stop any time I wanted to."

"LET ME ASSURE YOU," said Sanji, addressing the friends and relatives at the wake. "Had I detected anything pathological, or overwrought, or even suspicious about her manner, I would not have stood by idly. But there she was, looking so beautiful, and charming, and full of life when she talked that way. I always gave in. Of course, I had known she had a weakness in the lungs from the time we got married. But lately there had been no sign of trouble. In fact, I can't think of anything irregular that might have endangered her health. And that's why I felt safe, no matter how crazy her little dramas may have seemed. I felt certain she would be all right.

"Take last night. The house was in perfect order. There was no sign of her having gotten upset and losing control of herself. She was dressed as beautifully as an actress in a play, and she had made up her face with extra care. There she was, lying on the floor with her eyes closed and looking so beautiful and sweet, and so totally at peace. There is no reason why Fuyuko ought to have died. I'm convinced she thought she was going to live."

Everyone in the room waited for Sanji to continue.

But he fell silent, and inching away from the casket on his knees, he chose a spot in the corner of the room. He sat in a formal posture, his hands resting on his thighs and his mouth clamped tightly shut. It was hard to believe he was the same man who had spoken until now at such length.

It appeared that it was time for the guests to have a word to say. But they were at a loss to know where to begin, and a long silence ensued. More than anything, their silence spoke of the confusion they felt in the face of Fuyuko's sudden and unexpected death.

"Ahem. . . ."

At last an elder member of the group of the room spoke.

"So that's how it was? It's not anything I readily understand, mind you. Whatever made her think she could draw into a shell like that and expect her little world to fit into the larger scheme of everyday life?"

No sooner had he spoken than, as if by prearrangement, each person sought to express an opinion in turn.

"I suppose she couldn't live without creating a hypothetical world of her own. She constructed a big armchair out of the projections of her mind, and by lounging in it and ensconcing herself in its unworldly embrace, she sought to keep herself warm and safe from the demands of a cold and indifferent world. What she didn't realize was life had already given her a warm and comfortable chair. Too much champagne taste, if you ask me. But once people get that way, there's not much that those of us on the sidelines can do or say. We could have told her she was letting herself get divorced from real life, but what good would it have done? It wouldn't have sounded bad to her at all."

"Well, I'd call it a love of danger. Or, a love of dangerous games. It was precisely because life was so safe and sound for her that she started those crazy little dramas. But once she became reckless in the way she went about expressing her love, she ceased to be aware of the danger she was in."

"She set up conditions of her own making. But rather than living within those conditions and letting herself be governed by them, she couldn't resist the temptation to rewrite the rules of the game. But what happened? When she discovered, belatedly and quite by accident, how binding the rules were, she was already beaten. Seen from Fuyuko's point of view, it was simply a matter of having miscalculated and making the wrong move. What started out as no more than an innocent pastime turned into something a hell of a lot more dangerous, however."

"At first everything was a game. Fuyuko created her own shadow play. She filled it with her own cast of characters, and when she tired of them, she was ready—poof—to get rid of them. I'd call it whimsy, pure and simple. Still, the shadows had come to life in the meantime, and they were not about to retreat from the stage because Fuyuko was no longer interested in them. To stop a game, one has to expend the energy needed to call it quits. That's where the issue of will power comes in. In the end Fuyuko made the unhappy mistake of getting herself into a position in which she could no longer exercise her own will. She was like the person who announces in the pink of health that he'll be brave and commit suicide if he has a stroke and is paralyzed. But the determination to end it all gets fuzzy once paralysis sets in. By the time Fuyuko reached the decision that it was time to shut off the gas, the poison was already circulating through her system. The mental brake that was supposed to kick in failed to work. Or, to put it another way, it was at the moment when her life hung in the balance that the gas got to her. The weak condition of her lungs was probably one more factor that she failed to appreciate fully."

"As a general rule, isn't it often the case with all of us that we are unable to express ourselves and say 'no' in difficult situations? Each of us knows this is wrong, and it's not how we intend things to work out, but we can't help ourselves. We just go along. It's the sort of predicament we find ourselves in when, let's say, a popular song becomes a hit tune and sweeps the public by storm. Why, take the case of 'Mars' Song.' . . ."

No sooner had the words "Mars' Song" been said—the title tossed out as a topic for discussion—than the room exploded in a great roar. Everyone struggled to make his or her voice heard. Eyes turned red. Spit flew through the air. No one spoke in turns anymore. Each had a private monologue, advocating a particular point of view without the least concern for the opinion of anyone else and directing it toward no one in particular:

"This is top, top secret, but can you guess how many nails it takes to produce a pair of infantryman's boots?" "Stated in the broadest terms, it's a loss of national proportions. Think what would have happened to Italy if Enrico Caruso had been sent to the Ethiopian front and not come back alive?" "When you're fired from one of those catapult machines, at first your back is slammed smack-dab against the rear wall. But the second you are launched into the air, it's the frame of the body that goes flying forward. Your brain and your guts still feel glued to the back of the seat. No, it's not that I've ridden in one. But I know. I have a cousin in the navy." "Tell me quick. How many times does five sen go into fifty billion yen?" "What puzzles me is, if there's a news story to be covered on those stone buddhas, why hasn't the newspaper sent me abroad to do it?" "Anybody got a map? A good map? You can't plan a battle without a decent map!" "You tell me. What is it they mean by the popular phrase 'The Defense of Culture'? . . ."

Suddenly a terrible cry rent the air. It emanated from the corner of the room, and so agonized was the sound, it defied description. Everyone gasped and fell silent. The passion of each and every one for his or her opinion had been broken, and like a wave breaking on the shore, the resounding cry washed whitely over the room, its bubbles bursting on the floor and soaking quietly into the tatami mats. There was a lapse of four or five seconds before anyone realized it was Sanji who had cried out in pain.

"No, no, no, no. . . ."

He was doubled over, moaning.

"It's all my fault. I'm the one who's to blame."

Brushing aside the barrage of shocked queries and protestations to the contrary with a wave of his hand, he sat up straight. Once again, his posture was very formal.

"The problem is that I didn't love Fuyuko enough."

"What? . . ."

"I'd be less than honest if I refrained from saying this, but as I sat here listening to all of you carry on about your silly theories, I began to hate you. All that you are interested in is Fuyuko's death and what caused it. You are interested only in showing off your clever explanations — and at the expense of her life and my grief. Of course, I . . . I . . . yes, I'll admit it . . . I too was amused by her little dramas.

"But, tell me, who in the world is going to waste time playing games pretending to be deaf and dumb so long as life has meaning and that meaning reaches to the core of one's existence — yes, down to the most minute crack? There must have been something missing in the life that Fuyuko and I shared together. There had to be an unseen crack somewhere in this house — a sort of void that I failed to detect and I let go unfilled. To make matters worse, it never occurred to me to look. Poor Fuyuko . . . I didn't love her enough.

A single tear glistened as it ran down the bluish side of Sanji's cheek. But he continued to sit as erect and formal as ever, and he did not break down and cry. Not one of us had seen him like this before. It was not so much a matter of what he said but the forlorn and unreceptive tone of his voice. It was the voice of a man who has been set adrift in the world alone, and everyone was thoroughly taken aback. There was a heavy, labored measure to the way we breathed. The air seemed to congeal like wax and seal off the possibility of anyone adding a word more of either complaint or protest.

Finally a long, plaintive sigh broke the silence in the room. Obiko had gotten up, and going over to Sanji, she threw her arms around his shoulders.

"No, Sanji, you mustn't say that. When you start to talk that way in front of others, words fall apart, and they will never feel right again. Remember how important they are and keep them deep inside yourself. It really hurts Obiko to see you like this. . . . Poor Sanji . . . and poor Fuyuko."

Sanji gave no sign of responding. He sat there, his eyes staring straight ahead. Obiko slipped away and plunked herself in front of the casket. The chrysanthemums arranged in a vase on the funeral altar shook as she sat down. Two or three petals fell to the top of the incense stand.

Someone suggested Obiko should act more ladylike.

"Oh shush! What makes you think you have a right to say anything?" she retorted, looking defiantly over her shoulder in the direction of the speaker. There was a noticeable change in her tone of voice. It was vehement in a way that it had never been.

"Go ahead and talk about 'Mars' Song.' I know how much you like it, but I bet you haven't the foggiest notion what it's all about. All right, go ahead, if that's how strongly you feel. Why don't you sing it for all of us? All right now, all together . . . why don't we all sing 'Mars' Song'?"

As for myself, I had propped my back against one of the exposed pillars at the side of the room and had sat motionless throughout the wake. I had not offered so much as a single word, let alone a comment or a speech; and as for what the others had to say and the commotion they made in announcing their opinions, it had all grazed past my ears and faded into oblivion. I paid them no mind, choosing instead to focus my attention on Fuyuko's face as I saw it now for the last time. I let my eyes pursue it like a vision that floated in the air. It was a beautiful face, and it was made up with exquisite care, just as Sanji had said. I was struck in particular by the sight of her lips, the bright red hue of the lipstick having faded to a more somber shade in the dim and uncertain light of the room. . . .

The door on the opposite side of the room slid open. Someone stuck his head inside and was looking for Sanji. There was a very serious expression on his face. Sanji stood up and, with a silent nod to his guests, excused himself. Meanwhile, everyone stayed seated, absentmindedly waiting for him to return. It was as though we had been momentarily struck dumb and had forgotten why we were there.

Sanji was back almost immediately. He stood at the edge of the sliding door, his tall frame looking that much taller dressed in the funeral garb of a black silk kimono and its long jacket imprinted with the Aioi family crest. He held a piece of paper in his right hand. The paper was of a cheap, inferior bond, and it was pale red in color. Sanji's hand shook as he held it.

Everyone recognized at once the significance of the piece of paper in Sanji's hand. For it was one of the "greetings" sent out to all young men in this land, regardless of rank or station in life. It was the call to arms that corralled them for the hunt and, amidst rousing choruses of "Mars' Song," saw them off to faraway fields where the smell of gunpowder filled the air. Every eye in the room was glued to it — this unfeeling announcement, the fateful notification. In a flash, we were welded into a single emotion. The air in the room was now hotly charged, and by comparison, Sanji's remarks seemed almost matter-of-fact, if not perfunctory.

"Here are my marching orders. I had guessed I'd be called up, and I was prepared to go in any event. Now that Fuyuko is gone, there is nothing to keep me from going. I am saddened by the thought I shall not have the time to mourn her properly, but given the circumstances, I have no choice. The first order of business for tomorrow is to take care of having her body cremated and then see to it that the ashes are buried. At any rate, I have a five-day reprieve. I'm to report to the induction camp in Utsunomiya in the morning, five days from today. I anticipate my father will come to Tokyo to take care of closing the house."

Each person in the room struggled to put his or her feelings into words. But we bit back whatever colorful phrases we might have had in mind in the face of the transparently colorless way in which Sanji spoke. By having looked at the letter in advance of us, he had already filtered out any sign of his true emotions.

IV

Following the wake and the cremation of Fuyuko's body, I attended the funeral that the family conducted as a small, private service at Sōjiji Temple in the Tsurumi section of Yokohama. After the funeral, I left Obiko at the house in Kamata, where she planned to go through Fuyuko's personal effects, and heading for the Ginza, I returned to the apartment house alone. The next morning, namely, very early this morning, I was roused from bed, someone having come to call me to answer the phone in the lobby of the apartment building.

"I apologize for the sudden call. . . ."

The person on the other end of the line was one of the relatives who had attended Fuyuko's wake.

"Do you remember the name of the inn in Nagaoka? Yes, Nagaoka on the Izu Peninsula. . . . That's right, an inn where Sanji stayed before. . . . They say he left Tokyo last night. We were notified just now, and that's all we know. Yes, Nagaoka. The problem is . . . well, it appears Obiko has gone with him. Yes, that's what I said. Obiko. I'm sure they'll be back in no time, and there is nothing for us to worry about. Of course, we'd have nothing to worry about at all if they hadn't gone in the first place. Sanji can say all he wants about having 'a little breathing spell' before getting down to serious business again, but this is no time to be taking things lightly, especially since it comes right after this crazy business with Fuyuko. For Sanji to take off like this, and for no apparent reason . . . why, it gives me a fright. First of all, he has to report to Utsunomiya, doesn't he?

"No?! You don't think he might possibly . . . ? No, no, I'm sure that's not it. . . . But if for some small reason or other he shouldn't get back in time, then we'll have real trouble on our hands. That's why, as I was about to say, if you are free, we wonder if you would go to Nagaoka for us. . . . You know, just to see how things are? Yes, it would be so good of you to go. . . . Really? As it is, none of us can get away because of work. We would genuinely appreciate it. Tell Sanji everybody is worried. . . ."

And so it was that I found myself seated on board the Tōkaidō train ready to take the morning express to Izu.

Because I find it pointless to spend time second-guessing what may or may not be true, and what moreover probably cannot be comprehended at any rate, let me intervene at this point in the story and delay until such time as I have reached Nagaoka any discussion of questions that may arise concerning the propriety of Sanji's and Obiko's behavior in abruptly having gone off to Izu together unannounced and unchaperoned. For the moment, I prefer to take the botheration of an unwanted chore and look upon it instead as the occasion for an unexpected pleasure trip that I tell myself I decided upon on the spur of the minute. As a matter of fact, the more I think about it, the more convinced I am that this trip is not such a bad idea after all.

Enough of the stagnant air in my sunless apartment. Instead of struggling in pain at my desk, how much better to sit back, relax, and let the gentle zephyrs that pour through the train window wash from my face the wrinkles that the gloom of my room has etched across my furrowed brow.

Yet, it was all too good to be true. I found my hopes were dashed even before the train pulled from the platform. A unit of swordless enlistees, clean-shaven as barbers and dressed in khaki-colored uniforms, were rushing about the platform. They moved busily to and fro in a sea of little paper flags waved by wellwishers there to see them off. Other groups joined in, and soon every-one was clapping, engrossed as the crowd was in creating a great commotion. As the train gave a short blast on its whistle, the cry of "Banzai!" went up from the throng. As well as — ah, ah, here we go again! — a rousing chorus of "Mars' Song." . . .

What will ensue in the hour when you, Mars, rise and gird for battle?
"How bold!" "How valiant!" they sing. . . .

Voices were lifted in song even in the car of the train that I had boarded. Indeed, total strangers began to sing in unison, and those who refrained sat looking at the floor in embarrassed silence. As the train gathered steam, the singing died away, but here and there passengers struck up random conver-sations, their remarks going back and forth independently of each other, their exchanges sounding ever so much like the vain pronouncements that had stirred the air at Fuyuko's wake. It was as though the topics to be discussed had been agreed upon in advance, and no one tired of rehashing them at great length.

Someone had taken the mood of the streets and, like a lunch sold in a balsam box at any railroad station, packed it on board the narrow confines of the passenger car. Anything and everything that spoke of the season of Mars had been squeezed in, leaving room for nothing else. And just when it appeared that the gentle breezes blowing through the windows might unwittingly clear the air and rarefy the atmosphere at last, what should happen but the train pulled into another station. There — on the platform at each and every stop — another chorus stood ready and waiting for us. We were not to escape and, as if to heat up our ardor and once more solidify the mood aboard the train, the band proceeded to strike up the refrain of "Mars' Song."

I sat in the far corner of the car feeling as if I were about to die from asphyxiation. I reached for the overhead rack and pulled from my bag several books that I had brought along to read. A small booklet, its pages threaded together in the traditional manner, slipped from among the bound volumes and landed in my lap. How, I wondered, had it managed to lodge itself there—this chapbook of verse by the Tenmei poet Ōta Nanpo? I returned the other books to the bag and settled on it as the perfect companion for the jug of saké I purchased when the train pulled into Yokohama Station. Turning to the introduction, my eyes happened upon a passage in which Nanpo writes from the city of Edo to his literary counterpart in Kyoto, the poet Hatanaka Kansai. The passage is in Chinese, written in the five-word line typical of the "ancient style."

"Your letter of the tenth / just now reached my hand / I have read its particulars / I can only exclaim: how / refined, and ever more so! . . ."

No matter in what age Ōta Nanpo may have lived, here was a man who truly knew the meaning of refinement in life. Better than anyone, this awesome master understood the singular importance of keeping one's true genius to oneself. That was enough for him. And as for how he dealt with the demands of making his way in the world, it sufficed him to make do with his secondary talents, letting works drop from his pen like blossoms from the trees and his person pass through the dust of the earth yet remaining all the while untouched by its soiling hand. Indeed so adroit was Nanpo at the art of disguising himself in his works that we cannot find even a trace of him left behind in the flowers that are his works. By that act, what a rare and distant flower he has become!

"How refined, and ever more so!"

But I digress and am carried further astray from the novel that I am trying to write. By now the second bottle of saké that I had purchased when the train stopped at Atami Station was nearly empty.

Given the season aboard the train we were on, surely the sane thing was to add one's voice to the chorus of "Mars' Song," was it not? And if sanity lay in joining in, didn't that mean my brand of sanity was insanity?

As the rays of the sun grew stronger, I could see the spit of the passengers fly through the dusty air of the passenger car as they spoke. The color of khaki suddenly flashed past my eye. Someone had knocked a pair of soldier's gaiters from the overhead rack. Across the aisle, a child had pulled a toy sword from its sheath and was brandishing it about.

Ah, ah . . . *"How refined, and ever more so!"* How Nanpo's phrase echoed through my mind! Everything about the train looked quite mad. And, now, ever more so. . . .

We pulled to a stop. I looked up and saw we had arrived at Mishima Station. I hurriedly got off the train and rushed down the stairs to the exit. I grabbed a taxi at the entrance to the station and headed for Nagaoka.

My guess about the location of the inn had been correct. Talking to the innkeeper at the door, I learned that Sanji and Obiko had arrived late last night. That had not inhibited them from getting up early in the morning, however; and though they appeared in a great hurry, nonetheless they seemed to be enjoying themselves. They had checked out, he said; but he knew where to reach them because he had called ahead to the boat landing at Mito. They had asked him to charter a boat, as they planned to go sailing in the waters off Shizuura Cove.

"They're probably out in the boat right now. They also said they wanted to get on the road as soon as they returned to shore. A car is to pick them up at Mito at four o'clock. You should be able to catch them, if you go to the boat landing and wait."

My watch showed a little before three. I left the inn, and hopping on a bus that cut through the town, I headed for the boat harbor at Mito.

A seawall ran along the righthand side of the highway where I alighted from the bus. Directly below, along a narrow strip of sand at the bottom of the wall, the clear waters of the cove lapped the beach. The water glimmered in the afternoon sun, as it stretched all of the way across to a long spit of land where a stand of tall trees checked one's view. The trees created a lush, natural backdrop for the inlet. On the placid waters of the bay, under a sky unspoiled by so much as a speck of cloud, an excursion ship putted along, emitting little white puffs of smoke from its smokestack.

Across the highway was a row of houses, the eaves of each roof closely abutting those of its neighbor. Next to the houses was a shop that offered tea and a place to sit. The words "Bay Cruises — Departures and Arrivals" were painted on a signboard in big, imposing letters.

I stepped inside the dirt floor of the shop. To one side was a small glass case containing boxes of caramel candies and cheap pastries. A rectangular table and benches to sit on had been set out for customers to use. No one was about; and no one replied when I called for service. Presently a woman emerged from the rear of the shop. She appeared to be the boatkeeper's wife.

"The charter is due in shortly," she said, in reply to my question.

She stood by the entrance and chatted with a neighbor who happened to come along. Then she disappeared inside, this time to emerge with an aluminum pot and teacups, which she put on the table. She was off once more, and it seemed unlikely she would return anytime soon.

I sat down on a bench and took out a cigarette. My mind seemed lost in a daze, although I also had the distinct impression that something vague and indefinable was brewing inside me. I felt confused in the face of it, overtaken by the restless and irritable feeling that comes when one has misplaced an exceedingly simple object and cannot find it. Still, nothing readily suggested itself.

But then, it came to me. What I perceived was the onset of the change in the seasons. Autumn was coming.

Ah, ah, the seasons! Surely the season that I experienced there and into which I would have longingly immersed myself as though lowering my limbs into a soothing tub of hot water was not to be confused with the season of "Mars' Song." No, it was something altogether different.

I stood up, and taking the pair of binoculars from the bag I had put on the bench, I stepped outside. I clambered down the steps of the seawall to the narrow strip of beach.

A breeze blew intermittently across the bay. Far out from the shore the fishing boats had formed a semicircle and were working together as a team. As the water broke on the shore at my feet, it made a crisp, bubbly sound like spray spouting from a mineral spring. It was almost as though the waves that moved across the bay existed solely to smooth out its surface and, by leaving no trace of their ripples, they left it as unwrinkled as a fine piece of silk.

I happened to turn and look to the north. There was Mount Fuji on the horizon, although given its great size and shape, I cannot imagine how I had managed to overlook it until now. Its outline was etched against the sky, where it seemed to float and dominate the landscape. How could I possibly have missed it?

Of course I have never cared much for the shape and image of Mount Fuji. To tell the truth, although it has never been a favorite of mine, in my dislike of it, I have never gone so far as to equip myself with whatever mental armor might be required of a man who, taking up the challenge, argues against Mount Fuji and thereby articulates just what it is about the shape or what the shape represents that makes it less than appealing. Still, I was not about, for want of such equipment, to change my mind and suddenly be impressed because, in this particular instance, the mountain had caught me off guard, and it happened to look every inch as majestic as the clichés would have it be.

I turned my binoculars toward the bay and focused on the outer shoals in order to get Fuji out of sight as quickly as possible. The fishing boats were still at work, their formation drawn like an arc on the surface of the water. On the side of each boat, the crews had stripped to the waist and were straining at the ropes of the net. What was the day's catch? I wondered. As they pulled in the heavy tow line that closed the open end of the huge underwater net, the fish were caught inside and were unable to escape.

Just then I saw a small sailboat round the tip of the inlet and head toward me. It skirted the outermost ring of the row of fishing boats and proceeded in the direction of the beach. I could see it clearly now. Sanji and Obiko were on board.

The boat dropped speed and drifted on the tide. The captain stood at the stern, and with his left hand, he pressed a glass-bottom barrel against the surface of the water. Bending over the barrel to block out the light, he used it to study the bottom of the bay. From the way he worked a long pole that he held in his right hand, I guessed he was using it to spear an octopus.

Sanji and Obiko laughed excitedly as they watched him work. Not unlike fish freshly taken from the water, they looked so healthy and full of life. Why was there cause to worry about them?

Obiko looked especially lovely. The more I studied her in her yellow dress, the more it struck me as the perfect match for the clear skies and blue waters of the bay. . . .

. . . yet, as I looked at her and Sanji, I could not help feeling there was something inappropriate about the way I was training a pair of binoculars on them. They had no knowledge of it, but in doing so I had singled them out within the larger context of life and was treating them like objects to be observed and watched carefully. The binoculars allowed me to magnify their arms and legs. They made it possible for me to see every gesture and move-ment the two of them made. It was as though I were peeping through a crack to spy on them. I could not help but feel there was something reprehensi-ble — even forbidden — about what I was doing. There was something eerie, if not unlucky, about the entire business. I lowered the binoculars.

But there it was again — Fuji writ large across the landscape. It was as though it were glued against the sky.

I took up the binoculars only to be confronted once more by the over-sized faces of Sanji and Obiko. What was I to do? I felt frustrated at not having a better place to direct my attention. I stuffed the binoculars into my pocket.

By and by the boat began to move again and head for the shore. Sanji and Obiko had seen me, and standing on tiptoe, they were waving their arms back and forth.

The prow of the boat lifted out of the water. A gentle tapping sound reverberated across the bay, as the boat suddenly picked up speed. The cap-tain must have decided to use the outboard motor. They were headed straight my way.

"Hey!" shouted Sanji as he jumped into the water and wadded ashore. "You should have gotten here sooner." I could tell he was genuinely glad to see me.

"What are you talking about? You didn't even tell me you were going to go to Izu."

"I guess I didn't, did I? . . . How'd you find us? . . . So that's what they said? . . . Even though there's nothing to worry about . . ."

"I wasn't worried . . . and I certainly wasn't worried like they'd have you think. . . ."

"I decided I'd use the two or three days left to really enjoy myself. There are so many things I'd like to do that I've gotten greedy and am trying to do them all. I really should have thought to invite you along, though."

"But coming by yourself would have been a lot easier, wouldn't it?"

"Well . . . that's true. Still, to come alone seemed frightening somehow. I had a feeling that just at the point when I'd get most involved and be totally absorbed in enjoying myself, suddenly I'd feel a terrible emptiness and it would cast a pall over everything. I was really glad Obiko was willing to come along."

A plank had been extended from the far side of the boat to the shore. Obiko came charging down it, hoisting the hem of her skirt as she ran.

"It's been an out-and-out marathon keeping up with Sanji," she said, struggling to catch her breath." We've been competing to see who can do the most. And just when it seems we've both run out of steam and it's impossible to do anything more, we come up with a new idea. It's been one challenge after the other. I'm the one who had the idea of chartering a boat. So off we go, heading out to sea. But before we can reach the mouth of the inlet, Sanji here announces he's had enough. What he really wants to see isn't the ocean after all, but the mountains! . . ."

"I don't deny it. It's just as Obiko says. Only, I couldn't keep up the pace if Obi weren't along."

"How far down the peninsula do you plan to go, anyway?" I asked.

"Nothing's planned. We've hired a car to drive us to the top of Amagi Pass and then over to the other side of the mountains. We'll stay one more night at wherever it is that we reach late tonight. For one thing, there aren't any deluxe hotels on this side of the peninsula, and I'm in the mood to stay in a place that is really first class. We can't stay more than one night, though. I have to be back in Tokyo by tomorrow evening because the fellows at work are throwing a party for me. After that, it's off to Utsunomiya, where I'll see my family first. How about it? Care to join us tonight?"

"Sorry, I'm not the sporting type like you two. I'll leave it to Obi to keep up with you."

"Even little Obiko doesn't know what's next," said Obi, speaking coyly of herself in the third person. "All Obiko knows is that somehow or other it feels all right. Sometimes, though, Sanji gives her a real scare. When we were out on the boat, he said he was going to jump overboard and go swimming in the ice-cold water. And he was on the verge of doing it too. Once we get to the mountains in the car, I know he won't be satisfied until he has the driver take a few of the hairpin curves at top speed."

"Danger doesn't seem dangerous anymore, that's all. I figure I'm safe all the way from here to Utsunomiya, no matter what happens."

The boatkeeper's wife was standing atop the seawall looking for us. A Pontiac was parked in front of the shop.

"Have you ever seen the aquarium?" Sanji asked me, pointing to a small island along the shore. It was no distance away.

"Once we take off, why don't you go and have a look at it? I'd go with you, but aquariums aren't the sort of thing that interest me any more."

Sanji jumped ahead and scaled the steps to the highway. I noticed he was not carrying the camera he always brought with him when he traveled.

"No pictures, huh?" I asked. "What's happened to your Kodak?"

"You know, I asked myself the same question just a little while ago. I completely forgot about it. It's as though I suddenly stopped thinking about the whole business of taking photos." The long lashes of his eyes batted ever so faintly. But because he was wearing a hat with a brim that cast a shadow across his face, I could not read his expression.

The door of the Pontiac swung open. A pair of suitcases and two over-coats were piled on the seat inside. Sanji climbed in after Obiko.

"Well, we're off."

"This is it then. Good-bye, and go in good health and spirits. Remember, no matter how far you go, don't fail to come home. We're all waiting for your safe return."

Sanji paused and looked at me. "Thank you," he said, bowing in my direction.

The car started to move. Sanji stuck his head out the window and bowed one more time. Meanwhile, Obiko had reached across him with her right hand, and letting her fingers flutter back and forth in the open window, she waved good-bye. The Pontiac turned and disappeared around a bend in the road.

SEVERAL MINUTES LATER I found myself standing at the entrance to the aquarium that Sanji had pointed out. It was on a spit of land that, less island than wartlike protuberance, projected into the bay and then curved back to the shore to create an enclosed body of water. The island rose to a point, where a rock outcropping served as an observation deck with a view of the entire aquarium. The spot where I am standing at this very moment is said platform. . . .

Though the light in the sky has faded considerably, Mount Fuji remains sharply outlined against the horizon, looking ever so much like a raised paper figure embossed on a greeting card. But I have turned my back to it and am watching the schools of fish as they swim in the water below.

The aquarium is out-of-doors, having neither roof nor glassed-in walls, and the way the clear blue autumn sky shines on this corner of the bay makes the water transparent as a sheet of glass. Partitions have been erected to separate the fish into their respective species; meanwhile, the change in the tide on the outer shoals insures the aquarium is constantly supplied with fresh seawater. Because the tidepools inside never stagnate, the fish show no signs of being anything less than their usual, healthy selves.

In one pool a school of young tuna is circling, their scales gleaming with a bright, metallic glow. They swim with great vigor and without fear of predators, as they cut a broad swath through the water with the greatest of ease. It looks almost as though they are stirring a great vat of blue dye as they make their grand sweep of the enclosure and bring to the surface the deep indigo of the bay.

Sightseers call to the attendant to throw out some bait. The pieces of mackerel that had been in his bucket until just now hang momentarily in the air before they plummet and hit the surface of the water. And as they do, the tuna leap. With a flash of the silver tails of the tuna, the bait disappears.

At the other end of the pool, the tourists crowd around a man dressed in white pants and shirt. He is holding a sturdy bamboo pole to which a line is attached: he steadies the pole against the pit of his stomach by bracing it with his right hand. . . .

. . . at the end of his line is a large, spindle-shaped piece of wood that floats in the water like a buoy. The man takes a big breath, and by synchronizing the timing of his breathing with the upward motion of his right hand, he yanks in the line. The buoy dances in the air, but only for so long as it takes him to reach across with his left hand and grab it. This is the way he practices casting a line to the tuna. . . .

After repeating the exercise several times to show the sightseers how it is done, he offers the pole to the crowd. At first everyone hesitates and is reluctant to step forward, but at last two or three volunteer to give it a try. They cannot hold the pole steady, and they soon lose control of the buoy line. Everyone is laughing.

Meanwhile, in the adjoining tank, a lone fish that resembles nothing so much as a thin silver streak moves stealthily through its enclosed space. . . .

I STOOD LOOKING BLANKLY at the spectacle as it unfolded before me. Each enclosure offered its own show, and as I stood on the platform, I let my eyes move from one compartment to the next. . . .

But how could I have found the aquarium even the least bit interesting?

Yes, I was willing to concede the setting engendered a feeling of what one might call peace of mind, but was there anything indicative of a deeper, inner fulfillment? Was there anything that penetrated to the core of one's being and sought to fill its empty cracks? No, absolutely not. There was nothing like that.

The flawless sky . . . the fish bursting with the boundless energy of their oily flesh and flesh alone . . . the sightseers detoxified and made picture perfect . . . all of them were elements in a still life that had come together in a highly serendipitous arrangement. Given the perfect symmetry of the setting and the air of happy mutuality that enveloped it, everyone felt transformed somehow, and in the process each and every one of us had lost sight of our usual, workaday selves. Suddenly everyone forgot how dumb he or she could be or ceased to recall the contrary and asinine ways in which we often behaved. For a brief instant, we saw ourselves as very different from the way we really were. We led charmed lives, our senses lulled by the sight of ourselves as we wished to be.

But look at the strange and laughable creatures we were! Be it Sanji, or Obiko, or the khaki-colored crowds on the railway platforms, or the passengers on the train, or even myself. Once I began to see how silly people looked, there was no limit to how preposterous we appeared. Not one of us was acting particularly eccentric or bizarre, or even inscrutable, yet there we were, looking strange and abnormal as could be. Moreover, that I should see such plain and ordinary people as ourselves look so peculiar struck me as yet another odd and ironic touch.

Why was it that in the season of "Mars' Song" the shadows we cast across the face of the earth were off-center, and they no longer fell into their proper places? It was as though we had become the poorly magnified subjects in a great lantern-slide show where the light from the projector had grown too dim and cloudy, even murky; and as a result, our images had gotten distorted and bent out of shape.

What was missing? What was needed to set people straight again? To make them pure, precise, strong, and beautiful once more? Back at the boatkeeper's stand I had identified autumn as the source of the seasonal change taking place around me. Here too, standing on the rise overlooking the aquarium, I felt as though I were in the presence of something very real that ought to be clearly identifiable. Yet as I stood before it and tried to define it, my mind became confused and muddled. I grew nervous and restless. I was unable to maintain my usual sense of composure.

But, presently, it came to me. Albeit belatedly, but with a quiet persistence, it filled my being down to the tiniest crack.

I felt the full measure of my dimwittedness. How dumb of me to have taken so long to guess. How stupid of me to have marked so much time in the face of something so patently obvious. I felt terribly ashamed of myself. My face was bright red.

A philosophy. A worldview.

Ah, ah . . . that's what was missing. A worldview. My throat went dry and began to burn. I perceived I was not alone in my thirst. My parched throat participated in a far greater thirst.

I climbed down from the observation deck.

Alongside the fish enclosures was a two-story, Japanese-style pavilion. A part of the downstairs had been transformed into a Western-style café. Wood flooring had been installed, and tables and chairs set out on the floor. The café was open to the outside, and souvenir and postcard stands had been set up under the eaves of the pavilion.

A bridge extended ramplike to a tank that housed the porpoises. It appeared the porpoises were a popular attraction, and a crowd had gathered to watch.

A porpoise stuck its head out of the water. It had two small nostrils at the tip of its slick and smoothly rounded nose. When it snorted, the valvelike lids at the apertures opened and closed.

When the keeper tossed it food, the porpoise dove to the bottom of the tank and skillfully caught the fish in its mouth. It looked ever so much like a military police dog in training. I became more and more disgusted as I watched. There was something asinine, even mildly obscene, about the stunt—as when a stray dog lies down on its back and, pawing the air with its feet, reveals the spotted underside of its belly.

I headed for the café and, sitting down, asked the waiter to bring a beer to my table.

Just then a rowdy party of four or five people came barging in. They sat at a table on the opposite side of the room. They began to talk in loud voices and, all at once . . .

Ah, ah . . . what in hell are they shouting about?

Not the same old story here too?!?

In one corner of the room was an old-fashioned gramophone with a horn. The waiter had put on a record and was cranking the machine.

Ah, ah . . . what in hell does he think he's doing?

"Turn it off!"

My voice was virtually a snarl, and it seemed to echo angrily around the room. I had thought out loud. Yes, without thinking, I had said what was on my mind: "No more 'Mars' Song'!"

The people on the far side of the room suddenly turned and glared at me. The look of sharp disapproval in their eyes was almost palpable, and it pierced me like a barbed skewer. There was no mistaking, moreover, the air of moral rectitude they assumed. It smacked of the imperious and belligerent self-righteousness that comes to those who, waiting upon power and authority, adopt its airs as their own.

I became so irritated I could no longer bear to stay where I was. I downed the last of my beer and stood up. As I headed for the exit, I felt certain I could hear the sound of a commotion in the making. Doubtless someone was pointing a finger at my back and having something to say.

MOON GEMS

≈ 1945 ≈

I

New Year's Day, 1945.

I rose early and went into the city to a certain Hachiman Shrine. I went to greet the new year and to receive a lucky arrow as a souvenir. As I stood in the crowd that had gathered at the shrine and was bathed in the light of the rising sun as it spread across the cold, windy sky, I composed a crude *kyōka* verse.

> *Though their gabled peaks*
> *Are enshrouded in the first mists*
> *Of the new year,*
> *As ever we entrust*
> *The sum of our hopes to the gods.*

I returned to my lodgings at the edge of Tokyo and propped the arrow against the wall of the *tokonoma*. It and the three branches of a holiday green that earlier I had arranged in a cheap vase became my sole concession to celebrating the new year in my otherwise drab bachelor apartment. Nursing my government ratio of saké, I yielded once more to the temptation to compose another dubious *kyōka* verse—in honor of the saké, described in fixed epithets of old as dispelling all care with the sweep of its "jeweled broom," and the *senryō,* a holiday green that, bearing its felicitous red berries in the dead of winter, is worth a "thousand *ryō.*" The poem was the best that an amateur like me could do; no doubt the great *kyōka* poets of the past would chuckle at my feeble imitation of their great Tenmei style.

Sweet elixir of the jeweled broom
And holiday green bedecked in red,
'Tis a senryō spring!
How its light pours forth, glittering
Like a thousand thin pieces of hammered gold.

My visit to the shrine and the receipt of a lucky arrow had been a matter of whimsy; and I had felt no need to celebrate simply because today was the first day of a new year. Yet I was possessed of a secret longing and wished to secure for it a propitious resolution. The desire? I am under no obligation to keep it secret: I longed to learn how to ride a bike, and the sooner the better! It was in December of last year that I conceived the idea of taking bike lessons. I was determined to proceed with my plan.

By nature I am disposed to the quick and convenient although there is nothing about my person even vaguely suggestive of agility. My hands move only to let a ball tossed gently my way fall to the ground. Let a trolley stop across the street, and my legs will not carry me the few yards to board it in time. Given this state of affairs, I must admit I had little hope of initiating any movement that might prove equal to the harsh realities of the times in which we live. My profession too is devised to eliminate the need for nimble hands and feet, and so it has been my destiny to let them be content with inactivity.

Indeed were one to seek the mathematical equivalent of this thing that is myself, it would be an exercise in the calculation of the square root of minus one. I think of myself as inhabiting not the face of the earth but rather a space one foot under, living in shame. I know I must rise and, casting off this state of ignominy, crawl out upon the ground, there to climb to the height of a single foot and make my mad dash through the reality that impinges upon all of us.

Were this longing to assume concrete form, nothing would suit my needs better than the self-propelled mechanism of a bicycle. I could manage the cost of a used one; it would require no gasoline, and it ought to be comparatively easy to operate since bikes are ridden by women and children too. What is more, the fulfillment of my wish lay readily at hand. I had only to obtain the bike and, with a contemptuous look over my shoulder at the crowds on the commuter trains, be off to negotiate the city. Moreover — the benefits are too many to enumerate here — by and by my small coup might attract a particle of attention and lead to the desired movement. . . . My heart leapt at the thought, but I had yet to master the rudiments of the vehicle.

Some time ago a friend gave me a letter of introduction to a certain corporation. He was determined to have me play a role in what he called "the vital operations of our day." His intentions were well meant, and I rejoiced at this stroke of good luck. Thinking that at last I had found a way out of the snake hole in which I lived, I set out late last year to call upon a gentleman who held an important post in the company.

It would be more correct to say that what I met was not the man but his boots. As he lounged in his chair with one leg extended casually over the other, the room was so overwhelmed by the sight of his spit-polished, oxblood red leather boots — so tight-fitting as not to show a single crease, so spanking new as to reek still of a live steer — that the man's face seemed disproportionately small and insignificant by comparison. Poor fellow. It was as though he and his face had been relegated to the rear of the room.

Admittedly, there was good reason why I might be impressed by his boots. For what I coveted second only to a bicycle was a fine pair of boots.

Need I recite the litany of their praises? When the air raid siren sounds in the middle of the night, how much simpler it would be to ease one's feet into a pair of boots rather than fumbling in the dark with puttees and getting them on inside out. Or, rather than tiptoeing in shoes along the side of a muddy street, stepping gingerly from one dry spot to the next, imagine how carefree one could be in a sturdy pair of boots! I could strut right down the center of the street. What's more, boots are essential footgear for riding a bicycle. They look smart, and one pedals better. There is no fear of brushing against an object and scraping an ankle.

It may sound odd for me to speak so extravagantly of a pair of boots when I have yet to attempt the bicycle, however. Indeed it is a bit like eating the icing without ever tasting the cake. As befits the used bike that I desire, I shall have to content myself with a pair of plain, even faded, black leather boots. . . . And even that is a fantasy I only halfheartedly believe will materialize.

Nonetheless, the man's boots had appeared on the scene to make sport of the unprepossessing pair I only dreamed of owning. There they were in front of me, solidly blocking my way. I ceased to recall what errand had brought me to the man's office in the first place. There was nothing for it but to submit to the beautiful shine of his boots, however intimidating it might be.

The résumé being examined by the face at the far end of the boots was virtually blank. I had but one line to record about myself, and it served as the sole distinction that set me apart from the ranks of the unemployed and uncouth. It was an unvarnished statement of my abilities that read, presumptuous as it may sound, "writer by trade." It did not appear to be of much help to him, however. The organization of the firm was divided, he said, into two groups — those who handled the goods and those who did the paperwork. His manner suggested he would work me into the latter category.

"No," I replied. "I'd appreciate your putting me in with those who handle your company's product. That's why I've come."

I was being completely sincere. I knew that if I worked in clerical operations, I would be forced to deal with endless scraps of paper, each printed in a blurring profusion of figures and letters. I did not want that. "Training in the service and delivery end of our firm," the man continued patiently, "begins with recruits of seventeen and eighteen years of age."

"But couldn't you let me do their job?"

No sooner had I asked than there flashed before my eyes a vision of young men dashing about the city proudly conducting company business on their bicycles! If only I had known how to ride a bicycle I might have pressed my case. But I felt a twinge of embarrassment, and it appeared to have crept into my voice. My request sounded weak.

It was then that "Boots" cut me to the core.

His tone was pleasant enough, but he emitted a crude chortle as though he pitied me. He was every inch a man dressed in boots, and he possessed a sharp, discerning eye. I should have known better than to come, but I now felt too devastated to speak. I blushed and backed out of the room.

Thus the search for a job undertaken so spuriously came to an abrupt end after only a three-minute interview. I had squandered the goodwill of a friend; I had wasted three minutes out of this man's busy day; and in seeking the favor of both and pleasing neither, I had set myself to a good deal of unnecessary trouble. I felt obliged to remonstrate with myself since this wretched state of affairs was due solely to my inability to ride a bicycle. As long as the bicycle eluded me, I was destined to fail again should I decide in an impetuous moment to crawl from my hole and seek a place for myself in the "vital operations of our day." To be found wanting in this way again would only deepen my shame and entomb me forever one foot underground. And how unhygienic that would be.

For lessons of any sort, the younger the age at which one starts, the better. And how much more so for operations requiring manual dexterity. To be quite honest, I have reached an age that can hardly be called young any-more . . . and a state in which, having started down the path that inevitably links the human life span to the course of physical time, I am helpless to reverse matters. Still, inasmuch as I can tie my obi and am still free to walk about, it is imperative that I mount a bicycle and learn to ride it without further delay.

Today, namely, New Year's Day, is the occasion of my first lesson.

To the rear of my lodgings is a small vacant lot. There, one used bike and an instructor await me. The person who has volunteered to give me lessons is a little girl who lives in the neighborhood.

"*Oji-san,* what's taking so long? Aren't you ready yet?"

I can hear her calling me from outside my window. She has called me two or three times now.

I hurry to finish my saké, and pulling on my tired puttees and worn-out canvas shoes, I rise.

In a moment such as this, who has time for comic verse?

II

Those familiar with the layout of the older, densely built-up parts of downtown Tokyo will recall how, if one followed the covers of the drainage ditches along a back alley, at the point where the alley narrowed and appeared to dead-end, often one discovered a large vacant lot. The lots could be quite extensive in size, such as the ones used by dyers to stretch panels of kimono cloth on drying frames. Today these large lots can be found only in a few neighborhoods on the edge of the city. The back lot of which I speak, while not a dyer's lot, is one of the few still left.

For quite some time it had been vacant, and it saw little human traffic except in the hot summer months when a sumo ring was improvised and the children of the neighborhood came in the evenings to practice wrestling. Thus it was a lively spot until the fall. By this time of year, however, the ring had been plowed under, and alongside the vegetable patch planted by the neighborhood patriotic association, small foxholes had been dug in the ground as bomb shelters. Fortunately, there was just enough space to practice riding a bicycle, and the plowing along the edges had the salutary effect of softening the earth so that I was unlikely to injure myself in a fall.

My lodging house was situated to the back of the east side of the lot, and a small rise overlooked the lot to the south. To the north was the alley that led to the street where the trolleys ran; to the west were the rear entrances to the seven or eight houses that ran businesses that fronted on the main street. The bicycle shop was one of them.

The shop had long since ceased to be open for customers, and its proprietor, now a civilian conscriptee, commuted each morning to an armaments plant located quite some distance away on the Chūō train line. All that remained in his shop were two used bikes. The fact that I was allowed to borrow one was due to the largess of this man who, despite his nearly fifty years, looked healthier and heavier — does one dare ask why? — than the rest of us. Although the bike might be better described as dilapidated than used, on account of its age and rickety condition, that lowered the price and made it a sensible purchase for a beginner like myself. The owner and I agreed that, once I had mastered the bike, he would let it go — "at a special discount" — for monthly installments of ten yen. I could not have asked for a better bargain. Besides, he had a daughter, age fifteen; it is she who has volunteered to take me on as her pupil.

A spiteful person, seeking to find fault with this innocent and soft-limbed child, might possibly detect that her left leg appeared to be a fraction shorter than her right. In fact, "lame" was what some boors in the neighborhood called her, and that explained for them why she had not been impressed into service in the civilian girls' work corps.

Yet her handicap was not so great as her detractors suggested.

Admittedly, she dragged her left foot a bit when she attempted to move in a hurry, but under normal circumstances the limp was scarcely noticeable, and it did not seem to bother her in the least. To the contrary, once she mounted the bicycle, which was her natural forte, she would throw her hands in the air, and like a cherry petal fluttering upon the breeze, she would go round and round in circles, cutting an arc on the ground that grew progressively smaller. She possessed the fundamental and unquestioned poise of an equestrienne. Indeed anyone who has ever had the opportunity to observe the girl as she rode her bike will surely agree it constituted her true set of legs.

A description of the events of my first lesson on New Year's Day brings no honor to my name. There is no question that the girl's instruction was thorough and without fault. But since I was new to the task, I spent much of my time sprawled on the ground rather than mounted on the seat of the bike. The vehicle disdained me as a clumsy beginner, and no matter how often I rose undaunted by a spill — or how much I attempted, first, to mollify the bicycle or, growing impatient, to conquer it by force — it dumped me on the ground like so much unwanted furniture. I found myself at a loss to know how to deal with its stubborn frame, and though I begged and cajoled, it remained unmoved and would not yield to my entreaties. I perspired. My clothes got muddied. The palms of my hands became scratched and cut. At times I collapsed on the ground as I struggled to catch my breath. And, as if that were only the beginning of my torment, there came children who, gathering from every quarter of the neighborhood, formed a circle around me and the bike. They watched, talking and laughing noisily all the while.

There were so many that one wondered where they had been hiding until now. A Frenchman whom I once knew would throw his hands into the air and shout, "*Des gosses, des gosses,*" when exclaiming at the endless hordes of children who descended upon him wherever he traveled in Japan.

Likewise, on this day a great number appeared even though it had already been arranged for many of the children in the neighborhood to be evacuated to the countryside. I did not welcome the sight of them. It was bad enough to be the object of their attention, but the final blow came when the little girl on whom I relied as my teacher suddenly joined their ranks and, gleefully clapping her hands, laughed at the sight I was making of myself. She grabbed the bike, and letting her foot glide over the crossbar, she began to ride. In her hands the old, recalcitrant machine appeared to breathe new life, and it went round and round just as she directed. I lifted my weary body from the ground and brushed the dirt from my clothes.

"Enough for today. Enough, enough. . . . "

I persevered with the lessons, nevertheless. I went to practice in the back lot whenever weather permitted. Still, I made no progress, and I had no good news to report. I remained as clumsy as ever. Likewise, the bicycle continued to make sport of me. At least I had mastered the art of falling off without injury, and I suffered less.

As for the children, they no longer rushed to the lot to watch. The weather had turned cold, and their interest waned. Occasionally, the mother or father of one of them passed through the lot, but the adults were always in a hurry, and they gave no heed to my lessons. The little girl was ever so patient in teaching me the fundamentals of her art, but since she was under no obligation to stay continually by my side, I spent many hours struggling with the bicycle by myself.

Confronted alone, it assumed a monstrous and almost lethal air. As I spat dirt from my mouth, I knew I was engaged in a terrible life-and-death struggle. I had long since ceased to understand why I had chosen to spend an hour of every waking day with it or what purpose originally I had in mind in imposing this task upon myself. What I knew was the hour had encroached upon my life, pushing its way into the time I had once spent comfortably sleeping, my legs spread wide upon my bed. Now here I was, riding a bicycle that propelled me in the direction of violent, almost murderous action. It obsessed me, and forgetting all else, I rode until I fell to the ground utterly exhausted.

Ludicrous as my behavior may have seemed to an outsider, the back lot was a quiet place removed from the clamor of the world, and I felt little embarrassment in practicing there. Although the cliff to the south of the lot served as a shortcut through the neighborhood, now that it was winter the north wind whipped across it, and few darkened the path where withered bamboo grass clung as best it could to the frozen and exposed earth. No one, that is, except an old man who passed along the top of the cliff from time to time.

Though I say old, there was nothing remotely aged about the man. He was tall; his back, straight; and a soft black felt hat made his silky white hair seem almost youthful. He wore a great black frock coat over a suit of imported black tweed of the sort that had been available in Japan before the start of the war. On his feet, however, were a pair of low clogs that looked terribly worn. Sometimes he carried an umbrella or a leather Kodak bag as he walked at a brisk clip and cut through the dry leaves of the bamboo grass. For the moment, let me identify this gentleman as, simply, Mr. Gūka, "the Lotus."

Gūka is a poet of great renown. His residence is located five or six blocks away, at the end of a quiet lane. He calls it "Liaison House." Even the most common of men, who may know nothing of what Gūka has accomplished in poetry in the last few decades, have heard rumors about the Parnassian existence of the Master of Liaison House — of how, loath to waste even a word of vituperation upon the sleazy claims of our society, he has sealed his gates and refused categorically the traffic of the mundane. I too rank among the common lot who have heard them. Lacking any true profession, I have maintained appearances by proclaiming myself a "writer by trade," but all that I have authored is of questionable value, totally and completely; and since I am congenitally given to laziness and am no more than an impoverished dilettante, too indolent to rouse myself for a trip to the library to peruse a copy of Gūka's *Complete Works,* I have been content with only a secondhand acquaintance with his accomplishments. As the world would have it, the Lotus lives alone and is said to be engaged in the composition of a work that he chooses to keep from all eyes. He handles all of his daily chores, and on the occasion when some philistine dares to wander through the front gate and trespass upon the front yard, it is Gūka who goes to the door and sends him away with the words "The Lotus is not at home."

If indeed this is his wont, I would not presume to peek through the trellis or tread the perilous space before his door, even though I live nearby;

nor have I the curiosity. Whenever he has come my way on the street, I have expressed my respect inwardly. I have never taken the liberty of addressing him or been so frivolous as to doff my cap. Because we have never met and he passes by the lot on his constitutionals unmindful of my lessons at the bottom of the cliff, likewise I have continued to ride my bike with blithesome disregard for whatever his opinions in the matter might be.

One matter troubles me, however. And it relates not to Gūka's poetry, but to his clogs. I have heard that in better times he paid meticulous attention to the details of his dress and insisted on the rule that clogs be worn only with kimono. It is not clear at what point in the chronology of his career there was a switch and he began wearing clogs with Western attire, but my random guess is that the innovation is of recent origin and it is indicative of a sudden increase in Gūka's spiritual energies. As the color of his suit of clothes faded and the clogs became chewed and worn, he began to move forward — in the area of literature to be sure — at a pace equal to the speed of light. At first the combination of a suit and clogs belonged to the realm of eccentric dress, and no doubt the world has had its laugh at his expense, but today fashion runs far behind him, breathless in an effort to catch up with the leisurely pace of Gūka's clogs. How true it is that one can never be too vigilant, especially given the speed with which poets advance.

But as for myself, his junior, I run even farther behind a world that can scarcely keep up with Gūka. I have only begun to take bicycle lessons and to approach distantly the mastery already achieved by a child of fifteen. I feel profoundly ashamed of myself.

And yet, although there is virtually no connection between my life and Gūka's, one could perhaps claim that the relationship between his clogs and my bicycle is not entirely tenuous. The course that he has run in a decade I must compress into a few hours.

There is a Chinese maxim to the effect that cold and impoverishment make a man brilliant and agile. As for being cold and poor, there is no question: I am second to none. But when it comes to brilliance or agility, I have no confidence whatsoever. . . . Were there a saying that cold and impoverishment make a man weary and dumb, how appropriate it would be for me!

As I stood at the foot of the cliff and gazed up at Gūka, was it merely false pride or a sheer inability to admit defeat that prompted me to say to myself, "Damn you, Gūka"? From time to time I have raised my eyes and studied the face of the Master of Liaison House. Was it an illusion? Did I not see him stop and take a look at me? Perhaps a link exists between us after all.

Yet, while his clogs fly across the face of the earth like the eight swift stallions of Emperor Mu of the Chou, I have yet to succeed in using my bike to describe a circle a yard wide on the ground. To close the gap between us, I needed to extemporize, and in my limited way, I had conceived a plan of action. It was exceedingly simple: a regimen of deep breathing exercises in the morning.

On the days when I woke early, I went outside at dawn and aerated my lungs. The little girl was still asleep, and Gūka had yet to appear. I alone possessed the back lot. The city still lay darkly frozen in the cold, predawn hour. But the clouds began to bank and swell in the early morning light to the east, and like a body warming itself from its inner core, they turned a bright, flaming red and began to roll across the sky. Catching the wind as it whipped into my face, I threw out my chest and took a deep breath.

From the distant sky, at a point where the first rays of the sun separated the land from the darkness, there arose three stripes—one blue, one white, and one red. They resembled neither wind nor light, and like a powerful life force—some strange constellation of *ch'i*—they let their colors dance and entwine as they raced across the sky. And, like the shards of a rainbow that had been flung across the horizon, they took deliberate aim and poured into my mouth. No sooner had their cold seared my tongue and entered my lungs than my body became cool, and the impatience and irritation within me seemed to issue from the soles of my feet and disappear. This is what is known in the Chinese art of wizardry as the rule of *t'ai-su nei-ching,* or the Inner Spirit of the Primordial Element. And what had I gained? My body became lighter, which is a most convenient state for a cyclist. For a novice like me, who is unschooled in the secret arts of Taoism, the experience lasted only a matter of seconds. Yet in the brief moment in which it occurred, I had set my sextant, so to speak, and by getting a fix on their parameters, I was able to gauge not only how Gūka made his mad dash through terrestrial time but also the élan with which the little girl rode a bike.

Chance yielded another discovery. I happened upon the practice of riding the bicycle late at night.

These were the hours when the world lay asleep, although it was hardly a day and age when people's heads rested heavily on their pillows. When the sirens wailed, I, like everyone else, kicked back the covers and jumped up, pulling on my puttees in the dark (inside out, no doubt). Rushing outside with fire ax in hand, I would crack the ice in the rainwater barrels. But if by chance the air raid ended without mishap, instead of crawling into bed again, I chose to stay up and practice riding the bike. Somehow or other, I seemed to do better, and I would deceive myself into thinking that, having practiced for fifteen minutes at night, I had compensated for an hour of wasted effort during the day.

Still, one needed moonlight to practice, and for the first time I discovered how bright the moon can be. There is a famous *kyōka* verse in which the poet Ōta Nanpo suggests that a person "dare not ask more" *(mōshikane)* of life than a full rice bowl and a moonlit night — only to add, in a facetious double entendre, that "maybe more money" *(mōshi kane)* might be something else worth asking for. But, however welcome extra cash might have been, surely there was not a soul living in wartime who was not grateful first and foremost for a full bowl of rice and the moon at night. Food was scarce, and houses were blacked out early in the evening. The darkness was so thick that one stumbled in an air raid to find a foxhole.

One night, after awakening from a brief sleep, I stepped outside to find the moon had risen, and the back lot was flooded with light. The moonlight seemed to have rejuvenated the old bike somehow. Even the places where the black paint had chipped away from the metal glowed with the look of the original lacquer. And the frame possessed a sturdiness that it had lacked until now. The chrome fixtures looked more solid, and while they shone with an iciness that looked cold enough to freeze and snag off a finger, a jewellike sparkle danced about the grips where the moonlight fell across the handlebars. Grasping at the light, I climbed aboard and let myself slip onto the saddle.

As I rode, the wheels of the bike streamed round and round like sprays of water circulating in a fountain. They spun and gained momentum until before long I began to wonder where the bike would carry me. Oh, ancient and iridescent stones that glow in the darkest of nights! Oh, gems of the moon! How rare you are! And how difficult to obtain! The clusters of jewels that filled the small hollow of my hands amounted to nothing more than beams of moonlight that danced about the handlebars. How wonderful it would feel to master the bicycle . . . at least half as well as the little girl . . . faster . . . one fraction of a second faster . . . it has been misery struggling with you, bicycle . . . let me ride smoothly, gracefully, naturally . . . we are no longer here . . . it is long, long ago . . . once upon a time . . . a poet from the West was saying . . . long before anyone else . . . *"Nothing is more likely to propel us headlong down the path to barbarism than a single-minded obsession with spiritual purity. . . . "*

"*Oji-san,* hold on. Hold on tight."

To my surprise, my instructor had come into the lot and was calling to me from behind. She urged me to keep going. I felt so confident. Going round and round . . . round and round . . . unless one hand loses its balance . . . no, no. . . . I fell to the ground with a thud.

III

We had far more snow this year; seldom was a winter so bitterly cold. Moreover, the number of air raids was greater than ever, and the heavens were often enveloped in flames. My determination notwithstanding, it was simply not possible to continue with my lessons each night.

January and February came and went, and by the beginning of March, I had grown accustomed to riding the bike. Physical object that it was, still, it came to treat me with consideration. Even if I had not reached the point where I could ride with no hands, as long as I maintained my balance, I managed to stay on board for nearly an hour.

Besides, the bike was in the process of becoming my own. I had spoken with the bicycle man, and per our earlier agreement, it would be mine for monthly installments of ten yen. I made my first payment at the beginning of March. According to him, I also needed to pay an additional ten yen each month for maintenance—a sure indication of how antiquated the bicycle was. But it was the only conveyance I possessed, and I dared not suggest it might not be worth the additional charge.

One night during the first part of March, the wind blew hard as the hour grew late, and at the height of the gale, the air raid sirens began to whir. Everyone in the neighborhood was immediately up and out of bed. We had come to cultivate a sixth sense about air raids, and this did not seem to be a typical drill. A crowd had gathered by the time I reached the lot, and people were hard at work in anticipation that we would be under attack. Belongings were carried to the small air raid shelters and piled in a heap. The radio crackled in the driving wind. A fire hose had been stretched across the ground; a hand pump was at the ready.

The horizon turned bright red in the direction of the downtown section of the city closest to us, and as we watched, the fire spread rapidly in our direction. We could see it burning madly out of control as the wind picked up and fanned the flames. Nor were the flames confined to downtown Tokyo. Soon pockets of fire broke out to the right and left of us. The sky lit up, illuminated by an ominously bright light that made the faces of those of us who had gathered at the vacant lot and even the color of our clothes stand out clear as day. Sparks fell from the sky and twirled about our heads.

I walked back to the rear door of my lodging house, where I usually parked my bicycle, and stood ready to defend the building. The fire buckets were filled with water. I had no family heirlooms to remove from my room. Besides, I assured myself, the fires that had broken out nearby would not spread within our reach. Preventive measures would work, and the flames would be confined to a limited area. Still, it was premature to relax one's guard.

Suddenly I realized the little girl was standing beside me. She had stolen up from behind, and leaning on the seat, she let the bike press against my side. She said nothing as she looked deep into the sky. She seemed unafraid, but what vague foreboding caused her shoulders to tremble ever so slightly? It was then that I understood for the first time what it meant for her to have a foot that was not entirely normal. She was no longer the little girl who rode a bicycle with the greatest of ease. She was a young lady who would go through life handicapped, sadly enough, by a bad leg.

I forgot my usual ineptitude and resolved then and there that, should a crisis arise, I was prepared to sacrifice to the flames the one and only set of possessions that I had in this world, namely, the collection of old and rare books that I kept in my apartment. To save this child, I would put her on my bicycle and ride to the ends of the earth.

Fortunately, it was not necessary for me to carry out my resolve that night. The fires in the vicinity had gone out by daybreak, and our quarter had not reported a single casualty. Moreover, that the color of the sky over the downtown sections of the city gradually paled and faded away was not due solely to the dawning of a new day. The flames had died down just about everywhere. I heaved a sigh of relief at the thought that the people fighting the flames had been victorious in their efforts.

"We've won, *Oji-san,* we've won! I promise I'll give you another lesson," shouted the little girl as she ran toward her house. Her step was smooth and self-assured; she had reverted to being the little acrobat of the bicycle.

"What's this?" I thought to myself. "Doesn't she realize how worried I was about her?" She had already turned her back toward me as I threw my hands into the air and offered her a silent blessing. One wanted no less than to wish her well.

"Yes, we've won. I'll ask for your help again soon."

I returned to my room and collapsed on the floor. I had not meant to fall asleep, but it was nearly noon when I awoke. The neighborhood seemed changed. The sky had cleared, but something in the air made one feel irritable and nervous. The relief I had felt at daybreak had disappeared, and an inde-scribable feeling of anxiety swept over me. I could not bear to sit still, and leaving the house, I grabbed the bike. On its own accord it headed in the direction of the city and the shrine I had visited on New Year's Day.

This was my first excursion. Never would I have believed it would happen on a day like this, and lost in thought, I sped along untroubled by the mechanics of operating the bike or the fact that I was madly pedaling away in an old pair of canvas shoes.

I still had not obtained a pair of boots. Perhaps it was for the best. That would have meant the fulfillment of all of my dreams, and I would not have known what to do with myself.

Presently I found myself in the vicinity of the shrine. I cannot remember the details of what I saw there or along the way. Nor would I have wished to. The shrine had been obliterated.

This was no time for *kyōka*. Indeed, there never again will be an occasion when the shrine might be described in comic verse or anything else.

I hurriedly retraced the route by which I had come. As I entered the lodging house, I realized my clothes were covered with a thick layer of gray dust. I grabbed a brush, and standing in the doorway, I beat the ash from my shoulders. I choked on the odor that filled the air.

A scene floated before my eyes. It was not the one I had witnessed on the road to the center of the city. It was from a passage I read a long time ago in a book . . . a description of the cremation grounds at Toribeno in Kyoto. Larks danced in the sky, and the sun shone brightly in the springtime, but columns of smoke drifted slowly from the pyres in the fields, and an acrid smell hovered over the grasses and mingled with the shimmering heat. That was the smell that had permeated my clothing. I stopped, and letting the brush hang idly by my side, I fell into a wooden silence. My sadness knew no bounds.

I became anxious about the welfare of Mr. Gūka and his mansion. On the way to the city I had passed the street that ran behind his house. Relieved to see everything in order, I had not troubled myself about his welfare. But hadn't flames shot up the previous night from the area where he lived? From the rear the property may have appeared to be safe, but wasn't it possible the front had been hit? I turned and started out again, this time on foot. I climbed the path running from the back lot to the top of the cliff and took the shortcut through the adjoining neighborhoods. My feet hurried along only to come to a grinding halt. The quarter visible from the top of the cliff, the section where Gūka's mansion was located, had been leveled.

Night had begun to fall, and the dull light of the sun made the whole area look like the bottom of a ravine. Here and there victims of the air raid had fire hooks, and they were turning over the smoldering ashes in an effort to salvage what they could. There was no sign of Gūka.

An elderly woman was sifting through the rubble that lay behind Gūka's mansion. From time to time she looked up, as though she were aware of the presence of someone standing absentmindedly nearby. Eventually she approached me, and as though inviting an explanation, she studied my face in silence.

"This was Mr. Gūka's residence, wasn't it?" I said.

"Yes, it was. As you can see, it burned to the ground."

"What happened to Mr. Gūka? . . ."

"He's safe. He escaped in time."

"I see. And his belongings? . . ." No sooner had I asked than I was embarrassed at the frivolousness of my question.

The old woman's reply was firm, as though to emphasize her point.

"No, Mr. Gūka was not the type to bother with possessions. This section of the neighborhood was the last to burn, but even if there had been time, he was not likely to have bothered. He carried out a manuscript wrapped in a cloth bundle, and that was it. He walked to the small rise across the way, and he stood there and watched the house burn. Yes, he stood there until it burned to the ground. Until about dawn. He watched it to the end."

I knew nothing of the old woman, but I found the matter-of-fact way in which she described the fire both forthright and refreshingly different. At the same time, her reply reinforced my feeling that I had asked a question that was utterly irrelevant. There was nothing more for me to say.

"Someone came for him early in the morning. I'm a neighbor, and I have known Mr. Gūka for many years. He lived alone, you know, and is a quiet, retiring sort. When he finally got ready to leave, there was a little bread in the house, and since I know he is partial to bread, and I even had a little butter, I gave it to him. He was delighted. I expect he'll be back tomorrow."

My mind was no longer concentrating on what the old woman said. Instead, there rose before me the vision of a man stripped of everything but his manuscript, standing on a rise, blown by intemperate winds, and bathed in a shower of sparks, as he quietly watched his house collapse in flames. I sought to capture and keep within me this vision of a great poet, weary with age but undaunted by time.

If a man draws a bow, let him draw it boldly. The bow that Gūka has drawn in the belles lettres of our day is no ordinary one.

I thanked the old woman as I turned to leave.

I went to the vacant lot that evening, and wiping my bike clean of the dust that had collected on it from earlier in the day, I gave it a polishing. The hour was still early, but the neighborhood seemed quieter than usual. People had turned off the lights in their houses and closed out the world. It appeared the little girl would not be joining me tonight. The heat of the flames that had ravaged the city hung in the air, but the moon rose in the sky, bathing the back lot in a cool, white light.

The mad winds had ceased to blow. The days were getting warmer. Had life been otherwise, we would have counted the days until the cherries blossomed. Polishing the bike bolstered my spirits, and I composed in my mind a *kyōka* that I titled "Love Song for a Bicycle."

Although there was no reason why the bike should have responded to a good polishing, after working at length, I found it began to emit a small shine. Perhaps it was the brightness of the moon. Instead of parking the bike under the eaves once I had finished my work, I straddled the seat and began to glide about the lot. In a single breath I went round the lot five or six times, cutting a sweeping arc across the earth.

My movements were light and supple, or just as I felt after I did my deep breathing exercises in the mornings. Finally, I had got the hang of it.

To tell the truth, my infatuation with the bicycle has begun to wane a bit, even as the bike is about to become my own.

Were someone to express a genuine desire for an old, used bike, I would be ready to make a present of it.

THE LEGEND OF GOLD

≈ 1946 ≈

"Now I ask you, sir. How can people expect to be served white rice in times like these? There's none to be had no matter where you look. Besides, I wouldn't serve it even if I did have it on hand. It wouldn't feel right if I did. Yes, I know. The Chinaman across the street has got white rice. He's got it, and he doesn't think twice about offering it to his customers. You name it, he'll serve it. Vegetables over rice. Meat with rice. A bowl of steamed rice to go with the main dish. But not at this shop. No, sir, I'm sorry, but we can't do that for you.

"So just what is it that *we* can do? I knew you'd want to ask. Well, it's not much. As you can see, this is about the best we have to offer. How about. . . ?"

With that, what came sailing over the top of the counter but a plate with slices of white bread on it. Out came a cup of coffee with cream and sugar. There was a piece of custard cake with bits of ham baked into it. And a plate piled with doughnuts made with real egg yolks. Take any one of them — the bread, the coffee, the cake, the doughnuts — there was not a single item that you'd find served just anywhere these days. In the world in which we live, they are all as rare and hard to come by as a bowl of freshly steamed white rice. You'd think people would be grateful. . . .

But for so long have the inhabitants of this island worshiped the god of rice and offered the firstfruits of every harvest at his altar that even now, when times have changed and his intermediary here on earth has been separated like chaff from the grain and driven out as an impostor, still nothing, but nothing, has been able to dislodge white rice from its time-honored position in the popular mind. It has retained its uncanny sticking power in the psychology of everyday life, silently holding sway over the heart and mind of each and every citizen. Indeed so dark and mysterious is its hold that to want something else — be it bread, or cake, or doughnuts—is to violate an unspoken taboo. Yes, there is a silent malediction that puts a curse on anything seeking to take its place.

Small wonder, then, that the heart and mind of this sensible business-woman should be troubled at the thought of having stricken rice from the list of dishes she has to offer her customers. She knew she could brag all she wanted about white bread and black coffee, but in the end, if she did not serve rice, her words sounded like just so much hot air. Such was her logic. It explained her windy disclaimer as well as the touch of false modesty that prefaced each plate as she passed it across the counter to her customers.

SUCH IS THE STORY at this spot here in Yokohama. It is late in December of nineteen hundred and forty-five, and the restaurant stands, like its numerous counterparts, in the middle of the ruins of a bombed and burnt-out city. The shop is a shack made out of sheets of corrugated metal that have been hastily slapped together. The customers shuffle in, pale shadows of their former selves, their figures moving along the wall like the silhouettes of people living in caves who hover over the flickering light of a small fire. We are packed together, all seated in a row and pressed so close that it is virtually impossible to tell one customer from the next. Everyone is silent, our hands and mouths moving noiselessly as we eat. I too number among the cast of shadow figures performing in this silent motion picture. I sit at the far end of the counter, perched precariously on an unstable and makeshift stool. Lighting a cigarette, I seek to enjoy a brief moment of rest.

FOR A MOMENT'S REST is a rare commodity in life amidst the ruins. I know, because some months ago I was burned out of my apartment in Tokyo, and I have been on my feet ever since. I have had to keep moving, and in the process I have spent much of my time standing. Quite literally, I had been standing on trains for seemingly months on end, caught as I was between the hordes of people relocating from one part of the country to the next and the mountains of luggage that they brought on board and piled in the aisles. Like everyone else, I have been hard-pressed to find a square inch in which to breathe, let alone stand. Indeed I have been jettisoned about the country without so much as a chance to sit down and catch my breath.

Such was the case at a little past noon last August 15, when, far from Tokyo, I stood in the aisle of an overcrowded train headed for Toyama. Just as the train cut through the Kurikara Pass [itself the sight of a bloody rout long, long ago], a rumor began to circulate among the passengers, and I learned for the first time that an important broadcast had been made only moments earlier. Suddenly an elderly gent who was standing in the aisle ahead of me lost his balance and let the large gunny sack slung over his back shift and come flying my way. Indeed he had been swaying precariously under the not inconsiderable weight of the sack for some time now, and it was only a matter of when the load would shift and he would lose control of it. The sack hit me square in the chest. It made a thudlike sound, and with that, the watch that I carried in my breast pocket stopped, the time it kept having now ground to a crashing halt.

Of course, if the truth be told, my watch had never been quite right since the night of the bombing raid when I was burned out of my apartment in Tokyo. I had pretended to myself that it worked, and I had kept it running by carefully winding it three times a day without fail. Yet with this latest blow, the watch grew increasingly temperamental. Even an additional winding each day did not suffice to keep it from hesitating. Yes, I admit, there were even times when, in order to extract its compliance and to get its hands moving again, I went so far as to take it out of my pocket and give it a good shaking.

But what of it? It appears that everyone's watch is broken nowadays, there being nowhere to turn to find the standard by which to tell the correct time. Consequently, I have taken to setting my watch via a process of, first, scrutinizing the weather outside and, then, comparing it with the physical state I happen to be in at the moment. Depending on what I find, I have advanced the hands on the watch or set them back, according to whatever seems appropriate. I have not felt it was wrong for me casually to set them at random, telling myself, "Why, this feels about right." In short, given the conditions under which we live at the moment, a broad and generous approximation has been my answer to the question of how to determine the hour of each passing day. That's right — my solution has been a kind of formula in which I let the course of my own inner chemistry define the parameters of physical time.

In the days and weeks that have come and gone in the wake of August 15, this eccentric watch has been my sole companion. Unreliable as it may be, it has kept me company; and I have reciprocated by keeping it safely tucked inside my breast pocket as I have dashed about the country, from one part to the next. I traveled to all of Hokuriku, and to Kinki, and even to Shikoku.

Everything was in ruins, no matter where I went. It was a terrible sight, yet the more I saw of the destruction, the less it pained me to know I had joined the ranks of those who, by virtue of having been burned out of their houses, had become the homeless and disenfranchised of society. As a matter of fact, I had ceased to think at all about what people meant when they spoke of someone like myself as a displaced person. Indeed so total was my loss that I no longer knew who I was or what I had once been, when it came time to recall events of the not so distant past, or how I had felt or reacted at the time. I found that I had no memory of them. They might as well have belonged to another — perhaps previous — lifetime, for that is how remote they had become in terms of my present circumstances.

That is because in the season and landscape that are total destruction, time and place stretch forth like an endlessly flat and unvarying plain. Indeed it is as though the very meaning of change was lost, and like a river that bears no water, one ceased to know of the variety that comes in life from alternating waves of joy and sadness. Everything had become a flat, dry riverbed. Such was the state of my life, and in that static and unchanging condition, I was like a flake of ash that had fallen from a burning ember. When the wind blew, I scurried. Whipped by its force and driven from one place to the next, I drifted. From Toyama I headed to Fukui. From Fukui I moved to Tokushima.

At no stop along the way was there a train station left intact. The buildings had been blown away in the bombing raids; only the tracks remained. The station platforms had been leveled to the same flat surface of the adjoining streets. And each time I saw a locomotive lumber in — the cars top-heavy with their load of passengers, the train swaying from side to side as it slowed to stop and take on still more people — I would gasp at the sight of it and want to sink into the ground beneath me. So exhausted was I that the thought of standing up on yet another train was more than I could bear. But in that instant — in the crucial second when it was time to rush forward and climb aboard, or otherwise be left behind — what kept me among the living and made my feet move across the face of the earth was something no more profound than the sound of my watch, which, functioning however badly out of sync, still counted the time of this world, its insistent tick-tick-tick sounding ever so much like an admonition to stick to life and not give up. . . .

Now, IF I AM TO TELL YOU why I was so rootless and given to running about the country, moving hither and yon, then I shall have to confess to being a man possessed of three secret desires, none of which I have revealed to anyone before.

The first concerns the watch of which I have already spoken.

By birth I am a person whose physical health has not always been the most reliable, and it has had its moments of being erratic and unpredictable. Accordingly, it has not always been wise, or even convenient, for me to rely upon the state of my health as the sole, or best, indicator of whatever information one might require in order to determine the correct time of day. Consequently, I thought I might be better off to locate a dependable repairman in some remote corner of the land and have him fix my watch. That way I would be free to rely on my watch, and that would save me at least the trouble of taking it out of my pocket every now and then to give it a good shaking. This was the first of the three wishes I hoped to fulfill.

As for the second, it concerns the matter of a hat. Because I had been foolish enough to let my favorite black felt go up in flames the night that my apartment in Tokyo burned, I ended up wearing what I had worn the night of the air raid, namely, the army cap that I happened to have on my head at the time. The cap was all that was left to me in the way of a hat, and as to the spectacle I made of myself as I went about in such strange-looking gear, I cannot begin to guess. But I could hardly bear the thought of having to go about dressed in something so totally odd and inappropriate. I thought how nice it would be were I to locate a shop where a sporty touring cap or, better yet, a real hat with an indented crown and a brim was for sale. In short, what I wanted was the kind of hat worn by a real human being. That was my second wish.

As for the third, I am almost too embarrassed to mention it. I say embarrassed because it concerns my feelings for a certain woman who had been the object of a not inconsiderable infatuation on my part. I had meant to tell her of my feelings, but alas, I had allowed far too much time to slip by, and I had never summoned the courage to tell her straight out how strongly I felt. Moreover, by not having spoken up, I never learned how she felt about me. I have continued to live in total ignorance as to the status of our relationship. As a matter of fact, it would be safe to say that my longstanding desire for her has been no more fixed or any more predictable than the continually precarious state of my physical health.

Nonetheless, word reached me that, although her house had burned in the air raids and her husband had died in the war, she herself managed to come through unscathed. Moreover, I learned she had left Tokyo to seek refuge with relatives who lived somewhere in the western part of Japan. That was all I knew, and that was why I set forth to scour the countryside — from Hokuriku to Kinki to Shikoku — searching in vain to find her. Without so much as a real clue as to her whereabouts, I traveled from one prefecture to the next, calling at places where she was reputed to have family. Come what may, I simply had to know what became of her. That was my third wish.

Still, I have yet to see the realization of even one of my three dreams, however modest they may be. To the contrary, all of my best intentions appear to have gone astray. Take the case of the watch. I would have sent it out and had it fixed, but if one is not careful these days, he may very well find his watch has been returned as repaired, but only after all of the works inside have been replaced with inferior parts. That is because the task of finding a reliable repairman in today's world is not unlike that of finding a truly honest man. Indeed it may well be as difficult, if not impossible.

Or take the case of the hat. Go to a haberdasher's shop in any part of the country these days, and it will be only too happy to supply you with a military cap. For that's all they have. In today's world, obtaining a hat worthy of a real human being is not unlike trying to find a man with a real head on his shoulders. Like the watch, the matter of finding an appropriate hat for my head was a problem that would not be amenable to an easy solution.

And as for the all-important issue of the woman who was missing from my life, what did I have to say for myself? She seemed to have disappeared without a trace. Was it that she had gone into hiding somewhere, and she was secretly avoiding me? No matter how earnestly I tried or how frantically I raced about the country, I had no success in locating her. As a matter of fact, I uncovered nothing — not even a clue or a fleeting glimpse caught, perhaps, as we passed in a crowd. I was like a man grasping for straws, the scintilla of my hopes gone, so that after three, going on four months of being on the road, I remained empty-handed. With nothing to show for my troubles and convinced I would never find her, I gave up and returned to Tokyo. I was crestfallen and in despair.

Since then, I have been lodging at the house of a friend who lives on the outskirts of the city. Until some better arrangement presents itself, it is the best I can do. Perhaps the most that I can say of my current situation is that it resembles, however superficially, the circumstances once described by the great haiku poet Bashō. Returning to his humble abode in the city of Edo after one of the many pilgrimages he made deep into the countryside, he wrote, "My hermitage! No sooner have I settled in than I am ready to head for the open road."

I was back in Tokyo at last, and the first order of business lay in getting myself cleaned up. I gave my underwear a thorough laundering. I raked up a pile of pine needles, heated the bath, and doused myself from head to toe with copious buckets of scalding hot water. For what I brought back from my travels amounted to nothing more than the soot on my face and the lice that covered my body.

Yet, as I scrubbed myself clean, what called forth the fatigue that comes to a body weary from travel and that left me feeling limp and utterly spent was not the pained recognition of having been unable to fulfill even one of the three wishes on my list. Nor did the weariness arise from the disgust that I experienced at the sight of my filthy, lice-ridden body. Nor was it even the sheer physical exhaustion that had come from the overcrowding on the trains, the lack of a decent inn anywhere, or the chronic shortage of food. No, it was none of these. To the contrary, the cause lay in something altogether different.

It was a thought that came to me one day in the course of my travels. It was an insight that struck me all of a sudden, and having opened my eyes, it has weighed on my mind ever since. Indeed it is an issue so ponderous that it concerns the destiny of each and every one of us living through this moment in history. Namely, I speak of the fast one that has been pulled on us, the outrageous sleight-of-hand that has been used in the application and promotion of the so-called Concept of Guilt [and the definition thereof as the "Repentance En Masse of the Hundred Million"] that is currently being foisted on the public with regard to the events of the recent war. For surely as we live, it sits in judgment upon us all, its authority unquestioned. Indeed so rigorous and pervasive is the imposition of this concept that, irrespective of any serious discussion of guilt or innocence, the presumption is that everyone has something to hide — that, for having been party to the fray, one carries a secret scar beneath one's breeches, whether a heinous blot on one's record or a mere knick on the shins. No, no exceptions will be tolerated, and no one permitted to speak to the contrary. However blameless and free of marks upon one's person, no one shall be allowed to emerge as clean and unscathed. It is the "doings of fate" by which we are all to be scarred in the same broad stroke. Because that is what the "Concept of Guilt" has come to mean.

But at least by dousing myself in water hot enough to scald the flesh off my back and by washing away the lice and the soot, I managed to feel refreshed for the first time in months. The stiffness in my neck and shoulders, which were weary with the weight of my heavyheartedness, began to abate a bit, and a sense of well-being — even lightness — started to return. And now that I had given a bit of thought to the matter, it might very well be that I am wrong, and I err in my weighty interpretation of the so-called Concept of Guilt. For surely what most people define as guilt or sin is nothing so abstract or complex. To the contrary, for them it is something that is very concrete and easily identified. Why, come to think of it, might they not say guilt is like soot, which rains from the sky? Or like lice, which spreads from too close contact with one's neighbors? To be sure, it is something tangible, even material, so that like sacrifice in an ancient Vedic ritual, it can be bought, burnt, and offered up as a quick and easy absolution of one's sins. . . .

ONE DAY as the year was drawing to a close — yes, the day of this very morning — I set out for a walk down what remained of the streets and neighborhoods of Tokyo. Lately I have been in exceptionally good health, although I am at a loss to explain why this should be the case. My complexion has taken on more color, and I have even gained a pound or two. As a matter of fact, my health is the best it has been since I was a child and I began to remember such matters. Everything was functioning well.

My watch too has ceased to act in a temperamental fashion, and it is no longer necessary to take it out and give it a good shaking. And, as if that were not curious enough, it now suffices to wind it only three times a day.

Of course, were one to delve into the source of the new and unusually fine state of my health — or, conversely, to look back at the reasons for its poor condition in the past — wouldn't we find the difference lies in the new and powerful supply of energy that has been released inside me? Until now this energy has been a latent force that lurked within my weak and sickly constitution, but at long last it has come to the fore, and now it is asserting itself for the first time. Need I point out, moreover, that this time around its belated emergence as a source of vitality and power has nothing to do with the watch I carry in my breast pocket or any positive influence it exerts on me now that by some means or other it has managed to keep time more accurately? Clearly the cause of the change lies in something far more extraordinary. I know what I am about to say may sound very pompous and smug, but that it does is a reflection of the newly found confidence that I have gained by being able to look at matters from the vantage of hindsight. . . .

Namely, my conclusion is this: can we not say that heretofore modernity has been an understudy in the drama of history, and it has been anxiously awaiting its chance to appear on the stage? Until now it has been made to stand in the wings, unheard and unseen, its potential cloaked in the heavy curtains of possibility. As of this moment, however, suddenly there has been an opening, and it has stepped into the limelight to take its place on center stage. It is announcing to the world that "believe it or not, ladies and gentlemen, thanks to the marvelous invention known as the 'Introduction of Time,' it is possible at last to bring you all that you've been waiting for!" That was the sort of madcap scenario I had in mind. It was my answer to the question of why there had been a sudden increase in the quality of my health and well-being. Surely, it had to be the reason, or at least something very close to it.

Suddenly, everything about a city that had been familiar to me and everything about the state of my health and my life struck me as radically new and different. I strutted about the streets of Tokyo in a lighthearted mood, and when the urge came upon me to get a bite to eat, I stopped in my tracks, and taking the watch out of my breast pocket, I spun the hands on the dial and reset them at exactly twelve noon. It was as though I had become the pendulum of a clock that swung over the land and that measured its hours and minutes. Indeed were one to compare my time with the precision clocks at the observatory in Greenwich, surely he would find — would he not? — there was no significant deviation. In short, given the way things had worked out according to my new definition of time, what need had I to spend a minute more searching for a reliable watch repairman or an honest human being?

The section of Tokyo that I happened to be walking through is famous for its bookstores that specialize in old and rare books. Ever since the night when my apartment burned and I had consigned a veritable mountain of books to the flames, I had gotten away from reading and collecting the printed word. There had been any number of other things to worry about. But as time went by and my love for books began to return, I found myself gravitating once more in the direction of this section in downtown Tokyo where the used booksellers are located. Still, once I got there, I discovered there was virtually nothing I really wanted to read or buy no matter what store I entered. I was repelled in particular by the rather foul and smutty smell of some of the more inane titles currently on the market. I decided to turn down a side street and take off in the direction of a different part of town.

As I sauntered along, I came upon a corner shop selling men's haberdashery. Out in front of the store were some brand-new touring caps. My first thought was the hats were there for purposes of display, but when I inquired inside and learned they were for sale, I did not hesitate. I purchased one immediately. Quite some time had passed since I discarded the cap that I had worn in the air raids, but lacking a decent substitute, I had decided that my notion of a proper hat was satisfied, at least for the time being, by putting nothing on my head at all. Now, suddenly, a suitable replacement presented itself quite by surprise. Not only was it brand-new, but the hat fit just right,

and it looked good on me too. And though, like most everything else manufactured in this country of late, it did not represent the best in quality, still
it felt right when I picked it up and popped it on my head.

Thus it happened that two of my three wishes were granted. As for the
third . . . alas, my memory has grown so dim, I fear I can hardly remember
what it was. . . .

They say love cannot survive prolonged separation. However passionate
my feelings may have been, the length of time that I spent divorced from the
object of my affections had grown so long and the prospect of my learning
of her whereabouts so scant, it was becoming increasingly apparent I simply
might not be able to sustain my sense of devotion for very much longer. My
patience had worn thin, and my watch could no longer calculate the extent
of the separation — the period of time was simply too great. So that, whereas
I had long thought of love as an affair dependent upon only oneself and a
matter solely internal to the heart and mind of the person involved, it began
to dawn on me that I had been operating under an illusion. In the end, love
is but one of many external events that happens in one's life. It is an event
that takes place in the world outside one's self, and it is acted upon by forces
that all too often lie beyond one's control.

So what was I to do?

To hell with love, I told myself. I thought it best to content myself with
the renewed state of my health, a watch that ticked merrily away, and the
look and feel of a brand-new hat. Perhaps it was the aura of pride and
respectability they lent me; at least they made me feel better. Besides, at the
very moment that I am standing here in the middle of the street, the one and
only thought that occupies my mind — and does so to the exclusion of all
else — is, to put it as simply and forthrightly as possible, the desire to sit down
and have a decent cup of coffee.

I hopped on a train and headed for Yokohama. It was only yesterday that I
learned the name of this new place to eat. . . .

I am seated at the counter at the far corner of the room, barely visible
and floating, as it were, on a cloud of cigarette and coffee fumes. There is a
vacant stool next to mine, and the customer who has just now entered the

shop and who is deftly threading her way among the tables, is about to plant herself on the chair next to mine. The legs of the cheaply made stool emit a sharp screech as the woman, getting situated and making herself comfortable, leans in my direction. She is dressed entirely in red from head to toe, and her powdered bosom fills the air with its oily perfume. Like a ripe flower ready to drop its petals, it comes perilously close to spilling into my lap. . . .

Yet when I looked up at her face, what did I see but the person who has been the object of my relentless search across the length and breadth of the land. Yes, it was the face that I have sought in vain for these past months in spite of many a hardship on the open road. Yes, hers was the face that I had nearly forgotten yet somehow managed to remember.

"Of all the . . . " It was the woman who took the initiative in starting a conversation. "I always wondered what had become of you." At the same time she straightened in her chair and then leaned back to get a better look at me, she inched closer. With her knee practically touching mine, she called to the woman who owned the restaurant.

She spoke as though she knew her well and did not hesitate to impose. She proceeded to order one of everything on the menu. Then, opening her handbag and producing a pack of Lucky Strikes, she took out a cigarette and put it to her lips. The large purse was still halfway open, and I could easily see its contents. It was stuffed with packs of cigarettes, bars of chocolate, as well as other items not produced on the domestic market. I tried not to be obvious, but when she caught my eye wandering, she announced I was welcome to "anything at all." She would be only too happy to share.

Before I had time to wonder if I knew what to say or whether I could get my mouth to move and come forth with an appropriate reply, I realized I had been undone by this unexpected rendezvous. I found myself shot through with a sudden and renewed burst of passion for the lost object of my love. It was like a second bout of fever that returns with even greater virulence, and it left me unable to collect my wits or get my nerves under control. No external event was this. To the contrary, as the fevered delirium of my past infatuation returned with renewed intensity, I felt my entire frame burn as though it had become a veritable pillar of fire.

Never before had this woman spoken to me, or treated me, in a manner so intimate and uninhibited as she did now. I was taken completely by surprise, and I had no idea what to do next. Finally, I succeeded in stammering out a word or two, and phrasing my speech in the courtly tones of the past and of a time that reflected the nature of our previous acquaintance, I asked her where she now "resided."

"Here in the 'Hama," she replied, tossing the phrase out in a dry, matter-of-fact way. Her voice sounded casual enough; still, I thought I detected a certain pained expression in its tone. "Couldn't you guess?" she seemed to say in an offhanded and unspoken chastisement of my having asked what was blatantly obvious.

Judging from the way she spoke and the manner in which she dressed and handled herself, there was nothing to make one think that the woman came from a "good family." Neither was there any sign of her having been a sad victim of the war — namely, a widow left without a husband or a place to live. Perhaps it was sheer imagination on my part, but what resonated in my ear when she enunciated the word "'Hama" was not Yoko*hama,* but a place that sounded a lot more like "Hommoku," or the part of town that had been taken over by the Occupation Army and set up as a red-light district. The thought shocked me; and though I heard what she said, and I saw how she looked as she sat there beside me, still my mind steadfastly refused to believe it. I was prepared to doubt the validity of my own eyes and ears before questioning anything else.

That is because, when it comes to the matter of my memory of this woman — of the mental image that I had constructed of her in my mind — there is but one face that I see and only one voice that echoes in my ears. It is a cameo portrait of her that I formed long, long ago. Yes, I speak of a time so far in the past that it stands separated from us in time by the distance of exactly one year.

As I remember it now, it was a night late in December of 1944 and at a time when the air raid sirens had yet to sound with either the frequency or the urgency that later we came to expect as a matter of course. I was sharing a bottle of saké with a friend — an old friend who also happened to be the husband of the woman. We were at their house — a house built high on a hill — and we sat up most of the night drinking and talking. By daybreak my friend had collapsed in a drunken stupor, and I decided to take my leave and go home.

As I got up to go, the woman — namely, the wife of my friend — insisted on seeing me off. We climbed to the top of the hill, and in order to make certain that I did not miss the cutoff on the path leading to the streets below, she stood outside in the cold morning air for the longest time and watched me as I made my descent down the long slope. It was only by grabbing hold of the trunk of a pine tree and leaning out over the edge of the path that she could follow me as I made my way down the hill.

"Watch your step as you go.

"Now turn to the left.

"Yes, now to your right."

That was all she said. But her directions were so patient and full of care, and she tendered them in the politest and most elegant of voices. It was almost as though I had been her lover that night, and having plighted our troth in a grand and secret affair, we were sharing the sweetness and sorrow known only to those who love but are destined to part. It was a classic tale — just as in days of yore. My heart was strangely stirred; and my feet, unsteady as they were, hurried blindly on their way as I headed down the hill.

Let there be no confusion, however. My encounter with the woman today is not a case of mistaken identity. The face that I saw before me — and the voice that I heard in this restaurant that had been hastily constructed at a burnt-out site here in Yokohama — was none other than the face and voice that I had seen and heard that rare and wondrous morning a year ago. The sight of her now and the sound of her voice rekindled all of the sweet memories of the fateful day when last we parted. I was filled with great longing for the way life had once been.

PRESENTLY, WE WERE READY to leave the restaurant. As if by unspoken agreement, we left together and headed in the direction of the train station at Sakuragi-chō. She took hold of my arm as though it were the most natural thing in the world for her to do, and stealing an inquiring look at the profile of my face, she laughed and said I looked "as pale as ever." Perhaps she meant to be funny. Or to make fun of me.

Without her having said it, I already knew the blood in my veins had begun to run cold. I felt the flesh shrink from my bones. I was shaken by a violent chill — my hands and feet going limp, my breathing becoming labored. The state of my health had taken a sudden and decided turn for the worse.

And if that were not bad enough, my new hat got twisted askew, and my watch fell silent. The latter ceased to tick at all, its hands no longer moving.

As we neared the station, the woman, who until now had let her body press against mine, suddenly bolted from my side. She did it with no more than a gentle shove, but it was clear that I was being brushed aside, and she went running on ahead. I tottered, and it took a moment for me to catch myself and get my feet planted squarely on the ground once more.

That was when I happened to look up. I looked across the way to see the powerful figure of a soldier moving toward her. His face shone from out of the crowd as he stood head and shoulders above everyone, his height monumentally tall, his color strangely dark.

The black soldier wore a lightweight pink silk muffler tied jauntily about his neck, and the firm and neat row of his teeth sparkled and gleamed gemlike when he opened his mouth and shouted something in words that I could not decipher.

And there, clinging to the thick chest of the powerful man, were the arms of the woman dressed in red. She was like a butterfly resting on the trunk of a tree, and she clung to it as securely as she could.

Her back was turned to me. But her faceless silence spoke, and I knew she had nothing more to say to me. There would be no final "adieu." There would be no lingering reservations — no moment of hesitation — in which, for even a second, she might turn and look back. She was gone from me forever.

And what — pray tell — was I to say in calling after her?

"Watch your step as you go"?

"First to your left, and now to your right"?

In truth, there are no words that one might say at a time like this. I was so ashamed, I thought I would die on the spot.

Comprehending nothing, I ran straight for the center of the square in front of the train station, where a great whorl of people churned through the entrance to the station.

The faster I ran, the more the blood in my veins began to circulate. The muscles in my arms and legs started to swell and regain their strength. The terrible chill subsided, and as my step and grip grew stronger and my breathing less irregular, I felt myself return to normal.

Before I knew it, my hat had snapped into place, and my pocket watch had begun to tick merrily away.

THE JESUS OF
THE RUINS

≈ 1946 ≈

Under the blazing sky of a hot summer sun, amidst choking dirt and dust, a cluster of makeshift stalls has sprung from the land, and like a weed that grows in a clump, it has sent out its tendrils to cover the earth. The stands are partitioned by screens made of reeds, each pressing so hard upon the next there is scarcely room to breathe, let alone move. And as for the occupants, if there are those who flog their various and sundry household goods by simply setting them out on the ground, and those who spread kimonos or things to wear across tables, by far the vast majority are people with food to sell. They operate out of their carts, openly taking out white rice and serving it to the public in defiance of the law.

"Last chance! Last chance!" they cry. "Today's the last day! Tomorrow's too late."

The faces of the men turn beet red under the broiling rays of the sun as they shout at the top of their lungs, and oily beads of sweat drip from their brows. And, to the chorus of the men's voices, the women vendors add their ear-splitting cries, the noisy crescendo of the marketplace rising to a fever pitch. The spectacle of so many people furiously shrieking and shouting is a powerful, even frightful sight. Indeed it is a scene that is almost bloodthirsty in its relentlessness.

For today is July 31, 1946, and come tomorrow, the first of August, official notice has been served that the market is to be closed for good. Everyone stands on the brink of being put out of business.

And, even if that were not the case —

This is Tokyo's Ueno, the most pugnacious part of town, where tempers and nostrils flare, and every inch of territory — even the space under a train trestle — is guarded jealously. Yes, it is just the sort of place where, not so very long ago, there was a bloody row in which the locals took on the gendarmes of the law.

It is also what comes in the wake of war and its fire: a city in ruins, the burnt-out shell of a metropolis. Its creatures have hatched out of the debris, and now they survive by the sheer tenacity with which they came into the world and by which they cling to life.

In truth, they live as though in their original naked state, all looking alike and possessed of nothing more than the shirt on their backs. Yes, were it not for the flimsiness of the fabric one could hardly discern male from female, the men identifiable only by the tattoos visible on their shoulders and backs; the women, by the rounded swell of their chests.

Each lurks within the shadow of his or her reed stall, hiding there and harboring a unique brand of venom. For the denizens of the marketplace are as ready as ever to reach into the crowd and sink their teeth into a potential customer. Indeed they have so devised the business of selling food that they need only to rattle a plate to make the cheapest of yen notes fly forth from someone's tired pocket. It is like a trap or a clever springlike device in which the clatter of dishes sets up a hollow sound that echoes all the way down to the pit of the empty stomach of every customer and makes him or her want to eat.

Yet look at the customers —

They too are not about to be outdone, each and every one a perfect match for the hawkers. Wild-eyed and frantic, the whites of their eyes all bloodshot, they too are poised, their mouths lunging for food almost before there is time to race into a booth and polish off a filthy plate in a single gulp.

The business of the marketplace is the transactions of beasts, the winners in the game of profit and loss being decided in a single bite. It is a dog-eat-dog world; and no matter how much one creature feeds or is fed upon, the time never comes when either party announces he or she has had enough. No, it appears there will never be a time in which they will lift their heads and, momentarily studying the sky, decide to take a breather.

No, it appears there will never be a moment when a cool breeze might arise from one quarter or the other.

A MAN SLAPS A POUND of sardines on what passes for a grill and lets the fish sizzle. The sardines are already red around the eye, and a sheet of corrugated metal is no great shakes as a griddle. Nonetheless, the foul, rancid smell that fills the air when the oily fish hits the hot metal—an odor rank enough to turn the stomach of any ordinary mortal—appears only to whet the vulgar appetites of the crowd, and all the more shamelessly. The great unwashed come running, and like flies, they swarm over the stall.

Yet real flies know better, and fearing the heat of the flame, they keep their distance, content merely to buzz about noisily. They head downwind of the breeze that carries the smell of the oily sardines and the stench of the sweaty crowd, and they decide to settle on the stall next door. Alighting atop the dark, round, and uncovered objects that have been set out on the counter for sale, they swarm over them and turn them completely black. . . .

Aside from the woman who works at the stand, no one is about. Apparently there has been a momentary lull in her business. . . .

"Get 'em while they're still nice and warm! Fresh *o-musubi*. That's right. *O-musubi* for only ten yen apiece. And made from polished rice too!"

Were it not for her verbal advertisement, who would have known what it was she had for sale? Sure enough, the dark, round objects set out on the counter were *o-musubi*. They were balls of rice, and each had been wrapped in a thin sheet of dried seaweed.

Yet the seaweed had none of the sheen or crinkle of a reliable brand. It was of a cheap, inferior sort that, when pressed against the warm, moist surface of a ball of freshly steamed rice, merely went limp and looked more like wilted *shiso* leaves than seaweed. Moreover, it was torn in spots, and as a result, the rice showed through the tears. The rice was white all right, just as the woman had loudly proclaimed in her promise of polished rice, but once the grains had dried out and started to stick together, they looked as though they had been glued in place. There was no trace—nay, not even a lingering whiff—of the steam or the heart-warming smell that arises when freshly cooked rice is scooped from the pot and pressed into firmly shaped balls.

To the contrary, were there any suggestion of steaminess—and the feeling of fecundity that fills the air when one lifts the lid from a tub of freshly steamed rice—surely it was not to be found enveloping the *o-musubi* that had been set out for sale. No, it emanated instead from the woman who sold them. . . .

J UST HOW OLD is she, anyway?

All that can be said with certainty is she had yet to acquire any real age in life and was still very much a young woman. She had filled out, the flesh on her limbs radiating with the voluptuousness of youth, its heat almost palpable as it glowed on her sunburnt skin. And through the peachlike fuzz that covered her arms and legs shone the blush of the crimson that coursed so richly through her veins and that, in rising to the surface, brought to her complexion its fresh and healthy fragrance. Her arms and legs were full, almost bursting with an excess of energy; and when she threw back her head and shoulders with a defiant look, her breasts flashed like the tips of pointed daggers as they pressed against the fabric of her sliplike chemise.

She had hiked up the hem of her already short skirt as she sat in the booth, and without the slightest hint of shame, she lifted one leg and let it rest on the other in full view of the crowd. It was a pose that seemed to suggest she was inciting her own body and, by egging it on, aroused herself to a state of sexual desire.

Yet, really, was there any other position for her to assume, given a body so free of strain or artifice? There she was, arrayed in her most natural mode of expression, even to the point of looking almost base or ugly. She made one think. Given a world in which the physical nature of human beings was allowed to manifest itself regardless of its surroundings, just how far might we go in letting ourselves give expression to the inner chemistry of our bodies? Why, wouldn't naked desire want to push its way to the fore and make itself known to the world in the same sort of wild and uncivilized way in which the girl presented herself here? In short, wouldn't debauchery come to constitute a new and wholesome morality? And flesh, a new and competing source of illumination and enlightenment in the world? For so intense was the glow of the girl and her body, and so blinding was its glare when it struck the eye that even the sun at high noon began to pale by comparison. Yes, even a force as powerful as the sun assumed an artificial hue and looked almost sedate in its hazy efflorescence. . . .

From time to time the woman belted out her cry, hawking her wares, but her voice never assumed the cutthroat and gangsterlike tone of her male competitors. They were professional salesmen, and they had learned how to make their sales pitch sound like an adult throwing a temper tantrum. By contrast, the woman's cry remained unabashedly her own, and by virtue of that fact, it was natural, and it revealed a lingering touch of innocence.

"Step right up and get a freshly made *o-musubi*. Only ten yen apiece. . . ."

JUST THEN a commotion broke out in the stall next-door that was selling sardines. The crowd began to stir.

"You filthy . . . "

"Don't touch me. Yeah, you. You heard me. Don't even get near me. Keep your dirty paws to yourself."

"Get out of here. Get the hell out of here, and I mean now."

The crowd was thrown into an agitated state, with everyone shouting at once. A man came rushing over to the stall. He was dressed in a pair of shorts and military boots. He appeared to be a patrolman who had been hired by the market to keep an eye on things.

"You're back, huh? I thought I told you to clear out," he said in a gruff voice. "You don't listen, do ya?"

"Hell, you're so filthy, who'd want to lay a hand on you? All right, you'll stay out of here from now on, or you'll be as good as dead if I find you around here again. Got it? 'Cuz I'll bash your head in. Now git the hell outta here."

The man in the boots might as well have been driving off a stray dog, his voice having become a veritable hiss. Words were a powerful whip that he used to lash at his victim.

Yet what shot from the torrent of abuse that the man rained upon the ground — yes, what shot out from the stall or, more precisely, from between the legs of the customers standing there — was surely no dog.

It was a boy.

A living, breathing human being.

And insofar as appellations of gender or age may apply, yes, he was male . . . and a child. . . . In short, just a boy.

Yet, in point of fact, he defied description. Here was a creature for whom there was no proper name, because the taxonomy of his kind had yet to be invented. . . .

It was as though an old suit of clothes had been abandoned by the wayside. It had gotten dirty and foul from lying in the dirt, but then one day who should come along but some wild and crazy sprite. The sprite took a liking to the clothes, quickly donning them, upon which the old suit suddenly sprang to life. Yes, there it was, a set of rags, and it was standing on its own two feet. Fanned by the breeze, it began to walk about, acting ever so much like a human being who was out for a stroll.

Behold, the boy was black as the sludge in a ditch, and it was impossible to tell at a glance where the ragged edge of his clothes ended and the flesh underneath began. He was so caked in dirt and filth, he looked as if he were covered in scales. To make matters worse, his head and face were covered in unspeakable boils. The boils oozed with pus that, baked to a crust in the terrible heat of the sun, had dried and begun to reek with an awful smell. Indeed, the stench was so potent that it seemed to reach out and attack one's nostrils. Even those who worked in the marketplace had begun to complain, and surely they had never been known to flinch at the thought of handling anything foul or rotten. . . . Not even the immovable object of the man in the military boots was unfazed. He too could hardly bear to stand next to the boy.

So that, while the former soldier sounded tough, and his voice rumbled like a resonating gong, he contented himself with taking a few steps back and motioning for the boy to get moving.

Yet in backing off and simply using threats instead of actually taking the boy in hand, he suggested by his manner that, were there a cowering dog in the marketplace, surely it was none other than himself. And, like a dog that is easily frightened by the specter of whatever lurks in the shadows, it appeared he had decided to confine his barking to a safe distance.

WHAT WAS IT about the boy? He had only to step into the center of the thoroughfare, and a look of sheer panic spread across the faces in the crowd. It was a reaction shared by all—one read it in the eyes of vendor and passerby alike. Every man and woman was on guard, knees bent, their bodies ready to spring into action at a moment's notice. But, somehow, like the hireling in the military boots, their legs failed them. It seemed as though they were powerless to move. Whatever had caused each and every one of them to assume an unexpectedly frozen pose, and with a conformity that was universal?

Fear. It goes by no other name. Albeit a lawless mob, this was a crowd that knew trouble when they saw it coming their way.

True, it had been a while since they experienced what it was like to live in fear and trepidation of something far more powerful than themselves. They had known the feeling, but they had driven all thought of it from their minds, and now they acted as though the terrors of the not so distant past had never really happened. Why, if one tried counting back only a mere five years, to a date as close in time as 1941, and asked them to recall the events of their lives in those fateful Shōwa years, surely that was to ask them to cross a mental divide that, in terms of its historical significance, measured not five but a full five thousand years!

Besides, now that they had lost their way in a land ravaged by war and fire, and they had wandered into the labyrinth of the marketplace that grew out of the ruins, what need did they have to think of the past, anyway? It was as if no one had survived from the last century and, no, there had never been an era in the history of modern Japan when people had paraded about smugly wearing the look of His Majesty's loyal subjects—when the land had been populated by a race of so-called Neo-Confucian gentlemen who were only too happy to be of unquestioning service to the empire. No, not a soul from that day and age appeared to be alive. They had all vanished—down to every last man, woman, and child.

They were errant seeds, their feet planted on the spot where they happened to land. They had sprouted out of the ground, and with the force of a weed that reaches maturity overnight, they were now fully grown. They were the "new leaf" that had been turned over. They were the "newly created society." They were all of the new this-and-that touted in the press of late. They were billed as a "brand-new" product: the local specialty and the showcase item of today's "new moment in history."

Such were the people milling about the marketplace. Down to a man they had the look of moral delinquents and social outlaws who knew no yesterday and know no tomorrow. And as for what Heaven might have to say, they cared not a whit — for they feared it no more. The business at hand here on earth was making money, and the art of making money lay in their skill at duping their neighbors. By taking advantage of people and their ignorance, they knew how to skin them alive and make a hearty meal of them. Yes, their fellow human beings were to be the source of their sustenance.

Besides, no one had been appointed as the new leader for them to follow and serve, and since the old calendar of imperial events and obligations was now no longer in force, what difference did it make whose reign it was or what was today's date?

Likewise, if one did not recognize the law, then why give a damn about rules and regulations, anyway? Or care about whomever it was who claimed the right to enforce them? If it is not one official line, then surely it is another. To hell with them all, the faces in the crowd seemed to say, their nostrils flaring defiantly. Yet, in spite of all their talk and bravura, what did one find when the time came for these people to get down in the dust and hammer out a price for their goods? Namely, that everything was contraband. In short, in the entire lot of food and clothes and whatever else they have for sale on just about any street corner in the city, there is not a single item worthy of being called bona fide or legitimate. What's more, the currency with which these goods are bought and sold is of equally dubious value, since the government bureaucrats who manufacture the money do not hesitate to mint more and more stacks of devalued yen notes. . . .

Consequently, for all the talk of "the new ways of living" and "the dawning awareness of newly emergent peoples," what is it really worth? Is it something truly new and genuine? No, not in the least. So much for talk of "the contemporary lifestyle" and "the modern consciousness." For in point of fact people have yet to take one step beyond the here and now, and the most quotidian prescriptions of what they think life is about. It appears that, just as in the last century, they are still self-absorbed in the lusty appetites of their baser emotions, and their lives are consumed by the myriad transactions that are part and parcel of running a business and making a living. There has been no change. Only now, by being caught in the throes of being busier than ever before, they have failed to ask what the all-important and much touted "today" really means. Today marks, in fact, the end of time as we have known it heretofore.

But, alas, this precious moment is about to slip away, and it will be already too late when people look up and finally take notice. They will come to their senses only to find that the surface of reality is as unbroken as it was before, the fabric of their lives looking as though, no, there had never been a hole in it — no, it had never been rent or torn. Everything would remain the same, as if there had never been any change after all. The damned hole — the spot, the little rip, the "oh-did-I-do-that?" cigarette burn — that by virtue of its foolish and irritating presence challenges us and allows time to enter into our lives would be gone forever. . . .

But, suddenly, standing there in the void was the boy, catching everyone at an unguarded moment. Dirty, foul-smelling, and glowing with an other-worldly black sheen, he revealed himself in all of his ugly glory. He stood in the midst of the squalor and stench of the marketplace, and he outshone it in his filthiness. He arrested every eye; and in his doing so, did not the denizens of this lowly place — these vulgar and undaunted types who never flinched in the face of anything — secretly turn inward and, taking a long look at themselves and the state in which they lived, suddenly realize they were no different? Startled at the mirror image of their own ugliness, they shuddered. And as each inwardly raised a bootless cry for help, a great shock wave passed through the multitude.

One could hardly bear to look at the boy because of the unspeakable rags and boils that covered him. Still, there was nothing about his person, neither in his posture or his deportment, that spoke of the beggar or the petty thief. Nor was there any sign of physical illness, mental imbalance, or other infirmity. No, there were none of these, although, given the circumstances, he might well become a bank robber . . . or a murderer . . . or whatever monstrosity one might care to imagine.

Yet given — hmm — the comparatively normal shape of whatever part of his face was visible through the sea of pus and boils — and the correctness with which he carried himself, keeping his back straight as a rod — and the way his shoulders had begun to fill out, it appeared he possessed a surprisingly solid physique. One guessed his age was somewhere between ten and fifteen. In short, he was at the peak of his growing years. The healthy development of his bones and the lack of any malformation in the extremities served to insure his growth into a healthy, unstunted adult male.

Still, there remained something physically soft and supple about him. No doubt his boyishness accounted for the touch of arrogance that he gave off as he walked down the street. He thrust out his chest. He never looked back. And he paid no heed to the crowd as it swirled around him. "Why all the fuss?" his body seemed to say, as he moved silently and singularly through the throng, his gaze coolly fixed on a point far in the distance. He was like an actor who makes his grand entrance down the ramp, gliding to the center of the stage with the greatest of ease. How calm and collected he was! Surely it was by no mean feat that he carried himself with such aplomb, and doubtless the naturalness of his step derived in great measure from his profound sense of self-reliance. He depended on no one; and without such confidence, he should not have been able to make his feet advance so adroitly. As for whither he came or where he was going, that was something no one knew.

But then, the marketplace was a recent development, and no one knew where any of the people here had come from or to what tribe, or subspecies, they belonged. They simply milled about with no apparent direction. Some moved one way; the others, another. Thus, when a lone boy — a boy possessed of an air of authority and looking ever so assured of his ultimate destination — stepped into their midst, the mere lightness of his step was reason enough to bring a startled look to their faces. How nimble he was on his feet! Indeed so great was the impression he had made on the crowd, people were immune to further surprise. By now they would not have been fazed in the least were he, like a specter that appears momentarily in broad daylight, to snap his fingers and with equal suddenness — poof! — vanish into thin air.

B UT THEN, something unexpected happened.
Paying no more heed to the sardines on the grill, the boy turned from the stall and started into the crowd. But just as he was about to make his exit and it appeared to all eyes that he would disappear into thin air, suddenly he

reeled about, and darting past the reed partition, he shot into the neighboring stall. From seemingly nowhere, he produced a brand-new crisp and seamless ten-yen note and slapped it on the counter.

Seizing one of the rice balls that was black with the flies that had settled on it, he opened his mouth and bit into it, flies and all. His hand moved so fast that no one could intervene, and by the time the woman at the stall started to her feet, shouting something in shocked surprise, the merchandise had already been consumed.

And now, with the same lightning speed, the boy directed the thrust of his hand toward the woman. As she started to stand, he flew at her, his body dancing wildly toward her, and he pushed her back against the bench. Grabbing at her, he reached for the exposed flesh of her thighs, and making it the object of his embrace, he attacked it with the same determination with which he had sunk his teeth into the *o-musubi* ball of rice. As his face smacked full force against the side of the woman's leg, it made a slapping sound loud enough that it could be heard beyond the confines of the stall. Crying out in shock and pain, the woman jumped up and tried to free herself.

"What do you think you're doing? Damn you, you little brat. . . ."

But the boy was not about to give up, no matter how hard she struggled to disengage herself.

By now the man in the military boots had come running. This time he was brandishing a long, thin bamboo stick.

"Damn you, you little beast. . . ."

Yet the fact that the man did no more than curse suggested, once again, the sight of the boy's boils and dirty rags kept him at bay; and holding himself at arm's length, he merely leapt about, circling the pair and letting the woman bear the brunt of having to contend with the boy. By doing no more than lashing the air with the bamboo stick and making it crack like a whip, not only did he avoid having to touch the boy but—by not laying a hand on him—he also saved himself the trouble of pulling the two apart.

The bodies of the boy and the woman were united as one, and as their entwined form emerged from the stall and spilled into the street, they teetered back and forth, ready at any moment to fall to the ground.

B UT THEN their bodies shifted, and suddenly the pair came crashing headlong in this—or shall I say *my?*—direction.

It just so happened I was standing in front of the adjoining stall at that very moment. The stall next to the woman's was run by a seller of sweets and candies, but the candyman could be persuaded to reach into the false bottom of the kerosene drum that held his wares to produce a pack or two of contraband cigarettes. I had prevailed upon him, and I had just now lit a match and was about to light one of the cigarettes I had purchased.

I was in danger, of course; and I immediately adopted a stance of being ready to grab hold of and roll with the lump of flesh as it tumbled toward me. Otherwise, I would be crushed underneath when the boy and the woman toppled to the ground.

A single lump—or clump—of flesh had been formed by the union of the two bodies. I had to think fast, and making a quick decision, I chose to embrace the half where the skin would be soft and pleasant to the touch rather than the half covered in rags and boils and pus and, no doubt, lice. Yes, how much better to latch onto the gentler part. . . .

What I mean is—and I am embarrassed to say this—but from the time I had approached the booth of the candyman, I too had seen the meaty thighs of the woman's legs, and I could think of nothing else. I was mesmerized, yet no matter how much I might be overcome by the sight of a beautiful pair of legs, never—no, never—would I throw caution to the winds and rush forth to embrace them in full view of the public as the boy had just now done. No, it was something I simply could not do, and the reason lies solely in the fact I do not possess one iota of the spunk and courage demonstrated by this young man. It is just that simple. . . .

Yet, given the unexpected stroke of good luck that was now about to come tumbling my way, what need had I to be shy about standing in the shadow of the boy's glory? By basking in the virtuous light of his courageousness, why not make happenstance the happy occasion in which I saw to the fulfillment of my basest desires? Yes, it was terrible of me. And as if that were not vile enough, let me add that the thought occurred to me to be even nefarious enough to push the boy aside and attempt to take the woman solely for myself. Once he was out of the way, I could direct my attention to her backside and seize her from the rear. . . .

But punishment was about to be meted out to me right on the spot. For no sooner did I find myself unable to check the motion of the woman's body by use of my passive strength than, believe it or not, her powerful hips came flying my way, and with a high-spirited upper cut, she sent me sailing through the air. It was with a resounding thud that I found myself thrown to the ground.

My knees and elbows were badly scraped. I bit back the pain, and when at last I managed to get to my feet, I found the boy was now nowhere in sight. He had vanished without so much as a shadow or trace of his former presence. As for the woman, she was shouting at the top of her lungs about something or other that I found impossible to comprehend. She was livid as hell, and the force of her anger — as well as the heat of her glare — was clearly directed at me. Standing alongside her was the man in the military boots, slashing at the air with his bamboo stick. He was intent upon intimidating me into submission, as he towered over me and sought to block any avenue of escape.

I gathered from what the woman said that, in the confusion of the moment, the light from the tip of my cigarette had somehow or other pressed against her back, and it had burned a large hole in her blouse. Yes, a hole . . . a singed spot . . . a cigarette burn. . . .

A crowd had formed. It was in a nasty mood, and it was clear I was the object of its anger. People assumed I had been the one who had grabbed the woman by the leg and attacked her. (Actually, it is true that I had been party to the whole sordid affair.)

My face turned bright red. My embarrassment was due in part to being at the center of a crowd in broad daylight, but I also shuddered at the thought of what new indignity was about to come my way. Driven by the desire to flee as fast as I could, I scanned the wall of people lined up in front of me. Aiming for the weakest build and the least attentive face, I saw my opening and charged headlong. I shunted the man aside, and weaving my way through the now disordered ranks of the crowd, I ran like mad. I was desperate to get outside the marketplace.

Just beyond the narrow confines of the market lay a broad avenue where streetcars ran. I kept running until I reached it. Only then did I stop to catch my breath. I turned around and looked behind me. To my great relief, I could see that no one had come in pursuit.

Yet when I looked once more in the direction of the streetcar tracks, I realized everyone was staring at me. There was a look of stern disapproval on every face.

No wonder. I was covered in mud from the top of my head to the tip of my toes. My elbows and knees were scraped and bloodied from where I had fallen on the ground. Moreover, one adopts a certain air on entering the marketplace, and I had yet to shed it. I must have looked bizarre and out-of-place.

By nature I am a proud and vain sort of person who spends much of his time and energy keeping up appearances. Even on the occasion when I have rubbed shoulders with the shameless types who populate the marketplace or I have been smitten by the sight, for example, of a pair of good-looking legs like the ones on the woman at the *o-musubi* stand, I have always been careful not to reveal the slightest suggestion of anything vulgar or base in the way I present myself. I have put on airs, inasmuch as one can these days. By making myself appear ever so prim and proper, I have advertised myself to the world as a paragon of refinement.

Yet once things had reached this pretty pass, what did I have to say for myself? I looked worse than the most shameless denizen of the marketplace. I was an outcast who ranks as the lowest of the low.

But forget the revealing light of day. Forget the eyes that stared at me in rebuke. They are hardly worth mentioning, even if it is true that I felt totally embarrassed. More important, what did I have to say for myself? What excuse could I offer to assuage my own wounded sense of pride? My vanity was hurt at the thought of how utterly difficult it was for me to speak to my own defense. What was there to say on my own behalf?

I brushed the dirt from my clothes. I wiped the blood from my scratches. I tied the laces of my shoes. And, feigning an air of nonchalance, I started to walk away. But my feet would not cooperate. They were clumsy and would not move with the ease that I demanded of them.

And speaking of feet . . . how was it that the boy managed to move with such composure when he made his way among the blackguards of the market? How deftly, how subtly — or, rather, how boldly and with what unfettered grace — he parted the crowd as he passed through it! From what distant reach of heaven or what bowel deep in the earth had he come? For surely he had been sent to the marketplace on a divine mission, had he not? He had come to this newly created site, and it was here that he made himself manifest to its people. "I am the progenitor of a new race that shall plant its seed and flourish in this vast and empty plain." That was what he seemed to say — just as he also threatened to push from the ring any contender who dared to step forward to challenge his authority over the arena of the marketplace.

For who else was prepared to stand side by side with the naked camp of the poor and outcast? Who else but the boy would succor the multitudes who knew no law and who were dressed only in the garments of their naked shame? Is it not written that the Messiah is always with the poor and the oppressed, and that God loves those who do not know the Law? If such is the case, might it not be that the young boy stood far closer to the divine than one might think? Might it just not be the case that he ranks among the very first of men — that, yea, he is to be the leader of a new breed of humankind that dwells in the place of ruin and sends out its tendrils to cover the earth? Indeed it may very well be the case that he has been singled out to play the role of the Son of Man who is come to save us. The signs are all unclear, and I feel uncertain in going so far as to suggest he has been chosen as our lord and savior, as the name Christ implies. Yet surely I am not wide of the mark in saying he is at least our Jesus, and a very human Jesus at that. Yes, am I not on target in calling him "the Jesus of the ruins"? "The Jesus of the Burnt-Out Shell of Japan."

I never cease to be amazed that the denizens of the marketplace are a tight-lipped lot who keep their mouths shut and have little to say. But how much more so in the case of the boy! He is doubly silent, what with never having uttered a single word. Come to think of it, I suspect it is his acts that are his true words. They are his sole means of communication.

What's more, were we to examine each and every act he has undertaken and how he has sought to express himself in each and every case — be it the act of "hand over a sardine," or the gesture of "gimme a rice ball," or the feat

in "let me at her thighs" — inevitably we would find in each and every instance they are cast in the imperative voice. His acts are commands and,
inasmuch as each and every one of them is delivered like an order from on
high, surely they possess some sort of deeper, theological meaning. Doubtless
they speak of things that are comprehended only by theologians and the like,
and which we vulgar mortals cannot hope to grasp.

Truly, the boy's every act is a metaphor and has parallels to be found in
the words and deeds of Jesus of Nazareth. Indeed, were someone to observe
the boy's daily comings and goings in detail and then go so far as to write
them down and compile a permanent record, would we not have before us a
new set of teachings on life in the promised land that constitutes no less a
testament than Jesus' Sermon on the Mount?

Yes, now that I thought of it, it seemed to me the boy possessed great
majesty, his physical appearance notwithstanding. It is no ordinary mortal
who can stand before the world adorned in robes so thoroughly tattered and
a body so encrusted with boils, pus, and, no doubt, lice too. It takes the
authority of a king and, even then, only the most regal and stately of rulers.
I too have been stirred by the secret desire to transform myself into something
more impressive, to take my vulgar body and garb it in the best of fashion;
and I have suffered not inconsiderably, my sense of pride and vanity
wounded, given my current lack of means. In fact, it appears the day when I
shall be able to don the raiments of a king and be arrayed in splendor is a
time that not only has not come but also seems so distant in the future that
I may never see it.

In the meantime, then, for me at least, the enemy is this Jesus.

And if in our tug-of-war for the woman at the *o-musubi* stand the worst
disaster to befall me was to scrape a hand or a knee, what of it? My losses
were light. It is probably best that I forget the entire matter and not dwell on
it. At last I began to calm down and pull myself together.

By the time I had cooled off, I had walked as far as Ueno Hirokoji. I
stood at the broad intersection there and waited for a streetcar headed for
Yanaka, a section of Ueno that was not far away. Yet when there was no sign
that a car would be coming along, and it looked as if I would have to wait
quite a while, I decided to go on foot. The quickest route to Yanaka lay over

Ueno Hill. The grounds of the Tōshōgū Shrine were atop the long incline. I could cut through the shrine precincts and then head down the other side of the hill to Yanaka. Indeed, going to Yanaka had been the reason I had set out this morning and the reason I had come all the way to Ueno.

IT WAS ONLY THE OTHER DAY that I had been to Yanaka on another errand. As I was walking back to Ueno, I happened to pass a temple that is the grave site of Dazai Shundai, a noted scholar of the Confucian classics who lived in the Edo period. Both the temple and the surrounding neighborhood had been lucky during the war, and they had escaped the terrible fires that had ravaged so much of Tokyo. The rows of houses that line the streets of Yanaka looked much as they had when they were originally built.

I entered the temple grounds through the main gate, and skirting around the main sanctuary, I headed for the cemetery in the rear. That I should do this — namely, decide on the spur of the moment to stop and take a look at Shundai's grave — had nothing to do, of course, with anything so conventional as wishing to pay my respects to Shundai by washing the headstone of his grave. To tell the truth, I have no reason whatsoever to mourn the man buried there, because, when it comes to the matter of Confucianism and the study of its texts and its teachings, I consider myself a total outsider. In fact, I could care less about them or for that matter anything about Dazai Shundai and his school of Neo-Confucian scholarship. I do not even think much of the personality of the man as it is recorded in the history books. Frankly speaking, Dazai Shundai is a figure altogether alien to me and my interests.

What had arrested my eye was the memorial stone erected at the site of his grave or, more important, the inscription that had been done in brush and then carved onto the stone. In short, my interest in Shundai lay solely in his epitaph. Both the words of the memorial and the characters in which they were written came from the pen of no less a figure than Hattori Nankaku, the greatest master of Chinese verse as it was practiced in Japan in the eighteenth century. It is Nankaku who is to be credited with having laid the foundation for the great revival of interest in Chinese poetry and belles lettres that flourished among the citizens of the city of Edo; and, as a latter-day child of that time and place, I count myself fortunate to be an heir—however distant—to the great literary tradition that he fostered. When it comes to the spirit of Nankaku and his works, I consider myself neither stranger nor alien.

That the arts and letters flourished and witnessed a great renaissance in the city of Edo in the mid- and late eighteenth century during the three successive eras known as Meiwa, An'ei, and Tenmei and that the writing of poetry reached an unprecedented degree of sophistication in the form of the "Tenmei Style" was due in no small part to the efforts of Nankaku, who, several decades in advance of anyone else in Japan, set about disseminating to the general public a knowledge and appreciation of the verse of the great masters of the T'ang dynasty. It was to the works of the T'ang that the practitioners of Tenmei poetry and prose turned for their inspiration, and there can be no question that the Chinese verse produced in Tenmei—albeit a distant echo of an earlier, far greater age—owes a considerable debt to T'ang poetry for its own thoroughly fashionable, cosmopolitan, and altogether up-to-date air. I dare say the spirit of the T'ang masters has become the fundamental source for all of the subsequent literary scholarship in Japan that is worthy of the accolade of "modern" or "sophisticated."

Fortunately, the memorial tablet had escaped damage in the war, and Nankaku's inscription was perfectly intact. Yet even in surviving the flames when so much else was in ruins, given the amnesia of the times, thought of it had slipped from public memory, and the tablet was now in danger of falling into oblivion. Yes, as far as the world was concerned, it was almost as though it no longer existed. For my part I wished to do something to preserve the words of Nankaku's memorial before it became too late and they were lost for all time. The day that I happened upon Shundai's grave, I made a mental note to myself to return. This time I would be prepared, and I would take a rubbing from the stone. I had set a date, and I had readied the necessary materials.

The day circled on my calendar is, of course, none other than today. And here I was. I was ready, and I was on my way. As a matter of fact, in one hand I held a small cloth bundle. Wrapped inside the bundle were rubbing paper and ink as well as two hard rolls that will have to suffice as my lunch for today's outing.

A rubbing is, to be sure, a nullity and an imperfection. For once the paper is pulled from the stone, it becomes nothing more than a secondhand acquaintance with a lost age — a pale copy, yea a mere tracing, taken from the annals of the history of arts and letters.

Yet even a leftover has a life of its own, does it not? And weren't there plenty of cracks in the walls of my temporary and ever-so-humble abode? And wasn't a rubbing just the thing to keep up appearances and paper over the worst of the holes in my life? . . .

Now, WHERE WERE WE? I know — I was making my way up Ueno Hill and was about to reach Kiyomizu Hall, the first of the outbuildings at the Tōshōgū Shrine, when I happened for no particular reason to turn around and look behind me.

Who should I see following me up the hill but the boy from the marketplace! He was still several blocks away, but it was clear he was headed in my direction.

No, there was no mistaking him. It was the boy all right. He was dressed in rags, and his face was covered in boils.

Yet what need had I to pay attention to him now that I had gotten back to the business that brought me here in the first place? I had already wasted too much time loitering on the way. Besides, from the top of a broad and open space like Ueno Hill, the boy did not look much like Jesus. He had changed, and curiously enough, here on "Mount Ueno" he lost the Jesus-like aura that had come so naturally to him when he had moved through the crowd in the marketplace. Here, he was simply a lone animal on the prowl for its supper. No longer the progenitor of a new race, he had become instead — in the words of the New Testament — the sole survivor of a generation of swine who, possessed by the devil, had flung themselves over a precipice and perished in the waters below. He alone had survived and was left to wander along the side of the mountain or by the edge of the sea. That was how he looked, and whatever fascination he may have held for me initially was now gone. I turned away. I paid him no mind and pressed on about my business.

This far up Ueno Hill there were no shops set out with things to sell, and only rarely did I encounter anyone who was out for a stroll. There was no danger of being tempted by the sight of a pair of women's legs here, however wanton and frivolous my thoughts might be.

As I passed through the torii that gave entrance to the shrine precincts, I turned around once more and casually looked behind me.

Sure enough. There he was. The enemy was behind me, but this time he had narrowed the distance, and now it was only a matter of his being ten or fifteen yards away. There was no question about it. He was following me.

What I saw was the face of the enemy, and the look on it was no joke. No longer the last of a dying breed of swine, the boy had become a wolf thirsty for blood.

There was a murderous glint in his eye. His teeth, which were exposed for me to see, glistened in the sun. Even the pustules on his face were flush with the red glow that comes from having imbibed the blood of prey recently taken. The rags that stuck to his skin bristled like the hairs on the back of a wolf. His eyes, his mouth, his face—they all spoke of the powerful thirst for the hunt.

But why of all people had the enemy set his sights on me? Did he hold a grudge because of the incident at the marketplace? I saw no reason why he should. I could care less about it. Or was he out to waylay me and take my money? Yes, I had a wallet, which I carried shoved deep inside my pocket. But, as for its contents, they were so negligible as to be hardly worth the trouble.

Or was he simply out for blood? Were that the case, he would have even less to chew on, given the fact that I am probably more anemic than the undernourished condition of my wallet. . . .

Yet the logic of a human may not be that of a wolf, and what made sense to me may not have been equally comprehensible to the boy. Whatever the case, it was all too apparent—the fearsome reality of it was now staring me squarely in the face—that the enemy, having stalked me this far, was ready to pounce.

I tried to remain calm. I told myself to slow down and walk as nonchalantly as possible.

By now I had reached the front of the Tōshōgū Shrine. There was no more need to turn around and look. I knew the enemy was closing in. It was only a matter of time before he would strike. I could feel him behind me, the poised energy of imminent attack tangible against the tensing muscles in my neck and shoulders. No one else was in sight. There were a few large trees here and there, but they did not amount to anything that one could rely on for cover. The sun beat down as relentlessly as ever. I was soaked to the skin. I felt as though I were swimming in an oily pool of sweat.

At last I came to the rear of the shrine. If only I could make it to the path that led down the other side of the hill, at least there would be houses in the neighborhood. But it was already too late. With a precision that was almost painful, my ears registered every move the enemy made, be it the sound of his labored breathing or the grinding and gnashing of his teeth. He was only a few feet away. In one flying leap, he would be on top of me, sinking his teeth into the nape of my neck. That is just how close he was.

I began to panic. I tried to reach the row of houses up ahead. Yet, by quickening my pace, I merely drove myself farther into the open—and right into the enemy's trap.

It was a field where tufts of weeds grew out of the red clay soil—or just the perfect place for the site of a bloodletting. At least I knew not to cry out or to break into a mad dash. The enemy would jump on me for sure.

Yet wasn't I equally foolish in doing nothing? The enemy had me cornered no matter what, and he was about to go for the jugular. The time in which I might have suddenly spun around and adopted a stance of engaging him head-on had long since passed, however. All that I had in my hand was the small cloth bundle. And inside was only the broadsheet of paper on which I planned to trace a pale copy of a lost, great age from the history of the art of poetry.

Alas, a blank sheet of paper is far too transparent and insubstantial a thing to be of much use in times like these. And here I was calling upon it to serve as a weapon in mortal combat with a wolf. How could it possibly prevail against a vicious set of claws and teeth? I was trapped, and I was desperate.

When I came to the biggest tree I could find, I decided to turn and confront the enemy. As I spun around, he too made his move and came lunging at me.

Yes, what kicked the earth and came flying through the air, only to crash on top of me, was a hideous clod — a sickening, foul-smelling clump — of rags and boils and pus and, no doubt, even lice. I raised my hands in front of me in order to break the full force of his attack. I felt his claws . . . I felt his teeth . . . as they tore into me. I heard my shirt rip. I felt his nails dig into the flesh of my arms.

Everything became an incoherent blur after that. We had become a single, solidified mass that fell down and rolled across the ground. Yes, I had become one with the hideous clump of rags and boils and pus and, no doubt, even lice.

The struggle went back and forth in total silence, but at last I was able to grab hold of the boy's wrists and hold him down. His hands were as powerful as they were agile, but I also discovered to my surprise how soft they were to the touch. Yes, his skin was as fine as could be. His hands had the texture of a youth somewhere between the ages of ten and fifteen.

How I did it I shall never know, but by summoning forth the last ounce of life left in my body, I managed to get a lockhold on the boy, and I succeeded in pressing his arms to the ground. There, staring me straight in the eye, was the face of the enemy. Yes, it was a dirty face covered in pus and sweat and grime. It was a tormented face too — a face that had been twisted out of shape as the boy, gasping for air, struggled to catch his breath.

And in the split second when I stared at him and he at me, his face being right there before my eyes, I felt a terrible shudder pass through the core of my entire being. It was an experience bordering well-nigh on ecstasy.

For what had I seen? No, it was not the dirty face of a boy or the mangy head of a wolf. No, it was not a face that belonged to just any man either. To the contrary, it was the incarnation of the pain that had etched itself upon Veronica's veil. It was the living, suffering face of Jesus of Nazareth as he made his way along the road to Calvary. I knew it immediately, the recognition of it having come to me in a piercing flash of insight.

The boy was Jesus, the Son of Man; and he was also Christ, the King and Messiah. Surely the enemy had been sent to bring me this message of salvation.

I know that I am unworthy, and as a person without so much as a single redeeming merit, I rank among the lowest of the low. Nonetheless, by virtue of possessing at least a touch of the coarse and common disposition that is enchanted, if only in passing, by the sight of a good-looking pair of legs such as those on the woman at the *o-musubi* stand, had I not revealed something of my true self and thereby found favor with God? And had not God therefore sent me his bearer of the good tidings of the gospel? My hands and feet began to shake in fear and awe of what had happened to me.

And in that unguarded moment, the enemy slipped his wrist free from my hand and delivered a powerful uppercut to my jaw. I fell flat on my back.

And, in that selfsame second, I saw the small cloth bundle fly through the air and land on the spot next to where my head hit the ground. The bundle fell apart, spilling its contents. Out came the paper, so crumpled it was now hopelessly bent out of shape. Out came the two pieces of hardtack, which rolled in the dirt.

The boy scooped up the bread; and then, grabbing the paper, he threw it, dirt and all, right in my face. With that, he was off. He headed over the hill and disappeared.

When afterwards I got to my feet, I found there were teeth and fingernail marks the length of my arms and legs. And when I went to brush the dirt from my pants, I reached into my pocket and found it was empty. My wallet was gone.

THE FOLLOWING MORNING, I left my apartment and set out once more to the marketplace in Ueno. Perhaps it was the aftereffect of having worked up a sweat in a fight the day before, but I felt curiously refreshed. Even my head felt somehow revitalized, my thinking having become a bit more clear and tidy. And, as for the unfinished business of taking a rubbing from the memorial stone in Yanaka, I gave it nary a second thought.

No, it was because I was in hopes of seeing the face of Jesus one more time that I made my way to the marketplace. And if in passing the *o-musubi* stand I also happened to catch sight of the woman with the good-looking legs, so much the better. Yes, if only I might have one more chance . . . that was the sort of outrageous thought that I had in mind.

But overnight the topography of the marketplace had been altered forever.

"CLOSED EFFECTIVE AUGUST 1."

That was the official edict, although it was probably no more reliable than many of the pronouncements issued by officialdom.

But, astonishingly enough, this time it was being put into effect.

The area had been cordoned off along the street where the streetcars ran. Ropes stretched from one corner to the next across the alleys that gave access to the interior, and two or three military policemen dressed in white summer uniforms were stationed at the corner of each alleyway.

So blank was their stare and so firmly were their feet planted to the spot, they looked like stakes or pylons that had been hammered into the ground. There was a fixity to them that suggested they would not be moved nor just anyone be allowed to pass through.

A crowd had gathered a short distance away. By craning their necks and struggling to peer down the alleys, people were trying to see what had happened to the quarter. I too mixed in, and by peeping around the erect, white pylons at the entryway to the marketplace, I managed to find a gap through which I could see inside.

The center of the market area was completely deserted. It was now a cold, white desert, and there was no indication — nay, not even the shadow — of anyone moving about. It was as though the earth had opened up and swallowed the river of the great unwashed that had flowed through the streets and stalls of the marketplace until only yesterday.

Alas, never again would I have the means whereby I might see the face of Jesus or the good-looking pair of legs on the woman at the *o-musubi* stand! Indeed were it not for the wound marks of the boy's teeth and nails that remained so vividly and freshly imprinted upon my arms and legs, I might have thought the events of the previous day were altogether too unreal to believe. Yes, without solid evidence to the contrary, I might have been tempted to think it had all been a dream — the work of an aberrant figure who, by forcing his way into my fantasies, had come to attack me.

Until only yesterday stands had lined the alleys of the marketplace like a wall. But what about today?

All that remained along either side of the streets were the long, empty rows of stalls constructed of flimsy reed screens. Stretching as far as the eye could see, they resembled a huge stable equipped with countless berths and mangers. But it was a horseless livery. Not a horse was in sight.

Peering still farther inside, one saw an open space. It looked freshly swept. It was as if someone had taken a stiff broom and given it a vigorous sweeping.

Still, the surface was marked by a spot here and there. It was as though something had traipsed across it and left behind its traces. They were the marks of an unidentified being that had walked upon the face of the earth and left its telltale imprint. As a matter of fact, the traces looked ever so much like footsteps — yea, even hoofprints — that a strange creature, having wandered into the desert, left as its tracks in the sand.

THE RAPTOR

≈ 1953 ≈

I

"The canal." So this was it.

Here, its path cut from the land, was where the abundant waters flowed.

Coming from the center of the city, where the streets were lined with dirty little shacks each built hard upon the other, one came to a bridge. Crossing the canal, one immediately came upon a great concrete causeway. It stretched far into the distance.

There was nothing vaguely suggestive of a house where people might live. Only warehouses. Long, gray warehouses. They were like walls that lined both sides of the highway. They seemed to go on forever.

"Hmm . . . now where?"

So unrelentingly uniform were the gray walls that one could only guess at which corner to turn.

"This feels right."

With that the canal suddenly swung into view again. It too had taken a turn as it twisted through the landscape.

And there, in an open space right at water's edge, stood "the house." There it was, all by itself.

From a distance it resembled nothing so much as an old, dead bush.

Caught here and there in what corresponded to the branches of the bush were the pages of a newspaper. Yes, it had to be newspaper, and if that were a sign, surely somebody had to live there. To be sure, the place was not totally out of touch with the land of the living.

Moving closer, one saw it was a house, after all. It was a single-story, wood-frame structure like most people live in.

Newspaper had been pasted over most of the windows.

But other windows had been boarded up or simply left open to the elements. In other words, not a speck of glass had gone into the construction of the house.

Approaching it still closer, it appeared to have not one, but two stories. But there was no sign of an entrance or a door.

If one considered the side of the house facing the canal as the front, then at a corner to the rear was a small window that served as a receiving area. Still, the window amounted to no more than a square that had been cut into the siding. A shelf had been attached on the outside. Sitting on the shelf were two large brown paper bags.

It was a bright and sunny morning, yet peeking through the window revealed nothing. Everything was pitch black inside. There was no sign of anyone on the premises.

But the paper bags were open at the top. By peering over the edge, one could see they were filled with packs of cigarettes.

Hundreds of packs of cigarettes in little boxes. There was no mistaking them. Each of the smartly designed boxes was machine-printed. The word c-i-g-a-r-e-t-t-e-s was spelled out in English.

But the brand name was written in a strange and indecipherable script.

This was no domestic product. But neither was it an imported brand. It made one wonder: Who was the manufacturer? In what country—and at what cigarette factory—had the cigarettes been made? There seemed to be no way to tell.

"In other words . . . "

They had to have been manufactured right here at the house.

"Hmm, I wonder if this building is some sort of special cigarette factory?"

Kunisuke had finally located "the house by the canal." He had come all this way through a veritable maze of confusing streets and unmarked intersections to find only this small receiving window and two brown paper bags filled with packs of cigarettes.

"HELLO? Anybody there? Hello?"

No matter how many times he tried to rouse someone inside, there was no reply. The interior of the house was as silent and dark as when he peeked through the window the first time.

If no one was around, then what about the cigarettes in the brown paper bags? Kunisuke was curious. Were the cigarettes in the smart-looking packs really cigarettes after all? Perhaps they had been made to look like an expensive brand of tobacco when, quite the contrary, they contained a strange and unknown substitute. Perhaps someone was playing a trick on him.

Kunisuke reached into one of the brown paper bags and pulled out a pack. He tapped the bottom, and as the silver wrapper popped out, the glare from the light falling on the pretty, heavy-duty foil blinded him momentarily. He peeled back the wrapper. There—just as one would expect—were ten neatly rolled cigarettes in two rows of five apiece.

But even before Kunisuke finished peeling back the foil, a distinctive aroma filled the air. It reached out and attacked his nostrils. It penetrated to the pit of his stomach. It made his head spin.

He was completely taken aback. No question about it. This was very fine tobacco. He knew it all right because, when it came to the subject of choice tobaccos, he considered himself something of an authority. But why hadn't he known it right from the start? He should have known, but he had chosen instead to question the cigarettes, to consider them dubious. Naturally enough, he was embarrassed, and his face turned red. Shame on me, he thought, for having doubted anything so fine.

Just then there was a screeching sound. It was the sound of a tightly closed door being opened. A cut had been made in the siding by the window to create a secret entryway to the house. As the door swung open, a man stuck out his head from inside.

Kunisuke hastily stuffed the opened pack of cigarettes into the paper bag. He stumbled as he nervously stepped back from the shelf. The man at the door was a lummox. He looked big enough to be a prize fighter, and his ears had been battered out of shape. There was an angry scowl on his face as he stood in the doorway and stared straight at Kunisuke. He said nothing as he kept his eye trained on him.

Kunisuke became confused. He could hardly speak because of the piercing gaze that was being directed his way.

"Well, sir, it was K who told me about this place . . . ," he stammered at last.

The man still said nothing. His eyes scanned the figure at the door a second time.

Kunisuke repeated himself. "It was K who told me. . . . He said you'd have work for me if I came. That's why I'm here."

At last the man spoke.

"So you're the one he calls 'Kuni'?" The tone of the man's voice was far gentler than Kunisuke anticipated it would be.

"Yes, sir, that's me, Kunisuke. Are you 'Mister E'?"

The man said nothing. But surely he must be "E." Kunisuke interpreted the man's silence as wordless confirmation of the fact.

The man stuck his hand inside the small receiving window and pulled out a large burlap bag. He stuffed the two brown paper bags in the sack and thrust it in Kunisuke's face.

"Throw this over your shoulder and get going."

"But where, sir?"

E pulled a slip of paper from his pocket. This too was thrust under Kunisuke's nose.

It was a map illustrating the streets at the heart of the city. On it was the name of a tobacco shop as well as the name of the office building where the shop was located. Wrapped in the map were a number of large bills. Was it his pay, perhaps? Kunisuke could only guess at the amount, but it was no small sum.

"You mean all I have to do is to deliver this bag?"

"That's it for today at least. And pick up the cash that's due on the goods. So long as you're back before dark, there's no need to hurry."

Yet instructions appeared to be the least of the man's concerns. To the contrary, his attention was now riveted to the spot where Kunisuke stood. His eyes flashed at the sight of a small dog—no, it was no more than a pup—and the way the puppy was prancing about as it tried to entwine itself around Kunisuke's legs.

Kunisuke had almost forgotten the puppy. Reaching down, he took him into his arms and proudly announced,

"This is my pet."

The man said nothing as he headed into the house, but Kunisuke was right behind him. His voice sounded almost desperate at the prospect of being left outside. "Hey, Mister, please don't leave. . . . K said I could talk to you about a room for the night. . . . He said . . . "

But E had already disappeared, and now that the door had been slammed in Kunisuke's face, it was too late. Kunisuke's plea echoed woodenly, falling as it did on the house's clapboard siding. He consoled himself that everything would work out in the evening when he returned, for surely they would have a place for him to stay the night. Slinging the burlap sack over his shoulder, and cradling the puppy in the crook of his arm, he turned in the direction of the city and set forth from the house on foot.

I T WAS LAST NIGHT that Kunisuke learned of the curious house by the canal for the first time. He had gone for supper at the same run-down restaurant that he always patronized in his neighborhood. He went last night, as he did every night, for the simple reason he had nowhere else to go and nothing else to do.

Until two years ago, Kunisuke had been employed by the National Tobacco Monopoly Corporation. He had been one of the workers, although not on the floor where the cigarettes were made. No, he had worked — and this had been his preference — at the scientific study of the leaf, happily doing research on the species of plant known to the world as "tobacco." He had been happy at his job, but then one day he was summarily fired, and he was given only the vaguest of reasons. The Corporation said it was on account of what they called the "Red Purge." That was why, they said, they were obliged to let him go.

It had been Kunisuke's philosophy that, because tobacco was a product enjoyed by all, its study and research ought to be directed, especially in the areas of its practical applications and uses, toward furthering what he called "The Happiness of All the People." As a consequence, he felt it incumbent upon himself and the Monopoly Corporation to produce for the public the very best cigarette possible. To his way of thinking this was the best way to make everyone happy, but his moderate and liberal "ideology" ran counter, he was told, to the policies of the Monopoly. In particular, it appeared the Corporation had taken a dislike to his use of the phrase "The Happiness of All the People." And insofar as it had been appointed to exercise exclusive control over the market, doubtless the Monopoly would not be satisfied until it, and it alone, monopolized the definition of whatever happiness was meant to be.

Kunisuke had found the company's logic hard to comprehend, but what of it? It hardly mattered now. He had lost his job, and the condition known as unemployment had taught him the full measure of his dimwittedness. He had learned a bitter lesson, and it was not one that would be easy for him to forget.

Nevertheless, he had managed to make ends meet by taking odd jobs such as working for fly-by-night publishers or subcontracting on translation jobs of a questionable, if not sometimes downright illicit, nature. At least he had not been forced to find cheaper accommodations in the suburbs. He had been able to stay in the city, and he still occupied the room that he had rented at a lodging house in a more obscure corner of town.

Yet, of late, even this margin of comfort had grown perilously thin. Since the end of the month the old woman who owned the rooming house had served notice that he would have to move, and she had done so repeatedly. As a result, Kunisuke now had to spend the better part of each day roaming about town in order to avoid being at home and running into his landlady. Besides, he was not the type to dig in his heels and refuse to move. By nature, the role of the irate boarder was an act alien to his nature. Given a choice, he much preferred to play the part of the feckless soul who, moving from place to place, wanders happily through life.

And so it was last night when he stepped from his apartment with the air of the happy wanderer. He had seated himself at the far end of a table in the old, run-down restaurant in his neighborhood. There he sat, nursing a cup of cheap saké all by himself, when suddenly he felt something brush against his pant leg. Whatever it was, it felt soft and furry, and it tickled as it entwined itself about his feet.

And what did he find when he looked under the table?

A puppy. It was prancing about as it tried to catch his attention.

And where had it come from? Clearly of indeterminate stripe and no bigger than a minute, it appeared that, having gotten lost, the puppy had wandered into the restaurant. It had not rained, but the little fellow was soaked to the skin, the fur on his back being all wet and plastered down. By standing on Kunisuke's shoes and pawing at his pant leg, he tried to climb into Kunisuke's lap. Kunisuke could feel the warmth of the dog's tummy as it pressed against his legs, and that made the poor fellow seem all the more pitiful. He took the leftovers from his plate and tossed them on the floor.

And then, as if lighting a beacon in a sea of darkness, he reached for a cigarette. Pulling the cigarette from the pack, he struck a match.

But, uh-oh, there was only one — no, not even one — cigarette left. What remained was only the black, stubbed-out tip of a cigarette, the still un-smoked half of a butt that he had saved and stuffed back into the pack.

It was like a picture of the current state of his life. He had no job, and he did not know where to turn to find one.

But what sort of work was he looking for, anyway? He pursued the thought, yet it went nowhere. It was as if all of his prospects had gone up in smoke and turned as black as the tip of a burnt cigarette. They had been stubbed out, leaving behind only the butt end of his hopes, which, albeit half alive, smoldered deep within his breast pocket.

"Need a job?"

From nowhere, he heard a voice. A stranger had sat down at the table directly across from him, and he was looking straight at Kunisuke. He had on a hunting cap that was pulled down over his eyes. He was so thin and bony it was hard to guess his age. He looked neither young nor old.

"What? . . . " replied Kunisuke, taken by surprise.

"You're looking for a job, aren't you, my friend?"

"Well, yes, but . . . "

"What type of work are you interested in?"

"That's the problem. I'm not really sure.

"Huh. In that case, what type of work do you think you can handle?"

"Well, just about anything so long as it has to do with cigarettes. . . . "

Suddenly, the man reached into his pocket and took out a piece of paper and a pencil. With startling rapidity, he drew a map.

"Try this place first thing in the morning."

THE PLACE ON THE MAP was the house by the canal. The stranger's explanation about the location had been brief, almost laconic; and once it was clear Kunisuke knew the way, the man struck a match and held the map to the flame. He dropped it in an ashtray and watched it burn until it was finally reduced to ashes. Kunisuke asked for the man's name, but he identified himself only as K.

"Call me K."

And when Kunisuke wanted to know whom he should ask for when he went to the house by the canal, K identified him only as E.

"Call him E."

"Ask E, and he'll fix you up with a live-in arrangement as well."

Kunisuke tried to imagine why the man called himself K. Was it an abbreviation, perhaps, for a name like "Kei"? But when he asked, the stranger simply dipped his finger in beer that was spilled on the table and traced out the letter "K." And what about the name of the man whom he was to contact at the house? Kunisuke wondered. Would K have traced out a similar reply — the letter "E"?

With that K stood up, and paying his bill, he disappeared out the door.

Kunisuke hardly knew what to think. Yes, it was true the stranger had come at the right time and with the welcome news of a job, but what evidence did he have of a solid offer? — why, absolutely none. The sole proof that the stranger had even been in the restaurant amounted to no more than a slip of paper, now reduced to ashes, and the initial capital letter of a name that had been traced in bubbles of beer atop the table. It was not much to rely on. Kunisuke was not at all confident anything would come of the matter, and thinking it best not to make too much of K's offer, he decided against laying any new plans. For tonight at least, he would wait and see. He deliberately let time pass and let the hour grow late before he headed back to the lodging house.

No sooner had he reached his room and started to take off his jacket than he was startled to find the puppy tucked inside. Had he inadvertently scooped up the little fellow and carried him home? Or had the little fellow, by taking advantage of a moment in which Kunisuke had let his thoughts wander, concealed himself inside the jacket? At any rate, the puppy was light and fluffy, and having burrowed his way into the inside pocket of the jacket, he was now sound asleep. Moreover, inasmuch as this unexpected piece of baggage was a living, breathing creature, Kunisuke felt that he could not turn it out into the streets. There was nothing to do but move over and share his small pallet, however narrow the bed might be for the two of them.

When he woke this morning, he found the little fellow was already awake and lying on top of him. The puppy looked ever so much like a toy dog, given the way he cocked his head from side to side and opened his big, round eyes and studied Kunisuke's face with a wide-eyed and puzzled look. But, clearly, the puppy was no toy. It was real enough. And, no question, it was very much alive.

What is more, Kunisuke could now say as much for the house by the canal. The previous night it had consisted of no more than a set of directions on a burnt scrap of paper. Like the puppy, it really did exist, and it was located at the very spot that K had indicated on the map. Kunisuke had just come from the house, and he had verified its existence with his own two eyes.

The puppy was his all right, but as for the house by the canal, now that was a different matter. It had yet to open its doors and invite him in. Nonetheless, he felt that, by virtue of the job he had been given, at least he had gotten a foot in the door toward establishing contact with the residents of the house. Surely that was worth something, even if the work he was asked to do consisted only of shouldering a burlap bag filled with packs of cigarettes. At least as far as today was concerned, he felt he had little reason to complain. Following the map that E gave him, he made his way to the heart of the city's bustling business and shopping district. He quickly identified the office building he was looking for. The tobacco shop was in the basement, where it had a large store frontage. The people working in the shop seemed to know why he had come. They simply took the goods, and in exchange, they handed him payment in a sealed envelope. Kunisuke could only guess what was inside, but it was clear that the people at the shop trusted him. Why else would they have given him money without so much as asking for a receipt? It had been all so simple. His work for the day was done.

Yet, just as he was about to turn and leave, he happened to notice one of the employees step to the counter at the front of the shop. The man had emerged from the rear of the store, and he was carrying what was surely one of the two brown paper bags that he, Kunisuke, had delivered only minutes before. Kunisuke watched as the clerk upended the contents of the bag into a large glass jar atop the front counter. The little packs of cigarettes set up a soft patter as they slithered into the container, each one falling quietly on top of the others.

Was it legal, Kunisuke wondered at the sight of what the clerk had done, to sell cigarettes that were of unknown origin and manufacture? Or still more to the point, was it legal for a customer to let his curiosity get the better of himself and take the risk of buying them?

But, no, the real question in Kunisuke's mind had little to do with what others might say or be curious about. Above all it was a matter of his own burning desire to taste one of the cigarettes. He had to try one. Without hesitation, he marched to the counter.

But what was happening? There was the jar all right, and it was being filled with packs of "Peace" cigarettes. But why was he so excited? Peace was a well-known domestic brand, wasn't it? One could find it at any store in town. What did he expect?

Perhaps he had been mistaken. Perhaps it was a different brown paper bag that the clerk brought from the back of the store. Maybe it wasn't the one he delivered after all. But it had to be. He remembered the bags had been torn along the top. Each bag had a tear on the top edge in the shape of a crescent. And he knew he had seen the crescent-shaped mark on the bag when the clerk carried it to the front of the store. For a brief second Kunisuke stood in the middle of the floor feeling dazed and wondering what to do next. Nothing seemed to make sense.

But, just in case, he decided to buy one of the packs of Peace cigarettes in the jar. Leaving the shop, he turned in the direction of the crossroads of the city.

I T WOULD BE quite a while before evening.

Kunisuke chose a coffee shop on the street, and taking one of the Peace cigarettes from the pack he bought at the store, he lit it and inhaled a puff of smoke. Nothing different about this Peace. It tasted the way Peace always did.

But then something very peculiar happened. The puppy, who had been lying quietly in Kunisuke's lap, sat up on his haunches. His nose began to twitch, and as he squinted his eyes and sniffed the air, he tried to follow the train of smoke as it emerged from Kunisuke's lips. It was obvious the puppy was enjoying himself, so that no matter how many times Kunisuke petted him and tried to get him to lie down, the little fellow kept jumping about. He was like a rubber ball that bounced in Kunisuke's lap.

Now that Kunisuke thought of it, hadn't it been a Peace cigarette that he smoked this morning as he lay awake in bed? And, hadn't he — just for the hell of it — blown a puff of smoke in the puppy's face? He had meant it as a joke, of course, but what did the little fellow do? He had screwed up his nose and given Kunisuke the saddest look. He had even tucked in his tail and run away from him.

From the time they left the house by the canal until just now when they entered the coffee shop, Kunisuke carried the little fellow in the crook of his arm, and to keep him happy, quite naturally he made a point of never letting the smoke from his cigarette drift in the direction of the puppy's face. Still, the puppy always looked unhappy when Kunisuke had a cigarette.

Kunisuke could not help wondering. Did the little fellow's reaction here in the coffee shop mean the cigarette that he was smoking was somehow different from the regular brand of Peace? Just to double-check, he inhaled once more, and holding his breath, he let the smoke roll slowly over his tongue. It tasted like a Peace cigarette all right. It was the same, regular flavor. But what had become of the aroma of fine tobacco of which he had a whiff this morning, when he stood by the receiving window at the house by the canal and dared to open one of the packs of cigarettes? It was almost as though it had never happened. Still, he knew it was no lie.

But the puppy would not be deterred. He sniffed all the more furiously at the smoke from the cigarette as he bounced about Kunisuke's lap.

Suddenly Kunisuke remembered he had put a pack of Peace cigarettes in his pocket as he was leaving the lodging house this morning. He took out a cigarette and lit it. It was the last one.

No sooner had he taken a puff than the puppy put his head down on Kunisuke's lap. Looking ever so much as though he wanted to crawl into a hole and hide, the little fellow buried his nose inside Kunisuke's jacket.

Kunisuke was completely taken aback. What was happening? Not only could he not explain it, but he began to wonder if, as a supposed authority on all there was to know about tobacco, he was losing his touch. He tried comparing the two cigarettes once more. He took a puff of the Peace cigarette he bought at the store. Then he took a puff from the Peace that came from the pack in his pocket. There was no difference in the way they tasted, but what a change in the puppy's attitude! Kunisuke found it all quite mysterious.

But, no, he chose not to think any further. It was "just one of those things" that happens, wasn't it? Rather than spend time speculating about a matter he could not hope to divine, wasn't he better off simply not to think at all? Yes, that was it. He would go on living in a daze.

But meanwhile — as he sat in the coffee shop letting his mind wander absentmindedly — he happened to look down and see, much to his surprise, that his hands were in constant motion. They were moving independently of his control, and he watched as they took the map that E had given him and proceeded to tear it into little pieces. Moreover, they struck a match, and lighting the paper on fire, they let it burn in the ashtray. It was really quite amazing; the movements of his hands were a perfect match for the display that K had put on last night at the restaurant! Weren't they moving in unconscious imitation of what K had done? There, right before his own eyes, the pieces of the map were going up in flames. They sent up a pale column of blue smoke that, vanishing into thin air, left no trace of the actions that earlier in the day he had carried out under orders from K and E.

Kunisuke did not understand why, but somehow or other he felt he had become closer to the two men by virtue of what he had done this morning. Now he was on their side. Only, he had no clue as to what it meant to say he was on their side or what the world they lived in was really like. For him, it was an unknown world. It was knowledge that lay beyond his ken, no matter how hard he tried to reach out and grasp it. As a result, he was at a loss to know how his actions this morning were related to the unknown world of which they were undoubtedly a part. What was the connection? And what meaning did it possess?

By now the puppy had snuggled inside his jacket and was sound asleep.

K UNISUKE had killed a fair amount of time at the coffee shop. When he decided it was time finally to get up and leave, the puppy was already a step ahead of him. The little fellow had opened his eyes and was looking about as though he were on the alert. At exactly the same moment, the glass door of the café opened and in walked a man wearing a hunting cap. Kunisuke recognized him immediately.

"Hey, it's K."

Just like that. There was K standing in front of him. K sat down even before Kunisuke could offer him a seat.

"What a surprise. I didn't expect to see you here."

"You can bet on it, my friend. Whenever your mind starts to wander, I'll be there."

"My mind wasn't wandering. I was thinking, that's all."

"The truth is there isn't a real thought in your brain. You sit here with your head full of all sorts of vague doubts and suspicions. You question who so-and-so is and why he did such-and-such. You test one scheme after another, mentally trying to figure out what will work and what it is worth to you. But it's all nonsense. Yes, it's sheer stupidity. It's precisely because your mind is full of such doubts that you can't tell the taste of one cigarette from the next.

"Of course, seen from our point of view, you too are a total unknown. We don't know a thing about you, my friend. But did we question you? Did we doubt you? Did we test you first to see how you'd do? No, right from the start we accepted you as you are."

Once it was pointed out to him, Kunisuke had to admit that what K said was true. Take E, for example. Hadn't he immediately entrusted him with a sack of goods, although it was only the first time they ever met? Or, what about the people at the tobacco shop? The clerk who paid for the goods had not even asked for a receipt. All of the transactions rested, did they not, on the fundamental principle of trust in humankind.

It was all so obvious. Were it the case that everything rested on trust, Kunisuke wondered, what would happen were one to become so cynical that it was no longer possible to trust humankind and be trusted in return? Did it mean he would lose the discriminatory powers of his senses as well—lose them even to the point where he could no longer tell the taste of one cigarette from the next?

Perhaps he had come to the city and lived too long at its crossroads. Perhaps after having been buffeted by its strong winds and being enveloped in its clouds of swirling dust and dirt, he had changed—just as any person would—and now he went through life with a permanent scowl etched on his face. Perhaps he had grown numb and his senses dulled to the point where even the choicest tobacco now tasted like any old Peace.

"I appreciate the goodwill that you and E have shown me, K. It makes me happy to know you really believe in me. Only, what I don't understand is . . ."

"What you don't understand, my friend, is the way we talk. We have our own language, and you'll have to learn it if you want to understand the words we use. You'll have to start giving yourself lessons."

With that, K produced two small books and placed them on top of the table. One was a grammar; the other, a dictionary. Both were titled, in English, *Futurese: The Language of Tomorrow*.

But what was "Futurese"?

"I appreciate it, but . . . " Kunisuke had no idea what K was talking about.

As he picked up one of the books and started to open the cover, the puppy lifted his head and began to growl. It was a low, insistent growl. It was as though he were warning of impending danger.

K had already gotten to his feet.

"Quick, stash the books under the table. I'm being followed. If anyone asks, you've never heard of me. Got it?"

K dodged behind the table and disappeared out the back door of the shop.

At the same time, two sinister-looking men came sailing through the front door. They scanned the room. And, with an air of thwarted expectation, they muttered something to the waiter. Either the waiter did not understand, or they could not get their point across, but in no time they turned and went out the front door. It appeared the waiter never knew that K had been in the coffee shop.

Kunisuke quietly slipped the books into his pocket. He stood up, and trying to look as nonchalant as possible, he made his way out the door.

He came to the grassy lawn of a public park, and finding a bench in the sun, he sat down and opened the two books. Never before had he seen letters shaped like those he found printed inside. Starting even from the alphabet chart on the first page, the books struck him as virtually impenetrable.

There was a side to Kunisuke's personality, however, that welcomed the challenge of learning a language he did not know. He struggled with the strange, new alphabet, knowing that a bit of frustration was inevitable at first. There was explanatory material in English, which he read with great care. There was logic to it, and he found himself gradually drawn into the book. It was really quite fascinating.

The grammar did not seem so complicated after all. It appeared that each word had a very precise meaning, and a clear and distinct sound to it. When he used the phonetic table in the notes and tried pronouncing the words, he found they echoed with a clear, bell-like ring. There was not the slightest suggestion of anything vague or ambiguous. To the contrary, the words struck his ear as having a powerful rhetorical effect. How fortunate people would be, he thought, to possess a language constructed of words like these. What an incredible stage for the human spirit! What a setting in which spirit might manifest itself and give full expression to its movement! Kunisuke had no idea when, or where, or by what people the language of tomorrow was currently spoken, but the image that rose in his mind was of an orchestra about to sound the opening bars of a magnificent symphony. The enunciation of each word was music to his ears.

First, he memorized the alphabet and practiced pronouncing it. Then, he started on the text. With the turn of each page, he found himself becoming more and more immersed in the language.

By and by the sun faded on the lawn, and as the sky clouded over, the first few drops of a gentle rain began to fall. The puppy, who had been having fun rolling in the grass, trotted over. He grabbed Kunisuke's pant leg and gave it a tug.

"Oh, that's right. . . . " Kunisuke remembered he was supposed to be at the house by the canal before dark. He got up from the park bench and headed for the bus stop.

The light in the sky had faded by the time the bus reached the vicinity of the canal. The rain had let up for a while, but dark clouds still hovered over the horizon.

This time, when Kunisuke stood outside and made his presence known via the small receiving window, the door opened almost immediately. E stepped out.

Kunisuke handed him the cash he had collected when he delivered the cigarettes, and he returned the empty burlap bag. E merely took them and said nothing. He turned and started into the house. But rather than lock Kunisuke out, he motioned with his chin for him to come inside.

Kunisuke now saw the interior of the house for the first time. The house was suffused with a dim, white light of a shade and color that defied description. It closely resembled moonlight, although the moon did not shine in from the outside. There was a concrete floor, and deep inside the room was a large table around which a group of people were gathered. At the center of the table was a large candle. It was shaped much like the kind of votive lamp one saw on a Buddhist altar. The lamp appeared to be the source of the strange and eerie light that filled the room.

There was no time to determine what was happening, however. Right in front of Kunisuke's nose was a set of stairs. E motioned toward it with a sidelong glance.

"Take the stairs. At the landing turn right and walk to the end of the corridor. Along the wall to the left you'll find another set of stairs. Take it to the third floor. That's your room.

"In the room, there's a window. It's a hole that's been cut to the outside. To close it, take a sheet of newspaper and tack it across the hole. There's a newspaper on the bed."

Kunisuke climbed the narrow flight of steps. To the right of the landing was a corridor that ran along the lefthand wall. There appeared to be a room on the other side of the wall, and there was a door to it. Along the righthand side of the corridor was a railing, and peering over it, Kunisuke could vaguely make out part of the concrete floor down below. He could also see the turn at the end of the hall, because enough of the light from downstairs reached to the second floor.

When he had examined the house from the outside this morning, the roof looked lower than in most two-story dwellings. It had never occurred to him to think there might be a third floor. Nonetheless, the house was clearly larger on the inside than its external appearance suggested. Sure enough, to the left of the end of the corridor was a second set of stairs. It consisted of three short steps. A black door loomed in the dark at the top of the stairway.

Kunisuke pushed open the door. It was pitch black inside. He struck a match and found the room was no bigger than a walk-in closet. It had an extremely low ceiling.

There was no sign of a light fixture. Nor was there any furniture or decorations on the walls. Only, a part of the wall had been hollowed out and a plank attached to it to create a narrow bench. Was this what E had meant by a bed? A newspaper was rolled up and lying on top of the bench.

Opposite the bed, a small hole had been cut into the wall. But it was an air vent at best, and it looked more like the hollow in a tree than a window. Kunisuke's match went out as he stepped over to take a look at it. He stuck his neck through the hole, and taking a peek outside, he discovered the moon was not visible after all. To the contrary, it was raining again, and the rain was coming down hard. He could see the canal below as its inky waters coursed darkly through the night. He did not know why, but he liked this view of the canal from the third-floor window.

Groping his way across the room to the bed, he sat down and lit another match. This time it was to light a cigarette.

But the instant he sat back and inhaled a mouthful of smoke, he gave a start.

"Hey," he shouted in disbelief, "this is no ordinary Peace!"

No, not on your life, it wasn't. The flavor was completely different. And, the aroma that filled the air was identical to the fragrance of the fine tobacco of which he had a whiff this morning. The puppy leapt out of Kunisuke's jacket and, sniffing excitedly, began to race about the floor.

Yet how was it possible for the pack of cigarettes in Kunisuke's pocket to be any different from the one that he had bought at the tobacco shop? It simply could not be. Kunisuke reached into his pocket and fished out the small pack of cigarettes. He lit another match and held the pack to the light. As he inspected the package a second time, he was shocked to find that it looked completely different. It wasn't a pack of Peace cigarettes anymore. It had been radically transformed, and embossed across the smartly designed box were a set of letters written in a strange and indecipherable alphabet. They were the same set of letters he had seen this morning when he peeked into the brown paper bags.

Humph. He might not know what they meant, but the letters were no longer "the unknown" that they had been this morning. No, they were a perfect match for the letters of the alphabet that he had studied so assiduously as he sat on the bench in the park. He hurriedly reached for the dictionary.

"Damn!?!"

The match went out as he started to flip through the pages — and just when it was so important! There was only one match left in his box of matches. He struck it, and flipping rapidly through the dictionary, at last he came to the word he was searching for.

"What the hell is going on?"

There it was, along with its equivalent spelled out in English.

"P-e-a-c-e."

The match flickered and went out.

Kunisuke decided that for tonight at least he would leave the window as it was. He would not fuss with it. As for the newspaper, he unfolded it and used it to cover his face. He stretched out on the narrow plank of the bench, and in order to make himself fit, he lay on his side and pulled his knees to his chest. Clutching the puppy, he soon fell sound asleep.

II

"Asshole."

Kunisuke woke with a start. He was sure someone was speaking to him.

But this was no dream. The voice was real all right. He heard it through the wall at the spot right beside his ear.

"You asshole. I told you 'no' before. I won't permit it."

Although the voice spoke with authority, it sounded to Kunisuke like it belonged to a young girl.

"It's not a matter of permission, yes or no." This time a man was doing the talking. "What you don't understand is that I'm absolutely crazy about you. Believe me, you can depend on it. It's the best thing in the world for the two of us. That's why I feel I have the legitimate right to treat you any way I like."

Kunisuke recognized the man's voice immediately. It was E. But the tone of his voice was so pleading and gentle that it was hard to believe it emanated from a man as big and brawny as E.

Suddenly the air reverberated with a sharp, stinging sound. It sounded as if someone's face had been slapped. Yes, it must have been the sound of the girl's hand as she reached out and flexed it like a whip. Still, nothing seemed to come of it, and there followed a long silence. Presently, Kunisuke heard a door opening. Someone stepped into the corridor that led downstairs. He could hear footsteps recede into the distance. That was all there was to it.

It was toward daybreak when the hole in the wall began to glow with a whitish light. When Kunisuke got up and peeked outside, he could see the rain had stopped, but the wind had picked up and it was blowing hard. He remembered he was supposed to cover the hole to keep out the wind. There were some tacks scattered on the floor beneath the window. No doubt someone else had stayed here before and used them to pin a sheet of newspaper over the hole.

But when Kunisuke reached for the newspaper on the bed, he was startled by what he found printed on the front page.

"What in the . . . ?" His eyes were glued to the page.

This was not just any old newspaper. To be sure, there was the usual jumble of print on the front page, but the typeface was completely different, and it was set in the strange alphabet that he had seen in the books on the language of Futurese. The print ran every which way—up and down, back and forth, on a diagonal, even upside down. It was scattered across the page, looking as if the letters had been haphazardly thrown at random. They did not appear to form words, let alone sentences. Blank spaces were inserted here and there, with each of several large, white squares being big enough to accommodate a news photo or a cartoon. The newsprint itself was soft to the touch, yet it was also sturdy enough to resist tearing when Kunisuke rubbed it between his fingers. What's more, the paper was semitransparent. It had the properties of a paper-thin piece of isinglass.

Kunisuke tacked it over the hole. Immediately the wind stopped blowing in, and the light that entered the room through the blank, white squares looked filtered. It was as though it were passing through a fine mist.

Presently, the blank spaces began to glow bright red as if they had burst into flame. Probably the sun had come up. Kunisuke convinced himself that each red spot was like the small firepeep one might find on a stove or a furnace. As a matter of fact, the room was beginning to feel nice and cozy. The puppy had gotten up, and giving his legs a stretch, he began to prance about the floor. Kunisuke removed the pack of cigarettes from his pocket, and giving it a whiff, he found it retained the same wonderful aroma that it had had last night. The letters were of the same strange design, and the cigarettes, the same atypical brand. The newspaper and the pack of cigarettes were mysterious all right, but there was no longer any question in Kunisuke's mind. Beyond the shadow of a doubt they were real, and like it or not, they were part of the real world.

SO FAR SO GOOD, but starting from today, what sort of life was in store for him now that Kunisuke knew about the house, the cigarettes, and the newspaper with the strange alphabet? A great shudder passed through him, and he felt as though he were a warrior girding his loins in preparation for battle. If, as was surely the case, the cigarettes were manufactured here on the premises, he needed to get himself properly informed. And being informed meant it was essential for him to see the raw material of the tobacco leaves from which the cigarettes were made. Despite his considerable knowledge of cigarettes and tobacco, nothing in his past had prepared him for a moment like this. That so fine a tobacco leaf existed was a fact that surpassed his wildest imagination. For him to grasp to the fullest the meaning of the new life that lay ahead of him, he had to start first and foremost with the experience of actually touching the leaves. He needed to take a sheaf of the fine tobacco and hold it in his own two hands. He had to see it with his own eyes.

His hunch was that the leaves were kept under lock and key in a storage area on the first floor. It was just a hunch, but he was convinced the secret to the house, and to its inner workings, was be found somewhere downstairs. But here he was a newcomer, and why should a newcomer be allowed to see something so secret — and right off the bat, to boot? Who would permit such a thing?

"It's not a matter of permission, yes or no."

Isn't that what E had said? Kunisuke heard him say it through the wall this morning. The phrase still echoed in his ear.

Did he not love cigarettes? And had he not made the study of tobacco the focus of his work in life? Here was a grade of tobacco that exceeded anything he ever imagined. What possibly could be wrong with wanting to hold a leaf of it in his hands — just to touch it and feel what it was like? To look into the matter of this rare tobacco and study its properties — wasn't that precisely what he ought to be doing? And, after all, if that's what he liked, didn't he have every legitimate right?

No, this was not a matter of mere curiosity on his part. It was something far more serious, and it might well involve considerable risk. This time around the slapped face might be his own, and E would probably be the one to deliver the blow. But Kunisuke felt he had to take the chance. He had made up his mind, and throwing caution to the winds, he pushed open the door of his room. In a single stride, he descended the short flight of stairs to the hall corridor.

The house was quiet as a tomb. Kunisuke peered over the railing and took a look at the floor below. There was no sign of anybody having gotten up or moving about. He made his way along the narrow corridor, but as he was about to reach the landing at the top of the stairs, the door facing on the hallway suddenly swung open, and a young girl stepped out. Kunisuke came perilously close to bumping into her.

There she was, standing in front of him. She looked more like a boy, dressed as she was in culottes and riding boots, and standing stiff as a ramrod.

But the face that blossomed like a flower from the circle of white lace at the collar of the riding jacket was richly soft and feminine.

Still, there was an air of naked and unbridled power about the girl—a strange and powerful synergy that called to him. She held a whip in one hand, as if she were always on guard and prepared to resist attack from any quarter. He was certain it had been her voice—"Asshole!"—that had awakened him early this morning. Perhaps it had been the crack of a whip, and not the back of her hand, that had sent a sharp, stinging sound reverberating through the air.

Still, if the sound had originated on the second floor, why had it been so clearly audible in his room on the third? And through a wall, no less? It made no sense unless, of course, the rooms shared the same ceiling. His room appeared to be on the third floor, but—wait—in point of fact it was not. In other words, the room on the second floor had been divided, and a raised floor installed in one half of it to create a loft. The loft corresponded to his room.

Kunisuke had it all figured out in no more time than it took to bat an eye. He stepped back, and acknowledging the girl's presence with a polite nod, he waited for her to pass. But she did not move. Keeping whatever thoughts she had to herself, she silently gestured for him to go first. It was a clear and unmistakable signal not only for him to "get moving!" down the stairs, but no doubt she intended to drive him from the premises as well. To hesitate one moment more meant the lash of her whip would come flying his way for sure. In fact, Kunisuke thought he almost heard it crack over his head.

Inside Kunisuke's jacket, the puppy was cringing, his little body shaking like a leaf.

Kunisuke clambered down the stairs as fast as his feet would carry him. At the same time, the door at the foot of the stairs swung open. Propelled by the force of his own momentum, he found himself flying headlong outside, and no sooner did he turn and look back than the door was slammed in his face. Everything was precisely as the young girl commanded. He had been ordered out, and now he was lying on the ground.

E stuck his neck through the receiving window.

"Do like yesterday."

That was it. Not a word more. E tucked his head inside. He had left a burlap bag and a stack of bills sitting on the shelf beneath the window.

"Here I go again." There he was, starting all over for a second time. Did it mean, he wondered to himself, that the people in the house still refused to recognize him as a fellow member of their own humankind? He did not know what to think.

Kunisuke slung the burlap bag over his shoulder, but as he started for the city, he happened to glance back at the window of his room. No matter how one looked at it, the sheet of paper tacked across it had to have come from an ordinary newspaper, and that was that. What else could it be but a page from a newspaper that one saw every day?

And what about that pack of Peace cigarettes he had in his pocket last night? There was one cigarette left. But Kunisuke no longer felt the urge to take it out and look at it. He felt certain there was no point in checking. He knew only too well that by now the cigarette had reverted to looking like any old Peace.

DOING AS HE WAS TOLD, Kunisuke passed the day — namely, "today" — much like "yesterday." First, he went to the tobacco shop in the office building at the heart of the city. The details of his routine at the store were an exact copy of what he had done the day before, and it need hardly be said that, for his evening pleasure, he purchased one of the packs of Peace cigarettes from the jar on the front counter. Next, he headed for the crossroads of the city and decided to stop for a while at the same coffee shop.

Only, today K did not appear. What's more, Kunisuke made no attempt to take out his pack of cigarettes and have a smoke. He had no desire. He had reached the point where the ordinary brand of Peace no longer satisfied him. How could he possibly like it anymore? The flavor did not measure up to his high standards. Come to think of it, he had lost his appetite as well, even though he had not eaten anything that qualified as a real meal since yesterday morning. He wasn't hungry, but still he and the puppy would need something to eat. He bought some cheese and crackers and headed for the grassy lawn of the public park. Munching on the crackers, Kunisuke opened his two books and set about teaching himself the language of the future.

As luck would have it, however, along came a policeman who was making the rounds of the park.

"What book is that?" he demanded to know, sounding as if the law entitled him to exercise control over everything that appeared in print.

Kunisuke decided on the spur of the moment to say the book was about the Pali language.

"Pali?"

What kind of language was that? And where was it spoken? And why was a young man like him studying it? The policeman fired a round of questions at Kunisuke, interrogating him as if he were a criminal.

Kunisuke patiently explained that Pali was a dead language from long, long ago. He was studying it for use in his research on Buddhist philosophy and Buddhist texts written in Pali.

The policeman looked reassured. Perhaps the fact that Pali was a dead language made the difference. Or he thought that Kunisuke was a follower of the Buddhist faith. He made a great show of respect for Kunisuke before heading on his way.

Presently, it was dusk. There was no sign of rain tonight, and the sunset had been beautiful. Kunisuke made his way back to the house by the canal. Once again, he was admitted inside, but only as far as the stairs that gave him access to his room on the third floor.

THE ROOM DID NOT APPEAR to have been tampered with. Aside from the sheet of newspaper that he had tacked across the window in the morning, there was no difference in appearance from the previous night except the moon was out. The moon had just risen, and its light shone through the blank, white squares on the page of the newspaper. It bathed the room in a soft white light that seemed to move in little waves that rippled across the floor.

Kunisuke knew he had seen this kind of light before. No — it wasn't even a matter of struggling to remember where. Hadn't he seen it last night, right here on the premises? As a matter of fact, hadn't he seen it tonight as well? Only moments before, when he was downstairs, he had seen it radiating from the center of the big table in the middle of the room. It was a soft white light

produced by the device that resembled a Buddhist altar lamp. No question
about it. Moonlight had to have been the source of inspiration for invention
of the fluorescent, light-emitting device that sat on the table downstairs.

Kunisuke sat down on the bed and let the waves of pale white light that
enveloped the room wash over him. He experienced the same sense of intox-
ication that came from inhaling the aroma of an incomparably fine brand of
tobacco. . . .

But, no, it was not the moonlight or even the thought of unquestionably
fine tobacco that moved him. No, there was a room on the other side of the
wall, and who knew who might be there. But it was a silent abyss and a place
of unfathomed mystery. Who knew when the whip might lash out and cut
the air with its rasping sting? It was almost as though his ear had become
attuned to the sound. He was waiting for the whip to rend the silence.

What was it about the girl's whip that had the power to inveigle him
and tug at his imagination in a way that even the taste of a special brand of
tobacco could not? For surely he knew what an incomparably fine thing a
first-class cigarette could be, because in point of fact he was sitting there
smoking one right now. Not once had he experienced the pain of being
smitten by the cruel lash of a whip, but it called to him nonetheless. And it
called to him in a powerful way.

He envisioned the hand that held the crop, the arm flexing backward,
the circle of white lace at the throat of the young girl as she poised herself
and got ready to strike. He could see it all now as he reconstructed in his
mind the image that he had seen when he ran into her at the top of the stairs
this morning. She stood before him as a living representative of that species
of humankind called girl. And for a brief while, he ceased to think about the
plant called tobacco. . . .

It might well be that the girl was standing on the other side of the wall
and was ready to crack the whip over his head. Hadn't she pointed it at him
and threatened to use it this morning? Wasn't that proof enough the whip
was about to become part of his life? Surely a karmic connection was in the
making here. The image of the female phantom with the whip haunted him,
and for a brief, ephemeral moment, Kunisuke was lulled into a happily se-
dated, almost mesmerized, state of mind. Meanwhile, the puppy had fallen

fast asleep in his lap. The little fellow no longer bothered to perk up his ears and pay attention as he had done before.

L ITTLE BY LITTLE the room grew brighter. It seemed as if the rays of the moon were concentrated on the sheet of newspaper tacked across the hole that served as a window.

When Kunisuke looked up and began to study the light in a vague and absentminded way, he noticed to his surprise that little black dots were moving across the surface of the page. They began to congregate into groups. What was it? Some sort of joke in which "movable type" actually moved and reset itself? But, no, that was ridiculous. . . .

What were the dots, anyway? Little bugs? Or was he seeing spots before his eyes? No, he told himself, they were letters, and they were definitely in motion.

Just then the light of the moon grew stronger. As it spread across the entire page, Kunisuke became convinced the dots were letters that belonged to the strange alphabet of the language of the future. They moved every which way—diagonally, in reverse, or at random. There seemed to be no order to their movement whatsoever. But then, quite precipitously and as though working in unison, they gained speed, and like an army of ants falling into formation, they began to line up and become neat little rows of type. The lines soon extended into paragraphs, and the paragraphs into columns. In practically no time the letters had typeset the complete text of a newspaper article. Not only that. The blank, white squares began to fill in with a news photo, and then a cartoon. . . .

Letting the puppy slip from his knees, Kunisuke stood up in utter disbelief. What in the world was going on? The sight of the moving letters filled him with an unspeakable feeling of horror. Words froze on his lips, and he found himself unable to cry out. Had he taken leave of his senses and gone mad? He doubted his own sanity.

Still, he managed to pull himself together. Getting as close as he could to the window, he took a deep breath and inspected every minute detail on the surface of the page. No, he was definitely not seeing things. He had only to touch the paper to know the dots were really letters. They were moving, and the news was being freshly printed right before his eyes. Letters formed into words; words, into phrases; phrases, into whole sentences.

Naturally, there was no reason why anyone would be able to read and decipher the meaning of a whole page of text after having studied the letters of the strange, new alphabet for only two days. In spite of his limited knowledge, Kunisuke could still pick out an occasional word, and he was able even to unscramble the meaning of a phrase or two. Given their clarity of resolution, the photo and the cartoon spoke for themselves.

The face of the man in the news photo was one he had seen before in magazines and newspapers. He was a famous politician. Kunisuke consulted his dictionary and did his best to decipher the article that appeared under the man's picture. He was not confident about the details, but he did feel he succeeded in grasping the main point.

"At 2:35 P.M. today . . . the sudden and unexpected death of a leading statesman . . . in a fatal automobile crash . . . cause of accident to be determined . . . assassination plot suspected . . . police investigation under way . . . possible indictment of suspects believed to have political or ideological motives . . . an act of high treason . . . a 'thought crime' . . . "

How much time had he spent plodding through the article? By now the moon appeared to have gone behind the clouds, and the print on the page became too indistinct to read. Kunisuke was terribly exhausted. His head began to spin, and stumbling toward the bed, he collapsed on it face down. He slept as though he had fainted and fallen unconscious.

THERE WAS NOT A PEEP from the adjoining room the following morning. Not from the time when Kunisuke woke up until the time when he left the house for the day. He did not encounter the young girl in the hallway, either.

His orders were exactly the same: "Do like yesterday!"

Although Kunisuke followed the schedule that had been established for him, he found it hard to concentrate on where he was going, because his mind was preoccupied with the events of the previous night. He missed a turn, and for a short while he lost his way.

How strange it was! The more he thought about the previous night, the more mysterious it became.

And speaking of strange, what about the suspicious-looking votive candle on the table downstairs? It dawned on him that the lamp, which appeared to operate on the same secret principle as moonlight, was designed for reading news written in words that, by all rights and purposes, ought not to exist in today's world. After all, how could one think of a newspaper written in tomorrow's speech when it was still only today? Were his thinking correct, then what did it have to say about the people who lived in the house by the canal? Surely they had already mastered the language of the future, and with the aid of the lamp, they knew how to decode its news. Just what sort of people were they, anyway?

Or, more to the point, just who was the young girl supposed to be? Now, there was a question that piqued his curiosity. It struck him as a real mystery—something even more forbidden than the tobacco leaves that he had yet to see.

But what of it? What did all this endless speculation on his part about the house, its people, and the girl have to do with the city and the streets down which he was ambling at this very moment? Why, absolutely nothing at all. Kunisuke stood at a fork in the road. He was lost in a daze.

He was an hour behind schedule when at last he reached the main thoroughfare of the downtown business district and the office building where the tobacco shop was located. He proceeded with his daily routine exactly as he had on the previous two days.

The sky had cleared, and it was now a deep, faultless blue. The weather was perfect for stretching out on the grassy lawn of a public park and studying a new language. The same policeman came by, but this time he greeted Kunisuke with a friendly nod. In the evening Kunisuke boarded the bus and rode home to the house by the canal. Today too, the sunset was spectacular.

The bus was packed with people on their way home from work. The evening edition of the city paper was out, and the eyes of everyone on the bus were glued to the front page. The passengers seemed terribly upset. There was even one agitated fool on board who was talking out loud and shouting at everyone.

When Kunisuke stole a glance at the paper that the man seated next to him was reading, he saw a large photograph. It was the picture of a famous politician. His eye caught a fragment or two of the story beneath it.

"At 2:35 P.M. today . . . the sudden and unexpected death of a leading statesman . . . in a fatal automobile crash . . . cause of accident yet to be determined . . . assassination plot suspected . . . police investigation under way . . . possible indictment of suspects believed to have political or ideological motives . . . an act of high treason . . . a 'thought crime' . . . "

Why all the fuss? The news came as no surprise. What was the point of getting upset a day late? It was news he already knew. . . .

Kunisuke sat bolt upright. What was it that he had just said to himself about not being surprised? Wasn't the edition the passengers were reading *tonight's* paper? And didn't the article refer to the time as 2:35 P.M. *today?*

But it was last night when he had read the article. How was it possible for last night's paper to have carried news of an event that did not happen until today? Kunisuke was dumbstruck.

In short, a newspaper written in a language yet to be conceived by today's world—indeed news written in words and phrases that could not and ought not exist today—had to be tomorrow's newspaper. "The Newspaper of Tomorrow." It seemed so obvious. But Kunisuke was convinced he was the only person on the bus who knew the secret.

Naturally, he blanched at the thought that he, and he alone, possessed this secret knowledge. Luckily for him, the bus was thrown into a state of confusion, and no one noticed the look of embarrassment that appeared on his face. Yet had there been an eagle-eyed detective on board—yes, the sort of gumshoe who knew a guilty face when he saw one—surely he would have understood in a flash what was happening. He would have identified Kunisuke as a collaborator in the death and assassination of the prominent political leader, and there would be no chance of Kunisuke's getting off lightly. No sir, not on your life, he wouldn't. He would be made to pay for his crime. Kunisuke could feel the sweat from his armpits trickle down his side. And when at last he found himself standing at the curb, his mind was a total blank. He could not for the life of him remember when it was or where it was that he had gotten off the bus.

SINCE HE KNEW THE NEWS about the assassination plot the night before, that meant the people at the house by the canal had known it too. And didn't they know it even earlier? Given his limited comprehension of the language of the future, he had been able to read only bits and pieces of the next day's news. But to their well-trained eyes, reading the news must have been easy, and they could read farther into the future than he. They might even know about the events of the day after next or those still farther ahead in time.

Seen from the point of view of the established order of today, the ability to read the language of the future—or, that is to say, to know the events of tomorrow before they happen—had to constitute a criminal act that made a person guilty of willfully undermining and destroying the existing code of law and order in society. Indeed it constituted an act of treason that surely belonged to the category of so-called thought crimes. Yes, that's what they would call it. "Isms." "Ideological crimes." "Crimes of the mind." That's what it was; and, yes, come to think of it, wasn't it possible to say that all words were ideologies? Yes, that every word is a philosophy. The words written the night before had come true, hadn't they? And now they were unerringly spelling out the facts of today. It was a case of words manifesting themselves as realities. Until now, Kunisuke had never really understood what people meant when they talked about the inevitability of history. Surely this was it, wasn't it?

In short, the newspaper at the house by the canal was writing the history of tomorrow. As for the fate of the political leader who had died today, his story had been foretold the previous night in the pages of the newspaper at the house. And as for who had collaborated in generating the news of his assassination, it was the windows at the house that would have to be implicated. Yes, the windows were the ones likely to be indicted—because, in this case, to have known of the incident in advance was virtually synonymous with having fabricated it. Yes, that's what this incident was all about: inventing the events of tomorrow! Seen from the point of view of today's social order, why, the act was tantamount to insurrection. "Insurrection." Yes, that's what they would call it, insurrection pure and simple.

And wasn't that precisely what was happening at the house by the canal?

Weren't the people there not only manufacturing a Peace that was not the usual Peace, but weren't they also distributing it to the city? Yes, the Peace that they manufactured was the Peace of tomorrow, and because theirs was a brand that was infinitely superior to ordinary Peace, eventually the day would come when everyone in the city would rise up and embrace it for its peerless aroma and taste. And when that day finally came, what an event—what news!—it would be.

From the point of view of the sensibly moderate and liberal philosophy that Kunisuke always entertained about cigarettes, the answer was clear. If the quality of the product was better, then the happiness of all the citizens of the city would be that much greater. Conversely, seen from the vantage point of today's order, his ideas smacked of rebellion, and that made them all the more pernicious.

So that's how it was. The people in the house by the canal were rebels and insurrectionists. And, he was one too. By slinging a sack of Peace over his shoulder and making deliveries, he had become a party to their conspiracy. A cold chill ran down his spine.

But what did he have to fear? He had set out to find a job that accorded with his desire to promote not only a fine tobacco but also the happiness of all people, hadn't he? Why should he be confined by rules and regulations established by the Monopoly Corporation? Now that he was engaged in work that, quite serendipitously, fulfilled his own ideals, what reason was there to fear a company that had already given him the boot? Why, none at all, of course.

Still, his feet hesitated.

"They're after me."

K had said he was being followed the day before at the coffee shop, and Kunisuke saw firsthand how two mean-looking characters had tracked K down at the coffee shop. Perhaps they were after him too, he thought. Take the policeman who nodded to him in the park only a few hours ago. Had he known the contents of the two books were not Pali at all, but the language of tomorrow, surely he would have been only too happy to chase after him and slap a pair of handcuffs on his wrists. He had seemed friendly enough, but the ruthlessness of the police when they felt wronged and wanted revenge was not a matter to take lightly. It was a terrible force, but one that he would have to reckon with. Kunisuke felt certain the policeman was already at his back. He was positive he could hear the sound of footfalls approaching from the rear.

The situation was far worse than he imagined. What seemed at first like someone approaching from behind was, in fact, the sound of feet pounding the ground in hot pursuit.

"Rebel."

The words echoed through the warrens of the city.

"They're after me."

Kunisuke broke into a mad dash. But where to? He felt that fear and anxiety were written across his face. And even if they were not, surely people could tell from the way he was breathing so heavily. He also knew that if he returned to the house wearing the weight of his cares in so visible a fashion, the people there would know too, and E would never forgive him. There was no doubt in his mind that E's sanctions would be far harsher than any policeman's manacles.

One minute he ran like crazy; the next, he stopped and hesitated — only to find his feet were ready to take off again in a mad dash. Before he knew it, he had crossed the bridge and reached the house by the edge of the canal. Now that he was on this side of the canal, he ceased to hear the sound of footfalls ringing in his ears. The sun had set some time ago, and the quiet, steady flow of the water in the channel seemed to relegate the city to a point far in the distance.

Kunisuke heaved a sign of relief and slackened his pace. He was more than an hour behind his regular schedule. How was he going to explain his tardiness? At any rate, he was drenched in sweat. How could he possibly report to E and let him see how discombobulated he looked? The sweat had permeated through his jacket and his pants until they were soaking wet. The puppy too was looking pale and overheated. Kunisuke pulled out a handkerchief, and first he gently wiped the little fellow's face and back. Then, he wiped himself off. By that time he had pretty much stopped perspiring.

But E did not appear when Kunisuke, having arrived at the door to the house, finally screwed up his courage and called to him through the receiving window.

REPUDIATION.

Wasn't that it? Repudiation. A shock wave passed through him like a bolt of electricity.

Yet when he pushed at the siding by the window, the door swung open without a hitch. It was uncanny the way it opened so easily.

The "votive lamp" atop the table continued to glow with the pale light of an overcast moon, but there was no sign of anyone on the premises. Had they all disappeared? No, that couldn't be.

Kunisuke felt certain he heard something moving behind the wall of a room that lay deep within the house. It sounded as though a great crowd had gathered, although not so much as a single speck of dust stirred in the air. A synergy—a special tension in the air—was being generated somewhere deep within the building. No, it was not simply a matter of physical bodies being hard at work. It was energy of humankind—an intense concentration of commitment and effort that knew no laxity. It was work. Labor. Some sort of grand endeavor was in progress. Of that much he was certain.

Kunisuke felt undone. He felt as though he had had the stuffing knocked out of him. The terrible fear and anxiety he experienced until only seconds before suddenly seemed unimportant, even tawdry. It was beneath contempt, if not worse, in comparison with the monumental struggle that was in progress deep within the house. For the first time in his life Kunisuke knew what it meant to feel cheap and insignificant as a human being. He slunk away, trying to keep the sound of his steps from drawing attention to himself. Making himself look as inconspicuous as possible, he climbed to the top of the stairs.

He was back in his room at last. The intense concentration of energy that churned the air downstairs did not reach to the top floor. As for the window in his room, it was only dimly lit by the light of the moon. The moon was out tonight, and it cast a faint light across the newspaper page. But it was still too low in the sky to be able to read what was printed on the page.

Kunisuke was exhausted. He collapsed in a heap on top of the bed. Letting his back lean against the wall, he propped himself up and gradually caught his breath.

By and by, more rays of light began to filter through the window and spread across the room. When he looked at the window, he noticed the print on the page had begun to shift position, albeit ever so slightly. It seemed to him that it was ready to switch into action any minute now.

He recalled the pack of cigarettes he had bought this afternoon. He reached for his pocket. The box was labeled, as was always the case, "Peace."

BUT WHAT ABOUT this pack of Peace cigarettes? Now here was a matter that had escaped his attention. Although he had not stopped to think about it, there was good reason to believe the Peace in his hand was not really the right brand after all. That is because, unbeknownst to him, there had been a minor slip-up at the tobacco shop.

Yes, it was true that today, as on the other two days, he had witnessed the clerk bringing the newly delivered brown paper bag to the front of the shop, and he had watched as its contents had been emptied into the jar on the counter. And, yes, it was true that, as he turned to leave, he made a point of buying one of the packs in the jar. But, in the same instant that he stepped to the counter and was about to make his purchase, another customer came rushing up, and they collided headlong. It was then that Kunisuke committed the mistake of averting his eyes from the jar. In that brief, unguarded moment, the clerk had reached in and fished out a pack of cigarettes at random. By the time Kunisuke turned and looked at the jar again, the pack was sitting on the counter in front of him. The jar was already more than half full of packs of Peace that had been poured in earlier, and now they had mixed with those that had just been added. But how was it possible to distinguish which packs were which? It simply could not be done. Even if the mathematical probability of getting a new pack was greater, there remained the outside chance that the clerk's hand happened to fall upon one of the packs at the bottom of the jar. It was not clear whether the pack that was now in Kunisuke's hands was an old or a new Peace. What's more, Kunisuke was unaware a discrepancy had occurred.

Kunisuke took the box from his pocket. Hrumph. That's strange, he thought to himself. The packaging and printing were different from the house brand; they looked like the design on a regular pack of Peace. But by now he firmly believed the cigarettes were surely the same as those that he had been asked to deliver. Besides, his attention was drawn to the letters moving at the window — or to whatever incident from tomorrow's news was about to be spelled out in tonight's paper. He did not bother to take a second look at the pack. He pulled out a cigarette, and paying no heed, he put it to his lips and lit it.

"Ech. . . . "

Inhaling a single puff was sufficient to leave him gasping for air. As the smoke passed down his throat, it reeked of something burnt and charred. He spat and tried to get rid of the bad taste.

The puppy gave a yelp and jumped out of Kunisuke's jacket. The cigarette emitted a foul and noxious smell that immediately filled the room. Little black flecks of what looked like soot floated in the air. They rose to the ceiling. They spotted the walls. They hurled themselves against the newspaper at the window in an all-out attack on the pale light of the moon. And, in that instant, the movement of the letters on the newspaper page ground to a crashing halt. There was something palpable, even tangible, about the darkness that enveloped the room. It hung over it like a heavy curtain.

With that, a great commotion broke out downstairs. Kunisuke heard the sounds of voices cursing and feet racing about as they reverberated and reached all the way to his room on the third floor. It seemed as if all hell had broken loose. A riot? A coup? Who could tell? But it was all too obvious that the work in progress downstairs had been brought to a forcible halt.

What was he to do? Kunisuke was in a state of panic. As he started to get up from the bed, suddenly he felt the sting of a whip slash at his back. It came from directly behind him and at precisely the spot where he had been leaning against the wall. It seemed to tear at his back and cut his flesh to the bone.

"Traitor."

It was the voice of the young girl.

There was a gaping hole in the wall. The bench snapped into its upright position. Kunisuke fell to the floor, and he began to roll like a ball, turning head over heels, until finally he fell headlong into the adjoining room.

III

I t was like sinking in water.

He rolled until he came to a spot resembling a vast sea of kelp that grew out of the floor and covered it completely. Something soft had sucked him into its wet embrace, and it kept him from falling any farther. Kunisuke managed to get a hand down on the floor, and using it to flip himself over, he tried to float on his back like a swimmer. But no sooner had he righted himself than he looked up to see what resembled a boat.

"A yacht!?! . . . "

At first he was sure it was a yacht, but once he was able to get a good look at it, he realized that the boat was not a boat, but a hammock. A hammock had been hoisted in the air, and it hung close to the ceiling. It was near the wall that adjoined his room and at a spot located directly over his bed. Sitting astride it was the girl with the whip.

Kunisuke realized the room he had been assigned on the third floor amounted to not much more than a locker or a closet in the girl's room.

And, didn't that mean, of course, he was little more than a prop or a tool that had been set aside for the girl's future use?

The ceiling of the room curved in the shape of a dome. A faint ray of light emanated from the center of it, and as best as he could tell, it flickered as the hammock swayed back and forth. That the room felt as quiet and unruffled as the waters at the bottom of the ocean was due, no doubt, to the soft, lambent quality of the light.

"Slave!" "Traitor!"

The lashings of the girl's tongue rang out to the accompanying sound of her whip. As she let the whip crack in the air, Kunisuke felt the full measure of its cruel sting.

He was furious. He could hardly contain the anger that welled inside him.

"Slave? Why a slave?" he shouted back. "You say, 'traitor,' but who's a traitor?

"I'm a human being, I'll have you know. I work here. I do a decent job, and every day I get paid for what I do. That may not mean much to you, but I have my rights as a human being. Besides, what entitles you to insult me like this? Quite frankly, Your Highness, I find your tyrannical behavior intolerable!"

A dull, leaden sound like the distant roar of the ocean shook the room. Where had it originated? It was so loud Kunisuke could hardly hear himself think. It was the voice of the young girl, who, tossing her head back and roaring with laughter, made fun of him from the great height of her hammock. It was a dry, sarcastic laugh, and it rang with the unmistakable force of a man's voice.

"Asshole! Wasn't the cigarette you were smoking one of those meant for slaves? See what its foul and dirty odor has done. You've made a complete mess of tonight's work. It's a total rout. So don't tell me. Anyone fool enough to bring slave cigarettes onto the premises and who pollutes the air with their stench deserves to be called a traitor."

"Slave cigarettes?"

Humph. So it had been his Peace cigarette that had produced the terrible smell. Perhaps it was a cigarette meant for slaves after all. But did that make it his fault?

"I didn't know, Your Highness. I didn't realize, that's all. Quite innocently, I . . . "

Once again, the young girl reeled back in the hammock and roared with laughter.

It dawned on Kunisuke that this was the second time he had addressed the girl in the hammock as "Your Highness." It appeared it was his use of this phrase that made her laugh so hard.

But just what did he think she was? A *queen?* Still, he could think of no other way to address her.

"Your Highness, you say I've done something terribly wrong, but what could you possibly mean? I'd like to know what it is that you say I've done wrong.

This time the girl did not laugh. Without so much as a single word, "Her Highness, the queen" simply raised her whip, and aiming in the direction of the floor, she let it snap. In the second the tip of the lash licked the ground, the bed of kelp leaves parted. A great rent had formed in the ocean floor.

L IGHT BEGAN TO POUR IN from below, and it illuminated the mouth of the hole. What had looked like kelp leaves were really sheaves of broadleaf tobacco that, like rugs in a pile, were thickly stacked, layer upon layer, around the perimeter. One could see they had fallen one on top of the other and built up an instant floor. But what was more important, they gave Kunisuke something to hold onto, since he was in serious danger of slithering over the edge. They were tentative support at best, but by latching onto a sheaf or two of the tobacco leaves, he was able to maneuver himself into a position where he could peer into the space below without falling in. A vast pit stretched before his eyes.

Fire! . . .

But, no, there were no flames. Only light. Rows of windows filled the pit with light that shone with the brilliance of the moon. At one window there was a hole, and great puffs of ash-colored smoke belched into the room, spewing it with soot and emitting a foul and nasty odor. As the smoke poured in and attacked the light, people swarmed over the window and did their best to dispel it. What an unbearable smell! What ugly gray soot! No sooner had Kunisuke gotten a whiff of it than he knew it had come from the Peace cigarette he had lit in his room. Yes, right from his cigarette. There could be no other explanation. In which case, he was the cause of the tumult unfolding right before his eyes. His negligence was the source of it all.

And, as if that were not lesson enough, something else was there to remind him of the terrible thing he had done — namely, the beautiful fragrance right at the tip of his nose. It came from the tobacco leaves to which he now clung for dear life. The light shining from below reflected on the leaves and made it possible for him to see their texture clearly and distinctly. The leaves were of unquestionably fine quality. What a startling surprise! And what mockery they made of his previous knowledge of the plant!

At the same time, he noticed that the bundles were coming undone as the leaves slid apart, one by one. In fact, one sheaf had already slipped out of his hand and plummeted through the hole. He too was on the verge of being sucked over the edge. He would be next, falling head over heels through the hole.

A heavy-duty conveyor belt had been set up below and was being extended to the mouth of the hole on the second floor. Like a waterfall, the leaves cascaded over the edge and were carried along the belt, each leaf tumbling one after the other. At the end of the line sat a huge machine, ready and waiting. Down below, a crowd of people was swarming over the machine or, more precisely, over the part of the machine that appeared to be its controls. The workers labored in silence and without ever stopping to take a break.

Kunisuke knew in an instant the machine was designed to cut and roll cigarettes. Everything about the house was as he predicted. It was a cigarette factory, after all!

Still, it was hard to believe a building so narrow could house so mammoth a machine or so many people. It defied all imagination. What's more, he could hardly believe the huge machine or the gang of workers could work with such fury yet not raise a single speck of dust or stop even to cough. How could it be?

But, no, the taskmaster of the house was a powerful synergy, and it brooked no complaint from man or machine. The tension in the air was palpable. It was in complete control, and it explained why those who participated in the mechanical operation of the powerful contraption were not permitted a second in which to take a break or relax their concentration. Indeed the proof of the fact, and the trademark of the entire operation, lay in the finished product of the steady stream of little, white cigarettes that poured from the giant machine. Kunisuke had only to look and see for himself. The leaves that came tumbling down the conveyor belt at one end spewed forth from the other like a fountain of white beads. On and on came the newly and neatly rolled cigarettes, rolling out of the machine and, instantly and endlessly, falling into neat little rows.

Yet, when it came to the contrast between the tidy white rows of cigarettes and the sight of the black smoke belching from the hole in the window — or the contrast between those who labored patiently alongside the machine versus those who struggled feverishly to stamp out the soot at the windows—there was no comparison at all. It was as if the two events were not taking place in the same room. That is how alien they appeared to be.

It was also undeniably clear the machine had dumped a pile of waste on the floor that looked like dirt or mud. The pile consisted of cigarettes that had been cast aside as rejects. An embarrassing blemish on the good record of the established order of the house, the remnants were also an index of the degree to which the machine had been made to malfunction.

Kunisuke tallied the figures in his head and came up with a quick estimate of the ratio of rejects to the volume of smoke billowing through the hole in the window. It worked out to be just about equal.

In the end, he was forced to recognize one incontrovertible fact. The rumbling noise that he had taken for the distant roar of the ocean was no breaking wave but the sound of a terrible upheaval that had erupted as a result of the cigarette he had smoked. Like a sudden and unwelcome guest trespassing on the premises, the foul and nasty smoke had intruded upon the established order of the house and unleashed a horrendous uproar.

"Got it all figured out, kiddo?"

The young girl's voice rained about his ears like a clap of thunder.

Yes, he had figured it out. And that was not all. For when he scrutinized the machine even more carefully, he realized the power supply was unlike any electrical system he had seen in the past. Quite the contrary, it was operated by a light-producing device that glowed with the light of the moon. The device was the source of the extraordinarily powerful charge that not only supplied power to the lamp downstairs but also served as the driving force for the machine.

Black soot continued to stick to the one spot at the window, and it was proving extremely difficult to remove. But at last the air in the room began to clear, and soon the workers who had been battling the smoke were back at their stations by the machine. Once again everyone was squarely at work on the assembly line. The light in the room grew appreciably brighter, and the machine began to churn out cigarettes at an ever more energetic pace.

Hey—and how about that!! Once the black smoke no longer threatened to cloud any of the windows, the newsprint on the pages tacked across them moved into full swing. The letters of the strange alphabet began to gyrate and fly about at bewildering speeds. They moved up and down. They intersected with each other on the page.

The gyrating letters no longer came as a surprise to Kunisuke, but he still found it difficult to comprehend how their motion was related to the operation of the machine and its production of cigarettes. What was the connection? It was not readily apparent.

B<small>UT WHAT WAS THE POINT</small> in thinking about it? There it was, a concrete and observable fact, taking place right in front of his eyes. The systematic, step-by-step production of tomorrow's cigarettes activated the movement of the strange alphabet, which, in turn, recorded what happened on the assembly line. The movable type on the newspaper page was like a musical score, and the music to be performed was being composed in the letters and words of the language of tomorrow. The news of the politician's assassination had made it only too clear, hadn't it? The score would be played out tomorrow in the form of very real and specific news events. There was no doubt about it. Without fail, a new order was in the making. It was being created in this place, and it would manifest itself the next day as the history of tomorrow. And if, just if, all of the citizens of the city reached the point where they too learned to read and comprehend the meaning of the letters and phrases written on the windows, then the day would come when they would appreciate the full flavor of the cigarettes being manufactured at the house. Believe it or not, the drama unfolding here and now in the setting of the house constituted a single frame from the future newsreel of history, and it was being experienced a priori!

It also meant the dark and medieval smudge at the one window bore the fingerprint of the criminal who was guilty of having soiled it. It was his handiwork, and what's more, the dirt — which had been rubbed so heinously across a page out of tomorrow's history — would appear as one of the more insidious news events to be reported in tomorrow's paper. A chill ran down Kunisuke's spine. So that explained it. That was why the work for the night had turned into a "total rout," just as the young girl said. And, as for the person who had caused all of the trouble — yes, the offender who had soiled everything with the imprint of his dirty little hand — why, the guilty party was none other than himself, wasn't it?

Still, both the production line on the floor and the newspaper pages at the windows pushed ahead with making cigarettes and printing the news by simply ignoring the soot as a blemish that was an inevitable part of any business. In the world of business, a blotch was a blotch. One simply wrote it off. The history of tomorrow was like the proverbial iceberg. A tip might break off and float away, but the larger story would carry on. It was what would be recorded as the history of the day after tomorrow or the day after that. It was the inevitability of history, wasn't it?

It struck Kunisuke as a terribly cold and competitive order, and he saw his worth as a human being cast aside as something that was totally useless. Wasn't it obvious he had failed to live up to expectations? And that he was like one of the rejects the machine had dumped in a pile on the floor?

TRASH.

The thought of it cut him to the core more cruelly than the lash of the girl's whip had ever done.

A HAND EMERGED from the top of the machine. It raised a finger in the air and pointed at Kunisuke. It was like the tip of an arrow aimed at his heart.

"Oh, no."

They had seen him for sure. Kunisuke ducked and tried to bury his face in the pile of tobacco leaves. But the finger was pointed directly at him, and it seemed to cry out for action.

"There's the bad guy. He's the bastard who did it." That was what it seemed to say.

Were he to fall onto the conveyor belt and go plummeting into the pit below, that would be the end of him for sure. He would be taken captive and executed as a traitor. The people who worked at the house were like locusts. From inside the machine, and from every corner surrounding it, they flew from their stations. They swarmed over the room. They fell like rain on the floor. They formed a circle and were ready to carry out his sentence. Somebody would be called to yank him down and drag him to the scaffold. The moment of reckoning was at hand.

Yet it was not to be. No, it was E who emerged from the machine. First, his hand appeared over the side. Then, he hoisted himself on top of what was probably the control tower of the machine. But he did not look this way, thought Kunisuke. E stood atop the machine, and waving his arms, he turned to the workers. He was shouting at them, and while Kunisuke could not catch what he said, he knew E called to his audience and spoke with great authority. Yes, it was with the same synergy that already galvanized the room. There was something razor-sharp about the way E talked, as though he were cutting straight to the heart of the problem. No doubt he was giving orders.

The circle disbanded, and like pieces of glass in a kaleidoscope, the workers scattered only to regroup into a new configuration. This time they adopted a defensive position. Not a person was out of place. Everyone was poised for the kill. They had only to wait for the enemy to appear.

So great was Kunisuke's curiosity that he forgot the danger he was in. When he went to peek over the edge of the hole, the leaves shifted and blocked his view. They came fluttering down around him, piling one on top of the other. Everything grew dim, then dark, until finally he could see nothing at all. It was as though a cloud had appeared to obscure the face of the moon. Yes, that's what it was — clouds.

Indeed so light, compact, and seamless were the leaves that they flowed like water through his hands when he reached out, and finally grabbing hold of one, he tried to get a better look at it. No, he wasn't at the bottom of the ocean. He was too high up for that. He was way up in the clouds, he realized. He was way above the spectacle of the lower depths that he had been looking at until now.

"How about it, small fry? Guess by now you've learned your place, huh?"

There was something flippant, even common, about the tone of the young girl's voice. How had he ever mistaken her for royalty? How could he have called her "Your Highness, the queen"? He did not know what to think of her now.

Yet, when he looked up, there she was reigning over him. The hammock hung in midair like the crescent moon, and her legs dangled over the sides. Her leather boots were a perfect match for her breeches, and they shone with an eerie blue sheen. It was as if they had been polished from the inside, and the shine had penetrated all the way through. From the polished surface of her sleek leather boots he could almost smell the soft, white fragrance and glow of her skin.

"Who the hell is she, anyway?" he asked himself.

But, no, the question that had formed in his mind was altogether different. What he really wanted to know was the sort of body she concealed underneath those boots and breeches. Her voice and the words that rained down on him from the unattainable heights of the hammock were like bits and pieces of flesh that she doled out like chunks of meat. "Here, take this," she seemed to say in an incredibly vulgar tone of voice. In the quasi-light of the clouds that enveloped him, the words became muffled, and it sounded as though she were standing next to him and whispering something in his ear. But it was a gross and salacious overture, and the tone of her voice came through loud and clear. It was a powerful narcotic that, as it pierced to the core of his lust, stuck out of his hide like a giant needle.

To know one's place. Had he not known it before, he did now. Were he to reestablish himself and find a foothold once he wandered into the clouds and lost his way, he had but one leg to stand on: the power of sexual desire.

That was when he recalled the conversation he had heard through the wall. He no longer remembered E's exact words, but were he to express what he felt now that he operated under the influence of the powerful stimulus of the girl's voice, surely he would give vent to it by paraphrasing the same passionate love call that E had used. Indeed the words were already on his lips, and they now echoed about the room.

"Okay, bitch. Get ready. I'm coming in the hammock with you."

The girl roared with laughter as she had before, and it was the same dry and cynical laugh of a man.

"So! So, at last you're beginning to make sense and get things right. Good for you! You know, I'm the one and only woman in this house. Or to put it more correctly, I'm the female slave. And that means when the men who work here need a helping hand, I'm the one who comes to the rescue—

or at least to the rescue of those who are just dumb enough and good-looking enough to be worth my trouble. If you want to get down on your knees and beg me for help, that makes you just one more name on my list of supplicants. All the boys here have the same bright idea. You're not going to be any extra trouble at all."

With that, she cracked the whip. It snapped over Kunisuke's head, the tip of the lash licking the side of his cheek. It felt like hardly more than the flick of a finger, but it stung with great intensity. Kunisuke leapt in pain, and grabbing the end of the whip, he held on with all his might. As it reeled back, he was pulled through the air. He was jerked upward, and propelled higher and higher, he made a flying leap into the hammock. He landed right on top of the girl.

How bitter cold it was in the hammock! No, cold was not the word — it was a place utterly devoid of warmth. It was a place in which pain was all. The girl's legs, in their breeches and leather boots, were like the powerful jaws of a vise, and they held him sideways in their grip. It was hard to believe there was any flesh on them. They were like metal shafts that ran the length of the girl's thighs, and when she squeezed them together, they threatened to shatter his joints.

A beam of light pierced the retina of Kunisuke's eye and left him momentarily blinded. Was he inside the hammock? Was the girl with him? He could no longer tell.

To make matters worse, he was denied any chance to cry out and give voice to his pain. The girl (he guessed it was the girl) bit at his lips, pressing her mouth so tightly to his that he could scarcely breathe. Her lips were sharp, thornlike barbs, and they came at him with a greedy, blood-sucking sound. Kunisuke gritted his teeth and sought to fight back the pain. The girl's caresses were perfect torture.

His torment bordered, if anything, on ecstasy. Kunisuke was not a pederast, but for a split second he doubted he was with the girl and wondered if her embrace was not the same as the love between two men. And in that millisecond, he lost all feeling. Not only the awareness of his sexual desire, but all consciousness as well.

It seemed as if the ocean had roared in the distance once more. Perhaps it was the sound of his own long and plaintive moan that had sought to register itself and resounded only within the inner chamber of his ear. But, no, he was mistaken. The sound grew louder. It was a rumbling noise, and rising from far below, it came in waves that engulfed the room all the way to the rafters. A revolutionary coup appeared to be under way in the world below the hole in the tobacco leaves. He was numb from head to toe, but a part of him was conscious of the sound, although he could not say where.

For all of a split second, he let the lockhold on his jaw relax; and in that momentary lapse, his teeth, which until now had bit back the intense pain, parted ever so slightly. Suddenly, something red-hot forced its way into the space between his lips. It was the girl's tongue, and it was a torch of fire. He threw back his head to unleash the pain that shot from the seared lining of his throat, and in that instant, his arms and legs spilled over the edge of the hammock. Doing a somersault in the air, he started to fall head first . . . down . . . down . . . down . . . and, as he tumbled, a great fissure opened in the strata of whatever it was — clouds? broadleaf tobacco? — that moved in endlessly shifting layers beneath him.

Kunisuke was caught in the leaves, and hanging precariously over the edge of the crevice, his feet dangled in midair. Directly below, a full-scale riot had broken out. A battle was under way. On all sides of the giant cigarette machine, people were slugging each other. They cursed, and they shouted, and as the fight went back and forth, it became impossible to tell friend from foe.

Still, Kunisuke was certain he knew who his "brothers" were. They were the ones taking the terrible beating. Hadn't he learned just now in the hammock the meaning of pain? He felt an emotional bond with those who were on the losing side of the battle, and it derived from his newly found understanding of what it meant to be the person who gets hurt or slapped. It was a perception that bordered on love.

The machine was already covered in blood, and he felt the blood had been spilt from his very own veins. Where had the enemy who was attacking his brothers come from? he wanted to know. They were wielding clubs and had gone on a rampage. What's more, from outside the building he could hear the rumble of more trucks on the way. Dressed in uniforms and geared for battle, the enemy soldiers came in endless waves. They poured into the building via the blemish — or, more precisely, via the hole in the window that had been tarnished and stained. Kunisuke saw it all. Taking aim at the soot spot, the soldiers hacked their way in. Then came a second wave of troops, trespassing the premises. The invaders were clearly intent on destroying the order of tomorrow that had been created in the house.

The blemish on the window acted as a marker or guide for the enemy. Yes, it had been his blunder after all. The person responsible for indicting his own brothers was none other than himself. Feeling utterly demoralized, he felt his grip loosen, and with that he saw himself slide through a break in the cloud.

In that fleeting second he heard the puppy yelp. Where had the little fellow been all this time? And how could he have forgotten him?

Kunisuke plummeted like a dead weight into the midst of the confusion that engulfed the work floor. And when he hit the ground with a thud, he lay there, knocked out cold.

IV

When he came to, the sun was out. It was bright red, and it was shining in his face. It was morning. Something soft and gentle was licking his cheek. Yes, there it was, the puppy's tongue, pink and wet. Kunisuke lay sprawled upon the floor by the door to the house. When he got to his feet, and looked around inside, he discovered the building was totally deserted. There was no sign of anyone.

What in the world had happened to the gigantic machine? And the swarms of people he had seen last night? He knew he had seen them, that much was for sure. But where had they gone? But, no, even if they had evaporated into thin air, as he looked about the room, he could not believe it was large enough to have accommodated so many people. The ceiling was too low; the walls, too close together; the space, not deep enough. At best, one might squeeze in a table for five or six people, but no more. The house was a shack. An old, dilapidated shack.

Did it mean he had dreamed it all? No, that couldn't be. No, that was absolutely impossible. But, if the events of the previous night did not happen, then what was he doing, standing here?

In fact, everywhere around him were the traces of the disturbance that had taken place last night. The door, the partitions between the rooms, the windows—everything had been bashed in, and the downstairs was now thrown open to the elements. The table had been upended. The chairs, legs broken, were scattered about. The place was a complete shambles. The stairs to the second floor had been knocked loose and broken off halfway up. The railing along the upstairs corridor had fallen off. The door to the room on the second floor was gone, blown who knows where. Through it, he could see all the way to the back of the roof, from which several planks were missing. The hammock was still there, hanging limply overhead, but it was in tatters. And what of the young girl? Not a trace. The closet that served as his room had virtually disappeared too. And, as for the piles of tobacco leaves, what about them? All that fluttered about his head as he looked up at the second floor were flecks of lint. It appeared that, in the wake of the horrific spectacle of the previous night, only he and the puppy were intact.

"This place is a wreck."

He was a mess too. The welts that covered the back of his hands were stained with blood. The elbows of his jacket were ripped. And, what was wrong with the puppy's leg? The little fellow was limping. Kunisuke scooped him up and stepped out the door.

His eye fell on three cigarettes that had fallen by the doorsill. They were Peace cigarettes. He picked them up and slipped them into his pocket.

And, as he went to reach into his pocket, he felt something dry and crinkly inside. He pulled it out and found a piece of paper in the palm of his hand. It had been rolled into a ball and was looking badly wrinkled. Printed on it in very small letters was the strange alphabet of the language of Futurese. It must have been a page that he had torn from one of the books that K gave him. Kunisuke stuffed the piece of paper back in his pocket for future reference.

Outside, the waters of the canal shone with a brilliance that made his eyes hurt when he looked at them. As the sun danced across the water, the light scattered into a thousand pieces that then ricocheted off the surface. It was like a rope. It pursued him and sought to entwine itself about his feet.

Although his feet felt as heavy as lead, Kunisuke started walking, and as he gained speed, he broke into a headlong dash. His feet carried him along at such a clip that, when he came to a sudden halt, he felt for sure that he would fall flat on his face. And then, as if it were the most natural thing in the world for them to do, his feet turned in the direction of the bridge and headed for the city. This had become their habit of late. It was a habit of which Kunisuke had ceased to be conscious, however.

The city looked no different than usual. Except — and it was perhaps here that he was overreacting — there seemed to be extra police stationed at the police boxes on the way. And, by the time he reached the streets at the heart of the downtown business district, he was convinced he was right. No, he was not imagining things. More patrolmen were on the streets and stationed at the police boxes. As a matter of fact, they were heavily armed, and they were keeping an eye trained on all pedestrians. Indeed, there was even something mean and barbarous about the way they looked at people. They had a certain bloodthirsty synergy to their stare that reminded Kunisuke of the "invaders" who had trespassed the premises of the house the previous night.

Just as he started to cross at one street corner, the puppy, who had been tucked inside his jacket, began to stir. The little fellow perked up his ears. He was on the alert for something.

A crowd had gathered in front of the corner store, and people were pushing to get near a radio that had been set out on the street. Kunisuke stopped, and desperate to know what was going on, he joined the throng. The static on the radio was terrible, but he could tell an important news bulletin was being issued to the public even if he was unable to catch every word. The newscaster spoke in a phony, pompous tone of voice as he delivered the news, the fragments of which filled the air.

— police apprehend a gang operating a large-scale, international ring manufacturing contraband cigarettes

— fugitives still being sought

— major conspiracy lurks in the background

— investigation expected to grow in size

The people in the crowd had probably read the news in the morning paper or heard it on the radio, and now they stopped to confirm it once more. Of course, the investigation had nothing to do with them, but by making the crisis seem important, they appeared to be enjoying themselves and thereby dispelled some of the tedium in their everyday lives. Given so obedient an audience, the announcer hastened to toss out one final tidbit of news. This time his voice rang out loud and clear.

"Ladies and gentlemen, the following report has just been received . . . at an undisclosed location in the city, an armored division of police has apprehended eight fugitives sought in connection with the investigation. As the suspects were about to be placed under arrest, police came under heavy fire from a large band of more than one hundred rebels launching a counter-attack. A pitched battle is in progress. The number of dead and wounded has risen to twenty-three. . . ."

A stir of approval passed through the crowd. Some applauded the news, while others remonstrated in protest. It was impossible to tell what side people were on. A scuffle broke out, and the police came running over. Kunisuke was breathing heavily by the time he managed to squeeze through the sea of shoulders and slip from the crowd. The news event that had been destined to occur had happened at last.

"Fugitives from justice!"

No question. He was one of them. And, sure enough, the long arm of the law would be quietly closing in on him. He felt sure he could hear the footfalls of his pursuers as they approached from behind. Yet, if he was to be arrested, where were the fellow "conspirators" who were supposed to come to his rescue? Or who, in order to get him back, were prepared to launch "the pitched battle" that the radio announcer talked about? He doubted there was anyone at all. He felt the color drain from his cheeks. He quickened his step and crossed to the opposite side of the street. Standing momentarily in the shadow of a building, he looked back to see if he was being followed. No, he had no reason to believe someone was after him. As a matter of fact, neither the police nor the crowd paid him the slightest attention. They passed by, ignoring him completely.

So there he was. A man on the run with no one to pursue him. Had they already counted him as one of the twenty-three dead and wounded and written him off as a nameless and forgotten casualty? Alas, "casualty" seemed to be the word that fitted him best, or at least that was how he felt. What a dark and wretched state of mind he was in.

In no time he had been pushed along the street by the crowd, and before he knew it, he was back in the vicinity of the office building where he had gone to deliver the cigarettes. Suddenly he was overcome by a terrible urge to take a look at what had become of the tobacco shop. He was prepared to risk everything. He walked into the building and marched right to the entrance.

The store was shut tight as a drum. A patrolman was on duty by the front door, but what was there to be afraid of? He was not about to be intimidated. The policeman gave him only a perfunctory glance and, suspecting nothing, abruptly looked the other way.

It was then that Kunisuke noticed a sign taped on the door.

"Business Holiday—Closed Temporarily."

To close and to take a holiday struck Kunisuke as a synonymous, if not redundant, way of describing a temporary state of affairs. Still, the sign spoke of something that would not last indefinitely. In that case, perhaps it was possible to believe the predicament in which he found himself at the moment was not destined to go on forever. There would be nothing final or decisive about it. Instead, it was a temporary, liminal state. And inasmuch as the store closing was only temporary, the day would come when it would reopen, and as a part of its regular business, it would restock its shelves and openly sell to the public the cigarettes that he had been delivering. He could even foresee a time when once again he would sling a sack over his shoulder and go back to work. In other words, he saw the sign as a promise that implied that the unfortunate interval known as the present would intervene for only just so long. The meantime was only temporary, and the happy day would come when everyone in the city might, as a matter of course, openly smoke and freely enjoy the taste of fine tobacco.

"The Happiness of All the People."

Now that he thought of it, he had heard that sweet-sounding phrase somewhere before, hadn't he?

How could he have forgotten? Hadn't it been his own philosophy? To be so forgetful about his own ideas compounded the impatience he felt with the present, and it only made him all the more miserable. Yet, compared to the wretched souls who were being treated as fugitives and casualties, how liberating it was to think his own discomfort was only temporary. There was nothing to stew about. The stress he felt began to dissipate a bit. Inside his jacket was the puppy, and the little fellow's tummy began to growl. Poor fellow, he must be hungry! It was well past noon. After checking to see how much money was left in his pocket, Kunisuke decided to start with the café where he had been the day before. He headed down the street toward the coffee shop.

Radios blared to the public at places here and there at the crossroads. Perhaps there had been a lull in the more sensational developments, but fewer people were listening to the news. The maniacal atmosphere that had gripped the city earlier in the day had disappeared. Perhaps it is an ironic fact of life that no matter how great an event, if people cannot experience it firsthand and see it with their own eyes, it may as well have never happened. It was hard to believe how calm and quiet the streets were.

A smartly dressed couple came along walking arm in arm. They were totally absorbed in conversation. Then came a second couple, and a third. As he passed them going the opposite way, Kunisuke happened to overhear what the young woman was saying to her boyfriend. Perhaps her emotions had got the better of her and she could no longer contain herself.

"I'm crazy about you," she said to her boyfriend. "Hold me real, real tight tonight, will you."

It was a beautiful voice that rang with the pure distillation of sexual desire. The couple had passed him, but he turned around to take a second look. He watched from the rear as the man and the woman quickly faded into the distance and disappeared around a street corner. They had been like a mirage — a walking vision of what a brief moment of happiness was meant to be.

"'Hold me real, real tight tonight, will you.'"

Kunisuke repeated the girl's words. In whose arms was she to be embraced and held ever so tight? The man's? Or the embrace of the thing called love?

Suddenly he heard the sound of the whip crack. And, just as quickly, he felt all the welts on his body — all the places where he had been branded by the strange embrace in the hammock the previous night — spring to life. Every joint ached with pain, and his arms and legs went numb again. He felt the culottes and boots of the young girl bear down on him once more, and by applying themselves full force, they were about to crush him in their powerful grip. He struggled to take control of his voice and cry out for help. And, in the midst of his pain, he experienced once more a feeling that bordered on ecstasy. It transfixed him. It left him stupefied. He was rooted to the spot.

He came to a complete stop that lasted one . . . two . . . three . . . full seconds.

By the time he came to his senses, Kunisuke discovered he was practically at the coffee shop; and as the door of the café came into view, he heard an awful crash. It was the sound of the glass door breaking and splintering from the inside. Three or four men came flying from the shop, grappling with one another.

At the center of the fracas was a man who had fallen to the pavement. As he lay on the ground, the others stomped and kicked him unmercifully. Then they grabbed him by the collar and pulled him to his feet. They slapped a pair of handcuffs on his wrists. It was impossible to see his face, however, because his hair was badly disheveled.

But when the man looked up, Kunisuke was shocked to see it was K.

From the pale blue veins at the side of K's forehead ran a thin trickle of blood. Kunisuke felt as if he too had been kicked and beaten, but as he went to cry out, someone pushed him from behind. Suddenly there was a crowd on the street, and people rushed over and blocked his way. Now the police were on the scene, and K was surrounded. Did K know Kunisuke was there? Kunisuke had no way of knowing. When a policeman raised his hand and gave the signal, a small van that was painted black and looked like a cage pulled to the curb. K was shoved inside. The vehicle set off down the street at breakneck speed.

A FTER THE CROWD dispersed, Kunisuke was left standing alone, nailed to the spot in front of the picture window of the coffee shop. He was stunned, and what he saw reflected in the plate glass was a face — a face down which ran, starting from the pale blue veins at the forehead, a single trickle of blood. It was K's face, wasn't it? But, no, that couldn't be. It had to be his own. . . .

If there was blood on his face, then surely someone in the crowd would have spotted it and pointed him out, wouldn't they have? But then, he wasn't so sure. Given the people in this city, was there anyone who gave a damn about another person spilling a little blood? Hell no. . . .

But why in the world did his reflection in the window look so much like K's? Come to think of it, perhaps the reason he had headed for the coffee shop had very little to do with the puppy. Yes, it was true the little fellow had been hungry, and his tummy had started to growl. But Kunisuke wondered if the real reason did not have a lot more to do with K than with the puppy. Hadn't he felt a secret urge to get in touch with K? And hadn't he been desperate to know how to handle himself from here on out? Never in his wildest dreams did he imagine he would actually meet K under circumstances like these. But now he felt certain K had come to the coffee shop because he knew Kunisuke was in need of him. K always responded to his needs, didn't he? Surely K would have known what was best for him to do. Yes, K would have given him sound advice. K's orders were always short and to the point. Likewise, his movements were always swift and nimble. In terms of time, it never took K more than three seconds to do anything.

It was all too clear. If on the way to the coffee shop Kunisuke had not stopped in his tracks for all of three seconds, he would have met K in time, and K would have taken care of the business at hand immediately. K would have been out the door of the café before the enemy had reached out and grabbed him. K would have given them the slip, and his escape from their hands would have qualified as one of the world's great disappearing acts. There was no doubt about it in Kunisuke's mind. He would have seen K get away for sure. It was his tardiness that had been the decisive, even fatal factor, and the responsibility for having taken too long lay with him and him alone. Wasn't he the one who deserved to be arrested, not K?

Still, if fate ruled that K was to be arrested, Kunisuke wondered if perhaps there was a message, if not an important lesson to be learned in the unhappy predicament in which he now found himself. Perhaps fate was providing him with insight into his own destiny. Wasn't K's fate fast becoming his own? In that case—and K was, after all, the one who got caught first—

what else might Kunisuke be expected to feel but a touch of jealousy at what had happened to his good friend K?

A waiter came out of the café with a broom. He began to sweep up the broken glass that had fallen on the ground in front of the shop, and pretty soon he was dusting up a storm. Kunisuke beat a hasty retreat to avoid getting something in his eye. Predictably, his feet headed for the public park. The park was a place in which he could stop and catch his breath; and today, more than ever before, he felt a compelling desire for the gentle warmth of the sun and the soft touch of a grassy lawn. Yes, the park provided a place in which he could breathe freely.

Yet no sooner had he sat down on the bench than he was on his feet again. He jumped up as if he had been pricked by a thorn. He had seen the all too familiar face of the patrolman. The policeman was standing in the shadow of the trees across the way.

"Damn!?!"

It had not occurred to Kunisuke to think of him. Here was the enemy, and he was probably not about to adopt the conciliatory air of the previous day. He would be suspicious, and he would eye Kunisuke as one of the gang of rebels. He would be relentless in tracking him down.

So the park was a trap too. The enemy would be on top of him in no time. The cop was almost to the bench, and what made things worse was the ominous grin on his face. Suddenly their eyes met, and sensing danger, Kunisuke got up and started to run. The policeman looked mildly puzzled, but he followed Kunisuke just the same.

At first, it was like a game. But Kunisuke lost his sense of composure. The more desperate he felt, the faster he ran. Likewise, the faster he ran, the more determined the policeman became, and the more he pursued Kunisuke.

The puppy squirmed inside Kunisuke's jacket. It was as if he had fallen into water and was struggling to stay afloat.

Kunisuke was in a genuine fix by now, and there would be no turning back. He cut diagonally across the lawn. He made his way among the flower beds. He ran through a grove of trees. He came to a high hill. It blocked his path, but up, up, up he ran until he reached the top of a do-or-die precipice.

A pond was directly below. The water looked as if it had been waiting all along for someone to come and take a plunge.

And in the instant when Kunisuke faltered — his foot catching on a root of the tree at the edge of the cliff, his body tottering on the brink — he gasped and — "oh, no" — the puppy spilled from his jacket. The little fellow skidded down the side of the cliff and came to a stop within an inch of the pond. Landing in the midst of a clump of weeds, he was on his back, his feet pawing the air.

And, just as suddenly, Kunisuke felt a hand reach from behind and clamp itself squarely on his shoulder. The long arm of the law was as heavy as a set of chains, and he could feel the weight of it down to his bones. He was flipped around to face his pursuer.

"What in hell do you think you're doing?"

"What made you run like that?" the cop fired back, demanding an answer.

Kunisuke was both gasping for air and shouting at the same time. "Run? What's wrong with that? There's no law that says you have a right to stop a person for taking a little exercise. If you're going to take me in, I want to see the warrant for my arrest. Come on, show it to me."

The cop was momentarily at a loss for words, but then he announced Kunisuke would be taken into custody.

"You're under arrest for being caught in the act of flight."

"What? 'The act of flight'? That's the dumbest thing I've ever heard! . . ." Kunisuke was so agitated he could hardly speak.

To run had been an admission of guilt, hadn't it? By running away hadn't he announced to the world that he was a fugitive from justice?

Meanwhile, his reaction was almost unconscious, but he kept his right hand stuffed into his pocket. As for what was inside, and what he clutched so determinedly in the palm of his hand, why, it was the crumpled piece of paper on which were printed the strange letters of the alphabet of Futurese. Were the officer to find it on him, it would be incontestable evidence, and it would be used against him.

Suddenly the enemy reached over and pulled Kunisuke's hand from his pocket. The policeman pried open Kunisuke's fingers one by one.

But what lay crumpled in the palm of Kunisuke's hand was a cigarette. It was one of the three cigarettes that he had bent over and picked up this morning as he went out the front door at the house by the canal. What a relief! Kunisuke was glad to find it was not the page that he had torn from the dictionary.

What relief? What in hell was he thinking? What evidence could have been more damaging than possession of a contraband cigarette? He felt the policeman grab his wrists and hold them down forcibly. Click. He saw the handcuffs snap in place, before his own eyes.

The handcuffs had a cold, metallic ring that rankled to the very core of his being. Yet, paradoxically, Kunisuke also felt himself begin to calm down. Some place deep inside him had come to accept his fate, whatever it might be. Once this new resolve solidified, it was as hard as ice.

"Okay, you got me. There's nothing more I can do but make a complete turnabout in the way I've been living. Once things reach this point, a person has to shift and decide to move in an entirely new direction. Get to the point where one cannot go farther, and that's when a whole new life begins. . . .

"But, Officer, before we go, how about letting me have a puff? I haven't had a cigarette since this morning. Be a good joe and give me a light, will you?" Kunisuke's voice was a mixture of pleading and bravado.

Kunisuke plunked himself at the foot of the tree. Taking the cigarette from the palm of his hand and clenching it between his teeth, he thrust the tip of it into the face of the enemy. There was an edge to his voice—a certain synergy—that seemed to say he would not be budged from the spot until the cop did what he wanted and lit the cigarette. The enemy said nothing. He gave Kunisuke a light.

Kunisuke sat back and extracted a long, slow puff from the cigarette. He let the smoke fill his lungs.

No, this was no ordinary Peace. Its extraordinary aroma and its exceedingly fine taste rolled over his tongue and washed down his throat. When he exhaled through his nose, the smoke began to float in the air. It traveled along the ground. It mingled with the grasses. It wafted on the breeze. It filled the sky even to its farthest extremity. There—far, far above the dust and dirt of the city and its crossroads—the puff of smoke began to unfold like a drifting layer of incense. It was like the vision of a fragrant paradise made manifest here on earth. For a brief moment, Kunisuke felt as though he were living in a dream.

He stopped to look at what was happening next to him. The policeman had let his hands drop limply to his side. His nose was pointed in the air, his nostrils extended. He wore an absentminded look on his face, his eyes vacantly following the mistlike trail of smoke.

"Here, my friend, why don't you take a puff too?" Kunisuke's voice sounded both friendly and commanding, as he handed the cigarette to the policeman.

The policeman almost seemed to leap at the cigarette as he pressed it to his lips. A smile spread across his face, as if he were the luckiest guy in the world. His eyes narrowed into a glint, as he concentrated on drawing the full flavor of the tobacco from the cigarette. In no time he was enveloped in a cloud of smoke.

"Excellent," he said, almost in a whisper.

But by then he caught sight of his fellow officers as they advanced through the shadows of the forest and rushed to his aid. Suddenly his face reverted to its stern and uncompromising look. He was back to being the enemy again. He stubbed out the cigarette and carefully deposited the butt in his pocket.

"I'll take this Peace as evidence!" he announced.

Kunisuke stood up. He was surrounded by police. The puppy, who had been wagging his tail as he watched from the edge of the pond, looked terribly sad. Poor fellow—the sight of him struck Kunisuke as so sad and lonely. It made his eyes smart with tears.

The police marched Kunisuke off to the edge of the park, where a paddy wagon was waiting. It was painted black and shaped like a cage. Kunisuke was shoved into the back. Immediately the van took off at breakneck speed.

There were no windows in the van. Kunisuke was squeezed between two enemy guards, who sat on either side of him. He had no idea where or in what direction they were going.

But by being a little observant, he was able to make a calculated guess. That is to say, he could tell from the sounds coming from outside that the van was taking the same broad avenue that the bus regularly used, and it was headed for the canal. He fantasized that, just as when he rode the bus, he was once again on his way home to the house by the canal. By and by, he was able to tell from the dampness in the air that blew through a crack in the rear door that the van was in close proximity to the canal.

But the van did not cross the bridge. It appeared to make a sharp turn at the foot of the bridge, and now it was traveling along the quay. Kunisuke was convinced they were at a point alongside the canal that was directly across from the house.

The wagon pulled to a stop. He was kept blindfolded as he was taken from the rear of the van, but he could definitely hear the sound of rushing water. He could also tell that the whole area had been cordoned off and was under tight security; the presence of the police was almost palpable. He was made to walk, and presently he heard the sound of a steel door opening. Once the door clanged shut behind him and it was locked from the inside, the blindfold was removed. Everything was pitch black. He was led down a narrow set of metal stairs that gave access to an underground cell block in which every cell was lined with bars. After a complete body search, his handcuffs were removed. But no sooner were his hands set free than he was thrown behind bars.

Was it merely a figment of his imagination? Once he entered the cell, he felt he was back in his old room on the third floor of the house. Yes, it looked just like the room that he had been assigned at the house by the canal. Perhaps it was the cramped space. Or the low ceiling. Or the lack of any light fixture or decor. Or the square-shaped air vent that had been cut into the outside wall. They all matched his garret room back at the house by the canal.

Except, in this case, the air vent in the wall had been positioned at a height that was much higher from the floor. In fact, his fingers could barely reach it. Furthermore, it was covered with a formidable set of bars.

The prison was underground, and since the elevation of the window was surely lower than the surface of the canal, doubtless it would be impossible to have the view of the canal that he had enjoyed from his third-floor window. No, he was certain it was out of the question — even if he were able to stick his neck between the bars and take a peek outside.

Kunisuke stood beneath the window and pressed his ear to the wall. He listened as carefully as possible. It seemed to him that he could hear the sound of water flowing on the other side. It sounded far away, but it moved in time to the beat of his pulse, breathing in syncopation, as it were, with his own breath.

"The channel flows on!" he told himself.

The simple act of putting his ear to the wall and hearing the waters as they coursed through the canal served to confirm that he was still alive and part of the living, breathing world. True, here he was, incarcerated behind bars and totally cut off from his fellow man. Yet even in this predicament he saw no need to give up and admit defeat.

He sat on a plank that had been attached to the wall and served as a bench. He let his eyes scan the space that had become his new quarters, and he discovered it was not entirely to his displeasure.

As was his habit, he sat back, and naturally his hand reached for the pocket where he always carried his cigarettes. As his fingers fished through his pocket, what did they find but the piece of paper printed in the strange-looking alphabet of Futurese and the two cigarettes left from this morning.

What else did he expect? It was perfectly natural for them to be in his pocket, wasn't it?

Yes, it felt natural enough, but there are times when what feels perfectly natural and what happens as a matter of course ought not to be so natural after all. Surely this was one. At the time when the authorities conducted a thorough body search, they seized both the paper and the two cigarettes as highly incriminating evidence. How could they possibly be in his pocket?

One could only guess that, instead of being locked inside the dirty desk drawer of a petty jailer, the evidence had preferred — quite naturally and as a matter of course — to jump right back into Kunisuke's pocket.

By now Kunisuke had grown accustomed to surprises like these; he had even come to think of them as perfectly natural. As a matter of fact, when he looked down at his hands, what did he see but one of the cigarettes hooked between his fingers. To make doubly sure there was no mistake, he checked to see what was printed on the label. Sure enough, it was just as he thought. There were the letters that spelled out the word "Peace," and they were printed in the strange alphabet of the language of the future. This too was no surprise. His sole regret lay in his not being prepared by having failed to bring a match. How could he light the cigarette?

But, no, far more regrettable was the chagrin he experienced at not having the puppy with him. The poor little fellow—if only he were here!

Kunisuke heard footsteps on the cell block. The guards were probably making their rounds. He could not see them, but their voices drifted within earshot.

"How about that bastard they brought in earlier today? Boy, wasn't he a showman?!?"

"And a real tough cookie too. He sure pulled a fast one."

"Did you see the way he handled himself when he got out of the wagon? I'm telling you it was a sight to see. It was one humdinger of a stunt."

"But what I want to know is who'd be fool enough to dive into the canal wearing a blindfold and a pair of cuffs? Somebody was caught off guard for a second. The guy saw his opening, and in he went. Head first, no less."

"He didn't let so much as a bubble come to the surface, either. He must've swum along the bottom and climbed out on the other side of the canal. Now there's a lucky stiff for you."

"The canal's their territory. Let 'em get within reach of it, and you'll never see 'em again. Hell, they don't pay us enough here to make it worthwhile to dive in after them. Besides, it's dangerous. Who wants to end up floating face up in a ditch for next to nothing?"

"Hell, they're so tightfisted around this joint they don't give us a thing. With all the talk about cigarettes, you'd think they'd hand out one or two. But not these tykes."

"Let's get back to the guardroom. At least we can get a cup of something hot to drink. . . . "

The footsteps receded into the distance. It appeared the guards were talking about K. Yes, Kunisuke was convinced K had to be the topic of their conversation. He was elated at the thought that K had made a successful getaway. A great burden had been lifted from his shoulders. He felt his spirits begin to rise.

But, wait, that was only a part of it. He felt as though the story about K was virtually the same as his own. Only, the canal had never been the reality for him that it had been for K. There was always a feeling of distance that separated him and the canal, and that was why the thought of taking the plunge and jumping into it had never occurred to him. What made K different from him was the way in which they handled themselves, and the difference lay in the fact that regardless of the obstacle—be it a blindfold or a pair of manacles— when K had a flash of inspiration, he translated it into action immediately. For K, there was always another, yonder side to the canal. K believed in it, and you could be pretty sure he had made it safe and sound to the other side.

Ah yes, the far and yonder shore! Kunisuke craned his neck and tried to see what lay beyond the square-shaped air vent of his cell. But the bars blocked his vision and resolutely refused to let him see outside. What's more, they seemed to deny the very idea of the canal. They ruled it out as an impossibility or something that did not exist, and like a blindfold, they left Kunisuke to sink into the dark depths of despair.

K UNISUKE HATED the bars. He would never be able to make himself like them. Of course, they were something that ought not be. Nonetheless, their presence explained in large measure why to his surprise he had taken a liking to his new quarters.

The shadow they cast on one small square of the floor soon spread until it filled the entire room. It was already night by now, and the darkness in the cell was as black as pitch. Whatever distinction existed between the color of the bars and the surrounding darkness was lost in the depth of the night. It was all the same now.

Nonetheless, Kunisuke struggled to see, and peering into the darkness, he sought to identify the canal and to determine the color of its waters. After a while, he noticed a spot on the wall that seemed to light up and glow with an intensely red color. A single shaft of light shone into the cell, and passing between the bars, it fell on the wall. It was almost as if the spot of light were ready to burst into flame. The beam of light did not resemble the shaft of moonlight that one saw in everyday life, but it was the light of the moon nonetheless. And for it to penetrate the thick darkness that enveloped the cell, it had to be extraordinarily powerful.

Kunisuke took the cigarette in his hand and touched the tip of it to the spot of light. The cigarette lit. At first only a pale column of smoke rose languidly in the air, but as it turned bright blue, the smoke began to pour from the tip of the cigarette like water spraying in a fountain, and the room was filled with the aroma of fine tobacco. The moonbeam redoubled its glow, and shining more intensely than ever, it shone with a force that seemed powerful enough to snap the bars in half.

That was when Kunisuke caught sight of strange drops that dripped down the bars. Were the bars sweating on account of the heat that the light generated? Or had the night air condensed into tiny droplets of dew? Or perhaps—just perhaps—the bars had been splashed by the inky waters of the canal.

But, no, it was none of these. Drop by drop, the liquid trickled down and coalesced into viscous beads. The descent of each bead was long and slow. It was like time being measured in drops of oil that, when poured, drip ever so slowly while they tick away the seconds and minutes of each hour. Kunisuke got up and moved closer. He stood directly under the window and tried to see as best he could what was happening.

The drops were like pearls that, in the fierce glow of the light of the moon, turned a dark, ruby red. They looked as though they were oozing from the bars.

Kunisuke stood on tiptoe. He stretched his arm as far as possible and let his hand reach as far as it would go. Still, his fingertips barely managed to touch the bottommost rung. When he withdrew his hand and took a good look at the sticky liquid on his fingers, he was shocked to find it was blood.

No question about it. It was blood. The bars had absorbed such an excess of human blood that the intense light of the moon appeared to make them sweat with it. So thoroughly had they sucked the life from their prisoners that they were like a hot grill on which juices sizzled and ran. They dripped with blood, measuring out time second by second; and, as the drops fell one by one, ticking away the minutes, they seemed to speak of the historical meaning of time as it is spent living behind bars. It was like an inexhaustibly long tale that, no matter how many times it is told, never comes to an end. It went on and on and on—this endless dripping and spilling of blood. Kunisuke put all of his strength into his fingertips, and when he pushed against the bars with all his might, they cracked like pieces of hard candy and let a new supply of blood drip forth. Yet at no time did his prodding appear to make them flinch. No, nothing fazed them. The bars would not be moved.

Kunisuke lowered his hand. It was covered in blood all the way to his wrist. He used the sleeve of his jacket to wipe it off. The sleeve was now dyed several shades of crimson where it absorbed the blood on his hand — except for one thin line that continued to trickle down his finger. At some point he had nicked his finger. This blood was his own, and it stubbornly refused to clot. The bloodstains on his hands were becoming a mixture of the blood of others and his own. Even as he found himself isolated from the outside world by being locked behind bars, he still possessed a real and immediate sense of what it meant to be part of history. He was a participant in history. He stood in its midst and shared in its suffering.

But the bars at the window were unflinching. They would stand in obstinate defiance for as long as it took to render null and void the meaning of history as it has been created and invented by human beings. Or so long as it took to take a fine tobacco and, by depriving it of its fine aroma, invalidate any claim it had made to superiority. How was it that the energy and power inherent in the blood of humankind was no match for the energy and power of the prison bars?

Kunisuke flew into a rage. He got up from the floor and took a flying leap at the bars. He clung to them and made them endure the full weight of his body as his legs dangled in the air. He shook the bars and tried to break them loose. But they brooked no interference, and he was thrown to the floor. He flew at them again and was repulsed. He repeated his futile attack time and again. He became obsessed to the point that he could no longer tell how many times he had lunged at the bars in an attempt to attack them and dislodge them by force.

Meanwhile, he became aware of a second presence in the prison cell that, like himself, was hurling itself repeatedly against the bars. Was it his shadow? Or was he seeing things?

But wait . . . how could it be? There he was, the little fellow. Unbeknownst to Kunisuke, the puppy had found a way into the cell. The little fellow was covered in blood. He was limping badly too, but it made no difference. He leapt into the air and hurled himself against the bars with all his might.

But their struggle had no effect. Kunisuke collapsed on the floor in a pool of sweat.

At some point, he had stripped off his jacket. There beside him on the floor was the crumpled piece of paper. It was the page torn from the dictionary. It had fallen out of his jacket pocket.

As he lay on the floor, Kunisuke reached over and picked up the piece of paper. He threw it at the bars with all the strength he could muster.

It hit the window with a hollow, weightless sound. But just as it was about to fall to the ground, it stuck to one of the bars. The blood had acted as an adhesive that held it in place, and as the light of the moon washed over the little crumpled ball, the paper began to unfold and spread itself across the bars much like it had been pasted there.

Kunisuke watched carefully. Did it mean the letters of the strange alphabet of the language of Futurese were about to switch into action? He waited with bated breath to see what sort of announcement would be forthcoming. What would it say?

To his chagrin, the letters did not move. To the contrary, they started to fade until there was almost no trace of them. All that remained was a single blank sheet of paper that glowed with an eerie white light as the moonlight filtered through it. Words had ceased to exist, or at least words as humankind had known them. Here was a show of force, was it not, of how dreadful the bars could be. Here was their curse, and they cast an awesome spell. It was their verdict and their final rendering of the sentence that henceforth there will be no more tomorrows. The unit of time known as tomorrow would cease to exist.

But, no, wasn't it a far simpler message? Wasn't it a statement to the effect that the energy he had expended, and the puppy had expended alongside him, amounted to nothing more than time spent totally in vain? Wasn't it the case that their efforts were useless? That all action was inaction, was it not? Kunisuke lay on the floor, the strength in his body spent. He felt as though he had collapsed in the middle of a great desert. And there was the puppy beside him. The little fellow had let his tail curl, and he wore a bewildered and frantic expression on his face. It was a look of utter despair and frustration.

But then from somewhere inside — and Kunisuke could not say where — a rhythmical beat began to fill the room as he lay sprawled on the floor. Did it originate within his own body? No, that wasn't it. He could feel the beat as it was transmitted from one thick wall of the prison to the next and as it traveled along the floor. Surely it was the rhythm of all human beings who, extracting every ounce of energy that can be squeezed from the human frame, take to their feet in revolt even if they are repulsed time and again. It was the beat of the movement of all those who continually hurl themselves against an undefined and inexplicable force. In other words, hadn't Kunisuke come to understand at long last that the energy of his own movements was synonymous with a great rhythmical beat of which he had been unaware in the past?

There on the other side of the thick wall of his cell was someone else, and his neighbor was engaged in the same ceaseless motion. No, there was far more to it. Across many a wall, in many an adjoining chamber, there were countless small, stout cells in the underground reaches of the prison. And in those cells, an equally infinite number of human beings were immured, each isolated from the other and kept under lock and key. But these people had come together through the act of hurtling themselves against the bars. They were battling away, exhausting themselves to the very last drop of their energies. There could be no doubt in Kunisuke's mind as to the certainty of this fact. Perhaps the young girl with the whip, and E, and all of the other people who had gathered at the house by the canal counted among the incarcerated human beings who were engaged in the same struggle. The whole gang had to be here. He was here, wasn't he? So it was that he and the puppy were not alone. He put his ear to the floor and listened as closely as he could.

The rhythm was pleasing to the ear. Perhaps it sounded all the more beautiful because his movements — his own hurtling against the intractable — was racked with pain. The music was a silent song. It did not express itself in words, but he knew that whenever it had arisen, people were laboring on behalf of the life they wanted to create. Come to think of it, the rhythm was the sound he heard the night before at the house on the far shore of the canal.

He had seen the people swirling over the giant machine. Silence reigned, but he was certain he had heard the same musical beat in the background. It was the sound of humankind at work. In short, the sound of Labor.

Given the circumstances in which he now found himself, his definition of work had been radically altered. It now consisted of the act of rising up and dashing oneself against the iron bars of the prison. What's more, the people from the house by the canal were participants in the same kind of labor.

Kunisuke remembered he had several bills in his pocket. They were the leftover portion of the daily wages he had received from E. Just as he had labored outside the prisonhouse, shouldering a sack of cigarettes each day, here too he must not give in and abandon the work that lay before him. To lose it, to let himself be distracted, would mean the loss of his life and livelihood in the here and now. Borne along by the rhythm and summoning all of his strength, he got up from the floor.

Suddenly, from the direction of the cell block corridor came the sound of feet racing down the hall. He could hear hoarse, husky voices shouting to each other. Soon the footfalls were within reach of his cell, as a horde of guards massed in front of the bars at the door. The keys clanged in the lock as one of them attempted to open it. The enemy was back, and Kunisuke braced himself for the onslaught.

But the door refused categorically to open. Both the key and the lock would not turn. The door was locked, and locked it would stay. It had sealed itself against the outside.

"Shit." The enemy began to bray like wild animals. Seen from his side of the bars, the guards had become, ludicrously enough, the ones who were the prisoners.

"Vive la république!"

From somewhere, a voice cried out. It appeared a new republic was about to come into being. It was a republic of the energy of work. The laboring force within the walls of the prison had coalesced to become a state of its own. A Republic of Energy.

Kunisuke turned and looked at the white sheet of paper glued to the bars of his cell window. And, in what he intended as his final cri de coeur shouted in response to the synergy of all the other voices in the prisonhouse, he summoned the last ounce of strength from his body and lunged at the blank, white page at the window.

Coming still faster was the puppy, who, taking a flying leap, also hurled himself headlong at the bars. He danced higher and higher until, what do you know, he hit the bars and disappeared out the window.

And right behind him came Kunisuke, hurtling through the air . . . moving toward . . . toward . . .

Toward what? All of a sudden there were no more bars to stop him. There was nothing to check the force of the flying leap that carried him straight out the window. He came perilously close to tumbling the long way down to the ground, but somehow he managed to save himself by grabbing hold, however tenuously, of the iron fence that rose in the air across from the window.

RISING FROM FAR BELOW and soaring high into the sky, the palings of the fence encircled the prison. Beyond them and reaching farther in the air stood a concrete wall. The wall was so high, in fact, that it checked one's line of vision and made it impossible to see beyond it. Still higher in the sky was the moon, its light so bright that it illuminated every corner as far as the eye could see.

It was readily apparent that the only one hanging on the fence was Kunisuke. Doubtless all the other people — each having flown from his or her prison window — had made an agile escape, and they had long since disappeared. An emergency alert went off belatedly, the sound of the siren now filling the prison yard. It sounded like a terrible wail of pain that arose from the underground.

There was no sign as yet that the enemy was about to come as far as the fence to apprehend him. He was free to struggle on his own, and at last he succeeded in inching his way to the top. From there he could look up and see the concrete wall across the way. But it was far too tall, and the distance between the fence and the wall was far too great for him to cross it in a single leap. He despaired of ever being able to escape from where he was. All seemed to be lost. He sat atop the fence and let his feet dangle in space.

It was then that a tiny figure appeared atop the concrete wall. It was such a small figure, but given the brightness of the moon, Kunisuke immediately identified who it was. It was the young girl with the whip. And, hey, there was the puppy right by her side! The girl stood tall, her shoulders thrown back in a proud, even haughty, manner. She was like a queen surveying the stars from her castle parapet. Or a whore, who, standing in the dust at the public crossroads, awaits her next customer.

The sight of the young girl reawakened memories of the terrible physical torment that he had known the night before. As he found himself once again hanging in midair, his feet dangling with no place to go, he was reminded anew that suffering is an inevitable part of love. Ah, the whips of love! It was a simple fact, but it was brought home to him with great poignancy.

Whereupon something grazed past his eye. It was as though a shadow had fallen across the earth. Had the sky clouded over? No, that couldn't be it. The moon continued to shine with singular intensity. Whatever was it that had severed the light and seemed about to come crashing down on top of him?

It was the shadow cast by the young girl. Yes, that was it.

The small and insubstantial shadow had started to grow. It moved down the side of the wall. It flowed over the palings of the iron fence. In the twinkling of an eye, it spread across the entire horizon. As it raced and swooped, it unfolded a mighty pair of wings far too grand for a human shadow.

Yes, it actually appeared to have wings.

The girl had become a beautiful, birdlike shadow. To her usual outfit of culottes and leather boots that always made her legs look so straight and tall, she had added a great manteau. She let the wind catch in its folds, and as it billowed, the sides flapped winglike on the breeze. She dared to raise her whip heavenward, and letting the tip of it flick across the face of the moon, she gave the command. There, high in the heavens, her shadow was transformed into a great, blue bird of prey. It became a raptor, a hawk — an *Accipiter gentilis* — that raced across the sky with an awesome, jetlike roar. It rose so high and unfettered in the air that its wingspan threatened to eclipse the light of the moon.

Just then, as it passed over the iron fence, the tip of its wing extended down far enough to touch the tallest paling. It passed within Kunisuke's reach. And in that instant, he leapt and was lifted effortlessly to the top of the concrete wall. . . .

"Hey—"

But, no, the girl and the puppy had vanished from sight. He was alone atop the wall, and what he saw as he surveyed the world beneath his feet were the waters of the canal. They shone like a river of light that shimmered as little waves broke and rippled across the surface.

On the far shore of the canal, he could see a single speck of light. A bright but inconstant flame, it was like a beacon that flashed in the night.

The raptor let its shadow play upon the waters as it circled one more time and wove a final, intricate dance in the air. But then, it trailed away, and moving in the direction of the light—poof!—it disappeared without a trace.

Using the beacon from the far shore as his guide, Kunisuke poised himself at the edge of the wall. He sprang into the air, and letting his body dance momentarily upward, he piked and dove the long way down to the canal. And when he surfaced and began to swim, his hand cut a brilliant swath through the waters.

II

Critical Essays

On "Mars' Song"

Written late in 1937 and published in January 1938, "Mars' Song" must be read against the backdrop of its times to be fully appreciated. In July 1937, an incident ominously similar to the military fait accompli that had precipitated Japan's seizure of Manchuria in 1931 occurred on the outskirts of Beijing, and Japanese forces invaded China. By August, Beijing had fallen, and Shanghai was under siege. By the end of December, Nanjing lay raped. At home, news of Japanese military advances was met by a rising chorus of popular support that found its voice in "The Bivouac Song" *(Roei no uta)* and the lyrics of its opening stanza, "Oh so bravely, 'Off to Victory'" *(Katte kuru zo to isamashiku).*[1] The winning entry in a nationwide song-writing contest, the song sold more than sixty thousand copies within a fortnight of its release in the fall of 1937 — a remarkable figure in a day and age in Japan when records were played on gramophones, found more commonly in public establishments than in private homes. Sound trucks plied the streets playing the song and drumming up support for the war.

Gone was the backlash against military highhandedness at home and adventurism abroad that had come a year and a half earlier in the wake of the attempted coup of February 26, 1936, when junior army officers in Tokyo assassinated Cabinet members and tried to seize control of the government.[2] The pendulum of public opinion had swung back toward the hawkish; or as Ishikawa's metaphor has it, the "season of 'Mars' Song'" (I, 577) was at hand. Call him the Roman Mars or the Japanese Hachiman, the god of war had been unleashed, and a bellicose chorus of support for victory in

China swept the land. For Ishikawa, the jingoistic fever that arose from every street corner, whistle-stop, and café was like the choking, acrid smoke that comes when a fire is about to burst into flame, and he predicted it would not only stifle any contrary point of view but also permeate its way into the most minute "cracks" of everyday living. Moreover, the time was fast approaching when no one would be clearheaded enough or strongminded enough to check its progress. In short — to use the allegory that is developed in the second part of the story — no one would reach for the stopcock and, by shunting off a lethal gas at its source, alter the course of history and save the country from tumbling headlong down the fiery path to death and destruction. War with China had yet to be declared officially, and the domestic political situation still remained somewhat fluid, but by the fall and winter of 1937-1938 Japan was about to embark upon the perilous point of no return in its protracted "Fifteen-Year War."[3]

As *watashi*, the first-person narrator of "Mars' Song," stands on a rise one warm autumn day and surveys the aquarium that is his microcosm for the country, he remarks that the "lantern-slide show" (*gentō;* I, 577) of Japan has gotten sorely out of focus. What is to be done, he asks, to set people straight again? How are they to be made "pure, precise, strong, and beautiful once more" (I, 577)? He hardly knows how to answer this difficult, life-or-death question. But he senses that a stupefying — even suicidal — force is at work in the land, and although he too is nearly overcome and baffled by it, for him the fundamental corrective to the "malaise of our times" (I, 551)[4] lies solely and unambiguously in the vehement "NO!" that he hurls in the face of "Mars' Song" as he begins his tale — "I rise from my chair and, turning in the direction of the popular refrain . . . I shout 'NO!'" (I, 552) — as well as the equally emphatic *"Yamero!"* (I, 578) with which he ends it — "Turn off the damn music."[5]

"No More 'Mars'!"

Although the war against China is never referred to directly in "Mars' Song," the singularly most important message that Ishikawa has to convey to his readers is his stance of unequivocal opposition. This is done at the outset, and in a defiant tone, via the invective "NO!" that the first-person narrator *watashi* directs toward the sound trucks and crowds that noisily congregate outside the window of his Ginza apartment. Moreover, his message is reinforced immediately by the quick trip that he makes to the cinema, where, after nodding off momentarily, he is startled awake by the sounds and sights of a battle in progress. Although the locale of the war, as well as the nationalities of its combatants, go unnamed, we can easily surmise—as doubtless Ishikawa's contemporaries readily did—that the China coast is being bombarded and Japanese forces are occupying the Chinese countryside.[6] Moreover, as the newsreel camera zooms in and focuses on the two Chinese boys who have been commandeered by the Japanese military for a close-up fraternization shot, *watashi* reads in their silent and unsmiling faces the vehement but speechless echo of his own protest and powerlessness. Feeling utterly ashamed and frustrated, and no longer willing to remain a passive spectator to a propaganda film (or a participant in the collective unconsciousness that is, he reminds us, the nature of moviegoing), he slinks—doglegged and shamefaced—from the theater.

Later in the story, he will be repulsed and depressed once again by what he sees as the rapid and wholesale militarization of Japanese society. Taking the morning express from Tokyo Station to the Izu Peninsula, he sets out on a leisurely excursion only to find, contrary to his own air of calm detachment, that the rest of the nation is working itself into a frenzy. The signs of a war-in-the-making are everywhere: the color of khaki, as more and more recruits are drafted and reservists are called back into uniform; the flag-waving crowds; the relentless brass bands; even the sight of a child brandishing a toy sword. Moreover, as the overheated atmosphere aboard the train makes only too clear—in a brilliant contrast between images of heating up and cooling down, and of coalescence and dilution (an example of the rhetorical flourish at which Ishikawa excels)—there is less and less of the calm and rational or the free and easy, or even a gentle breeze to clear the air and suggest that the wisdom of cooler heads might prevail. Indeed, a chronic airlessness, death by asphyxiation, and the concomitant last gasp for a breath of fresh air (or "breathing spell"—*ikinuki*—

as in the case of Sanji's trip to Izu; I, 569) are recurrent images that speak not only of the claustrophobia of the times but also of *watashi*'s mounting sense of alienation and paranoia.

Watashi is a man of pronounced opinions on everything from Mount Fuji (never his favorite!), to binoculars (far too dehumanizing!), to *kyōka* comic verse ("How refined, and ever more so!"). At times he can be bitingly sarcastic, such as when he compares the trained porpoises at the aquarium to military police dogs and, by inference, his fellow human beings. Indeed it is via his outspokenness that we come to feel we know him well and to appreciate the humanistic and cosmopolitan values that lie at the heart of his iconoclastic opinions. At the same time, it comes as no surprise that his outspokenness is the cause of dirty looks and finger pointing directed toward him at the aquarium café. He knows only too well that a "commotion is in the making" (*zawameki ga kikoeru;* I, 578) and that he is a likely target for "those who wait upon power and authority" (*ibu wo tanomu mono;* I, 578). There is a price to pay for going against the tide to become the rare dissenting voice, especially at a time when "Mars' Song" is omnipresent.

Finally, in this connection, it is important to note that while, on the one hand, *watashi* is bold and explicit in his opinions, "Mars' Song" also demonstrates a pronounced orientation toward the use of indirection and ellipsis. We have already seen how, in a stroke of stylistic economy or camouflage, Ishikawa evoked more with less by deleting or suppressing the names and places from *watashi*'s account of the propaganda film shown at the movie house. When we turn to the allegory of the curious suicide and death of Fuyuko, moreover, we find that understatement, which is everywhere in evidence, has been elevated beyond a rhetorical technique to the status of a metafictional strategy. Not surprisingly, at this point in the story the ever vocal *watashi* is relegated to the sidelines, his role being limited — at least temporarily — to that of interlocutor to Obiko and silent witness at the wake. In his stead emerges Fuyuko, who, less person than ghostly presence, delivers sotto voce a cautionary tale on the price to be paid for adopting a play-it-safe attitude of see, hear, and say no evil in a time of national crisis and hard choices. If Fuyuko's tale is any indication, the price to be paid for speaking out — and for being so insane as to register one's protest — may be high. Yet as time will show, the costs are not nearly so dear — or so fatal — as those incurred by looking the other way and having nothing to say at all.

The High Price of Feigning Ignorance

As the story-within-the-story begins, *watashi*'s cousin, Obiko, has appeared at his Ginza apartment with the startling news that Fuyuko has probably committed suicide. A freewheeling and spendthrift *moga*, or "modern girl," Obiko had gone to her sister's house to borrow money only to find the doors locked and the smell of gas leaking from a crack at the back door. Instead of breaking in, however, she is overcome by shame and embarrassment at the thought that Fuyuko has done something impetuous (just as she herself has done in arriving with an inopportune request for money). She sends the maid away; and dismissing the gas as the smell of scallions rotting in the trash, she leaves, feigning ignorance of what has happened at the house. She struggles to convince herself that Fuyuko has no reason to die and that doubtless she has saved her sister — and herself, for that matter — from having to make embarrassing explanations and apologies to the neighbors. It is a myopic, short-term point of view, however; and even she is never fully persuaded of its effectiveness or its wisdom. Obiko merely runs away, haunted all the while by the specter of her sister's death. It is a horrific thought, and it pursues her like the train barreling down the tracks at the railroad crossing at Kamata Station.

Alas, what may have saved Fuyuko's face will not save her life; and by the time Aioi Sanji, Fuyuko's husband, returns home late from work, the house in Kamata is filled with gas, and Fuyuko lies dead in the family room. Her clothes are neatly arranged about her person — "dressed as formally as an actress in a play" (I, 563) and, in a pointedly ironic note, her face "made up . . . with extra care" (*nen'iri ni keshō shite;* I, 563). There is no sign of foul play or accident. Nor is there any apparent reason why Fuyuko should have chosen to kill herself. As an element of suspense — or more precisely as an interpretative puzzle — the question of her death becomes the focal point of the wake held the next day. In a sense, we the readers are invited to join the discussion and search for an explanation. Why has Fuyuko died? The conundrum is couched, moreover, in the form of a rhetorical question taken from the writings of an unidentified Western dramatist: "What is the price to be paid for pretending to be deaf or dumb?"

Although childbearing was the expected norm, if not a patriotic duty, for newlyweds in their day, the childless Fuyuko and Sanji have led a modern urban lifestyle in which Fuyuko pursued her love for the foreign theater and Sanji, his career as a successful newspaper photographer. The year before, however, Fuyuko had begun to act out a series of little dramas (*mane;* I, 562) in which she feigned temporary blindness, deafness, and even unconsciousness, while Sanji was called upon to play the role of doctor and miracle worker. He had been a willing partner at first, but as time passed, the increasingly complex dramas became more dangerous. At the wake he is reminded of the cryptic remark Fuyuko had made, in quoting the Western dramatist, to the effect that to feign an illness or handicap is an act that, carried to extremes, just might prove deadly. *"Tsunbo no mane wo suru mo ii ga, do wo kosu to inochi ni kakawaru."*[7] Whatever had she meant?

Initially, Sanji brushes aside the line that Fuyuko had quoted him as not meaning much ("It means what it says, doesn't it?"), but then his worst fears materialize when he discovers that in enacting her latest drama — a neatly orchestrated suicide by asphyxiation — Fuyuko has miscalculated and killed herself. He blames himself for not having been more vigilant and suspects the possibility of an "unseen crack" (*mienai sukima;* I, 566) in their seemingly happy marriage.[8] Still, ever the literalist, he does not attempt to read between the lines to consider what meaning may lie behind Fuyuko's cryptic remark or her reckless behavior; and the story never does spell out the answer for him, or us, leaving it only to be inferred. But surely one cause of Fuyuko's unspoken anxiety concerns her husband, who, as a junior officer in the army reserves, is about to be called to serve at the front — as was the case with large numbers of reservists who were recalled to active duty after the China Incident.[9] Fuyuko can hardly bear to hear, much less speak, of it. Enacting her private minidramas, she seeks to tie him more tightly to her and to divert attention from the harsh and inevitable reality that Sanji will shortly be sent off to war and death. She feigns ignorance of her true concern, and she does it to the point where she can do it no more.

Although the relatives at the wake recognize a diversionary tactic at work in Fuyuko's thinking, they are not at all sympathetic toward her theatrical behavior. For them, Fuyuko is guilty of having allowed herself to become "divorced from real life" (*seikatsu wo yūri shite iru;* I, 564). The reality uppermost in their minds is the current escalation in the nation's preparations for war, as even the most casual mention of "Mars' Song" reveals. The room becomes charged, with everyone assuming the role of instant authority or source of insider information on the war. Even their limited insight into Fuyuko's death is colored by a wartime mentality that foreshadows the "luxury-is-the-enemy" *(zeitaku wa teki)* slogans of self-restraint and patriotic service that became the focus of home front propaganda during World War II.[10] To their way of thinking, Fuyuko should have been self-sacrificing not to her private fears or dramas but to the national cause.

Sanji is offended by the smug and moralizing tone of the relatives' remarks, while *watashi,* who has sat glumly on the side, feels frustrated that nothing has been said in appreciation of Fuyuko's life. He had felt a special kinship with Fuyuko because of her love of literature; moreover, he is struck by the beauty and grace — indeed, the artful deliberateness — with which she has made her exit from life. Simultaneously, he is appalled by the relatives' unbridled enthusiasm for "Mars' Song" — just as he had been horrified the night before when Obiko interrupted her sobs to rush to the window to shout "Banzai!" to a passing sound truck. In fact, no one dares *not* to congratulate Sanji when, irony of ironies, official "greetings" arrive saying he must report for active military duty. Here is a man who has lost the love of his life only the night before, but the relatives are delighted (or, perhaps, feel mutually constrained to appear delighted) at the news of Sanji's induction into the army. Only *watashi* dissents, the novel adopting his perspective by referring to the supposedly felicitous red letter as "the call to arms that corralled [all the young men in the land] . . . and saw them off to faraway fields where the smell of gunpowder filled the air" (I, 567–568). Or where, as Obiko comments earlier, "too many people who don't want to die are dying every day" (I, 559).[11]

The relatives become quite concerned two days later, when Sanji uses his "five-day reprieve" (I, 568) to head for the Izu Peninsula, a favorite vacation spot. How does it look for a man so recently bereaved to take off on a pleasure trip? And in the unchaperoned company of a young girl no less, especially one as modern and independent as Obiko? Perhaps Sanji has become unhinged by Fuyuko's suicide. At a minimum, a spending spree that includes chartering a boat and then a car as well as staying overnight at a deluxe hotel smacks of a failure to observe a proper period of mourning and a lack of seriousness at a time of national crisis. Or, more important—and surely this is the source of the relatives' apprehensions—it hints at possible dereliction of duty vis-à-vis Sanji's obligation to report to the army. While the relatives may not approve of Obiko traveling in Sanji's company because, typically of them, they are concerned with the matter of appearances, it would be inappropriate for us to read "Mars' Song" as a clandestine romance or, more extremely, a whodunit in which Sanji and Obiko have schemed to eliminate Fuyuko. Such readings are unwarranted. The story clearly rejects extramarital affairs on either Sanji's or Fuyuko's part as the cause of Fuyuko's suicide; the ratiocinative elements of the plot are directed not toward the evolution of a secret affair between Sanji and Obiko, but toward the interpretative puzzle of Fuyuko's death; and the tone of the friendship between Sanji and his sister-in-law is of asexual innocence or at most sibling affection and rivalry.

Watashi is dispatched to Izu to check on Sanji—a busybody task that he does not welcome. There is no impropriety; the cousins would have happily included him from the start. He notes, however, Sanji has atypically left his camera behind in Tokyo, as though to suggest that Sanji is done with his past as a professional photographer and recorder of life; and the frenetic and almost fearless excesses to which Sanji is given in a rare moment of extravagance and recklessness are indicative of a man who feels he may not have long to live, let alone enjoy life. When, in the tersely worded parting where the two men say good-bye and go their separate ways—Sanji over the mountain, *watashi* to the aquarium—it is with the tacit recognition and unspoken pain that it may well be the last time they see each other. The unstated pathos of the scene would not have been lost on an audience reading it in 1938. In saying, "We'll be waiting back at home," *watashi* sends a double message of hope for Sanji's safe return not simply to Tokyo the following evening, but from the killing fields far away.[12]

"What's Missing?"

In the story's coda, the view-of-the-aquarium scene, *watashi* elaborates on the image of the "malaise" or "injury" introduced at the very beginning of "Mars' Song." In it, he offers his meditation on why people in Japan are prone to the kind of self-deception and false pretense that characterizes the behavior of nearly everyone—whether those associated with Fuyuko's suicide or the anonymous crowd he sees at the aquarium. Why is it they cannot look unblinkingly at the harsh facts of life in the fishbowl that is Japan? He hypothesizes that "the gaping mouths raised in song" to the war god as well as the "open and inflamed . . . wound" on the body politic,[13] are the product of a terrible deficiency, or "great thirst" (I, 577)—an image that, coincidentally, resonates with the story's many references to "cracks" or "voids" in the quality of everyday life. Something vital is missing; and the word that he seizes upon for what is lacking in Japanese society is *shisō* (I, 577):[14] "philosophy," "worldview," or "Weltanschauung" (although probably not "ideology," given Ishikawa's lifelong iconoclastic, anarchistic, and anti-ideological posture). The word is ambiguous in most Japanese contexts, and *watashi* does not develop his use of the term either fully or specifically. But, surely, in "Mars' Song," *shisō* implies an overarching essentialism or anchoring principle that people might choose as a source of identity and self-definition in their lives. Because of this ontological void, people are awash. Not unlike fish kept in an enclosed tank by the sea, they are highly vulnerable to the alternating waves of hysteria and compliance that sweep through their lives.

As *watashi* laments, people are naive and unquestioning ("they forgot how silly he or she could be"; I, 576). They are only too ready to sink into a sea of "happy mutuality": namely, a photogenic image of Japan as a carefully posed and airbrushed composition of the mountains, the sea, and themselves. It is the picture-postcard view—an "orientalism" manufactured for domestic consumption—that they might buy as tourists traveling on the Izu Peninsula and that induces amnesia about the harsher, sillier aspects of their everyday lives. They lack "the mental armor that they need to take up the challenge and argue" (I, 572) against patriotic symbols such as Mount Fuji,[15] which is presented as dominating the physical and mental landscape of the country in a seductive and oppressive way. People are subject to manipulation, and unbeknownst to themselves, they behave like the tuna that stalks its own enclosure or the porpoises trained like military police dogs.

"Facts" versus "Fiction"

"Mars' Song" appeared in *Bungakkai* but was banned within a week of the magazine's distribution. Unsold copies were seized, and the magazine was ordered to cease publication temporarily. Eventually, Ishikawa and his editor, Kawakami Tetsutarō (1902–1991), were hauled into Tokyo District Court, where they were fined thirty and fifty yen, respectively—a considerable sum at the time and one that neither could hope to pay. Only through the intervention of Kikuchi Kan (1888–1949), then doyen of Japanese letters and editor-in-chief of the prestigious literary journal *Bungei shunjū,* were the fines paid and the two men released. Later Ishikawa would claim he had been in "an optimistic mood . . . that, as I was writing ['Mars' Song'], I felt . . . something on this order would get by *(kono gurai wa ikeru).*"[16] Perhaps he believed the story would pass or survive the censors and, like Fuyuko, thought his little drama would have no unforeseen consequences only to discover he had miscalculated. Nonetheless, as his remarks suggest, Ishikawa was cognizant he was publishing in the face of social sanctions that discouraged outspokenness as well as a longstanding system of government censorship that, by its policy of postpublication suppression, was designed first and foremost to promote, through the twin pressures of lost time and money, a propensity for self-censorship on the part of writers and editors. Ishikawa's remarks indicate he had weighed the possibility of his story being seen as potentially offensive. In addition, the work itself demonstrates his awareness of the way in which social and government pressure can tempt a person to self-censorship and make of him or her an accomplice of silence. Obiko rules out the thought of Fuyuko as a suicide in the same instant that she wonders what people will say; and when *watashi* thinks aloud at the café, he reports that his vehement demand to turn off "Mars' Song" has been made spontaneously or "without thinking" *(omowazu;* I, 578). That is, he has spoken without censoring his thoughts or calculating the costs of freely speaking his mind.

Ishikawa's modest ipso facto explanation of the suppression of "Mars' Song" as simple naïveté or accidental miscalculation is no more convincing than the relatives' arguments concerning the disastrous outcome of Fuyuko's little drama. Nor is it possible to believe the story would have eluded the censors had Ishikawa been more prudent or skillful at "the art of disguising himself in his works" (*sakka no shōtai ga mienai*; I, 571) after the manner of Ōta Nanpo (1749-1823; a.k.a. Shokusanjin), whom *watashi* touts as the "awesome master" of the mystification style *(tōkai-buri)* of the Edo period. Indeed, in discussing this work critics and scholars have tended to draw attention to the ways in which Ishikawa employs the dissembling techniques of indirection and understatement used by the writers of Edo to circumvent censorship and defy the authorities.[17] But however much *watashi* sings Nanpo's praises as a paragon of cool detachment who excludes "the dust of the earth" (I, 570) and his own personal affairs from his works, it is all too apparent that Ishikawa does not follow his example in writing "Mars' Song" —or at least he follows him only to the extent that allegory can be said to mystify at the same time that it highlights. For, in point of fact, Ishikawa makes no attempt to veil or hide his message of dissent in this work. To the contrary, with his radical "NO!" he announces it boldly, and given the extraordinary nature of the times, he says he is prepared to pull into the novel the flotsam—the "facts" (*jijitsu;* I, 554)—of quotidian life. Yet—and herein lies the paradoxical nature of this work—by introducing Fuyuko, or "Winter's Child," he also weaves a tale that, despite its many "facts," is after all a metafictional device that surely emulates, if not equals, "the blossoms" that once dripped from Ōta Nanpo's facile and mystifying pen.

In the opening salvo of "Mars' Song," there is a great deal of talk about a dichotomy between facts and fiction, and of how *watashi* is unable to produce a Parnassian prose (in the manner of Valéry and the Symbolists), as he sits before the rickety tabula rasa of his writing table, eminently poised to create an original and transcendent work of fiction divorced of "all ties to terrestrial sentiment and its attendant distractions" (I, 552). As in the case of Fuyuko and her dramas, however, the immediate and absolutist demands placed upon those living in the noisy, warmongering days of "Mars' Song" eschew the luxury of fiction making. The times insist on facts, and hard facts at that. Thus, when talk turns to "Mars' Song" at Fuyuko's wake, everyone is obsessed with facts—down to the minutiae of the number of nails in an infantryman's boot or the jolt registered by the catapult mechanism in a kamikaze plane. To be sure, the value of facts has been aggrandized by the heightened aura of secrecy that inevitably surrounds every bit of news and information that circulates in a nation at war, and especially one where facts are tightly controlled by the government and the military. *Watashi* disparages facts. First, he is suspicious of their factual content, which is often more rumor than truth. But, more important, his distaste for facts in literature, or fiction, reflects his preening and posing as a modernist, antinaturalist writer bent on creating a transcendent prose (as well as his aforementioned desire to adopt the cool, detached air of a Nanpo). Finally, his antifactual bent expresses his contrarian stance as a social critic. The world is a sea of facts; what is needed for a change is some genuine thought—a comprehensive worldview that will put all the facts into proper perspective. But, alas, his thirst is not to be quenched, and unable to fulfill his own prescription for fiction of "producing even one novelistic sentence" (*ichigyō no shōsetsuteki bunshō wo mo erarenu;* I, 552), he tells us with great reluctance he will allow "his pen to deviate" (I, 554) to take up the "facts" of Fuyuko's story.

Authorial intent is a matter fraught with difficulty, but clearly the tergiversations in the introductory passages of "Mars' Song" concerning the priority to be given to fact or fiction raise the welter of issues that surround an artist called upon to address, whether by choice or by circumstance, the political concerns of the day via the medium of artistic production. The value of the pure prose to which *watashi* aspires lies in its intrinsic separateness from the noisy concerns of quotidian care and daily life, yet it is also by virtue of its separation that it runs the risk of being denounced as divorced from reality—in short, of being too escapist and out of touch with current affairs. At the same time, to jettison the transcendent embrace of fiction in order to address social realities (and fight facts with facts, so to speak) entails the likelihood of being misunderstood as having capitulated to resisting war on war's terms—namely, hard facts—and having produced a work that is mere reportage or the self-absorbed blathering of a confessional "I-novel."[18]

The dichotomy of facts versus fiction—or, to state the matter differently, the issue of politics versus art—had been a topic of perennial debate in Japan ever since the rise of proletarian realism in the late 1920s and the increasing polarization of writers in the 1930s into the camps of political activists, on the one hand, and apolitical aesthetes, on the other. Identifying himself as an iconoclast and an anarchist, Ishikawa had resisted the supremacy of politics over art as advocated by the former at the same time he deplored the socially disengaged attitudes of the latter. For Ishikawa, the modernist writer had a role to play as both creator of pure fiction and social critic, and he needed to find a way to combine or synthesize the artistic and political voices in his work or, to put it another way, to combine elements of *ga,* or elegance, with *zoku,* worldliness.[19] In 1936 he had raised these issues in his first novella to receive major recognition, *Fugen* (trans. *The Bodhisattva,* 1990),[20] in which he expresses allegorically his longstanding love for and disappointment with the revolutionary underground (as embodied in the sublime Yukari, who metamorphoses into a fulminating she-demon) as well as the failure of artists working in both traditional and contemporary forms (as represented by the Noh dramatist Terao Jinsaku or the novelist manqué Iori Bunzō) to create a literature relevant to a period of national crisis. By 1937 and the outbreak of the War in China, the issue was even more pressing, and no longer would the position of literature in service to politics be cast in terms of the relation of art to left-wing thought. Instead it would be redefined as service to the nation, the creation of a "national literature" *(kokumin bungaku),* and ultra-nationalism. Now that the proletarian opposition on the left had largely fallen away and many of its followers had converted to apolitical or right-wing positions, modernist writers such as Ishikawa became the last bastion of resistance. With "Mars' Song" he offers us a fusion of quotidian fact with metafictional allegory that addresses his twin priorities of artistic creation and social relevance.

Hindsight of a Half Century

From the perspective of fifty years later, we see only too clearly how the invasion of China embroiled Japan in a hopeless war in Asia and then the

Pacific, and how the further acceleration of national mobilization programs begun after the seizure of Manchuria in 1931 culminated in military control over civilian politics a decade later. The rousing call-to-arms played on and the consequences went unheeded. And if, in the years since 1945, many have debated the cause and effect of Japan's march to war, Ishikawa's message delivered from the eye of the maelstrom in 1937-1938 is unequivocal and highly instructive. It was a time in which to speak out and say no, as he did. To pretend otherwise, to sink into "the empty crack of unconsciousness" (I, 552) or to feign deafness in the face of "Mars' Song," was to pursue a course of inaction that, while perhaps forgivable as all too human, would prove fatal for Japan. Moreover, while we can only guess what lies in store for Sanji, for example, the deleterious effect of death and destruction inflicted on China, even if only glimpsed in the newsreel, is already apparent for those who, like *watashi,* had eyes to see what war, masquerading as liberation, pacification, or amity, really meant.

Not only does "Mars' Song" rank as one of Ishikawa's most forceful works, it is one of the most powerful antiwar statements to appear in Japanese — if not world — prose fiction. It is exemplary of the small body of "resistance literature" *(teikō no bungaku)* written by Ishikawa Jun, Nagai Kafū, Kaneko Mitsuharu, and other writers of prose and poetry;[21] and, as such, it belongs to those circles of wartime dissent and nonconformism in Japan that, albeit never broadly or powerfully organized, included maverick journalists; imprisoned and underground leftists and communists; some Christians, especially the Holiness Church of the nonestablishment wing of the Japanese Christian movement; as well as some Buddhists and followers of the "New Religions."[22] Furthermore, one must recognize "Mars' Song" as representing the incipience of a pacifist literature in Japan, since pacifism, which had its earliest advocacy at the time of the Russo-Japanese War of 1904-1905, did not achieve widespread recognition as a political and philosophical position until Japan's defeat in World War II and the A-bombing of Hiroshima and Nagasaki in particular.

Seen against the onset of the "dark valley years" of the second decade of the Shōwa era, "Mars' Song" is both a warning and a prophesy of what issues in the wake of the wholesale militarization of society. Moreover, it is Ishikawa's rumination on why this sorry state of affairs had come to pass. And, finally, it is the chronicle of his *bunjin,* or literati mentors, and the spiritual resources that are the roots of the intellectual independence by which the lone protester in the story—the seemingly unheroic but intrepid *watashi*—"pen-points" the locus of his sanity (*watashi no shōki wo pen-saki ni tsukitomeru;* I, 553) in a world madly out of joint.

On "Moon Gems"

The half-written poem at the beginning of "Mars' Song" and the chapbook that falls serendipitiously from the overhead rack on the train to Izu remind us that *kyōka* comic verse and the example of its chief practitioner in the Tenmei style, Ōta Nanpo, played an important inspirational role in Ishikawa's life during the next seven and a half years of war and privation. It was to them that he turned for sanity, humor, and refinement — or what we might call Ishikawa's fundamentally seriocomic and ironic outlook — as well as strategies for literary and professional survival at a time when freedom of expression was severely restricted and the government moved to put "Japanese Literature in Service to the Nation" with the formation of the *Nihon bungaku hōkokukai* after 1942.[1] In "Moon Gems" *watashi* tries his hand at *kyōka* once again, and he cites Nanpo's famous verse on the special pleasures of a moonlit night and full bowl of rice (II, 314).[2] What more — *"mata mōshikane"* — might one want of life? he seems to ask in an ironic, if not facetious, echo of Nanpo's rhetorical question.

"A Moonlit Night and a Full Ricebowl"

A great deal more, to be sure. For by April 1945, when "Moon Gems" was written, the consequences of Japan's "single-minded pursuit" (*ipponyari;* II, 315) of the war god were all too obvious: the rationing of everything from food, to saké, to boots; the blackening out of all lights at night; the prioritization of "operations vital to the times" (*tōsei yūyō no jitsumu;* II, 303, 305); the mobilization of civilians as armaments workers and firefighters; the construction of communal gardens and bomb shelters; and the ever more frequent air raids that culminated in the heaviest attack to be launched against Tokyo, namely, the saturation bombing of the night of March 10 (*sangatsu jōjun no aru yoru;* II, 316) — a historical fact described here in terms of both the leveling of downtown Tokyo and the burning of Gūka's mansion. At age forty-six, Ishikawa had little to call his own besides a collection of Edo period books and a reputation as Akutagawa prize winner from a decade earlier. He had few prospects of getting published as a nonparticipant in efforts to support the war through either literary or civilian service.[3] Furthermore, his poetic prognosis for the war, as given in the *kyōka* verse that he has his alter ego *watashi* compose by the light of the rising sun on New Year's Day 1945, is hardly optimistic. The intent of the gods remains obscure, the gabled peaks of the Shinto shrine — and by extension those who reside in high places — being enveloped in a cloud of mist.[4] Finally, when *watashi* is sent to visit "Boots" — a military man assigned to what remains of Japan's industrial base — he knows his "three-minute interview" (II, 305) is doomed from the start. By nature, *watashi*/Ishikawa is simply not agile enough — or shall we say "facile" enough? — to make himself be of use.

Yet it is not the litany of physical loss and destruction or of victimization by the war that we hear from him. To the contrary, it is the loss of any semblance of personal and intellectual freedom that is the source of *watashi's* most poignant regret. Everything has been hedged in; and caught in a liminal state, he sees himself as "not inhabiting the face of the earth, but a space one foot under *(chika isshaku),* living in shame" (II, 302). A "writer by trade" (*chojutsu wo gyō to suru;* II, 304) with no means left by which to support or express himself, he has become a man entombed, a live but nearly silent witness to his times and his powerlessness. He longs desperately to emerge from the underground, as it were, and "making his mad dash through the reality that impinges upon us all" (II, 302), he hopes to initiate or join some sort of "movement" or "coup" (*undō;* II, 303). Despite the seditious sound of the word, which for reasons of censorship or — more likely — poetic license is left undefined, *watashi* is about to set himself in motion and take up, however belatedly in life, the art of riding a bicycle. He has lined up a used bike, an instructor, and a safe place to practice; and we the readers are called to share in his *acte gratuit*. Is it an exercise in futility, mere physical locomotion, or spiritual transcendence? Considering the transformations the dilapidated bike undergoes—ranging from an elegant steed in the hands of the young girl to revolving freshets of water sparkling in the moonlight (or even cherry blossoms arcing on the breeze), it is an allegorical "vehicle" worthy of a master of comic verse. Indeed, *watashi*'s antic struggles in the back lot bring a knowing smile to our lips, for in finding the smallish space in which to be free, he mounts a protest against his times and the "unhygienic" (*fueisei;* II, 305) existential state in which he finds himself. His motions may be circular and his triumph pyrrhic, yet seen in the right light, they shine with the intensity of rare and otherworldly "moon gems" (*meigetsushu;* II, 314).

"Study Abroad in Edo"

During the Fifteen-Year War very few Japanese intellectuals sought asylum abroad. There was no émigré tradition in Japan, its absence being abetted by the country's geographic, historical, and linguistic isolation. Even the most prominent Japanese writers lacked genuine bilingual facility, not to mention the international reputation and connections whereby they might have taken leave of their native land; moreover, if doors abroad had ever been open to them, surely after December 1941 they were resolutely closed. By and large, it was the avenue of "inner emigration" that served as the escape hatch for Japanese writers and intellectuals who held to dissenting opinions.

To withdraw from society and delve in the past, or history, as a socially sanctioned refuge or a cover for advancing ideas at variance with or designed to subvert the powers-that-be, has been a time-honored pattern of resistance in the eremitic tradition of East Asian letters. It has its roots in Taoist and Buddhist thought, and as an ethos for writers and artists working in opposition to established academic styles of poetry and painting, it evolved into the Southern Sung concept of the *wen-jen* (Jpn: *bunjin*), or literatus.[5] Introduced into Japan in the Edo period (especially in the form of the rejection of Neo-

Confucianism in Ming China by Yüan Hung-tao [1568-1610] and the Kung-an School),[6] the literati tradition laid the groundwork for a cultural renaissance and revolt against Tokugawa orthodoxy in the Tenmei era (1781-1789). Tenmei constitutes, alongside Genroku and Bunka/Bunsei, one of the three pinnacles in the cultural history of the Tokugawa period (1600-1867). It also marks the historical juncture at which the arts broke from their traditionally Kansai — or Kamigata — origins and, shifting to the eastern capital, took on the more permissive and expansive style of life in the rough-and-tumble city of Edo. But more importantly and personally for Ishikawa, Tenmei constituted a mental bulwark against the atavistic, no-exit situation in which he found himself. Writing in retrospect, he draws a sharp distinction between the dark valley years of the war and Tenmei. He boldly calls Tenmei the genesis of all that is "modern" *(kindai)* in nineteenth- and twentieth-century Japanese history and thought, and he affectionately dubs his period of stasis and inner emigration as his years of "study abroad in Edo" *(Edo ryūgaku):* "Since it was impossible to get out of the country during the war, I decided to make my living off domestic products and study abroad in Edo. As a result, I discovered Japan's modern age in the decades between the eras known as Meiwa and Bunka [1764-1817]. The quality of everything produced after Bunsei [1818-1829] falls off considerably, however. Even as Tokyo burned, I found it more exciting to spend my time with my Edo contemporaries than to be out looking at the ruins" *(Ransei zatsudan* [On a Day and Age When the World Was in Chaos], in *Isai rigen* [XIII, 165 – 166]).

For Ishikawa, Tenmei was a time when a panoply of *kyōka* poets, *share-bon* novelists, *ukiyoe* artists, *nanga* painters, and patrons of the arts — Ōta Nanpo, Santō Kyoden, Suzuki Harunobu, Watanabe Kazan, and Tsutaya Jūsaburō, to name a representative sample of what he calls "the happy few" (XIII, 445) — formed a series of coteries, or *kyōka-ren,* in which by setting aside the social distinctions of Tokugawa feudalism and, furthermore, "secularizing" *(zokuka)* the traditional canon of Japanese literature,[7] they recreated themselves as "disguised Genjis" *(yatsushi Genji)* and "glorified Komachis" *(mitate Komachi),*[8] in a legacy that is known to us today via the special genre of woodblock prints known as *surimono.*[9] The anonymous atmosphere of the "underground" literary salons in Tenmei provided a protective guise — a smokescreen of mystification *(tōkai-buri)*[10] — for sallies against a feudal system that had grown reactionary and incompetent in nearly two centuries of Tokugawa rule. We shall return to the modernity of these "sophisticated" artists, especially with reference to the historical figure Hattori Nankaku (1683-1759) and the groundwork he laid for the cultural flowering of Edo, in Ishikawa's story "The Jesus of the Ruins."

The grand master of the *kyōka* coteries was Ōta Nanpo.[11] Simultaneously a samurai bureaucrat and a literary light whose precocious talents had been recognized at age nineteen by the early scholar of Western learning and painting Hiraga Gennai (1728-1779), Nanpo flourished until 1787, when the arts came under fire as a result of the severe economic retrenchment policies of the Kansei Reforms (1787-1793). Although in latter years Ishikawa was to rethink the high esteem in which he held Nanpo, there is no question that this "awesome master" *(osorerubeki tatsujin;* I, 570), as Nanpo is described in "Mars' Song," was a significant force in Ishikawa's thinking during the war years. Writing in 1942 on Nanpo, or Shokusanjin, he says,

> I was possessed by the desire to write a treatise on the literature
> of Shokusanjin, along with an account of his life. This, the best
> of Edo's writers, had stirred my thoughts for some time, and I
> was unable to apply myself to anything else. . . . I decided to
> deal with his verse in my own way, focusing solely on his litera-
> ture and giving no heed whatsoever to his life. . . . I decided the
> very best means to quantify the movement of his spirit was to
> focus on the deviational angle of this vexingly shadowless gentle-
> man whose works fired the imagination of an entire generation.
> Suddenly an idea awakened inside me: . . . I would adopt his lit-
> erary techniques as my own . . . I would follow his lead and pro-
> duce my own *kyōshi* ["mad poems" in the Chinese manner] or —
> drawing upon the *Manyōshū* and the *Kokinshū,* and standing the
> spirit of *haikai* on its head — create my own versions of *kyōka* in
> the Tenmei style. Doubtless such talk is the beginning of mad-
> ness, but then it is probably not possible to participate in the es-
> sence of Shokusanjin's spirit without driving oneself slightly mad

in the process. (from *Yuki no hate* [The Last of the Snow; II, 282–283])

Ishikawa's high estimate of Nanpo derives, as we see here and in the paean delivered to him in "Mars' Song" (I, 570–571), from Nanpo's antiestablishment stance and iconoclastic humor, his cultivated air of aloofness, his uncompromising adroitness at playing the game of public versus private personae *(omote/ura)*, his disdain for personal revelation, and his ability to generate fictions or fabrications that have an artistic integrity independent of the author's life. As a member of the avant-garde of Japan's modernist movement who sought to advance the twentieth-century novel beyond the self-referential style of the Japanese I-novel, Ishikawa surely found Nanpo's "shadowless" transparency to be enviably cool and, at the same time, not a little bit crazy. Nanpo was, finally, a kindred spirit who had known the constraints of censorship and political pressure.

Kafū as Gūka

Yet more than Nanpo, it is the modern writer Nagai Kafū (1879–1959) who provides *watashi* with the most immediate example of a "role model" of noncompliance and the inner émigré. Kafū had established a reputation for challenging authority, whether in the form of intense antipathy for the Meiji oligarchs or his perennial battles with the censors over the erotic content of his novels. Moreover, he deplored the war in China and the Pacific. After publication of his story "The Decoration" (*Kunshō;* trans. 1964) was banned in December 1942, he confined his literary production to keeping a diary to which he confided his criticism of the Japanese military and his resolve to cut himself off from society.[12] In "Moon Gems," he is introduced as a renowned poet, the name Gūka, or "Lotus [Flower]," being a play on Kafū's nom de plume of "Lotus Breeze" and "Liaison House" *(Renshikan),* a parody of "Eccentricity House" *(Henkikan),* the name of Kafū's Western-style residence located in Azabu, Tokyo. *Watashi* does not know Gūka personally, and he has never darkened the door of Gūka's "liaison" stronghold, but he lives nearby, and he experiences an unspoken affinity for the independence of mind that Gūka represents.[13] Like Kafū, Gūka has been "loathe to waste even a word of vituperation on the sleazy claims of society" (II, 310), and sealing his gates against the world, he devotes himself "to the composition of a work that he chooses to keep from all eyes" (II, 311), namely, the diary that Kafū published after the war as *Danchōtei nichijō* (Gut-wrenching Days at Eccentricity House).[14] It is Gūka's constitutionals to the rise that overlooks the vacant lot and *watashi*'s bicycle practice down below that link the two men in silent cognizance of each other. Moreover, *watashi* makes a point of noting Gūka's odd combination of a tweed suit and cape worn with Japanese clogs. It is a description, as a matter of fact, of what Kafū regularly wore and of the deprivations brought on by the war. But, more important, Gūka's odd combination of Western clothes and native footgear is symbolic of his nonconformity to popular tastes and conventions of propriety, if not protest against nationalistic notions of single-minded purity in dress.[15]

Above all, it is a certain fleetfootedness that *watashi* admires most in Gūka. The world may laugh at Gūka's clogs as unfashionable, but as *watashi* notes, "One can never be too vigilant, given the speed with which poets advance" (II, 312). His view is a modern, Romantic notion of the artist as vanguard of social change and fashion who operates at a higher level of energy or insight than his contemporaries. Gūka outstrips lesser mortals; indeed, given his costume, he verges on the ethereal transcendentalism of a Taoist immortal, or *sennin,* who can transverse time and space at will.[16] *Watashi* aspires to this lightness. Witness, for example, his practice of Taoist breathing exercises in which he inhales the *chʿi* of three stripes of blue, white, and red that streak across the morning sky (*ao, shiro, aka, sanjō no ki;* II, 313).[17] He cannot help but feel slightly envious, moreover, at the ease with which Gūka's "clogs fly across the face of the earth like the eight swift stallions of Emperor Mu of the Chou" (II, 312). If only he could emulate Gūka's aplomb in life and art, and in a matter so trivial yet so frustratingly important as simply staying mounted on the seat of a bike! The desideratum of nonchalance as seen, first, in *watashi*'s admiration for the ever-transparent and awesome Nanpo and then in the urbane figure cut by Kafū comes to constitute a social stance, if not the symbolic articulation of a fundamental philosophical outlook that occurs with increasing frequency in Ishikawa's works and is best described by the phrase "Edo cool." Levity in life is not only sane policy, it is moreover a powerful antidote to "a single-minded obsession with spiritual purity." As *watashi* notes, quoting the wisdom of an unidentified Western poet, "nothing is more likely to propel one headlong down the path to barbarism" (II, 315) than the single spear *(ipponyari)* of repeatedly and aggressively pressing one's only strong suit or weapon.[18]

In a final metaphor, *watashi* likens Gūka to a great archer — "If a man draws a bow, let him draw it boldly" (II, 321).[19] It is an image that evokes the cool intensity of the Zen marksman who aims without aiming, or Minamoto Yorimasa, who exercised the *nue*-demon by twanging his longbow. The implication is that if one is to resist one's times, let him or her be bold in doing so. The episode is drawn, moreover, from the night of March 10, when, during the saturation bombing of Tokyo, fire spread and eventually engulfed "Eccentricity House." It is said Kafū carried out his diary as the sole item that he chose to save among many valuable possessions and rare books, and he watched stalwartly as his residence of twenty-six years was reduced to a pile of ashes. As time went by, the story of his unruffled stoicism became legendary, Ishikawa's rendering of it here also having had a hand in its retelling and dissemination. It became a lesson in detachment and unsentimentality over material possessions as well as one facet of an evolving postwar portrait of the modern Japanese intellectual as a solitary and steadfast individual who, as writer and critic, stands outside society.

The Larger Issues

The unhappy story of how the majority of Japanese writers embraced the war in Asia and the Pacific has been told in Donald Keene's brief essay "Japanese Writers and the Greater East Asia War."[20] It is a cautionary tale that reminds us how intellectuals can be wrong or easily swayed, and for want of dispassion and responsibility as social critics, many let literature devolve into propaganda, if not saber rattling. Yet even if it is argued that bellicose voices were dominant among writers in Japan and resistance was limited, to say that *"almost everyone was involved"* (Keene's italics)[21] is to establish a blanket rule that is too broad and not entirely just. First, it ignores the extent to which resistance was suppressed via statist controls, (even though this is an issue that is the subject of some debate).[22] Moreover, it fails to address the all-important qualifier of almost-everyone-but-not-all and in the process to blur what is a far more constructive distinction, namely, how to separate the rare goat from the herds of sheep, or the doves from the hawks, as it were. It is to give undeservedly short shrift to the independent few who, rather than capitulate to ultranationalism, chose incarceration (Kurahara Korehito, Miyamoto Yuriko), death (Tosaka Jun, Ōzaki Hotsumi), political asylum (Ōyama Ikuo, Dan Tokusaburō), or solitary resistance within society (Nagai Kafū, Tanizaki Jun'ichirō, Kaneko Mitsuharu). Of these, perhaps only Kafū and Tanizaki are well known. Other writers such as Abe Tomoji, Funabashi Seiichi, Satomi Ton, Yanagi Muneyoshi, and Yanase Masamu merit attention as well.[23]

To retell their stories is a time-consuming and complex task because, one, it is necessary to examine each case in scrupulous detail, and two, the growing discourse on resistance in the half century since World War II has become simultaneously more precise and elastic as it now covers a wide range of stances from solitary witness to nonconformity, to selective opposition, to acts of refusal, to outright protest. Moreover, its theories reference a variety of historical contexts from French *résistantialisme* to "Good Germans" to writers of samizdat literature.[24] Generally speaking, the degree to which acts of resistance are "public" and "intentional" has been seen as key, as James Scott cogently argues in *Domination and the Arts of Resistance*.[25] Even so, there is much slippage in knowing how to evaluate intent and — still more fugitive — the ways in which intent plays itself out in the agora of everyday life. "Charismatic acts" of outspokenness with their "irreducible element of voluntarism" are easy to identify. It is "offstage" and "infrapolitical" communication via what Scott calls "hidden transcripts" that has yet to be fully articulated.[26]

Furthermore, the context of the discourse on resistance has been overwhelmingly European or Western. Aside from Keene's pioneering essay and Edward Seidensticker's *Kafū the Scribbler*, both of which date from the mid-1960s, little has been done in English on the subject of Japanese writers and the war. Indeed it is surprising how little work has been attempted, since

Japanese scholars have pursued the topic with periodic regularity.[27] Poshek Fu's *Passivity, Resistance and Collaboration,* a recent study of Chinese literary resistance in the face of the Japanese occupation of Shanghai, has made a fresh start from a new and different quarter,[28] but the longstanding eremitic tradition in East Asia of noncompliance through withdrawal from society, passive resistance, and the use of mystification, evasion, and nonverbal strategies makes it especially difficult to tease out what will be defined as public versus private acts of resistance. One is often at a loss to know whether the intent of retreatism or feigned conformity is tactical cover or political accommodation, if not collaboration. Is a shadowless transparency à la Nanpo, for example, subtly scripted insouciance, self-serving duplicity, or a bit of both? To put the matter baldly, to move toward a definition of resistance that is more globally inclusive is to wrestle with the bugbear of "oriental inscrutability," which, while an egregious cultural stereotype, nevertheless has also been a time-honored modus operandi for circumvention and subversion of authority in East Asian cultures. Keene touches on this in his essay in discussing the proverbially vexing "vagueness of the Japanese language,"[29] just as Seidensticker is bedeviled in *Kafū the Scribbler* by the issue of how to "read" Kafū's wartime diary, *Danchōtei nichijō,* given the revisions and editorial emendations that Kafū made after the war. (In a "Postscript on the Diary," he exonerates Kafū of aspersions he may have cast on Kafū's integrity.)[30] Issues of ambiguity and exegesis of texts are ones that we shall have to deal with here too. But a comprehensive history of the important handful of writers who resisted in Japan will have to await close readings of individual authors, such as this book attempts in the case of Ishikawa. As for the still larger issue of the epistemology and hermeneutics of reading resistance in Asia, or even globally, that is research that will take far more time and scrutiny.

As Scott points out in *Domination and the Arts of Resistance,* because "the shared discourse of the hidden transcript [is] created and ripened in the nooks and crannies of the social order," it often results in "an instantaneous mutuality" between writer and audience.[31] Nonetheless, even a coded "NO!" raised in the face of peer group and political pressure is a lonely position to maintain. It does not offer the blandishments of "constructive" criticism. Nor is there any assurance that one's message has been successfully conveyed or received, because feedback is minimal or nonexistent. Readers' reactions may also have to be veiled. As Ishikawa wrote in 1936 in an essay titled *Seijiteki mukanshin* (Political Apathy) that has gone virtually unnoticed,[32] social criticism in literature, and political satire in particular, is predicated upon the presence of an audience that, however small, is receptive to its message, however guarded. When, in "Mars' Song," *watashi* takes us to the theater and has us stare into the faces of the two Chinese boys commandeered for the newsreel, like him we know their deafening silence literally roars with the vehemence of his own protest. Or as the conventional Japanese phrase has it, "Those in the know know" *(shiru hito zo shiru).*[33] As for those who do not, they remain clueless.

Ishikawa in the "Dark Valley"

The evidence in the case of Ishikawa Jun is overwhelmingly clear, and it has been made much easier to examine by his outspokenness. Albeit a junior figure in the world of Japanese letters, he dared to speak against the war in China; and although he lacked financial independence of any consequence, he managed to sustain himself as a writer without any significant lapse into political accommodation—a matter to which we shall return momentarily. But, first, to state briefly the broader argument: during the seven lean years from 1938 to 1945, Ishikawa wrote little fiction.[34] He produced only one novel, *Hakubyō* (Writing in White; 1939), a roman à clef that takes as its hero the modernist architect Bruno Taut (1880–1938), who fled Nazi Germany in 1933 and who, after three years in Japan, questioned the validity of residing in a country that had grown increasingly ultranationalist.[35] Moreover, the handful of short stories that Ishikawa wrote are largely on Taoist themes *(Kijutsu, Tekkai, Hi Chōbō, Korobi sennin, Chō Hakutan)* and are flights of fantasy to the "purple-colored land" (II, 241) of China in the days of the Taoist immortals. By far, the bulk of Ishikawa's literary production during the war was as an essayist. His critical tour de force on the Meiji period writer Mori Ōgai *(Mori Ōgai;* 1941) established a standard for style in writing literary criticism that is greatly admired even today; and atypical of Japanese writers, he set forth his theory of prose and the novel in *Bungaku taigai* (All about Literature; 1942). Nonfiction represents the only other genre in which he worked. He produced a biography of the *bunjin* painter and samurai official Watanabe Kazan (*Watanabe Kazan,* in both adult and children's versions; 1941, 1942)[36] as well as an account of the life and military defeat of the fourteenth-century warrior Nitta Yoshisada (*Yoshisada-ki;* 1944). Both can be read as accounts of antiestablishment "failed heroes;"[37] moreover, the originality of Ishikawa's treatment of the materials sets them apart from the vast lot of historical novels, which were the sole growth industry in Japanese literature during the war years — a development that left Ishikawa ambivalent or distressed.[38] Finally, he took up the avocation of writing *kyōka,* the heterodox form of *tanka,* at a time when *tanka* was being revived as the preeminently Japanese and imperial mode for poetic expression. There are many Japans within Japan; and Ishikawa's championing of Edo and the Tenmei literati also represents his counterbalance to the orientalism promoted by officialdom or the concept of a "national literature" *(kokumin bungaku)* in which writers were called upon to effect their "return to Japan" *(Nihon e no kaiki).*[39] Note also that Ishikawa's vision of Edo is not the conventional characterization of the city as the gay and decadent Yoshiwara demimonde, or the "downtown" disposition of the feisty *Edokko,* or child of Edo. To the contrary, it is the Parnassian world of the *kyōka* versifiers whose salons once lined the banks of the Sumida River and were washed in its cool and gentle breezes.

> I constructed my hermitage in such a way that, were someone to break in and take a look inside, there would be nothing material to find — only spirit; what's more, had someone come along to introduce the element of time, I would have broken out of its shell immediately. During the years when the world was taken up with the contraption called the war, even a clumsy type like myself managed to survive and avoid becoming a murderer in print. To die? Hell no, to live as long and as comfortably as possible became my aim. That, and that alone, was the secret source of my success. (*Mujintō* [Vimalakirti's Inexhaustible Light]; II, 426)

Ishikawa's works are free of "the sort of inflammatory writings by almost every recognized author" with their "endless cries for the annihilation of America and England."[40] There is no indication that he contemplated writing a novel in support of the Greater East Asian Writers Congress as his contemporary Dazai Osamu (1909–1948) did, for example,[41] or that he experienced anything but contempt for the one government-sponsored conference on literature that he did attend and that he left abruptly.[42]

A blemish on a pristine record is all the more visible, however. It is possible to identity isolated passages that are not without a touch of xenophobia;[43] moreover, sensitive to what might be viewed as "faking it politically" *(seijiteki gomakashi)*, Ishikawa took the initiative in 1960 in reprinting and calling public attention to what he considered to be three potentially embarrassing "Fragments from the War Years" *(Senchū ibun)*.[44] The first and third address his doubts about the merits of the historical novel that flourished during the war years.[45] They are of no particular interest to us here, but the second, "On Neighboring Cultures" *(Zenrin no bunka ni tsuite)*, his review of the Manchurian National Treasures Exhibition mounted at Ueno in 1942 to celebrate the tenth anniversary of the founding of Manchukuo, bears examination because it represents what Ishikawa calls "his shame as a novelist" (XIV, 14). While in tone and content the essay is clearly skeptical about what the exhibition has to offer, and Ishikawa takes pains to construct a forthright—even bold—argument that Japan's connections to Manchuria are solely political in origin and not the result of any abiding cultural affinity between the Tungus and Japanese peoples: "It is only after the Russo-Japanese War that our political relationship with Manchuria began to spread like sparks from beneath our feet . . . and only since the Manchurian Incident . . . that the relationship has grown in direct proportion to the expansion of political power" (XII, 638), nonetheless the essay then proceeds to draw a conclusion that, looking in retrospect in 1960, Ishikawa found to be startlingly embarrassing as propaganda and accommodation to the worldview of Japanese imperialism: "Namely, the simple and self-evident hypothesis—and one that inevitably will be demonstrated—sets up Japanese culture as 'king' of its related cultures" (XII, 638).[46] "I should have had the courage to write it differently," he wrote in 1960. "Even in telling a lie," he adds, "there is a right way to do it" (XIV, 14).

A far more troubling passage appears, however, in a short piece titled "Literature Today" *(Bungaku no konnichi)*, published in January 1941.[47] Not included in the three fragments resurrected for commentary in 1960 and absent from all three editions of Ishikawa's *Complete Works* published during his lifetime, the article begins as a defense of prose and repeats ideas presented the year before in Ishikawa's work on the theory of the novel, *Bungaku taigai.* Something of a hodgepodge, it appears to have been written in response to two contradictory ideas widely circulating in Japanese literary circles at the time, namely, the rigorous call for creation of a national literature *(kokumin bungaku-ron)* and the view of literature as powerless in the face of political exigencies *(bungaku hiriki-setsu).*[48] It is clear that Ishikawa subscribes to neither view: instead he advances the argument we have already heard from him that, because literature is concerned with "movement" rather than fixed positions, writers operate in the vanguard of their times. This is true even if their work is misunderstood, and all "beautiful things" *(utsukushii mono)* are destined to die. But then, in a passage that once again seems to leap from the page, Ishikawa adds abruptly, "With regard to Germany and Germany alone, it is for certain that Hitler is a dazzling leader *(migoto na shidōsha).* In order for him to be so in the present, the necessary conditions had to be in place in the past. And if, by some small chance, he should fail, one can imagine it will be a beautiful thing" *(man'ichi kare ga shippai toshite mo sore wa utsukushii mono da to sōzō sareru;* XII, 612).[49]

We recoil today from any reference to Adolf Hitler as dazzling or brilliant, although it is a fact that he had admirers outside of Germany until the final onset of war in Europe. The passage calls out for correction, as does misinformation in the following paragraph concerning Thomas Mann's "reportedly having left Germany on his own, and without speaking ill of the Nazis thereafter."[50] Nonetheless, *"migoto"* is a word that can be used as sarcastic euphemism (e.g., *"migoto na shippai,"* a brilliant mistake); and the passage is ambiguous with regard to the way in which Ishikawa imagines Hitler's possible failure as a "beautiful thing." Is it that he anticipates Hitler's demise, just as he offers faint praise for Hitler's inevitable moment in history? And by speaking about Thomas Mann, is he conveying information that there are writers who have abandoned their homeland as well as those who do speak ill of the Nazis, the case of Mann being the supposed exception rather than the rule? The repeated use of hypothetical caveats *(kansuru kagiri, shippai toshite me, sōzō sareru)* and the terse ambiguity in which the passage is cast further undercut the ostensible praise. They also appear to allow Ishikawa to push the envelope of an unstated counterargument against advocacy of any relevance that Hitler and his successes may have for Japan, just as he is quick to delimit Hitler's leadership skills as being useful for "Germany and Germany alone." Writing at a time when Germany was winning on a number of military fronts in Europe, Ishikawa nods in the direction of propaganda, while fending off any suggestion that fascism may be suitable for Japan, or perhaps anywhere other than Germany. As he goes on to add cryptically, "In reality, the various conditions will not come together and fall into place in any hurry" (IX, 612). Although it is virtually impossible to reach a definitive conclusion concerning the intent of this passage, surely it must be read in the context of the "mess" *(gotagota)* in which, as the article says, literature existed during the war. As the article concludes, writers live, caught as they are, "in the uneasy state of the relationship between Ideal and Reality" (XII, 614).

It has been argued that Ishikawa momentarily wavered in his commitment to an antiwar, antiestablishment position when the pressures exerted on writers by the state were at their greatest in 1941-1942,[51] or that, in the faint praise of one critic, he succeeded in "sitting pretty" throughout the war, by staying out of harm's way and "smiling happily as he hopped on a white crane with red crest à la the paintings of Kano Sanraku . . . and soared off to the heavens."[52] It is altogether possible to see "Moon Gems" as a mini-reenactment of the conflicted feelings that Ishikawa experienced, tempted as he was by the prospect of a decent job and a real pair of boots, on the one hand, and equally determined to emulate Kafū and his hygienic constitutionals by taking up bike riding, on the other. At the same time, insofar as the world is concerned, learning to ride a bike is a pointless gesture. *Watashi* is limited to moving in circles, the arc of his "movement" metaphorically circumscribed by the very narrowness of the negotiable space in the vacant lot. Moreover, mastery does not come easily. He must call on a mere child (who is handicapped in her own way), Taoist breathing exercises, and the secret, transforming power of moonlight to see himself through. But by and by he learns to stay astride the bike, and in a moment of pure play in the midst of national catastrophe, he is restored to the unfettered and childlike innocence of his instructor. Indeed his tenacious struggle with the bike becomes something of a love affair. As a depiction of survival in a no-exit situation, *watashi*'s story reveals striking similarities to the existentialist themes that European intellectuals developed in response to their own experience of repression and resistance during World War II. As Ōe Kenzaburō notes, in an observation on Kafka and Ishikawa as the two figures who most influenced his generation of postwar writers and himself personally,[53] it is the power of the imagination to transform reality that is the salient feature of this work, which ranks as his favorite. Like the moonlight that beautifies the dilapidated bike in the solitary hours in which *watashi* practices, imagination is the *"mōshi"*—the "if" of Nanpo's pun on the pleasures of a full rice bowl, a full moon, and—just maybe—a pocket filled with money to spend. In the rare, translucent light of his imagination, *watashi*'s praxis takes on not only new life but also a gemlike sparkle. Allegory mediates outspokenness, and as we saw in "Mars' Song," it advances Ishikawa's tale beyond the quotidian arena of political rhetoric. It lifts it to the realm of art.

Light at the End of the Tunnel

To be right, or even appear to be right, on every moral issue is doubtless an improbability; moreover, to insist on the possibility that one can always be right is to flirt with what has been called "the vanity of . . . *l'insupportable justesse.*"[54] Nonetheless, as is argued here, via a combination of outspokenness and mystification Ishikawa succeeded remarkably in sustaining an independent voice vis-à-vis the powers that be. It was a feat about which he would remain modest, as the hindsight of "Fragments from the War" suggests.

While the war years were a long, lonely, and dismal period in his career, it appears he was also was blessed with "moral luck"; moreover, he had friends, especially Ebina Yūji, the son of Ebina Danjō (1856–1937) who had been president of Dōshisha University and pastor of the famous Reinan-zaka Church near the American Embassy in Tokyo. Yūji is representative of what is called in Japan the liberal or "soft" wing *(nampa)* of the Japanese Protestant movement. His friendship with Jun dates to the so-called lost years of Ishikawa's life circa 1929-1931, when it is held Ishikawa was involved in underground political or artistic movements (as yet to be identified). Ebina considered himself a "patron and *oyabun* [boss]" to his anarchist friends in the 1930s,[55] and when he worked for a shipping firm that transported military supplies between the Bōshū and Izu peninsulas during the war, he supplied Ishikawa with meat, fresh vegetables, and saké from time to time. "Occasionally, [Yūji and Jun] would spread a sumptuous banquet for themselves at Ishikawa's apartment — somehow finding space in a room knee-deep in rare editions of Chinese verse by Dōmyaku Sensei [Hatanaka Kansai] or the poetry of Apollinaire."[56]

On the night of May 25, 1945, however, Ishikawa was burned out during a bombing raid that left him with only "one hundred yen and five cigarettes" (XIV, 166), and he sought refuge at the Ebina residence in Funabashi, Chiba. Given that Funabashi was the site of a major army installation and Ishikawa was likely to attract the unwelcome eye of the military police, the Ebinas called upon a relative and former governor of Hokkaidō, who arranged for Ishikawa to go out on fieldwork for a quasi-government foundation *(gaikaku dantai)* surveying living conditions in *burakumin,* or outcast, communities. It was in the course of his tour of remote villages in Hokuriku, Kinki, and Shikoku, and specifically aboard a train headed for Toyama, that Ishikawa first heard the news of Japan's surrender on August 15, 1945. The war was over, and Ishikawa was about to launch himself into what would become the most feverishly active period of his career: the immediate postwar years.

On "The Legend of Gold" and "The Jesus of the Ruins"

" The Legend of Gold" (*Ōgon densetsu;* 1946) and "The Jesus of the Ruins" (*Yakeato no Iesu;* 1946) rank among Ishikawa's most famous and commonly anthologized works. Representative not only of his brilliance as a stylist, especially as past master of the garrulous style *(jōzetsu-tai),*[1] they are also powerful evocations of the immediate postwar milieu in which Ishikawa rose to prominence, alongside Dazai Osamu, Oda Sakunosuke (1913-1947), and Sakaguchi Ango (1906-1955), as one of the first of the "après guerre" novelists and a member of the so-called libertine school *(burai-ha)* of writers.[2]

Salvation in the Ruins

As the title of one of the stories suggests (and the English cannot fully convey), Japan has become the *yakeato,* or "burnt-out shell," of its former self.[3] People have been left homeless, train stations leveled, and life reduced to "an endlessly flat and unvarying plain" (II, 326). In chronically short supply, food has become the new national obsession. Indeed the mere mention of it — whether white rice, doughnuts, or the almost loving description lavished on a desiccated and fly-covered rice ball — is surely a ploy on Ishikawa's part to whet the appetite of his hungry contemporaries and lure them into exploring his many ruminations and asides on the meaning of the new age of *sengo,* or postwar.[4] At their most basic level of interpretation, these two stories chronicle the state of physical and mental prostration in which Japan found itself after August 15, 1945. They speak of a time of unparalleled destruction, deprivation, occupation — and even personal or national humiliation if, for example, one chooses to read "The Legend" as a tale of "victor's justice" in which the G.I. gets the girl, so to speak. Such is the conventional view of the immediate postwar years held by many Japanese; and it explains, if only in part, the perennial fascination that these stories hold for their readers and anthologizers.

Yet reading "The Legend" and "The Ruins" as mere chronicles of postwar life in the dark days of 1945-1946 constitutes too superficial an appreciation of a writer who seven years earlier was perspicacious enough to foresee the all-consuming fire latent within "Mars' Song" and whose style is characterized by a high degree of polysemy. For just as *yakeato* is a disfiguring "burn," or even a humiliating "brand" on the landscape of Japan, it also signifies the promise of what comes after the flames subside. Seen in this light, ruination is something akin to a biblical refiner's fire or the torch of the ancient tiller who sweetens the land through a technique of slash-and-burn. Indeed it is the importation of the millenarianism of Christian metaphor into these two stories that is the most telling signifier of Ishikawa's efforts to lift narrative out of the realm of reportage and elevate it to the status of metafictional exploration of the theme of *yakeato* as saving grace or promised land. With the title of "The Legend of Gold," for example, Ishikawa establishes a chain of association between the denizens of Yokohama and the lives of the Christian saints as recorded by Jacobus à Voragine (1230-1298) in his medieval classic *The Golden Legend (Legenda aurea);* and in "The Ruins" he taps the messianic hopes of the New Testament as subtext for the story's many allusions associating the wild child of Ueno with Jesus, the Christian Son of Man, and Christ the Savior (II, 475-476, 478, 480, 482). It is a curious juxtaposition of images, Ishikawa's "illumination" of his text by means of Christian iconography coming as something of a surprise to foreign readers, just as it has to generations of Japanese.

In Ishikawa's paradigm, the dross of the past has been radically burned away, and in this rare and unprecedented existential moment of Japan as tabula rasa, the country has entered a historical divide from which it can be envisioned as utterly divorced or liberated from its feudal past. Moreover, Ishikawa perceives a new and unformed vitality at work in the land, and he invites us to contemplate his teleological vision in which "modernity" (*gensei; genzai no yo; kannō;* II, 329) is about to assume its place on the stage of Japanese history.[5]

As Ishikawa correctly divines in having *watashi* focus on the two most prominent black markets (*yami'ichi*) of postwar Kantō, the barracklike shacks in the vicinity of Sakuragi-chō Station in Yokohama and the reed stalls that line the back alleys of Ueno in Tokyo, it is there — in what he rarefies as "the marketplace" (*ichiba*) — that the contest for the hearts and minds of a new Japan is about to be wagered and fought.[6] It is there too that the two characters of "the woman in red" and "the wild child of Ueno" appear to challenge *watashi;* and by the unsettling encounters he has with them, he/we are forced to contemplate anew the meaning of the postwar period as setting for both personal drama and broad social allegory. What manner of "Legend" is Ishikawa setting out to create? And who is about to emerge deus ex ruina to be anointed saint and/or savior of *sengo?*

Total devastation as fertile potential is the existential and literary philosophy that Ishikawa shares with his so-called fellow libertines, although they did not join forces to form a coterie or publish a literary magazine. "To live [is] to de-moralize" (*Ikiyo ochiyo*), wrote Sakaguchi Ango in his much-touted essay "On Decadence" (*Daraku-ron;* 1946).[7] Only through consciously and actively embraced acts of demoralization — of "sinking" or "falling" — can the social hierarchy and moral constraints of the past be abandoned and a spirit of creative liberation unleashed in the postwar era. This deliberate embrace of what comes naturally is what Ishikawa identifies in "The Ruins" as "debauchery [as] wholesome morality" (II, 469);[8] it is what the woman in red comes to personify; and it is the natural providence granted to the wild child of Ueno, born as he is outside the parented, cosseted, and inhibiting confines of human social organization. Similarly, in his seminal essay "The Literature of Possibility" (*Kannōsei no bungaku;* 1946), Oda Sakunosuke called for the literary equivalent to this social iconoclasm, namely, the abandonment of the traditional lexicon of Japanese literature in order to produce a new art that articulated what had not been previously known, thought, or expressed.[9] Or to state the matter in Ishikawa's symbolist idiom of the blank page as the writer's sole point of departure, to give expression to a wholly new, unstructured age is "to think with the pen" *(pen to tomo ni kangaeru)* and thus push language beyond its existing perimeters.[10]

Reading the Legend

"The Legend" begins in medias res: the "momma-san" at the makeshift restaurant has launched into a tour de force apologia on the scarcity of white rice, while *watashi,* perched on a stool across the counter from her, lets his thoughts run to the last twelve months of his life. Who is speaking to whom in these opening lines is knowledge we acquire only as we read along, however. In the original text, the momma-san's monologue is not set off as direct speech, and her identity as speaker and businesswoman is initially withheld from us, or at least only hinted at in the first few lines.[11] In addition, almost immediately thereafter, she is overridden by a second unidentified voice ("Out came the coffee . . . the cake . . . the doughnuts"). It too goes unidentified, and it speaks in the broad, sweeping tones of a social commentator ("Nothing, but nothing, has been able to dislodge white rice"). Commencing in medias res, withholding identification of the initial speaker(s), and superimposing a narratorial voice that comments on the text like a talking head or a roving microphone are techniques that we have come to recognize as the idiosyncratic signature of Ishikawa's style. In "The Ruins" and *The Raptor,* they will be developed to a high art.

Today, we are told, it is late in December 1945, and *watashi* has sat down to take stock of his life. Ishikawa creates a powerful sense of immediacy by focusing on specific dates and events — be it January 1, 1945, for a bike lesson in "Moon Gems" or July 31, 1946, as the last day of operation for the marketplace in "The Ruins" — and he evokes an instant air of contemporaneity by treating them as historically present. Events may be past, even preterit, but they are invariably "now" or "today,"[12] and as if played by a video cassette player with its freewheeling mechanisms of fast forward or reverse, each mise-en-scène is presented as synchronic with the next. By flashing us back and then forward, *watashi* is about to present us with his reckoning of profit and loss in the past year. It has been a tumultuous year to say the least, but in the months since the end of the war, he has succeeded in obtaining two of his wishes — a watch that runs and a properly civilian hat. He is now contemplating the third. His wishes appear modest, but as symbols the watch, the hat, and the woman take on allegorical significance of "cosmic" proportions.

That *watashi*'s timepiece hesitated and nearly died in the last days of the war comes as no surprise, given the state of suspended animation in which he had lived "one foot underground" (II, 302) as well as the further loss of identity that he has experienced as a burned out and displaced person. He is desperately in need of giving his life and his watch "a good shaking" in order to get himself moving again. As for the traditional ordering principle of Japanese time, "the old calendar of imperial events and obligations" (*seisaku;* II, 471),[13] it is now defunct, its "intermediary here on earth [having] been separated like chaff from the grain and driven out" (*kamigakari ga tataki-dasareta ato;* II, 325).[14] *Watashi* has no regrets, although the loss of an absolute standard means that everyone's watch is broken, and there is no repairman to whom anyone can turn. The postwar age is one of do-it-yourself existentialism, and in the days and weeks that follow the end of the war he develops a feel or approximation for a sense of time that is distinctly his own by comparing the "state of his inner chemistry" with the external world.[15] Time is treated as relative and arbitrary, and should the need arise, *watashi* is not averse to spinning the hands on the dial of his watch and resetting them — as he has done only moments earlier in hopping abroad a train in Tokyo and heading for the restaurant in Sakuragi-chō. In short, he has become "the pendulum of a clock that swung over the land."[16] As he grows more self-confident, his watch ticks with a degree of accuracy that rivals even the clocks at Greenwich, another arbitrarily agreed upon convention of timekeeping. The discovery of *watashi*'s own existential time is closely linked, moreover, to the onset of a sense of physical well-being, his health always having been erratic in the past. As his sole companion and alter ego at the time of Japan's defeat, the watch was what kept him alive with "its insistent tick-tick-tick sounding ever so much like an admonition to stick to life and not give up."[17] Ever since it has beat like a pulse. It may wane, but it never deserts him.

A similar allegorical reading applies to *watashi's* second wish, the donning of a new and decent piece of headgear. If there are no serviceable watches in Japan, there are no civilian hats either. The dearth is indicative of the final breakdown of a war-driven economy, just as it is also a metaphor for the lack of any real head — either in the form of a new postwar mentality or a qualified civilian leader — in a society that has been so heavily regimented. *Watashi* jettisons the military cap that he wore during the air raids, but it is not until shortly before he goes to the restaurant — "yes, the day of this very morning" (II, 329) — that he chances upon a touring cap as replacement for the favorite "black felt" *(kuro no sofuto)* that he had consigned to the flames along with a collection of rare books when his apartment burned to the ground. A touring cap hardly qualifies as "a hat with an indented crown and brim," but it is enough to signify *watashi's* formal return to the status of true civilian and real human being *(ma-ningen;* II, 327).

If the beginning of *watashi's* postwar reincarnation is announced by his watch and hat as symbols for the restoration of time and dignity, it is also amplified by another important, but highly cryptic, moment — namely, the bath or delousing scene that occurs directly after his return to Tokyo. Generally speaking, "The Legend" is a very tightly written and densely constructed narrative, and this compression is never more in evidence than in the passage in which *watashi* sheds his sooty, lice-ridden wartime life and ruminates on the meaning of Japan's defeat. More than at any time since August 15, it dawns on him that the relief he felt at the news of the war's end — albeit thudlike and with the force of an old man's gunny sack (II, 326)[18] — is tied to the weighty issue of how responsibility for the war is to be meted out. To make matters worse, he is depressed by the official response to the issue that is currently being foisted on the public in the form of what he identifies elliptically as "the outrageous 'Concept of Guilt'" *(tohō mo nai tsumi no kannen;* II, 328). Since the passage does not identify the concept per se, nor does it tell us who is imposing it "on the whole of the world,"[19] its meaning is likely to be unclear to the reader, and no doubt that is doubly the case for those of us approaching it more than half a century later. But, surely, Ishikawa's contemporaries would have recognized *watashi's* abstract reference to the "Concept of Guilt" as the catch phrase of the autumn of 1945, or namely, the call from the media and officialdom to the "hundred million" *(ichioku)* Japanese to engage in an act of "penitence en masse" *(sōzange).*[20] For *watashi,* it is an outrageous, even repugnant thought, and he is deeply discouraged at what he sees as a return to the kind of collective mindset and group action that he had found so disturbing in "Mars' Song."

At first inspection, one might be tempted to interpret this delousing scene not only as an abnegation of responsibility on *watashi's* part but also as a petulant, even self-serving, display of his innocence — look, my hands (shins!) are clean, he seems to say. But to do so would hardly be fair, because we know the protagonists of "Mars' Song" and "Moon Gems" as well as Ishikawa himself have ample grounds for claiming noninvolvement and resistance to the war. But exempting himself from the concept of guilt currently in vogue is only one part of *watashi's* worries. What weighs most heavily on his mind is that the public has adopted the position — or at least is about to be sold a bill of goods — that the war, and responsibility for it, is attributable to "the doings of fate" *(unmei no shoi)* and "all are to be scarred in the same broad stroke" *(tare mo mukizu ni wa nogareōsenai yō;* I, 328).[21] If in the Fifteen-Year War the hundred million subjects *(ichioku kokumin)* of Japan had been urged to make their hearts beat as one *(ichioku isshin)* or at the eleventh hour to "pulverize" themselves down to every man, woman, and child *(ichioku gyokusai)*[22] in the name of unquestioning obedience to the emperor, then in postwar Japan the same shopworn call has been resurrected in the name of a new, yet now ironically pacific, exercise in national unity. For just as the populace was uncritical in marching lockstep to the cadences of "Mars' Song," likewise it is unthinking in donning sackcloth and ashes in a formalistic display of guilt and repentance. As a result, no one gives thought to the real causes of the war. The locus of responsibility is likely to be left ambiguous, and an act of mass contrition becomes no more than a *tatemae* gesture or is construed as having granted a general amnesty. Still worse, expiation of guilt may become nothing more than the offering up of a sacrificial object or physical substance as in an ancient Vedic ritual *(kodai Indo no shinkō no yō ni busshitsu ni chigainai);* and the sooty, lousy business of war treated as natural phenomenon or unlucky contagion (*furikatte kuru mono . . . densen shite kuru mono;* II, 329).[23] To speak out on this issue, to be vociferous in the defense of his own innocence, and to insist that he was not and will not be party to the mindset of the hundred million is to break the mold of thinking en masse and to promote a much-needed diversity of opinion. To have *watashi* question the "Concept of Guilt" as well as a host of other current events germane to the postwar era constitutes Ishikawa's new, or renewed, posture of resistance. For, more than anything in "The Legend" and "The Ruins," he fears that postwar life will be allowed to become business as usual, and the all-important "tear" or "rent" (*yabure-ana;* II, 471) in the fabric of historical time that sets the meaning of the postwar moment apart from the timeless traditions of the past will be overlooked or misunderstood.

Enter the Woman in Red

Restoration of his sense of time and dignity as well as ablution of his soot-covered, lice-ridden life are relatively easy tasks for *watashi,* but fulfillment of his third and last wish proves far more intractable and illusory. He has been infatuated with his friend's wife, and the memory of her has been with him ever since they parted the year before. In fact, it had driven him to search the land for her after he learned she had been widowed and left homeless. To be reunited with her constitutes his third wish, but what restitution means is far less clear than in the case of the watch or the hat. Although *watashi* speaks of love and passion (*koigokoro; renbo no netsubyō;* II, 330, 331), "The Legend" is not a love story, and he does not entertain a vision of what life might be like once the two are reunited. Surely the point of *watashi's* reunion with the woman in red lies elsewhere.

For if the end of the war signals a return to a new kind of normalcy, at the same time it also implies a radical transformation. Indeed the love of *watashi's* life has changed so irrevocably that he can hardly recognize her, or to borrow a metaphor from Ishikawa's novel *Fugen,* his "swan maiden" has molted and become a "fire-eating emu" (I, 417).[24] Her attire in red (*akazukume no yōsō;* II, 331), her pocketbook full of chocolates and Lucky Strike cigarettes, and even the way she enunciates her address as "here in the 'Hama" all point to the fact that his paragon of wifely or courtly virtues has taken up the life of a prostitute working the Hommoku area of Yokohama, a section of the city requisitioned by the Allied Forces, where a "special" or red-light district (*tokubetsu chitai;* II, 332) caters to foreign soldiers.

Watashi is utterly taken aback, but he does not moralize, because he detects something powerfully vital about the woman. Not content to be a "sad victim" (II, 332) of the war, she has embraced life in the new postwar age wholeheartedly. (One is reminded of other fictional heroines from the immediate postwar years, such as the daughter in Dazai's *Shayō* [1947; trans. *The Setting Sun,* 1961], although Kazuko's embrace of women's liberation and her apotheosis from former aristocrat to single mother and feminist comes later and with more difficulty.)[25] In the process of her transformation, the woman in red has discarded the courtliness of speech and classic refinement of romance,[26] or the best aspects of Japan as it used to be. The physical flame of *watashi's* love for her is rekindled nonetheless, and he waxes nostalgic. In particular, he is reminded of her solicitude the cold December morning when she patiently guided his descent down the hill from her mountaintop home. Her words — "first to your left, and now to your right" — echo in his ear. It is with an air of renewed camaraderie that the pair step from the restaurant.

But at mention of how pale he looks, *watashi's* confidence begins to fade, and when the woman abandons him to run in the direction of an American G.I., he knows he has lost her forever. The ever voluble *watashi* is left speechless, and overcome by feelings of mortification and shame (*hasshi-uru kotoba tote wa naku, tada shinu hodo hazukashiku;* II, 334),[27] he leaves us to define the meaning of his feelings in a passage that, heavily understated, is another example of Ishikawa's use of compression in key scenes. Of course, *watashi* is shocked at having been brushed aside, but what is the cause of his ensuing silence and sense of shame in particular? Does his tongue-tied humiliation arise from having been bested in an international contest for the woman's hand, because, as she says "mockingly, teasingly" (*azakeru yō ni, karakau yō ni;* II, 333), he is as pale as ever, and as a vanquished Japanese, he may no longer be man enough for her? And is it further acerbated by the inference that as a latter-day "Madame Butterfly" (*chō ga ki ni tomaru yō ni;*

II, 333), she is guilty of having betrayed him, especially in crossing national and racial lines? She has, after all, turned her back on him, and her body language offers no final adieu (II, 333).[28]

A closer reading of the passage reveals, however, that *watashi's* befuddlement arises ultimately from the pained realization that he himself is unable to offer her a final word of parting. She had wished him fond farewell the year before and seen him safely on his way, but why is it that at this crucial moment he has no benediction to offer her? He longs to tender some final comforting phrase, yet the words will not come, and the rhetorical question is thrown to the audience: "And what was I to say in calling after her?" (*Watashi wa nan to yobikakeyō;* II, 333). Both *watashi* and the woman stand at the threshold of a new age for which the language of past proprieties is wholly inappropriate, if not grossly inadequate, given the degree of independence, aggressiveness, and sheer chutzpah that will be necessary "to live and fall" in life amidst the ruins. Just as toward the end of "Moon Gems" *watashi* came to see his question concerning the safety of Mr. Gūka and his possessions as irrelevant and mildly embarrassing, here too he discovers it is better to say nothing at all. And so it is that he awakens in this final scene to both the question and the answer to his third and final wish. He comes to reject a lingering attachment to the past or a sentimental yearning for its courtliness. It is an insight that makes his pulse quicken, his hat right itself, and his watch tick ever more resolutely. Life in postwar Japan has become a whole new existential game. His head no longer suffers the ignominy of a make-do army cap. Nor is time caught in a parlous state of suspended animation. He is free to throw himself into the fray at last, just as the woman has done in advance of him. His wordless echo of her words — "watch your step as you go; first to your left, and now to your right" (II, 333–334) — is heartfelt and genuine, and it is chastened of sentimentality. Such is the all-important tone of the passage. Furthermore, that *watashi* plunges into the crowd at Sakuragichō Station is not to be taken as a sign of a regressive desire to bury his shame in a collective identification with his own kind and, by inference, as condemnation of the woman as a social outlaw. Surely that would be out of character for *watashi,* who opposes solutions undertaken en masse and who sees the individual promise latent in the ruins.

Enter the Wild Child

"The Ruins" takes us to the most "pugnacious" (*hanaiki no arai;* II, 467) part of Tokyo, or what Sakaguchi Ango called in his inversion of the characters for Ueno, the "*Nogami* Jungle."[29] It commences with a hot-as-blazes scene — the eye of the sun beating down brutally on us — that seems to anticipate the opening frames of Kurosawa Akira's classic cinematic rendition of postwar Tokyo, *Stray Dog* (*Nora inu;* 1949).[30] Moreover, the scene unfolds in one long gasp of a sentence that runs to eight sentences, and three paragraphs, in this translation.

Ueno is a microcosm of both the poverty and the vitality of postwar life, its reed stalls likened to "a clump of weeds" (*zassō no . . . hitokatamari;* II, 467)[31] that has emerged from the hot, arid wasteland. As the new and ad hoc economic and social framework of postwar Japan, it is a lawless, illegitimate society that respects neither the traditional source of authority — *ten,* "Heaven" or, by extension, the imperial order (*ten wa motoyori osoreru koto wo shirazu;* II, 471) — nor whatever rule-enforcing body is to take its place (*torishimari kisoku wa sono suji demo ano suji demo kuso wo kurae;* II, 471).[32] As *watashi* surveys the anarchical marketplace — his identity suppressed fully a third of the way into the narrative — he alternates between excitement over what this "precious today" (*taisetsu na konnichi;* II, 471) represents and despair that his fellow man will fail to see its potential, obsessed as the public is by "the quotidian prescriptions" (*konnichiteki kitei;* II, 471) of making money and obtaining food. Life, *watashi* fears, has become "the transactions of beasts, the winners in the game of profit and loss decided in a single bite."[33] Not only is there no cool breeze (II, 468) to stir the air, the marketplace is operating at a fever pitch now that it stands on the brink of extinction. Today is July 31, 1946, and word has it the black market is to be closed.

Enter the "wild child," or *furyōji,*[34] who circles the food stalls like a stray dog ready to pounce on a grilled sardine or a fly-covered *o-musubi* ball of rice. A lone wolf (*ippiki ōkami*),[35] he lives beyond the pale of society, surviving by his quick wits and tenacious grasp. The black marketeers despise him as a beggar, even though he is the spitting image of themselves; and scorning the sight and smell of his "rags and boils and pus and, no doubt, even lice" (II,

473, 476, 477, 480), they sic the man in the military boots on him. None-theless, an air of mystery, even charisma, surrounds the boy, and *watashi* is fascinated at how, as in a fairy tale, the "set of rags" (*boro;* II, 470) has sprung to life and is disporting itself with regal detachment and wordless self-confi-dence (or just the kind of aplomb or "Edo cool" that a child of Edo such as Ishikawa Jun would admire!). The boy is a one of a kind, the word for his new breed of postwar Japanese not yet having been invented. Not only is he the sole survivor of a generation that collectively suicided itself in the war, but as the "progenitor of a new race" (*shuzoku no senzo wa ore da;* II, 475), he is the incarnation of the future. He may not look the part, but in Ishi-kawa's version of the naked emperor's new set of clothes, he wears the "rai-ments of a king" (*ōja no seisō;* II, 476), and waxing poetic, *watashi* endows the most reviled and despised of men in the marketplace with the messianic qualities of a King of Kings. He is the "Son of Man" (*hito no ko;* II, 475),[36] and his silent "acts" are not unlike divine commands or unspoken parables on the order of Jesus' Sermon on the Mount (II, 476). *Watashi* sees the boy as an analog or *mitate* version of the historical Jesus,[37] a man of humble origins and teacher to the salt of the earth. And as if the analogy of this youth of Japan as its Jesus were not startling enough, he wonders if the boy might not also be its Christ and savior. *Watashi's* heavily freighted paean to the precocious boychild is a curious amalgam of Christian millenarianism and eighteenth-century Enlightenment — or libertine — notions of a natural supe-riority that obtains to those born outside the constraints of society. No doubt there is also an element of tongue-in-cheek as a parody of American mission-ary policy, which saw postwar Japan as fertile ground for converting Japanese to Christianity, as well as an expression of Ishikawa's ambivalence concerning where the wild-child generation will ultimately lead Japan. Anarchical char-acters touched by the divine or a nativist purity surface with regularity in Ishikawa's fiction, Sata in *Aratama* (The Bad Boy of the Gods; 1963) being the most fully developed example of this type of bête noire born of the underbelly of Japanese society. Ishikawa appears to be mesmerized by them even as he fears their onslaught.

The wild child is the antithesis of everything that *watashi* represents. In point of fact, we know very little about *watashi,* although his narrative style

and self-appointed excursion to Yanaka indicate a man of considerable intellectual breadth and antiquarian interest in the history of Japanese art and
philosophy. His special interest lies in the *bunjin*, or literati, tradition, which
came to Japan from China in the seventeenth century as an antidote to the
Neo-Confucian orthodoxy *(shushigaku)* of the Tokugawa Shogunate and to
which we were introduced in "Mars' Song" and "Moon Gems" via *watashi's*
praise for Ōta Nanpo and *kyōka* verse written in the Tenmei style. Likewise,
here in "The Jesus of the Ruins" reference is made to names as unknown to
the Japanese reader as to the foreign in a brief discussion of the comparative
merits of two Edo period scholars of the Chinese classics, Dazai Shundai
(1680-1747) and Hattori Nankaku (1683-1759), both of whom were pupils
of Ogyū Sorai (1666-1728), a figure well known to Japanese intellectual
history for his rethinking of the Chinese classics.[38] The comparison is not
spelled out in detail, because *watashi's* treatment of the topic is never developed beyond a statement of dislike for Shundai and his feeling of karmic
affinity for Nankaku (*Hattori Nankaku naraba . . . watashi to manzara en no
nai koto mo nai;* II, 477). But the reason for his preference is both signifier
and pretext for developing the consistently anti-Confucian stance that runs
through the story. Not for him is the Neo-Confucian conservatism of Shundai, for example. He announces that anything associated with Confucianism
is alien to his tastes (*watashi wa keigaku no mongaikan;* II, 477); earlier he
had been vocal in his dislike of Japan as a twentieth-century "nation of Neo-
Confucian gentlemen" (*kunshi-koku;* II, 470).[39] By contrast, he speaks with
enthusiasm of the "refined" and thoroughly "sophisticated" (*shōsha naru;
shareta;* II, 477) calligraphy and intellectual accomplishments of Nankaku, a
popularizer of Chinese, especially T'ang period, verse among the general public of Edo. As a matter of fact, it is in order to preserve Nankaku's epitaph
that he sets out for Yanaka with rubbing materials in hand.

An air of futility hangs over the enterprise, nonetheless. He recognizes
that no one may know or care about the significance of Nankaku versus
Shundai, the amnesia of postwar life (*seken no hito no bōkyaku;* II, 477)
having erased any memory of the two men from the public mind. Moreover,
in what constitutes an implied metaphysic on the nature of the creative
spirit, *watashi* suggests that a work of art ceases to exist simultaneous to the

completion of its creation and is its own epitaph, so to speak. Even in the a posteriori act of appreciation and preservation, the object remains "a nullity and an imperfection," or what he identifies by the oxymoronic term *zanketsu* (II, 477).[40] What the audience (and the artist, for that matter) sees in a completed masterpiece is nothing more than the "remaining absence" of the artist's spirit having been at work. Hence, in a tone that is at once flippant and serious, he states that the rubbing he is about to take from the stone is at best "a pale copy, yea a mere tracing, taken from the annals of the history of arts and letters" (*shibun no rekishi no zanketsu;* II, 477). It will help him nonetheless to "keep up appearances," he says, and paper over the draughty cracks — literally, "holes" — in his lodgings.[41] Underlying the notion of the highly fugitive nature of artistic creation that Ishikawa presents here is his belief in an élan or energy that operates within history and manifests itself in the creative work of artists and writers who are its vanguard. The concept of "the movement of the spirit" *(seishin no undō)* is central to Ishikawa's aesthetic of vitalistic or automatic creativity.[42] Once the élan vital of the creative act is exhausted, spirit moves on. It leaves only its posthumous trace or epitaph.

Although something of a caricature of an intellectual, *watashi* is not so bookish or antiquarian, however, that it is beneath him to procure a pack of contraband cigarettes or ogle the thighs of the woman at the *o-musubi* stand. He may be refined and have pretensions to high culture, but he himself is not without a touch of the unbridled. That he is attracted to the wild child reflects, moreover, a desire to experience firsthand — albeit none too closely! — the pulse of the newest and most vital force in the ruins. Still, he is ambivalent about what the boy really represents. When in a moment of vanity he wonders whether it is the boy or himself who deserves more kingly attire, he announces in an abrupt and cryptic remark, "The enemy is this Jesus";[43] and when the boy pursues him up Ueno Hill, he denounces him as "a wolf" (II, 478) that is bloodthirsty for his anemic wallet. In the face of brute force, he is made poignantly aware of how vulnerable he is as an intellectual and artist. He cannot win in a fight against it. He has only the small bundle containing the tools of his trade as a writer. "A blank sheet of paper," he laments. "And here I was calling upon it to serve in mortal combat with a wolf. How could it possibly prevail against a vicious set of claws and teeth?" (II, 479).[44] Perhaps the pen is not as mighty as the sword, after all?

A wrestling match ensues between cultivated artiste and naturalistic wolf boy (or high and low culture — *ga* and *zoku* — to state the matter differently). It reveals, first, that the difference between the two is marginal, or only "paper thin," as the Japanese axiom *"kami hito'e"* has it.[45] They are mirror images of each other, and as intellect and beast confront each other face to face, *watashi* discovers, on the one hand, his own feet of clay and, on the other, the boy's Christ-like capacity for carrying the sins of the world on his shoulders (*itamashiku mo Veronikku ni utsurideta tokoro no, kugen in michita Nazare no Iesu no, ikita kao;* II, 480).[46] Behold the boy is both the Son of Man and the Christ who brings *watashi* a "message of salvation" (*watashi no tame ni sukui no messēji wo motarashite kita mono;* II, 480). What we have here is not "born-again" religious experience or a mock version thereof, but rather *watashi's* realization that salvation in postwar Japan is contingent upon not only embracing the most vibrant impulse in the marketplace but also putting the high culture of his erudition in the service of its beatification. The two forces may not understand each other, but they are inextricably bound in a fusion of body and mind, power and intellect, demos and elite. One is in need of the other's unreflecting dynamism; the other, in need of the former's witness and narratorial powers. The tandem nature of action and intellect is a perennial theme in Ishikawa's works, whether it be the interplay of the bodhisattvas of praxis and wisdom, Samantabhadra and Mañjuśrî, the symbiosis that he establishes between Jeanne d'Arc and the chronicler of her deeds Christine de Pizan in *Fugen, watashi's* struggle with the recalcitrant but manumitting bicycle in "Moon Gems," or his wrestling with the meaning of *sengo* via the metamorphosis of a courtly widow into the woman in red in "The Legend of Gold." That he has wrestled with these issues is clear in this story from the stigmata that the Jesus boy leaves behind as scratches and nailmarks impressed on *watashi's* arms and legs, the "traces" of *watashi's* encounter with the divine.

The following day the black market is closed, and human "pylons" (*kui no yō ni;* II, 481) are brought in to bar the entrance. The rows of reed stalls look like an abandoned stable with individual berths and mangers. Using the cinematographic technique at which Ishikawa excels, or what we might call "I/eye-am-a-camera," *watashi* describes the location for us as though he were a cameraman working a movie set on an outdoor soundstage. Dolly back, and we are given the broad shot; dolly up and zoom in, and the lens focuses on a patch of raked earth at the heart of the marketplace. It may well be the manicured sands of a *kare-sansui* garden at a Zen temple or a stretch of desert in the Palestine Hills. Across its surface an undefined force has pressed its footprints and leaves us to ask what we see in them. Are they merely the hooves of a wild beast that stalked the earth? Or are they proof of something more, that is, the passage of the wild child who, as the embodiment of all the naked and unharnessed energy of *sengo*, appeared apparitionlike to reveal its potential? Or was it a Jesus, who, bolting the manger of his childhood, is now a full-grown son of man heading for forty days in the wilderness? Ishikawa leaves us to conjecture, but surely something divine, even fabulous, has taken place, and as the stigmata of the nail and teeth marks on his arms and legs bear witness (*namanamashiku nokote iru ha no kizu, tsume no kizu;* II, 482), *watashi* knows the vision of the previous day is not a figment of his fertile imagination. However, the movement of the spirit is as fugitive as it is welcome. It appears in the most unlikely places; it revitalizes; it invigorates; and in the twinkling of an eye, it disappears into thin air, leaving behind the traces of its "remaining absence."

Modernity to Center Stage

The topos that unifies "The Legend" and "The Ruins" is the chiliastic promise of the postwar age as embodied in Ishikawa's concept of "today" as the "Introduction of Time" (*jikan no dōnyū;* II, 329), or to state the matter more broadly, the emergence of a true sense of modernity in Japanese life, art, and history. It is introduced in *watashi*'s important asides on current events, although its elaboration is decidedly minimal, given once again the terse, abstract, and highly compressed way in which Ishikawa handles these passages. As *watashi* strolls past the bookstores in the Kanda section of Tokyo (*furu-honya no machi;* II, 330), he comments first on "the rather foul smell of the more inane titles currently on the market"—a reference, no doubt, to "the literature of the flesh" (*nikutai bungaku*) that flourished immediately after the relaxation of morals censorship.[47] His interest lies elsewhere, however, and the topic shifts to a consideration of the dramatically improved state of his physical health, which he attributes to a force greater than even the life-saving effect of his watch. As a matter of fact, he proceeds to spin a minimetaphor of Japan as a stage on which a barker has stepped forth to announce the debut of a heretofore unseen star, who, having had to wait behind "the curtains of possibility," is now about to assume center stage (*kō naranai izen no yo ni wa kannō no tobari no kage de deban wo matte ita mono;* II, 329).[48] Like his health, this new talent has been a latent force *(sensei)* that has revealed its manifest powers *(gensei)* only since the end of the war.[49] The barker's voice is pointedly set off in the text through the sudden insertion of honorifics and the use of the distal form in the verbals, and he announces that, "believe it or not, ladies and gentlemen, thanks to the marvelous invention known as the 'Introduction of Time,' it is possible at long last to bring you all that you've been waiting for!" (*masaka jikan no dōnyū itashi-*mashita *o-kage wo motte shubi yoku kannō ni o-konomi no katachi no keshiki wo atae-*mashita; II, 329).[50] The actor or force is not identified per se, but it has the power to make *watashi* see everything in a new and different light (*subete kotoatarashiku, monomezurashiku;* II, 329). Clearly time—as teleological rather than linear and as the staging area for the "movement of the spirit"—has become the basis for *watashi's* newly found optimism.

In "The Ruins," however, the arrival of the postwar age is sounded more stridently when *watashi* registers his complaint that his fellow Japanese have failed to notice the significance of "today" as the rare existential moment that marks the "end of time" of an age that deserves to die.[51] Their notion of today, he scolds them, consists of nothing more than the empty clichés touted in the press about all the new this-and-that. Moreover, by allowing themselves to be overwhelmed by the age-old business of making a living, people have become busier than ever (*kyū ni yotte . . . kyū ni mo mashite ima isogashiku;* II, 471). As a result, they are in serious danger of forgetting how terrible the past was—even a past "so close in time as 1941" (*tsui saikin no Shōwa jūrokunen koro;* II, 470). In the process, they have failed to appreciate the epoch-making breakthrough achieved by the creation of the "damned hole" *(manuke no yabure-ana)* that, commencing from August 15, 1945, separates the prewar period from the postwar. More than anything, *watashi* fears the window of opportunity that has opened and permitted the introduction of real time, or Ishikawa's circumlocution for modernity, is about to close, because everyone will fail to notice it — and when finally they do, it will be far too late (*ukkari ki ga tsuku yō na manuke no yabure-ana wa doko ni mo aite inai no darō;* II, 471).[52] As reference to a series of tears, rents, and burn holes in this story makes clear (*yabure-ana,* II, 471; *yake-ana,* II, 474; *kabe no yabure,* II, 477) — in a manner reminiscent of the repeated "crack," or *sukima,* imagery in "Mars' Song" or the polysemous use of *"yakeato"* in this work — there has been an important historical divide or hiatus in Japanese history. It is a caesura in time, or what is called the "zero hour" (Stunde Null) in the case of postwar Germany. *Watashi* raises a Candide-like call for his readers to pay attention to its significance in more than the superficial terms in which change is being purveyed in the media. He urges them to stop and think: how is postwar Japan to cultivate its garden, reduced as it is almost to a wasteland, in new and creative ways?

The awakening of a modern consciousness, that is, the critical passage between what Tönnies demarcated in *Gemeinschaft und Gesellschaft* (1877; trans. *Community and Society,* 1957) as sacred and secular society, is the idea that lies at the core of Ishikawa's modernist thought, and it is spelled out in its fullest form in the reference in "The Ruins" to Hattori Nankaku, the Edo period calligrapher and popularizer of T'ang poetry. For implied in *watashi's* aside on Nankaku is his chronology of Asian intellectual and literary history in which he locates the roots of the modernist impulse in the T'ang dynasty (618-907). The T'ang is generally considered to be China's most international age, and Nankaku was responsible for disseminating to the general public via his commentaries and translations a knowledge of what Ishikawa calls the modern and sophisticated outlook of the T'ang poets, who came into vogue during the liberal years of Meiwa, An'ei, and Tenmei (II, 477). In speaking of his "study abroad in Edo" during the war, Ishikawa sees Tenmei as the starting point for what we might call a modern or Gesellschaft mentality. Furthermore, this modernist impulse is about to resurface in contemporary times after having been held in check (or so one infers) by the rise of the retrograde Neo-Confucian state during Japan's years of so-called modernization from Meiji through the second decade of the Shōwa era and the end of the war. Ishikawa's romp through history is far too kaleidoscopic, but it attempts to identify modernity as an ongoing liberating or revolutionary energy or movement rather than understand it in terms of specific acts of social change or objects of material culture. It also valorizes Edo, or at least its most progressive aspects, as more modern than the Japan of the first half of the twentieth century.

When "The Legend" and "The Ruins" appeared respectively in March and October 1946, Japan was in the throes of dramatic change—the emperor's renunciation of divinity in January, the opening of the Far Eastern Tribunal in May, agrarian reform in October, the promulgation of a new constitution in November. Already a postwar establishment was emerging from the chaos of August 15, 1945, and the initial Yoshida Cabinet moved to stabilize the economy by, first of all, closing the black markets. While it is probably precipitous to read "The Ruins" as Ishikawa's lament for a "failed revolution" in Japanese society as some critics do,[53] the anonymous footsteps imprinted on the sands of time that appear at the end of the story provide sufficient reason to give us pause. What do they signify? Whose traces are they? And what do they say about Ishikawa's judgment of the state of postwar Japan a year after the unleashing of its newly founded modernity?

Ishikawa's answer is moot. He had used Buddhist iconography in *Fugen* to argue there would be no bodhisattva to intervene and save Japan after 1936.[54] Perhaps a decade later he is warning once again against entertaining millenarian hopes, saying that Japan will not see the miracle of the avatar and is better off not to believe it will. At the same time, he appears to suggest that some sort of change or deliverance is possible, or in the making. It will not come from external sources such as the Allied Occupation, which at best is a new and different set of rules, but still no more than a policing action. Instead, Japan's salvation lies in profound changes that must occur within the hearts and minds of each and every denizen of the marketplace and that begin at the most rudimentary levels of society. It may become a reality, or it may end as an illusion. The élan vital that Ishikawa posits as running like a kinetic force through history is, by his own definition, an ineffability. It is not quantifiable or tangible, although it may assume a shape — even don a set of rags. One recognizes its presence when it appears; and it may even leave its telltale traces. It is to this fugitive vision and its paradox that Ishikawa turns next, in his exploration of today and tomorrow in *The Raptor,* his first legend of Japan at peace.

Postscript to "The Legend"

It is one of the ironies of Ishikawa's career that a writer banned for his outspokenness in "Mars' Song" should have also come under the censorship of the American Occupation. "The Legend of Gold" had appeared uncensored in *Chūō kōron* magazine in March 1946, but three passages were cited for deletion at the time of its inclusion in a collection of Ishikawa's postwar short stories scheduled for publication November 20, 1946 (as the colophon indicates), and submitted for prepublication review by the SCAP Civil Censorship Detachment. (Censorship review prior to publication was the practice until September 1947, when the Occupation authorities shifted to postpublication.) The original monograph submitted to CCD by Chūō kōron-sha, with the passages marked in blue pencil, can be found in the Gordon W. Prange Collection of Occupation Censored Materials housed in the East Asian Section of McKeldin Library at the University of Maryland, College Park.[55] Of the notations made by an anonymous censor on pages 169, 179, and 182 of the text and on the cover (Document No. 6250, SCAP Civil Censorship Detachment, J-Z332, checked 1-14-47), the first calls for deletion of the reference to white rice and, in particular, its availability at the "'Chinaman's shop across the way'" that appears in the opening monologue delivered by the "momma-san" at the restaurant in Sakuragi-chō. The second, also marked "delete" in English, calls for removal of the brand name of Lucky Strikes and its replacement with the generic term "tobacco" (written in Chinese characters), as well as elimination of *watashi*'s description of the contents of the handbag opened by the woman in red, especially of those "items not produced on the domestic market," that is, American chocolates and cigarettes. The third deletes any reference to the American G.I. and the Japanese woman's rush to embrace him. It is an extensive cut of three sentences, which runs to nearly half a page of text and which would make it impossible for the reader to understand why *watashi* is abandoned by the woman. As a result, the overall integrity of the story collapses.

In conjecturing about the nature of the censor's objections regarding this passage, Japanese sources have tended to focus on the story's reference to the soldier as "strangely dark" or "black" (*ayashii made ni iro no kuroi . . . heishi; kuroi heishi;* II, 333) as the source of its offense.[56] But the soldier is not presented in the story in a stereotypical or derogatory light, and because the censor's cuts are made without explanation, no definitive answer is possible. It seems plausible to conclude, however, that the color of the man's skin is not at issue. Rather it is the depiction of fraternization between Occupation personnel and a Japanese national both in the form of gifts of PX goods and relations between the sexes that are "unspeakable" acts under Occupation rules and censorship policy.[57]

Censorship of "The Legend" is doubly ironic when one considers, moreover, the unabashed candor with which Ishikawa refers to the emperor and the imperial system in both it and "The Jesus of the Ruins." Less than a year before, a turn of phrase such as the rice god's "intermediary on earth" having been separated from his post "like chaff from the grain" (II, 325) or a frank statement of the public's uninhibited lack of respect for the authority of "Heaven" (II, 471) would have courted a serious charge of lèse majesté. Now, faced with censorship for the second time in his career, and this time by the liberating forces of the Occupation, Ishikawa chose to pull the story rather than make cuts or revisions. As an act of resistance, however, he retained *The Legend of Gold* as the portmanteau title that was printed on the cover of this first anthology of his postwar fiction. Hence, when the monograph *Ōgon densetsu* appeared early in 1947 sans the offensive story, the title called attention to the missing text by virtue of its "remaining absence."

On *The Raptor*

One has only to see an actor gesticulating with a cigarette in an old movie — *The Women* (1939), *Casablanca* (1942), and *All about Eve* (1950) rank among Hollywood's smokier titles — to recall how ubiquitous smoking was in the not so distant past and how elaborate the grammar, if not innuendo, of its gestures. But, like ashtrays and lighters now consigned to roadside tag sales, in recent years cigarettes have largely disappeared from coffee tables across the United States. Of all the social movements generated in the northern hemisphere of the Americas since the 1960s, abstinence from tobacco ranks as the most quantifiable shift in mores, and one that is all the more remarkable given the financial and psychological hold exercised by *Nicotiana tabacum* since its cultivation began as a major cash crop and a social habit nearly five hundred years ago.

"Gotta match?"/*Matchi arimasu ka*

Tabako, or "the smoking grass" as the Chinese characters record it, did not reach Japan until a half century after Columbus. Never demonized as it was initially in Europe and the Near East, it was consumed on a par with tea and saké by both sexes and all ages. Recognizing it as a ready source of income, the Tokugawa Shogunate moved quickly to establish control over its domestic production. Indeed government monopoly over, first, cut tobacco for the long, small-bowled *kiseru* pipes then in fashion and, later, rolled tobacco in modern times has been the norm in Japan, except for a brief era of privatization in the Meiji era and since 1985, when the government-run Japan Salt and Tobacco Monopoly *(Nihon senbai kōsha),* established in 1904, was partially deregulated.[1]

Although tobacco consumption has declined in Japan in the last decade and smoking in public is noticeably curtailed, cigarettes have been and remain an important prop in the social discourse of Japanese life. This was especially true during the hard times of the war and the immediate postwar period. *Watashi* smokes in "Mars' Song"; he envies the woman in red in "The Legend of Gold" for her Lucky Strikes; and he buys black-market cigarettes in "The Jesus of the Ruins." Without a doubt tobacco was everyman's luxury item, whether in the form of imperial issue to the troops during the war or a pack of Peace after it. In the case of the latter, the simple blue and white pack contained ten cigarettes and was imprinted with the word "PEACE" in English. Appearing on the market in 1946, it heralded the arrival of the postwar era and replaced or rivaled brands with nationalistic-sounding names such as Yokuhō and Shikishima. Moreover, in 1952, to commemorate ratification of the peace treaty signed in San Francisco the previous fall and in anticipation of the end of the occupation that spring, Peace was upgraded and reappeared in more expensive packaging. The word "cigarettes" in English was added to the brand name along with a gold and white art nouveau logo of a dove descending with an olive branch in its beak. Until the arrival of Hi-Lite filter tips two decades later, Peace reigned supreme over all brands on the domestic market.

Peace is also the topos and the central metaphor for *The Raptor (Taka),* and we can imagine Ishikawa Jun, an inveterate smoker who died of lung cancer at age eighty-eight in 1987, turning over a freshly minted cigarette as he sits at his writing desk circa 1952-1953 and contemplates the timely question of what brand of domestic tranquillity—or Peace in both its commercial and historical senses—is about to be consumed and enjoyed in the new tomorrow of post-Occupation Japan. The outlying streets of Japanese cities are still lined with "dirty little shacks each built hard upon the other" *(kitanai koya no tatekonda shigai;* IV, 359), reminiscent of the airless reed stalls in "The Jesus of the Ruins," and the unrelieved gray of concrete causeways and rain-stained warehouses is broken only by the emergence of "the canal," a waterway constructed so as to cut through the urban wasteland like the river of time. Ishikawa is about to dip his pen into waters that will serve not only as a landmark for his young narrator, as Kunisuke wanders in search of a newer and better Peace, but also as a point of departure for Ishikawa's own rhetorical flourish: "Here, cut from the land, [courses] the abundant flow" (*Koko ni kirihirakareta yutaka na mizu no nagare;* IV, 359),[2] whereupon our author proceeds to spin a tale that is sleek and cigarettelike in its minimalism — yes, it is long, white, and tubular, with a burning tip at the end! — yet kaleidoscopic at every turn in the road and every twist in its layered use of imagery.

Given the preponderance of abstract and surreal images in this novella, it is tempting to read it as a work of pure fiction, a Kafkaesque labyrinth, or even a psychedelic novel. There is no question that Ishikawa admired the French symbolists,[3] and through his patronage of the young writer Abe Kōbō (1924-1993), he came to share Abe's taste for Kafka as well.[4] We would be mistaken, however, to think of *The Raptor* as simply a novel of dreams and symbols or a nightmarish state of mind, and nothing more; moreover, there is no reason to believe that Ishikawa flirted with drugs or knew of the cannabis republic envisioned by Hemp Liberation. To the contrary, *The Raptor* clearly references its own times — the "Red Purge" of 1950 being the most obvious allusion to a contemporary historical event[5] — and it takes as its plot an allegorical culture war between two competing views of the postwar era, or "peacetime," represented, on the one hand, by the newly emergent status quo defined, marketed, and controlled by the Monopoly, "the enemy," and the police — or what might be termed the conservative "reverse course" establishment that began to emerge in Japan in 1947-1948 — and, on the other, by remnants of left-wing visionaries who promoted the utilitarian dream of "The Happiness of All the People" (*bannin no kōfuku;* IV, 363). And doubtless it resonates with an awareness of the famous *Mēdē jiken* — the May Day Incident of 1952 — in which an antigovernment demonstration escalated into a veritable pitched battle with the police in which two demonstrators died, two thousand were injured, and more than a thousand were arrested.[6] This is the struggle presaged at the end of "The Jesus of the Ruins," where the authorities intervene to exert control over the anarchical demos and close down the black market. It is to this historical turning point — when the Christ-like wild child wanders "into the wilderness" of the years of postwar reconstruction ahead — that Ishikawa returns as he sits back and, taking a whiff of the new "Peace" and its heady ecstasy, envisions a long-term view of Japan and the ensuing battle between utopian and dystopian forces.

A Radical Shift

Beginning with *The Raptor,* Ishikawa would cease to use the stylistic and narrative devices of the *watashi* pieces that characterized his wartime and early postwar literary production. Gone is the garrulous prose championed by modernist writers in the 1930s and 1940s. In sentences remarkably short and streamlined, *The Raptor* reflects the sea change that took place in prose style internationally in the 1950s, when brevity became the hallmark of post-World War II writing. By 1949, Ishikawa had begun a series of *otoshibanashi,* or stories with a punch line or twist *(ochi),* and in 1951 he began his parodies of world-famous works of juvenilia for adult readers.[7] By virtue of their story-telling style, they required a prose that was both more colloquial and less convoluted. Moreover, as Ishikawa's style became more streamlined, his production turned prolific. By the 1960s, his novels *Aratama* (The Bad Boy of the Gods; 1963) and *Shifuku sennen* (The Millennium; 1965) ran to over four hundred pages each. His longest work, the mammoth *Kyōfūki* (Record of a Mad Wind; 1981), extends to nearly a thousand.

Gone too is the first-person narrator. It is about this time that Ishikawa began to publish also as an essayist, writing under the nom de plume "Isai" ("the *ikyoku* or *kyōka* poet at his desk"). Entrusting his political and social opinions to a series of "propos" *(hitsudan),* he wrote in the manner of the French writer and aphorist Alain.[8] By developing parallel careers as novelist and essayist, and by separating "terrestrial facts" *(chijōteki jijitsu;* I, 554) from fiction in accordance with the prescription for the novel that *watashi* describes in "Mars' Song," he now set both himself and direct commentary on current events outside his stories and novels. If in "The Jesus of the Ruins" he had foreshadowed this change and experimented with the suppression of the first-person narratorial voice by allowing *watashi* to appear only belatedly, and moreover he had used the omniscient and cinematographic pan shot to great effect in the final scene, then in the opening paragraphs of *The Raptor*, he merges the two devices of anonymous speaker and roving dolly, and we are made to look at the world of the canal and its strange ramshackle house through the paradoxical "I-am-a-camera" eye of the third-person central character, Kunisuke.

As the novel begins, we stand at a liminal point on the periphery of the city, and like the lens of a handheld camera, our eyes move clumsily over the concrete labyrinth and landscape of urban alienation. The topography has been stripped of local color, and even if one sees the Sumida River and its godowns as a probable model for the canal and its environs,[9] the names, dates, and signboards of anything Japanese have been ostensibly erased. We have entered a real but also imaginary, even hallucinatory, land and, relying on only the vaguest of directions provided the night before by the mysterious stranger named K, we proceed tentatively toward the bramblelike structure that stands on the other side of the canal. Nothing is as it appears to be (not one story high, but two; no door, but a cut made in the siding), and it is not until Kunisuke is announced as the third-person central character (*Ima, Kunisuke ga wakarinikui michi wo yōyaku tazunete kita;* IV, 360) that we realize, via a quick grammatical flashback in which we mentally rewind and double-check the possible first, second, and third personae, that the scanning eye and narrating voice belong to neither ourselves nor the novelist, but this curious young man. Such is Ishikawa's skill at exploiting what linguists call the "empty categories" of Japanese—namely, its penchant for ellipsis of subjects and pronominal anonymity—that the story creates a roving eye/I that wanders in a dazed and subjectless stream of consciousness—and in a way that is not easily done in English.[10] (Invariably, English forces an identifiable actor upon the translation, if only the neutral "one" who comes to the bridge and crosses it.) Ishikawa makes it impossible to discern categorically whether, in recognizing the canal or wondering where to turn (*unga to yobubeki darō; sa; tsumari;* IV, 359), it is Kunisuke, ourselves, or the author who is thinking out loud. Or is it thinking *to ourselves*? Alas, English also obliges the translator to demarcate direct from indirect speech. Mental and verbal thoughts handled unobtrusively in Japanese by the particle *"to"* must be segregated by the crooked fingers of opening and closing quotation marks in English.

Moreover, surrealistic elements replace the terrestrial concerns of the *watashi* pieces. If in "Moon Gems" the moon endowed *watashi's* bike with an iridescent beauty, in *The Raptor* it is the science fiction votive candle (*gandō;* IV, 371) and light-generating device (*hakkō sochi;* IV, 378) that not only sets the typeface in motion on the futuristic newsprint windows (shades of computer screens thirty years in advance of their time!) but also drives the powerful machine that produces the vision-inducing cigarettes of the new Peace. One of the beauties of this tale is its ability to expand the horizons of our imagination at the same time it asks us to suspend quotidian logic. Some of its more dramatic moments—the ocean of tobacco leaves, the chase through the park, the surprise return in the prison cell of the cigarettes to Kunisuke's pocket, and the great aerial dance of the blue hawk at the end—defy reason, but we accept them as distillations of a beauty that is as lyrical as it is unreal, and we allow ourselves to press forward with the story.

Finally, *The Raptor* shifts from a preoccupation solely with "today." Although the narrative remains eminently in the present, and it unfolds in the short and highly compressed time span typical of an Ishikawan plot—after all Kunisuke's saga of the discovery and destruction of the house by the canal occurs in only three days—the existential focus of the novel is not on today, but on the world of tomorrow, as exemplified by the language of Futurese (*ashita-go,* or *myōnichi-go;* IV, 369) and the exploration of what Kunisuke calls "unknown worlds" (*michi no sekai;* IV, 368). The function of literature as a visionary art that anticipates the future is a credo that we have already heard from Ishikawa. Like the "language of tomorrow," the text of *The Raptor* is intended to become "an incredible setting for the movement of the spirit" (*ikanaru seishin no undō no ba;* IV, 370). It emerges here as the desire not only to make language convey what has not been imagined or articulated before, but also actively to create and embrace the unknown world of the future.

Revitalization of language and the imagination are concepts that date from Ishikawa's period of inner exile, when he began to detail his vitalistic

theory of prose as movement *(undō)* rather than fixed positions or philosophies *(shisō)* in such critical works as *Bungaku taigai* and *Mori Ōgai*.[11] In his
strikingly idiosyncratic interpretation in the latter, for example, he argues that
Ōgai's breakthrough as a modern novelist dates from his story *Tsuina* (Exor-
cising Demons; 1909) and the unfinished novel *Kaijin* (Reduced to Ashes;
1911-1912) in which Ōgai, by following his "night thoughts" *(yoru no shisō)*,
focused on the imaginative possibilities latent in a single word, *"Shinkiraku"*
(The New Pleasures) — the name of a teahouse that Ōgai had yet to visit.
Much like the play on the word "Peace" in *The Raptor*, "new pleasures"
becomes a trajectory into an "unknown world" *(michi no sekai; XII, 160-
161)*. Similarly, Ōgai — and his alter ego and narrator Setsuzō — makes the key
word "Newspaperland" *(Shinbun-koku)* the centerpiece of the novel-within-
a-novel in *Kaijin*.

> Setsuzō was seized by the idea of trying to write at this late hour.
> He sat up in bed and began working in the notebook he had
> bought for taking notes at the university. His pen dashed across
> the page quite independently of himself. Even he was struck by
> how odd it was. . . . In no time he had a title to the piece:
> "Newspaperland."
>   . . . Newspaperland was a satire calculated to draw blood.
> . . . Setsuzō, who had been impressed by Poe's "The Devil in the
> Belfry," decided to cast his account of Newspaperland in the sim-
> ple declarative style of a gazetteer. That was how he would de-
> scribe the way the country looked. He would describe it just as it
> was, without embellishment. That made each and every satirical
> line all the more venomous.
>   It was a land that possessed nothing but newspapers, and its
> citizens consisted of three species: those who provided the scoops,
> those who then gleaned and wrote the news, and those who
> bought and read the papers. It goes without saying that those
> who generate the news are often synonymous with those who
> write it and/or those who read and buy it. . . . As for those who

cannot write of things as they are . . . why, they often write about themselves! (pp. 75-76)

Since it was now nearly dawn, Setsuzō thought it best to stretch out and get a little rest. He closed his eyes, but sleep would not come . . . That was when the idea of what to write came to him. There would be a radical change of government in Newspaperland. A powerful political leader would appear on the scene and would attempt to destroy the newspapers by means of a coup d'état. . . . The conversations taking place among groups of people or the commotion on a streetcorner . . . the fragments of the story began to fall in place as they came to him in their fine detail and rich colors. As he pursued them in his mind, he gradually felt consciousness slip away. Before long he was sound asleep.[12] (pp. 84-85)

To quote Ōgai's *Reduced to Ashes* is not to suggest *The Raptor* is a derivative work. But just as Ōgai was inspired by Edgar Allan Poe's satire on the time-obsessed citizenry of "the borough of Vondervotteimittiss" in "The Devil in the Belfry" and even translated it into Japanese,[13] the influence of "Newspaperland" as a kernel of inspiration for Ishikawa is so obvious—from the key word to the coup d'état—that it cannot be ignored. It is the germ of an idea for Ishikawa's exploration of the "unknown world" of the new peace as it is about to be written in the pages of tomorrow's newspapers. Interestingly enough, it is also about the time that Ishikawa was writing *The Raptor* that he began to refer to his works as *jikken shōsetsu*, or experimental novels.

The Nation's Helper

Kunisuke, or the "Nation's Helper," as his Everyman name implies, is the type of naive and impetuous young man who, filled with dreams of peace and a better world for all, is likely to be found in the pages of a bildungsroman (which Ōgai, incidentally, intended *Reduced to Ashes* to be). Yet *The Raptor* is not a novel about personal progress, and just as Kunisuke has no last name, he is not developed in detail. Ishikawa is clearly not interested in a psychological portrayal. We know only that, as a civil servant, Kunisuke had been purged from his job at the Tobacco Monopoly (*senbai kōsha;* IV, 363) two years earlier. On the surface, he remains unjaded and leads the life of a "happy wanderer" (*ma no nuketa hōrōsha;* IV, 363). But that he is often taken by surprise or lost in a daze (*azen to shite; bō to shinagara, bonyari shite iru;* IV, 367, 368) is due in part to his naïveté. It also derives from the fact that, after having been squeezed from the system with no place to go, he has begun to entertain doubts about himself and his fellow human beings. In fact, he has become something of a reject or cipher, the transparent and mirrorlike quality of his personality being reflected in all of the Ks of the story: the lost *ko-inu,* or puppy, who snuggles his way into Kunisuke's jacket to become his alter ego and watchdog, and the anomalous K, crimp and conspirator, who introduces Kunisuke to the house by the canal. (And, perhaps even the *kyurotto* — culottes — girl?) Kunisuke becomes increasingly dependent upon K for his self-definition; and later, when K is beaten and apprehended by the police, he will see K's bloodied face in the café window as a reflection of his own.

Only gradually does Kunisuke come to understand the enigmatic nature of the house by the canal. At first his interest is purely academic, as when he peeks into the bags of pretty cigarettes or pursues the study of Futurese, but his initiation accelerates once he commits the faux pas of smoking the wrong brand of Peace on the premises. All hell breaks loose; and like Dante peering into the Inferno, he has his first glimpse of the underground factory at work — work done by "slaves" (*dorei;* IV, 386) who labor like automatons along the assembly line of the giant cigarette machine. The factory is described as a place of tremendous "synergy" (*kiai;* IV, 384, 389, 392, 405, 423) — a word that occurs frequently in Ishikawa's novels at this time — in which the energy, or *ki,* of each worker calls to the others in a highly communalistic and synchronized operation.[14] We might liken the house, moreover, to a beehive ruled by a "queen" (*joō;* IV, 387), the title that Kunisuke unthinkingly bestows upon the girl with the whip. Like a queen bee, she too is a slave to the work in progress, but as the sole female on the premises, she reigns over E and his faceless crew, and everyone from E to Kunisuke desires to service her or seek her solace.

Fuyuko in "Mars' Song" and the woman in red in "The Legend of Gold" have been remarkable figures in Ishikawa's works to date, but it is with the appearance of the girl with the whip in *The Raptor* that we note the emergence for the first time of a powerful female figure in Ishikawa's fiction. She will control Kunisuke's destiny, meting out reward and punishment at the house and serving as his savior at the end, when he is stranded on the palings of the prison fence. Much to her delight and Olympian laughter, he addresses her as his queen; at the same time he sees her as a peculiar composite of both decidedly feminine (white lace at the collar of her riding jacket) and masculine traits (standing stiff as a ramrod). He entertains a paradoxical and ambivalent attitude toward her, alternating between moods of attraction, submission, and defiance. Even at the end, when he recognizes her atop the high concrete wall in her great cloak, he refers to her as "a queen surveying the stars from her castle parapet" or "a whore who [stands] in the dust at the public crossroads [awaiting] her next customer" (IV, 413). He is at her mercy once again, and it may be tempting to see her as representing "the modern woman [who has] become increasingly Other, unreachable, even demonic" in the evolving postwar *sararī-man* social organization of Japan, in which "men are entrapped and continually reminded of male powerlessness."[15]

Yet, while it is true that the girl with the whip belongs to the genealogy of the "man-woman" *(otoko-onna)* who, dressed in the garb of the dominatrice, has appeared with increasingly regularity in Japanese fiction since the Taishō period,[16] and she numbers among the powerful S&M seductresses and bitch goddesses who populate Ishikawa's later novels, rather than being a source of alienation for either E or Kunisuke, she draws them to her like a magnet. Her leather boots and barbed tongue are like a narcotic; and just as they touch and fondle the beloved broadleaf tobacco, the two men long to get their hands on her. She is the embodiment of the classic male stereotype that dichotomizes woman into queen or whore, or superior or inferior goods. But it is her role as tobacco muse and symbol of house authority that really whets their appetite. For authority is both terrifying and tantalizing, and this is especially true in the case of a female leader. In spite of their devotion to her as faithful yeomen, E and Kunisuke entertain subversive fantasies of wresting power from her. By stripping her of her breeches or jumping into her hammock, they fantasize they will cut authority down to size through sexual conquest. For her part, she must keep them in line by denying any special favors or rights arising from claims of love and affection they may place before her.

Like a Zen master with a stick, she must school and enlighten them. When the girl laughs and asks Kunisuke if he knows his place within the hierarchy of the factory, she makes it abundantly clear: she sends him packing one morning with the mere thrust of the crop of her whip, and she greets his insubordination in the hammock with a viselike embrace that is sheer torture and borders on what Kunisuke imagines to be "like the love between two men" (IV, 394). It is clear the girl will not let her authority be questioned, and is careful to regulate the potentially explosive activities of smoking and sex on the premises. Even when Kunisuke is away from the house and his attention is drawn momentarily to a woman on the street who speaks of "the pure distillation of sexual desire" — "'Hold me real, real tight tonight, will you?' " (*Komban daite ne;* IV, 401) — the queen of the hive snaps him to his senses with the distant sting of her whip and makes him witness the harm he has done to his good friend K on account of having loitered on the street for all of three seconds. We find that the girl's transgression of gender boundaries in this story enhances her authority, which employs both feminine and masculine wiles to establish and maintain control. Rather than alienating them, she wins the love and respect of her men.

Meanwhile, Kunisuke is branded as a traitor for having smoked the wrong cigarette. Moreover, he realizes he is no better than trash or the brown pile of waste extruded from the malfunctioning cigarette machine (*kuzu,* IV, 391; *haibutsu no yama,* IV, 389), when the reactionary forces of "the ordinary Peace" are unleashed and seek to destroy the factory by clouding its windows with smoke and soot. Because he fears repudiation (*kyōzetsu;* IV, 383) from the factory workers, he identifies with them as his "brothers" and fellow insurrectionists (*kyodai,* IV, 395; *muhonnin,* 382). He recognizes that just as the factory's cigarettes have the power to open a window on a better world and spell out the news of tomorrow, the pollution of an ordinary and retrograde Peace — the slave cigarette of the enemy (*teki;* IV, 395) — besmirches all that comes into contact with it. A terrible upheaval ensues (*ihen;* IV, 385).

When he awakens the following morning, Kunisuke wonders if what
has happened is no more than a terrible nightmare. But the house is in a
shambles, and going into the city, he hears a radio broadcast announcing
the wholesale arrest of an international ring of contraband cigarette dealers.
Shortly thereafter he is witness to K's arrest. He himself is incarcerated
when, in a moment of paranoia, he flees from a policeman patrolling the
park. Because Kunisuke believes the factory labors on behalf of the happiness of all people, he is unconvinced of his guilt, but the harsh reality of
the prison speaks all too clearly of the "historical meaning of time as it is
spent living behind bars" (IV, 410). In short, "there would be no tomorrows" (IV, 412).

He is trapped in a no-exit situation, but when he hears the silent chorus
that travels along the floor and arises whenever "people were laboring on
behalf of the life they wanted to create" (IV, 413), he throws himself into the
struggle to test whether "the energy and power inherent in the blood of
humankind was no match for the energy and power of the prison bars" (IV,
411). Suddenly, deus ex machina, the puppy returns; his cigarette lights; the
rhythm in the walls gives rise to a call for "a republic of the energy of work"
(*rōdō suru enerugī no kyōwa-koku;* IV, 413); and, voilà, he is transported
beyond the confines of the prison. In a soaring denouement, and the sole
reference in the novella to the word that is its title, *"Taka"* (*The Raptor*), a
goshawk or *aotaka* (IV, 415; literally, "a blue hawk") appears high in the sky.
It is a peregrine falcon, scientific name *Accipiter gentilis.* The blue bird of prey
alludes to, simultaneously, the girl with the whip (cloaked in a manteau not
unlike Gūka's cape), Maeterlinck's "bluebird of happiness" *(shiawase no aoi
tori)* — a popular commercial message in postwar Japan — and, lest we forget,
the logo of the white dove on blue background, bearing an olive branch while
plummeting bomberlike, on each and every pack of Peace cigarettes. The
sudden entrance of the hawk serves to remind us — in a passage that juxta-
poses whip with olive branch, terror with happiness, hawk with dove — that
the business of living in peace while courting the cause of social and political
change is a labor of love fraught with pain (*ai no kutsū;* IV, 414). To be sure,
it is an act that is far less dovish and rather more hawkish than one may care
to believe.

Of Hawks and Doves

If there is something nightmarish about *The Raptor,* nonetheless an overall sunny disposition prevails from the first bright morning to the flickering beacon at the end, and we are assured even in Kunisuke's darkest moment of incarceration that the channel flows on (*unga wa nagarete iru;* IV, 407). *The Raptor* is, as suggested by a series of Isai essays that Ishikawa wrote contemporaneous with publication of the novella, both an attack on authority, which "is ignorant of tomorrow" (XII, 94), and an anthem "pour les lendemains qui chantent" (*utau ashita no tame;* XII, 279-293).[17] One of the more famous essays relevant to the discussion here is the introduction that Ishikawa penned for Abe Kōbō's *Kabe* (The Wall; 1951). Including such signal works as "*S. Karuma-shi no hanzai*" (The Crime of Mr. S. Karma), *Kabe* was the first collection of novellas that Abe published as a a professional writer, and it won for him the prestigious Akutagawa Prize for Literature. Ishikawa writes,

> In life there are such things as walls. There they are, the bastards. And we would be sorely mistaken — yes, absolutely wrong — to think they stand for anything so fine as an idea or a philosophy (*shisō*). They are walls, pure and simple. Incontrovertibly hard and immovable objects, that's all. And why do walls exist? — no, by no account is it because of a need to partition space. For what necessity have we to take this narrow world of ours and, by dividing it further, check the light of the sun and send its rays traveling down still narrower corridors? But the walls go up. Solid walls. From time immemorial, they have been our impediment — as well as an outrage against the forward motion of human progess. They have been the source of fixed positions and the annihilation of the human spirit. . . .
>
> The first person to speak with real intelligence about walls was Dostoyevsky. What is the point, he asked, of knocking oneself silly by rushing at the edge of a wall and dashing one's head against it? Turn and go around it. It's a concept so simple it's brilliant. It is what we call a "revolution." . . . It makes one wonder

why human beings hadn't thought of it sooner. According to
Dostoyevsky's insight . . . walls are arrayed in our lives to mark
the arrival of turning points. . . . When walls and pro-wall people conspire, they throw up barriers in every conceivable direction. The enemy unleashes its overwhelming power in an unflag-
ging assault on the movement of humankind. . . . Yet walls are
not the limits of movement. . . . They are the point of departure
where life as a human being begins. . . . They are the possibilities. We might even call them the source of liberation in life.
(*Abe Kōbō sho Kabe jo* [Introduction to Abe Kōbō's *Wall*], in *Isai
jōzetsu* [XIV, 158-161])[18]

The Raptor can be read, and usually is, as championing a left-wing
libertarianism over the narrow and hidebound authority of a "reverse course"
establishment. The status quo with its monopoly, media, police, and prisons
is, after all, the enemy of the novel. The decisions of the bureaucratic and
anti-Red Monopoly Corporation are arbitrary and tendered without explanation; the police patrol not only the streets but also the content of what a
young man may read in the park. Only a religious text or a dead language is
deemed safe by the big brothers of thought control. Meanwhile, the crowds
on the streets and the turnkeys at the jail are reluctant underlings in a system
that tells them what to think and is by no means generous. In comparison
with the sterile and dusty image of the crossroads *(chimata)* of the city, the
world of tomorrow that lies on the far side of the canal is suffused with the
soothing light of the moon, the sound of an unambiguous and symphonic
language, and an informed perspicacity. Even in the prison, Kunisuke sees the
vision of a new world that is about to come into existence — a republic of the
energy of work in which all of the oppressed join forces to become a state of
their own.

At the same time, the house by the canal is far from a savory place. The
highly regimented insurrectionists working at the secret tobacco factory share
much in common with the armed enemy that they resist, and they too enforce absolute loyalty and secrecy on their comrades. Moreover, when Kunisuke is incarcerated for having joined them, he recognizes that his prison cell

is, ironically enough, the mirror image of his spartan garret room; and when in the final scene the girl with the whip stands atop the wall beyond the prisonyard, he is reminded that, whatever her sexual attractions, she is a harsh taskmaster and a very demanding if not brutal love object. If the house by the canal represents a workers' republic of shared purpose and energy, the workers pay a high price to be its inhabitants.

Looking back over the decades that have passed since Ishikawa Jun wrote *The Raptor*, we can see that the spectacle of synergy, power, and control that he has Kunisuke witness — both on the streets of the city and down the hellhole beneath his fragrant bed of tobacco leaves — is a metaphor that foreshadows, on the one hand, the furor of private enterprise and sacrifice when even as early as the 1950s Japan Incorporated geared itself up for the economic miracle and, on the other hand, the communalistic loyalty and fatal orthodoxy extracted by antiestablishment forces such as, for example, the *gebaru* cadres of Marxist-inspired youths in the 1970s. As we peer deeper into the abyss, we catch sight of Ishikawa's fundamentally iconoclastic and anarchical disposition that yields to neither the regimentation of the Monopoly nor the communal cooptation of the individual in the name of brotherhood. The organizational strategies at both ends of the political spectrum, right and left, are not dissimilar. In time the "New Peace" will devolve into the "Old Peace," the rebels will become the establishment, and tomorrow will fade into today. Moreover, as Ishikawa cautions, all words are ideologies (*kotoba ga shisō;* IV, 381), and authority of whatever "order" (*chitsujo*; IV, 381) — to use the multivalent term he employs in *The Raptor* and elsewhere for social organization — is prepared to issue its prohibitions against whatever it perceives as ideological crime or political incorrectness (*shisō-han*; IV, 381). A vicious cycle begins anew as utopia falls into dystopia, which in turn sows the seeds of new countervailing visions.

Ishikawa is acutely aware of the "inevitability" or "eternal return" of history (*rekishi no hitsuzen;* IV, 381) at the same time he believes in the supraquotidian tide, or canal, that transcends it. He is continually fascinated by the vitalistic synergy generated by the dialectical interaction of control and liberation as it is set in motion and played out by seemingly different yet fundamentally authoritarian forces and ideologies. Like Jean-Paul Sartre writing in *Les Mouches* (1943) that *"la vie humaine commence de l'autre côté du désespoir,"*[19] Ishikawa speaks independently yet nearly contemporaneously of what the critics identify as one of his perennial themes, namely, "the departure from futility" *(zetsubō kara no shuppatsu)*. That much of life lies in starting over amidst the shards of broken dreams and myths is not a happy tale to tell. Getting a grip on the next departure is no easy business either, and one often needs a touch of serendipity. The girl with the whip appears to lend her shadow to the man who clings to the dream of happiness and peace for all, and it is by a hawk that our dovish protagonist is transported beyond the palings and walls that confine him.

In the end, the house by the canal is destroyed. Or shall we say it reverts to being the old, dead bush that we stumbled upon three days before? If "The Jesus of the Ruins" was silent concerning the meaning of its ending, *The Raptor* is no more or less explicit concerning the upheaval that overtakes the house and leaves it in shambles. Like the "traces" left in the sand by the Christ-like wild child, all that remains of Kunisuke is the brilliant swath that his hand cuts through the inky waters that rise from the rich tide of history and the abundant flow of Ishikawa's pen. As Kunisuke swims toward the beacon emanating from the yonder or Other Shore *(mukōkishi;* IV, 415),[20] is he heading back to the house or pursuing yet another vision?

NOTES

Passages cited from the four short stories and one novella in this anthology as well as other writings by Ishikawa Jun are identified in the critical essays and notes by volume number (roman numeral) and page number (arabic numeral) as they appear in Ishikawa's complete works: Ishikawa Jun, *Ishikawa Jun zenshū* (Tokyo: Chikuma shobō, 1989-1991). This definitive edition, in nineteen volumes, was compiled after the author's death in December 1987. It represents the most exhaustive gathering of his writings, superseding a thirteen-volume edition issued by Chikuma in 1968, with a fourteenth volume added in 1975.

Introduction

1. The fourth Akutagawa Prize for Literature was awarded jointly to Ishikawa Jun for *Fugen* and Tomizawa Uio (1902-1970) for his short novel *Chichūkai* (The Mediterranean Sea). *Fugen* was championed in particular by three of the eight members on the committee: Yokomitsu Riichi, Sasaki Mosaku, and Murō Saisei. In Murō Saisei's words, "*Fugen* . . . grasped the spirit of modern novelology . . . and it is the kind of novelistic novel that, for one who lives with the noisome question of what it is to be a novelist, cannot be put aside. I have decided to give my absolute support to this work out of a strange feeling of destiny. Of the works reviewed, none [except this one] have in any way touched my life. . . . In spite of the fact that some members of the committee feel dissatisfied with this novel, apparently all have perceived its rare and irresistible qualities." See Murō Saisei et al., "Akutagawa Ryūnosuke-shō keii," *Bungei shunjū,* vol. 15, no. 3, (March 1937): 425.

2. See my discussion of "Larger Issues" and relevant notes in the essay on "Moon Gems." Steven Rabson's *Righteous Cause or Tragic Folly,* which went to press late in 1997, represents the first major study in English of war and antiwar poetry written in Japan since the Sino-Japanese War of 1894-1895. It is a new and welcome addition to this understudied area of scholarship; moreover, it contextualizes its material

within the genre of war poetry in world literature. Steve Rabson, *Righteous Cause or Tragic Folly: Changing Views of War in Modern Japanese Poetry* (Ann Arbor: Center for Japanese Studies, the University of Michigan, 1998).

3. See Donald Keene, "Modernism and Its Foreign Influences," in his *Dawn to the West* (New York: Holt, Rinehard and Winston, 1984), vol. 1, pp. 629-719, as well as Robert Torrance's insightful review of *Dawn to the West* and its treatment of modernism: Robert M. Torrance, "Modernism and Modernity," *The Journal of The Association of Teachers of Japanese,* vol. 22, no. 2 (November 1988): 195-223. For other works in English on Japanese modernism, see Dennis Keene, *Love and Other Stories* and *Yokomitsu Riichi, Modernist* (Tokyo: University of Tokyo Press, 1974 and 1981, respectively).

4. *Bungei fukkō* typically refers to the period 1930-1935, which witnessed a revival or renaissance in Japanese literature when long-established writers such as Shimazaki Tōson and Nagai Kafū published after a long silence, and the first generation of young writers from the Shōwa era made their debut. Innovation within Japanese literary circles was cut short by the outbreak of war in China in 1937. After 1937, and especially after 1942, literature came under strict government control.

5. Suzuki Sadami's numerous works related to the subject of modernism include *"Seimei" de yomu Nihon no kindai* (Tokyo: NHK Books, 1996); *Nihon no "bungaku" wo kangaeru* (Tokyo: Kadokawa sensho, 1995); *Modan toshi no hyōgen—jikō, gensō, josei* (Tokyo: Hakujisha, 1993); and *Shōwa bungaku no tame ni* (Tokyo: Shichōsha, 1991). Suzuki is editor of the definitive edition of the *Ishikawa Jun zenshū*. He has also jointly edited a ten-volume anthology of modernist short fiction, the first of its kind in Japan. See *Modan toshi bungaku,* ed. Unno Hiroshi, Kawamoto Saburō, and Suzuki Sadami (Tokyo: Heibonsha, 1989-1991). The volumes that Suzuki edited are *Modan gāru no yūwaku* (vol. 2), *Tokai no gensō* (vol. 4), *Puroretaria no gunzō* (vol. 8), and *Toshi no shishū* (vol. 10).

6. The text of the "Appeal" *(Chūgoku bunka daikakumei ni kanshi gakumon geijutsu no jiritsusei wo yōgo suru apīru)* of February 28, 1967, was reprinted in the magazine *Chūō kōron,* vol. 82, no. 6 (May 1967): 318-327, along with a statement of why the four authors issued the joint appeal.

Ishikawa's testimony before the Tokyo District Court—a commentary on the relationship between humor and eroticism in Japanese literature from the time of the *Kojiki* (Record of Ancient Matters)—is found in the *Ishikawa Jun zenshū* (XVI, 549-554). The *Shitabari* trial refers to Kafū's novella *Yojōhan fusuma no shitabari* ([What Was Visible] through the Sliding Door of the Four-and-a-Half-Mat Room). Nosaka sought to challenge existing censorship laws by publishing a work of literature by one of Japan's great literary lights that had been suppressed in the prewar period. Nosaka's challenge was unsuccessful.

7. Ōe Kenzaburō, "Kaisetsu—wakai sedai no tame no kakū kōen," in *Shinchō Nihon bungaku (33): Ishikawa Jun shū* (Tokyo: Shinchōsha, 1972), pp. 426–436. See note 53 in the essay on "Moon Gems."

8. For more on Mayor Motoshima, see Norma Field, *In The Realm of a Dying Emperor* (New York: Pantheon, 1991), pp. 177–264; also Ian Buruma, "Against the Japanese Grain," *New York Review of Books,* vol. 38, no. 2 (December 5, 1991): 32–36. For a discussion of the fallout over the Smithsonian exhibit and the exhibit's cancellation, see Philip Nobile, ed., *Judgement at the Smithsonian: The Bombing of Hiroshima and Nagasaki* (New York: Marlowe, 1995), and for an overview of the literature, see Richard Minear, "Hiroshima, HIROSHIMA, 'Hiroshima,'" in *Education about Asia,* vol. 1, no. 1 (February 1996): 32–38. For information on the controversial Nanjing exhibit, see Nicholas Kristof, "Today's History Lesson: What Rape of Nanjing?" *New York Times,* July 4, 1996, p. A4.

9. Sugihara Chiune or Senpo (1900–1986). See Hillel Levine, *In Search of Sugihara* (New York: The Free Press, 1996). Levine's book attempts to reconstruct Sugihara's life, especially the period when he headed a Japanese consulate in Kovno, Lithuania, in order to understand what factors in his background motivated Sugihara to offer exit visas to Jews seeking to flee the Russians and the Nazis. Levine sees Sugihara's altruism as different from "the heroism of Raoul Wallenberg of Sweden [who] was sent under diplomatic cover to Hungary, especially to rescue Jews" (p. 3) and from Oskar Schindler, who was ethnic German and a member of the Nazi party (p. 4). He also argues, albeit it in a less-than-successful analogy drawn between Sugihara and the forty-seven masterless samurai of Chūshingura fame, that "what appears to be uncharacteristic behavior of an obedient Japanese civil servant is actually, more historically and profoundly, quintessentially Japanese" (p. 259).

10. Ienaga Saburō (b. 1913). Frank Baldwin writes in the "Translator's Note" to his translation of Ienaga's classic history of the Pacific War, *Taiheiyō no sensō,* "Ienaga has made explicit and activist commitments to building and preserving the postwar society of civil liberties, disarmament and peace. In the turbulent decade after Japan regained its sovereignty in 1952, the new political order was threatened by conservative and rightist forces determined to turn the clock back" (p. vii); he is "a historian who has helped to prevent collective amnesia" (p. viii). See Ienaga Saburō, *The Pacific War: World War II and the Japanese, 1931–1945,* trans. Frank Baldwin (New York:

Pantheon Books, 1978). More recently, Ienaga has successfully fought several cases concerning state authorization of textbooks before the Japanese Supreme Court. For information on Ienaga's campaign against the Japanese Ministry of Education's control over the content of school texts, see Ienaga, *Sensō to kyōiku wo megutte* (Tokyo: Hōsei daigaku shuppankyoku, 1973); or *Dai-sanji Ienaga/kyōkasho sokō: hyōgen no jiyū to kyōkasho* (Tokyo: Kyōkasho kentei sokō wo shien suru kenzoku renraku-kai, 1995).

On "Mars' Song"

1. See Ikeda Yasaburō, *Nihon no kashō: senji kashōshū* (Tokyo: Victor Records, 1971), vol. 12, p. 23. The lyrics of the song were by Kozeki Yuji, the music by Yabuuchi Kiichirō; the song-writing contest was sponsored by the *Mainichi* newspaper. The lyrics are as follows:

> *Katte kuru zo to isamashiku / chikatte kuni wo deta kara wa / tegaradatezu ni shinaryo ka / shingun rappa wo kiku tabi ni / mabuta ni ukabu hata no nami*

> Oh so bravely "Off to Victory"/ Insofar as we have vowed and left our land behind / Who can die without first having shown his true mettle / Each time I hear the bugles of our advancing army / I close my eyes and see wave upon wave of flags marching into battle

> *Tsuchi mo kusaki mo hi to moeru / hatenaku kōya fumiwake / susumu hi-no-maru tetsukabuto / uma no tategami nadenagara / asu no inochi wo dare ka shirō*

> The earth and its flora burn in flames / As we endlessly part the plains / Helmets emblazoned with the Rising Sun /And, stroking the mane of our horses / Who knows what tomorrow will bring—life? [or death in battle?]

In Ishikawa's story there is a clear and evident parody of *Roei no uta* as *Marusu no uta* as well as an obvious reworking of the popular song's opening line *"Katte kuru zo to isamashiku"* as *"Iza tate, Marusu, isamashiku"* (What will ensue, Mars, when you rise? / "How bold!" "How valiant!") in the third line of *watashi's* opening poem. This is evident from the use of the extended predicate *te* form and repetition of the key word *"isamashiku"* (valiantly). It is not possible to establish a one-to-one equivalency, but doubtless *Roei no uta* served as the source of inspiration for Ishikawa's signifying a body of martial music endemic to Japan in 1937. Furthermore, we know Ishikawa was familiar with the pacifist writings written after World War I by the French essayist Alain (Émile Chartier, 1868-1951), whose "propos" he would emulate in a series of *hitsudan*, penned after 1950 under his own nom de plume, Isai. See Émile Chartier, *Mars; ou la guerre jugée*, 1921; trans. Mudie and Hall, *Mars; or, The Truth about War* (London: Jonathan Cope, 1930). Alain's title may have been the inspiration for Ishikawa's reference to the Roman god of war in his parody of *Roei no uta* as *Marusu no uta*.

Likewise, the incendiary prophecy of smoke about to burst into flames, or the seemingly innocuous but fatal wisp of smoke that plays about the mouth of the battleship gun barrel, reflects the scorched-earth claims of the second stanza of *Roei no uta* ("The earth and its flora will burn"), as well as perhaps the famous passage from Romain Rolland's novel *Jean-Christophe* (1912; vol. 10), which Rolland also used as the frontispiece to his famous antiwar treatise *Au-dessus de la mêlée* (1915; trans. C. K. Ogden as *Above the Battle*, 1916). While a university student at Tokyo gaigo gakkō (now Tokyo gaigo daigaku) from 1917 to 1920, Ishikawa read Rolland's *Jean-Christophe* cover to cover in the summer of 1918; as a teacher of French language at Fukuoka Higher School in 1924-1925, he used *Au-dessus de la mêlée* as a standard reading text. The oft-quoted lines from *Jean-Christophe* read:

> L'incendie qui courvait dans la forêt d'Europe commençait à flamber. On avait beau l'éteindre, ici; plus loin, il se rallumait; avec des tourbillons de fumée et une pluie d'étincelles, il sautait d'un point à l'autre et brûlait les broussailles sèches. A l'Orient, déjà, des combats d'avant-garde préludaient à la grande guerre des nations. L'Europe tout entière, l'Europe hier encore sceptique et apathique, comme un bois mort, était la proie du feu. Le désir du combat possédait toutes les ames. A tout instant la guerre était sur le point d'éclater. On l'étouffait, elle renaissaiat. . . .

Roei no uta enjoys wide circulation in Japan even today. It is played regularly in pachinko parlors, where its spirited rhythms now urge patrons to press forward in challenging the pinball machines. Note also in postwar Japan the song has been immortalized by a popular play on words on its opening line in which *"katte"* is interpreted as "to shop" *(kau)* rather than "to win" *(katsu)*. Hence, "Oh so bravely, 'Off to shopping'" — doubtless the contemporary Japanese equivalent of "When the going gets tough, the tough go shopping."

2. Namely, the famous February 26 Incident, or *Ni-ni-roku jiken*. See Ben-Ami

Shillony, *Revolt in Japan: The Young Officers and the February 26, 1936 Incident* (Princeton: Princeton University Press, 1973). Edwin O. Reischauer considered the period of 1936 to 1938 to be pivotal in what he called the "change of mood" that tilted Japan toward ultranationalism. See Edwin Reischauer, *The Japanese* (Cambridge: Harvard University Press, 1977), p. 100. It is interesting to note that while Ishikawa sees the emergence of "the season of 'Mars' Song'" (*"Marusu no uta" no kisetsu;* I, 577) as "seasonal," he distinguishes it nonetheless from the natural order and the ordinary progression of the seasons. (See the scene at the boathouse, where he experiences "the coming of autumn"; I, 572). He treats "Mars" as an aberration — the imposition of human affairs upon the usual transitions of the natural world.

3. The Fifteen-Year War, *jūgonen sensō,* is a term widely used in postwar Japan to describe Japan's militarization from the time of the seizure of Manchuria, a decade before the United States' involvement in the Pacific and Atlantic theaters of World War II after December 7, 1941. For more on the undeclared war against China and the domestic political situation, see Malcolm Kennedy, *A Short History of Japan* (New York: Mentor Books, 1963), pp. 263-266.

See also Carol Gluck, "The 'Long Postwar,'" in *Legacies and Ambiguities,* ed. Ernestine Schlant and Thomas Rimer (Washington: The Woodrow Wilson Center Press, 1991), p. 76. Gluck argues Japanese "progressive intellectuals have reminded people of the 'Fifteen Year War,' but the American view, and revisionist views held by Japanese officials and conservative politicians since the 1980s, have shifted the focus to the War in the Pacific theater. This has . . . meant the elision of the China War, which relegated the victims of Japanese aggression to the prologue of a story that ran dramatically from Pearl Harbor to the atomic bombs."

4. *"Jidai no kizuguchi ga soko ni pakkuri warehajikete ita,"* rendered here as "the malaise of our times, open and inflamed like a wound." The "mouth" of the wound (*kizu*-guchi) is a powerful image in the original, especially since it resonates with the chorus of voices that "mouths" the praises of the war god (I, 551).

5. *"Watashi wa tachiagatte haruka ni gaitō no ryūkōka ni mukai* NO! *to sakenda"* (I, 552); *"koko demo mata, ano rekōdo . . . 'yamero'"* (I, 578). Note that *watashi*'s opposition to "Mars' Song" is stated in English, as there is no term of negation in Japanese (*iie, iya, hantai*) that has the nay-saying force of "no" in English. The use of the English can hardly be construed as an attempt to mystify the government censors, however. "No" would have been simply too well known to any Japanese. "No" here has the same force as the imperative voice of *"yamero":* literally, [you] stop or desist [from some action, in this case "Mars' Song"]. But "Stop it!" in English has a petulant

tone that does not convey the forcefulness of the Japanese. In ordering the waiter to refrain and not play the record, *watashi* also implies enough is enough: "No more 'Mars' Song!'"

6. At no point does the text identify the parties involved in the naval bombardment or the land occupation of the countryside. But the rural village is characterized by "a riverbank lined by willow trees," a typical depiction of a Chinese country village. Moreover, the text makes a point of noting that the nationalities of the occupying soldiers and the two local boys differ, although without identifying either by national origin. The boys find themselves caught between the rock and the hard place, as it were, of dealing with "the foreigners' camaraderie and [the obvious plight of] the rivers and mountains of their homeland" (I, 553). The reference to the mountains and rivers — *sanka* — harks back to the famous poem "Spring Prospect" by the T'ang poet Tu Fu to the effect that, come war and destruction, only the hills and streams remain to sustain one's spirits in dark and unhappy times: or, in Japanese, *"kuni yaburete sanka ari."*

It may well have been that, by 1937-1938, references in print to events or locales detailing troop movements were verboten. See Gregory Kasza, *The State and the Mass Media in Japan, 1918-1945* (Berkeley: University of California Press, 1988), pp. 170-171, which cites a long list of "forbidden contents" issued in August 1938 as a directive to media organizations by the Book Section, Criminal Affairs Bureau, Home Ministry. Furthermore, it is only in this passage of "Mars' Song" that *fuseji* (suppressed words) were used by the publisher to strike potentially objectionable language from the original January 1938 text. For details on this, see Suzuki Sadami's exegetical notes in the "Kaidai" in *Ishikawa Jun zenshū* (I, 673); for a discussion of the uses of *fuseji*, see Jay Rubin, *Injurious to Public Morals: Writers and the Meiji State* (Seattle: University of Washington Press, 1984), pp. 29-31.

As Steve Rabson points out, expression of sympathy for the vanquished Chinese and other Asians or protest on their behalf was rare in the wartime works — even antiwar works — by Japanese. Rabson, *Righteous Cause or Tragic Folly,* pp. 6-8. "Mars' Song" is an exception.

7. Literally, "it may be all right to pretend to deafness, but if taken to excess, [the pretense] may endanger [one's] life."

8. There is repeated reference in "Mars' Song" to the *sukima,* cracks or gaps, in the lives of the characters and the society in which they live. See Okamoto Takuji, "Sensōki no Ishikawa Jun," *Waseda daigaku kōtōgakuin kenkyū nenshi,* no. 16 (January 1972): 1-4. See also Noguchi Takehiko, *Ishikawa Jun ron* (Tokyo: Chikuma shobō,

1969), pp. 198-199. In addition to recognizing the "cracks" as a void or space *(kūhaku)* in the lives of those living in the season of Mars, Noguchi argues they constitute an unfilled negative space not yet permeated by the all-pervasive "Mars' Song." "The very act of maintaining one's own inner void was one form of resistance, and for those who did not resist, they soon found the military chorus had invaded even the spiritual dimension of their lives and trampled it underfoot" (p. 199).

9. "Mobilization and expansion of the Army on a war footing had started shortly after the outbreak in July 1937, when two of the divisions scrapped in 1925 were revived and several reserve divisions were formed. More reserve divisions were created in 1938, the other two divisions disbanded in 1925 were restored, and a divisional reorganization was begun." Kennedy, *A Short History of Japan,* p. 267.

10. The remarks of Gregory Kasza in *The State and the Mass Media in Japan, 1918-1945* are germane here:

> Given the penetration of mobilization policies, the resistance of the mass media was feeble on the whole, and the fundamental reason was patriotic support for the country at war. War reinforces the myth that the state alone represents the public good, while "private" associations stand for selfish concerns that properly yield to this public good and its alleged spokesmen. . . . The state rarely had to unsheathe its brute power to win compliance from its subjects. Its moral authority in wartime was the major reason that so much destruction could be wreaked upon private individuals. (pp. 270-271)

11. *"Sore wa mokka kono kuni no wakamono wo katte, tarekare no sabetsu naku 'Marusu no uta' no gasshō no uchi ni, shōen no nioi ga suru haruka enpō no gen'ya e karitateru tokoro no unmeiteki na kamikire de atta"* (I, 567-568). *"Ima mitai ni, tōku de shinitakunai hito ga mainichi takusan shinde'ru toki ni"* (I, 559).

12. *"Genki yoku itte kitamae. Soshite, donna tōku e itte mo kanarazu kaette kitamae"* (I, 575). "No matter how far you go" *(donna tōku e itte mo)* is ambiguous enough to embrace the double meaning of how far down the Izu Coast or to a distant land such as China.

13. See note 4 above. The image of the mouths raised in song and of the "mouth" of the wound is amplified by reference to the "great thirst" — *nodo ga ōkiku kawaite iru* (I, 577).

14. As its translation as "thought," "philosophy," "worldview," "Weltanschauung," and "ideology" suggests — and as common usage of the word in Japanese reveals —

"shisō" is a term of broad and amorphous meaning. In some contexts, it refers to left-wing or specifically Marxist-Communist thought, without going so far as to identify the particular "ism." Such "isms" were classified as *kiken shisō,* or "dangerous thought(s)." A term originally coined in 1904 by the literary critic Ōmachi Keigetsu in his attack on Yōsano Akiko's famous antiwar poem "My Brother, Thou Must Not Die" *(Kimi shinitamō koto nakare),* it referred to ideas "'which [quoting Ōmachi] disparage the national family.'" See Jay Rubin, *Injurious to Public Morals,* pp. 57-58. Later, it came to refer to radical ideas, both left and right, although left-wing views were more typically characterized as "dangerous."

In Hasegawa Nyōzekan's *Nihon fasshizumu hihan* (Critique of Japanese Fascism; 1932) and Kawaii Eijirō's *Fasshizumu hihan* (Critique of Fascism; 1934), Japanese fascism is analyzed and attacked for lack of *"shisō"* (systematic thought). See Hirai Atsuko, *Individualism and Socialism: The Life and Thought of Kawai Eijirō (1891-1944),* (Cambridge: Council on East Asian Studies, Harvard University, 1986), pp. 152-169. Whether Ishikawa's thinking was influenced by the critiques of these two prominent liberalists *(jiyūshugi-sha)* is unclear. In this passage it is the general public, rather than the militarists, whom *watashi* finds wanting in philosophical roots or consistency.

15. *". . . Fuji ga ukitatte ita. Shikashi, zunō ni tatakai wo idomubeki nanimono motanu kono yama no keiyō wo ganrai watashi wa konomanai tachi nanode"* (I, 570). Furthermore, one observes that by spelling "Fuji" in *katakana* here and not referring to it as "Mount Fuji" *(Fuji-san)* Ishikawa seeks to neutralize and objectify the "sacred" status of one of the most typical patriotic symbols for Japan.

16. Odagiri Hideo, Ishikawa Jun, Korin Nao, et al., "Shōwa jūnendai wo kiku," *Bungakuteki tachiba* (Tokyo: Keisō shobō, 1972), pp. 92-108 (reprinted in Ishikawa Jun, *Isai zadan: Ishikawa Jun taidan shū* [Tokyo: Chūō kōronsha, 1977], pp. 197-219, as "Muishiki no sentaku" [Unconscious Choices]). In this series of interviews about writers' lives during the difficult decade of the "Shōwa Tens" (1936-1946), Ishikawa is interviewed by Odagiri Hideo, a literary critic who edited a two-volume anthology of "banned works" collected from the history of modern Japanese literature, *Hakkin sakuhinshū* (Tokyo: Hokushindō, 1957). "Mars' Song" was selected for inclusion in volume 2 (pp. 125-146) of Odagiri's anthology.

ODAGIRI: In 1938 you wrote "Mars' Song," and it was immediately banned. Considering the circumstances at the time, didn't you anticipate that to write in such a vein would definitely result in the work being suppressed?

ISHIKAWA: Yes, but that was still 1937. "Mars'" appeared in the January 1938 edition, but it was actually in print by December 1937. So, we are talking about December 1937. At the time, things were considerably different from the way they became afterward. I was in an optimistic mood that this sort of thing was still okay. So, when the work was banned, I realized they had changed. I realized the situation had reached the point where even "Mars'" was unacceptable. But at the time I was writing it, I had a feeling inside me that something on the order of this work would pass. And I think the people at *Bungakkai* were also thinking it would get by. We were still feeling optimistic. Things weren't as terrible as they later became. That's why I probably thought it would pass.

ODAGIRI: But December 1937 was the time when people like Miyamoto Yuriko, Nakano Shigeharu, Tosaka Jun, and so on, were banned from writing. It was half a year after the onset of the Sino-Japanese War, and just at the point when the government began to step up its control [over literature] with renewed vigor. . . . [Odagiri refers to the *Jinmin sensen jiken* of December 14, 1937.]

ISHIKAWA: That's why I had the feeling I'd give it a try for what it was worth. Will it pass, or won't it? It wasn't a time yet when you thought about being cautious, or anything—you could still forget about being on your guard.

ODAGIRI: Nevertheless, it is a very bold and brave work. When it comes to works written in a vein as vehemently critical of militarism as it is—with the exception of examples from "proletarian literature"—I can't think of anything else. It's in a class by itself. That's why I've been puzzled for some time now wondering what the author's intention was in writing such a work. Did he have some sort of scheme in mind?

ISHIKAWA: How shall I put it? Perhaps I was naive in my outlook and predictions. I had the feeling something on the order of "Mars'" would probably pass. At least I think that's what I thought. (Ishikawa Jun, *Isai zadan,* pp. 204-205)

For a curiously opposite point of view, see Kawakami Tetsutarō, "Ishikawa Jun den," *Gendai Nihon bungakkan (31): Ishikawa Jun* (Tokyo: Bungei shunjū, 1969), p. 16. Kawakami was the editor of the January 1938 edition of *Bungakkai.* In a brief account of Ishikawa's life (one of the few early accounts), he complains that, although the editorship of *Bungakkai* circulated among the contributors to this coterie magazine sponsored by the Bungei shunjū publishing company, the publisher forced him—

"just to be mean" — to assume responsibility with the authorities for having published "Mars' Song." The work was banned, he says, for its purportedly "antiwar thought" *(hansen shisō)*. Rereading the work thirty years later, however, he argues that in fact Sanji's holiday represents a state of "perfect liberty." Just as the famous literary critic Kobayashi Hideo (1902-1985) once typified Yoshida Shōin (1830-1859), the Tokugawa period patriot imprisoned and executed for advocating Japanese parity to the West, as representing a similarly liberated state of mind (one of, in Yoshida's words, "waiting for the call" of history), likewise for Kawakami, "Mars' Song" is "to the contrary, not an example of antiwar thought at all, but the story of 'a man [Sanji] who is now resolved to be ready at all times to put himself in the service of his country.'" This seems farfetched; moreover, Kawakami's idiosyncratic interpretation ignores the story's explicitly antiwar statements, and it erroneously elevates Sanji to the role of protagonist. Others have argued that what the censors found most objectionable about "Mars' Song" was Sanji's cavalier attitude toward his impending military duties, as represented by the frivolous trip to Izu. To my knowledge, no record of the censors' ruling remains, however.

17. Ōta Nanpo was also known by his sobriquets of Yomo-no-Akara, Negoto Sensei, and Shokusanjin. He was the leading *kyōka* poet in Edo literary circles and author of numerous *sharebon,* or pun books.

"*Tōkai-buri,*" "in the mystification style," is derived from the verb "*tōkai suru,*" literally, "to wrap in darkness," to obscure or mystify. The mystification style refers to the use of verbal false scents and smokescreens to avoid censorship or to introduce a facetious meaning or hidden agenda into a text. In writing for an audience that readily discriminates between what is said for the sake of appearances (*tatemae:* facade or pretext) and what is genuinely intended (*honne:* real story or text), a writer may employ the proverbial trail of smoke (*kemu ni maku,* "to envelop in smoke"), a form of verbal interaction commonly used by Japanese as a diversionary, delaying, or intimidation tactic. Kikuchi Shōichi is an example of a critic who emphasizes the importance of mystification techniques in Ishikawa's works. See "Mitate gesakukō," *Sengo no ronri* (Tokyo: Yūzankaku, 1948), pp. 142-170.

18. *Shishōsetsu,* the "I-novel" or confessional novel characteristic of the naturalist writers. Moreover, the recantations, or *tenkō bungaku,* of former left-wing writers and thinkers that appeared with increasing frequency after the late 1920s often took the form of the first-person confessional narrative in which the author, in an excess of *jiishiki* or self-consciousness, describes the process of his disillusionment with anti-establishment thinking.

19. Ishikawa would develop the concept of translating the courtly *(ga)* into the worldly *(zoku)* or the sacred into the secular, to use Tönnies' paradigm of Gemeinschaft and Gesellschaft, in both his prewar and postwar writings on *haikai* verse, Edo culture, and the art of *yatsushi,* or the aristocratic descent into the plebeian. In his famous essay on "Edobito no hassōhō ni tsuite" (On the Ways of Thought of the People of Edo; 1943), he argues the secularization *(zokuka)* or *haikai*-ization *(haikaika)* of ideas constituted the special genius of the denizens of Edo. In the postwar period, he writes:

> [This is] a new mode of expression based upon the tension that exists between the literary and the colloquial so as to give new life to old words and, simultaneously, not to permit excess license to contemporary speech. . . . Although the operation called *haikai*-ization may originate in the desire to overcome the commonplace, inevitably it must descend to the level of the mundane. The search for new heights in the depiction of beauty begins with the establishment of a setting for the aesthetic life in the middle of the mundane. (*Isai seigen;* XIII, 443-444)

For more on this subject, see William J. Tyler, "The Agitated Spirit: Life and Major Works of the Contemporary Japanese Novelist Ishikawa Jun" (Ph.D. dissertation, Harvard University, 1981), pp. 165-180.

20. *Fugen* (I, 321-428). Ishikawa Jun, *The Bodhisattva, or Samantabhadra,* trans. William Jefferson Tyler (New York: Columbia University Press, 1990). The notion that prose belongs to a realm apart from everyday living is enunciated in the opening lines of the novel: "For the breezes that stir the pages of the novel are far different from the gusts of the mundane world . . . [let us] brush from our wings the dust of the floating world and the dregs of human sentimentality" (p. 1). For a discussion of this work, see the critical essay appendixed to the translation, "Art and Act of Reflexivity in *The Bodhisattva,*" pp. 139-174.

21. This view is represented, for example, by Odagiri Hideo, who, as mentioned in note 16, includes "Mars' Song" in his two-volume anthology of banned works. See Odagiri, *Hakkin sakuhinshū.* Nagai Kafū's diary of life during the war years, *Danchōtei nichijō,* points to what Donald Keene calls Kafū's "silent protest" and "absolute integrity." See Donald Keene, "Japanese Writers and the Greater East Asian War," in *Landscapes and Portraits* (Tokyo: Kodansha International, 1971), pp. 315-316. Kaneko Mitsuharu's most famous antiwar poem is *Same,* (Sharks).

Prominent works in the history of pacifist literature include Bertha Suttner's *Die*

Waffen nieder (1889; trans. *Lay Down Your Arms,* 1892); Ludwig Quidde's *Caligula* (1894); works by Tolstoy, a source of inspiration to many in the pacifist movement; Romain Rolland's treatise *Au-dessus de la mêlée* (1915; see note 1 above), his play *Liluli* (1919), and his novel *Clérambault* (1920); and the antiwar poetry of poets enduring gas and trench warfare in World War I as well as Erich Maria Remarque's classic *Im Western nichts Neues* (1929; trans. *All Quiet on the Western Front,* 1929). These works, like the post-World War II writing on the Holocaust or Hiroshima and Nagasaki, address the brutality, waste, and inhumanity of war; moreover, works such as Joseph Heller's *Catch-22* and Kurt Vonnegut's *Slaughterhouse Five* speak of the inanity of military logic and organization. The cruelty directed toward enlisted men by Japanese officers appears in works such as Tayama Katai's *Ippeisotsu* (1908) and *Ippeisotsu no jūsatsu* (1917), short stories by Kuroshima Denji, and Noma Hiroshi's *Shinkū chitai* (1952; trans. *The Zone of Emptiness,* 1956). Examples of works that deal with the dilemmas of resisting authority in fascist regimes are the film drama *Mephisto* and Antonio Tabucchi's novel *Sostiene Pereira* (1994; trans. *Pereira Declares,* 1995). The special quality of Ishikawa's "Mars' Song" lies in its allegorical focus on the way in which war infiltrates and alters civilian life.

22. Dōshisha daigaku jinbun kagaku kenkyūjo, *Senjika teikō no kenkyū—Kirisutokyōsha, jiyūshugisha no ba'ai* (Tokyo: Misuzu shobō, 1968), 2 vols. This pioneering study by Dōshisha University represents one of the first thorough attempts to document domestic resistance to Japanese militarism during the war, especially by Christian groups or Japanese influenced by Christianity or liberal thought.

On "Moon Gems"

An earlier translation of this story appeared in Van Gessel and Tomone Matsumoto, eds., *The Shōwa Anthology* (Tokyo: Kodansha International, 1985), vol. 1, pp. 45-62. The translation here is a revision of the earlier version. I wish to thank Mr. Hiroaki Sato, poet and Japanologist, for his helpful comments.

1. *Nihon bungaku hōkokukai* is usually translated as "Japanese Literature Patriotic Association" but means, literally, Japanese Literature in Service to the Nation. The organization was inaugurated by the Japanese government on May 26, 1942. For a brief discussion of this organization, see Keene, *Landscapes and Portraits,* pp. 308-309, which draws upon information in Hirano Ken, "Nihon bungaku hōkokukai no seiritsu," *Bungaku,* vol. 29 (May 1961): 1-8. Keene suggests that writers joined ("One

important obligation was to join . . . "; p. 308), and many actively sought participation in the organization (p. 301), but Ishikawa reports that anyone already a member of *Bungei kyōkai,* the professional association of artists in Japan, was enrolled automatically. He too was enrolled but remained inactive.

A scathing portrayal of—and *watashi*'s stormy exit from—one of the major international conferences organized by the Association is given in Ishikawa's short story of July 1946 *Mujintō* (Vimalakirti's Inexhaustible Light; II, 426-427). It was probably the Greater East Asia Conference of November 5-6, 1943, that he attended. One of the speakers—most likely the *tanka* poet Saitō Ryū (see Keene's description of this conference, p. 304)—is described in scurrilous phrases as "a tottering old man . . . who wore a sword . . . he was said to be a man with a criminal past and buddy-buddy with the whole gang who were engaged in the business of killing people" (p. 427). This work was written after the war, however. Also see note 42 below.

2. "*Yo no naka wa itsu mo tsukiyo ni kome no meshi sate mata mōshikane no hoshisa yo.*" From Ōta Nanpo's *Shokusan hyakushū* or his earlier *Manzaishū.* See *Iwanami koten bungaku taikei (57): senryū kyōkashū,* ed. Hamada Yoshikazu (Tokyo: Iwanami shoten, 1958), vol. 57, p. 469.

3. In 1944 Ishikawa was called to join a *keibōdan* designed to maintain security and fight fires. He later wrote he was called out "to see the fires" from time to time (*Senchū ibun* [Fragments from the War]; XIV, 15). A passage in the short story of 1946 *Mujintō* says that *watashi* suffers from "pleurisy" *(kyōmakuen).* Ishikawa's age (he was forty-two when Japan attacked Pearl Harbor, for example, forty-six the year the war ended) and poor health may have been reasons for his being deferred from military or civilian service.

> And then there came the morning of December 8 [1941]. Yet I could not bring myself to look upon the events of this day as the crisis that the radio— "This is a national emergency!"—was shouting about. National emergency? A crisis of state? I could only lament that in this country, for which I felt a boundless affection, vistas were too narrow and a sanctuary nowhere to be found. Had I lived between the Sung and the Yūan, or between the Ming and the Ch'ing, would I not have sought my hermitage in the wild woods and made it the setting for the last of my days? Alas, the only refuge left to me was the inflammation of my lungs. Pleurisy became my modest hermitage. (*Mujintō;* II, 241-242)

4. "*Miyashiro no chigi ni kasumi no hatsugoromo omoi no take kami ni kaketsutsu*"

(II, 301). Note that in the half-written poem at the beginning of "Mars' Song" the gods are referred to as "somnolent . . . the voice of wisdom ha[ving] fallen silent, utterly silent" (I, 551).

5. For more information on *wen-jen,* or *bunjin,* see Cheng Ching-mao, "On Bunjin: The Literati of the Edo Period," in *Studies on Japanese Culture* (Tokyo: Japan P.E.N. Club, 1973), vol. 1, pp. 6-7. See also Cal French, "Bunjinga," in *Kodansha Encyclopedia of Japan* (Tokyo: Kodansha International, 1983), vol. 1, pp. 210-211.

6. "The formulas of Ming and Ch'ing aesthetics were transmitted to this land, and for a brief while they dominated the concept of cultivated living in Edo. This is why we can conjecture that the literati of An'ei and Tenmei looked to Yüan Hung-tao as their spiritual source" (in *Membō ni tsuite* [On Countenances], in *Isai hitsudan* [Isai's Propos], October 1950; XII, 14). For further information on Yüan, see Yüan Hung-tao, *Pilgrim of the Clouds,* trans. Jonathan Chaves (Tokyo: Weatherhill, 1978).

7. Anonymity of authorship (i.e., a fabricated author for a fabricated text) and secularization *(zokuka)* of the canon (i.e., translating abstract ideas or texts into the argot of contemporary times and everyday life) are key concepts in Ishikawa's analysis of the "metaphysics" *(keijijōgaku)* that underlie the *kyōka* movement and that he developed in essays written during the war, such as *Kitō to norito to sanbun* (Christian Prayers, Shinto Chants, and Prose; May 1942), *Sanbun shōshi* (A Short History of Prose [in Japan]; July 1942), and *Edobito no hassōhō ni tsuite* (On the Ways of Thought of the People of Edo; March 1943). Although for many years these essays were not included in Ishikawa's complete works, they can now be found in volume 12 of the most recent *Ishikawa Jun zenshū.* For more information, see Tyler, "The Agitated Spirit," pp. 165-180.

8. Deriving from the verb *"yatsusu,"* meaning "to disguise," *"yatsushi"* refers originally to the act of a highborn person traveling incognito; meanwhile, *"mitate"* refers to drawing analogies or making like sets and often, in the case of *mitate* poems or prints, to a likeness that exists between a lesser, even ignoble, object and a higher or more illustrious one. Just as *"yatsushi"* implies the aristocratic descent into the plebeian (i.e., the courtly Genji becoming an Edo townsman), *"mitate"* is the discernment of the noble in the lesser (e.g., the Yoshiwara courtesan seen as Ono-no-Komachi, the Heian period poetess and the most beautiful woman in Japanese history).

9. *Surimono,* literally "printed things," are a subgenre of *ukiyoe* woodblock prints that are smaller in size and often include *kyōka* as text. See Roger Keyes, *Surimono* (Tokyo: Kodansha International, 1984); and Joan Mirviss, *The Frank Lloyd Wright Collection of Surimono* (Phoenix: Phoenix Art Museum/Weatherhill, 1995).

254 ≈ NOTES TO PAGES 188-190

10. See note 17 to the essay on "Mars' Song."

11. See note 17 to the essay on "Mars' Song."

12. For Donald Keene's high opinion of Nagai Kafū, see note 21 in the essay on "Mars' Song." See also Edward Seidensticker, *Kafū the Scribbler* (Stanford: Stanford University Press, 1965), pp. 157-170, 347-349, for a discussion of Kafū's wartime diary, *Danchōtei nichijō*.

The reasons for the prohibition of "The Decoration" *(Kunshō)* have not been identified. The Home Ministry began blacklisting writers in March 1938 without full legal authority by instructing publishing houses regarding which authors were to be disinvited from submitting manuscripts. See Kasza, *The State and the Mass Media in Japan, 1918-1945*, p. 183. It is not clear whether Kafū had achieved blacklist status in 1942 or on what grounds "The Decoration" was found objectionable. The story—in part a Toulouse-Lautrec evocation of chorus girls relaxing between acts in their communal dressing room—tells us the narrator is a regular visitor backstage at a variety hall in Asakusa, Tokyo. Not only does he have special permission to pass through the stage door, he takes along his camera. One day he happens to photograph an old man who delivers food ordered by the women. The man has never had his picture taken before; moreover, everyone is surprised to learn the aging and unimportant-looking "delivery boy" had once been decorated for valor in the Russo-Japanese War of 1904-1905. He appears with his war decoration, and when one of the chorus girls hastily sews it on a military uniform currently being used in a stage production, the man poses for the camera for the first time in his life as the proud soldier that he once was. Only the narrator notices the decoration has been sewn in the wrong place on the uniform, and as the text comments, no one—including the old man—seems to care what military regulations require in such matters of protocol. When the narrator returns to the music hall ten days later with the developed photograph, the old man has disappeared without a trace. No one seems to know or care what has become of him. The old man can be seen as a heroic anachronism from the Russo-Japanese War. Yet in the current day and age no one knows or cares about proper military decorum. The protocols of the past have been replaced by a devil-may-care attitude. See the translation of "The Decoration" by Seidensticker in *Kafū the Scribbler*, pp. 329-335.

13. The conversion of the names Kafū into Gūka and *Henkikan* into *Renshikan* is also a play on the classical phrase *"gūdan renshi"*: "though the lotus be severed, its threads remain attached," that is, like minds may not be joined physically but they are connected in spirit. Hence, Ishikawa not only parodies the name of Kafū's house but also echoes the classic phrase and concept of shared intellectual affinity by incor-

porating it into the characters that comprise "Liaison House/*Renshikan*" and Gūka's name.

Note also that Kafū was instrumental in keeping Ōta Nanpo and his works before the Japanese public in the first half of this century, when the artistic accomplishments of Tenmei were overshadowed by scholarly and popular attention directed toward early (Genroku) or late (Bunka/Bunsei) Edo culture and art. Kafū was, as Ishikawa later became, one of the few practitioners of *kyōka* in the twentieth century.

14. See Seidensticker, *Kafū the Scribbler*, pp. 79–80. The title of the diary defies easy translation. Seidensticker translates it as "Dyspepsia House Days." *"Danchō"* refers to the gut-rending emotion that comes when one is utterly heartbroken or, even more literally, to the belly slashing of *seppuku*, when one commits ritual suicide out of either protest or despair.

15. It is significant that *watashi* pays close attention to what Kafū/Gūka wears, especially on his feet. *Haki-daore*, or a fatal weakness for shoes, has been the hall-mark of extravagance and the particular weakness of people from Tokyo or, more specifically, *Edokko*, the natives of Edo and later the modern capital. It stands in contrast to the penchant for expensive clothes, *ki-daore*, and for good food, *kui-daore*, the weak point or source of ruination for the natives of Kyoto and Osaka, respectively. In Edo, shoes make the man, or at least add the distinctively Edo touch to one's wardrobe. As metonymy for Kafū's spirit of independence and eccentricity, his peculiar outfit of "clogs with Western attire" not only serves Ishikawa's artistic purposes but also symbolizes the shift in Kafū's approach to researching and writing the novel in the case of his *Bokutō kitan* (1937; trans. *Strange Tale from East of the River*, 1965). In this novel, which is influenced by the novel-within-the-narrative structure employed by Gide in *Les faux-monnayeurs*, Kafū goes in search of material in the Tamanoi demimonde, the poorest of Tokyo's red-light districts. He wears a pair of clogs in order to fit in with the marginalized but free-spirited denizens of the quarter.

Note also that in Ishikawa's short story *Chō Hakutan* (Chang Pai-tuan; 1941), in which a Zen Priest steals a pair of shoes belonging to the Taoist immortal Chang Pai-tuan, Ishikawa includes an aside in which *watashi* reports that his only pair of shoes was stolen. *Watashi* must also make do wearing clogs with Western attire (II, 268, 275).

16. Katō Kōichi sees "Moon Gems" as a parody of Chinese tales about Taoist immortals in which *watashi*, in pretending to be a *sennin*, rides a bike rather than a

cloud. He looks to texts by the Taoist philosopher Chuang-tzu as sources for Ishi-kawa's composition of the story. Katō Kōichi, *Kosumosu no chie* (Tokyo: Chikuma shobō, 1994), p. 21.

17. Although the terms of reference in this passage are deep breathing exercises and Taoist wizardry, it may be that an additional interpretation is possible. As he stands facing the dawn of a new day and fills his lungs with fresh air, *watashi* says he is inspired by the three stripes of blue, white, and red *ch'i* or *ki* that streak across the sky. Is he inspired perhaps by the tricolor of *liberté, égalité et fraternité?* Or even — to read a play on words in the *"sanjō no ki"* of the text — might the three stripes be the red, white, and blue on the *Seijōki,* or "Star-Spangled Banner," representing an anticipated liberation by the Americans? The order of the colors differs, and the promise of a breath of fresh air is camouflaged as Taoist *ch'i,* but in almost direct proportion to the pounding that Allied bombers deliver Tokyo, *watashi* takes heart and succeeds in winning the affections and final mastery of his old bike.

18. I have been unable to identify categorically the source of this quotation from "a poet of the West," which reads: *"junsui seishin no ipponyari da to, kore yori hayaku yaban no hō ni tsurete iku mono wa nai"* (II, 315). It appears to be a very free translation — indeed one might call it an inspired rendition into Japanese of a difficult abstraction — of Alain's famous dictum *"Rien de plus dangereux qu'une idée, quand on n'a qu'une idée."* See Émile Chartier, *Système des beaux-arts* (Paris: NRF Gallimard, 1920). While *watashi* pursues mastery of the bike with tenacity, he recognizes the bike is only a means to an end — that is, the maintenance of the "hygienic" state of his mental health — and it is not an object for which one expends "purity of spirit" or develops a "single-minded obsession." Implied in this quote is a critique of the con-cept of "purity of spirit" *(junsui seishin),* a phrase used commonly by Japanese mili-tarists and devotees of the Japanese spirit, or *Yamato damashi,* to describe unmitigated devotion to a cause or idea, especially the war. The critique is also emphasized by the choice of *ipponyari* ("a single spear") with its double-entendre meaning of "one-track" mindlessness. Appeals to the spiritual beauty of unadulterated sincerity *(seii)* or purity *(junsui)* have a long history in Japan as the rationale or legitimation for extremist behavior — good or bad, right or left. As the psychiatrist Doi Takeo once remarked, often purity serves as a culturally institutionalized rationalization for immature social behavior. Ishikawa suggests blind or fanatical behavior ultimately leads to barbarism. While *watashi* is devoted to his bike lessons, he is not concerned with being "pure" in the pursuit of his spiritual enterprise, and the bike makes mockery of him when

he becomes too tenacious. He is prepared, moreover, to give the vehicle away once he achieves an approximation of mastery.

19. *"Yumi o hikaba masa ni tsuyoki wo hikubeshi"* (II, 321). The phrase "to draw a bow" has the additional meaning of "to oppose, challenge, or throw down the gaunt-let in opposition."

20. Donald Keene, "Japanese Writers and the Greater East Asia War," *Landscapes and Portraits* (Tokyo: Kodansha International, 1971), pp. 300-321. This essay first appeared in the *Journal of Asian Studies* in 1964 under the same title.

21. Ibid., pp. 300, 302. " . . . unless I mention the actual names it will not be possible to gauge the magnitude of the literary reaction. I earnestly request, however, that it be remembered that *almost everyone was involved"* (p. 302); " . . . that almost everybody was involved and, if guilty, equally so" (p. 300).

22. The statist process that saw to the diminution of free expression and the imposition of an official line was "crescive," taking place over time and affecting newspapers, fiction, films, and radio at different rates of speed and at different times. See Kasza, *The State and the Mass Media in Japan, 1918-1945,* pp. 122, 270-271. Also see Patricia Steinhoff, "Tenkō," in *Kodansha Encyclopedia of Japan* (1983), vol. 8, pp. 6-7, for a brief description of the "various forms of coercion, both physical and psychological, used to achieve *tenkō* or recantation of left-wing thought." A more moderate view of the level of repression is taken by Richard Mitchell, who argues that pressures in Japan were less extreme than in Germany and closer to those in Italy. Richard Mitchell, *Censorship in Imperial Japan* (Princeton: Princeton University Press, 1983), p. 364. Discussion of the history of *dan'atsu* (oppression) in prewar Japan is beyond the scope of this book, but see Hatanaka Shigeo, *Oboegaki—Shōwa shuppan dan'atsu shōshi* (Tokyo: Tosho shinbun, 1965), for a publisher's retrospective on the situation.

23. Kurahara (1902-1991) and Miyamoto (1899-1951) were imprisoned during the war because of their association with the Communist party and their refusal to recant; Tosaka Jun (1900-1945), educator and philosopher, was arrested in 1938 and died in prison just before the end of the war; the journalist Ozaki Hotsumi (1901-1944) was executed for his involvement in the Richard Sorge spy ring (see Ozaki's famous letters from prison, *Aijō wa furu hoshi no gotoku.* [Love is Like a Shower of Stars; 1941-1944], in *Ozaki Hotsumi zenshu,* vol. 4 [Tokyo: Keisō Shobō, 1979]; Ōyama (1880-1955), a scholar and politician, fled to the United States in 1933, where he taught political science at Northwestern University until 1947, when he was reinstated as professor at Waseda University; Dan (1901-1977) sought refuge in France. Dan was the first to introduce the story of the French resistance to Japanese

audiences, with the publication of *Teikō—rejisutansu* in 1949. It was followed by sequels, *Zoku teikō* and *Teikōsha*, in 1950 and 1951, when Japan saw a boom of interest in books published on the French resistance movement. Keene discusses the case of Tanizaki and Kafū in *Landscapes and Portraits* (pp. 313-316). Kaneko (1895-1975) was one of few major poets to write antiwar poetry, especially his anticolonial, anti-imperial, and anticonformist poems *(Awa, Same, Tōdai,* and *Ottosei)* appearing in the collection titled *Same* (Sharks; 1937). For an introduction to Kaneko, see Donald Keene, *Dawn to the West,* vol. 2, pp. 358-363; and for Kaneko's autobiography, Kaneko Mitsuharu, *Shijin,* trans. A. R. Davis (Sydney: University of Sydney East Asia Series, 1988). Steve Rabson also discusses briefly the arguments concerning Kaneko and the "zone of falsehood" *(kyomō chitai)* that Sakuramoto Tomio, writing in the year following Kaneko's death, alleged surrounds Kaneko's antiwar position. According to Rabson, "Much of the debate turns on whether Kaneko intended the popular wartime slogans appearing in the original versions of [his wartime] poems to be read satirically or not." See Rabson, *Righteous Cause or Tragic Folly,* p. 216. In his autobiography, Kaneko notes the consistent resistance of his fellow poets Tsuboi Shigeji and Okamoto Jun. Rabson also mentions the Okinawan poet Yamanokuchi Baku (pp. 10, 221-222), while Donald Keene mentions the case of two external émigrés: Hijikata Yoshi and Sano Seki, "important figures in the modern drama [who] went abroad in the mid-1930s" *(Dawn to the West,* vol. 1, p. 899, n. 3).

For more on Abe Tomoji (1903-1973) see Mizukami Isao, *Abe Tomoji kenkyū* (Tokyo: Sōbunsha shuppan), 1995. Mizukami examines in detail Abe's essays on humanism and his fictional works written between January 1936 when Abe joined *Bungakkai* magazine and November 1942 when the Japanese army targeted him and other writers to be conscripted. He surveys the *zadankai,* or recordings of coterie debates, in which Abe's liberal voice came increasingly under attack from Hayashi Fusao and *Bungakkai* members who actively supported the militarists after May 1938 (pp. 268-279). He discusses *Fuyu no yado* (A Place for the Winter; 1936) and *Kofuku* (Happiness; 1937) as protest novels; and, especially germane to the perplexing issue of how to read wartime literature is his handling of two stories that "Abe was made to write at the directive of the military news bureau" (p. 301) for inclusion in *Gunjin engo bungei sakuhinshū* (Anthology of Literature Backing the Troops; 1942). Mizukami argues Abe's treatment of the emperor in *Miezarumono* ("The Invisible") as a Christ figure constitutes a "humanizing" subversion of imperial authority, and that *Tomo ni ikin* ("Suviving Together") serves as a protective "alibi" for the liberties taken in *Miezarumono* (pp. 304-305).

The most famous antiwar/resistance statement by Funabashi Seiichi (1904-1976) is his short story *Daivingu* (Diving; 1934). The outspoken opinions of Satomi Ton (1888-1983) and Yanagi Muneyoshi (1895-1961), especially their criticism of the prowar position assumed by fellow members and former progressives of the White Birch School of Literature *(Shirakaba-ha)*, was brought to my attention by the Japanese critic and commentator Tsurumi Shunsuke. For more on Yanase Masamu (1900-1945) and his torture and imprisonment, see Ide Magoroku, *Nejikugi no gotoku—gaka no Yanase Masamu no kiseki* (Tokyo: Iwanami shoten, 1996). The critic Hirano Ken also discusses authors belonging to the "movement for artistic resistance" *(geijutsuha-teki teikō)* and writers of historical novels during the war. See Hirano Ken, *Shōwa bungaku-shi* (Tokyo: Chikuma sōsho, 1963), pp. 232-252.

Other important names that deserve recognition are Kawai Eijirō, Kawakami Hajime, Kiryū Yūyū, Masaki Hiroshi, Kiyosawa Kiyoshi, Hatanaka Shigeo, and Yanaihara Tadao. While not writers of fiction, as philosophers, educators, journalists, and editors, they were outspoken in print or in trouble with the authorities. For details on Kawai, see Atsuko Hirai, *Individualism and Socialism: The Life and Thought of Kawai Eijirō* (Cambridge: Council on East Asian Studies, 1966); for Kiryū Yūyū and his magazine *Tazan no ishi,* see the Dōshisha University study *Senjika teikō no kenkyū,* vol. 2, pp. 241-254; for Yanaihara Tadao, see Nobuya Bamba and John F. Howes, *Pacifism in Japan* (Kyoto: Minerva Press, 1978), pp. 199-219.

24. In its original use, the term "resistance" was applied to nonconformist and subversive activity carried out in France and other countries occupied by Germany during World War II. Even in these countries, the term has been subject to redefinition. See Tony Judt, *Past Imperfect: French Intellectuals, 1944-1956* (Berkeley: University of California Press, 1992).

> After the war, it suited almost everyone to believe that all but a tiny minority of the French people were in the Resistance or sympathized with it. Communists, Gaullists, and Vichyists alike had an interest in forwarding this claim. By the end of the forties, amidst growing disenchantment with the Fourth Republic, there emerged a new sensibility critical of résistantialisme and cynical about the whole wartime experience. . . . After 1958 and the return to power of the Gaullists, a modified résistantialisme became once again the order of the day. (pp. 45-46)

Resistance in Germany, like Japan, was a matter of resisting an internal regime rather than an external aggressor. The half-century anniversary of the fall of Nazi Germany has led to considerable discussion of how resistance has come to be defined in the case of Germany. For a handy review of relevant titles, see Gordon A. Craig, "Good Germans," *The New York Review of Books,* vol. 39, no. 21 (December 17, 1992): 38-44. Craig discusses a trend toward the inflated use of the term "resistance"; he covers the variety of stances assumed by resisters, and he advances the argument for the intentional and public nature of opposition as being key in determining true resistance.

25. James C. Scott, *Domination and the Arts of Resistance: Hidden Transcripts* (New Haven: Yale University Press, 1990). Although Scott's analyses derive chiefly from anecdotal evidence drawn from peasant and slave resistance movements in Europe and the American South, respectively, his research as a social scientist in Southeast Asia (and with Malay peoples in particular) gives his book greater breadth than works dealing solely with twentieth-century European culture. In Scott's view, "Any political refusal, in the teeth of power, to produce the words, gestures and other signs of normative compliance is typically construed — and typically intended — as an act of defiance. Here the crucial distinction is between *practical failure* to comply and *declared refusal* to comply. The former does not necessarily breech the normative order of domination; the latter almost always does" (p. 203). Scott further distinguishes between acts of defiance that "are relatively 'raw' and those that are relatively 'cooked.'" "Cooked" declarations are more likely to be nuanced and elaborate, because they arise under circumstances in which there is a fair amount of offstage freedom among subordinate groups, allowing them to share a rich and deep hidden transcript (p. 216).

26. Ibid., pp. 20, 217, 183, xii. Grumbling, euphemization, gossip, rituals of reversal, and Bakhtian fêtes constitute the immense "offstage" political terrain of "infrapolitics."

27. See notes 16 and 22 to the essay on "Mars' Song," where I have cited Odagiri Hideo's anthology of banned works published in 1957. See also in this connection Hanada Kiyoteru, Sasaki Kiichi, and Sugiura Minpei, comps., *Nihon teikō bungaku-sen* (Kyoto: San'ichi shobō, 1955), and the two volumes of research done in the late 1960s by the Dōshisha University study group on nonconformist activities pursued by Christian and liberal groups. Considerably more work has been done by Japanese scholars since the 1970s.

Published sources in English are Ienaga Saburō, *The Pacific War: World War II and the Japanese, 1931-1945,* trans. F. Baldwin (New York: Pantheon Books, 1978), which is a translation of Ienaga's famous *Taiheiyō sensō* (Tokyo: Iwanami shoten, 1968). See in particular pp. 85-87, 101-105, 120-122, 203-221; the endnotes are an especially rich and detailed source of information upon which Thomas Havens, *Valley of Darkness*

(New York: W. W. Norton and Company, 1978), and Ben-Ami Shillony, *Politics and Culture in Wartime Japan* (Oxford: Clarendon Press, 1981), draw heavily. But these three works by historians focus on resistance as only one aspect of the larger issue of "what the war experience meant for ordinary people" (Havens, p. 7).

Ienaga offers the following helpful definition of resistance in the case of Japan:

> A general classification would include (1) passive resistance and (2) active resistance. Under the former may be subsumed (a) "perfect silence," a refusal to endorse the war in any way, and (b) ignoring the war and continuing one's nonwar professional work. The second category may be further subdivided into (a) legal resistance and (b) illegal resistance, with the latter including refusing induction into military service, secret dissident activities within Japan, resistance in prison, and overt antiwar activities abroad. The extremes in each category were perfect silence and illegal resistance; people in these polar modes were able to oppose the war clearly and unequivocally. The other categories include numerous gray areas. Many individuals had to pretend tacit approval of the war in order to avoid repression. The distinction between these modes of resistance and opportunistic cooperation with the government was very fine. The dissidents were frequently placed in ambiguous situations in which an outsider cannot judge their real motives. (p. 204)

Ienaga cites *Fugen, Marusu no uta,* and *Sorori-banashi* (The Story of Sorori Shinzaemon; 1938) as examples of resistance works by Ishikawa, whom he places in the category of passive resistance. "Works like those of Kaneko [Mitsuharu] and Ishikawa were positive statements skillfully camouflaged in complex styles" (p. 205).

For an unpublished dissertation in English on Japanese writers and the war, see Yoshio Iwamoto, "The Relationship between Literature and Politics in Japan, 1931–1945" (Ph.D. dissertation, University of Michigan, 1964). Iwamoto's dissertation discusses three major groups of writers on the political left, center, and right during the Fifteen-Year War, but his attention is particularly drawn to proletarian writers who did not recant ("only four—Kobayashi Takiji, Kurahara Korehito, Miyamoto Kenji, and Nishizawa Ryūji—chose to remain unalterably faithful to communism either through death or indefinite prison terms," p. 81) or to those who moved to a centrist position, such as Nakano Shigeharu. A minor figure, Hashimoto Eikichi, is also cited as an exemplar "who produced a small body of novels *(Tankō, Chūgi, Asa)* that might be designated as resistance literature" (p. 159). Iwamoto's dissertation is the only source in English to discuss writers who combined political and aesthetic issues in the 1930s, especially after the collapse of the proletarian movement, and who can be loosely identified as belonging to the "Newly Arising Aesthetic School," or *shinkō geijutsu-ha*. This movement consisted of the "Neo-social School" *(shin-shakai-ha)*, represented by writers Asahara Rokurō, Kuno Toyohiko, and Ryūtanji Yū, as well as those associated with *Kōdō*, or *Action*, magazine, such as Funabashi Seiichi and Abe Tomoji, who took up the clarion call of Gide and Malraux in coming to the *"défense de la culture"* in the face of the rise of fascism (p. 185). The term is *bunka no yōgo* in Japanese; it is, incidentally, mentioned in "Mars' Song" when the guests break into their simultaneous monologues about the war at Fuyuko's wake. Ishikawa Jun is also briefly mentioned by Iwamoto (p. 248).

A more recent dissertation is Zeijko Cipris, "Radiant Carnage: Japanese Writers on the War against China," (Ph.D. dissertation, Columbia University, 1994). It surveys reactions across the political spectrum by fourteen writers, including Ishikawa Jun. (It also includes a translation of *Marusu no uta* titled "The Song of Mars," pp. 192–223, as well as one of Ishikawa Tatsuzo's *Ikite iru heitai* as *Soldiers Alive*, pp. 224–396.) Cipris seeks to set the nature of Japanese writers' responses within the context of "Japanese vs. Anglo-American imperialism" (pp. 9–14) and to address larger questions, such as how writers of any country respond in wartime or what constitutes a "literary" response to the experience of war. In his concluding chapter, he attempts an assessment of the writers he has reviewed. He singles out "Kuroshima Denji, Oguma Hideo, Kaneko Mitsuharu, and Ishikawa Jun" as numbering among the few who produced "works of intellectual and aesthetic distinction" (p. 189). He shares Donald Keene's view that the level of repression in Japan was comparatively "less extreme" but disagrees with Keene's overall evaluation: "On balance, it seems fair to characterize Japan's literary response to the war as 'normal': neither courageously defiant nor entirely submissive, and relatively free of the bellicose rhetoric often associated with wartime literature" (p. 188).

28. Poshek Fu, *Passivity, Resistance and Collaboration: Intellectual Choices in Occupied Shanghai, 1937–1945* (Stanford: Stanford University Press, 1993).

29. After the war, "poems which . . . had seemed pro-war . . . could also be interpreted as anti-war." Or conversely, during the war, "the convenient ambiguity of the Japanese language saved many seemingly frivolous works from the disapproval of the wartime censors." Keene, *Landscapes and Portraits*, pp. 300, 309.

30. Seidensticker, *Kafū the Scribbler*, pp. 347–349.

31. Scott, *Domination and the Arts of Resistance*, p. 223. The degree to which

Ishikawa's metaphors for resistance anticipate Scott's discourse on the distinction between onstage and offstage communication, the "cracks" in which hidden transcripts reside, as well as the "tracks" and "traces" such transcripts leave behind is striking.

32. This essay on satire—and the rare passage in which Ishikawa actually identifies himself as a satirist—does not appear in any edition of the *Ishikawa Jun zenshū* before the most recent. Neither has it been discussed in the critical literature on Ishikawa.

"In the first place, satire *(fūshi)* is a strange flower that blooms only in a land with a full quotient of good conscience. Does that mean there is no margin left for satire to show its face in the culture of this country, where conscience limps along, running out of breath?" (XII, 569). This essay, which ran in three installments in the June 17, 18, and 19 editions of the *Chūgai shōgyō shinpō* newspaper, lends credence to the point of view that Ishikawa had satire in mind when he was writing *Fugen* in the spring of 1936 and when he wrote "Mars' Song." The opening lines of this essay—"The other day I stood atop a certain hill looking at the ocean" (II, 566)—evoke a scene that closely resembles the "view from the aquarium" in the coda of *Marusu no uta*.

33. *Shiru hito zo shiru* can also be used as a moral imperative, that is, "those who know ought to know better," or as a call "to know thyself." In the context here, I refer to those who are able to comprehend and decode messages conveyed ironically, such as words said tongue-in-check, false euphemisms, facetious remarks, and so forth.

34. It appears Ishikawa began to experience difficulty composing a sustained work of fiction around the start of the war in China. I have already spoken of the dilemma surrounding facts and fiction that is posed in "Mars' Song." Moreover, in the fall of 1937, Ishikawa published in *Shinchō* magazine a long third-person narrative, *Risō—shimo fumite kempyō itaru* (Ice Follows Frost; I, 497-548), only to make atypically a number of revisions at the time of its publication as a monograph. It is also clear from perusal of the "Author's Preface" to each of the six installments of *Hakubyō* (II, 754-758) and a temporary switch in title to *Tōhō no kaze* (A Wind from the East) that the novel evolved with difficulty.

35. The life of the famous modernist architect Bruno Taut and his last month of residence in Japan provide the tightly ordered time frame—July 31 to September 1, 1936—and the story line for this novel. Taut appears as the expatriate Dr. Kraus, who fled Germany three years earlier. Japan is an unlikely asylum for a pro-Soviet, anti-Nazi refugee, however much Taut may have endeared himself to the Japanese with his "rediscovery" of indigenous Japanese architecture as seen in farmhouse construction, the Ise Shrine, and the Katsura Detached Palace in particular, which Taut considered

the epitome of Japanese architecture (see Bruno Taut, *Nihon-bi no saihakken,* 1935). As the novel begins, Taut is preparing to emigrate to "Persia." As a matter of fact, Taut left Japan in 1936 for Turkey, where he consulted on the design of the new capital in Ankara until his death two years later. His bold decision to depart from Japan stimulates the other characters — Isshiki Keiko, a young Japanese woman from Kobe of partially Jewish ancestry; Tsutsumi Kingo, a young furniture maker and sculptor; the artist Sakari Daisuke, trained in Europe and married to a German woman; and the Russian émigré couple Sonya Liipina and Georgii Ardanov — to wonder why they continue to stay in a Japan that is less and less to their liking.

Albeit a cryptic work that poses more questions than it answers, *Hakubyō* enjoyed a following among young intellectuals in liberal circles, and it has been much esteemed by critics who see it as a revolutionary attempt at the *roman pur* and resistance literature. See Tyler, "The Agitated Spirit," pp. 152-165. Note that the novel derives in part from the "facts" of Ishikawa's life because of his contact with Taut and with Mme. Bubanov, a long-term Russian resident in Japan, who is probably the model for the character Sonya Liipina (XII, 563).

36. See Shiozaki Fumio, "Senjika no Ishikawa Jun — Watanabe Kazan ni okeru fu no jōnen," *Kindai bungaku shiron* (Hiroshima daigaku kindai bungaku kenkyūkai), no. 15 (November 1976): 26-45. Mikasa shobō commissioned Ishikawa to write a biography of Watanabe Kazan on the occasion of the one hundred fiftieth anniversary of Kazan's birth — which saw the publication of several monographs on this famous samurai artist. As Shiozaki documents in a carefully researched article, Watanabe had been a hero of the liberal "peoples' rights movement" in mid-Meiji, but over time — and especially during the war years — the story of Watanabe's rise from poverty was coopted for use in conservative morals education. There is no question, however, that Ishikawa treats Kazan as an example of the martyrdom of a farsighted thinker living in a reactionary age (see Ishikawa's postscript to the 1964 republication of *Watanabe Kazan;* XI, 185); moreover, as Shiozaki points out, Ishikawa's recension of Watanabe's life undermines the myths advanced in the texts for morals education *(shūshin kyōiku).* But, because he suspects that Ishikawa's book did little to change the tenor of the times, he sees *Watanabe Kazan* as a wasted or "minus" work for Ishikawa. Nonetheless, it paved the way for Ishikawa's study of Mori Ōgai and Ishikawa's passion in the postwar years for revolutionary change.

37. Keene, *Dawn to the West,* vol. 1, p. 1098. Keene alludes here to Ivan Morris' concept of the "failed hero."

38. The writing of historical novels flourished during the war years. For some it

was an avenue into escape and inner emigration; for the majority, it was an occasion for patriotic literature. In his biography of Mori Ōgai, Ishikawa takes pains to demonstrate that the three so-called *shiden* or histories of the lives of Shibue Chūsai, Hōjō Katei, and Izawa Ranken that Ōgai wrote from 1916 to 1918 are, in fact, novels, and they approximate his own ideal of what the historical novel should be. Furthermore, Ishikawa's *Sanbun shōshi — ichimei, rekishi shōsetsu yose* (A Short History of Prose, i.e., Stop Writing Historical Novels; July 1942, XII, 621-629) laments the "low level to which prose has been dragged by what is now called the historical novel." Such novels have become a "[Takizawa] Bakin phenomenon" in which empty "rhetoric" *(yūben)* predominates.

39. *"Nihon e no kaiki"* was coined by the leading poet of free verse, Hagiwara Sakutarō (1886-1942), in 1938. Hagiwara called for Japanese writers to abandon the West as their spiritual *furusato*, or hometown, in favor of a "return to Japan." At the same time, he was careful to distinguish his call from the "army's marching bugles" and "the orders of ultranationalism." His ideological position remained unclear, however. Is calling for a return to Japan a xenophobic reaction against the West? Or a rearguard action to draw a line in the sand and stave off further cooptation of literature by the jingoists? See Hagiwara Sakutarō, *Hagiwara Sakutarō zenshū* (Tokyo: Shinchōsha, 1960), vol. 4, pp. 477, 480.

40. Keene, *Landscapes and Portraits*, p. 302.

41. Ibid., pp. 312-313. Also see William J. Tyler, "Honne to tatemae: Ishikawa Jun Marusu no uta to Dazai Osamu Sekibetsu," *Hikaku bungaku nenshi* (Waseda daigaku hikaku bungaku kenkyūshitsu), no. 30 (March 1995): 126-142, which discusses in detail the mystification strategies that Dazai and Ishikawa used in writing *Sekibetsu* and "Moon Gems," respectively, in the spring of 1945. While there is ample evidence internal to the novel *Sekibetsu* to believe that Dazai was intent on undermining the Japanese slogans he was commissioned in advertise, the line between subversion of the text and accommodation of the authorities is often so blurred as to make discernment of Dazai's true opinions difficult. The work is marked, moreover, by a certain "phoniness" (or *kiza*, to use Dazai's favorite word of disapprobation) not to be found in "Moon Gems." Note that the stigma of political complicity never adhered to Dazai in spite of his writing a novel commissioned in support of the war effort — a factor offset perhaps by his suicide in 1948 and his early canonization as an antiestablishment hero among postwar youth. Ishikawa and Dazai met for the first time during the war (see Ishikawa, *Isai zadan*, p. 246); in the immediate postwar years they were treated as fellow *burai-ha*, or "libertine school" writers.

42. See Ishikawa's short story *Mujintō* (II, 426-427), in which *watashi* describes the conference (probably the Greater East Asia Conference of November 5-6, 1943) in sarcastic detail. "There are limits even to whimsy. I had enough, and I left in a great hurry. By the time I got outside I could hardly breathe. It was a very, very depressing business. No matter what it takes, since then I have stayed away from any sort of blackheartedness that seeks to militarize all towns and villages" (p. 427). *Mujintō* was written and published after the war (July 1946). As a story narrated by *watashi,* it may also be partially or wholly fictional. Also see note 1 on "Moon Gems."

43. In *Mori Ōgai,* for example, in discussing Ōgai's translations of Western literature, Ishikawa announces that "Japanese literature was never dependent on the wisdom of the West for its development." While Japanese writers may have "devoured the shenanigans of Westerners . . . at no point did they ever shed one drop of blood in the arena of influence from the West" (p. 193). A similar reference to the wisdom of the West as complex and annoying *(shichimendōkusai)* appears in the brief essay *Seikatsu to kotoba* (XII, 645); and Anatole France, whose works Ishikawa translated as a youth, is called a "hairy barbarian" *(ketōjin;* XII, 668) in *Rekishi shōsetsu ni tsuite* (On Historical Novels; August 1944). The only derogatory reference to the British and the Americans appears in *Kami no kanashimi.* "To put it in concrete terms, we are the gods *(kami),* and the British and the Americans are the beasts *(kedamono).* When it comes to beastly things, that is something we leave to the enemy. That way, we don't have to worry at all" (XII, 660). *Kedamono* is printed in *katakana;* the passage may well be a tongue-in-cheek takeoff on wartime slogans. In *Kitō to norito to sanbun,* he writes that "their gods are full of promises, but not once have they come down to the real earth. . . . That France today has had to grasp at the straw of such gods is a great pity. It is a defeated nation, after all" (XII, 449). The fall of France appears to have caused Ishikawa considerable pain, as this essay (which mentions a revival of Catholicism and the popularity of Charles Péguy in Vichy France) and *Bungaku no konnichi* (XII, 613) suggest. The foregoing covers all of the potentially offensive passages that I have identified. Although Ishikawa is disingenuous as a writer whose methodology derives in part from interaction with foreign sources, on the whole the list is relatively innocuous, especially considering Ishikawa's penchant for stylistic obstreperousness. His shift away from Anatole France dates from the 1920s; in the seven years since "Mars' Song" and the production of approximately a thousand pages of fictional and nonfictional material, the incidence of xenophobic remarks is very low.

44. *"Seijiteki gomakashi"—*"faking it politically" or "political accommodation" — is Ishikawa's term in *Senchū ibun* (Fragments from the War Years; XIV, 14). Ishikawa

does not go so far, however, as to call his fakery or accommodation a form of *"bubun kyokuhitsu,"* the standard term in Japanese for "perversion of the truth."

45. The two essays on the historical novel discussed in "Fragments" are *Sanbun shōshi — ichimei, rekishi shōsetsu wo yose* (A Short History of Prose, i.e., Stop Writing Historical Novels; July 1942, XII, 621–629) and *Rekishi shōsetsu ni tsuite* (On Historical Novels; August 1944, XII, 662–669; XIV, 22–30). Only the text of the latter is reprinted along with *Zenrin no bunka ni tsuite*.

Especially in the case of "A Short History of Prose" (in Japan), Ishikawa felt he had allowed himself to become overly exercised *(sakkidatte; seikyū-sugite)* in his attack on the deleterious influence of the Edo period writer Takizawa Bakin and the abuse of the term "historical novel" during the war. He cites the overheated tone of his essay as symptomatic of the overall state of frustration he experienced during the war. "As a matter of fact, I was really looking at another enemy in taking on Bakin. And that was the 'moral principles' that the military government issued. Perhaps it was the double punch of being slapped in the face with 'morality' *and* 'service to the nation' that brought my anger to the boiling point" (XIV, 13).

46. Writing in 1960 in "Fragments from the War Years," Ishikawa castigates himself for a lack of courage.

> Near the end of my essay I wrote to the effect there could be "no unification of the [related] cultures," and I hint at a position that naturally undermines my own earlier "hypothesis." Judging from the times in which I was writing, it is probably possible to look at this passage from the point of view of the big historical picture and not find it obnoxious. Yet when it comes to the hypothesis that I first erect, I must say that is an example of my faking it politically *(seijiteki gomakashi)*. Read in a favorable light, the passage is not without a touch of irony. But given the way it is cast, accommodation *(gomakashi)* looks a lot like ingratiation *(geigō)*. What does "a simple and self-evident hypothesis — and one that will be inevitably demonstrated" mean, anyway? One can never say that as a mode of expression there is anything "simple or self-evident" about it. What I should have written was "this is a vague and hopeless mess of a hypothesis that has no chance of ever being proven." (XIV, 14)

"On Neighboring Cultures" begins with Ishikawa's describing his fatigue and disappointment as he leaves the exhibition hall. He had come in hopes of finding a point of "spiritual negotiation" (XII, 635) between Japanese and Manchurian culture, only to discover that, historically speaking, the nations are too remote to have anything of real significance to share. Furthermore, the majority of the treasures in the exhibit are post-Sung artifacts of Chinese origin or influence, and little can be identified as indigenous to Tungusic culture. In spite of the "mountains" of publications (XII, 637) now available in Japan on the subject of Manchuria, it is still not possible for him to see the historical and cultural relevance of the Tungus to Japanese culture. As a nation of horse riders, the Tungus have been oriented westward; any connection with Japan has come through war and "the expansion of political power" (XII, 638).

It is at this juncture that Ishikawa jumps to his hypothesis on Japan as the "king *(ō)* of the related cultures" of Asia: "*Sunawachi, Nihon bunka wo kankei sho-bunka no ō toshite tateru to iu, kanarazu jitsugen subeki tanjun meihaku naru katei de aru*" (XII, 638). The sense with which he uses the term "king" is not entirely clear, but the view of Japan as a kingdom that exists within the hierarchy of China's empire — and of regional Asian kings *(ō)* who are subservient to the Chinese emperor *(tei)* — is a worldview of long standing in Asia. As Donald Keene suggests, it is a view "not unlike the opinions of the eighteenth-century dilettantes whom Ishikawa so admired" (Keene, *Dawn to the West,* vol. 1, p. 1098). Albeit a parochial view of the world, it is not imperialistic in the modern sense. Moreover, as Ishikawa points out in "Fragments from the War Years," the essay proceeds to deconstruct itself by arguing that, because China is Japan's only source of contact with Tungus culture, only the Chinese — and not the Japanese by inference — are qualified to judge the validity of the "hypothesis and reality" of the relationship between Japan and Manchuria (*migi no katei to sono genjitsu ni tsuite wa, wareware no tōmen subeki hihyōka wa kanarazu ya Shina no hitobito darō;* XII, 639).

The essay ends with cautionary statements to the effect that Japan must exercise care in the tone that it adopts vis-à-vis the Chinese (XII, 640); Asian cultural unity is unrealistic, especially in the case of Manchuria, whose "peoples . . . we have just met for the first time" (XII, 641); finally, if there is to be interaction, it is incumbent upon the Manchurians to take the initiative "via the procedure of communicating through the Japanese language" (XII, 641). While the latter can be viewed as an example of the "linguistic imperialism" that Japan practiced in Asia, at the same time the three provisos can be seen as subverting the overall intent of the exhibit, namely pan-Asianism, or more specifically pan-Japanism.

Clearly, the "Japan as king" passage must be read within the context of the entire essay. This is a point discussed and defended in detail in Izawa Yoshio, *Ishikawa Jun no shōsetsu* (Tokyo: Iwanami shoten, 1992), pp. 111–116. *Zenrin bunka ni tsuite* appeared in the November 1942 edition of *Shinchō* magazine.

47. Aoyagi Tatsuo was the first scholar to unearth and call attention to *Bungaku no konnichi*, which is not mentioned in Ishikawa's "Fragments," is not included in earlier editions of his *Complete Works*, and did not become readily available until the appearance of the new *Ishikawa Jun zenshū* published 1989-1991. See Aoyagi Tatsuo, *Ishikawa Jun no bungaku* (Tokyo: Kasama shoin, 1978), pp. 81-86, 89.

The essay begins as a defense of literature, and it replays a number of Ishikawa's views with which his readers are familiar. Experience is not what confines literature, but it is the starting point for its movement. Reality is a harsh taskmaster, because literature does not exist in abstraction or isolation from real life; and if, in history, people have thought literature a pariah to be eliminated, they have been proven wrong time and again. Writers work in the vanguard of their surroundings, but their fate may be to go unappreciated in their own time. As a matter of fact, such is the "fate of beautiful things" (XII, 610). "Beautiful things are destined to die" (XII, 611). The chief source of interference with literature is politics. A writer's heart ought to be always with the masses who have little power, as they are the source of his creative energy. It is at this point that Ishikawa introduces the provocative statement about Hitler.

48. *"Kokumin bungaku-ron"* means literally "the theory of a national literature" but is actually a euphemism for the creation of literature concerned with empowering Japanese readers with nationalistic sentiment; *"bungaku hiriki-setsu"* is literally "the thesis [arguing] literature's lack of power [in the face of politics]." Aoyagi discusses the way in which Ishikawa's essay appears to speak to these two major but different camps of thinking in Japanese literary circles during the war. *Ishikawa Jun no bungaku,* pp. 82-84.

49. The entire passage reads: *"Doitsu ni kansuru kagiri, Hitora wa migoto na shidōsha in sōi nai. Genzai kare ga sō de aru tame ni wa, katsute hitsuzen no sho-jōken ga atta. Kongo, man'ichi kare ga shippai shita toshite mo, sore wa utsukushii mono da to sōzō sareru. Kō iu kantan na koto ni wa, bungakusha wa dare mo kechi nado wo tsuke wa shinai. Tada Hitoraizumu wa doko ni demo yūzū dekiru to iu yō na kangaekata ni, doko no kuni demo, genjitsu no sho-jōken ga awatete tobitsuite wa ikanai dake da"* (XII, 612).

The essay was first published in the January 1941 edition of *Bungei jōhō* magazine. It was republished in the Shōgakkan monograph edition of *Bungaku taigai* and other essays in 1942, but it was deleted from the Chūō kōronsha edition of 1947.

Keene refers to this passage, citing it from the Shōgakkan edition of 1942 (see Keene, *Dawn to the West,* vol. 1, pp. 1098, 1110, n. 212). Citing Keene as his source of information on the passage, Cipris comments that "perceptive and nonconformist though he was, Ishikawa seems to have succumbed to at least one intellectual fashion of the day. . . . A romanticized image of Hitler as a bold man of action and a demystifier of political complexities appears to have exerted considerable fascination over a number of Japanese intellectuals of the period." Cipris, "Radiant Carnage," pp. 70, 410, nn. 11, 12. Cipris' support for the popularity of a romanticized image of Hitler is taken in part from Iwamoto Yoshio's discussion of Itō Sei's novel of 1941 *Tokunō Gorō no seikatsu to iken* (Life and Opinions of Tokunō Gorō). See Iwamoto, "The Relationship between Literature and Politics in Japan, 1931-1945," pp. 245-246.

While not seeking a whitewash of this troubling passage, I argue for a more careful and nuanced reading. Also I am reluctant to place Ishikawa in the same category with Itō Sei (1905-1969), who "compose[d] some of the most xenophobic utterances to issue from the pen of any major writer" (Keene, *Dawn to the West,* vol. 1, pp. 675-676) or to see the full-blown fascination with Hitler shown by Itō's alter ego in *Tokunō* as being on a par with Ishikawa's remark in this brief passage.

50. It is true that Thomas Mann left Germany in 1933 for self-imposed exile in Switzerland. It is also probable that Ishikawa did not have access to the news that Mann became an outspoken opponent of fascism. See Thomas Mann, *Order of the Day* (1942).

51. See Okamoto Takuji, "Sensōki no Ishikawa Jun," *Waseda daigaku kōtōgakuin kenkyū nenshi,* no. 16 (January 1972): 1-17. Okamoto argues the second half of 1942 represents the greatest and most dangerous "period of crisis" in which Ishikawa wavered under social and political pressure (p. 10). Writing in 1972, however, he did not have access to all materials relevant to reviewing Ishikawa's writings from the war years. Nonetheless, he presents a convincing case for treating Ishikawa as a model of resistance.

52. *"Ichihayaku sensō wo taihi shita sumashiya."* See Honda Shūgo, *(Sōhō) Senji sengo no senkōsha-tachi,* p. 286. The word *"sumashiya,"* translated here as "sitting pretty," defies ready translation. The nuance is somewhat negative. It suggests a person who manages to stay above the fray in a cool and self-satisfied way.

53. Ōe Kenzaburō, "Kaisetsu — wakai sedai no tame no kakū kōen," *Shinchō Nihon bungaku (33): Ishikawa Jun shū,* pp. 426-436.

> I reached the years of my youth in the postwar period through experiencing the reality of Japan's defeat as well as looking at postwar democracy at a time when the direction for that path seemed ever so clear. And, in my case, the first works of so-called postwar Japanese literature and those that moved me more power-

fully than any other were the works of Ishikawa Jun. How many times did I and my friends who were my peers in age sit around discussing the world of Ishikawa Jun!?! . . . We sought out everything he wrote; we imbibed it as though intoxicated; the words of praise poured from our lips. We had only one other author, or book, about whom we felt equally intense. That was Kafka, or should I say his novel *The Trial*. (pp. 426-427)

54. Noel Annan, "Secret Sharers," *New York Review of Books*, vol. 44, no. 14 (September 25, 1997): 23.

55. Ebina Yūji and Tamura Jōji, *Taidan: Ōta Juria to bokushi nisei* (Conversation: Two Second-Generation Ministers on Ōta Julia), p. 35. I am indebted to Inoue Katsuya, professor, Dōshisha University, for bringing this article to my attention. It was xeroxed and given to him by Ōshima Shōichi, Dōshisha professor emeritus and nephew of Ebina Yūji. The *taidan* or conversation between Ebina and Tamura—both "second-generation Protestant ministers"—appeared in an unidentified Japanese Catholic magazine in 1973-1974 (?), but the bibliographical source is not identifable from the xeroxed materials. In his conversation with Tamura, Ebina says, "At the time, I was sort of—what shall I call it?—patron or *oyabun* to the anarchists. Why, my anarchist friends and I had taken over and occupied half of my old man's house. People like Tsuji Jun, and Ishikawa Jun—the novelist—were always coming to visit and stay. Yes, we were loud and noisy, but we weren't engaged in any active 'struggle' like the Red Army types we hear about today." Ebina also asserts that, after Ishikawa was burned out of his Tokyo lodgings, he lived with the Ebinas for approximately three years. It was at the Funabashi residence that "Jesus of the Ruins" was written, as well as "all of his immediate postwar pieces" (p. 36).

56. Kawakami Tetsutarō quotes Ebina in Kawakami Tetsutarō, "Ishikawa Jun den," *Gendai Nihon bungakkan (31): Ishikawa Jun*, p. 20. Also see Ishikawa's short story *Kanro* (II, 337-368).

On "The Legend of Gold" and "The Jesus of the Ruins"

1. *Jōzetsu-tai*, the garrulous style, was a prose style that enjoyed currency in Japanese (and world) literature in the 1930s. Characterized by long sentences, often with minimal punctuation and paragraphing, it had an especially strong following among modernist and experimental writers. In the case of Japanese novelists, it may also be

seen as a reversion to a narrative style that predates the introduction of Western punctuation and has the look of the continuous texts of classical *monogatari*.

2. *"Apure-gēru"* was a term borrowed from French letters, where it was used to describe the first generation of writers on the literary scene after World War II. Dazai, Ishikawa, Oda, and Sakaguchi are often cited as the "first wave" of writers on the postwar literary scene in Japan. *Burai-ha* is literally "school of 'ruffians' or 'rogues' " but is more commonly translated as the "libertines." The term was coined by Dazai in reference to himself and his literary peers. See Okuno Takeo, *Burai to itan* (Tokyo: Kokubunsha, 1973), pp. 16-18. The libertinism of these writers was reflected in their shared pattern of obstreperousness and iconoclasm toward authority and traditional values as well as lifestyles characterized by hard drinking and sexual liberality. *"Shin-gesakusha,"* writers of the new burlesque school, is another term applied to members of this group because of their interest in Edo period *gesaku* fiction, their claim to be writers of modern-day versions of said "frivolous" works, and a tendency to cloak their opinions in the mystification style *(tōkai-buri).*

3. *"Yakeato,"* "burnt-out shell" or "burned site, remains, or ruins," may refer to a specific ruin or more generally to a *yakenohara,* torched fields. English words such as "ruins" or "debris" give no indication of the cause or means of destruction, and no single English word links destruction specifically with the work of fire. Given the context of the war and the heavy use of incendiary weapons and the atomic bomb against Japan *"yakeato"* also carries the nuance of "bombed sites."

"Yakeato" can also be written with the characters *yake[ru]* and *ato* (or *nochi*), indicating the progression of a fire and what comes "after" it, or *yake[ru]* and *ato* (or *kizu*), "burn mark" or "scar" in the sense of the more commonly used word *"yakedo"* or *"yakedo no ato,"* a physical burn on the body. *"Yakeato"* can also be thought of as the mark that comes from a branding iron, as in the case of the word *"yaki'in,"* "brand" or "stigma." See the Glossary for the variant usage of these characters.

In "The Jesus of the Ruins" Ishikawa makes repeated and conspicuous use of the varied and polysemous meanings and characters for *"yakeato."* This is also done with the word *"ato,"* by playing on its possible meanings of "trace(s)," "afterward," "site," "remains," and "scar."

4. *"Sengo"* is an abbreviation of *"haisen chokugo,"* or "immediately after the defeat in war."

5. *"Gensei":* "the force of the present, manifest power, modernity"; *"genzai no yo":* "the contemporary world"; *"kannō":* "possibility, potential."

6. Until the late 1980s it was possible to see vestiges of the hastily constructed,

tin-roofed promenades in the Nogé area adjacent to Sakuragi-chō Station in Yoko-hama or the Okachimachi section of Ueno. Even today the aura of a hot cash economy hangs over the electronic and computer discount stores at Akihabara in Tokyo. It has been argued by Japanese commentators that it was in the black markets of the immediate postwar years that the Japanese economic miracle was born and the future captains of Japanese industry received their baptism by fire in the school of excessive competition *(katō kyōsō)* and total market share.

7. *Ikiyo ochiyo,* "to live, to fall." Sakaguchi's *Daraku-ron* appeared in the April 1946 issue of *Shinchō* magazine. In an oft-quoted passage, he writes: "Japan has lost and *Bushidō* gone down to defeat, but the Mother of Truth called Decadence has given birth to a new class of true human beings. Is there any handy shortcut to saving humankind other than a proper application of the rule that 'to live is to de-moralize'? . . . Human beings degenerate. The righteous samurai and the holy woman degenerate. No one can stop the process of degeneration, nor will anyone be saved by doing so. People live, and they fall into decline. That we are degenerate and de-moralized is not because we lost the war. No, we sink because we are human; we fall only because we are alive." *Sakaguchi Ango zenshū* (Tokyo: Chikuma shobō, 1990), vol. 14, p. 520.

8. *"Kenzen na dōtoku to wa intō yori hoka no mono de naku"* (II, 469).

9. See Oda Sakunosuke, *Teihon Oda Sakunosuke zenshū* (Tokyo: Bunsendō shoten, 1976), vol. 8, pp. 115-129.

10. *"Pen to tomo ni kangaeru"* (XII, 285). Adapting the phrase *"penser à mesure que la plume écrit"* from the French critic and essayist Alain (Émile Chartier), Ishikawa refers to his style of writing as a process of "thinking with the pen" in his long essay on literature *Bungaku taigai,* published in 1942. For further discussion, see Tyler, "The Agitated Spirit," pp. 16-17, 140-145.

11. The woman is not identified immediately as speaker, but there are telltale indications that the passage is both direct speech and the statement of a shopkeeper, probably female, addressing a customer, through the recurrent use of honorifics (*o-kome, gohan, o-mise, Shina-san*) and the humble pronominal *"temae"* in *"temae-domo no mise,"* "our humble shop" (II, 325). Certainly Japanese readers would pick up on these clues. I do not wish to read a theory of Japanese culture as nonessentialist into the ellipsis or withholding of information that occurs here. To the contrary, ambiguity is introduced to catch the reader off guard; and by commencing in medias res, Ishikawa prepares the way for the introduction of new and improbable imagery.

12. The frequent use of "today" in Ishikawa's works in which many events are past yet represented as present — or more or less past than other events — poses a problem

for translation into English, a language that, having perfect tenses, is fussy about the chronological order of events and even the chronology of events within events. English usage also regularly embraces the historical present as a means of writing about the past, but the historical present tense is not an entirely satisfactory vehicle for conveying the fluidity of tense or aspect in Japanese.

13. *"Seisaku"* is literally "New Year's Day" and, by extension, the old Chinese lunar calendar. The term is used idiomatically here as *"seisaku ni hōzubeki mono ga ataerarete inai,"* "since the old calendar of imperial events and obligations [is] no longer in force." *"Seisaku ni hōzuru"* refers to the ancient Chinese custom of instituting a new reign name or calendar with the ascension of an emperor to the throne. Because the future status of Hirohito was unclear at the time in which this story is set (his renunciation of divinity was January 1, 1946), I have interpreted Ishikawa's remark as referring to the absence of a national leader and the abeyance of the traditional regimen of imperial obligations.

14. *"Kamigakari"* refers to the "intermediary" or Shinto medium who speaks to and for the god(s) of the firstfruits of the harvest, that is, white rice. As is so often the case with Ishikawa's use of compound verbs (*tataku + dasu* in this case), word play is involved, with *"tatakidasu"* referring, first, to the threshing of rice and, second, to the driving out or expulsion of a person or thing from a group.

15. *"Seiriteki jikan no keika jōkyō kara butsuriteki jikan no memori"* (II, 326).

16. *"Kono fūdo ni okeru furiko ni natta ambai de"* (II, 329).

17. *"Watashi wo chijō ni hikitodometa no wa, futokoro no tokei no, kuruinagara kachikachi to, sore ga mada da mada da to iu fū ni"* (II, 327).

18. It is altogether possible to read this scene as a metaphor for the country shedding the weight of the war.

19. The entire passage (II, 328) reads: *"Konnichi no yo no naka no ue ni oshika-busatte iru tokoro no tohō mo nai tsumi no kannen."* The *"yo no naka"* refers in this case to Japan, on which the outrageous concept of guilt is being imposed.

20. *"Ichioku,"* or one hundred million, refers to the size of the population of Japan, and by extension it becomes a metaphor for "all the subjects/citizens in the land"; *"zange,"* or penitence, is done by all or in unison *(sō)*. See Glossary under *ichioku*.

21. The full passage (II, 328) reads: *"Tare mo mukizu ni wa nogareōsenai yō na unmei no shoi da to iu koto."*

22. *"Ichioku kokumin," "ichioku isshin,"* and *"ichioku gyokusai"* were all slogans used to promote unity and sacrifice on the part of the Japanese public during the war; in

fact, *"ichioku gyokusai,"* the "breaking or pulverizing of the jewel of the hundred million," was the clarion call raised in the last days of the war, when all Japanese were expected to defend the homeland even to the point of extinction. The phrase *"ichioku sōzange,"* or the "repentance en masse of the hundred million" (see note 20 above), was the postwar media's ironic adaptation of these wartime slogans.

23. The entire passage (II, 329) reads: *"Tsumi to wa susu no yō ni furikatte kuru mono, shirami no yō ni densen shite kuru mono, kodai Indo no shinkō no yō ni tsumi wa busshitsu ni chigainai."*

24. See Ishikawa Jun, *The Bodhisattva, or Samanthabhadra,* pp. 120, 158-159. The beatification and then debunking of characters, especially of heroic women representing a historical ideal, such as Joan of Arc as the fallen liberator of France, or the character of Yukari as representative of the failed hopes of the left-wing underground movement in Japan in the 1930s, is a perennial theme in Ishikawa's works. After *watashi* waits a decade to see the maiden of his dreams, he discovers she has been sullied by the passage of time and the harsh life in the political underground. His "swan maiden" has molted and become a *yasha*-demoness or a fire-eating emu. A pattern of toppling idols from their pedestals applies to Ishikawa's life as well. Over the years, Nanpo, Gide, and Kafū would fall from the high estimation in which Ishikawa once held them. This comes perhaps as no surprise, given Ishikawa's high standards and the strong antiauthoritarian bent to his life and works.

25. Dazai Osamu, *The Setting Sun,* trans. Donald Keene, (New York: New Directions, 1956). "*The Setting Sun* is memorable especially for the character of Kazuko, who is determined to defy social convention and abandon traditional morals by her bold gesture of bearing an illegitimate child." See Keene, *Dawn to the West,* vol. 1, pp. 1060-1062.

Kurosawa Akira's film *No Regrets for Our Youth* (*Waga seishun ni kui wa nashi;* 1946) is another portrayal of a strong female protagonist created during the early postwar years. See Donald Richie, *The Films of Akira Kurosawa* (Berkeley: University of California Press, 1970), pp. 36-42.

26. *Watashi* refers to the way people spoke in the past as courtly—*mukashi dōri ingin ni* (II, 332)—and he likens his parting from the friend's wife to a secret rendezvous as found in classical Japanese literature. "It was as though I had been her lover that night, and having plighted our troth in a grand and secret love affair, we were sharing in the sweetness and sorrow of all lovers who are destined to part" (*Watashi wa michi naranu chigiri wo kawashite kaeru kinuginu no koibito de demo aru ka no yō ni;* II, 333).

27. "There are no words that one might say at a time like this. I was so ashamed,

I thought I would die on the spot" (*Watashi no hasshiuru kotoba tote wa naku, tada shinu hodo hazukashiku;* II, 334).

The issue of *watashi's* "*hazukashisa*" (which can be variously translated as "shame," "embarrassment," "humiliation") is key to interpretation of the denouement of this story. The critic Noguchi Takehiko, for example, also notes the centrality of this word and elaborates on its significance. Noguchi, *Ishikawa Jun ron,* pp. 229-233.

> Why is it that the central character in *Ōgon densetsu* becomes "deathly embarrassed" when he sees the woman cleave to the black soldier? Why is it the feeling that he entertains is not "despair" but "shame"? . . . The ideal woman to whom *watashi* entrusted his dreams during the war years metamorphoses into a prostitute who caters to foreign soldiers and reeks of the oily perfume of her red, Western-style dress. It is obvious that the central character, who is "embarrassed to the point of dying," is ashamed of the hopes in which he has enveloped himself. As for all the pretty dreams to which he had entrusted his own raison d'être during the war and all the inalienable and priceless hopes he had entertained, he is terribly ashamed of having carried this baggage into the postwar era, and he wants to purge himself of it. In the new chaotic conditions of postwar, what once seemed suffused with light and hope has now become nothing more than a scrap to be tossed onto a trash pile. This is the consciousness that lies at the heart of Ishikawa Jun's new departure. (p. 232)

A different reading—and one that I reject here—is given in Kawanishi Masaaki, "Mashin e," in *Subaru: Ishikawa Jun tsuitō kinen-gō* (April 25, 1988): 259-271. "The shame that occurs within *watashi* is probably neither public nor private shame. Wouldn't it be better to call it 'cultural shame' *(bunka haji)?*" (p. 271). The writer does not elaborate, however, on what this term means.

28. Ishikawa uses the word "adieu" here, borrowing it from the French and writing it in Japanese.

29. See his reportage on the differences between the Ueno and Shinjuku "jungles" in "Tōkyō janguru tanken" (June 1950), *Sakaguchi Ango zenshū,* vol. 17, pp. 200-240. See also Suzuki Sadami, "Yakeato no Iesu," *Nihon bungei kanshō jiten* (Tokyo: Gyōsei, 1987), vol. 14, p. 146.

30. See Richie, *The Films of Akira Kurosawa,* pp. 58-64.

31. Note also that the term "clump" or "cluster"—*hitokatamari* or, simply, *katamari*—is repeated several places in the story in reference to both the motley crowd of

people in the marketplace and the appearance of the boy as a clod or clump of rags, boils, pus, and lice. The shared reference serves to emphasize the affinity of the crowd with the boy.

32. *"Ten wa motoyori osoreru koto wo shirazu"*: "As for what Heaven might have to say — they cared not a whit." Heaven, or *ten,* is used here not in the religious or astronomical sense, but to refer to the imperial institution, *tennō. "Torishimari kisoku wa sono suji de mo ano suji de mo kuso wo kurae"*: "Why give a damn about rules and regulations, anyway? Or care about whomever it was who claimed the right to enforce them? If it is not one official line, then surely it is another. To hell with them all" (II, 471). This impertinence is directed at either the postwar Japanese government or the Allied Occupation, or both *(sono suji de mo ano suji de mo)* or at any regulating force that attempts to impose order on the marketplace.

33. *"Hitokuchi in shōbu no kimaru kedamono no torihiki"* (II, 467).

34. *Furyōji* is a delinquent child or children.

35. *Ippiki ōkami,* a lone wolf, is a term frequently used to describe a masterless samurai, social loner, or maverick-type character in popular Japanese culture.

36. Messianic references to the boy are first introduced when *watashi* considers him "the progenitor of a new race" *(shuzoku no senzo;* II, 475). He further wonders if the boy possesses qualities — his identification with the poor and the lawless, for example — that are not like those of a messiah *(meshiya* — also a play on the homophonic word for an inexpensive eatery, *meshiya?)* or make him related to the divine *(zongai kami to enko no fukai mono). Watashi* then proceeds to refer to him as the "Son of Man" *(hito no ko;* II, 475) and Jesus, but not as the Christ at this point. Of course, *hito no ko* is polysemous. It can also mean somebody's/nobody's child, a reference to a child's ambiguous or illegitimate origin. Note that the boy is never referred to in the story as the "Son of God" *(kami no ko).*

Other references to the New Testament and the life of Jesus are (1) the parable of the lost generation of swine *(buta no ei;* II, 478) from Matthew 8:31, (2) the extrabiblical account of Veronica's veil (II, 480), and (3) the final allusions to a stable and to Jesus' temptation and forty days of wandering in the desert. Although never a follower of Christianity, Ishikawa took a lively interest in Catholicism and its influence on French literature, especially the poetry of Paul Claudel (1868-1955) and the biting satire of Gide's *Les caves du Vatican,* the story of a false pope, which Ishikawa translated into Japanese in 1928.

37. For a discussion of *mitate,* see Tyler, "The Art and Act of Reflexivity in *The Bodhisattva,*" pp. 148-152.

38. *Shushigaku,* the study of the thought of Chu Hsi, or Neo-Confucianism, was the orthodox philosophy of the Tokugawa Shogunate as propagated by the Hayashi School. Dazai Shundai, "together with Hattori Nankaku . . . was considered one of Ogyū Sorai's most brilliant students. In contrast to the more literary Nankaku, Shundai excelled in the field of political economy. In his *Keizairoku* [Discussions of Economics; 1729] he emphasized the important role that economic affairs play both in public and private life. . . . He later grew critical of Sorai's scholarship, and taking up the question of individual morality that Sorai had ignored, he advocated that one's expression of morals should be controlled by the principles of *rei,* or external etiquette, regardless of one's inner feelings." Ōnishi Harutaka, "Dazai Shundai," in *Kodansha Encyclopedia of Japan* (1983), vol. 2, p. 80. "As the Sinologist par excellence of his time, [Ogyū Sorai] communicated a love of all things Chinese to his disciples and perhaps also a touch of intellectual snobbery, which made the most of his own acknowledged mastery of the Sinological sphere, while deprecating the importance of things Japanese. It is this attitude which carried over to his leading disciple, Dazai Shundai, a thorough-going Sinophile, who represents the highwater mark of Chinese influence on Tokugawa thought." Tsunoda Ryusaku, William Theodore de Bary, and Donald Keene, comps., *Sources of Japanese Tradition* (New York: Columbia University Press, 1958), p. 424. Hattori Nankaku's "greatest achievement lies in the mood he established for the popularity of Chinese verse in mid-Edo." His *Tōshisen kokujikai* (Selected T'ang Poems with Japanese Annotation) "was a bestseller in its day." See Mori Tadashige, *Wakan shika sakka jiten* (Tokyo: Mizuho shuppan, 1972), p. 670.

39. "*Kunshi-koku*" is a nation or land of *kun-tzu,* or gentlemen trained in the Confucian classics. (Note that *kunshi-koku* is not to be confused with *kunshu-koku,* or monarchy, although a Confucian state may also be monarchical or imperial.) The tone of this passage — "*zenseiki kara ikinokori no, rei no kunshi-koku no tami to iu tsuratsuki wa hitori mo miatarazu*" (II, 470) — is sarcastic.

40. "*Zanketsu,*" a "remaining absence," is not a term found in most dictionaries but the *kanji* and their meaning are readily comprehensible to the average Japanese. See Glossary.

41. "*Kagū no kabe no yabure wo tsukurou ni wa chōdo yoi*" (II, 477).

42. For more on *seishin no undō,* see Tyler, "The Agitated Spirit," pp. 16-17.

43. "*Teki wa Iesu de aru*" (II, 476).

44. "*Tada no shiroi kami de shika nai tokoro no, usui perapera shita mono de aru. Watashi wa kono usui hakushi wo totte ōkami no sòga to tatakawanate wa naranai*" (II, 479).

45. *Kami hito'e,* only a shade of difference; literally, the thickness of a single sheet

of paper. This refers to a situation in which the line between a dichotomy such as life and death, good and evil, sanity and insanity is no more than a hair's breadth. There is also a pun here on "the fine line between god *(kami)* and man *(hito)*."

46. *Watashi* sees in the face of the boy the pain and suffering that was etched upon Veronica's veil. Veronica's veil refers to the cloth with which a woman, often called Veronica, wiped the sweat- and blood-stained brow of Jesus as he struggled with the cross on the road to Calvary. The veil retained the imprint of his face, and as a holy relic, it is enshrined at St. Peter's Church in Rome. As an example of stigmata, moreover, it is thought to bleed or weep from the memory of Christ's suffering.

47. The immediate postwar years saw a sudden explosion in the publication and popularity of erotic literature because of the easing of prewar morals restrictions and the chaotic state of the times. The most representative of these works is Tamura Taijirō's *Nikutai no mon* (Gateway to the Flesh; 1947). For a cogent discussion of this "landmark in postwar popular culture," see J. Victor Koschmann, "The Japanese Communist Party and the Debate over Literary Strategy under the Allied Occupation of Japan," in *Legacies and Ambiguities,* ed. Ernestine Schlant and Thomas Rimer, pp. 177–178.

48. The key words indicative of the compression and abstraction in this passage are *"kannō no tobari"* (curtains of possibility) and *"deban"* (one's turn). They set the stage, so to speak, for the theatrical metaphor that is implied and then developed by the barker's announcement. Because of the similarity between Ishikawa's terminology and James Scott's paradigm from *Domination and the Arts of Resistance,* one is tempted to describe this scene as a case of the "offstage" or hidden transcript of Japanese history now going public and assuming center stage (see notes 25, 26, and 31 to the essay on "Moon Gems").

One might also read "The Legend" and "Ruins" as examples par excellence of what Victor Koschmann calls the "dialectical modernism . . . occupying centerstage during the early postwar years" as advanced by writers associated with the postwar journal *Kindai bungaku* (see Koschmann, "Debate over Literary Strategy").

> The *Kindai Bungaku* writers seemed to agree that tasks such as rooting out the emperor system through democratic revolution and fully airing the problem of war responsibility had to be carried out internally, in the minds of individuals, as well as externally in the political arena. This conviction led them to the ideal of modernity, which was intimately associated with the development of autonomous subjectivity *(shutaisei),* and also to the conception of European culture as the exemplar of that modernity. (p. 182)

While Ishikawa was not a member of the *Kindai bungaku* group, many of his ideas resonate with the thinking of this progressive, left-wing group that advocated social revolution but was not prepared to submit to the political orthodoxy of the Japanese Communist Party (ibid., p. 164). One may even wish to read *watashi's* cosmic wrestling match with the wild child as a metaphor for the dialectic struggle of intellect versus flesh, although in this case it is probably not to be construed as the struggle between a European-style identity and a native one.

49. *"Kyojaku de atta mukashi no sensei toshite kakurete ita mono ga ima yōyaku gensei toshite arawareta"* (II, 329).

50. Although a "barker" is not introduced per se, and no quotation brackets are included to indicate direct speech, both the context and the inclusion of honorifics and verbals in the distal *masu* form set this passage off as a voice addressing an audience about the wonders of the "Introduction of Time." The introduction of time into Japanese life has now made it possible for the appearance of the "manifest power or spirit" of the new, postwar age.

51. *"Sore hodo taisetsu na konnichi to iu mono ga jitsu ni wa tsui horobubeki kono yo no jikan de atta"* (II, 471).

52. *"Manuke no"* is used typically as a pejorative adjective meaning "idiotic" or, literally, "missing a proper interval, beat, or space." Given the context here of the sudden foreclosure of the possibility of change, it may also have the sense of "hole through which the interval of change slips in or away."

53. See, for example, Suzuki Sadami, "Yakeato no Iesu," in *Nihon bungei kanshō jiten*, vol. 14, pp. 142-143.

> "The Jesus of the Ruins" takes up the time when the initial anarchical phase of the immediate postwar era was coming to an end. It is based on the idea or philosophy of possibility as the starting point for a world in which human desire is revealed in its most raw and naked state. As the work unfolds, the writer weaves into the story his bitter awareness that the idea has ended only as an idea. It has proven to be a mere possibility. . . . The work combines the portrait of a filthy youth covered in boils with that of an intellectual who loves all that is elegant and refined. Through their brief encounter, the motif of the salvation of the world is introduced. It dissipates like a single beam emanating from a phantom light.

54. Tyler, "The Art and Act of Reflexivity in *The Bodhisattva*," pp. 144, 165.

55. I am indebted to Frank Joseph Shulman, formerly Librarian, East Asian Collec-

tion, McKeldin Library, for providing me with a photocopy of the relevant pages from the original monograph and CCD file copy of the anthology of short stories that was submitted by the publisher, Chūō kōronsha, for censorship review. Pencil marks appear in the text where they bracket and cross out three passages (pp. 169, 179, and 182) and note "delete" in English at the top of each passage. There is also the insertion of the characters for *"tabako"* on p. 179 to replace the American brand name, Lucky Strikes. The colophon gives the dates of printing and distribution as November 15 and November 20, 1946, respectively. The date of censorship review is January 14, 1947.

Marlene Mayo states that "The Legend" was "cut for magazine publication in *Chūō kōron,* March 1946, and subsequently deleted in full, apparently by his publisher, from a book by the same title at the end of the year." At the same time, she footnotes Donald Keene to the effect that "Ishikawa's 'Golden Legend' made it into print [at the time of magazine publication in March], unscathed, but was omitted from the November anthology when the censors subsequently decided it was derogatory to the occupation (*Dawn to the West,* 967)." In the same footnote, Mayo also cites Jay Rubin as giving a third account: "Rubin says that lines at the end, which depicted a Japanese woman running down the street toward a tall, black soldier, were chopped off; he also attributes the latter omission of the entire story from the anthology to a decision made by the publishers, possibly in protest against the previous censorship ('From Wholesomeness to Decadance,' 92)." See Marlene J. Mayo, "Literary Reorientation of Occupied Japan: Incidents of Civil Censorship," in *Legacies and Ambiguities,* ed. Ernestine Schlant and Thomas Rimer, pp. 144, 157, n. 34.

A review of the magazine text reveals, however, that *Ōgon densetsu* appeared uncensored in the March 1946 issue of *Chūō kōron* magazine (printed February 23 and put on sale March 1; vol. 61, no. 3, pp. 95–100). Therefore, only the text in the book version of *Ōgon densetsu* ran afoul the Occupation's censor.

Note also that the two or three discrepancies that exist between the text of the March 1946 magazine story and the text that appears in the most recent *Complete Works of Ishikawa Jun* are only minor changes in grammar, typography, or punctuation. These changes probably date from the time of publication of the first edition of the *Ishikawa Jun zenshū* in 1961.

56. For example, Suzuki Sadami, principal editor of the definitive edition of the *Complete Works of Ishikawa Jun* in nineteen volumes, notes in his editorial comments on "The Legend" that "the passage about the black soldier who appears at the end of the work touched on an Occupation interdiction, and the title work did not see inclusion" (II, 764).

While policies internal to the American forces stationed in Japan were segregation-ist, and Japanese were quick to recognize the social inequalities practiced among Americans, the logic of why a "black" soldier would be objectionable to the censor for reasons other than fraternization is unclear. Admittedly, in 1946 the term "black" had not come into American English usage as acceptable nomenclature for addressing African (or then, Negro) Americans. But there is nothing derogatory in tone about the language used in Japanese to depict the soldier. To the contrary, he is twice referred to by the more respectful term for soldier, *heishi*, rather than *heitai*. Fraterni-zation with Japanese nationals was actively prohibited early in the occupation, and it appears the censor attempts to bring reality into conformity with official policy by excising an example of cross-cultural interaction.

The same can be said concerning the reference to the availability of white rice at "the Chinaman's shop across the way" — *"sorya mukōgawa no o-mise wa Chūgoku-san desu kara heiki nan deshō"* (CCD file copy, p. 169). Yokohama had a Chinatown from early in its history as a port; as citizens of an occupation ally, Chinese living in Yoko-hama may have been treated more liberally during the occupation, or at least were perceived as receiving preferential treatment by Japanese such as the businesswoman in this passage. Hence the touch of annoyance or jealousy, and even moral rectitude, to her remarks. Note that *"Chūgoku-san"* in this passage is changed in the later *zenshū* editions to read *"Shina-san"* (printed in *katakana;* in the March 1946 magazine text, *Shina-san* is used but written in *kanji*). Perhaps as a result of Japan's defeat in the war and a shift in postwar reference to China as *Chūgoku* rather than *Shina,* Ishikawa or his publisher switched to the use of *Chūgoku-san.* Given the wartime generation to which the woman belongs, however, *Shina-san* is probably more in character.

57. Fraternization was "a taboo listed in the key logs but not in the Press Code." See Mayo, "Literary Reorientation in Occupied Japan," p. 142.

On *The Raptor*

1. "Tabako," in *Dai-Nihon hyakka jiten: japonika* (Encyclopedia Japonica) (Tokyo: Shōgakkan, 1973), vol. 11, pp. 617-628.

2. The opening sentence not only serves to identify and describe the physical setting of the canal but also becomes a metaphor for the act of composition, as Ishikawa takes up his pen and begins writing his narrative.

3. For more on Ishikawa's interest in the Symbolists, see his essay *Kyōka hyakki yakyō,*

in *Isai seigen* (XIII, 439-453), in which he draws a tentative parallel between the Tenmei *kyōka* movement and French symbolism. See also Izawa Yoshio, *Ishikawa Jun* (Tokyo: Yayoi shobō, 1961), pp. 7-12, 39-48, 101-118; Jinzai Kiyoshi, "Ishikawa Jun to Vararei," *Bungakkai*, vol. 5, no. 1 (January 1951): 92-96; and Noguchi, *Ishikawa Jun ron*, pp. 66-82, 92-98. Izawa has been the chief exponent for treating Ishikawa's works as symbolist novels. Izawa, *Ishikawa Jun no shōsetsu*, pp. 157-164. Donald Keene also advances a similar point of view in Keene, *Dawn to the West*, vol. 1, pp. 1100-1101.

4. Abe sought Ishikawa's acquaintance in 1948. For a conversation between the two writers, see Abe Kōbō and Ishikawa Jun, "Ishikawa Jun no hito to bungaku," in Ishikawa, *Isai taidan*, pp. 47-56. For more on their shared literary orientation, see Sekii Mitsuo, "Abe Kōbō to Ishikawa Jun—sōseiki shinwa no hōhō ni tsuite," *Kokubungaku: kaishaku to kanshō*, vol. 36, no. 1 (January 1971): 47-52.

5. "Red Purge," *reddo-pāji* (IV, 363) refers to an Occupation crackdown on the Japanese Communist Party and suspected fellow travelers carried out between May and December 1950. In the initial phase of the purge, all members of the JCP's central committee and the editorial board of the *Akahata* (Red Flag) newspaper were removed from their posts. Subsequently, JCP members and those suspected of membership were banned from newspapers, broadcasting, communications, motion pictures, and the coal and steel industries. Over ten thousand people were dismissed from the private sector and nearly two thousand from teaching or government service. The purge greatly reduced the influence of the JCP in the postwar labor movement. See "Red Purge," in *Kodansha Encyclopedia of Japan* (1983), vol. 6, p. 285.

6. "Reverse course" is a term used to describe a shift in Occupation policy away from its initial orientation of demilitarization, disestablishment of the prewar *zaibatsu*-controlled economy, and democratization in 1945-1946 to one of actively rebuilding Japan as a bulwark in Asia, especially after the "loss of China" to communism in 1949 and the outbreak of the Korean War in 1950. See "Occupation," in *Kodansha Encyclopedia of Japan* (1983), vol. 6, pp. 51-55. "1947 [is] often described as [the year] in which American policy began a 'reverse course,' a radical shift from reformist policies aimed at destroying Japanese militarism to conservative policies with the object of avoiding a possible communist takeover" (p. 53). "A group of largely conservative but not dogmatic leaders thus supplanted the militarists, backed many of the American reforms, and won substantial electoral support for their policies of stabilization and democratization. As time went on, these conservatives, with strong American support, began to crack down on labor protest and undo some of the more visionary plans for changes in the industrial system. . . . Japan in 1952 was

a very different nation from what it had been in 1945. Whether even more change could have occurred without the alleged 'reverse course' is an open question that will require further investigation" (p. 55). Antigovernment and anti-American anger over the United States-Japan Security Treaty, which went into effect on April 28, 1952, exploded when permission to hold a May Day labor rally in front of the Imperial Palace was denied. "After the official dispersal of the rally in [nearby] Hibiya Park, about 300 demonstrators (mainly students) clashed with police . . . [who] were were armed with pistols and tear gas; the students, who were joined by several thousand participants from the rally, retaliated with sticks, poles and stones." See "May Day Incident," in *Kodansha Encyclopedia of Japan* (1983), vol. 5, p. 142.

7. Ishikawa published seven of these "stories with a twist, or *ochi,*" on the lives of literary and historical figures such as Li Po, Coxinga, Kiyomori, and Narihara between May 1949 and November 1956; the parodies of juvenilia *(Heidi, The Little Prince)* appeared at various times from 1951 to 1955.

8. The first character of "Isai," *i,* refers to a synonym for *kyōka,* namely, *ikyoku.* The second character, *sai,* meaning "desk or study," is commonly used in writers' pen names. My interpretation of Ishikawa's *gagō,* or nom de plume, is based on an interview with Ishikawa (May 1974). Some interpret it as "the barbarian in his study," a plausible reading and interpretation, since the usual meaning for the first character is "barbarian." See note 1 in the essay on "Mars' Song" for information on Alain and his propos.

Taka was not, however, Ishikawa's first novel written in the third person. *Hakubyō* (see note 35 in the essay on "Moon Gems") uses omniscient narration. The *watashi* parodies dominate the war and immediate postwar years, however.

9. While emphasizing the allegorical nature of the novel, Suzuki Sadami also suggests that Tokyo and the Sumida River are possible models for its landscape. "No locale is specified, but the setting appears to be downtown Tokyo, and the time, the period of chaos following the war. One imagines that the canal is the Sumida River. The center of the city is the Ginza and Nihonbashi." Suzuki Sadami, *"Taka,"* in *Nihon bungei kanshō jiten* (Tokyo: Gyōsei, 1987), vol. 15, pp. 117-126.

10. Edward Fowler introduces the concept of a diffuse, reporting persona in his discussion of narrative voice in the *shi-shōsetsu,* or I-novel, in his *Rhetoric of Confession* (Berkeley: University of California Press, 1988). While Ishikawa is an altogether different writer from the I-novelists of Japanese naturalism — indeed he is the very antithesis of them — I am enlarging upon Fowler's treatment of persona as the "roving eye;" and "I am a camera" is taken from the title of Christopher Isherwood's

work. Finally, I am intrigued by the similarities that can be drawn between the visuality found in Ishikawa's novels and the cinematographic techniques employed in the films of Kurosawa Akira. See, for example, note 30 to the essay on "The Legend of Gold" and "The Jesus of the Ruins" in reference to the opening shots of the film *Nora inu*. While Kurosawa (1910-1992) was Ishikawa's junior in age, both men grew up in the liberal atmosphere of Taishō period Tokyo and were exposed to the *"ana-boru"* (*ana*rchism versus *bol*shevism) controversy in Japanese intellectual circles in the 1920s. Threading their way through the thicket of political ideologies on the left, they came to identify with the ideas advanced by the Russian anarchist Piotr Kropotkin (1842-1921) on anarchy as a state of nature and mutual dependence. In his youth Ishikawa was attracted to the anarchist writings of Kropotkin, Mikhail Bakunin, and Nikolai Bukharin. See Tyler, "The Agitated Spirit," pp. 47-54. Kurosawa's homage to the Kropotkin-like figure of V. H. Arseniev (1872-1930), author and narrator of the popular Russian novel *Dersu Uzala* (see *Dersu the Trapper*, trans. Malcolm Burr [New York: E. P. Dutton, 1941]), is to be found in Kurosawa's film of 1975 of the same title. It is my opinion that the anti-ideological bias of anarchism has played an important part—along with Christian thinking—in shaping the concept of intellectual independence and the role of the liberal *(jiyūshugisha)* intellectual critic in Japan.

11. In *Mori Ōgai* (1941) and *Bungaku taigai* (1942), Ishikawa argues that prose is the unique setting for the advancement and play of the human spirit; it is through the act of constructing narrative, and thinking beyond the status quo, "even if by only one ten millionth of a second divided into still more infinitesimal units" (XII, 194), that intellectual progress is achieved. Dissatisfaction with language and its limits and the desire to make words into a more expansive and effective medium are recurring themes in Ishikawa's works. It is enunciated in his novel *Fugen* (see Ishikawa, *The Bodhisattva*, p. 26), and it is reiterated here in Kunisuke's fascination with the bell-like clarity and vigor of Futurese. Ishikawa returns to this theme in his novel *Hakutōgin* (Lays from the White-Haired One; 1957). The eccentric character Kozue Santarō, a polyglot who speaks eighteen languages, tells us that whatever is wrong with his life "is the whole damned fault of [the] Japanese [language]." The language, he says, is too nebulous, tending to the worst hodgepodging of ideas. It is anathema "for speaking of credos and living. It takes the backbone out of every idea" (V, 450).

Mori Ōgai is also Ishikawa's critical study of the works of the Meiji period writer. See note 38 in the essay on "Moon Gems." Ishikawa's use of the terms "night thoughts" and "unknown worlds" appeared first in this critical study (XII, 159-161).

For an English translation of *Tsuina,* see *Monumenta Nipponica,* vol. 26, no. 1 (Spring 1971): 133-138.

12. Mori Rintarō, *Ōgai senshū,* ed. Ishikawa Jun (Tokyo: Iwanami shoten, 1979), vol. 4, pp. 5-85.

13. Edgar Allan Poe, "The Devil in the Belfry," in *Collected Works of Edgar Allan Poe* (Cambridge: Harvard University Belknap Press, 1978), vol. 2, pp. 362-375. A satirical romp on the punctiliousness of Philadelphians, the story is set in an imaginary place — "the Dutch borough of *Vondervotteimittis*" — in which everyone is obsessed with keeping time and knowing what the hour is. The town is dominated by its clock tower, which, kept running in perfect order, has its citizens operating in lockstep punctuality. But one day at "only three minutes to noon . . . a very diminutive foreign-looking young man" (p. 370) appears over the horizon. He climbs to the belfry, and by causing the clock to strike an unprecedented thirteenth hour, he throws the town into a state of chaos from which it never recovers.

Setsuzō refers in this passage to Poe's story via a literal translation of the title, *Shōrō ni okeru akuma;* in October 1912 Ōgai published his translation of the Poe short story under the title *Jūsanji,* "Thirteen o'Clock." Setsuzō's story of a place called "Newspaperland" is clearly inspired by Poe's use of satire (such as naming the town "Wonder-What-Time-It-Is"); and in it Ōgai satirizes the writers of the naturalistic I-novel, who, unable to "write of things as they are . . . write about themselves." There is no record whether Ishikawa had read Poe's "Devil in the Belfry," but as a youth he was an inveterate reader of Ōgai's translations from Western literature. Although the Poe story does not appear to be a direct source of inspiration for *The Raptor,* it is obvious Ishikawa was inspired by the possibilities of weaving a tale constructed around play on a key word like "Vondervotteimittis," "Newspaperland" or "Peace." There are, as well, Setsuzō's references to newspapers, a coup d'état, and so forth, for which direct linkage can be established.

14. There is no ready equivalent in English for the word *"kiai."* It can be variously translated as "cheering on," "energy," "tension," but what is implied is a meeting and mutual challenging of *ki* (Chn: *ch'i*). Because the word figures prominently in *The Raptor,* I have pointedly used the word "synergy" (which was probably not in wide use in American English in the 1950s, however) not only to translate the term, but to call attention to it in the text. Ishikawa also uses the word in the novella *Shion monogatari* (1956), which was translated by Donald Keene as *Asters.* See Keene, *The Old Woman, the Wife and the Archer,* pp. 119-172. According to Keene, finding an appropriate translation for *"kiai"* posed a problem (interview of July 17, 1974); Ishi-

kawa also mentions Keene's comment on the difficulty of rendering it into English in "Gadan keiroku ni tsuite," in *Isai yūgi* (XIV, 462).

15. This is one of several theses advanced by Susan Napier in *The Fantastic in Modern Japanese Literature* (London and New York: Routledge, 1996), pp. 56-57. Napier's principal thesis is that "fantasy exists as a counter-discourse to the modern" in modern Japanese literature (p. 8). Moreover, she is concerned with how women have been presented as alien or dystopian in fantastic novels written since the end of World War II. "Women in prewar texts are generally seen as an alternative to modernity but in postwar literature they become a threatening part of modernity itself" (p. 16). Napier discusses Ishikawa novels (pp. 154-158) and touches briefly on *Taka* (pp. 155, 197).

16. Suzuki Sadami discusses the phenomenon of the "man-woman," or *otoko-onna*, in *Modan toshi no hyōgen—jikō, gensō, josei* (Tokyo: Hakujisha, 1992), pp. 26, 186-190. He reports the phenomenon of the woman dressed in culottes, carrying a whip, and acting the equal of a man began appearing in Japanese literature in the 1920s. He cites Kishida Kunio's *Muchi no narasu onna* (The Woman Who Cracks the Whip; 1931-1932) as an example. Napier also discusses "androgynous characters" and "the Taishō fascination with identity ambivalence." Napier, *The Fantastic in Modern Japanese Literature*, p. 119.

17. The relevant essays are "Kenryoku ni tsuite" (On Authority), in *Isai hitsudan* (XIII, 80-103; February 1951); "Geijutsuka no eien no teki" (The Artist's Eternal Enemy), "Utau ashita no tame ni" *(Pour les lendemains qui chantent),* and "Kakumei to wa nani ka" (What Is Revolution?), in *Isai rigen* (XIII, 249-263, 264-293, 321-335; March, April, and August 1952). For more on these essays, see Tyler, "The Agitated Spirit," pp. 201-202, 213.

18. See note 4 to this essay. One scholar notes Ishikawa's preface anticipates *The Raptor* by nearly two years and suggests Ishikawa's remarks are more relevant to Ishikawa's yet-to-be-written novel than to Abe's anthology. See Miyoshi Yukio, "*Taka* wo megutte," *Nihon bungaku*, vol. 3, no. 5 (May 1954): 11.

19. Jean-Paul Sartre, "Les Mouches" (Act III, Scene 2), *Théâtre* (Paris: NCF, 1947), p. 114.

20. *"Mukōkishi"* (IV, 408, 415) is literally, "the far shore." As in English, it can also suggest an otherworldly, yonder shore.

GLOSSARY

This glossary is not intended as an exhaustive list. It covers only key words, periods, titles, and names.

Abe Tomoji 阿部知二
aotaka 青鷹
Aratama 荒魂
ashita-go (also myōnichi-go) 明日語
ato あと・後・跡・痕・傷
bubun kyokuhitsu 舞文曲筆
Bungakkai 文学界
bungaku hiriki (-setsu) 文学非力
　［説］
Bungaku no konnichi 文学の今日
Bungaku taigai 文学大概
bungei fukkō 文芸復興
bunka no yōgo (-ron) 文化の擁護
　［論］
bunjin 文人
burai-ha 無頼派
chimata 巷
Danchōtei nichijō 断腸亭日乗
Dan Tokusaburō 談徳三郎
Daraku-ron 堕落論
Dazai Osamu 太宰治
Dazai Shundai 太宰春台
Ebina Yūji 海老名雄二
Edo, Edokko, Edo ryūgaku 江戸、
　江戸っ子、江戸留学
Fugen 普賢
Funabashi Seiichi 船橋聖一
furyōji 不良児
fūshi 風刺、諷刺
ga 雅
gensei, genzai no yo 現勢、現在の
世
gūdan renshi 藕断連絲
Gūka 藕花
haikai-ka 俳諧化
haisen chokugo 敗戦直後
haki-daore, ki-daore, kui-daore 履き
　倒れ、着倒れ、食い倒れ
Hakubyō 白猫
Hakutōgin 白頭吟
hansen shisō 反戦思想
han-shizenshugi-sha 反自然主義者
Hatanaka Kansai 畠中寛斎
Hattori Nankaku 服部南郭
heishi, heitai 兵士、兵隊
Henkikan 偏奇館
hitsudan 筆談
ichiba 市場
ichioku, ichioku gyokusai, ichioku
　kokumin, ichioku isshin, ichioku
　sō-zange 一億、一億玉砕、一億
　国民、一億一心、一億総懺悔
Ienaga Saburō 家永三郎
"ikiyo ochiyo" 生きよ落ちよ
ikyoku 夷曲
ippiki ōkami 一匹狼
Isai 夷齋
Ishikawa Jun 石川淳
Ishikawa Jun zenshū 石川淳全集
"iza tate, Marusu, isamashiku" いざ起て、
　マルス、勇ましく
jishuku 自粛

jiyūshugi 自由主義

jōzetsu-tai 饒舌体

jūgonen sensō 十五年戦争

"junsui seishin no ipponyari da to, kore yori hayaku yaban no hō ni tsurete iku mono wa nai" 純粋精神の一本槍だと、これより速く野蠻のはうにつれて行くものはない

Kaijin 灰燼

kami hito'e 紙一重

Kaneko Mitsuharu 金子光晴

kanō, *Kanōsei no bungaku* 可能、可能性の文学

"Katte kuru zo to isamashiku" 勝って来るぞと勇ましく

Kawakami Tetsutarō 川上徹太郎

keigaku 経学

keijijōgaku 形而上学

kemu ni maku 煙に巻く

kiai 氣合い

kiken shisō 危険思想

Kindai bungaku 近代文学

kōdōshugi-sha 行動主義者

kokumin bungaku (-ron) 国民文学［論］

kunshi-koku 君子国

kunshu-koku 君主国

Kurahara Korehito 蔵原惟人

Kyōfūki 狂風記

kyōka 狂歌

Marusu no uta マルスの歌

Meigetsushu 明月珠

michi no sekai 未知の世界

mitate 見立て

Miyamoto Yuriko 宮本百合子

Mori Ōgai 森鷗外

mōshikane, mōshikane 申し兼ね・若うし金

Motoshima Hitoshi 本島等

mukō kishi 向こう岸

Nagai Kafū 永井荷風

Nihon bungaku hōkokukai 日本文学報国会

Nihon e no kaiki 日本への回帰

Ni-ni-roku jiken 二・二六事件

Oda Sakunosuke 織田作之助

Ōgon densetsu 黄金傳説

Ōgyu Sorai 荻生徂徠

Ōta Nanpo 大田南畝

Ōyama Ikuo 大山郁夫

Ozaki Hotsumi 尾崎秀実

Renshikan 連絲館

Roei no uta 露営の歌

Sakaguchi Ango 坂口安吾

sassōtaru tōjō 颯爽たる登場

Satomi Ton 里見弴

seijiteki gomakashi 政治的ゴマカシ

Seijiteki mukanshin 政治的無関心

seisaku, seisaku ni hōzuru 正朔、正朔に奉ずる

seishin no undō 精神の運動

Senchū ibun 戦中遺文

sengo 戦後

sennin 仙人

sensei 潜勢

Shifuku sennen 至福千年

shinbun-koku 新聞国

shin-gesakusha 新戯作者

shinkō geijutsu-ha 新興芸術派

shin-shakai-ha 新社会派

Shion monogatari 紫苑物語

shiru hito zo shiru 知る人ぞ知る

shisō 思想

Shokusanjin 蜀山人

shushigaku 朱子学

Sugihara Chiune 杉原千畝

sukima 隙間
tabako 煙草、たばこ
t'ai-su nei-ching 太素内景
Taka 鷹
Tanizaki Jun'ichirō 谷崎潤一郎
teikō no bungaku 抵抗の文学
Tenmei 天明
tōkai-buri, tōkai suru 韜晦ぶり、韜晦する
Tosaka Jun 戸坂潤
Tsuina 追儺
tsumi no kannen 罪の観念
"Tsunbo no mane wo suru mo ii ga, do wo sugosu to inochi ni kakawaru" 聾の真似をするもいいが、度を過すといのちにかかはる
Watanabe Kazan 渡邊崋山
yabure-ana 破れ穴
yake-ana 燒穴
yakeato 焼け跡、焼け後、焼け痕 焼け傷、焼けあと

Yakeato no Iesu 燒跡のイエス
yakedo 火傷
yaki'in 焼き印
yami'ichi 闇市
Yanagi Muneyoshi 柳宗悦
Yanase Masamu 柳瀬正夢
"yo no naka wa itsu mo tsukiyo ni kome no meshi sate mata mō-shikane no hoshisa yo" 世の中はいつも月夜に米のめしさてまたまをしかねのほしさよ
yoru no shisō 夜の思想
Yoshisada-ki (also *Giteiki*) 義貞記
Yüan Hung-tao 袁宏道
zanketsu 殘缺・残欠
zeitaku wa teki 贅沢は敵
Zenrin bunka ni tsuite 善隣文化について
zetsubō kara no shuppatsu 絶望からの出発
zoku 俗
zokuka 俗化

SELECT BIBLIOGRAPHY

Abe Kōbō. "Ishikawa-san no koto." *Gendai Nihon bungaku zenshū geppō,* no. 17 (September 1954): 2-3. Tokyo: Chikuma shobō, 1954.

———. "Kaisetsu." In *Nihon no bungaku (60): Ishikawa Jun,* 514-524. Tokyo: Chūō kōronsha, 1967.

Abe Kōbō and Ishikawa Jun. "Ishikawa Jun no hito to bungaku." *Nihon no bungaku furoku,* no. 43 (August 1967): 1-9. Tokyo: Chūō kōronsha, 1967. Reprinted in Ishikawa Jun, *Isai zadan,* 47-56.

Abe Kōbō, Ishikawa Jun, Kawabata Yasunari, and Mishima Yukio. "Chūgoku bunka daikakumei ni kanshi, gakumon geijutsu no jiritsusei wo yōgo suru apīru" (text of joint statement of February 28, 1967). *Chūō kōron,* vol. 82, no. 6 (May 1967): 321.

———. "Wareware wa naze seimei wo dashita ka — geijutsu wa seiji no dōgu ka." *Chūō kōron,* vol. 82, no. 6 (May 1967): 318-327.

Andō Hajime. "Ishikawa Jun ron." *Petite Revue — Genshisha,* vol. 1, nos. 2-7 (October 1972-January 1975).

Aoyagi Tatsuo. *Ishikawa Jun no bungaku.* Tokyo: Kasama shoin, 1978.

Bamba Nobuya and John F. Howes. *Pacifism in Japan — the Christian and Socialist Traditions.* Kyoto: Minerva Press, 1978.

Booth, Wayne C. *A Rhetoric of Irony.* Chicago: University of Chicago Press, 1974.

Brock, Peter. *A Brief History of Pacifism from Jesus to Tolstoy.* Toronto: University of Syracuse Press, 1992.

———. *Twentieth-Century Pacifism.* New York: Van Nostrand Rheinhold, 1970.

Chang, Iris. *The Rape of Nanking.* New York: Basic Books, 1997.

Chartier, Émile [Alain]. *Mars; ou la guerre jugée.* Paris: NRF Gallimard, 1921.

———. *Système des beaux-arts.* Paris: NRF Gallimard, 1920.

Cipris, Zeijko. "Radiant Carnage: Japanese Writers on the War against China." Ph.D. dissertation, Columbia University, 1994.

Craig, Gordon A. "Good Germans." *The New York Review of Books,* vol. 39, no. 21 (December 17, 1992): 38-44.

Dōshisha daigaku jinbun kagaku kenkyūjo. *Senjika teikō no kenkyū—Kirisutokyōsha, jiyūshugisha no ba'ai.* Tokyo: Misuzu shobō, 1968. 2 vols.

Dyck, Harvey L. *The Pacifist Impulse in Historical Perspective.* Toronto: University of Toronto Press, 1996.

Field, Norma. *In The Realm of a Dying Emperor.* New York: Pantheon, 1991.

Fisher, David J. *Romain Rolland and the Politics of Intellectual Engagement.* Berkeley: University of California Press, 1988.

Fletcher, William M. *The Search for a New Order: Intellectuals and Fascism in Prewar Japan.* Chapel Hill: University of North Carolina, 1982.

Fowler, Edward. *The Rhetoric of Confession.* Berkeley: University of California Press, 1988.

Fu, Poshek. *Passivity, Resistance and Collaboration: Intellectual Choices in Occupied Shanghai, 1937-1945.* Stanford: Stanford University Press, 1993.

Gluck, Carol. "The 'Long Postwar.'" In *Legacies and Ambiguities,* edited by Schlant and Rimer. Washington, D.C.: Woodrow Wilson Center, 1991.

Havens, Thomas. *Valley of Darkness.* New York: W. W. Norton and Company, 1978.

Hirai, Atsuko. *Individualism and Socialism: The Life and Thought of Kawai Eijirō.* Cambridge: Council on East Asian Studies, Harvard University, 1986.

Hirano, Ken. "Nihon bungaku hōkokukai no seiritsu." *Bungaku,* vol. 29 (May 1961): 1-8.

———. *Shōwa bungaku-shi.* Tokyo: Chikuma sōsho, 1963.

Honda Shūgo. "Ishikawa Jun no sassōtaru tōjō." In *Monogatari sengo bungakushi,* 75-79. Tokyo: Shinchōsha, 1960.

———. *(Sōhō) Senji sengo no senkōsha-tachi. Tokyo: Keisō* shobō, 1971.

———. "'Yakeato no Iesu' no shōgeki." In *Monogatari sengo bungakushi,* 80-84. Tokyo: Shinchōsha, 1960.

Ide Magoroku. *Nejikugi no gotoku—gaka Yanase Masamu no kiseki.* Tokyo: Iwanami shoten, 1996.

Ienaga Saburō. *The Pacific War: World War II and the Japanese, 1931-1945.* Translated by Frank Baldwin. New York: Pantheon Books, 1978.

Ikejima Shinpei, Ishikawa Jun, and Shimanaka Hōji. "Ishikawa Jun no maki." In *Bundan yomoyama banashi (jōkan),* edited by Nippon hōsō kyoku, 101-123. Tokyo: Seiabō, 1961.

Ishikawa Jun. *The Bodhisattva, or Samantabhadra.* Translated by William Jefferson Tyler. New York: Columbia University Press, 1990.

———. *Le Faucon.* Translated by Edwige de Chavanes. Paris: Éditions Philippe Picquier, 1990.

————. Isai zadan: Ishikawa Jun taidanshū. Tokyo: Chūō Kōronsha, 1977.

————. *Ishikawa Jun zenshū.* Edited by Suzuki Sadami. Tokyo: Chikuma shobò, 1989-91.

————. "Jésus dans les décombres." Translated by Edwige de Chavanes. In *Anthologie de nouvelles japonaises contemporaines,* 197-212. Paris: NRF Gallimard, 1987.

————. "La légende dorée." Translated by Jean-Jacques Tschudin. In *Les ailes, la grenade, les cheveux blancs et douze autres récits (1945-1960),* 65-77. Paris: Éditions Picquier, 1986.

"Ishikawa Jun-shi, tantan to shōgen — *Yojōhan fusuma no shitabari* saiban." *Asahi shimbun,* Tokyo morning edition, February 22, 1975, 3.

Isoda Kōichi. "Buraiha no hangyaku ni tsuite — dandeizumu shikō." *Entaku,* vol. 5, no. 9 (September 1965): 15-20.

————. "Ishikawa Jun ron-gisōsha no seiiki." In *Bungaku, kono kamenteki na mono,* 119-140. Tokyo: Keisō shobō, 1969.

————. "Kizoku no seishin to tōkai no kōzū." *Kokubungaku: kaishaku to kyōzai no kenkyū,* vol. 20, no. 6 (May 1975): 41-46.

Isogai Hideo. "Ishikawa Jun." In *Shōwa bungaku sakka kenkyū,* 181-209. Tokyo: Yanagihara shoten, 1955.

————. "Shōwa jūnendai no bungaku — kakōteki hōhō no bungaku wo chūshin ni." *Nihon bungaku,* vol. 12, no. 9 (September 1963): 1-13.

Iwamoto, Yoshio. "The Relationship between Literature and Politics in Japan, 1931-1945." Ph.D. dissertation, University of Michigan, 1964.

Izawa Yoshio. *Ishikawa Jun.* Tokyo: Yayoi shobō, 1961.

————. *Ishikawa Jun no shōsetsu.* Tokyo: Iwanami shoten, 1992.

Jameson, Fredric. *The Political Unconscious: Narrative as a Socially Symbolic Act.* Ithaca: Cornell University Press, 1981.

Jinzai Kiyoshi. "Ishikawa Jun to Varerei." *Bungakkai,* vol. 5, no. 1 (January 1951): 92-96.

————. "Kaisetsu." In Ishikawa Jun, *Yakeato no Iesu,* 194-198. Tokyo: Shinchō bunko, 1949.

Johnson, Chalmers. *An Instance of Treason — Ozaki Hotsumi and the Sorge Spy Ring.* Stanford: Stanford University Press, 1964.

Judt, Tony. *Past Imperfect: French Intellectuals, 1944-1956.* Berkeley: University of California Press, 1992.

Kanaya Osamu and Ishikawa Jun. "Sorai to hūmannitē." In *Nihon no shisō (12): Ogyū Sorai.* Tokyo: Chikuma shobō, 1970. Reprinted in Ishikawa Jun, *Isai zadan,* 151-168.

Kaneko Mitsuharu. *Shijin*. Translated by A. R. Davis. Sydney: University of Sydney East Asian Series, 1988.

Kasza, Gregory. *The State and the Mass Media in Japan, 1918-1945*. Berkeley: University of California Press, 1988.

Katō Kōichi. *Kosumosu no chie*. Tokyo: Chikuma shobō, 1994.

Katō Shūichi. *Form, Style, Tradition*. Berkeley: University of California Press, 1971.

———. "Kaisetsu-Ishikawa Jun shōron." In Ishikawa Jun, *Bungaku taigai*, 267-272. Tokyo: Kadokawa bunko, 1955.

Katō Shūichi and Ishikawa Jun. "Kotoba no chikara." *Tosho*, no. 364 (December 1979): 2-7.

Kawakami Tetsutarō. "Ishikawa Jun den." In *Gendai Nihon bungakkan (31): Ishikawa Jun*, 4-22. Tokyo: Bungei shunjū, 1969.

———. "Kaisetsu." In *Gendai Nihon bungakkan (31): Ishikawa Jun*, 464-471.

Keene, Dennis. *Love and Other Stories of Yokomitsu Riichi*. Tokyo: University of Tokyo Press, 1974.

———. *Yokomitsu Riichi, Modernist*. Tokyo: University of Tokyo Press, 1981.

Keene, Donald. "Asters." In Keene, *The Old Woman, the Wife and the Archer*, 119-172. New York: Viking Press, 1961.

———. *Dawn to the West*. New York: Holt, Rinehart and Winston, 1984. 2 vols.

———. "Japanese Writers and the Greater East Asian War." In *Landscapes and Portraits*. Tokyo: Kodansha International, 1971.

Kennedy, Malcolm. *A Short History of Japan*. New York: Mentor Books, 1963.

Kikuchi Shōichi, "Mitate gesakukō." In *Sengo no ronri*, 142-170. Tokyo: Yūzankaku, 1948.

Koschmann, J. Victor. "The Japanese Communist Party and the Debate over Literary Strategy under the Allied Occupation of Japan." In *Legacies and Ambiguities*, edited by Schlant and Rimer, 163-186. Washington, D.C.: Woodrow Wilson Center Press, 1991.

Kristof, Nicholas. "Today's History Lesson: What Rape of Nanjing?" *New York Times*, July 4, 1996, A4.

Levine, Hillel. *In Search of Sugihara*. New York: The Free Press, 1996.

Matsuo Akira. "Ishikawa Jun — meichi to tōkai." *Kokubungaku: kaishaku to kyōzai no kenkyū*, vol. 18, no. 15 (December 1973): 140-143.

Mayo, Marlene J. "Literary Reorientation of Occupied Japan: Incidents of Civil Censorship." In *Legacies and Ambiguities*, edited by Schlant and Rimer, 135-161. Washington, D.C.: Woodrow Wilson Center Press, 1991.

Minear, Richard. "Hiroshima, HIROSHIMA, 'Hiroshima.'" *Education about Asia*, vol. 1, no. 1 (February 1996): 32–38.

Mitchell, Richard. *Censorship in Imperial Japan*. Princeton: Princeton University Press, 1983.

———. *Thought Control in Prewar Japan*. Ithaca: Cornell University Press, 1976.

Miyoshi Yukio. "*Taka* wo megutte." *Nihon bungaku*, vol. 3, no. 5 (May 1954): 7–13.

Mizukami Isao. *Abe Tomoji kenkyū*. Tokyo: Sōbunsha shuppan, 1995.

Murō Saisei et al. "Akutagawa Ryūnosuke-shō keii." *Bungei shunjū*, vol. 15, no. 3 (March 1937): 425.

Napier, Susan. *The Fantastic in Modern Japanese Literature*. London and New York: Routledge, 1996.

Nobile, Philip, ed. *Judgement at the Smithsonian: The Bombing of Hiroshima and Nagasaki*. New York: Marlowe, 1995.

Noguchi Takehiko. "Ishikawa Jun bungaku no kakumei densetsu." In *Gendai Nihon bungaku taikei (76): Ishikawa Jun, Abe Kōbō, Ōe Kenzaburō*, 415–438. Tokyo: Chikuma shobō, 1969.

———. *Ishikawa Jun ron*. Tokyo: Chikuma shobō, 1969.

Oda Sakunosuke. *Teihon Oda Sakunosuke zenshū*. Tokyo: Bunsendō shoten, 1976.

Odagiri Hideo, ed. *Hakkin sakuhinshū*. Tokyo: Hokushindō, 1957. 2 vols.

Odagiri Hideo, Ishikawa Jun, Korin Nao, et al. "Shōwa jūnendai wo kiku." In *Bungakuteki tachiba*, 92–108. Tokyo: Keisō shobō, 1972. Reprinted in Ishikawa Jun, *Isai zadan*, 197–219, under the title "Muishiki no sentaku."

Ōe Kenzaburō. "Kaisetsu — wakai sedai no tame no kakū kōen." In *Shinchō Nihon bungaku (33): Ishikawa Jun shū*, 426–436. Tokyo: Shinchōsha, 1972.

Okamoto Takuji. "*Hakubyō* shiron." *Kokubungaku kenkyū* (Waseda daigaku kokubungakkai), vol. 29 (February 1973): 108–119.

———. "Sensōki no Ishikawa Jun." *Waseda daigaku kōtōgakuin kenkyū nenshi*, no. 16 (January 1972): 1–17.

Okuno Takeo. *Burai to itan*. Tokyo: Kokubunsha, 1973.

———. *Gendai bungaku no kijiku*. Tokyo: Tokuma shoten, 1967.

———. "Ishikawa Jun no shōsetsu no gainen — gendai bungaku no kijiku (13)." *Bungakkai*, vol. 20, no. 3 (March 1966): 151–159.

Ozaki Hotsumi. *Aijō wa furu hoshi no gotoku*. In *Ozaki Hotsumi zenshū*, vol. 4. Tokyo: Keisō shobō, 1979.

Rabson, Steve. *Righteous Cause or Tragic Folly: Changing Views of War in Modern Japanese Poetry*. Ann Arbor: Center for Japanese Studies, University of Michigan, 1998.

———. "Yosano Akiko on War: To Give One's Life or Not — a Question of Which War." *Journal of the Association of Teachers of Japanese,* vol. 25, no. 1 (April 1991): 44-74.

Reischauer, Edwin O. *The Japanese.* Cambridge: Harvard University Press. 1977.

Richie, Donald. *The Films of Akira Kurosawa.* Berkeley: University of California Press, 1970.

Rolland, Romain. *Above the Battle.* Translated by C. K. Ogden. Chicago: The Open Court Publishing Company, 1916.

———. *Au-dessus de la mêlée.* Paris: Librairie Paul Ollendorff, 1916.

Rubin, Jay. *Injurious to Public Morals: Writers and the Meiji State.* Seattle: University of Washington Press, 1984.

Sakaguchi Ango. *Sakaguchi Ango zenshū.* Tokyo: Chikuma shobō, 1990.

Sasaki Kiichi. *Ishikawa Jun — sakkaron.* Tokyo: Sōjusha, 1972.

Satō Yasumasa. "Sengo bungaku ni okeru kami to jitsuzon — 'Yakeato no Iesu' wo megutte." *Kokubungaku: kaishaku to kanshō,* vol. 35, no. 1 (January 1970): 39-45.

Schlant, Ernestine, and J. Thomas Rimer, eds., *Legacies and Ambiguities — Postwar Fiction and Culture in West Germany and Japan.* Washington, D.C.: Woodrow Wilson Center Press, 1991.

Scott, James A. *Domination and the Arts of Resistance: Hidden Transcripts.* New Haven: Yale University Press, 1990.

Seidensticker, Edward. *Kafū the Scribbler.* Stanford: Stanford University Press, 1965.

Sekii Mitsuo. "Abe Kōbō to Ishikawa Jun — sōseiki shinwa no hōhō ni tsuite." *Kokubungaku: kaishaku to kanshō,* vol. 36, no. 1 (January 1971): 47-52.

Shillony, Ben-Ami. *Politics and Culture in Wartime Japan.* Oxford: Clarendon Press, 1981.

———. *Revolt in Japan: The Young Officers and the February 26, 1936 Incident.* Princeton: Princeton University Press, 1973.

Shiozaki Fumio. "Senjika no Ishikawa Jun — *Watanabe Kazan* ni okeru fu no jōnen." *Kindai bungaku shiron* (Hiroshima daigaku kindai bungaku kenkyūkai), no. 15 (November 1976): 26-45.

Suzuki Sadami. "Ishikawa Jun no kiseki." *Subaru — Ishikawa Jun tsuitō kinengō,* (April 1988, rinji zōkan): 190-199.

———. *Modan toshi no hyōgen — jikō, gensō, josei.* Tokyo: Hakujisha, 1992.

———. *"Taka." Nihon bungei kanshō jiten,* vol. 15, 117-126. Tokyo: Gyōsei, 1987.

————. "'Yakeato no Iesu.'" *Nihon bungei kanshō jiten,* vol. 14, 139-148. Tokyo: Gyōsei, 1987.

Torrance, Robert M. "Modernism and Modernity." *Journal of the Association of Teachers of Japanese,* vol. 22, no. 2 (November 1988): 195-223.

Tyler, William J. "The Agitated Spirit: Life and Major Works of the Contemporary Japanese Novelist Ishikawa Jun." Ph.D. dissertation, Harvard University, 1981.

————. "The Art and Act of Reflexivity in *The Bodhisattva.*" In Ishikawa Jun, *The Bodhisattva, or Samantabhadra,* 139-174. New York: Columbia University Press, 1990.

————. "Honne to tatemae: Ishikawa Jun 'Marusu no uta' to Dazai Osamu *Seki-betsu.*" *Hikaku bungaku nenshi* (Waseda daigaku hikaku bungaku kenkyū-shitsu), no. 30 (March 1995): 126-142.

Unno Hiroshi, Kawamoto Saburo, and Suzuki Sadami, eds., *Modan toshi bungaku.* Tokyo: Heibonsha, 1989-1991. 10 vols.

Watanabe, Kiichirō. *Ishikawa Jun kenkyū.* Tokyo: Meiji shoin, 1987.

Wilkinson, James D. *The Intellectual Resistance in Europe.* Cambridge: Harvard University Press, 1981.

Yoshida Seiichi. "Ishikawa Jun to Tenmei *kyōka.*" In Yoshida Seiichi, *Gendai bungaku to koten,* 259-275. Tokyo: Shibundō, 1961.

ABOUT THE TRANSLATOR

William J. Tyler teaches modern Japanese literature at Ohio State University. He has also taught at Amherst College and the University of Pennsylvania. His translations include *The Psychological World of Natsume Sōseki* and *The Bodhisattva,* also by Ishikawa Jun.

JOHN LOCKE

JOHN LOCKE

BY

RICHARD I. AARON

THIRD EDITION

OXFORD
AT THE CLARENDON PRESS
1971

Oxford University Press, Ely House, London W. 1

GLASGOW NEW YORK TORONTO MELBOURNE WELLINGTON
CAPE TOWN SALISBURY IBADAN NAIROBI DAR ES SALAAM LUSAKA ADDIS ABABA
BOMBAY CALCUTTA MADRAS KARACHI LAHORE DACCA
KUALA LUMPUR SINGAPORE HONG KONG TOKYO

FIRST EDITION (*in the 'Leaders of Philosophy' Series*) 1937
SECOND EDITION 1955
THIRD EDITION 1971

PRINTED LITHOGRAPHICALLY IN GREAT BRITAIN
AT THE UNIVERSITY PRESS, OXFORD
BY VIVIAN RIDLER
PRINTER TO THE UNIVERSITY

TO
WILLIAM AND MARGARET
AARON

PREFACE TO THIRD EDITION

MANY changes have been made in this edition. The original text is little changed; some minor corrections were necessary, footnotes are added to acquaint the reader with post-1955 developments, and references have been brought up to date. But the main additions are the appendices, all of which are subsequent to the second edition, 1955, though the present Appendix I will be found in the 1963 and subsequent impressions of this book. Appendix II, written by Dr. Charlotte Johnston, clears up the confusion about the two issues of the first edition of the *Essay*. Appendix III, written jointly by Dr. Philip Walters and myself, discusses Locke's account of number, and in Appendix IV I examine Locke's rationalism and its limitations. Finally in Appendix V I give an account of some of the very considerable literature written since the last War on Locke's political philosophy. Additions have been made to the bibliography.

I am grateful to my wife for helping in the preparation of this new edition, to Dr. Charlotte Johnston and Dr. Philip Walters for their co-operation, to Dr. D. O. Thomas for many fruitful discussions on Locke's political philosophy and to Mr. Ian Tipton for conversations on empiricism and empiricists. These are all colleagues at Aberystwyth so that the new material is in part a product of the Department.

I also thank Professor H. B. Acton, Editor of *Philosophy*, for allowing me to re-publish sections of the article on number which appeared in that journal in July 1956, and the Delegates of Oxford University Press for permission to republish parts of an article which I contributed to *Seventeenth Century Studies*, 1938.

R. I. A.

GARTH CELYN, ABERYSTWYTH

Midsummer, 1970

PREFACE TO SECOND EDITION

CERTAIN corrections have been made to the text of the first edition and the whole work has been brought up to date. This involved many changes, the most considerable being the new note at the end of Part I giving an account of Draft C of the *Essay*. I studied this manuscript at the Pierpont Morgan Library, New York, and thank the officers of that Library for their help.

R. I. A.

ABERYSTWYTH

June 1954

PREFACE TO FIRST EDITION

MY first aim in this book has been a sound exposition of Locke's writings. But this is not an easy task. Locke's extreme caution, his adoption of the 'historical, plain' method and rejection of the 'high priori' which gives the neat, orderly system, and finally his candour, which leads him often to introduce considerations directly contrary to the run of his argument, all combine to make his teaching difficult to expound. In his case, in particular, the temptation is great to begin with some well defined position in his works and then proceed to show what he ought to have said if he had been consistent, neglecting from that point onwards everything he actually did say. This practice is in no way harmful (so long as it does not pretend to be history of philosophy) and may provide much pleasant intellectual exercise. But it is not exposition of Locke's thought. I hope I have avoided this erroneous kind of exposition which has led so frequently in the past to a falsification of Locke's philosophy.

The book is divided into three parts. Part I is biographical, and I have here been particularly helped by the materials to be found in the collection of Locke's private papers now in the possession of the Earl of Lovelace. Fox Bourne's *Life of John Locke* (1876) is an excellent piece of work of which I have made the fullest use, but unfortunately he was unacquainted with the Lovelace Collection, except with that small part of it which had then been published. We await a new biography of Locke which will do justice to all the materials now to hand. The sketch of Locke's life in the pages which follow, while much too brief to be of final value, will, I hope, prove to be on the right lines. In Part I also I have examined—again briefly, for my space is very limited—the main influences which worked upon Locke, and here, in particular, I have tried to emphasize Gassendi's influence upon him, since this, I believe, has been unduly neglected by historians of philosophy.

Part II is an exposition of Locke's theory of knowledge, that is to say, of the *Essay*. In addition to expounding the text I have tried to fit the teaching into its proper background so as to acquaint the reader with the issues involved. Part III deals with Locke's teaching on moral philosophy, political theory, education, and religion. In the course of my exposition in Parts II and III I have touched upon many problems which I should have liked to develop more fully. My chief hope is that this book may lead others to examine some of these, and to deal with them in far greater detail than I have been able to do.

I owe much to previous writers on Locke. A bibliography is appended of those books and pamphlets which I have found useful. But I should like to mention two books here to which I am particularly indebted: first, that little jewel amongst Locke studies, Professor Alexander's work in *Philosophies Ancient and Modern*, and, secondly, the authoritative and excellent *Locke's Theory of Knowledge* by Professor James Gibson, a colleague in the University of Wales.

Many of my friends have deepened my obligation to them by further kindnesses in connexion with this book. Mr. Gilbert Ryle, of Christ Church, Oxford, read through Part II and gave me some most useful suggestions. Mr. Michael Foster, also of Christ Church, read the whole book through and sent me some pages of notes which I found invaluable. The book in its present state owes much to his careful criticism. Miss Rhiannon Morgan read the manuscript and the proofs and corrected many errors which I had neglected, and my sister, Mrs. G. J. Hughes, kindly helped with the laborious work of typing. My chief debt, however, is to Mr. J. L. Stocks, the Vice-Chancellor of Liverpool University, who is the editor of the series to which this book belongs. He advised me at the outset, and has since read the book through at every stage of its production. My obligation to him is very great.

I wish to thank the officers of the Aristotelian Society for permission to republish some paragraphs from an article on *Locke's Theory of Universals* which appeared in their *Proceedings*. I should mention also the kindnesses I have received from many libraries, in particular those of the University College at Aberystwyth, the National Library of Wales, the British Museum, and the University Library of Amsterdam. Finally, I am greatly indebted to the Earl of Lovelace and to his brother-in-law, Mr. Jocelyn Gibb, who has charge of the Lovelace Collection at present, for permission to consult the Collection.

                                                                R. I. A.

YNYSTAWE
June 1937

NOTE. All references to the Essay are to the fourth edition (1700) and those to Locke's *Works* are to the fourth edition (1740) unless otherwise stated. Except where otherwise stated italics are Locke's. Words in square brackets included in the quotations are not Locke's.

CONTENTS

PART ONE

PART TWO

PART THREE

PART I

I

EARLY YEARS

1632–67

THE writings of John Locke portray the spirit of his age. In them we find that balanced and tolerant attitude to life which characterized late seventeenth-century England at its best. The prevailing love of cool, disciplined reflection and the careful avoidance of excess are mirrored with fidelity on every page. But Locke had been born into a different world, a mad world of bitter conflict and narrow zeal, of exaggerated and wild expression of opinion, where men's feelings and emotions were given too great rein and reason was forgotten. Or so it seemed to Locke's own generation. Late seventeenth-century England abhorred the emotionalism of the Civil War period. It might tolerate and even welcome a measure of emotional appeal in poetry and literature, meant 'for entertainment' only. But in the serious things of life, religion, politics, and above all in the inquiry into truth in philosophy and science, no appeal to the feelings was to be permitted. The apotheosis of reason in the life of man was at hand. It is significant that one of the few occasions upon which Locke permits himself to interrupt the placid, steady flow of his thoughts in the *Essay* is when he attacks the 'enthusiasm' of the previous age with unwonted violence. To call a man an 'enthusiast' was to condemn him scornfully. It was 'enthusiasm' that led men to strange and absurd conduct and to an attempted justification of it by arrogant claims, 'founded neither on reason nor divine revelation, but rising from the conceits of a warmed or overweening brain'. Locke might well have regarded the passage of his own life as a passage from an age of Enthusiasm to an age of Reason.

I

John Locke was born at Wrington, Somerset, on the 29th August 1632, of good Dorset and Somerset stock. The house in which he was born no longer stands, but the house to which he was shortly removed and where he spent his boyhood, namely, Beluton, near the village of Pensford, about six miles south-east of Bristol, can still be seen, a small but pleasant country residence. Locke's parents, John Locke and Agnes Keene, were married in 1630 and John was their first son. The mother was thirty-five years of age when Locke was born and ten years senior to her husband. We are told that she was a pious woman and Locke speaks of her with affection.[1] But the greater influence seems to have been that of the father.

John Locke, senior, was a man of some ability. A county attorney, he had become Clerk to the Justices of Peace, but in 1642, though the west was mainly Royalist, he sided with the Parliamentarians and seems to have suffered in fortune as a consequence of the Civil War. He educated his two sons—the second was Thomas, who was born in 1637, and died early—with extreme care, and Locke himself in later life approved of his father's attitude towards him in his youth. 'His father', Lady Masham tells us,[2] 'used a conduct towards him when young that he often spoke of afterwards with great approbation. It was the being severe to him by keeping him in much awe and at a distance when he was a boy, but relaxing still by degrees of that severity as he grew up to be a man, till, he being become capable of it, he lived perfectly with him as a friend.' There can be no doubt of the later friendship between them. There is sufficient testimony to it in letters from Locke to his father written many years later when his father's health was broken. These are full of tenderness and affection. But in his boyhood Locke knew the severe discipline of a Puritan home. He was trained to sobriety, industry, and endeavour; he was made to love simplicity and to hate excessive ornament and display. Early in his life he learnt the meaning of

---

[1] She was still alive in 1652, for Locke, writing from Westminster, sends her his greetings. Cf. two letters from Westminster to his father in the Lovelace Collection. She probably died between 1652 and 1660.

[2] Quoted by Fox Bourne, *The Life of John Locke*, 1876, i. 13.

political liberty. He would hear his father expound the doctrine of the rightful sovereignty of the people through its elected Parliament—a doctrine for which the father was prepared to suffer. Locke's later experiences broadened and changed his outlook, but his fundamental attitude to life was determined for him once and for all in that simple home at Beluton.

In 1646 Locke entered Westminster School, then Parliamentarian under its headmaster, Dr. Richard Busby. The struggle between King and Parliament still continued and the boy, were he interested, could now view it from a point of vantage. He might even have been present at the execution of Charles I in Whitehall Palace Yard, in close proximity to his school, in 1649. But this is not thought likely. The likelihood is that Locke had little time during these schooldays for reflection upon the turbulent happenings in the world outside. The training he received was thorough, but, to modern ideas at least, somewhat limited in scope. It was confined almost wholly to the study of the Classics. In the upper forms there would be, in addition, Hebrew and Arabic and some elementary geography, but the staple fare of the school was endless Greek and Latin exercises. Locke thus became thoroughly acquainted with the Classics, an acquaintance which stood him in good stead later. But he himself in his *Thoughts Concerning Education* criticized unfavourably the methods adopted at Westminster. Too much time was wasted on languages. A knowledge of Latin was essential in his day, but Greek, he felt, could safely be left to the 'profess'd scholar', not to mention Hebrew and the Oriental tongues. The abiding impression left upon Locke's mind was that of the severity of the discipline at Westminster, as witness his letter to Edward Clarke, in which he describes the life at that 'very severe school', and suggests that a little time spent there might do good to Clarke's own son, making him 'more pliant and willing to learn at home'.[1] Locke must have been a fairly promising pupil, for he was elected King's scholar in 1647 with an annual allowance of '13/4 for livery' and '6o/10 for commons'.

In 1652 Locke was elected to a Studentship at Christ Church,[2]

---

[1] *The Correspondence of Locke and Clarke*, Rand, p. 336.
[2] This is presumably the election about which he keeps his father informed in

and henceforth for over thirty years he made Oxford his home.[1]
Here John Owen was just beginning to re-create order out of the
chaos which followed the Civil War. Oxford had been Royalist.
Its losses had been very heavy and its prestige had sunk considerably. John Owen, who was appointed Dean of Christ Church a
year before Locke took up residence and who became shortly afterwards Vice-Chancellor of the University, set himself energetically
to the work of restoration. He was an Independent divine, a close
follower of Cromwell. Like Cromwell he was tolerant (in spite of
one or two intolerant acts), and to his credit it can be said that he
never sought to force the University into Independent channels.
He retained teachers who were Anglican and Royalist in sympathy. Locke must have welcomed this spirit of toleration, so
much in accord with his own deep love of religious liberty.

It is somewhat remarkable, however, that the change from
Royalist control to Puritan in the University produced no corresponding change in curriculum. The Puritans persisted in the

the two letters written from Westminster in 1652 (Lovelace Collection). I may
here quote the second (with the kind consent of the Earl of Lovelace):
'Most dear and ever-loving father,
    'My humble duty remembered unto you, I have to my utmost done what lies
in me for the preparation both of my folk and friends for the election. Capt.
Smyth I find most ready and willing to lay out himself for the accomplishment
thereof. Neither is Mr. Busby any way wanting, he having spoken to the electors
on my behalf, and although my Latin oration be not spoken yet he hath promised
that my Hebrew one which I made since shall, which I would desire you to be
silent of for there hath been something already spoken abroad more than hath
been for my good. If I be not elected (but I have good hopes) pray send me word
what I shall do, for we hear that those will be very soon chosen. Pray remember
my humble duty to my mother and love to the rest of my friends and desiring
your prayers.

Sum

Westminster, 11 May   Tuus obedientissimus filius,
        1652   John Locke.'

The Students of Christ Church were elected at their school and held the
Studentship for life provided they did not marry. They were also required
normally to take priests' orders, though this condition was occasionally waived.
They took no part in the government of the College, unless specifically appointed
to do so, as when Locke was appointed Censor of Moral Philosophy. In the
middle of the nineteenth century a distinction was made between Junior (undergraduate) and Senior (graduate) Students, but this distinction was not known in
Locke's day. Cf. H. L. Thompson, *Christ Church* (1900), in the series on the
history of Oxford Colleges.
    [1] Locke was late entering Oxford. Probably the disturbances of the Civil War
period account for this fact.

same traditional subjects, Aristotelian in origin but scholastic in exposition. Locke would probably devote a year to rhetoric and grammar, another to logic and moral philosophy, the third and fourth being given to logic, moral philosophy, geometry, and Greek. As might be expected, he found this course both insipid and dreary. He later complained to Leclerc that 'he lost a great deal of time at the commencement of his studies because the only philosophy then known at Oxford was the peripatetic, perplexed with obscure terms and useless questions'. After four years at the University he took his initial degree and two years later the Master's. In the years immediately following initial graduation he would still pursue his college course, continuing with Aristotle's logic and metaphysics, whilst also widening his field of study so as to include history, astronomy, natural philosophy, Hebrew, and Arabic. His studies in these Eastern tongues brought him into contact with Edward Pococke, the teacher who seems to have influenced him most in these early years at Oxford. Writing of him later Locke remarks: 'I do not remember I ever saw in him any one action that I did, or could in my own mind, blame or think amiss in him.' It is significant that Locke should have found a teacher whom he so much admired amongst the Royalist section of the University, for Pococke was staunchly Royalist. The old Puritan ties were already beginning to loosen, and we are not surprised to find Locke welcoming the Restoration when it came.

By this time Locke had already spent eight years within the shelter of the University, and he had still to decide upon a career. There were various alternatives. He might continue the life of the Christ Church don. He already lectured in Greek and rhetoric and was appointed Censor of Moral Philosophy for 1664. But the life of the tutor did not content him, nor was it sufficiently remunerative. His father died in 1661 and the fortune which he bequeathed to his son, small though it was, helped him to make his position more comfortable. His Studentship, however, was uncertain and he seems to have wished for a more lucrative occupation, especially as he appears to have been contemplating marriage at the time.[1]

[1] There is ample evidence of this from the letter to his father quoted by Fox Bourne (i. 80–81), and from the drafts of the love-letters to 'Madam' in the

Some of his friends desired to see him in Holy Orders. But Locke hesitated. Writing to one such friend he remarks: 'I cannot now be forward to disgrace you, or any one else, by being lifted into a place which perhaps I cannot fill and from whence there is no descending without tumbling.' The vocation which attracted him most was that of medicine. He was drawn towards the new experimental inquiries in the natural sciences and to the application of these to human disease. But though he trained himself assiduously for this vocation, so much so that the thoroughness of his knowledge was acknowledged in later life even by such an expert as Sydenham, yet he never became a professional physician, preferring to practise in an amateurish and occasional fashion.[1]

Still a further alternative presented itself to him, the profession of diplomacy, for which he was well fitted. In November 1665 he accompanied Sir Walter Vane on a diplomatic mission to the Elector of Brandenburg, then at Cleves, returning to London in February of the next year. No sooner was he home than another diplomatic post of greater importance was offered to him, namely, a secretaryship under the new ambassador to Spain, the Earl of Sandwich. This offer he finally rejected, though after much hesitation. He returned to Oxford to continue his studies there. Dimly Locke had already realized his true vocation. It was not the Church, nor medicine, nor again diplomacy, but philosophy. And yet it was not speculation as such that appealed to him. He was always a man of affairs, practical to his fingertips. But he also believed that one great need of his generation was a philosophical understanding of the fundamental issues which faced it, and he found his true vocation in a diligent quest for such an understanding.

Already in these early years (that is to say up to 1667, when an event occurred which opened a new period in his life) Locke had

Lovelace Collection which belong to this period, 1658–61. They are full of the tender passion 'robbing me', as he says himself in one of them, 'of the use of my reason'. There are also lovers' quarrels and 'Madam' has made him understand 'that I am not to procure my satisfaction at the expense of your time or patience' (4 June 1659).
[1] It was not till 1674 that he took the Oxford M.B. degree. On Locke as physician cf. *John Locke, Physician and Philosopher* by Kenneth Dewhurst (Wellcome Library), 1963.

collected much material and reflected considerably on the problems of his day, as his private papers show. It was about this period, as he himself informs us in his *New Method of a Commonplace Book*, that he began to prepare those commonplace books which, together with the journals, make so substantial and important a part of the Lovelace Collection,[1] and which are really small encyclopaedias (before the days of printed encyclopaedias) composed by Locke himself for his own instruction and for purposes of reference. In the Lovelace Collection also and again amongst the Shaftesbury Papers for these years there are many writings on constitutional, political, religious, and moral problems. He discusses the Roman constitution, the new Restoration settlement, the place of the civil magistrate in ecclesiastical affairs, and the problem of toleration. But never in these early papers, it is interesting to note, is he concerned with metaphysical matters; nor do those problems of epistemology to which he was later driven here disturb him.[2] It is the practical affairs of state and society which were uppermost in his mind at the time.

II

Locke's main concern, then, up to 1667 was with the practical and social. None the less, he was already familiarizing himself with the views of leading thinkers both of the past and of his own day. The chief influences upon him in this early period must now be traced.

It might at first appear that Locke was little influenced by other writers. His references to others were few. Occasionally, to confirm his general position, he would quote an authority, such as Hooker; but this happened rarely. The naïve method of impressing the reader by piling quotation upon quotation, a method very common in the seventeenth century, he wisely rejected. Instead he attempted to demonstrate each point rationally, and to consider each argument on its own merits in complete independence of what had been said in the past. But he was not ignorant of the

---

[1] One of them bears the date 1661 on its fly-leaf.
[2] Unless some of the essays on the Law of Nature (Bodl. MS. Locke, f. 31) are held to be epistemological.

past and he was not uninfluenced by other writers. His common-place books and journals show how widely he had read, and those who are familiar with the background will perceive at once how greatly he was indebted to other writers.

I do not propose in this book to give any exhaustive account of the influences that worked upon him. There is indeed no end to the tracing of influences, especially in the case of one whose interests were so wide and catholic. It would doubtless be possible to find sources in Greek thought for much that he says, although there is little evidence in his works of any close and detailed study of a Greek author. It is clear that he had studied Cicero with much care. Cicero was an important influence on his thought, particularly as the critic of a materialist philosophy of life. But his immediate debt to the Middle Ages, as one might expect, is greater than any to Greece and Rome. The first philosophy which he had learnt was the scholastic; and it was only gradually, with infinite pains that he found it possible to free himself even partially from its leading-strings. His terms and his central conceptions were derived from scholasticism. He took over bodily its logical framework, its substance and accidents, its modes, its essences, its genus and species, its universals and particulars. His metaphysic also is scholastic in origin, his conception of God and of His relations to the rest of the universe, his conception of man, and of the place which is his in the hierarchy of being. It would be wrong, of course, to say that there was no advance—or, at least, modification—in Locke. He broke away from scholasticism. But it is equally wrong to suppose that he was uninfluenced by his early training. Locke did not start wholly afresh. He built on the traditional foundation bequeathed to him by the schools.

But the problem of Locke's indebtedness to scholasticism is one for the medievalist, and much work remains to be done in this field.[1] In the present section, however, I propose to consider the

---

[1] Küppers in *John Locke und die Scholastik*, Berne, 1894, and Krakowski, *Les Sources médiévales de la philosophie de Locke*, Paris, 1915, are far from satisfactory. Tellkamp, *Das Verhältnis John Locke's zur Scholastik*, Münster, 1927, is sounder work, but still leaves much unexplained. What, for instance, is Locke's relation to Aquinas, to Nicholas of Cusa, and, most interesting of all, to William of Occam?

influence upon him of two contemporary writers, whom Locke himself would have regarded as of far greater importance than any scholastic writers, namely, Descartes and Sir Robert Boyle. Of the two the greater influence was Sir Robert Boyle, and indeed Descartes's role was primarily that of liberator rather than teacher. Locke was not a Cartesian. I hope to show in this book that if he is to be grouped with any European group we must follow Leibniz in grouping him with the Gassendists. It is as a good Gassendist that Locke criticized Descartes. Most often his criticisms, it is not too much to say, re-echoed those already made by Gassendi and his followers. But though he was not a disciple of Descartes, he himself was very ready to admit his great debt to the French thinker. When, as the result of his Oxford training, he had lost faith in philosophy, his reading of Descartes restored it.

He probably began to study Descartes soon after graduation, and it did not take him long to realize that the new philosophy was far more important and more real than the arid hair-splitting of his Oxford logical exercises. In his first *Letter* to Stillingfleet he acknowledges 'to that justly admired gentleman (Descartes) the great obligation of my first deliverance from the unintelligible way of talking' of the schools.[1] And Lady Masham informs us: 'The first books, as Mr. Locke himself has told me, which gave him a relish of philosophical things were those of Descartes. He was rejoiced in reading these, because, though he very often differed in opinion from this writer, he yet found that what he said was very intelligible.'[2] Thus, it was Descartes who first taught Locke how to develop a philosophical inquiry intelligibly. His Oxford education had left him with a sense of despair as to the possibility of advance by way of reason. Descartes was his deliverer from this despair and pessimism.

But Locke does not follow his deliverer blindly. He criticized him, primarily on empirical grounds. And the sequel in the history of philosophy is interesting for, when the long and fruitful reign of Cartesianism came to an end in intellectual Europe, writers (for instance, Voltaire and the Encyclopaedists) acknow-

[1] *Works* (references to fourth edition), i. 381 (1801 ed. iv. 48).
[2] Quoted by Fox Bourne, i. 61–62.

ledged Locke as its critic, though the truth is that he was only one
of many critics. They hailed him as the founder of the empirical
school. Confining their attention largely to the first two books of
the *Essay* and neglecting shamefully the third and fourth, they
created there and then the erroneous view that the two schools
had nothing in common. This view prevailed until the middle of
the nineteenth century, when people like Tagart and T. E. Webb
in England, Hartenstein, Geil, and von Hertling in Germany discovered once again the rationalist elements in Locke's thought, in
a word, rediscovered the third and fourth books of the *Essay*. In
our own day the pendulum is in danger of swinging too far in the
other direction, for Locke is talked of as if he were a mere rationalist, owing everything to Descartes. This view is equally untrue and
needs to be corrected. Locke accepted much that Descartes taught.
Nevertheless, he was his constant critic, criticizing him in the light
of empiricism, that of Bacon and of Boyle on the one hand, and of
the Gassendists on the other.

Apart from the general inspiration which he derived from
Descartes Locke was chiefly indebted to him for the details of his
account of knowing. If iv. ii of the *Essay* be compared with
the opening sections of Descartes's *Regulae* the measure of his
indebtedness will be appreciated. And yet the *Regulae* was not
published until 1701, eleven years after the publication of the
Essay. Many manuscript copies of it were in circulation, however,
and it is not at all improbable that Locke had seen the work. One
is tempted to the view that he actually had the *Regulae* (or a note
of it) beside him in writing iv. ii, the likeness between the two is
so close. Following Descartes he shows how knowledge is essentially intuitive, but demonstration involves memory, and this
makes it not quite so certain as intuitive knowledge.

Yet while Locke was clearly in Descartes's debt for this important theory, it is well to remember that his mind would have been
prepared for the views set forward in the *Regulae* by other influences. The doctrine of the *intuitus* was not original to Descartes.
It was sound medieval doctrine, and can be traced back no doubt
to the νοῦς ποιητικός of Aristotle's *De Anima*, and to Plato's
Theaetetus. Moreover, it was as much part of the English as of

the European tradition. Roger Bacon expounded it in thirteenth-century Oxford and ascribed to it a divine origin, so also did the Cambridge Platonists three centuries later. It was by appealing to it that Cudworth overcame materialism. Locke talked of it frequently in the metaphor beloved of the Cambridge Platonists, as a 'candle'. Thus, while he had Descartes chiefly in mind in writing IV. ii, the theory he put forward was in no way alien to his own English traditions.

Further points in which Locke was indebted to Descartes might have been considered. Locke accepted Descartes's account of clear and distinct ideas, he used his argument of the *cogito ergo sum*, and joined with him in emphasizing the importance of mathematics. More important still, the language of Locke's 'new way of ideas' is borrowed directly from Descartes. But these and other matters are details which it is best to examine as we expound Locke's own teachings. What we must now do is to emphasize another point, namely, that in spite of this debt Locke felt himself in open opposition to Descartes. He always regarded the Cartesians with a certain amount of suspicion. Such doctrines as those of innate ideas, that animals are automata, that the essence of body is extension and of mind thinking, and that there is no vacuum, were most distasteful to Locke. Moreover, in a general sense, Locke disliked the whole tone of Cartesianism. It was too speculative, its method was the 'high priori' one which he was resolved not to adopt. In his *Some Thoughts Concerning Education* he held that a young man might like to read the speculations of Descartes on natural science, 'as that which is most in fashion', since he could thus 'fit himself for conversation', but he should not expect to find truth in them. The 'high priori' method gives 'hypotheses' only. If the young man wants something more substantial he must turn to 'such writers as have employed themselves [rather] in making rational experiments and observations than in starting barely speculative systems'.[1] He instanced the works of Boyle and Newton. Again, in his second reply to Stillingfleet, the Bishop of Worcester, who had argued 'that Descartes, a mathematical man, had been guilty of mistakes in his system', Locke remarked:

[1] § 193 and cf. also § 94.

'When mathematical men will build systems upon fancy and not upon demonstration, they are liable to mistakes as others.' This was the real ground of Locke's dissatisfaction with Descartes. He 'built systems upon fancy', instead of contenting himself with what could be proved demonstratively or at least made probable by 'rational experiments and observations'.[1]

Locke's reference here, clearly, is to the practice and method of the English scientists of his own age, and we now turn to consider their influence upon him in these early years. The greatest name is that of Isaac Newton, but he could hardly be described as an early influence on Locke. Locke admired him immensely. In the *Education*[2] he praised him for showing 'how far mathematics, applied to some parts of nature, may, upon principles that matter of fact justifies, carry us in knowledge of some, as I may so call them, particular provinces of the incomprehensible universe'. And in this he contrasted him to Descartes. But his acquaintance with Newton and with Newton's work came late. Newton was Locke's junior by ten years, and it is not probable that they met each other before 1680 or so. Nor again does Bacon of Verulam appear to have been a deep influence. Locke no doubt read his works. And when Bacon remarked that of the natural world man knows 'as much as his observations on the order of nature, either with regard to things or the mind, permit him, and neither knows nor is capable of more',[3] he was expressing a doctrine which became central in Locke's philosophy. (At the same time Bacon was inclined to hold that man was capable of greater knowledge of the natural order than Locke found it possible to admit.) But there is no evidence to show that Bacon was an influence on Locke's philosophical development.

The really important influence on Locke from the empiricist side was the group that gathered around Sir Robert Boyle, and which ultimately founded the Royal Society. Indeed, the most important influence of all was Boyle himself. Boyle, the son of an

[1] *Works*, i. 572 (1801 ed. iv. 427). Cf. further 'The Influence of Descartes on John Locke: A Bibliographical Study' by Charlotte S. Ware (Mrs. Arthur Johnston), *Rev. Int. de Phil.* (April 1950).
[2] § 194. Cf. 'Locke, Newton and the Two Cultures' by James L. Axtell in *John Locke, Problems and Perspectives* (ed. Yolton), 1969, pp. 165 ff.
[3] *Novum Organum*, Aphorisms, Book i. 1.

Irish earl, was Locke's senior by five years. He was a member of the 'Invisible College' which held its meetings at Gresham College, London, and which devoted itself to the 'new philosophy', meaning in particular the new natural philosophy that stressed observation and the application of mathematics to the study of natural phenomena. This 'College' had a branch at Oxford, and when Boyle went to reside there in 1654 he soon became one of its most prominent members. In 1663 the 'Invisible College' became the Royal Society and Boyle, who moved back to London in 1668, had much to do with its growth in its earliest years. He died in 1691.

From 1654 to 1668, then, Boyle was at Oxford and Locke must have known him for most of this period. When Locke visited Cleves in 1665 he sent letters to Boyle as to a close and much respected friend. At Oxford Locke helped Boyle in his experiments,[1] when away from him he sent him scientific information; writing from Lord Shaftesbury's residence his one regret is that he has no time for laboratory work, 'though I find my fingers still itch to be at it'.[2] Lastly, Boyle submitted his *General History of the Air* to Locke's judgement before publishing it.

This will be enough to show that the connexion between the two was an intimate one. It certainly left its mark on the younger man.[3] The physics of the *Essay* is the corpuscular physics of Boyle, and if the reader has any doubts in his mind as to what Locke means he may turn to Boyle's works for a fuller exposition of the same views. Of course, some of these doctrines might themselves have been suggested to Boyle by Locke, but Boyle seems to have been the leader. He is the master who taught Locke how to approach nature empirically and yet scientifically. We shall refer later to the particular points in which Boyle's influence is most clearly seen, for instance, the distinction between primary and secondary qualities. Suffice it now to point out the general agreement between them. In his preface to *The Origins of Forms and*

[1] Cf. Boyle's *Works* (1744), v. 136–63, where there is a register of the weather at Oxford kept for Boyle by Locke. [2] Ibid. v. 568 b.
[3] It has even been suggested (L. J. More, 'Boyle as Alchemist', in *Journal of the History of Ideas*, vol. ii, no. 1) that Locke accepted Boyle's alchemy, so great was his faith in him.

Qualities, according to Corpuscular Philosophy, published in 1666, when the co-operation between the two men was at its closest, Boyle truly summed up the central thesis of the *Essay* itself with regard to the natural sciences when he remarked: 'For the knowledge we have of the bodies without us being for the most part fetched from the informations the mind receives by the senses, we scarce know anything else in bodies, upon whose account they can work upon our senses, save their qualities: for as to the substantial forms, which some imagine to be in all natural bodies, it is not so evident that there are such as it is that the wisest of those that do admit them confess that they do not well know them.' Locke's views about human knowledge and its extent were also foreshadowed in Boyle. For Boyle taught that the extent of our certain knowledge is not great. Without revelation the human intellect could discover very little indeed. None the less, our faculties are sufficient for our needs.[1]

---

[1] Cf. ibid. ii. 190 *b*, and iv. 42 ff.

II

YEARS OF GROWTH (1667–89)

I

IN 1666 Locke first met Lord Ashley, afterwards Earl Shaftesbury. It was a chance meeting at Oxford, but for both men, and for Locke in particular, the event was fraught with important consequences. Ashley was already one of the most influential men in the country; his talents were many, and his practical ability admitted by all. How far Dryden's bitter satire upon him is justified it is difficult to say. But Locke admired him, whilst Ashley, on his side, recognized the learning and wisdom of the young man. From the middle of 1667 onwards Locke became one of his advisers and went to live with him in London. He first served him in the capacity of physician, and in 1668 he carried out an operation on his patient which saved his life. But it was not medical advice alone that Ashley sought from Locke. 'Mr. Locke', the third Earl Shaftesbury remarks,[1] 'grew so much in esteem with my grandfather that, as great a man as he experienced him in physic, he looked upon this as but his least part. He encouraged him to turn his thoughts another way; nor would he suffer him to practise physic except in his own family, and as a kindness to some particular friend. He put him upon the study of the religious and civil affairs of the nation, with whatsoever related to the business of a minister of state, in which he was so successful, that my grandfather soon began to use him as a friend, and consult with him on all occasions of that kind.'

Thus Locke found himself at the very centre of affairs and was obliged to make himself acquainted with all the major occurrences of the day in order to advise Ashley. In Oxford he had spent his time in the company of men of learning and of scientists. Now he dwelt daily with business men, politicians, and courtiers. It was a

---

[1] Quoted by Fox Bourne, i. 198.

completely new world for him, but he possessed wit, grace, and
learning enough to hold his own in it. One of his first tasks was to
help with the framing of a constitution for the new colony of
Carolina, of which Ashley was one of the founders and lord-
proprietors. (The whole constitution is attributed to Locke, since
a copy of it in his hand was found amongst his papers, but it is
very unlikely that he is the author of it.) Another task, of a very
different order, which fell to his lot at the time, was to find a wife
for Ashley's son, a sickly and none too intelligent boy of seventeen
or eighteen. This he carried out most efficiently, negotiating successfully with the Earl of Rutland for the hand of his daughter,
Lady Dorothy Manners. 'Sir', Ashley wrote to him on learning of
the arrangements for the wedding, 'you have in the great concerns
of my life been so successively and prudently kind to me, that it
renders me eternally your most affectionate friend and servant.'[1]
He did not entirely neglect scientific work. He busied himself with
medicine, co-operating with Sydenham, whose acquaintance he
had lately made. He was also drawn into the Royal Society, now
well established, and was elected a Fellow in November 1668,
though he never seems to have played a very prominent part in its
work. In 1671 he first bethought himself of the problems of the
Essay, and wrote two important drafts to which we shall refer
later. His many activities, however, began to tell on his frail constitution, and for the first time we hear of his being forced to leave
London for reasons of health. He spent some time in the provinces,
and then towards the end of 1672 crossed to France for a very
short visit lasting a few weeks only.

He returned to weightier tasks of administration, for already
in April 1672 Ashley had been raised to the peerage as Earl
Shaftesbury and was now appointed President of the Council of
Trade and Plantations. Still greater honours were to come, however, for in November, just after Locke's return, he was made
Lord High Chancellor. Advancement for Shaftesbury meant
greater work for Locke; and he was appointed Secretary for the
Presentation of Benefices with a salary of £300 and the care of all
ecclesiastical business which came under the Chancellor's control.

<hr>

[1] *Shaftesbury Papers*, ii. 176; Fox Bourne, *Life*, i. 205.

Shaftesbury, however, was soon dismissed from the office of Chancellor and Locke lost the secretaryship. But in October 1673 he was appointed Secretary to the Council of Trade and Plantations (of which Shaftesbury was still President) at a salary of £500 a year.[1] He retained this post until the Council was dissolved by royal mandate in March 1675. He thus gained much information which he put to good use later after the Revolution of 1688. His own financial position was secured by an annuity of £100 from Shaftesbury, though Locke himself seems to have contributed towards this annuity.[2] He continued to hold his Studentship at Christ Church.

In 1675 Locke's health deteriorated so rapidly under the pressure of work upon him that he decided to try a prolonged stay in France. We are fortunate in having, in the Lovelace Collection, journals giving a very full account of his journeys there.[3] He crossed to Calais and travelled leisurely through Abbeville to Paris, thence to Lyons, Avignon, and Montpellier, at that time a famous health resort. He reached it on Christmas Day, 1675, having spent almost six weeks on the way. He remained for over a year at Montpellier, finding many new friends, amongst them being Thomas Herbert, later Earl of Pembroke, to whom the *Essay* is dedicated. In March 1677 he returned to Paris and stayed there from May 1677 to June 1678. He made a point of meeting as many scholars and learned men as he could, and he also interested himself in the philosophical speculation of Paris at the time. His journals contain many references to French thinkers. In the one for 1678 there is a long note entitled *Méthode pour bien étudier la doctrine de M^r des Cartes*, discussing the best books to read in order to gain a satisfactory view of Cartesianism. There are references to Bernier, the leader of the Gassendists, of whom we must shortly say more, to Cordemoy and others. He also made the acquaintance of many celebrated physicians, and that with Guenellon, the Dutch physician, was to prove useful later in his life. Others whom he met were Nicholas Thoynard (who later, in

[1] Probably Locke was never paid for this work, cf. Fox Bourne, i. 293-4.
[2] Cf. *Locke and Clarke Correspondence*, 11 March 1692.
[3] Cf. *Locke's Travels in France*, 1675-9, ed. by John Lough, Cambridge, 1953.

his correspondence,[1] kept Locke well informed of happenings in France), Römer, Cassini, Thevenot, and Justel.

In June 1678 Locke left again for Montpellier, travelling thither through Orleans, Bordeaux, and Toulouse. He describes vividly the unhappy state of the French peasantry in the Loire basin. In October he is back in Montpellier whence he hoped to journey on to Rome, but 'old Father Winter, armed with all his snow and icicles, keeps guard on Mont Cenis and will not let me pass'. After a week's stay at Montpellier he returned to Paris, arriving there in November. Here he spent the winter, seeing the shows the city and court had to offer, and spending as much time as he could, we may be sure, in the company of philosophic and scientific savants. In April 1679 Locke left Paris for London with many regrets for the friends and entertainments he was leaving behind him.

His regrets can be understood, for the England to which he returned was one troubled by acute political unrest. The Stuarts, surely the most lacking in political sense of all reigning families, had managed once more to unite the majority of the nation against them. Charles, his brother James, and the Court, were solidly Catholic, whilst the nation was no less solidly Protestant. Shaftesbury, now the leader of the people and of the opposition, had been imprisoned in the Tower. But with the summoning of Parliament in 1678 the King gave way before the opposition. Shaftesbury was freed and restored to power as Lord President of the Privy Council. Locke was recalled into Shaftesbury's service. During the summer of 1679 Parliament tried unsuccessfully to pass the Disabling Bill 'to disable the Duke of York to inherit the Crown of England'. The King, however, dissolved Parliament and in October Shaftesbury was again dismissed from office. Shaftesbury now joined the Duke of Monmouth's party and Locke no doubt was engaged in making various secret inquiries on his behalf. But ill health soon drove Locke out of London for the rest of the winter and he was not able to return until the spring of 1680.

Another Parliament was called in 1680 which proved equally

---

[1] In the Lovelace Collection there is a big bundle of letters to Locke from Thoynard.

stubborn in its opposition to James's accession to the throne, and was again dissolved. A new Parliament was summoned at Oxford. On this occasion Shaftesbury stayed at the house of John Wallis, the mathematician who had taught Locke in his undergraduate days; whilst Locke himself returned to his Christ Church quarters. But the Oxford Parliament was shorter lived than any, being dissolved within a week of its opening, and Shaftesbury returned to London.

Locke, however, except for occasional visits to London, stayed on at Oxford throughout the next two years, and the journals become fuller and more philosophical. He was probably in London in July 1681 when Shaftesbury was arrested, to be tried and acquitted in November. For the most part, however, he lived the quiet life of the scholar, researching in medicine and in philosophy. Meanwhile, watch was being kept on him by the King's party, and this was increased when Shaftesbury was compelled to flee the country and find safety in Holland. In January 1683, broken-hearted no doubt by his failure to prevent the succession of the Duke of York to the throne, Shaftesbury died in Amsterdam in the presence of a few friends. Locke who had served him so well was far away in Oxford, but he was not wholly forgotten, if we are to believe a certain Thomas Cherry, admittedly an enemy, who wrote in a letter: 'I'll give an unhappy instance, which I had from the very person in whose arms the late Earl of Shaftesbury expired. He said, when he attended him at his last hours in Holland, he recommended to him the confession of his faith and the examination of his conscience. The earl answered him and talked all over Arianism and Socinianism, which notions he confessed he imbibed from Mr. Locke and his tenth chapter of "Human Understanding".'[1]

The information we have concerning Locke's activities during the years 1682 and 1683 is rather scant. The best sources are the journals. There are also letters to Thomas Cudworth, the son of Ralph Cudworth, the philosopher, and to Edward Clarke, but

---

[1] Quoted by Fox Bourne, i. 469. As the *Essay* did not appear for another seven years, either this story is false, or, what is not improbable, Shaftesbury must have seen IV. x in manuscript.

they give only slight information. It is clear that he was of set purpose secretive in his movements during these years, fearing persecution, a fear which he could well entertain. His intimate friendship with Shaftesbury and his political sympathies were known. As his fears increased, Locke decided that it would be wise for him to follow his master's example and flee the country. He was still in England in August 1683, for he wrote a letter to Clarke from London on the twenty-sixth of that month. But soon after that date he took ship to Holland, and by the 7th September, as we see from his journal, he was in Rotterdam, an exile from a land in which the forces he had always opposed were for the time being triumphant.

Locke spent his first Dutch winter in Amsterdam. In a letter to Clarke he says that he proposes to 'apply himself close to the study of physic by the fireside this winter'. He no doubt made a point of visiting Guenellon, now back in Amsterdam, and in January he was introduced to the theologian Limborch, who quickly became a very firm friend.

Philip van Limborch is a most interesting figure. He was the grand-nephew of Episcopius, a follower of Arminius, the famous professor of theology at Leyden. Episcopius had set himself up against the prevailing Calvinism of the Dutch people. He stood for full liberty of belief, and for a church broad enough to include within it men of all opinions. By 1610 Episcopius had founded a new sect, which presented a remonstrance to the States-General, the sect from this time onwards being known as the Remonstrants. In 1630 they opened their first church in Amsterdam.[1] Episcopius died in 1643. In 1668 Limborch was appointed pastor of this advanced community. When Locke arrived at Amsterdam fifteen years later Limborch had become one of the most important theologians in Holland. His name was known throughout western Europe. He was acquainted with the movements of English thought and counted some of the Cambridge Platonists amongst his friends. The portrait of him which still hangs in the

---

[1] The church and the various committee-rooms attached to it may still be seen on the Keizersgracht, not far from the house in which Descartes resided for some time. The council-chamber contains fine portraits of both Episcopius and Limborch.

Remonstrant council-chamber at Amsterdam presents him as a strong, heavily-built man, energetic, combining strength of character with that of body, but jovial also and alert. The longer Locke was in his company the deeper grew the friendship between them, and it was kept alive by frequent correspondence until Locke himself died. Of all the good things that Holland gave him the best was the companionship of Limborch.

Locke spent the summer and autumn months of 1684 touring the northern provinces and visiting the more interesting towns of Holland. These he describes in his journals. He writes many letters to Clarke, but these contain disappointingly little information about himself. From some references in them it would seem that Locke hoped to be back in England speedily, but the position at home was not improving. Indeed, the news from England could hardly have been worse. In November 1684 the King expressly asked Dean Fell of Christ Church to deprive Locke of his Studentship. The Dean tried to temporize, but the King would brook no delay. On the 16th November Fell wrote to say that 'his majesty's command for the expulsion of Mr. Locke from the college was fully executed'. It was an unpleasant blow, but Locke could do nothing. He spent the winter quietly at Utrecht, in the house of a painter, van Gulick.

But persecution was to assume a more severe form. In the spring of 1685 Charles II died, James came to the throne, and Monmouth attempted his inglorious rebellion. His defeat led to an inquiry and Lord Grey of Walk named Locke as one of Monmouth's helpers. From the evidence at our disposal it appears most unlikely that Locke supported Monmouth in any way. But when Skelton came out to The Hague to demand of the Dutch government the surrender of eighty-five Englishmen who had plotted against their King, John Locke's name was set down on the list of traitors. The Dutch authorities made no great effort to find the culprits, for they had scant sympathy with the Catholic English court. Thus the actual danger to Locke was probably never very great. But he was very much disturbed by the news, and went into hiding in the house of Dr. Venn, Guenellon's father-in-law. He took the most extreme precautions and even assumed a false name, Dr. van der

Linden. A later list of English suspects issued by the States-General in May 1686 no longer contained Locke's name, and all danger was past. Pembroke wrote to him from London to şay that the King was even prepared to pardon him if he chose to return. But Locke stayed in Holland and continued to be most cautious in his activities.

If he suffered in this way, he enjoyed one great consolation. The air of Holland suited him admirably, and his health improved every year. In December 1687 he was able to write to Clarke, 'As to my health, which I know you are in earnest concerned for, I make haste to tell you that I am perfectly, God be thanked, recovered and am as well I think I may say as ever I was in my life'.[1] This improved health, and the enforced leisure which was his, Locke put to good use. In his letters to Clarke he outlined his thoughts on education, and it was these thoughts which were later gathered together and published. Again, in the winter of 1685-6 he was introduced to Jean Leclerc, a native of Geneva, a man of considerable ability, who had travelled widely before accepting a chair in the Remonstrants' College in Amsterdam in 1684. When Locke became acquainted with him, Leclerc was preparing the first issues of his *Bibliothèque Universelle*, one of the first literary journals. In the July 1686 number appeared (in French) an article by Locke, entitled *Méthode Nouvelle de dresser des Recueils*, an account of how he set out materials in his commonplace books. To this journal he also contributed reviews. Here we have Locke's first publications (if we exclude certain immature poems published by him in his early Oxford days).[2] In the winter of 1685-6 also Locke composed a letter to Limborch in Latin on the subject of toleration which was published in 1689 under the title *Epistola de Tolerantia*. (In the same year it was translated by Popple and published anonymously as the *First Letter Concerning Toleration*.) Toleration was a question hotly debated at the time in Holland. Leclerc complains in the May 1687 issue of his *Bibliothèque* that one hears of nothing in Holland except of toleration, and this enthusiastic discussion of a subject, upon which he had pondered from a very

---

[1] *The Correspondence of Locke and Clarke*, p. 230.
[2] Cf. Fox Bourne, i. 50-52, and the bibliography below.

early period, no doubt helped Locke greatly when he finally decided to set down his own thoughts on paper.

In January 1687 Locke moved from Amsterdam to Rotterdam, living there nearly two years in the home of a Quaker merchant, Benjamin Furly. Writing to Limborch, he remarks: 'I grieve much that I am parted from you and all my other dear friends in Amsterdam. To politics I there gave but little thought; here I cannot pay much attention to literary affairs.' The politics which took up so much of his time were obviously English politics, and he no doubt moved to Rotterdam in order to be near enough to The Hague to take part in the plotting against James II which was now coming to a head. After some hesitation William of Orange had thrown in his lot with the English Whigs, and it seems fairly clear that Locke was one of his advisers, either directly or indirectly through Lord Mordaunt.

But he was not wholly engrossed in affairs of this nature. He was, as we shall later see, well advanced with his greatest work, the *Essay*; at the same time he had been reflecting on questions of political theory. He kept up a very full correspondence with various people, particularly Clarke. He visited his friends at Amsterdam, and was a member of a jovial, mum-drinking club at Rotterdam, the Lantern, which met at Furly's house. Also, in January 1688 an abstract of his *Essay* was given to the world in the *Bibliothèque Universelle*, and Locke had to busy himself with the printing of it.

In the summer of 1688 he was visited by Edward Clarke, and his wife and daughter Elizabeth. Clarke, no doubt, took this opportunity of meeting William of Orange. The revolutionary plans matured in the autumn of 1688 and in November William left for England. His princess remained in Holland till January, when William was able to report that the revolution had been carried out peacefully and that James had fled. Locke had been left to bring over Lady Mordaunt, and they crossed in company with the Princess of Orange, now to be Queen Mary of England, on the 11th February, landing at Greenwich the next day. Thus Locke's exile of over five years in Holland was brought to an end. He returned home stronger in body and more mature in mind, anxious now to submit to the judgement of the world the conclusions to which a lifetime's reflections had led him. He had greatly enjoyed his stay in Holland and had grown to admire the Dutch people. 'In going away', he writes to Limborch, a few days before he left Holland, 'I almost feel as though I were leaving my own country and my own kinsfolk; for everything that belongs to kinship, goodwill, love, kindness—everything that binds men together with ties stronger than the ties of blood—I have found among you in abundance. I leave behind me friends whom I can never forget and I shall never cease to wish for an opportunity of coming back to enjoy once more the genuine fellowship of men who have been such friends that, while far away from all my own connections, while suffering in every other way, I have never felt sick at heart. As for you, best, dearest and most worthy of men, when I think of your learning, your wisdom, your kindness and candour and gentleness, I seem to have found in your friendship alone enough to make me always rejoice that I was forced to pass so many years amongst you.'[1]

II

What now were the chief philosophical influences that moulded Locke's thought during this middle period? Here again the search for all the minor influences even amongst his own contemporaries would be endless. Locke learnt much in conversation, and he was a voracious reader. It is probable that no book of any worth published in England during his adult years passed unnoticed by him. Even in France and in Holland he kept himself well informed of English publications, and he also knew of the more important books published in those countries. An exhaustive comparison of Locke's works with those others which he read during these years is, therefore, out of the question. Moreover, even if all the likenesses which exist between Locke's thoughts and those of others were traced, we could still not be sure which works had really influenced him. In writers belonging to the same age, and growing

[1] The beautiful letter of friendship from which I here quote is to be found (in its original Latin) in the Limborch correspondence in the University Library of Amsterdam.

up in the same 'climate of opinion'—to use a phrase of one of Locke's contemporaries, Joseph Glanvill[1]—parallelisms of thought are inevitable. For instance, how much, if at all, is the author of the *Essay* indebted to Richard Cumberland's *De Legibus Naturae*, published in 1672? The thought in both, particularly in connexion with questions of moral philosophy, converges frequently. Yet the likeness between the two might well be explained by the fact that both men had the same cultural background, used the same methods, started from the same data, and faced the same problems. It is thus very dangerous to argue that since there are parallel passages in two writers belonging to the same epoch the one must have influenced the other directly.

Indeed, it is safer to talk of broad movements than of individual authors in dealing with this question of influences, and I propose to take here two contemporary movements which certainly did influence Locke greatly: first, the liberal-minded movement in theology typified by Cambridge Platonism and Latitudinarianism in England and by Arminianism in Holland; secondly, the Gassendist criticism of the prevailing Cartesianism in France. It is not difficult to show that these movements were the most important influences on Locke during this period.

The Cambridge Platonists were a school of erudite theologians flourishing in Cambridge in the middle of the seventeenth century. Their chief members were Benjamin Whichcote, Henry More, John Smith, and Ralph Cudworth. In their general standpoint they were opposed to more than one group. They criticized Hobbes's materialism; but they were equally severe on the dogmatism of the Calvinists and on the 'enthusiasm' of the sects. They were rationalist in outlook. For whilst they admitted that revelation was necessary to complete our knowledge, reason was to be trusted wholly within its own, admittedly confined, sphere of operation. There could be no conflict between reason and revelation; the one completed the other. Nor was there any authority to which appeal might be made beyond reason on matters within reason's own compass. Consequently, they were resolutely opposed

---

[1] To whom, incidentally, we might refer in illustration of our point here, since he has very much in common with Locke.

to any body of doctrine, such as Calvinism, which involved a revolt against reason, or an appeal from reason to inspiration or non-rational religious intuition. They held that reason was infallible; it was something divine in man, 'the candle of the Lord'; it enabled man to distinguish explicitly between truth and falsehood. On the other hand, just because they so clearly realized the high dignity, the finality, and the absoluteness of reason, they could not accept the Hobbesian interpretation of the world. They were progressive, and recognized willingly the splendid achievements of the 'new philosophy' in empirical inquiry. But they could not admit that the new science in any way justified the thorough-going atomistic and mechanical materialism implicit in Hobbes's system. In their very confidence in human reason they found justification for a religious view of the world. This confidence also made them broad-minded and tolerant. Each individual was a free agent, possessing sufficient reason to guide his life aright if he made proper use of it, and so each individual should be free to order his own life in accordance with his own reason.

Locke was naturally disposed to doctrines such as these, and no doubt he would know something of them before leaving Oxford. But on coming to London in 1667 he met Mapletoft, Tillotson, and Patrick, all three of whom were disciples of Whichcote. The latter himself came to London in 1668 as rector of St. Lawrence Jewry and remained there until 1681. Locke might very well have been among his congregation.[1] He had closer contacts, however, with another Cambridge Platonist, Ralph Cudworth, though we have no evidence that the two ever met. They were both Somerset men, born within twenty miles of each other, Cudworth being Locke's senior by fifteen years. The Clarke correspondence shows us that Locke knew the family well before he left for Holland, and there are letters between Locke and Thomas Cudworth, the son. In his old age, also, as we shall see, Locke found a pleasant refuge in the house of Lady Masham, the daughter of Cudworth, at Oates, and for some years Mrs. Cudworth, the widow of the philo-sopher, lived in the same house. So that even if Locke had not

[1] Lady Masham tells us that he approved of 'sermons he had heard from Mr Whichcote'. King, ii. 56.

discussed his philosophy with Cudworth himself, he had every opportunity of discussing it with those who best knew his philosophical position and temper.[1]

There are clear traces of the influence of this school upon Locke's work.[2] Much of the fourth book of the *Essay* might have been written by one of the Cambridge school. The argument in IV. x. 10 and what follows, where it is shown that God must be other than material, breathes the spirit of a Cudworth.[3] His chapters dealing with reason and revelation, and that on enthusiasm, are very much in line with Cambridge thought. Outside the *Essay* also, in his letters on toleration, and in his *Reasonableness of Christianity*, the influence of Cambridge Platonism is even more evident. He recommends the reading of Cudworth to the student in his *Thoughts Concerning Education*[4] and appeals to his authority on more than one occasion in the correspondence with Stillingfleet.[5] Locke, we shall find, shared the view of the Cambridge Platonists on the nature and significance of reason in human life, on the relations between reason and faith, on the paramount importance of practical conduct in true religion, on toleration, and on enthusiasm.

In all these matters Locke helped to carry forward the liberal tradition which the Cambridge Platonists had themselves inherited from still earlier English sources. Yet while it is correct to hold that Locke was influenced by Cambridge thought, it would be a great mistake to regard him as a member of this school. There are important differences between his final standpoint and theirs, and it is these differences which made Locke's works so very fruitful, whilst the works of the Cambridge Platonists were soon forgotten. I may mention, first, two of the more incidental differences. Most of the Cambridge Platonists believed in innate ideas, but Locke rejected them. Again, the Cambridge Platonists had room

---

[1] On the relations between Locke and Cudworth cf. further J. A. Passmore, *Ralph Cudworth*, Cambridge, 1951, ch. viii.

[2] A detailed account of the matter is given in chapter iii of Freiherr von Hertling's *John Locke und die Schule von Cambridge*. W. von Leyden in *Essays on the Laws of Nature* (1954) draws attention to the influence of Nathaniel Culverwel on Locke, cf. pp. 39–43.

[3] That Locke in this passage was directly influenced by Cudworth is clear from a note in the Journal of 1682. Cf. Aaron and Gibb, p. 118.

[4] § 193.   [5] Cf. *Works*, i. 498, 597.

for a world of real intelligible objects, wholly other than the world of sensible things. Now Locke sometimes talks of an 'intellectual world' and always holds that reason has a type of object which is permanent and eternal. But for Locke these intellectual objects, i.e. universal ideas, were merely the creations of our own mind. The Cambridge school, however, attributed to them a reality as 'essences' or 'Ideas' in the Platonic sense which Locke could not attribute to them. In this important respect their theory of universals is different.

But the fundamental difference between them is one of purpose and method. The Cambridge men were speculative theorists. Their aim was to show that a religious metaphysic and a theism were still possible, and, indeed, necessary, in spite of the changes in men's opinions since the Renaissance. They were apologist and on the defensive. Locke, on the other hand, was critical. He had no system to defend. Indeed, his task, as he explained, was to clear the 'under-rubbish' that had first to be removed if an adequate system was to be built. Thus Locke's attitude and purpose in philosophizing, particularly in the *Essay*, were fundamentally different from theirs, however much he may have shared their theological and religious outlook. It is when one studies works other than the *Essay*, the letters on toleration and the *Reasonableness of Christianity*, that one best realizes the measure of Locke's debt to them.

Cambridge Platonism, however, is only one manifestation of the liberal-minded trend in English religious and political thought and Locke was influenced by other manifestations of it. It is significant that 'the judicious Hooker', who himself belongs to the same tradition, is the author to whom Locke most frequently makes appeal (particularly so in the *Treatises on Civil Government*).[1] Again, in Locke's own youth a movement more influential than Cambridge Platonism had come into being, Latitudinarianism. At first the most important figures were Hales and Chilling-

---

[1] Hooker, though Royalist, interpreted government largely in the terms in which it was interpreted by Locke himself. In theology he defended reason as having equal authority within its own sphere with scripture. He also advocated toleration. Great respect was paid to his name in Locke's day, and this, no doubt, accounts in some measure for the frequency with which Locke refers to him.

worth. The latter's *Religion of Protestants*, 1637, left a deep impression upon the more thoughtful members of his own generation and the next. After the Restoration in particular liberal theologians and ecclesiastics in the Church of England were anxious to see the foundation of the Church laid on so broad a basis that all sincere believers in Christ, however they interpreted the Scriptures, might be included within it. The Christian creed consisted of a few essentials (they might even be reduced to one, that Christ is Saviour), and of very many non-essentials. The Latitudinarians argued that disagreement about the latter ought not to keep men apart. Conformity on non-essentials should not be demanded. 'Require of Christians only to believe Christ.' In Locke's own day the leaders of the movement were Tillotson and Patrick, to whom we have already referred, and Locke was on most intimate terms with both.[1] He was only too ready to accept views such as theirs, and in theological matters became Latitudinarian, as may well be gathered from his *Reasonableness of Christianity*. Still another influence upon him of an advanced liberal kind in theology was that of Episcopius, Limborch, and the Arminian Remonstrants of Amsterdam. The Latitudinarians themselves were Arminian in theology, so were the Cambridge Platonists, but in Holland Locke touched Arminianism at its fountainhead. Thus throughout this middle period Locke was in constant contact with the liberal Arminian school of theology, with men who desired to see established a broad and tolerant Church that would put no fetters upon human reason and would demand only such articles of faith as were deemed essential.

Before we turn to consider the influence of the Gassendist criticism of Cartesianism on Locke, a word should perhaps be said about the relations between him and Hobbes. When John Edwards charged Locke with putting forward views in his *Reasonableness of Christianity* very much akin to those of Hobbes the accusation went home. Locke does not try to hide his chagrin. He

[1] Tillotson in particular was a very great friend, as witness a letter to Limborch (11 December 1694) written on the occasion of Tillotson's death. Locke describes him as 'that able and candid investigator of truth' and adds: 'I have now scarcely any one whom I can freely consult on dubious points of divinity—I have, indeed, been deprived to my great injury and regret, of a friend, sincere and candid, and endeared to me by the intercourse of many years.'

pleads ignorance of the details of Hobbes's works, though it is very difficult to believe that he was wholly ignorant of them.[1] In connexion with one doctrine said by Edwards to have come direct from the *Leviathan* he remarks: 'I borrowed it from the writers of the four Gospels and the Acts and did not know that these words he quoted out of the Leviathan were there or anything like them. Nor do I know yet, any further than as I believe them to be there from his quotation.'[2] He links Hobbes with Spinoza as 'justly decried names' and declares that he is not 'well read' in either.[3] Finally, he condemns the ethical standpoint of the 'Hobbists'.[4] From all this it is clear that Locke was anxious not to be regarded as a follower of Hobbes. For in spite of Hobbes's show of orthodoxy, the real meaning of his philosophy was not hidden from his contemporaries. And Locke was convinced—as convinced as the Cambridge Platonists—that Hobbes's materialism was inadequate as a philosophy of life. 'That which is not body', Hobbes had said, 'is no part of the universe.'[5] On this fundamental issue Locke and Hobbes were in opposing camps, and that of itself is sufficient to explain Locke's animosity. On political questions also, as we shall see later, they were fundamentally opposed; and though Hobbes is not mentioned in the second *Treatise on Civil Government*, that book is obviously directed against his political views.

Hobbes's influence on Locke is thus primarily of a negative sort. He is aware of him and sometimes is obviously seeking to answer him. But in a positive sense the influence is slight. True, their method is identical, namely, the compositional. (For Hobbes

[1] Locke possessed a copy of the *Leviathan* in his library. It is listed amongst the books bequeathed to Francis Masham. Unfortunately the nine hundred books so bequeathed were dispersed in a sale a century or so later. In a notebook (now in the Lovelace Collection) in which he gathered together the opinions of various critics about the thinkers in whom he was interested there are three or four references to Hobbes, which shows that he was amongst the thinkers Locke regarded as important.

[2] *Works*, ii. 722 (1801 ed. vii. 420).

[3] *Second Reply to Stillingfleet*, i. 598; cf. *Remarks upon Norris*, § 16. (Locke had also various works of Spinoza in his library. He bequeathed some to Peter King and some to Masham.)

[4] Cf. *King*, i. 191: 'An Hobbist with his principle of self-preservation, whereof himself is to be judge, will not easily admit a great many plain duties of morality.'

[5] *Leviathan*, iv. xlvi. (middle of section).

reasoning itself was a computation of words, propositions, and syllogisms.[1]) But the compositional method was common to the age and not peculiar to Hobbes. Again Hobbes forestalled Locke in asserting that truth pertained to propositions rather than to terms or things,[2] and Locke may be indebted to him for suggesting this. I cannot, however, agree that Locke followed Hobbes in his nominalism, as is frequently argued, since Locke's philosophy, it seems to me, is never nominalist. Nor again should it be said that Locke borrowed Hobbes's account of the association of ideas and made it his own, for Locke's theory is very different from that of Hobbes. Professor Laird has recently pointed to certain parallelisms between the two writers;[3] but they are not such as to overthrow the view generally held, namely, that Locke's direct debt to Hobbes was very slight.

The second movement to be considered here is the Gassendist. The influence of Gassendi upon Locke, and indeed, upon English thought in general at this period, has been strangely neglected. Yet in his own day Locke was regarded by no less a critic than Leibniz as a member of the Gassendist party, and a similar view was put forward by Henry Lee in commenting on Book II of the Essay.[4] What Leibniz says is very important. The relevant passage will be found at the opening of his Nouveaux Essais, where Philalethes (who is Locke's spokesman) rejoices in the fact that new support has come to the Gassendists from England. 'You were for Descartes', he says, 'and for the opinions of the celebrated author of La Recherche de la Vérité, and I found the opinions of Gassendi, clarified by Bernier, easier and more natural. Now I feel myself greatly strengthened by the excellent work which an illustrious Englishman . . . has since published. . . . He writes obviously in the spirit of Gassendi, which is at bottom that of Democritus. He is for the vacuum and for atoms; he believes that matter might

[1] Cf. Elements of Philosophy, I. i. 2: 'By ratiocination I mean computation.'
[2] Cf. ibid. I. iii. 7, I. v. 2.
[3] Hobbes, p. 267.
[4] Anti-Scepticism or Notes upon each chapter of Mr. Locke's Essay, p. 41: '. . . he might as well have said, in Gassendus's words, Nihil est in intellectu quod non prius fuerit in sensu; for it comes all to that, even according to his own principles.' The attribution of this aphorism to Gassendi is itself interesting and instructive. He stood for a certain point of view which Locke also accepted.

think; that there are no innate ideas, that our mind is a *tabula rasa*, and that we do not always think, and he appears disposed to approve of most of the objections which Gassendi has made to Descartes. He has enriched and strengthened this system by a thousand beautiful reflections; and I do not at all doubt that now our party will triumph boldly over its adversaries, the Peripatetics and the Cartesians.'[1] Thus Leibniz, who was surely in a position to know, makes Locke a party man. For him Locke is a protagonist in the intellectual warfare then being waged between Cartesians and Gassendists, and belongs to the Gassendist party.

If Leibniz is correct, the supreme formative influence upon Locke's thought was 'Gassendi, clarified by Bernier'. How far is this view sound? In the first place it is well to remember that Leibniz wrote for European rather than English readers, and that he perhaps underestimated the strength of English influences. Cambridge Platonism and English Empiricism left their mark upon Locke's mind. And yet Gassendi is certainly as great an influence as any of these. The *Essay* becomes, in my opinion, much more intelligible if read alongside Gassendi's works; while Locke's steady opposition to Descartes and to the Cartesians both in the *Essay* and elsewhere, as, for example, in his *Examination of Malebranche*, is more easily explained if his relation to the Gassendist party is borne in mind.

Locke, no doubt, came into closest contact with the Gassendists while on his visits to France. But he must have been familiar with their point of view earlier.[2] For the first drafts of the *Essay* were written in 1671, and they already show the influence of Gassendi. The four years which followed 1671, as we saw, were crowded with political business, but in the leisure which his second visit to France gave him Locke was able to return to his philosophical reflections, so that the influences at work upon him on this visit must be reckoned as of very great importance. The reigning philosophy was then Cartesian, and Locke had an opportunity of studying it at first-hand. He was dissatisfied with much of it. He already

---

[1] *Nouveaux Essais*, i. i. (Erdmann, i. 204).
[2] He may have studied Gassendi with Boyle, who was also deeply influenced by his thought.

favoured the Gassendists, and it is not unlikely that he would soon seek out the acknowledged leader of the Gassendists since Gassendi's own death, namely, François Bernier. Bernier is mentioned by Locke in his journals on more than one occasion, although usually in reference to non-philosophical matters. These references also make it plain that Locke knew him personally. It is not at all improbable that he spent a great deal of time in his company, for Bernier was a man after Locke's heart. He was no mere philosopher. Like Locke he had been trained as a physician, but had never settled down to the life of a practising doctor. Instead he had wandered over North Africa and Asia, Syria, the Nile, Suez, and India. He wrote books on his travels which became famous in their day.[1] He was a gay companion, famed as a singer of 'bacchic' songs, and 'sought after by the most illustrious and distinguished persons of the time'.[2] Such merits would certainly count with Locke, who was always attracted by high spirits and joviality wherever they were to be found, and who loved to hear of travels in distant lands and of the curious and novel sights to be seen there. But Bernier was something more than an adventurer and wit. He was a philosopher of no small merit. And, in particular, he was the greatest enthusiast for Gassendi's philosophy then alive in Europe. In the very years in which Locke met him he was publishing an abridged (and occasionally modified) edition of the works of Gassendi which attracted a great deal of attention. It is unthinkable that Locke could have been long in his company without discussing Gassendi with him, and his interest in that philosopher must have been considerably heightened as the result of his acquaintance with Bernier.

Gassendi himself had died two decades earlier in 1655. He was born in 1592 in Provence. For some years he taught philosophy at Aix, but he also studied the new astronomy and natural science, particularly anatomy. He was a keen defender of the new learning and attacked the scholastic philosophy of the universities. He was best known as the critic of Descartes and the Cartesians. An estrangement ensued between the two philosophers, though they

---

[1] One was translated into English and published in 1671.
[2] Cf. *Nouvelle Biographie Générale*, vol. v.

were partially reconciled in 1648. His most important criticisms of Descartes may be found in the fifth set of objections to the *Méditations*. A complete edition of Gassendi's works was issued three years after his death.

Gassendi was much influenced by the Greek atomists and by Epicurus. In his philosophy he attempted to set forward an Epicureanism which could, as could no other system in his opinion, adequately explain the new world revealed by the sciences of his day. At the same time the Epicureanism proposed by him was to be purified of all its pagan elements, so that it could also express what was valuable in Christian thought. Accordingly, Epicurean atheism and the Epicurean doctrine of the soul were both rejected by him. But he reintroduced the physics, the psychology, and the ethics of the Greek school. He also restored the Epicurean doctrine that knowledge begins with sensation. 'Nihil est in intellectu quod non prius fuerit in sensu.' Nevertheless, he was no mere sensationalist, for he believed that intellect, an eternal and immaterial faculty, also plays its part in the gaining of truth. His moral philosophy was a hedonism for which the end of life was harmony between soul and body. He stressed the importance of liberty and was, in this respect, a worthy forerunner of the Encyclopaedists. He agreed with much of Descartes's philosophy, but criticized his view of matter, of space, of innate ideas, and of animal life. Like Locke, he found Descartes over-speculative. For Gassendi theory should rest upon sound empirical evidence. The collection of the latter alone, the *ars bene colligendi*, as he termed it, was insufficient. Speculation was also necessary, but it should always rest on observation and be constantly tested by it.

This brief account of Gassendi's thought is sufficient to show the close relation between him and Locke. But the reader should turn, for instance, to the first part of Gassendi's *Syntagma Philosophicum*, and to the section called *Institutio Logica*, so as to compare it with the *Essay*. The measure of Locke's debt to Gassendi will probably surprise him. Gassendi divides the *Institutio* into four parts, of imagination, of the proposition, of the syllogism, and of method. I have here space to quote from the first part only, and shall take the second of its eighteen canons to illustrate my point.

The canon runs: 'Every idea which exists in the mind originates in the senses.' Gassendi adds the following explanation: 'For whoever is born blind has no idea of colour, since he lacks the sense of vision whereby that idea is attained; whoever is born deaf has no idea of sound, since he lacks the sense of hearing whereby that is attained. And if any one were wholly deprived of senses (which, however, is impossible since all creatures have touch) he could not have the idea of anything nor could he imagine anything. Hence the celebrated saying "There is nothing in the intellect that was not previously in the senses", or again the intellect or the mind is *tabula rasa* on which nothing has been imprinted or depicted. Hence also the difficulties they find in proving their assertions who assert that ideas are impressed naturally and innately on the mind (*ideas a natura impressas*) and are not acquired by the senses.' Here surely is the foundation upon which Locke erects the first two books of the *Essay*.[1]

---

[1] If it were necessary, there is further evidence of Locke's having studied Gassendi's works in the fact that he quotes Gassendi's opinion of various other thinkers from time to time in the notebook in the Lovelace Collection, in which Locke gathered together such opinions. There is also a complete set of Bernier's eight-volumed abridgement of Gassendi's works amongst the books bequeathed to Peter King and now in the Lovelace Collection.

III

MATURITY (1689-1704)

I

LOCKE was fifty-six when he returned from Holland. He was already known in person to a large circle of friends and by repute to many others. But now he was to become a national figure, the prophet of the Whig party which had put William on the throne. His first publication was the *Letter Concerning Toleration* which appeared anonymously soon after his return.[1] (The measure of toleration granted later by the new government in 1690 was niggardly and ungenerous, and the opportunity for uniting all the sects into one broad comprehensive Church, as Locke and the Latitudinarians desired, was lost.) In 1689/90 appeared another anonymous publication upon which Locke had been working for some years, the *Two Treatises on Civil Government*. The first treatise is an attack on Filmer's *Patriarcha* (published posthumously in 1680), the second presents Locke's own positive contribution to political theory. The immediate purpose of the book is made explicit in the preface:[2] 'to establish the throne of our great restorer, our present King William; to make good his title, in the consent of the people . . . and to justify to the world the people of England, whose love of their just and natural rights, with their resolution to preserve them, saved the nation when it was on the very brink of slavery and ruin.'[3] In 1690 also Locke's greatest

---

[1] Jonas Proast criticized this work in his *The Argument of the 'Letter concerning Toleration' briefly considered and answered*, published in April 1690. Locke replied with his *Second Letter Concerning Toleration*, 1690. Proast replied in February of the next year, and Locke wrote his *Third Letter*, 1692. Twelve years later Proast returned to the attack and Locke began, but never finished, a *Fourth Letter On Toleration*, cf. below, p. 293, n. 1.

[2] It is regrettable that the splendid preface which Locke wrote for this book is so frequently omitted from modern editions. On the 1690, 1694, 1698, 1714, and 1764 editions of this work cf. J. W. Gough's edition of *The Second Treatise of Civil Government*, p. xxxix, Blackwell, Oxford, 1946. Cf. further Peter Laslett's edition of this work, Cambridge, 1960.

[3] The book, however, was not written in 1688-9, cf. the introduction to Peter Laslett's edition, Cambridge, 1960, pp. 45 ff.

work, the *Essay Concerning Human Understanding*, appeared. (I append a special note showing how the *Essay* was written.[1]) For the copyright of the *Essay* Locke received the sum of £30.[2]

During the years 1689–90 Locke resided in Westminster, London. He had been offered ambassadorial appointments by the King, but he politely refused them. Instead he accepted a post as Commissioner of Appeals that brought with it a salary of £200 per annum. When the London air affected his weak lungs he would retire to Lord Peterborough's house on the fringes of the town. But frequently he found it necessary to go farther afield to Oates in Essex, where he was sure of a welcome from Sir Francis and Lady Masham. From the Clarke correspondence we can see that he visited Oates very shortly after his return from Holland. He spent many weeks there in the summer of 1690, and again in October and at Christmas.

Lady Masham or Damaris Cudworth was now a young woman of thirty-two, and Locke had known her for at least ten years. She fully recognized Locke's worth and welcomed him warmly to her house, while he found in her steady friendship a comfort and support which proved invaluable to him in his declining years. Oates became his refuge and in 1691 he made it his permanent residence. 'His company', Lady Masham explains to Leclerc, 'could not but be very desirable to us, and he had all the assurances we could give him of being always welcome here; but to make him easy in living with us it was necessary he should do so on his own terms, which Sir Francis at last consenting to, Mr. Locke then believed himself at home with us, and resolved, if it pleased God, here to end his days, as he did.'

At this pleasant retreat, in addition to Sir Francis and his wife, lived Mrs. Cudworth, Esther, Lady Masham's step-daughter, and Francis, her six-year-old son. Other friends came to visit Locke. Already, in 1691, we read of visits from the Clarkes with their children, Edward and Elizabeth, and one also from Isaac Newton. Locke, no doubt, would be particularly happy to talk with Newton of his scientific work, although scientific subjects were not the only

[1] Cf. p. 50 below.
[2] The agreements between him and his publishers in connexion with this and subsequent editions are to be found in the Lovelace Collection.

ones discussed, for Newton by this time was even more interested
in Biblical criticism than in scientific inquiry. The years sped by at
Oates pleasantly and quietly, being only interrupted by occasional
visits to London. In 1693 appeared his *Some Thoughts Concerning
Education*, a book based largely upon the letters sent to Clarke
from Holland, in which Locke had outlined his ideal of a sound
education. During these years he was also busy on the second
edition of the *Essay*, which was already in demand, the first edition
having been exhausted by September 1692. The correspondence
with Molyneux, which had now begun, throws light on the task
he had to face in connexion with the preparation of this second
edition, while that with Clarke gives the gossip of Oates for these
years and much information about Locke's interests and properties
in Somerset. The second edition of the *Essay* duly appeared in
1694. Already the work was attracting attention. It had been in use
in Trinity College, Dublin, since 1692 and was not unknown to the
other universities. The public at large had given it a good welcome,
and although John Norris had criticized it adversely in 1690, his
was as yet the only dissentient voice. By this time the Whigs were
in full power and Locke could number amongst his friends the
leaders of the party. Edward Clarke was a great force in Parliament. Somers, who became Lord Chancellor, and Montague, afterwards the Earl of Halifax, were close friends of Locke and were
guided by his advice. Locke was one of the original subscribers to
the Bank of England (subscribing £500). In Locke's correspondence for these years there is also frequent reference to a small
club, called the 'College', of which he was a member, which interested itself in public affairs and worked for reforms. In particular
it concerned itself with the Coinage Act. The coin of the realm was
being constantly clipped and much counterfeit coinage was in
circulation. Already in 1692 Locke had made certain suggestions
in a paper added to his *Some Considerations of the Consequences
of the Lowering of Interest and the Raising of the Value of
Money*[1] and entitled *Of Raising our Coin*. And he co-operated
with his friends in the intervening years to work out an effective

---

[1] William Lowndes attacked this work and Locke replied in 1695 with his
Further Considerations Concerning Raising the Value of Money. He had already
made the main points set forward in this work in an earlier work published also

plan of action. In April 1696 it was finally decided to call in all debased coinage and to recoin it according to standard weight, the cost to fall upon the Exchequer. This reform was very much to Locke's liking, and the correspondence of the time makes it abundantly clear that he and the 'College' played an important part in bringing it about.

Another undertaking of these years was the anonymous publication of the *Reasonableness of Christianity* in the summer of 1695. In it Locke sought to define the one essential of true Christianity, namely, the recognition of Christ as the Messiah. This theme might not appear very provocative, but it produced some very bitter controversy. The last decade of the seventeenth century witnessed the sudden rise of Unitarianism, and when the *Reasonableness* appeared Locke was at once suspected of belonging to that sect. He was known to be friendly with Thomas Firmin, the leader of the anti-Trinitarians, and his demand for a simpler Christianity was interpreted as Unitarianism. John Edwards attacked Locke vigorously in his *Some Thoughts Concerning the Several Causes and Occasions of Atheism, especially in the Present*

in 1695: *Short Observations on a Printed Paper, entituled, For Encouraging the Coinage of Silver Money in England, and after for Keeping it Here.*

The detailed consideration of Locke's economic theories is not within the scope of this present work. Locke was a Mercantilist, and Heckscher, perhaps the leading authority on this school, thinks highly of his contribution. 'What places Locke in so unique a position is the fact that his philosophic training enabled him at times to attain a clarity of argument unparalleled among other mercantilist writers. At the same time, since his general outlook was mercantilist in every respect, one may obtain from him a clearer picture of this outlook than from any other writer, at least in those matters with which he deals.' Heckscher, *Mercantilism* (London, 1935), p. 203. The whole of Part IV, 'Mercantilism as a Monetary System', is very relevant. Locke's main concern was with the quantity theory of money, exchange relationships between countries and theory of international prices, the use and control of the precious metals, and usury. In addition to Heckscher, the following books may also be consulted: Angell, J. W., *The Theory of International Prices*, Harvard, 1926 (particularly ch. ii, 'English Thought before the Nineteenth Century', where a good deal of attention is given to Locke); Monroe, A. E., *Monetary Theory before Adam Smith*, Harvard, 1923; Keynes, J. M., *The General Theory of Employment, Interest and Money*, London, 1936 (particularly ch. xxiii, where Keynes argues that Locke's theories are still of great importance); Cossa, L., *An Introduction to the Study of Political Economy*, London, 1893, pp. 241–5; Stark, W., *The Ideal Foundations of Economic Thought*, London, 1943. Also articles on Locke by D.G.R. and J.B. in Palgrave's *Dictionary of Political Economy*, vol. ii. I thank Professor R. B. Forrester of Aberystwyth for information on this matter.

Age. Locke replied with a *Vindication*, in which he emphatically denied that he was of the anti-Trinitarian party. In 1697 a second *Vindication* appeared, in answer to Edwards's *Socinianism Unmasked*.

Throughout these years Locke continued to act as a Commissioner of Appeals, although there were frequent occasions when ill health prevented him from attending to his business in London. In May 1696 he was appointed a commissioner to the new Board of Trade and Plantations set up by Sir John Somers, at a salary of £1,000 a year. The secretary to the Board was William Popple, who had translated Locke's *Letter on Toleration*. Locke set to work with characteristic zeal and industry. He was clearly the guiding spirit of the Board during its first years. And if one recalls that this body was the forerunner of both the present Board of Trade and the Colonial Office, it will be understood that the work to which Locke now gave himself was of real administrative importance. From June 1696 onwards the Board sat daily, and through the summer months Locke was in constant attendance.[1] In 1697 he found the duties so heavy in his broken state of health that he tried to resign, but those in authority would not hear of his retirement, and he continued in the office, attending to it diligently whenever his health permitted, until 1700. After 1700 he avoided all public employment.

When attendance upon his health kept him at Oates he would turn to his literary work. It was during these last years of the century that Locke engaged himself in a prolonged debate with Stillingfleet, Bishop of Worcester. In his *Discourse in Vindication of the Doctrine of the Trinity* Stillingfleet sought for the philosophy behind the anti-Trinitarian movement and professed to find it in Locke's 'new way of ideas' as expounded in the *Essay*. In January of 1697 Locke replied in *A Letter to the Bishop of Worcester concerning some passages, relating to Mr. Locke's Essay*. Stillingfleet was ready for the fight and replied in April, to which

---

[1] In the Lovelace Collection is a big batch of private papers dealing with the various problems that had to be faced by the Commissioners. These should be of great value to the social and economic historian. Cf. further Peter Laslett, 'John Locke, the Great Recoinage and the Origins of the Board of Trade' in *John Locke, Problems and Perspectives*, pp. 137 ff.

Locke published his second reply in June. At the beginning of 1698 Stillingfleet published a further pamphlet 'wherein his [Locke's] Notion of Ideas is proved to be inconsistent with itself and with the Articles of the Christian Faith'. Locke replied in May 1698 (though the pamphlet was not published until 1699). We shall have occasion later to note some of the points at issue between the disputants. Many of the criticisms made by the Bishop were pertinent in the extreme, and Locke's efforts to answer them throw much light on his position in general. Other opponents, Thomas Burnet and Sergeant, wrote against the *Essay*, but Locke did not consider himself called upon to answer any of these attacks.[1]

In the winter of 1697–8 Locke was seriously ill. 'My time', he complains to Clarke, 'is all divided between my bed and the chimney corner, for not being able to walk for want of breath upon the least stirring, I am a prisoner not only to the house but to my chair, so that never did anybody so truly lead a sedentary life as I do'.[2] But under the constant care of Lady Masham and Esther, and through the ministrations of Elizabeth Clarke, now growing into womanhood, he strengthened sufficiently to return to his duties in London in 1698. This summer was made memorable by a visit from William Molyneux of Dublin, who spent some time with Locke. Molyneux had published a work on optics in 1692 in which he had praised Locke's work highly. A correspondence ensued between them which continued for many years; the tone, at first respectful, soon became affectionate. In 1698 the two were able to meet for the first time. Locke found very great pleasure in the visit, and Molyneux, to judge from the letter he forwarded to Locke on his return to Dublin, found true happiness in Locke's company. But this great joy was to be turned to sudden

---

[1] Burnet was answered by Mrs. Cockburn. Locke himself may have thought of writing a reply to Burnet, for his own copy of one of Burnet's pamphlets is filled with marginalia. (Cf. Dr. Noah Porter's 'Marginalia Locke-ana' in the *New Englander and Yale Review*, July 1887.) His copy of John Sergeant's *Solid Philosophy Asserted*, now at St. John's College, Cambridge, has also many marginal notes. Cf. Dr. J. W. Yolton's 'Locke's Marginal Replies to John Sergeant' in the *Journal of the History of Ideas* (October 1951). Apart from Stillingfleet the only critic of the *Essay* he replied to publicly was James Lowde, cf. the Epistle to the second edition of the *Essay*, 1694. Lowde's *Discourses concerning the Nature of Man* had just appeared.   [2] Locke to Clarke, 25 February 1698.

sorrow, for on the 11th October of the same year, a few weeks after his return from London, Molyneux died, and Locke was left to grieve the loss of a very worthy friend.

In his last years Locke's interests turned more and more to theology, as the letters to Limborch reveal. He had been busy for some time with the fourth edition of the *Essay*, but when this was published in 1700 he turned to the epistles of Saint Paul and wrote a paraphrase of Galatians, Corinthians, Romans, and Ephesians, together with full comments. He also prepared a preface in which he exhorts the reader to read each epistle through at one reading, and to try to understand the background and the particular circumstances in which each was written. These commentaries were prepared for the press by Locke himself, but not published until 1705–7. Together they cover almost as many pages as the *Essay* itself, and Locke's industry and vigour of mind in these last years are amazing.

In the intervals between his literary activities other matters required attention. His own needs were now few enough, 'a man out of the world', as he described himself, 'who lies abed and dreams'. But he busied himself with his friends' concerns, particularly with those of their children. Limborch's son came to England on a visit and Locke gladly made the necessary arrangements. Clarke's children went abroad and Locke knew of friends they should meet. Benjamin Furly's son sought a post in England. The third Earl of Shaftesbury, whose tuition Locke had once undertaken, had become a politician of note and Locke gave him good advice. Finally, his own nephew, Peter King, required greater and greater attention. King was already a member of parliament. He had profited from a sound legal training and was showing very great promise. Locke wrote to him frequently and his letters are full of wise advice and anxious care. In their turn all these people came to visit him at Oates, and their visits were like balm to his weary heart. He found a new friend too in the young Anthony Collins. Their correspondence only begins in May 1703, but in the last year of his life Locke found much pleasure in the company of this gifted young man, and when Collins was away from him wrote the most affectionate letters to him.

When the spring of 1704 came round Locke knew that his end
was near: 'in the race of human life where breath is wanting for
the least motion, one cannot be far from one's journey's end'. On
the 4th August he wrote his last letter to Limborch.[1] There was
still time, however, for one celebration on which he had set his
heart. Peter King had found a bride for himself in Glamorgan,
and Locke wished to welcome her to Oates. Part of the letter which
he wrote to King telling him what he was to order in London for
the feast may here be quoted: 'Four neats's tongues. Twelve par-
tridges. . . . Four pheasants. . . . Four turkey pullets, ready larded
if they be not out of season. Four fresh rabbits, if they are to be
got. Plovers, or woodcocks, or snipes, or whatever else is good to
be got at the poulterer's, except ordinary tame fowls. Twelve
Chichester male lobsters, if they can be got alive; if not, six dead
ones that are sweet. Two large crabs that are fresh. Crawfish and
prawns. . . . A double barrel of the best Colchester oysters. . . .
I desire you also to lay out between twenty and thirty shillings in
dried sweetmeats of several kinds . . . do not be sparing in the cost,
but rather exceed thirty shillings. . . . If there be anything that
you can find your wife loves, be sure that provision be made of
that, and plentifully, whether I have mentioned it or no.' The
feast was duly held at the end of September, presided over by
Locke himself aided by Lady Masham. How completely happy
he must have been amongst this merry crowd!

And, then, when the banquet was over, there was little left to do.
He was cheerful, but every day took its toll in increasing weakness.
As the month of October came to its end Locke's strength also
ebbed away. On the 27th, a Friday, he was very weak indeed; the
next morning he was a little better, and in the afternoon he rose
and dressed, and then sitting down while Lady Masham read the
Psalms to him, he presently closed his eyes and passed quietly
away. 'His death was like his life,' wrote Lady Masham, 'truly
pious, yet natural, easy and unaffected.'

He had had sufficient time to arrange for the disposal of his

[1] The letter is now at the Amsterdam Library, and it is good to see that the
hand that wrote it was firm and steady as the spirit inspiring it was serene.
(There is an entry into a book of accounts as late as the 24th October, four days
before his death.)

estate. He left behind him between four and five thousand pounds in all, most of which he bequeathed to Francis Cudworth Masham. He gave all his manuscripts and half his books to Peter King. (These are now the Lovelace Collection.) He forgot none of his friends, nor the servants who had waited on him, nor again the poor of Pensford and of Oates. He was buried simply, as he had desired, in the parish church of High Laver.

II

A modest epitaph of his own composition is inscribed on Locke's tombstone, and in it he advises the reader to turn to his written works if he would know what sort of man he was. The works reveal the philosopher, and undoubtedly their most characteristic virtue is what is sometimes called 'common sense' but is really prudence. The phrase 'a common-sense philosophy' is ambiguous. If it means a ready acceptance of the customary opinions of one's age, Locke's philosophy was no more 'common-sense' than, let us say, Descartes's, Kant's, or Bradley's. Of course, his own age influenced him, and admittedly Locke is not eminently original. But his debt was not one to the ordinary Englishman of the seventeenth century. It is well to remind ourselves of the fact that even to a highly educated man like Stillingfleet Locke's philosophy appeared new, revolutionary, and dangerous. That we today find it frequently obvious and almost commonplace is the measure of its influence upon us. If, again, a common-sense philosophy is one which accepts positions accepted everywhere and in every age by the ordinary, unreflective man, such as that the material world exists independently of the mind knowing it, that the spiritual is real, and the like, it is still to be doubted whether Locke's philosophy is a common-sense philosophy. For would this unreflective man agree with all the doctrines to be found in Locke's works, for instance, the distinction between primary and secondary qualities? Surely what is meant by us when we talk of Locke's 'common sense' is simply that he never allowed his argument to carry him forward to any extreme position. In other words, we refer to that wise caution, that prudence which the Encyclopaedists had in mind when they talked of *le sage Locke*.

Prudence is a virtue one finds on every page of Locke's work. It must have been obvious to him, for instance, that his view of material substance was most inadequate and that much of his teaching pointed inevitably to an idealism of some sort or other. But he never propounded such a doctrine. If Locke had lived to read Berkeley he would have regarded him, no doubt, as a brilliant thinker but lacking caution.[1] Again, he was as puzzled as any other philosopher by the mind–body relation and the occurrence of sensation. The physical and physiological concomitants of the sensation of white seem to be so little connected with it that Locke had to admit that the Occasionalist hypothesis was not wholly absurd. And yet he did not accept Occasionalism. It was too easy a solution of a grave difficulty, just as idealism was too easy an escape from the difficulties which our imperfect knowledge of things brought into being. On yet other occasions when the argument had shown him that there were some elements of truth in the position of the materialists, he would not accept materialism; or when, again, he saw the usefulness for science of Descartes's view that we might deal with matter entirely in terms of extension, he recalled to himself a factor neglected by Descartes, our experience of solidity, and rejected the Cartesian view. Being prudent Locke avoided premature syntheses; and this in part explains why he offered us no finished, rounded system of philosophy.

Locke, it is clear, was prudent by nature. Moreover, the spirit of the age and his own wide experience in the world of thought had deepened his caution. He was genuinely afraid of wild speculation. The same restraint that kept him from publishing his thoughts until late in life kept him free also from extravagances of any kind in those thoughts. He particularly despised the showman in philosophy, who takes pleasure in erecting the most unlikely systems so as to draw attention to himself. He put truth first, even if it meant being humdrum. 'That which makes my writings tolerable, if

---

[1] Locke did comment upon and reject idealism, but the idealism of Norris and Malebranche. We have (a) his *Examination* of Malebranche, and (b) his *Remarks* on Norris, together with (c) the MS. in the Lovelace Collection 'J.L. to Mr. Norris'. Mrs. A. Johnston in a work as yet unpublished has argued successfully in my opinion that all three MSS. are criticisms first of Norris, and that the *Examination* was never meant to be a full consideration of Malebranche's philosophy.

anything', he says to Molyneux,[1] 'is only this, that I never write for anything but truth and never publish anything to others which I am not fully persuaded of myself.' 'If I have anything to boast of', he says later to Collins,[2] 'it is that I sincerely love and seek truth with indifferency whom it pleases or displeases.' That is a proud boast to make, but in his case not a foolish one, for his works justify it. It is so also with his style. He never sets out to impress, he uses homely, unaffected language and avoids technical jargon so far as he possibly can. He is quiet, even prosaic; very rarely does he allow himself to become eloquent. He is sometimes verbose, a fault for which he apologizes on more than one occasion, but he was in no great haste and wrote for leisured readers. The private papers he left behind him testify to his great learning. He must have been one of the most learned men of his age. But he makes no show of erudition. His works also reveal the extent of his interests. Logic and epistemology, ethics and economics, politics, both civil and ecclesiastical, theology and Biblical criticism (not to mention medicine and physics), all come within his scope, and he treats them one and all as an expert. At the same time he was most modest in the claims he made for himself, and ever ready to admit himself in error. Such is the picture which the works reveal to us, a modest, simple, unaffected man, sincerely seeking for truth, catholic in his interests, and more than usually prudent.

Locke's correspondence, his private papers, and such memoirs as we have of him, written by those who knew him, confirm and complete this picture. Here we see the full man; all the characteristics already noted are present, but the emotional side of him, which is kept in check in his works, is freed. It is not surprising to read that in private life he was neat in his dress and orderly in his activities. (He seems to have kept strict account of every penny he ever spent, to judge from the notebooks left behind in the Lovelace Collection.) He disliked unnecessary display. He was modest. 'No man', said Lady Masham, 'was less magisterial or dogmatic than he, or less offended with any man's dissenting from him in opinion.' In eating and drinking he was temperate and, for reasons of health, even abstemious. His friends trusted his wisdom and his

---

[1] 30 March 1696.   [2] 17 November 1703.

good sense, and admired his intimate knowledge of men and affairs. Thus far the picture we have of him accords with the personality revealed in his writings. But the impression left upon one after a cursory reading of the *Essay* is of the cold, immobile philosopher. It is in this connexion, more than any other, that Locke's correspondence and private papers can help to correct our first impression. The absence of warmth and feeling in the works is intentional. There is ample evidence to show that the emotional side of Locke's nature was strong. Pierre Coste, who knew him well, tells us that he was naturally a hot-tempered man, but had learnt to control his feelings. Essentially, his nature was warm and generous. We may illustrate this side of his character by referring to his relations, first, with children, and secondly, with his adult friends.

Children attracted Locke greatly. He made himself the guardian and protector of all his friends' children. Esther and Francis Masham were, of course, especial favourites. He took much trouble with the Shaftesbury and Peterborough children. We know most, however, about his friendship with Elizabeth and Edward Clarke. And it is remarkable to what trouble he was prepared to go for their sakes. Edward used to stay with him for weeks at a time so that Locke might guide him in his lessons. Elizabeth seems to have been the greatest friend of all; he always writes of her as his 'wife' or 'mistress'. He is for ever scheming ways in which the education of the children might be improved. He was so fond of them that he found it difficult to find fault in them, and he was always ready to excuse their failings. Mrs. Clarke, in an amusing letter to Locke, finds it necessary to acquaint him with the true state of affairs. Of Edward she says: 'I fear you think him forwarder than he is. He is a sort of downright honest block-headed boy and what he has in him is pretty hard to find out.' Even Elizabeth needs correction. She 'seems to look mightily concerned when you tell her of a fault and like a little saint, but the next time it is forgotten'. Locke himself, after spending some weeks in coaching young Edward, has to admit that he is somewhat lacking in application, attributing the fault (and partly excusing it at the same time) to a certain 'saunteringness that is in his temper'. No domestic matters were too small to be reported to Locke, and the children must have regarded him as a third parent. In April 1696 he wrote to Clarke: 'I have been so long accustomed to take care of your son that it is now habitual to me.' The children on their side, it is good to think, were not wholly unappreciative of Locke's many kindnesses towards them, if we may judge by the beautiful letters, full of gratitude and tender solicitude, which Elizabeth penned to him in the last years of his life.

His amiability and tenderness become clear also in his relations with friends. Friendship was a necessity for him. 'To live', he wrote once to Esther Masham, 'is to be where and with whom one likes.' The company of others inspired him. The *Essay* was begun in a talk with friends. His letter on toleration was addressed to Limborch and was the outcome of talks with him. The *Thoughts Concerning Education* were originally letters to Clarke. There are some suggestions that his Biblical criticism at Oates was the fruit of conversations with Lady Masham. All through his life he sought the company of men of taste, of wit and humour. He liked his companions to be gay and jolly. He possessed an infectious gaiety of his own and sought for it in others. But he needed more than gaiety. His letters to his more intimate acquaintances, frequently intense, even poignant, are more than mere expressions of friendship. Fox Bourne truly remarked: 'He showed a lover's temperament.' The correspondence between Locke and Molyneux proves this. The respect of one true man for another grows into friendship and friendship into love. Their desire to meet each other increases with the passage of the years until it becomes almost a necessity. And then the quick and tragic sequel to their meeting and Locke's grief-laden letter to Molyneux's brother. Molyneux was certainly more to him than friend. So was Clarke. 'I love my country and I love you.' The letters to Limborch are equally warm and to the last are charged with affection. 'Vale vir colendissime et me, ut facis, ama.' One might quote from his letters to Thoynard and to Newton and others. But strongest of all are the letters to the youthful Collins in the very last year of his life. He was old now and nearing the end of his journey, and he had friends enough. But the passionate ardour of the man was uncooled and his need for human friendship still as great as ever. His love found for itself a new object. He almost flung himself at Collins. 'Pray pardon the forwardness wherewith I throw my arms about your neck.'

Locke, it is clear, possessed an inordinate strength of affection. True, the age demanded of the letter-writer courtesy and politeness even to the point of flattery. But there is more than politeness here. A powerful, emotional nature expresses itself in them. I stress this point because it has been neglected and because the purpose of the writings becomes clearer if it be kept in mind. Beneath their calm, unruffled surface there is a turbulent, fiery spirit, burning all the more fiercely because of the self-imposed restraint. Just as passionately as he loved Limborch and Collins and the rest, so he loved toleration, true religion, piety, justice, goodwill amongst men, and, most of all, truth. This Locke was not the cold, disinterested thinker we sometimes imagine him to have been. He was warm and passionate with life. But he knew how to keep the emotional side of his nature in check lest truth should suffer, and how to assume the impartial, objective air of the judge and the critic.

There are other facets of Locke's character upon which we might have touched, his homely humour—sometimes, particularly in his youth, a trifle forced and heavy—his unfailing courtesy, his patriotism, for he was a true Englishman. We might also have illustrated his deep religious piety. (As we have seen, he disliked too fierce an exhibition of religious fervour, as he also disliked intolerance and excessive dogma. But there is no denying the reality of his religious life and emotion. The humility and piety which shine through the *Reasonableness of Christianity* are the fruit of a truly religious spirit.) But it is time now to turn to an exposition of his doctrine which, in spite of its occasional verbosity, its incompleteness, and its apparent contradictions, has established Locke's name as the greatest in English philosophy.

Note 1

HOW THE *ESSAY* WAS WRITTEN

UNTIL recently very little was known of how John Locke wrote the *Essay Concerning Human Understanding*, but considerable new information has been obtained with the discovery of three drafts of the *Essay*, two written in 1671,[1] nineteen years before the *Essay* itself appeared, and the third in 1685. I have named these drafts A, B, and C respectively.[2] In addition to these three another draft has been recently discovered[3] in the Shaftesbury Papers at the Public Record Office (London). This, however, is a copy of Draft A with some slight though interesting variations.

Drafts A and B were discovered amongst Locke's private papers in the Lovelace Collection. This well-preserved collection contains all Locke's private papers at the time of his death.[4] They were bequeathed by him to his nephew, Peter King, the founder of the Lovelace family, and are now in the possession of the present Earl of Lovelace.[5] They consist, firstly, of hundreds of letters to Locke with occasional drafts of Locke's replies; secondly, of numerous notebooks, some recording his domestic arrangements and payments, others noting points of medical information, others again containing the titles of, and quotations from, the books he had read; thirdly, of two catalogues containing the complete list of books in his library at his death, a very valuable item; fourthly, of miscellaneous papers, including his agreements with his publishers and his will; fifthly, of journals kept of the years 1676–88,[6] which are full of information, biographical, medical, and philosophical; sixthly, of some forty manuscripts, being unpublished papers on various topics, early drafts and corrections of his published writings, together with the manuscripts of certain of his works. This rich collection of Locke's papers still remains for the most part unpublished. In the *Life of Locke* written by Lord King (1829) some of the more interesting manuscripts are printed together with

[1] *An Early Draft of Locke's Essay*, ed. Aaron and Gibb, Oxford, 1936; *An Essay Concerning the Understanding*, ed. Rand, Harvard, 1931.

[2] For Draft C, cf. Note 2 following.

[3] By Mr. Peter Laslett, cf. *Mind*, January 1952, pp. 89–92.

[4] For a list of the philosophical manuscripts in this collection, cf. the Appendix below, pp. 310–12.

[5] Since 1937 these papers, with the exception of a few MSS. including the book containing Draft A, have come into the possession of the Bodleian Library, Oxford.

[6] Excepting only that for the year 1679, which is in the British Museum.

many excerpts from the journals; but by the opening of the present century only a small fraction of the Collection had thus been published.

With the aid of the drafts, the journals, and Locke's correspondence, it is now possible to give a fairly consecutive story of how Locke's *Essay* was written. At the opening of that work Locke takes his reader into his confidence. The *Essay*, he remarks, arose out of a meeting of five or six friends gathered together to discuss a point in philosophy. They found some difficulty in proceeding with their discussion and Locke suggested a prior inquiry: the extent and limitations of the human understanding. He was asked to prepare a paper on this topic. 'Some hasty and undigested thoughts, on a subject I had never before considered, which I set down against our next meeting, gave the first entrance into this discourse, which, having been thus begun by chance, was continued by entreaty; written by incoherent parcels; and after long intervals of neglect, resumed again, as my humour or occasions permitted; and at last, in a retirement, where an attendance on my health gave me leisure, it was brought into that order thou now seest it.'[1]

This meeting of friends must have taken place early in 1671.[2] The paper which Locke wrote for the next meeting is not amongst those which he bequeathed to King, unless it be Draft A. This, however, is unlikely in view of the length of the draft (although it may be possible that the opening sections of the draft were the actual paper read to the society). One may guess at the contents of this paper. It argued, no doubt, that our knowledge is derived from our senses; and that whatever lies wholly outside the bounds of human experience is not knowable by us. After the meeting, in consequence, perhaps, of the criticisms of his friends, he found it necessary to strengthen his argument in various ways. Meanwhile, the conviction grew upon him that he had before him a problem of the greatest importance. And so he devoted a good part of the summer of 1671 to its solution, and wrote out Draft A. But he had no sooner finished it than he decided to begin again from the beginning. This is clear from the final page of the draft, which goes back to a matter considered at the outset, and reveals Locke's dissatisfaction with the opening pages. In the autumn of 1671 he tried again, this time writing his thoughts out in a neat and orderly manner and in a manuscript very obviously meant for the press. But Draft B also is unfinished, and it is unfinished in respect to the very

[1] *Epistle to the Reader.* [2] The Lovelace Collection enables us to follow Locke's thinking on epistemology even prior to the 1671 drafts. Von Leyden discusses the matter in *John Locke: Essays on the Law of Nature* (Oxford, 1954), cf. section 7 of his introduction.

problem which Locke set out to solve, namely, that of the extent and limitations of knowledge. Its incomplete state may be due to the fact that Locke had no time to proceed with it; but it is more likely that he did not then know how to finish it.

A comparison between Draft A and Draft B, and again, between both and the *Essay*, gives interesting results. Draft A contains Locke's first rough thoughts. He comes to the main problem, that of the extent of human knowledge, very early in the draft, but, as he proceeds, realizes that there are more and more prior problems to be solved. In Draft B he is concerned almost entirely with these prior problems and the main problem remains practically untouched. Thus Draft A, unlike Draft B, reveals some of Locke's thinking on the main problems of Book IV. On the other hand, it hardly touches the subject matter of Book I and only deals crudely with that of Book II.[1] Draft B, however, covers much of the ground covered by Locke in Book II and does it so well that Locke was able to take much of it over bodily into the *Essay*. None the less, there are some important differences.

If we compare Draft B with the *Essay* as published we may see wherein the former is lacking as compared with the latter, and what problems faced Locke during the nineteen years which elapsed before the *Essay* was fit for publication. Very little of Book I of the *Essay* is not already contained in Draft B. It is true that there are differences in order. In Draft B he first deals with innate practical principles, and the discussion of innate speculative principles is not so full. But no book of the *Essay* is so fully represented in the draft as Book I. When we turn to Book II we see that its scheme and a very great number of the details are already contained in the draft. That the fountains of knowledge are sensation and reflection, that ideas are divisible into simple and complex, are points common to draft and *Essay*. The former contains a great deal of the actual classification and also substantial accounts of space, duration, number, infinity, and relations, including moral relations. Yet there are some noteworthy omissions. Psychological considerations are few. In the draft he does not consider perception, neglects abstraction, has little to say about the mind's operations and the modes of thinking. Nor have the *Essay*'s chapters on pleasure and pain, and on power, any counterpart in Draft B.[2] Similarly, the discussion as to whether the mind always thinks and the detailed examination of solidity are absent from it. Primary and secondary qualities are distinguished in the draft, though I cannot trace the use of the word 'secondary'. Finally, the five chapters which

[1] On Draft A cf. also the introduction to Aaron and Gibb, *An Early Draft of Locke's Essay*.   [2] But see von Leyden, *Law of Nature*, p. 263 ff.

bring Book II to an end were not part of the original scheme as embodied in Draft B.

It is when we turn to Books III and IV, however, that we see the biggest omissions in the draft. In the latter the discussion on words is a digression apparently not at first intended. In the *Essay* Locke finds it necessary to devote a whole book to it, the third. The paragraphs taken over into the published *Essay* from Draft B become now considerably fewer. The whole problem of words, their imperfection and abuse, had to be reconsidered and re-examined in far greater detail. This is also true of the problem of universals and abstraction hardly touched upon in the draft. Book IV of the *Essay* again has very little corresponding to it in the draft. It is not too much to say that Draft B fails entirely to inquire into the limits and extent of human knowledge, though this was the main problem which the author had set before himself in 1671, as is clear from Draft A. Nor has Draft B any satisfactory theory of knowledge. With the exception of a few minor points, the all-important opening chapters of Book IV are absent in the draft. Locke was in search of a satisfactory theory of knowledge and of its object, but in 1671 he had not found it.

When writing these first drafts Locke was in the service of Ashley, and his leisure hours were few enough. This may explain why the *Essay* was not finished outright. Moreover, the years that followed were, if anything, busier, until, as we saw, in 1675 Locke was compelled for reasons of health to take a holiday in France. Now that he was freed from onerous political duties as adviser to Shaftesbury he returned to the problems of the *Essay*. Our sources of information from this point forward are the journals and correspondence. They throw a great deal of light on the growth of the *Essay* in Locke's mind. Already in 1676 we find him dealing with will, power, pleasure and pain, the passions, matters partially neglected in Draft B, with simple ideas of reflection, extension, faith and reason, and the idea of a Deity. Then in 1677 we find an essay on knowledge, its extent and measure, which is clearly in preparation for Book IV, also considerations of distance and space, of study, of error, of understanding, and a division of the branches of knowledge. In the 1678 journal the philosophical problems discussed are those of relation, space, memory, madness, together with many references to books he was then reading in French philosophy. Locke left Paris in 1679 to return to his post under Shaftesbury. The next two years were again so full of work of a political sort that he had no time for philosophy. In the journal for 1680 there is little reference to philosophical problems, but in 1681, it will be remembered, he returned to Oxford and once more found time for philosophy. In the journal for the year are notes on knowledge and on truth. In 1682 he is working on proofs of God's existence and on the relation (or absence of relation) between matter and thought. Already, also, he is preparing his attack on enthusiasm. 1683 was another restless year, and, as we should expect, his journal contains little philosophical matter.

From the Clarke correspondence we see that Locke spent the winter of 1684–5 working on 'my inquiry concerning Humane Understanding, a subject which I had for a good while backwards thought on by catches and set down without method several thoughts upon as they had at distinct times and several occasions come in my way; and which I was now willing in this retreat to turn into a less confused and coherent discourse'.[1] In the months that follow we find that parts of the *Essay* are ready to be sent to the Earl of Pembroke for his perusal.[2] By October 1686 the third book is ready and by December the fourth. Thus the whole *Essay* was finished by the end of 1686, though he again worked over it in the next two years so as to bring a little more order into it. 'For there are so many repetitions in it, and so many things still misplaced, that though I venture it confused as it is to your friendship, yet I cannot think these papers in a condition to be showed anyone else, till by another review I have reduced them into yet better order.'[3] A little farther in the same letter he adds an interesting remark: 'For being resolved to examine Humane Understanding, and the ways of our knowledge, not by others' opinions, but by what I could from my own observations collect myself, I have purposely avoided the reading of all books that treated any way of the subject, that so I might have nothing to bias me any way.'[4] This does not mean, however, that the teachings of the *Essay* were uninfluenced by other writers. We have already shown how deeply indebted he was to others. In 1687 and 1688 he continued, at intervals, to work on his *Essay*; thus we find him writing to Furly, on 19 January 1688: 'I am resolved to busy my thoughts about finishing my Essay "De Intellectu".' And he had already prepared the abridgement of the *Essay* meant for

[1] 1 January 1685.

[2] This no doubt was Draft C. Cf. Note 2.

[3] In this letter Locke mentions again the 'accidental discourse' which was the occasion of the *Essay* 'which is now five or six years' (so Rand, p. 177). But this seems an obvious slip: fifteen or sixteen is meant. If it is not a slip then there must have been another discussion in 1680 or 1681 which reawakened Locke's interest in this problem. I think this, however, unlikely.

[4] Cf. also James Tyrrell's letter to Locke in the Lovelace Collection, 18 March 1689/90 (Bodl. MS. Locke, c. 22).

Leclerc. When Locke returned to England after his enforced sojourn in Holland he had the *Essay* more or less ready for the press, and soon found publishers. Even in 1689, however, he still worked upon it; there is the reference to 'this present year, 1689' in II. xiv. 30 to prove this. In May 1689 he wrote his dedication to the Earl of Pembroke and in December he is able to report to Limborch that the printing of it is almost over. 'The die is cast and I am now launched on the wide ocean.'[1] Before the year was over the *Essay* was already on sale in the bookshops of London and Oxford, though the edition bore the date of 1690. There were two issues of this first (1690) edition, the one 'printed by Eliz. Holt, for Thomas Basset, at the George in Fleet Street, near St. Dunstan's Church' and the other 'printed for Tho. Basset, and sold by Edw. Mory at the sign of the Three Bibles in St. Paul's Church-Yard'. [I am grateful to Mrs. A. Johnston for this information.][2]

Note 2

DRAFT C OF LOCKE'S *ESSAY*

AFTER writing the drafts of 1671 other matters engaged Locke's attention, but he was able to make periodic revisions of his *Essay* and fortunately one such revision, dated 1685, survives and is now in the Pierpont Morgan Library, New York. This draft, Draft C, is not likely to prove as valuable as Drafts A and B. For, first, it is a draft of Books I and II of the *Essay* only; secondly, it contains comparatively little not already published, either in Draft B or in the 1690 text. Nevertheless, it shows the position at an interesting moment in the writing of the *Essay*. We see from the Clarke correspondence that by the spring of 1685 parts of a new revision of the *Essay* were ready to be sent to the Earl of Pembroke for his perusal. It is likely that more than one copy of the draft was made and that one was prepared for Edward Clarke. This would be Draft C, consisting of Books I and II. Book III was not ready till October 1686 and Book IV not till December of that year. Even then Locke was still dissatisfied with the *Essay* and spoke of the need for 'another review'. The chief value of Draft C is that it

---

[1] 3 December 1689.

[2] The sectional headings which appear in most editions of the *Essay* are Locke's. They are to be found in the First Edition, though not at the heads of the sections but under *Contents*. In the Second Edition they appear marginally at the head of the various sections.

shows us the state of Books I and II of the *Essay* in 1685 and, by comparison with the 1690 text, the nature of the changes which Locke still found it necessary to make in the final revision of the whole work. It is only regrettable that we have not the 1686 drafts of Books III and IV, for these would be likely to show larger advances from Draft B to C and from C to the 1690 text.

A word should be said about the history of Draft C. It was known to Locke scholars that such a document was in being a century ago, since it was referred to by Thomas Forster in 1830 as being then in his possession, but later its whereabouts had become unknown. In February 1952 Mr. G. K. Boyce of the Pierpont Morgan Library listed the document in the *Publications of the Modern Language Association of America* and this led to its identification (by Mrs. Arthur Johnston and Mr. Peter Laslett) with the missing draft.[1] In the Pierpont Morgan Library is a letter from Forster to H. B. H. Beaufoy of South Lambeth to whom he gave Draft C on 27 August 1849. In this letter Forster says:

'After I got home last week I recollected your having asked me to give you the history of the MSS. of John Locke and how they came into my father's hands, which I have since found. The copy of the Essay, which you have, seems to have been Locke's earliest thoughts on the subject and is for this reason very curious: he consigned it to the three persons named in the flyleaf, to the survivor of which, Mr. John Furly of Rotterdam,[2] it naturally came and he gave it or left it (I am not sure which) to my grandfather, as his nearest akin, together with a parcel of letters from Algernon Sydney, Locke and Lord Shaftesbury. All these became the property of my father on the death of his and were made mine by a clause in his will which gave me all his manuscripts.'

Draft C seems to have remained in the possession of the Beaufoy family until it was sold to the Morgan Library by the Rosenbach company in 1924.[3]

[1] *The Times Lit. Suppl.*, 25 July 1952, p. 492.

[2] Presumably Benjamin Furly. Furly's name is not found on the fly-leaf of Draft C.

[3] Draft C is about two hundred leaves long, with writing on rectos and versos. It has four blank leaves at the beginning, six at the end, and some blank leaves in the body of the work. The whole is bound in vellum, $6\frac{1}{4} \times 4\frac{1}{4}$ inches, with the figures '1.2' in ink on the spine of the volume. On the first leaf is written 'For Edward Clarke of Chipley Esq., James Tyrrell of Oakley Esq., or Dr. David Thomas of Salisbury' and on the second 'An Essay concerning humane understanding in fower books'. This is followed by the date '1685', apparently added later, in the same ink as some of the corrections made to the text. Following the date is a quotation from Cicero.

The document is in a hand very much like Locke's and yet possibly is a

According to the inscription on the first page the draft was intended for Clarke, Tyrrell, or David Thomas. Yet it turned up amongst the papers left by Benjamin Furly, a Quaker merchant who lived in Rotterdam, and in whose house Locke spent the greater part of his last two years in Holland. It seems probable that Locke brought the draft along with him to this house and left it there when he returned to England and that it never reached any one of the gentlemen mentioned in the inscription. If we accept the date 1685 on the manuscript —and we have no reason to doubt its authenticity—Draft C was written, probably in Amsterdam, almost two years before Locke moved to Rotterdam.

In what follows I give an account of Draft C, comparing it with B and particularly with the first edition of 1690. Draft C is not perhaps important enough to justify either a complete edition of it or a line to line collation with the 1690 *Essay*, but I have sought in this note to give some idea of its contents, and have chosen the points that are likely to be of most general interest to philosophic readers. As the interest is philosophical rather than bibliographical I have everywhere modernized the spelling and punctuation in quoting from the manuscript.

Book I. Little need be said about the correlation of texts in the case of Book I since here Drafts B, C, and the published text of 1690 agree so closely. Speaking generally, the ideas adumbrated in Draft B are more carefully stated in Draft C and given final form in 1690 although, it should not be forgotten, this process of making more precise and of elaborating went on for the rest of Locke's life as the second and fourth editions of the *Essay* show. Book I in the 1690 text is divided into an introduction and three chapters on innate ideas. The material of the introductory chapter is much the same in B, C, and 1690. Here and there will be found changes of wording, and some sentences and phrases are omitted. Thus at the end of the very first sentence in the chapter Draft B has: 'and which perhaps has been less seriously considered upon than the worth of the thing, and the nearness it has,

copyist's. Mr. Peter Laslett and myself who have together examined it would not care to be dogmatic about this point, for there are difficulties. Draft C is clearly a copy of another manuscript, and it is corrected. These corrections are almost certainly in Locke's hand. But occasionally the correction is such that it creates a doubt whether Locke also wrote what was being corrected. For instance, at one point the copyist apparently failed to understand a word and left a space; the word was added later and proved to be 'sensation'. Now it is difficult to understand how Locke in copying, if he was the copyist, could have failed to know that the word before him was 'sensation'. The context itself would at once suggest it. At the same time the hand is so very like Locke's that we hesitate to attribute it to an amanuensis.

seems to require'. But this is omitted in C and in 1690. Most often the material in B is elaborated. B 1–3, for instance, is elaborated into a chapter and the point thrown out in B 3 about the use of the word 'idea' becomes a complete section in C and in 1690. But 1690 too improves upon Draft C. Thus the last two sentences of I. i. 6 in 1690 are not to be found in C, and all that C has to correspond to I. i. 7 is the following: 'To this purpose have I ventured upon this bold Essay, to find out those measures whereby a rational creature, put in that state which man is in this world, may and ought to govern his opinions and actions depending thereon.' Very rarely, one finds in 1690 what is in B but not in C. Thus in I. i. 3 (1690) Locke remarks 'First I shall enquire into the original of those ideas, notions, or whatever else you please to call them'. Draft C omits 'notions' though Draft B includes it. But this is a rare occurrence and may in this instance be merely a slip.

The three chapters which deal with *innate ideas*, I. ii–iv, show remarkably little change in material in B, C, and 1690. On this point it is clear Locke's thought was the same in 1690 as in 1671. He thinks it wise to reverse the order of the 1671 argument, for whereas in B he begins with practical principles and proceeds to theoretical, he changes this order in C and in 1690. There are many minor changes and in I. ii 1685 is closer to 1671 than to 1690, though this is not so in I. iii and iv. But it is in I. iv only that we find any real differences in content between B and 1690, and here C agrees with 1690. For instance, the important section about substance, I. iv. 18, is not to be found in B but is present in C. But even in I. iv these differences are few. As to I. ii and iii, Locke had made up his mind about innate ideas in 1671 and from that point onward gave very little further thought to the problem.

Thus it is interesting, in view of subsequent discussions about the target of the polemic, that what Locke describes in I. iii. 15 refers to 1671 and not to 1690. He says that he had worked out his argument against innate ideas before having his attention drawn to Lord Herbert's *De Veritate*. But the 'When I had writ this' of this passage should not be taken to refer to 1690 or the years immediately preceding: they refer to 1671.[1] After 1671 he did not bother to find out whether anyone else had written on this matter. He merely restated the 1671 argument and left it at that.

But though the main argument remains the same the revision of

---

[1] The words in B 5 (Rand, p. 31) are: 'Since the writing of this, being informed that my Lord Herbert had in his book *De Veritate* spoken something of these innate principles, I presently betook myself to him.'

phrases and sentences is constant throughout the years. I may take
one instance of this from the section in which Locke blames those who
take things on trust (I. iv. 22 in 1690, 23 of the fourth and subsequent
editions) and who:

Draft B: 'misemploy the power they have to assent to things
which they ought to examine and blindly take them upon trust.'

Draft C (a first draft then corrected): 'misemploy the power they
have to assent to things which they ought to examine and which
they should not blindly with an implicit faith swallow.'

Draft C (corrected draft): 'misemploy their power of assent by
lazily enslaving their minds to an implicit faith in doctrines, which
it is their duty carefully to examine.'

1690: 'misemploy their power of assent, by lazily enslaving their
minds, to the dictates and dominion of others, in doctrines which it
is their duty carefully to examine, and not blindly, with an implicit
faith, to swallow.'

This elaboration, incidentally, whilst it causes the thought to be
more precise and sometimes advances it, makes too for diffuseness, as
the present instance shows.

The differences between the various drafts are far greater in the case
of *Book II*. Locke, from the beginning of it, is at once in deep waters
and the variations in the drafts reveal the extent of his difficulties.
Changes in the first four sections of II. i have to do with the nature of
sense-perception, of 'reflection', and of substance.

In Draft A Locke spoke naïvely of 'particular objects which give us
the simple ideas or images of things' but already in Draft B he has
learnt to speak more guardedly. 'Our senses conversant about particular sensible objects, do convey into the mind several distinct ideas
or images of things.' Yet what are 'ideas or images of things'? In C we
find 'several distinct ideas or representations of things', which is
changed in 1690 to 'several distinct perceptions of things'. Nor is this
all, for in the second edition, 1694, Locke added the following clause
to the sentence, 'which when I say the senses convey into the mind, I
mean, they from external objects convey into the mind what produces
there those perceptions'. These changes show that Locke is struggling
with many theories of perception and is not certain which to adopt.
He rejects a crude causal theory; it is not true that things, and particularly the qualities of things cause us to see them as they are; but
yet he does not wish to accept a mere phenomenalism, and least of all
an idealism.

Nor is he free from trouble in explaining the genesis of our knowledge of our own mental operations, the 'other fountain of knowledge'.[1] At first in B he speaks as if the operations of the mind themselves were the fountain, but in C and 1690 for 'operations' he substitutes 'the perception of operations'. In this section, however, C is on the whole closer to B than to 1690. He tries in C to explain what he means by the term 'reflection', '. . . these ideas being got by the mind reflecting on itself and its own actings'. But in 1690 he drops the word 'actings' and prefers the broader term 'operations', for as he explains, 'the term *operations* here I use in a large sense, as comprehending not barely the actions of the mind about its ideas, but some sort of passions arising sometimes from them, such as is the satisfaction or uneasiness arising from any thought'. The drafts and 1690 show that throughout Book II he is bothered by the relationship between (1) the object, which is the idea, (2) the same idea on its subjective side, and (3) the reflexive.

Most noteworthy, however, is the sudden introduction of the problem of substance. Locke's first point in Book II is that all knowledge is derived from sensation and reflection, but this is followed immediately in Drafts B and C by a second point, the weightiest consequence of the first. If all knowledge is derived from these two sources solely, then we can have no knowledge of whatever in an individual thing is imperceptible in sensation or reflection, and the substance of a thing, Locke supposes, is imperceptible. The passage in Draft C is worth quoting—much the same words will be found in Draft B:

'The understanding seems to me not to have the least glimmering of any idea which it doth not receive from one of these two, and as external objects cannot furnish the understanding with any ideas but of sensible qualities, because they operate on the senses no other way, and so we can have no other notion of them, nor the mind furnish the understanding with any ideas but of its own operations and the several sorts and modes thereof; hence it comes to pass that we have no ideas, no notion of the *substance* of body or any other thing, but it lies wholly in the dark, because when we talk of or think on those things which we call natural substances, as man, horse, stone, the idea we have of either of them is but the complication or collection of those particular simple ideas of sensible qualities which we use to find united in the thing called *Horse* or *Stone* (as I shall hereafter show more at large) and which are the immediate objects of our senses; which, because we cannot apprehend how they should subsist alone or one in another, we suppose they subsist and

[1] ii. i. 4.

are united in some fit and common subject; which being as we suppose the support of these sensible qualities we call *Substance*, though
it be certain we have no other idea of that substance but what we
have barely of those sensible qualities supposed to inhere in it.'

This passage is followed by another on the notion of spiritual or
mental substance. After 1685 Locke came to see that he had been too
precipitate in introducing the problem here, that it was better first to
make clear the different kinds of ideas which sensation and reflection
gave us. Accordingly the discussion of how the idea of substance is
gained is reserved for II. xxiii—the passage in C on spiritual substance
will be found almost word for word in II. xxiii. 5—the discussion of
how substances are named is reserved for III. vi, and that of the extent
of our knowledge of substances for IV. iii. But the procedure of the
drafts shows that Locke had realized the central importance of this
consequence of his empiricism as early as 1671, and the more he dwelt
upon it the greater became its importance in his eyes.

As to the remainder of the lengthy II. i many minor differences
between 'C and 1690 occur. I may confine myself to two points; first,
a curious clause in C which was dropped in 1690, namely, the mention
of an 'intellectual soul' in the passage in Draft C ·corresponding to
II. i. 6: 'He that attentively considers the state of a child at his first
coming into the world, or at least when the intellectual soul first takes
possession of the body . . .'. This last clause will not be found in 1690.
Secondly, the qualification made by Locke in II. i. 16 to the immediately preceding sections is an afterthought when writing C, and is
inserted there marginally. On re-reading he must have felt that his
doctrine at this point was too extreme and needed qualification.

II. ii–vi of 1690 follow C fairly faithfully, except for some rearrange-
ment and minor changes. The chapter devoted to solidity comes
later in C (ch. 21), but a discussion of the notion is found in the
chapter corresponding to II. iii. In Draft C the idea of time was first
introduced in the discussion of simple ideas of reflection.

The main difference between C and 1690 II. vii lies in the attention
paid to the idea of *power* in the former. In 1690 it is briefly noticed in
II. vii. 8, the main discussion being postponed, whereas in C several
pages are given to discussing the idea, some of which will be found in
the 1690 II. xxi. In both C and 1690 Locke asserts that reflection upon
our ability to think leads us to the idea of power, but also we are aware
of power, says C, in the power of 'the object of sensation . . . to produce
in us the ideas we receive of their several qualities'. It is not surprising
to find this modified in 1690 where he speaks merely of 'the effects that

natural bodies are able to produce in one another'. The reader may
like to compare II. xxi. I of 1690 with the passage in C in the chapter
entitled 'Of Ideas both of sensation and reflection' which corresponds
with II. vii of 1690. The latter runs as follows:

> 'The Idea of power I conceive we come by thus. The alterations
> which we every moment observe in ourselves or other things makes
> us take notice of the beginning and ceasing to exist of several sub-
> stances and of several qualities in those substances and several ideas
> in our minds, which changes since we cannot observe to be produced
> by nothing nor can conceive possible to be brought to pass without
> the operation of some cause that is able to produce such a change,
> the consideration of any thing as able to make any substance,
> quality, or idea to exist or cease to exist is the idea of its power. The
> way or efficacy whereby it is done we call action, as the alteration in
> the subject wherein it is made we call passion. Power then is looked
> upon and considered in reference to some alteration, and action is
> the efficacy of that power producing it.'

Following this paragraph will be found five further paragraphs dealing with power, impulse in body, and thinking, the material of these
paragraphs being not unlike parts of II. xxi. Further, in § 15 of Draft C
the important suggestion is made: 'And therefore I desire it may be
considered whether the primary and inseparable property of spirit be
not power, active power (for passive power everything has but God
alone), as that of matter is extension'.

II. viii is celebrated for its paragraphs on *primary and secondary
qualities*. As is clear from the published *Essay* Locke has difficulty
in speaking consistently of idea and quality in this connexion, and
confesses in II. viii. 8 to occasional confusion. This confusion is obvious
too in the Drafts. Apart from this the two most interesting differences
lie, first, in the explanation in C of why figure is included amongst the
primary qualities, and, second, in the less guarded way in which he
speaks in C of the action of body on mind. On these points I may
quote two passages. The first introduces primary qualities in C:

> 'Concerning these qualities we may, I think, observe those original
> ones in bodies that produce simple ideas in us, viz., solidity and
> extension, motion or rest, and number. And the extension of bodies
> being finite every body must needs have extremities; the relation of
> which extremities on all sides one to another being that which we
> call *figure*, figure also we may reckon amongst the original qualities
> of bodies, though the idea it produces in our minds be not altogether

so simple as the other we shall see when we come to consider simple modes.'

The second passage introduces secondary qualities:

'What I have said concerning colours and smells may be understood also of tastes and sounds and all other ideas of bodies produced in us by the texture and motion of particles whose single bulks are not sensible. And since bodies do produce in us ideas that contain in them no perception of bulk, figure, motion, or number of parts (as ideas of warmth, slowness, or sweetness) which yet 'tis plain they cannot do but by the various combinations of those primary qualities however we perceive them not, I call the powers in bodies to produce these ideas in us secondary qualities.'

Turning now to the psychological chapters in the middle of Book II, the celebrated Molyneux problem is absent of course from Draft C and from 1690, appearing first in 1694. At the end of what corresponds in C to II. ix. 7, while making no attempt to set out 'the order wherein the several ideas come into the mind' Locke does suggest that those things most deeply impress the mind and are most readily retained 'which do either most frequently affect the senses or else do bring with them pleasure or pain (the main business of the senses being to give notice of those things which either hurt or delight the body)'. The account of contemplation is fuller in C than in 1690, and fuller than in B.[1] Contemplating is a form of retention and we retain, he says, in two ways:

'1. either by keeping the idea which is brought into it actually in view, which the mind hath a power to do (though it seldom happens that the same idea is for any considerable time held alone in the mind, either from the nature of the mind itself, wherein if they be left to themselves—as in one who gets himself not to think of anything—the ideas are in continual flux, or from the nature of consideration, which consists not in one but variety of coherent thoughts, i.e. variety of ideas, or else through the importunity of other objects or ideas drawing the looking another way, or sleep, which at once in most men draws a curtain over all the ideas of the understanding). This way therefore of retaining of ideas in the understanding by continued view of any one may be called *Contemplation*.'

The other kind of retaining is memory, another difficult idea to

[1] Cf. Draft B, Rand, p. 72 (§ 23).

account for. Locke's description of the 'storehouse' of memory in Draft C is as follows:

'... the storehouse of our ideas, by the assistance whereof we may be said to have all those simple ideas in our understandings which though we do not actually contemplate yet we can bring in sight or make appear again and be the objects of our thoughts without the assistance of those sensible qualities which first imprinted them there'.

II. xi, 'Of Discerning and other Operations' of 1690 is broken up in C into four chapters, entitled *Of Discerning, Of Comparing, Of Composition,* and *Of Denomination and Abstraction* respectively. The first three are close enough in material to II. xi. 1–7 and need no comment, but the fourth on *Denomination and Abstraction* is much more detailed than II. xi. 8–11. Section 7 of Draft C is close to II. xi. 10 and 8 to II. xi. 11, but it would be as well to quote in full the first sections of this chapter for they light up the details of Locke's thought on naming and abstraction at this period. After 1685 he seems to have felt that this matter too needed far greater elaboration than he had given it, and so he cuts down the discussion on naming and abstracting at this point in order to give greater attention to it later in the *Essay*, particularly in Book III. Draft C is as follows:

'1. When the mind by the frequent occurring of the same sensible qualities has got a familiar acquaintance with those simple ideas they suggest which now by custom and frequent repetition begin to be well fixed in the memory, the next thing is to learn the signs or sounds which stand for them or else give them names, if there be nobody who knows and can communicate the names they have already. Words thus applied to ideas are the instruments whereby men communicate their conceptions and express to one another those imaginations they have within their own breasts; and there comes by constant use to be such a connexion between certain sounds and the ideas they stand for, that the names heard almost as readily excite those ideas as if the objects themselves which first produced them did really affect the senses.

'2. And because by familiar use we come to learn words very perfectly and have them in our memories more readily than some simple ideas and more certain and distinct than the greatest part of complex ideas, hence it comes to pass that men even when they would apply themselves to an attentive consideration do more usually think of names than things.

'3. This learning of names and affixing them to certain ideas begins to be done in children as soon as their acquaintance with and memory of several sounds[1] is sufficient to apply their organs of speech to the imitation of those sounds, and also to observe that such sounds are constantly annexed to and made use of to stand for such ideas.

'4. 'Tis true many words are learnt before the ideas are known for which they stand and therefore some, not only children but men, speak several words no otherwise than parrots do, only because they have learnt and have been accustomed to those sounds; but so far as words are of use and significancy, so far they consist in the connexion between the sound and the idea and the knowledge that the one stands for the other, and in the constant application of them.

'5. But names being only marks laid up in our memories to be ready there upon every occasion to signify our ideas to others or record them for our own use, and the ideas we have there being only taken from particular things, if every particular idea we take in should have a distinct name the names must be endless and more than we have need of. The mind therefore hath another faculty whereby it is able to make the particular ideas it received from particular things by a general representation of all of that sort become universal.

'6. For having received from paper, lilies, snow, chalk, and several other substances, the selfsame sort of ideas which perfectly agree with that which it formerly received from milk, it makes use but of one idea to contemplate all existing of that kind; whereby that one idea becomes as it were a representative of all particulars that agree with it and so is a general idea and the name that is given to it a general name. This is called abstraction, which is nothing else but the considering any idea barely and precisely in itself stripped of all external existence and circumstances. By this way of considering them ideas taken from particular things become universal, being reflected on as nakedly such appearances in the mind without considering how or whence or with what others they came there, but lodged there (with names commonly annexed to them) as standards to rank real existences into sorts as they agree with those patterns and to denominate them accordingly.

'7. By this means the mind, considering any of its ideas as representing more than one particular thing which do or may exist *in rerum natura*, makes universal ideas and gives an occasion for general or universal words.'

---

[1] At first he had written '. . . memory of the ideas of several sounds'. But 'of the ideas' is deleted.

Locke then proceeds to doubt whether beasts abstract, as he does in
II. xi. 10, and from this section onwards to the end of II. xi the text of
1690 follows the draft closely.

In the next chapter on complex ideas Locke is as explicit in C as in
1690 that modifications of simple ideas are 'found in things existing'
as well as are 'made within' the mind itself. Not all complex ideas are
'made'. An interesting point, however, is that at this stage Locke is not
quite sure whether simple modes should be classed with complex
ideas, but ultimately decides to group them with the complex. His
account of complex ideas is as follows:

'The complex ideas that we have I think may be divided into
these following sorts:

'1. *Simple Modes* for they are a sort of complex ideas consisting
of the repetition and combination of simple ones of the same kind.

'2. *Mixed Modes* which include in them several simple ideas without taking in that of substance into the combination, as law,
modesty, a lie.

'3. Ideas of *Substances* as water, lead, horse, man.

'4. Ideas of *Collective Substances* as army, crowd, herd of cattle.

'5. *Relation* as bigger, older, whiter, father, brother.'

The revolutionary changes in II. xii. 1 which cleared up the muddle of
the complex idea are not to be found here, neither are they to be
found in the 1690 text, they only appear in the fourth edition, 1700.
But Locke's difficulty in classifying ideas into simple and complex is
obvious enough in Draft C. II. xiii and xiv follow pretty closely the
draft chapters on space and duration, though II. xiv. 18–24, on the
measurement of duration, is much extended in C.[1] Minor changes in
II. xv, xvi, xvii, and xviii need no comment. II. xix in 1690 is entitled *Of
the Modes of Thinking*, but Draft C speaks *Of the Simple Modes of
Thinking*, and it is significant that Locke should have dropped the
adjective 'simple'. It was his original intention no doubt to bring the
psychological into line with the physical in his classification and speak
of simple and mixed modes. But the distinction of simple and complex
modes in the psychological sphere is confusing rather than helpful.
Can remembering, for instance, be spoken of as a repetition of one
and the same simple idea? If it could, would not our real concern be
with the simple idea? Yet in Draft C, more than in 1690, he tried to
conform to the distinction. The chapter in C opens thus:

'We have in the foregoing chapters considered several of the
simple ideas and their modes which from without excite the act of

---

[1] On ch. xiv cf. also B, §§ 103–23.

perception or thinking in the mind, which action of the mind when
reflected on we shall also find to have its different and various modifications. I have had occasion to mention some of them in the former
part of this book and therefore shall be the shorter here.'

The one 'action of the mind' has several modes and so the mode is, in
Locke's terminology, a simple mode. Already in 1690 these words have
disappeared and no effort is made to distinguish between simple and
mixed modes of thought, unless such a passage as II. xxii. 10 be held
to echo Draft C. For the most part the term 'modes' is used of the
operations of the mind in 1690 in a very loose sense and is almost
equivalent to 'kinds'.

The long chapter on Power, II. xxi, was considerably altered in the
second edition, 1694, but 1690 too differs a good deal from Draft C.
The first paragraph is much the same in both, and the second is an
afterthought in Draft C which is included marginally. The ethical
doctrine which follows varies considerably in Draft C, 1690, and 1694,
and any student of Locke's ethics will want to see the variants. I have
no space to consider them here, but turn instead to a consideration of
the chapter on Substance, II. xxiii. I shall compare Draft C with 1690,
but the reader should also look at Draft B 60, 61, 63, 94, and 97. The
numbering of the paragraphs in what follows is that of Draft C.

1. This agrees with II. xxiii. 1 of 1690.

2. And this with II. xxiii. 2 except that (*a*) in the last sentence C has
'supposed but unknown cause of the subsistence of those qualities'
whereas 1690 has 'supposed but unknown support of those qualities',
and (*b*) C has 'that imagined support' for the 1690 'that support, *substantia*' in the same sentence.

3 ·C runs: 'An obscure and relative idea of substance in general
being thus made we come to have the ideas of particular substances
by collecting such combinations of simple ideas as [having received
by our senses][1] we observe to exist together and suppose to flow from
the particular internal constitution or unknown essence of that substance. Thus we come to have the complex ideas of substances as
a man, a horse, sun, water, iron, upon the hearing of which words
everyone who understands the language frames in his mind the
several simple ideas which are the immediate objects of his senses,
which he supposes to rest in and be as it were adherent to that unknown common subject which is called substance; though in the
meantime it is manifest and everyone upon enquiry into his own
thoughts will find that he has no other idea of that substance, for

---

[1] Added later.

example, let it be of *gold, horse, man, iron, vitriol, bread,* but what he
has barely of these sensible qualities which he supposes to be inherent
in it with a supposition of such a substratum as gives as it were a
support to these other qualities or simple ideas which he has observed
to exist united together. Thus the idea of the sun is but an aggregate
of these several simple ideas, bright, hot, roundish, having a constant
regular motion at a certain distance from us, and perhaps some other,
as he who thinks and discourses of the sun hath been more or less
accurate in observing those sensible qualities, ideas, or properties,
which are in that thing which he calls the sun.'

4. 'For he hath the perfectest idea of any particular substance who
hath gathered and put together most of those simple ideas or qualities
which are causes of those simple ideas which do exist in it, among
which are to be reckoned its active powers and passive capacities, i.e.
not only those qualities which do actually exist in it, but such as are
apt to be altered in it or that thing is apt to alter in any other subject
upon a due application of them together. Thus the power of drawing
iron. . . .' For the continuation of this passage see II. xxiii. 7. Note how
in this paragraph both in C and 1690 Locke finds it difficult to decide
whether power is a simple or a complex idea. 'For all these powers that
we take cognizance of terminating only in the alteration of some sensible qualities in those subjects on which they operate, and for making
them exhibit to us new sensible ideas, therefore it is that those powers,
though in themselves properly relations, are reckoned amongst those
simple ideas which make the complex idea of any of those things we
call substances; and in this sense I would crave leave to call these
potentialities simple ideas when I speak of the simple ideas which we
recollect in our minds when we think of substances which are necessary to be considered if we will have true notions of and distinguish
these substances well one from another. And such powers as these we
are fain to make use of as the marks whereby we distinguish substances one from another; because the figure, number, bulk, and
motion of these minute parts being in corporeal substances that which
really distinguishes them, we have no faculty to discern the difference
of those minute parts and so cannot distinguish them that way. Therefore being excluded from a discovery of their different constitutions
by the several modifications of their original qualities we are fain to
content ourselves with the notice we have of their secondary qualities,
which are indeed nothing else but the powers they have differently to
affect our senses or other bodies by reason of the different bulk, figure,
texture, motion, and number of those minute parts whereof they
consist.'

5. 'For the power of being melted but not wasted by the fire, of being dissolved in aqua regia, are simple ideas as necessary to make up our complex idea of gold as its colour or weight; for to speak truly the simple ideas themselves we think we observe in substances, bating those primary qualities, are not really in them. They are but powers in them to make those alterations in us and produce such ideas in our minds; for yellowness is not actually in gold but is a power in gold to produce that idea in us by the sight when placed in a due light. And the heat which we feel its beams to cause in us is no more really in the sun than the white it introduces in wax. These are powers in the sun to make us feel warmth and the wax appear white, i.e. differently to change these simple ideas in man as so to alter the parts of wax as that they have the power to cause in us the idea of white.'

6. 'And this in short is the idea we have of particular substances, viz., a collection of several simple ideas which are united together in a supposed but unknown cause of their subsistence and union; so that by substance or the subject wherein we think they inhere we mean nothing else but the unknown cause of their union and coexistence.'

7. 'When I speak of simple ideas as existing in things, e.g. heat in the fire and red in a cherry, I would be understood to mean such a constitution of that thing as has power by our senses to produce that idea in our minds, so that by idea when it is spoken of as being in our understandings I mean the very thought and perception we have there: when it is spoken of as existing without us I mean the cause of that perception, and is vulgarly supposed to be resembled by it, and this cause, as I have said, I call also *quality*, whereby I mean anything which produces or causes any simple idea in us whether it be the operation of our own minds within, which being perceived by us causes in us the ideas of those operations, or else anything existing without us which, affecting our senses, causes in us any sensible simple ideas. These all, I say, I call qualities.'

8. 'Farther, because all the powers and capacities which we can conceive in things are conversant only about simple ideas and are considered as belonging to and making up part of the complex idea of that thing they are in, I call those also qualities and distinguish qualities into *actual* and *potential*. By *actual qualities* I mean all those simple ideas, or to speak righter, the causes of them that are in anything, e.g. the taste, colour, smell, and tangible qualities of all the component parts of a cherry. By *potential qualities* I mean the fitness it hath to change the simple ideas of any other thing or to have its own simple ideas changed by any other thing, e.g. it is

a *potential quality* of lead to be melted by fire and of fire to melt lead, i.e. change its solidity into fluidity, which potential qualities may again, if anyone please, be distinguished into *active* and *passive*. All that I desire is to be understood what I mean by the word *quality* when I use it, and if it be used by me something differently from the common acceptation I hope I shall be pardoned, being led to it by the considerations of the thing, this being the nearest word in its common use to those notions I have applied to it. By the word quality then I would here and elsewhere be understood to mean a power in anything to produce in us any simple idea and the power of altering any of the qualities of any other body. Thus the power in fire to cause in us the idea of heat I call *quality*, and the power likewise in fire to make wax or lead fluid I call *quality*.'

9. 'But having spoken at length of this (ch. 5) I shall only add that in *secondary qualities*, which probably consist in a certain number, figure, bulk, and motion of minute parts, if we had senses acute enough to discover and observe these they would then affect us after another manner, and the texture of the parts of gold and the motion of light from it would not then produce the idea of yellow in us but the perception of the bulk, figure, and motion of the constituent minute parts of gold and light.'

10. 'That this is so the increase of the acuteness of our sight by optical glasses (wherein the bulk of visible bodies seems to be augmented as 100 or 1,000 to one, i.e. our faculty of seeing is made 100 or 1,000 more acute than it was) seems to evince, for pounded glass or ordinary sand looked on by the naked eye produces in us the idea of white, but the same looked on in a good microscope loses the white appearance and the parts appear pellucid. So a hair that to the naked eye is of a flaxen or an auburn colour through a microscope (wherein the smaller parts of it become visible) loses that colour and is in a great measure pellucid with a mixture of some bright sparkling colours such as appear from the refraction of diamonds and other pellucid bodies. Blood to the naked eye appears all red; but by a good microscope wherein its lesser parts appear, shows (as is said) only some few globules of red swimming in a pellucid liquor, and how these red globules would appear, if glasses could be found that yet could magnify them 1,000 or 10,000 times more, is uncertain.'

11. This is as 12 of 1690, except that 1690 has one or two minor additions.

12. 'When then I say want of *faculties* and *organs* able to discover the figure and motion, etc., of the minute parts, and thereby the formal constitution of bodies and their qualities, is the cause why we have

not clear, perspect and adequate ideas of them, I do not say it would be better for us that we had faculties and organs fitted for such discoveries. God hath no doubt made us so as is best for the ends of our creation and our being here; and, though we have no perfect knowledge of things, yet we have enough to glorify him and discover the way to our own happiness, if we made a right use of that light he hath bestowed on us.'

13–20. As 1690 (§§ 14–21) but with some rearrangements and some minor changes.

21. A section in C is omitted from 1690. 'The ideas then we have peculiar to body are solid parts and a power of communicating motion by impulse. The idea of solid parts includes the idea of that extension which belongs to body, which is the idea of the distance between the extremes of solid and separable parts. For the extension that belongs to pure space is of inseparable parts without solidity whereof I think everyone has as clear an idea as of the extension of body, the idea of the distance between the parts of concave superficies being equally as clear without as with the idea of any solid parts between. So that extension in the largest signification as standing for the idea of distance of continued parts is not an idea belonging only to body.'

22. 'Let us then compare the primary simple ideas we have of *spirit* with those we have of *body* and see whether they are not as clear as those of *body*. For as to the substance of *spirit* I think everyone will allow we have as clear an idea of it as of the substance of body. Our primary idea of body is to me, as I have said, the union or cohesion of solid parts from which, as I suppose, all the other ideas belonging to *body* do derive themselves and are but modifications of. The primary idea we have of *spirit* is that of thinking, which if examined, I suppose is as clear and evident, nay possibly clearer than, that of the cohesion of solid parts.' The rest of this paragraph is 23 of 1690. Marginally in C, he adds a qualification, which appears as 24 of 1690, except that the last two sentences are not marginal in C and are different in minor but significant ways from 1690. They are as follows: 'So that perhaps how clear an idea soever we think we have of the extension of body, which is nothing but the cohesion of solid parts, he that shall well consider it in his mind may have reason to conclude that it is as easy for him to have a clear idea how [a substance he knows nothing more of or perhaps in][1] an extended substance may think as how the parts of a solid substance do cohere, so far is our idea of extension of body, which is nothing but the cohesion of solid parts, from being clearer or more distinct than the idea of thinking.'

[1] Added later.

23–28. The same as 28–32 of 1690 with some minor changes.

29. 'I say then by these steps we come to have such an idea of God and spirits as we are capable of, viz., finding in ourselves knowledge of some few things, and also a power to move and alter some things, and also existence and several other simple ideas or faculties which it is better to have than to want; having also the faculties in our minds whereby we can enlarge some of these ideas and extend them without bounds, e.g. if I find that I know some few things and some of them or all perhaps imperfectly, I can frame an idea of knowing twice as many things, which I can double again as often as I can add to number the same, also I can do of knowing them more perfectly, i.e. all these qualities, powers, causes, and relations, etc., till all be perfectly known, that is, in theory, or can any way relate to them, and thus frame the idea of infinite or boundless *knowledge*. The same may also be done of *power* till we come to that we call infinite and also of *duration*, existence from eternity, infinite and eternal being and so, in respect of place, *immensity*, by which way alone we are able to conceive ubiquity, the degrees or extent wherein we ascribe existence, power, wisdom, and all other perfections which we can frame any ideas of that sovereign being which we call God, being all boundless and infinite, and so frame the best idea of him our minds are capable of, all which is done by enlarging of those simple ideas (we have taken from ourselves by reflection, or by our senses from exterior things) to that vastness to which we can imagine any addition of numbers can come, which is the idea we have of *infinite* and *eternal*.'

30–31. These are similar to 35 and 36 of 1690.

32. 'Before I conclude this chapter it may not be amiss here to reflect how all our ideas of other things are restrained to those we receive from sensation and reflection. Since though in our ideas of spirits we can attain by repeating our own even to that of infinite, yet we cannot have any idea of their communicating their thoughts one to another, though we cannot but necessarily conclude that spirits which are beings that have perfecter knowledge and greater happiness than we must needs have a perfecter way of communicating their thoughts one to another. But our way of doing of it being only by corporeal signs, and the best and quickest of all other, by sounds, we have no idea how spirits which use not words can with quickness, nor much less how spirits that have no bodies, can be master of their own thoughts and communicate or conceal them at pleasure, though we cannot but necessarily suppose they have such a power.'

33. The same for the most part as 37 of 1690 but this section is added marginally in C.

As for the remaining chapters of Book II little need be said. II. xxiv copies Draft C but adds the last paragraph (3). II. xxv on *Relation* shows some differences of minor importance. It is interesting to compare in C and 1690 the opening sentences of II. xxvi *Of Cause and Effect, and other Relations.* C reads thus:

'In the notice that our senses take of their proper objects in external things we find that certain simple ideas do in several subjects begin to exist which before were not there and also that several particular substances do begin to exist, observing also that those simple ideas or substances are thus produced by the due application of some other simple ideas or subjects, which therefore being considered by us as conducing to the existence of that simple idea or substance, we frame the notion or idea of cause and effect, calling that which does operate toward the existence of any simple idea or substance cause and that which is thus produced the effect.'

It will be seen that the language of 1690 in opening this chapter is more guarded. Nothing of II. xxvii *Of Identity and Diversity* is to be found in C. There are differences between the account of moral relations in C and in 1690 of interest to students of Locke's ethical teaching, and six sections are added in C to II. xxviii. 20, which are not in the 1690 edition; but for the rest of this chapter 1690 follows C closely.

At the end of II. xxviii Locke in C adds his signature, apparently meaning to end Book II at this point. But he then adds two further chapters. The first corresponds closely to II. xxix and is entitled *Of Clear and Distinct, Obscure and Confused Ideas.* The second entitled *Of Real and Phantastical, Adequate and Inadequate Ideas,* corresponds to II. xxx and II. xxxi, though there are big differences. C has nothing corresponding to xxxiii *Of the Association of Ideas,* except that II. xxxiii. 19 is found little changed in the 1685 draft. To this section is appended Locke's signature 'Sic cogitavit John Locke'.

PART II

I

THE AIM AND PURPOSE OF
LOCKE'S WORK

PHILOSOPHY, Locke tells the reader in the epistle with which he opens the *Essay*, is 'nothing but true knowledge of things'. It is whatsoever a man knows when he knows truly—the whole body of knowledge, which Locke himself in the final chapter of the *Essay* divides into three parts, *physica* or natural philosophy,[1] *practica* or moral philosophy, and logic, the 'doctrine of signs'.[2] The aim of the philosopher is to erect as complete and adequate a system as he possibly can under these three heads. Locke and his contemporaries were ignorant of our present distinction between philosopher and scientist. Locke's researches into social and moral problems would, of course, be philosophical, but so also would his work in medicine. Newton, Boyle, and Sydenham were all philosophers to him, and, indeed, he would have regarded them as more deserving of that title than he was himself.

In his own eyes his chief work, the *Essay*, was not so much a part of philosophy as a preliminary to it. It is an examination of the instrument (the 'understanding', as he termed it) whereby we erect the philosophical structure. That it is preliminary work and no more is a point that needs to be borne in mind. Locke would have thought it strange had anyone identified the aim of the philosopher as such with his aim in the *Essay*. In the *Essay* he thinks his task is to prepare the ground for the builder rather than to erect the building. 'The commonwealth of learning is not at this

---

[1] Such 'natural philosophy' he tells us in IV. xxi. 2 includes the study of 'things as they are'. Amongst these 'things' are included the non-physical. 'God himself, angels, spirits, bodies, or any of their affections as number and figure, etc.' In modern terms it includes the natural sciences, but also mathematics, psychology, and even metaphysics.

[2] He calls it σημειωτική. On this word, see further, p. 209, n. 1, below.

time without master-builders, whose mighty designs in advancing the sciences will leave lasting monuments to the admiration of posterity; but everyone must not hope to be a Boyle or a Syden-ham, and in an age that produces such masters as the great Huygenius and the incomparable Mr. Newton, with some other of that strain, 'tis ambition enough to be employed as an under-labourer in clearing ground a little and removing some of the rubbish that lies in the way to knowledge.'[1] As it turned out, the *Essay* did provide some positive knowledge of its own, for instance, in psychology and again in logic. But to provide such knowledge was not its primary purpose. The primary purpose was solely to prepare the ground. To blame Locke for not producing a finished system in the *Essay* is like blaming the under-labourer who clears the ground for not erecting the building. Philosophy as such, he would think, should not be confused with this preliminary, critical work.

Accordingly, while the purpose of philosophy in Locke's opinion is the discovery of a systematized and adequate body of knowledge, and while its method is synthetical, the aim of his own work, the *Essay*, was the 'removing some of the rubbish that lies in the way to knowledge', and its method analytical. It involved an analysis of the human understanding, in the full consciousness that this was far from being the only concern of philosophy, was indeed only a preliminary concern. He makes his aims perfectly clear in the *Epistle to the Reader* and later in the *Essay*. In the first place, knowledge is hindered by 'vague and insignificant forms of speech' and by 'misapplied words, with little or no meaning' which are 'mistaken for deep learning and height of speculation'. Locke has primarily in mind, it is clear from the context, the type of person who, wishing to make a display of learning, uses a jargon of technical terms which he does not understand, and so instead of increasing knowledge manages only to increase confusion and ignorance. For such Locke rightly has nothing but contempt. However, it is not pedants such as these, unfortunately, who alone make use of vague words and express themselves in sentences whose meaning is not clear. Locke came to see that the commonest

---

[1] *The Epistle to the Reader.*

words and the most frequently used sentences are permeated with vagueness, which cause us to be misled only too easily. At first, Locke had not realized how big this problem of language was. But in the finished *Essay* he devotes a whole book to it, and though the analysis of Book III is no doubt crude and superficial, its author deserves all honour for drawing attention to the matter with which it deals and for emphasizing its importance.

From the first, then, Locke realized that vague and confused language was one great hindrance to knowledge, and that it was part of his duty to point this out. Another hindrance, he realized, was bondage to false methods. The search for the proper method of procedure was one whose importance all the thinkers of the seventeenth century agreed in emphasizing. They believed, as Descartes explained, that man possessed the power of knowing, but that frequently he failed to gain knowledge because his method of procedure was false. Locke, in particular, mentions two tendencies of his own day which led men to adopt false methods. There was first the tendency to believe that knowledge must originate in certain fundamental principles or 'maxims', which are innate, known prior to all experience. We gain as much true knowledge as we manage to deduce from these maxims. Locke rejected this view completely. He denied both that there is innate knowledge, and that all the knowledge we gain is the result of deducing truths from 'maxims'. The second tendency of his day which Locke deprecated was the tendency to regard the syllogism as the true and sole method of knowledge. The blind insistence of the schools upon the reduction of all argument to syllogism had done great harm to science in Locke's opinion, and on this point he attacked them vigorously. Man had power to know. But this power, Locke thought, was frequently limited and even made ineffective by theorists who insisted that knowledge should always proceed syllogistically and who refused to admit the validity of other methods, even though men of science in those very days were advancing rapidly by methods of a very different order. Locke conceived it to be his task to liberate reason and to point out the folly of those who would fetter it in this way.

But there is still a further hindrance to knowledge, Locke

realized, more deep-seated and more difficult to remove than either of the foregoing. Man's own unquenchable and boundless curiosity can itself become a hindrance. For man would know the unknowable, and when he fails, as fail he must, he becomes disheartened and sceptical and refuses to use his talents even in spheres where rightly used they might well succeed. 'Thus men, extending their inquiries beyond their capacities and letting their thoughts wander into those depths where they can find no sure footing, 'tis no wonder that they raise questions and multiply disputes, which never coming to any clear resolution, are proper only to continue and increase their doubts and to confirm them at last in perfect scepticism.'[1]

To help mankind to rid itself of this unfortunate failing, Locke set himself to determine the limits of human knowledge. Having once determined these, he hoped, men would not then rush forward to problems whose nature is such that they cannot be solved by human intelligence. 'If we can find out how far the understanding can extend its view, how far it has faculties to attain certainty, and in what cases it can only judge and guess, we may learn to content ourselves with what is attainable by us in this state.'[2] Man has been blessed with capacities and talents sufficient to enable him to live a useful and profitable life. Many conquests yet remain to him if he uses these talents intelligently. He may increase his knowledge of the natural world, deepen his understanding of social and moral relations, and enjoy a fuller communion with God than he does at present. 'Men may find matter sufficient to busy their heads and employ their hands with variety, delight and satisfaction, if they will not boldly quarrel with their own constitution and throw away the blessings their hands are filled with, because they are not big enough to grasp everything.'[3] Accordingly, Locke's chief purpose in the *Essay* is severely practical and utilitarian. In it he seeks to discover the limits of human knowledge so that we may order our lives and our inquiries wisely as best fits the nature of the capacities granted us, and not waste our time searching for knowledge of things lying for ever beyond our ken.

This threefold aim of the *Essay* is crystallized by Locke into

---

[1] I. i. 7.   [2] I. i. 4.   [3] I. i. 5.

one phrase: 'to inquire into the original, certainty and extent of human knowledge, together with the grounds and degrees of belief, opinion and assent.'[1] For if, first, we discover the 'original' of knowledge we shall be able to test the view that a mysterious innate knowledge exists, the source of 'maxims' and principles. Secondly, if we understand the true nature of certain knowledge we ought to be in a position to decide whether the syllogistic method is the sole method for gaining certainty. Moreover, we should not then be led astray by words and phrases whose meaning is not clear to us. Thirdly, if we know the extent of human knowledge we can know what problems it would be wise to leave untouched as lying beyond our capacities.

To complete our task, Locke points out, we need also to inquire into 'the grounds and degrees of belief, opinion and assent', that is, into probable knowledge. Not all knowledge is certain. Indeed, the conclusion to which Locke is driven is that very little knowledge is certain. All the more reason why an examination of probable knowledge should be included within the scope of the *Essay*.

The preliminary work that needed to be done, therefore, as Locke conceived it, was an examination of knowledge, both certain and probable. He undertook this task in the hope that thereby he might remove certain hindrances to knowledge that had obstructed it too long, vagueness and imperfections in language, false methods, and meddling with problems that the human understanding could not possibly solve. The method he proposed to adopt in his inquiry was the 'historical, plain method'. ('Historical' is here a synonym for experimental or observational.) And the field he was to examine was primarily that of his own experiences as a cognitive being. As we shall see, the actual procedure is both psychological and logical, and this because, in studying knowing, Locke found it necessary to study the objects known, namely, as he thought, ideas, together with the symbols standing for such ideas, particularly words. His examination of ideas is a curious mixture of psychology and logic, together with the introduction of some metaphysics, though ontological and metaphysical considerations are more apparent in the fourth book, when, for in-

[1] I. i. 2.

stance, an attempt is made to discuss the reality of knowledge. Thus, while Locke's goal is an account of human knowledge and of its extent, he finds it necessary to traverse many unexpected by-paths in order to reach it. It is this fact which makes the *Essay* so cumbrous, although it also adds considerably to its worth, since the various excursions he thus makes are never profitless.

Before we proceed to follow him in his quest we might add a word of criticism. No objection can be made to his desire to free men's minds from ambiguities and vagueness of language, or again from allegiance to false methods. But it may be questioned whether his third and chief resolve was a wise one—to determine the extent of human knowledge. How far is this possible? It is only fair to Locke to stress one fact which is sometimes forgotten by his critics, namely, that he has no doubts about the existence of knowledge. It is sometimes argued that Locke's whole procedure is vitiated since he assumes what he sets out to prove. He sets out to prove the fact of human knowledge and assumes it in so far as he uses knowledge in attempting to prove its existence. In examining the instrument, so it is argued, he is compelled to make use of that instrument itself. But all such criticisms, surely, miss an important point. Locke does not set out to prove the fact of human knowledge. He never doubts its possibility. He takes it for granted that we do on occasion know and know with indubitable certainty. But there is no proof of this in the *Essay* and no attempt to prove it. It cannot, therefore, be argued that he assumes what he sets out to prove.

The more effective criticism, however, centres upon another assumption which he makes, namely, that we can set limits to human knowledge. Can we really set up a precise and fixed barrier of such a sort that we can say, 'All problems this side of the barrier are soluble, those lying beyond are insoluble'? Can we determine the limits of knowledge beforehand? Locke's statement of the problem in the *Essay* is somewhat condensed. It is easier to understand his position if one examines it as set out in 1677 in the long note on study which he wrote into his journal for that year. In the course of this note he remarks:[1] 'This [to know what things

---

[1] King, i. 197–8.

are the proper objects of our inquiries and understanding], perhaps, is an inquiry of as much difficulty as any we shall find in our
way of knowledge, and fit to be resolved by a man when he is come
to the end of his study, and not to be proposed to one at his setting
out; it being properly the result to be expected after a long and
diligent research to determine what is knowable and what not,
and not a question to be resolved by the guesses of one who has
scarce yet acquainted himself with obvious truths.' From this
passage it is clear that Locke did not mean that when beginning
to inquire into any particular field of knowledge we can know
beforehand how far our knowledge will extend. The expert alone
'at the end of his study' is in a position to say that such-and-such
problems are wholly beyond our powers of apprehension.

But this further consideration cannot wholly free us from our
difficulties. For when are we 'at the end of our study'? When
are we in such a position that we can confidently say, 'This is a
problem which the human intellect will never solve'? In the above
note Locke sets before us three instances of problems insoluble to
our intelligence. First, 'that things infinite are too large for our
capacity'. Now in what sense is this statement true? It is certainly
true if we mean by 'things infinite' those things which a finite mind
like man's cannot understand. Then by definition finite minds
cannot know infinite things, that is to say, cannot know those
things which it cannot know. If more is meant than this empty
tautology it can only be that many matters are at present beyond
our understanding, that is, that we are not omniscient. This again
must be admitted, but, of itself, affords no proof that the problem
which I cannot solve today is such that I never shall solve it. The
second instance that Locke gives reads: 'the essences also of substantial beings are beyond our ken.' This we cannot discuss fully
without a prior discussion of what Locke means by the essence
of a substantial being, a discussion which will come later. But, on
the face of it, the question, 'What do I know of essences?' is only
significant if essences are within the realms of experienceable
entities. If they are wholly outside that realm then I shall never
know them, admittedly, but also the question whether I can know
them or not is absurd. Indeed, if I do know that these mysterious

entities are beyond my ken, that in itself is to know something about them. Of course, there may be entities and existences wholly beyond my knowledge, but then of these I neither have now, nor ever shall have, any conception whatsoever. Real essences, however, did mean something to Locke, little as he could explain them. And if we do know anything whatsoever about them, however slight the knowledge be, it is most dangerous to say that we shall never know more. Precisely the same general considerations apply to Locke's third instance, 'the manner also how Nature in this great machine of the world, produces the several phenomena, and continues the species of things in a successive generation etc. is what I think lies also out of the reach of our understanding'. Here again we must postpone detailed consideration. But we do know something about these natural phenomena. How then can we say that further knowledge is wholly ruled out?

Now if Locke's view was that we can set down limits to knowledge of a precise and definite sort, and that we can determine what problems are soluble and what wholly insoluble, then his position would be very difficult to defend. (We may, of course, say that we cannot know what lies beyond experience, but this, I contend, is not a significant limitation, especially when, as in the present case, the term *experience* is not confined to sense-experience, but covers all instances of awareness. To say that we cannot know what lies beyond experience is to say that the unknowable is unknowable, a tautology which cannot help us in any way.) Yet while in this precise sense we cannot hope to set limits to knowledge, in a more practical sense we certainly may assume that there are problems at present beyond us and likely to be beyond us for a very long time. And it is important to remember that Locke is thinking in practical terms. His interest here, as almost everywhere, is primarily practical. As a matter of logic we may not, strictly speaking, be in a position to deny the possibility of discovering a solution to the most abstruse problems, but practically we frequently find ourselves in a position, as the result of repeated failure, in which we feel able to say that it is most unlikely that this problem will ever be solved by us. What Locke is really saying here is that if we examine human knowledge we shall find certain problems which the mind has failed completely to solve, and having found them we shall be well advised not to waste further time and energy upon them. We should concentrate upon solving the simpler problems first.

In defence of Locke, therefore, as against the second criticism, it is necessary to emphasize his practical interests. It is significant that he concludes the passage from the note on study to which I have referred with these words: 'That which seems to me to be best suited to the end of man, and lie level to his understanding, is the improvement of natural experiments for the conveniences of this life and the way of ordering himself so as to attain happiness in the other—i.e. moral philosophy, which in my sense comprehends religion too, or a man's whole duty.' His contribution, he here implies, is pre-eminently practical in purpose. He will seek to discover those fields of inquiry in which the patient and diligent work of man's intellect is most likely to be rewarded whether by certainty or by probability, so that the sum-total of human happiness may be increased. And this is the most important task of the *Essay* in the eyes of its author.

As a final word, however, we should add that it is not primarily for reasons of this sort that the *Essay* remains a philosophical classic for us today. Its value for us lies rather in the fact that the task he set himself involved him also in a far-reaching analysis of the cognitive experience, and in many important psychological, logical, and metaphysical considerations.

II

THE POLEMIC AGAINST INNATE
KNOWLEDGE

LOCKE opens the *Essay* with an elaborate attack upon innate knowledge.[1] The matter is already introduced, though briefly, in Draft A of 1671.[2] There, having established his empiricism in the main argument, Locke adds a few additional paragraphs to meet two possible objections. The first is that knowledge may be gained innately. This objection is stated and dismissed by Locke in one section.[3] He admits readily that not all knowledge is sensory. Reason 'by a right tracing of those ideas which it has received from sense or sensation may come to the knowledge of many propositions which our senses could never have discovered'. Yet this is no innate knowledge, it presupposes ideas given in sensation or reflection. In a few brief sentences Locke shows the falsity of the innate theory. When, however, a few months later, he came to write Draft B, he must have felt that the claim to innate knowledge needed a fuller examination, and he devotes thirteen sections at the beginning of the draft to it. He is no longer defending his own position but attacking another. In spite of the protests of Gassendi and his followers, the theory of innate knowledge had gained in favour during the seventeenth century both on the Continent and in England, and Locke felt that the time was ripe for a thorough re-examination of it. The final statement of his argument in the *Essay* takes up the whole of Book I, excluding the introductory chapter. The main difference between it and that

---

[1] The polemic is usually termed 'the polemic against innate ideas', and, as we shall see, innate ideas are considered towards the end of Locke's discussion. But they are introduced incidentally. It is not so much ideas that we are supposed to know innately as certain principles, both speculative and practical, which lie as a foundation for theoretical and practical knowledge respectively. Accordingly, it is not necessary at this juncture to consider the use Locke makes of the term *idea*. We may postpone consideration to a more appropriate place, namely, the beginning of the next chapter.

[2] Even earlier in 1663/4 Locke discussed innate knowledge in *Law of Nature* (ed. von Leyden), Essays II–V.   [3] § 43. Aaron and Gibb, pp. 67–9.

of Draft B is that the latter begins with practical principles and proceeds to speculative, while the *Essay* reverses this procedure. In what follows I shall, first, summarize the argument of the *Essay*, then indicate for whom the attack was meant, and, lastly, estimate its value.

I

Locke begins by referring to 'an established opinion among some men' that there are innate principles 'which the soul receives in its very first being and brings into the world with it'.[1] Such principles are that what is, is; that a thing does not contradict itself; that the whole is greater than its parts, and so on. The first argument adduced for the innateness of the knowledge of these and the like principles is that we all agree about them. To this Locke replies that, in the first place, universal agreement in itself is no proof of innateness, and, in the second, not all people, strictly speaking, do agree about these principles. Indeed, not only is there no universal agreement about them but a large part of mankind has never once conceived them. Yet if they were truly innate, if they were 'naturally imprinted' on the mind, surely they would be in the thoughts of all. But they are not, for children and many adults know nothing of them. How, then, can we talk of universal agreement?

This brings up another point. It may be argued that we are all at least *potentially* capable of knowing these principles. If this means that we possess from the first a capacity to know them Locke agrees with this view. He accepts innate capacities. If it means more, as it usually does—if it means that the proposition 'What is, is' is in our minds implicitly, but not yet explicitly, Locke replies bluntly: 'No proposition can be said to be in the mind which it never yet knew, which it was never yet conscious of.'[2] If again it means that we shall know these principles when we come to reason, Locke answers that we shall also know that seven and five are twelve when we come to reason, but no one supposes this to be innate knowledge. Moreover, Locke adds, it is not by reasoning that we know these principles, though we use them in reason-

---

[1] I. ii. 1.   [2] I. ii. 5.

ing. 'Those who will take the pains to reflect with a little attention on the operations of the understanding will find that this ready assent of the mind to some truths depends not either on native inscription, or the *use of reason* [i.e. reasoning]; but on a faculty of the mind quite distinct from both of them, as we shall see hereafter.'[1] Obviously, the faculty referred to is the intuitive.

We cannot then argue from universal assent to the innateness of the knowledge of the principles. Nor again is it possible to claim for such knowledge any priority in time. Clearly the knowledge of the principles, abstract as it is, comes late. Sensation, recognition, seeing that red is not white, are all prior to our knowledge of the principle of non-contradiction. It is strange that the last named, none the less, should be singled out as a 'native inscription'.

But the argument, it will be said, is not from priority in time but from logical necessity. The principles are logically necessary and self-evident. Once we understand what the words in the proposition mean, for instance, 'What is, is', we must see it to be true. Now such necessity and such self-evidence, it is argued, can only be explained by holding that the principles have been inscribed innately upon the human mind, that knowledge of them is quite out of the ordinary and never acquired as other knowledge is acquired. To this Locke replies that admittedly the principles are self-evident. But so also are many other truths not usually regarded as innate, for instance, mathematical truths. Either these mathematical truths are also innate or self-evidence in itself is no proof of innateness. The principle 'What is, is' is necessary. Granted, but why? 'Not because it was innate, but because the consideration of the nature of the things contained in those words would not suffer him [the knower] to think otherwise, how or whensoever he is brought to reflect on them.'[2] In other words, however necessary and self-evident such principles are, Locke can see no argument in this fact for their being innate. He would be prepared to admit that as a class of objects known they make a group apart, though the analogies between them and propositions stating mathematical truths are many. But he cannot see that we need to presuppose

[1] I. ii. 11. In the first four editions the words *use of reason* are italicized.
[2] I. ii. 21. It is worth noting that Locke had already grasped this important truth in Draft B. Cf. § 15.

any peculiar, mysterious kind of knowing in order to explain our knowledge of them. They are known in the same way as we know any other knowledge. We intuit them, just as we intuit that two and two are four. The argument from self-evidence and necessity is shown to be as weak as that from universal assent.

Locke, therefore, concludes that there is nothing to show that principles used in speculation, such as identity and non-contradiction, are innately known. What now of those practical principles for which innateness was also being claimed? Locke begins again by asking whether there are any such practical principles about which we are all agreed. He finds it necessary to admit the existence of certain tendencies common to the human race. Common to all is 'a desire of happiness and an aversion to misery', but 'these are inclinations of the appetite to good, not impressions of truth on the understanding'.[1] As to moral principles as such, there is more agreement about speculative principles than about them, and yet not even the latter are known innately if our former argument is correct. It is very clear to Locke that the source of our moral principles is our own reason, or the education we have received from others, or the opinions of friends around us and the custom of the country in which we live. Locke believes that there are eternal, immutable laws of morality, but they are not known by any mysterious, innate knowledge, they are not implanted from the first upon our minds. Surely, if all men knew the moral principles innately we should not have the spectacle of whole nations breaking one or more of them and showing no shame in doing so, on the contrary, acting as if they were wholly unaware of the principle or principles concerned. Thus Lord Herbert of Cherbury must be incorrect when he argues in his book *De Veritate* that there are five practical principles which are known innately by all. Locke shows how easy it is to refute his position.

In a subsequent chapter Locke adds some further considerations in relation both to speculative and practical principles. If such principles are innate, the ideas out of which the principles are formed should also be innate. But they are obviously not so. '*It is*

[1] I. iii. 3.

impossible for the same things to be and not to be is certainly (if there be any such) an innate principle. But can any one think, or will any one say, that *impossibility* and *identity* are two innate *ideas*? Are they such as all mankind have and bring into the world with them? And are they those that are the first in children, and antecedent to all acquired ones? If they are innate they must needs be so?'[1] In the case of identity, for instance, in order to feel convinced that it is no innate idea, one need only recall that learned men ascribe wholly different meanings to the term, and that the less educated hardly ever use it.

Similarly, the practical principles contain ideas which cannot possibly be innate. One of Herbert's innate principles was 'God is to be worshipped'. Now the idea of worship is surely not innate. Is the idea of God? Locke shows how individual men and nations of men seem never once to have conceived the idea of God, and amongst those who have there is great disagreement as to the nature of the conception. But how could this be if precisely the same idea of God had been stamped upon the minds of men from the beginning? Surely, in this sense, there is no innate idea of God. Moreover, if there is no innate idea of him, it is unlikely we have innate ideas of anything else.

So there are no innate ideas, and if no innate ideas then no innate principles. The doctrine is wholly discredited. Why then do men persist in it? The answer must be that it gives a show of authority and finality which teachers and preachers can put to effective use. The doctrine 'eased the lazy from the pains of search and stopped the inquiry of the doubtful concerning all that was once styled innate; and it was of no small advantage to those who affected to be masters and teachers, to make this the principle of principles—that principles must not be questioned; for, having once established this tenet, that there are innate principles, it put their followers upon a necessity of receiving some doctrines as such; which was to take them off from the use of their own reason and judgement, and put them upon believing and taking them upon trust, without further examination; in which posture of blind credulity they might be more easily governed by, and made

[1] I. iv. 3.

useful to, some sort of men who had the skill and office to principle and guide them.'[1] The doctrine of innate ideas is thus seen in its true light as a buttress of obscurantism. The first step in the theory of knowledge must be an emphatic denial of it, even though there be reckoned amongst its adherents many worthy and learned men. Accordingly, in setting out his own account of knowledge, of its nature and extent, Locke begins by denying innate knowledge. He will only make appeal to 'men's own unprejudiced experience and observation'.

II

We must now inquire as to the opponents whom Locke has in mind in Book I. Against whom is the polemic directed? This is a question which has vexed many, and the answers given today are somewhat confusing. It is not difficult to understand the reason for this. The traditional answer accepted by all until the middle and end of the nineteenth century was that Descartes and the Cartesians were being attacked. But when scholars came to realize Locke's own debt to Descartes and rediscovered the rationalist elements in his writings, and when they examined Descartes on innate ideas more closely, they felt that this answer was unsatisfactory. But if Locke is not attacking the Cartesians, whom, then, is he attacking? The only person mentioned is Lord Herbert of Cherbury, but he is hardly the principal opponent, for the examination of his theory is somewhat of an afterthought, as is clear from the way in which it is introduced. The answer first proposed was that the Cambridge Platonists were the opponents Locke had in mind, and certainly some of them did uphold the theory of innate ideas in some form or other, though it is well to remember that others of the school rejected it. Von Hertling has shown conclusively, it seems to me, that the attack could not possibly have been meant for this school as a whole. Professor Gibson is very guarded in his statements, but thinks that if Locke had any particular group in mind it was the university teachers of his day. It is certainly true that Locke was thinking of these teachers, as is obvious, for instance, from the closing sections of Book I,

[1] I. iv. 24.

but I hardly suppose that Professor Gibson wishes us to believe that the attack was meant solely for them. The difficulty of finding opponents for Locke has been so great that it has been seriously suggested by some writers that Locke, in order to make his own views clearer, began by setting up a man of straw, presenting in a concrete and vivid fashion a theory of knowledge which no philosopher had ever actually upheld, and refuting it convincingly.[1] I find it difficult to accept the suggestion. The references to 'these men of innate principles' in the text are of such a kind that they seem to me to rule out this hypothesis. Moreover, Locke was not the man to waste powder and shot on imaginary opponents.

Is it possible to come to more definite views on this matter? I believe that it is, but only through returning to the traditional answer once again, and reaffirming it, with, however, certain important modifications. In the first place, the attack is aimed at Descartes and the Cartesians. But it is also aimed with equal force at various English thinkers and teachers, moralists and theologians of his own day who, whilst not direct followers of Descartes, agreed with him in holding a theory of innate ideas. I am well aware that the reassertion of the traditional answer even in this modified manner will be accounted heresy in many quarters, but certain arguments suggest the necessity of its reassertion, and I propose now to put these arguments before the reader.

The first point—and a very important one—is that this traditional answer was established by Leibniz and Voltaire. Leibniz connected the polemic with the Cartesians in 1696 in his first short paper on Locke's *Essay*. Again, in the *Nouveaux Essais* of 1703 he opens the whole discussion of innate ideas by grouping Locke with the Gassendists as against the Cartesians and finding in him one of their most eminent partisans. (I have already quoted from the passage in question.)[2] The theory of innate ideas is expressly mentioned as being a matter in dispute between the two schools, and it is assumed without further ado that Locke is attacking the Cartesians. Voltaire takes precisely the same view of the situation. In his letter on Locke in the *Lettres Philoso-*

---

[1] For instance, Cassirer, *Das Erkenntnisproblem*, ii. 230–1, leans to this view.
[2] Cf. p. 31.

phiques Voltaire praises Locke at Descartes's expense. He singles out for mention Descartes's impossible view of innate ideas and Locke's eminently successful attack upon it. He describes Descartes's theory in these words: 'He was certain that we always think and that the soul arrives in the body ready-provided with all metaphysical notions, knowing God, space, infinity, possessing all the abstract ideas and filled with fine thoughts, which it unfortunately forgets when the body leaves the womb.' Thus Voltaire also has no doubts whatever that Locke's attack is meant for Descartes. Now the evidence of these two men cannot be lightly turned aside. Leibniz had his finger on the intellectual pulse of Europe in Locke's own day and Voltaire was the prince of the learned men of the next generation. Both of them assumed without question that in Book I Locke was attacking Descartes and the Cartesians.

But if Locke had Descartes in mind, could Descartes ever have meant what Locke ascribed to him and what Voltaire, for instance, in the passage just quoted, also ascribed to him? In trying to answer this question it is first necessary to acknowledge—what I believe all commentators on Descartes are only too ready to acknowledge—that Descartes's theory of innate ideas is very vague and indefinite. I have not the space at my disposal to develop Descartes's theory in its full detail. I shall confine myself to one or two of the most important passages. There are the significant and explicit remarks which Descartes made in *Notes against a Programme*. First, in answer to the twelfth article of that programme, he says: 'I never wrote or concluded that the mind required innate ideas which were in some sort different from its faculty of thinking. . . . We say that in some families generosity is innate, in others certain diseases like gout or gravel, not that on this account the babes of these families suffer from these diseases in their mother's womb, but because they are born with a certain disposition or propensity for contracting them.'[1] And again in the same work in reply to another critic, he remarks: 'By innate ideas I never understood anything other than . . . that "there is innate in us by nature a potentiality whereby we know God"; but that these ideas are actual or that they are some kind of species different from the

[1] Descartes, *Works* (Haldane and Ross), i. 442.

faculty of thought I never wrote nor concluded. On the contrary, I, more than any other man, am utterly averse to that empty stock of scholastic entities—so much so that I cannot refrain from laughter when I see that mighty heap which our hero—a very inoffensive fellow no doubt—has laboriously brought together to prove that infants have no notion of God so long as they are in their mother's womb—as though in this fashion he was bringing a magnificent charge against me.' Descartes would likewise have laughed no doubt if he had lived to read Locke's polemic, but it is interesting in itself that the charge which Locke made later was already being made against him.

Now the above passages include an explicit denial on Descartes's part that he ever meant that children were born into the world with ideas, for instance, the idea of God, already implanted in their minds. What, then, would he have us suppose his theory of innate knowledge to mean? Two answers seem possible, and they might be supported by further quotations from Descartes's work. He seems to have meant sometimes merely this, that we have an innate faculty of knowing which he identifies with thinking. If he meant this then Locke would agree with him, for the latter admits, as we have seen, the existence of innate faculties. But, secondly, Descartes also seems to have meant that we are beings prone, as it were, to think in certain fixed ways and according to certain 'germs of thought' in the mind innately, though not in the sense that the child in its mother's womb is explicitly aware of these germs of thought. Some such view was suggested to Descartes by the necessity and universality of these truths. This view Locke attacked. He does not deny the element of necessity in such truths, but he does deny that this is an argument for calling them innate in *any* sense, even if all we mean to say is that we do not gain such truths in the same way as we gain other truths. It is frequently forgotten that Locke does attack this view of innate knowledge as well as the cruder kind which, in the passages quoted, Descartes claims should not be attributed to him.

But, now, is Descartes's claim in these passages justified? It is clear that in his own day he was supposed by some opponents to have taught that when the soul enters the body in the womb it already possesses the explicit knowledge of certain truths in addition to its possession of the faculty of thinking, and we have seen that Voltaire later did not hesitate to ascribe this view to Descartes. I should like to refer to a passage which commentators on Descartes neglect but which Voltaire, for instance, might very well have had in mind. Moreover, the passage is doubly interesting since it is part of Descartes's reply to Gassendi, who wrote the fifth set of objections to Descartes's system in 1641.[1] In the course of his criticisms Gassendi remarks that he finds it difficult to believe that the mind is always thinking, and particularly that the mind had thoughts in the womb, for he can find no evidence of this.[2] And his doubts here provide him with one reason for denying at a later stage[3] the existence of innate thoughts and innate ideas and for suggesting that all ideas are adventitious. Now Descartes in his reply finds the attribution of this view to him, that the mind has thoughts in the womb, neither strange nor unfair, but apparently acquiesces in it. 'You have a difficulty, however, you say as to whether I think that the soul always thinks. But why should it not always think, when it is a thinking substance? Why is it strange that we do not remember the thoughts it has had when in the womb or in a stupor, when we do not even remember the most of those we know we have had when grown up, in good health, and awake?'[4] Now, are these 'thoughts' which are in the womb innate ideas? Does he mean thoughts of God, of extension, and the rest? In fairness to Descartes we might point out that it is possible that all that he means here are such prenatal experiences as feeling hungry or cold, experiences whose existence Locke himself recognizes. But there is nothing to show that he had such experiences in mind, and the word *cogitationes* which he used here (translated 'thoughts') is more suggestive of Voltaire's *belles connaissances* than of prenatal experiences such as hunger. The passage does seem to provide a possible foundation, at least, for

---

[1] Incidentally, the reader who finds himself unable to procure a copy of Gassendi's work may gain some knowledge of his general position by reading his long and careful criticism of Descartes. Cf. Haldane and Ross, ii. 135 ff.

[2] Ibid. 141.   [3] Ibid. 153.

[4] Ibid. 210. Adam and Tannery, vii. 356, '. . . quid miri quod non recordemur cogitationum quas habuit in matris utero . . .'; cf. also the *Reply to the Fourth Objection*, ibid. 115.

the theory of innate ideas in the crudest form, and his opponents can hardly be blamed for assuming that Descartes was committed to it. Again, less eminent members of the Cartesian school were probably more definite in their avowal of the theory. It is well to remember that Locke was in an excellent position to judge of the dispute. He spent some years in the company of Gassendists and Cartesians and listened to their arguments.[1] He came away with the impression that some of the Cartesians (and perhaps Descartes himself) on occasion did hold that we are born knowing certain truths, and he attacked this view. He also realized, of course, that this was not the only form of the argument, that the theory of innate ideas was being put forward in addition as a very vague explanation of necessity and universality, and he pays attention (though perhaps insufficient attention) to this further aspect of the theory.

Thus there is very substantial evidence in support of the view that Locke was attacking Descartes and the Cartesians. But they were not the only people he had in mind. Those university teachers who still followed the narrow scholastic tradition held that knowledge begins with 'maxims' from which we deduce other truths syllogistically. These maxims, they held, were known innately and could never be doubted. Locke himself admits that they cannot be doubted, but not because they are innate. It is clear from the final chapter of Book I that Locke is attacking this scholastic view. Again, some of the Cambridge Platonists held to the doctrine of innate ideas, though never, so far as I can see, in its cruder form.[2] For instance, there can be little doubt that Locke was acquainted with the statement of the theory in the seventh chapter of the first book of Henry More's *An Antidote against Atheism* (1653), for the instances given at the end of this chapter are just those speculative principles which Locke himself

[1] He certainly knew their point of view intimately before he visited France, and in France he would become still better acquainted with it.

[2] Henry Lee, who published his *Anti-Scepticism* in 1702, was unaware of a theory of innate knowledge in the crude sense, and he was probably well acquainted with the English form of the theory. Discussing Locke's polemic in the preface of his book, he remarks: 'All which I think might have been saved, in the strict sense which he puts upon the word *innate*; for therein surely he has no adversary.'

discusses. But not all the Cambridge Platonists advocated the theory, and none of them, perhaps, was excessively enthusiastic about it.[1] However, it was felt that it was necessary to posit some sort of innate knowledge of God, and it is clear that, vague as the doctrine was, it was a very popular one at the time. Locke's polemic caused men to think out the matter afresh, and to speak more warily. And it is an interesting piece of information which Molyneux sends on to Locke in September 1696: 'He that, even ten years ago, should have preached that *idea Dei non est innata* had certainly drawn on him the character of an atheist; yet now we find Mr. Bentley very large upon it in his sermons.' So also on the Continent, it is instructive to note how very careful Leibniz is to dissociate himself from the Cartesian account, even though he still sees the need of a theory of innate knowledge.

The conclusion to which we seem driven, then, is that Locke's polemic was meant for the Cartesians, for the schoolmen, for certain members of the Cambridge Platonists, and for those others, Herbert and the rest, who advocated the theory of innate ideas in any way.

III

There remains the task of estimating the polemic's worth. Now if all it contained were the denial of the theory of innate knowledge in the strict, explicit sense, it could hardly claim to have great intrinsic value. This, however, is not all that it does contain, though, unfortunately, Locke was so enamoured of his criticism of innate ideas in the cruder sense that he over-elaborates it. The truth is that Book I is badly written. It emphasizes the relatively unimportant and neglects the important. Locke had found the Cartesians and others vaguely talking about thoughts in the womb and had realized that only their vagueness saved them from absurdity. He proceeds at great length to develop this point and to prove a position so obvious that one or two brief paragraphs would have sufficed. The result is that the balance of the polemic is lost. Insufficient attention is given to problems far more important than

---

[1] Robert South and Matthew Hale, not Cambridge Platonists, might be named as other writers whom Locke may have had in view.

whether a child knows the law of identity in the womb. Not that Locke wholly neglects them, for he is aware of them and does touch upon them, but without giving them the attention they deserve.

Bearing this in mind, we may proceed with the examination of the polemic. In order to make the matter clear it is first necessary to state precisely what Locke is, and what he is not, denying, for it is easy to be confused here. To begin with, Locke is not denying prenatal experiences. He recognizes that the child in the womb may experience hunger.[1] But such an experience is not different in kind from the post-natal experience of feeling hungry. Nor, again, does Locke deny what psychologists today term innate dispositions. He nowhere discusses such things as tropisms,[2] reflexes, and instincts. Once, when Pierre Coste mentioned instinctive knowledge in animal life as needing explanation, he replied a little tartly: 'Je n'ai pas écrit mon livre pour expliquer les actions des bêtes.'[3] His attitude here may be criticized. It is possible that much insight might be gained into the cognitive side of our nature by studying the lowlier forms of psychical activity. But in Locke's opinion, as in the opinions of his opponents, the theory of innate knowledge was meant to explain cognition at its highest and best, something far beyond the reach of animals. Indeed, it was just because this cognition was thought so excellent that it was necessary to introduce a fresh, non-natural faculty, pertaining to the inner essence of the soul of man, in order to explain it. Nothing that Locke says here in any way affects instinctive knowledge, if it exists, or, again, innate dispositions. He admits the latter, for instance, the innate disposition to seek the pleasant and avoid the painful. It is no theory of innate dispositions which he attacks in attacking innate knowledge. He is there concerned with what claims to be supra- rather than sub-rational.

It would be a complete misunderstanding, therefore, to suppose that Locke's denial of innate knowledge involves any denial either of prenatal experiences or of innate dispositions. But we must now

---

[1] Cf. *Essay*, II. ix. 5–6.
[2] Unless II. ix. 7 provides an instance.
[3] Fraser's edition of the *Essay*, i. 205, n. 2.

refer to a misunderstanding in this connexion which is even graver and far more serious in its consequences. It is frequently assumed that Locke's denial of innate knowledge is equivalent to the assertion that the one kind of knowledge which exists is sensory, where sensory knowledge means seeing colours, hearing sounds, and so on. Locke holds that all knowledge is acquired and none innate, and by acquired knowledge he is wrongly assumed to mean sense-experience, and nothing more. The outcome of the polemic against innate ideas according to this view is a pure sensationalism. Now there is nothing in the text to justify the very big assumption that is being made here. On the contrary, when he talks of our knowledge of the speculative principles in the course of the argument he obviously does not mean that this knowledge is sensory in the narrow sense explained above. From the context it is quite clear that he has something like the intuition of Book IV in mind. I cannot see that there is anything in Book I which contradicts the theory of knowledge put forward in Book IV (whatever be the case with Book II) though, of course, it is necessary to admit that this theory of knowledge is not at all explicit in Book I. But when Locke denies innate knowledge he is not saying that the only kind of knowledge is sensory.

This point needs to be emphasized. All knowledge is acquired, certainly, but it is acquired by intuition or demonstration. As we shall see later, with the exception of our sensitive knowledge of the existence of external objects, sensation, in Locke's view, is not so much knowledge as the provider of materials for knowledge, which latter is either intuitive or demonstrative. So far is Book I from being sensationalist in the narrow sense that it hardly admits that sensing is knowing. It is, indeed, a very grave error to hold that Book I is sensationalist and that Locke in denying innate knowledge is denying intuition and demonstration.

Just as Locke is denying neither prenatal experiences nor innate dispositions, so also he is not denying the possibility of rational knowledge by intuition or demonstration. What, then, does Locke deny and what does he assert? The polemic establishes two points. First, we ought not to talk of truths known innately unless we are prepared to go the whole way and accept the view that a child at birth knows the principle of identity. In other words, we ought not to use the term innate knowledge unless we mean innate knowledge in the strict sense. It has a plain meaning in English, and if we do not mean this we ought to use some other term. If, indeed, we are prepared to go the whole way, then Locke thinks our position absurd, and in this he is surely justified. In pointing out that Locke over-emphasized this side of the polemic one does not wish to deny either its soundness or its real value. Comparatively speaking, however, it is very much less important than the second point which Locke was also trying to make. The second point is this: We can explain all the knowledge the human mind ever gains in terms of sensation, intuition, and demonstration. Beyond these no appeal is ever necessary or even possible, so far as concerns human knowledge. A further type of knowledge, namely, innate knowledge, is superfluous.

To talk concretely we may consider the principle of identity. How do we know it? It is not so implanted in our minds naturally that we know it at birth in an explicit manner. Moreover, it is not there in our minds in a potential sense waiting to be actualized. This latter explanation is as unsatisfactory as the first. For knowledge is not sometimes a discovery and sometimes actualization of the potential within. Knowledge is always discovery. We discover by intuiting, by demonstrating, or sometimes, as Book IV will explain, by sensing. Actually we discover the principle of identity, Locke thinks, by intuition, and the mysterious fourth type of knowledge need not be dragged in to explain it.

Is this equivalent to a denial of the *a priori* in general? This term, *a priori* knowledge, which Locke himself never uses, is ambiguous, so much so that it is possible to assert that Locke both denies and asserts *a priori* knowledge. For if we mean by it a type of knowing which is other than all acquired knowing, if we mean by it a knowing of principles whereby we order experience, a knowing which is logically prior to that experience itself, then Locke emphatically denies such knowing. The only principles which Locke recognizes, namely, necessary relations between ideas, are themselves disclosed in experience in Locke's view (though this does not mean that they are disclosed to sensation

—or, again, by induction). On the other hand, if we mean by *a priori* knowledge a knowledge having an object, that carries with it universality and necessity, then Locke acknowledges the possibility of *a priori* knowledge. But the universality and necessity are in no sense inherent in the knowing mind, they are characteristics of that which is discovered. Thus Locke in denying innate knowledge is not denying the *a priori* in this second sense. At the same time, it should be immediately added that his analysis of knowledge of the necessary in Book I is most inadequate. He will not accept the view that innate knowledge is essential to explain necessary knowledge, yet at this stage of the argument he puts forward no alternative theory. We must wait until he has developed his theory of knowledge in the rest of the *Essay* before being in a position to judge the matter fairly. Book I, after all, is destructive and negative. Except by implication, it offers no positive theory.

Its value then consists, firstly, in showing the absurdity of a theory of innate knowledge in the crude sense; secondly, in suggesting that human knowledge can be explained in its entirety in terms of sensation, intuition, and demonstration. Both these points are valuable, particularly the second, but we have yet to see whether this second point is substantiated by the rest of the *Essay*. The practical bearing of the polemic too should not be forgotten; it aimed a shrewd blow at the obscurantism of the day in religion and morality and made fresh thinking in these fields essential.

III

THE NATURE AND ORIGIN OF IDEAS

No term is met with more frequently in Locke's pages than the term *idea*, and to understand his philosophy and his theory of knowledge it is first necessary to understand his usage of this term. It is, indeed, the central conception both of Locke's own philosophy and of English empiricism in general after Locke. Without this conception and the theory built around it both Berkeley's idealism and Hume's scepticism, it is not too much to say, would have been impossible. It therefore deserves serious attention, and I propose in this chapter, first, to explain the nature of Locke's *idea*; secondly, to discuss his account of its origin, together with the distinction between simple and complex ideas; thirdly, to discuss the further distinction between ideas of primary and those of secondary qualities.

I

Locke is aware of the importance of the term in his philosophy and so defines it carefully at the opening of the *Essay*. 'It being that term which, I think, serves best to stand for whatsoever is the object of the understanding when a man thinks, I have used it to express whatever is meant by *phantasm, notion, species* or whatever it is which the mind can be employed about in thinking.'[1] The idea then, for Locke, is 'the object of the understanding when a man thinks', where 'thinking' is used widely to cover all possible cognitive activities. He expressly includes within the connotation of the term, first, phantasms, that is to say, sense-data, memories, and images; secondly, notions, to cover the more abstract concepts; and, lastly, species, whether sensible or intelligible.[2] In the controversy with Stillingfleet he admits that he has no special liking

---

[1] I. i. 8. Cf. Descartes's 3rd Reply, A. T. 181: '. . . omni eo quod immediate a mente percipitur'. In the Stillingfleet Correspondence Locke acknowledges that he uses 'idea' as Descartes does. Similar accounts of idea are found in many contemporary writers, e.g. Malebranche.

[2] On sensible and intelligible species cf. Hamilton's edition of *Works of Thomas Reid*, Note M, 'On the Doctrine of Species'; cf. also article on 'Species' in the *Catholic Encyclopaedia*.

for the term *idea* itself but that after working with various terms he has found this the most convenient of all those which were possible.

One criticism which has rightly been directed against Locke in this connexion is that he has included far too much within the connotation of this one term. Sense-data, memories, images, concepts, abstract ideas differ from each other greatly, and to call them all by the same name is to invite confusion. Locke wanted a comprehensive term to embrace all the immediate objects of the understanding, but his use of the word *idea* in this exceedingly wide manner does lead to ambiguity.

It is frequently argued, however, that in his actual usage Locke goes beyond even these wide bounds, and sometimes means by *idea* not so much an object of thinking but the thinking itself, the perceiving of the object.[1] Were this criticism justified, Locke would certainly be guilty of a grave inconsistency, since his definition confines *idea* entirely to the objective side. But I doubt whether it is justified. It is perfectly true that Locke used the word *perception* to mean both the perceiving and what is perceived. But does he ever use the term *idea* to mean explicitly the perceiving as opposed to what is perceived? Of course, there is the whole group of ideas known as 'ideas of reflection', that is, the ideas we have of the activities and operations of the mind. But these are still objects for Locke, and the difficulty in connexion with them is the perennial one of how subject can be object to itself. Granted this, there is then no inconsistency in respect to such ideas; they also are still objective. When Locke does want to talk of the apprehending or the perceiving he usually speaks of 'having ideas'. I doubt whether a single unambiguous instance of the explicit identification of *idea* with the perceiving can be found.

On the whole then it would seem that in this respect Locke uses the term *idea* consistently and means by it the immediate object of perception and of thought. But further inquiry as to the nature of this object meets with grave difficulties. For, in the first place,

---

[1] This criticism is put forward by Reid, Gibson, Husserl, Ryle, and others. Cf. Gibson's *Locke's Theory of Knowledge*, p. 19: 'The idea for him is at once the apprehension of a content and the content apprehended.'

the idea is said to be 'in the mind', and yet its precise relation to the mind is not easy to determine. Of all the ambiguous phrases used by philosophers this phrase 'in the mind' is surely the most ambiguous. For the ideas are not themselves mind, nor yet are they non-mental, but they are supposed to possess, as Professor Alexander has explained,[1] 'a twilight existence' of their own between the mind and the physical objects of the natural world. In the second place, the confusion is increased by the fact that *idea* may mean two things. It is a representation, representing either an existence or a quality of an existence in the physical world outside, or, secondly, it is a universal, a logical content. We shall consider Locke's theory of universals later, and until it has been considered it is not possible to make the nature of idea as universal wholly clear. For the present we may confine our attention to idea as representation. But we note now that Locke also means by *idea* a universal, a logical content or meaning. We may refer at once to that interesting passage in the controversy with Stillingfleet. When Stillingfleet had found some difficulty in making clear to himself what ideas of matter, motion, duration, and light he possessed, Locke remarked to him: 'If your Lordship tell me what you mean by these names, I shall presently reply that there, then, are the ideas that you have of them in your mind.'[2] The idea of matter is what I mean when I use the word *matter*. But it is then extremely difficult to identify 'idea' in this sense of the term with any semi-psychical entity or any 'twilight existence'. We must return to this question later. But the fact that Locke uses the word in this dual sense is not likely to add to clarity of thought.

Now this varied and confusing use of the term *idea* is very largely the consequence of Locke's adoption of the representative theory of perception and knowledge, and it is necessary here to show in what sense he accepted this theory and to what use he put it. Knowledge of the real, the theory asserts, need an intermediary object between the knowing mind and the ultimate object. This intermediary object is the one immediately given or thought and represents the ultimate object. The immediate object when I look at this table is no physical entity but an idea which represents the

[1] Alexander, *Locke*, p. 32.   [2] *Works*, i. 565, 'Second Reply' (1801 ed., iv. 413).

table. I know physical entities and their qualities through the mediation of ideas and through ideas alone.[1]

In connexion with Locke's representationalism there are two extreme positions which we need to avoid. There is, first, the position of those who claim to find in Locke an enthusiastic advocate and, indeed, the original inspirer of the representative theory. On the other hand, there are those who argue that, despite appearances, Locke is a realist and not a representationalist. He may appear to be a representationalist occasionally, but this is not his true position. Both these views, however, may be shown to be defective.

For, while Locke does accept the theory of representative perception, he accepts it with no great enthusiasm. He is certainly not its originator. The view that he is responsible for it will not stand historical examination. It was held almost universally at the time, and held by opposing schools of thought, for instance, Gassendists and Cartesians. Locke was heir to it and it was an inheritance not wholly pleasing to him. If we take the theory in its crudest and most straightforward sense, that is, as meaning that we are acquainted with ideas which are exact copies of originals, then it is correct to say that in one important respect, namely, in respect of ideas of secondary qualities, Locke rejected the theory. Today its defects are perfectly plain. In the first place, given ideas only, how can we know whether they do adequately represent originals which we have never seen? To know whether the representation is correct or not one must first see the original. Locke himself seems to have been aware of this criticism, though it is not clear that he fully realized how devastating it could be. For in his *Examination of P. Malebranche's Opinion* he remarks: 'How can

---

[1] The full history of this theory remains to be written, but it is at least a synthesis (not necessarily made explicitly) of the medieval doctrine of *species* with that other doctrine, emphasized anew by Galileo and his successors, that things are not as they appear. In the medieval theory, for instance in Aquinas, the species is not itself the object, but that through which the object is known. With this at the back of their minds it was possible for seventeenth-century thinkers to talk of the idea as the object of perception and yet to assume that they were still in touch with the real external world. On the other hand, they insisted that the idea was the object perceived (and not that *through which* the object was perceived), for otherwise much that was central to their theory of perception, for instance the distinction between the ideas of primary and secondary qualities, would have been lost.

I know that the picture of any thing is like that thing, when I never see that which it represents?'[1] To know that the representations are faithful one would first have to see the originals and yet, if one saw the originals, seeing the representations would surely be superfluous. In the second place, the theory is defective because we have no right on the evidence before us to assert that these originals do exist. We only see the copies. How then can we possibly know that they *are* copies, copying certain originals which are never directly experienced by us? Without contradicting oneself it becomes possible to deny the ultimate object supposed to be copied by the idea, and the door is opened for idealism. Now how far Locke was aware of the full defects of this theory it is difficult to say, but there can be no doubt that he felt uneasy about its implications. The objections that he brings forward against his own position at the beginning of iv. iv reveal his uneasiness.

But if Locke felt even vaguely that the theory was inherently defective, why did he accept it? There is ample evidence in the *Essay* to show that he did, and to refute those others who think that Locke was not a representationalist. For instance, when at the opening of iv. iv he makes his doubts about representationalism clear, he immediately goes on to reaffirm it in the most explicit terms. ''Tis evident, the mind knows not things immediately, but only by the intervention of the *ideas* it has of them.'[2] One might argue that the account of sensitive knowledge in Book IV is inconsistent with his representationalism, and this may be so. Also Locke sometimes speaks loosely; for instance, he talks of ideas as if they were qualities in physical things, so that in having ideas we are in immediate contact with the external world. But for such loose talk, it is interesting to note, he apologizes beforehand: 'which *ideas* if I speak of sometimes as in the things themselves, I would be understood to mean those qualities in the objects which produce them in us'.[3] His philosophy is certainly representationalist; and it is significant that in the very same paragraph as that

---

[1] § 51. *Works*, iii. 465 (1801 ed., ix. 250).
[2] iv. iv. 3, and cf. also ii. xxix. 8: '. . . our ideas which are, as it were, the pictures of things'.
[3] ii. viii. 8; and for an instance of this loose language cf. ii. xxi. 1.

in which he apologizes for these lapses he modifies his definition of *idea* slightly so as to bring it more definitely into line with his representationalism: 'Whatsoever the mind perceives *in itself* or is the immediate object of perception, thought, or understanding, that I call "idea".'[1]

But, again, if Locke knew the defects—or some of the defects —of the theory of representative perception why did he accept it? The only possible answer is that he must have felt there was no other alternative. It is indeed most difficult for the realist, who wishes to maintain that there are physical objects in the external world independent of the mind knowing them, to avoid representationalism or some sort of perceptual dualism. *Prima facie* there is a great deal of evidence for ideas in Locke's sense. I see the moon the size of a florin, or to speak more precisely, I see a white circular patch looking as big as a florin looks at arm's length. I know (or claim to know) that the real moon is a sphere of large dimensions. But the moon cannot at the same time both be and not be the size of a florin, and if the real moon is not the size of a florin what is the object which I see of that size? If it be answered that it is an appearance of the moon then this is what Locke means by *idea*, and we are admitting the dualism. In the same manner, when we ask where the moon the size of a florin is, Locke, in spite of the unsatisfactoriness of the answer, could find no other than that it was 'in the mind'. The circular patch of white the size of a florin does not fill the space that the real moon fills nor, presumably, does it fill part of that space. It is not where the moon is, nor can we suppose that it is in the intervening space between the moon and my body. It cannot be on the retina of my eye, since the whole of the latter is much smaller than the size of a florin, and it seems absurd to think that there is a white patch the size of a florin inside my brain. What then can we say except that the moon the size of a florin is in my mind, meaning that it is in the same place as is the image of the moon which I now imagine? Perhaps, we ought not to ask, 'Where is the object I see?' just as we should not ask 'Where is the image I imagine?' since we thereby presuppose that these objects are somewhere

[1] II. viii. 8. (The italics are mine.)

in space. But if we do ask the question, there is certainly a strong *prima facie* case for the answer Locke and his contemporaries gave.

Locke accepts the theory of representative perception, then, not because he is over-fond of it, but because he finds it inevitable. It is in this tone that he always speaks of it, as witness the interesting passage in his second reply to Stillingfleet: 'Not thinking your Lordship, therefore, yet so perfect a convert of Mr. J. S[ergeant]'s that you are persuaded that as often as you think of your cathedral church or of Des Cartes's vortices, that the very cathedral church at Worcester, or the motion of those vortices itself existed in your understanding; when one of them never existed but in that one place at Worcester and the other never existed anywhere *in rerum natura*; I conclude your Lordship has immediate objects of your mind, which are not the very things themselves, existing in your understanding; which if, with the Academics, you will please call representations, as I suppose you will, rather than, with me, ideas, it will make no difference.'[1] He supposes that Stillingfleet would not quarrel with him in his representationalism. What was new in the 'new way of ideas', as is obvious from the correspondence, was not representationalism but the stress on sensation and reflection as the sole source of materials for knowledge, in other words the thorough-going empiricism.

Locke thought, then, that some sort of representationalism and dualism was inevitable. At the same time he does not accept the copying theory in its crudity; for him representation or idea does not necessarily signify copy. Moreover, as we have seen, some ideas do not appear to be representative, but to be logical meanings, complete in themselves and pointing to nothing beyond themselves, while, as will become clearer, even representations are to some extent universals as well. Thus, while Locke accepts representationalism as his own general standpoint, he modifies it considerably and criticizes it.[2]

From the foregoing it will be easily understood that ambiguities

[1] *Works*, i. 554; *Second Reply to the Bishop of Worcester* (1801 ed., iv. 390–1).
[2] On the further question, In what sense, if any, is the idea of reflection representative? cf. p. 130 below.

in connexion with the term *idea* can hardly be avoided. It follows that it is almost impossible for Locke to give a coherent and satisfactory account of the relationship between idea and mind. The former is object, the latter subject. Yet ideas are 'in the mind'. It has been suggested that this merely means that they are experienced by mind. But it must mean more than this, for the question of existence is involved. Locke opposes such objects to those that are 'without the mind' and independent of it. The latter exist in a real world of physical objects, but the former exist in the mind only. Consequently, *the mind* itself has a double meaning. It is the knowing, the experiencing, and the willing agent; but it is also the place of ideas. In the first sense mind perceives the ideas, in the second it contains them. This phrase 'in the mind' obviously requires the most careful handling, but, unfortunately, Locke uses it freely in the *Essay* without explanation and without examination. In the *Examination of Malebranche* he argues that the idea cannot itself be mind or spiritual substance (for the latter is usually taken to be unextended and so could never represent extended things). Nor, again, can it be a modification of spiritual substance (for then on my seeing white and black the mind would at the same moment and in respect to the same part of it be both black and white). The ideas are 'in the mind', he here holds, as being seen by the mind.[1] But that is precisely the difficulty. The mind does not see the real physical object. It sees an object which somehow exists in the mind, and yet it is not the mind itself, nor a modification of the mind. The phrase 'in the mind' is highly ambiguous, nevertheless it is essential to Locke's theory of ideas—just as Berkeley's very idealism rests upon it and would be impossible without it.

We conclude, then, that the term *idea* is used ambiguously by Locke and that it is not possible to give a single definition of it. On the one hand, it is a semi-psychical, momentary existence 'in the mind'. Yet what sort of existence it there possesses it is most difficult to say, being neither spiritual substance nor a modification of spiritual substance. The only point which is clear is its function.

[1] *Examination of Malebranche*, § 18; cf. also § 39 and *Remarks upon Mr. Norris*, § 2.

It represents an externally existing entity, although again that representation may not be exact in all particulars. On the other hand, Locke may also mean by *idea* a universal meaning, a term of a proposition, a logical content. It is clearly a most ambiguous word which Locke ought to have analysed with greater care. In studying the matter, particularly in the light of subsequent developments, one cannot avoid the intriguing, and surely not wholly foolish, reflection that if Locke had analysed this concept more rigorously and more adequately, the idealism of Berkeley might never have come into being.

II

The next question to be considered in connexion with ideas is one of origin. How does the mind gain its ideas? The first book of the *Essay* has shown that none of them is present innately. They are all acquired. 'Let us then suppose,' Locke says,[1] 'the mind to be, as we say, white paper, void of all characters, without any *ideas*; how comes it to be furnished? Whence comes it by that vast store, which the busy and boundless fancy of man has painted on it with an almost endless variety? Whence has it all the materials of reason and knowledge? To this I answer in one word, from *experience*: in that all our knowledge is founded and from that it ultimately derives itself.' Locke proceeds to analyse experience into sensation and reflection, and adds: 'These two are the fountains of knowledge, from whence all the *ideas* we have, or can naturally have, do spring.'[2]

We may postpone consideration of ideas of reflection to a more appropriate occasion, and turn immediately to ideas of sensation. In the opening sections of the *Essay* Locke has already remarked that he does not propose to inquire into the correlates of sensation on the physical and physiological side. He will not trouble 'to examine . . . by what motions of our spirits, or alterations of our bodies, we come to have any sensation by our organs, or any *ideas* in our understandings'.[3] Instead he proposes to adopt the

---

[1] II. i. 2.   [2] Ibid.   [3] I. i. 2.

'historical, plain method', that is, to accept facts as they are with-out seeking ultimate explanations. The fact he now accepts is that we do have ideas in sensations.

This is what he proposes to do in theory, but actually his pro-cedure as he develops his argument in the second book is very different. For the account of the origin of ideas rests upon a theory of sensation, never fully asserted in the *Essay* it is true, but none the less always implied. The description of sensation in II. i. 3 is very vague: 'Our *senses,* conversant about particular sensible objects, do *convey into the mind* several distinct *perceptions* of things, according to those various ways wherein those objects do affect them.' The keyword here is the word 'convey'. The senses convey perceptions into the mind according as they are affected by things outside. Locke himself, however, can see that this ex-planation is inadequate and tries again: 'When I say the senses convey them into the mind, I mean, they from external objects convey into the mind what produces there those perceptions.' The senses now convey into the mind not perceptions but something that can produce perceptions. Clearly Locke is none too happy in his account of sensation. But the kind of explanation which he wishes to give can be gathered from these remarks and from subsequent passages in Book II, especially the chapter dealing with primary and secondary qualities, where 'physical inquiries' become necessary 'to make the nature of sensation a little under-stood'.[1] The explanation which he seems to presuppose runs some-what as follows: In the world of nature are certain physical objects, composed of a very great number of corpuscles. These affect our sense-organs by emitting effluences or species which strike the sense-organs. This affection is then carried on to the brain, which in turn affects the mind. The consequence is the idea in the mind. Now Locke nowhere teaches this theory explicitly. He is too well aware of its difficulties.[2] In the *Examination of Malebranche,* where he actually discusses it, he is careful not to accept it out-right; none the less he is obviously more inclined to this explana-

---

[1] II. viii. 22.

[2] He gets nearest an explicit statement, perhaps, in II. viii. 13; cf. also IV. ii. 11–13.

tion of sensation than to any other of those which Malebranche puts before his reader. In so far as he does accept it, it is well to note, he makes three assumptions, which are never proved in the course of the *Essay*, first, that such physical objects exist, that is, he assumes a realism; secondly, that the brain being affected affects the mind, that is, an interactionist theory of the mind–body relation; thirdly, that perception is brought about causally by the action of physical objects on the mind through the brain.

But while Locke is compelled to base his account of sense-experience upon some theory of this sort, he is not really interested in speculations about the correlates of sensation as such, and so far as he can avoids them. His real interest lies in his attempt to establish his empiricist thesis. The theme of Book II to which he returns over and over again is man's dependence upon sensation and reflection for the beginnings of knowledge. He classifies ideas in order to show that all of them are ultimately derived from experience. He analyses them only so far as is necessary to prove the same thing—and this, incidentally, is the reason why Locke's analyses in Book II are frequently so inadequate. He digresses, but always returns to the main theme; and it is almost amusing to observe his anxious efforts to drag in his central thesis before closing some of his chapters. The whole purpose of Book II is the establishment of the empiricist position.[1]

Since this is so, it is important to make clear the nature of Locke's empiricism, particularly in view of the fact that this theory of his has in the past been sometimes expounded in unsatisfactory ways. I may mention two interpretations which are, in my opinion, particularly misleading. For the first, empiricism is identified with what may be called sensationalism in the narrow sense. According to this kind of sensationalism we know the external world in the act of sensing and know it *only in this way*. When I open my eyes and look around me my seeing is knowledge. I see the world as it is in its full reality. And as much as I ever shall know of it I know in this way. Now Locke's empiricism

---

[1] The last five chapters of the book, however, form an exception. There he discusses ideas from the point of view of their clarity and adequacy rather than of their origin. But these chapters are a sort of appendix and, as the drafts show, they were not an original part of Book II.

is not to be identified with sensationalism in this sense. It is true that Locke does say in Book IV, as we shall see, that we know the *existence* of things in sensing. But this is very different from saying we know the full nature of those things in sensing. It is true also that he does occasionally imply that we know in sensation many of the qualities of existing things and many coexistences of these qualities. But this again is very different from asserting that knowing is to be identified with sensing and that there is no knowing apart from sensing. So far from being the only knowledge we have of the external world, sensation, as Locke usually conceives it in Book II, provides no knowledge of that world. It provides the 'materials' for knowledge; it fills the mind with ideas. But knowledge comes later. This is the prevailing view of Book II and indeed of the whole *Essay*. It is only explicitly denied when the fact of existential knowledge compels Locke, in spite of his main theory of knowledge, to recognize that sense-perception (not to be identified with bare sensing) is itself a knowing. Even then it is only one sort of knowing and a rather doubtful sort at that. If sensationalism be defined in the narrow sense described above, it is surely false to identify Locke's empiricism with it. His empiricism is no sensationalism, and yet many who read Book II hastily and do not bother to understand Books III and IV, mistakenly write it down as such.[1]

We may pass to the second misinterpretation. Locke's empiricism is frequently identified with his compositionalism. This is the theory that we begin with simple ideas which are given us in the course of experience. We then take some of these and combine them into complex ideas, but all complex ideas are combinations of simple ideas first given in experience. Empiricism, according to this view, is the belief that all ideas are either simple in the sense of being given in experience, or compounds of such simples. Now this interpretation is more dangerous than the former because it is supported by a good deal that Locke actually says in the text. None the less, it is, in my opinion, unsound interpretation, and that because it confuses what is incidental to Locke's empiricism with what is essential to it. The compositionalism is

---

[1] Cf. also *First Reply to Stillingfleet*, *Works*, i. 363.

not itself the empiricism. It is the outward garb in which the empiricism appears. It is not difficult to show that Locke's distinction between simple and complex ideas is inadequate and, indeed, breaks down in the course of the *Essay*. But whilst admitting this, as one must, I wish to maintain that Locke's empiricism remains in its essentials untouched by such criticism. For it cannot rightly be identified with that distinction between simple and complex ideas, in which he tries to express it.

In setting forward the distinction Locke was once again accepting current fashion. The guiding concept of the age was that of composition. Since Descartes's day, at least, stress had been put on the need for analysing the complex into its simple parts. Things were assumed to be either simples or compounds and the task of the scientist was to reveal the elements out of which the compounds were made. Locke would be quite familiar with the method in the sciences, and when later he applied it to the study of mind and its ideas, there was precedent here also for his procedure. Indeed, Hobbes, as the *Elements of Philosophy* makes clear, had already used the method in this realm with a degree of thoroughness to which Locke never attained. Yet Locke too was committed to this theory and it provided the framework for Book II, even though the distinction between simple and complex ideas was finally more of a hindrance than a help to him. That the latter was in fact the case is clear on following Locke's argument. For, first, he failed to make the conception of a simple idea, and so the distinction between simple and complex, wholly clear to himself. Secondly, such distinctions as he was able to make between simple and complex ideas broke down as the work developed. Thirdly, the class *complex ideas* could not possibly contain all the ideas which according to this theory it was supposed to contain.

Locke failed to make the nature of the simple idea clear to himself largely because he meant by the term *simple idea* two quite distinct things: (*a*) the *given*, (*b*) the indivisible, the atom. Generally speaking, the simple idea is that which the mind receives;[1]

---

[1] Cf. II. i. 20–25. In receiving the simple ideas the mind is said to be passive (in accordance with traditional teaching). But Locke does not use the terms

the complex that which it makes, 'the workmanship of the mind'. But the simple idea is also 'the uncompounded', that which 'contains within it nothing but one uniform appearance or conception in the mind and is not distinguishable into different *ideas*'.[1] That is to say, it is the atom. And the atom may be the outcome of a process of abstraction rather than be a *given* of sensation. (*a*) and (*b*) are not synonymous, yet Locke means by the term *simple idea* sometimes the one and sometimes the other, and this fact does much to confuse his argument.

But whether the distinction between simple and complex be between what is given and what is not given or between the atomic and the composite, both distinctions break down as the argument proceeds. Frequently in the *Essay* complex ideas, as well as simple, are held to be *given*. 'Simple ideas', he remarks, 'are observed to exist in several combinations united together'.[2] But this surely means that the complex idea is given. And this is no chance passage. He constantly speaks of observing ideas 'going together'. I know that the simple ideas which together frame my idea of the table do go together because I have observed them to go together.[3] What then of the view that the simple alone is given? Again, Locke was compelled to admit that some ideas were simple and yet not atoms. We may take the instance of the ideas of space and time. 'Though they', he holds, 'are justly reckoned amongst our *simple ideas*, yet none of the distinct *ideas* we have of either is without all manner of *composition*; it is the very nature of both of them to consist of parts.'[4] Thus whichever view of it we take, the distinction between simple and complex breaks down. Not everything given is a simple idea and not all composites are complex ideas.

active and *passive* in any very consistent way. For instance, the text of II. i. 25 tells us that in the reception of simple ideas 'the understanding is merely passive', but in the heading of the same paragraph Locke says it is 'for the most part passive'. Again in II. vi. 1 perception is included amongst the *actions* of the mind. What Locke means, however, is fairly clear in spite of such inconsistencies. In sensing the mind receives and does not itself create. In that sense it is passive, although in another sense receiving is itself an activity. Simple ideas are given us, they are not creations of ours. Perceptions, as opposed to sensations, may, however, involve an element of judging, cf. II. ix. 8 and below, p. 134.

[1] II. ii. 1.
[2] II. xii. 1.
[3] Cf. II. xi. 7, xxii. 2, xxiii. 1, &c.
[4] II. xv. 9.

Thirdly, the class *complex idea* cannot possibly retain all that is packed into it. According to the compositional theory every idea which is not a simple is a composite idea made up of simples. But surely ideas of relation and general ideas are not composite in this sense. Locke himself came to see this and it is exceedingly interesting to note the changes which he made in the fourth edition when he had fully realized this fact. Two instances will suffice. In II. i. 5, in the first edition, he remarks of the simple ideas: 'These, when we have taken a full survey of them, and their several *modes* and the *compositions* made out of them, we shall find to contain our whole stock of *ideas*.' The fourth edition, however, drops the phrase 'and the *compositions* made out of them' and substitutes 'combinations and relations'. That is, relations are not compounded ideas but a distinct group. More significant are the additions in II. xii. 1. Here he alters the classification of ideas in certain very important respects. The difference may best be shown in tabulated form thus:

First Edition	*Fourth Edition*
I. Simple Ideas.	I. Simple Ideas.
II. Complex Ideas:	II. Complex Ideas.
(*a*) modes,	III. Ideas of Relation.
(*b*) substances,	IV. General Ideas.
(*c*) relations.	

In the fourth edition both ideas of relation and general ideas are considered as distinct classes of ideas. They are not compounded ideas. Incidentally, it is to be regretted that Locke did not rewrite Book II with this new classification in mind. Even in the first edition, however, Locke does not permit himself to be bound too closely by his classification. He conveniently forgets it when discussing ideas of relation and general ideas. In the case of ideas of reflection his thoughts about them are never guided by the simple–complex division.[1]

Locke, then, begins with the compositional theory in Book II, but as his argument proceeds it becomes less and less useful. He is not greatly perturbed at this, however, precisely because he does

---

[1] It is true that II. xix is entitled 'Of the Modes of Thinking' but the thought of that chapter is certainly not compositional.

not think compositionalism fundamental to his argument. The real purpose of Book II is not to show that all ideas are either simple or complex and that the latter are compounded of the former. The real purpose, as has been said, is to establish empiricism, and the foregoing is not empiricism.

What then is Locke's empiricism? It is the doctrine that the mind is originally white paper, upon which nothing has been written, the *tabula rasa* of earlier thought.[1] Upon it are imprinted ideas. Experience (that is to say, sensation and reflection) 'stocks' the mind. This is, of course, highly metaphorical language. It means that were we unable to sense and to reflect (or introspect) knowledge would be impossible for us. To the person blind from birth the word *red* no doubt conveys something. He has heard it discussed and may have sought to imagine its character. But what it cannot convey to him is what I now experience in looking at this red object. Ultimates are given to the mind in experience which cannot be suggested to it by description or definition, but must themselves be experienced. And Locke's point is that, whenever we think, our thought-content will be found to consist of material which may be different enough from these immediately experienced ultimates, but which is based upon them in the sense that had there been no experience, there could have been no such content in the mind. 'All those sublime thoughts which tower above the clouds, and reach as high as heaven itself, take their rise and footing here: in all that great extent wherein the mind wanders in those remote speculations it may seem to be elevated with, it stirs not one jot beyond those *ideas* which sense or reflection have offered for its contemplation.'[2] The ultimates given in sensation and reflection are essential as the basis of human knowledge. This is the essence of Locke's empiricism.

And if this is the doctrine of empiricism in its essentials may we not also take one further step in order to complete our elucidation of it? Locke's empiricism in this sense is surely independent of his 'idea-ism' and representationalism. The truth or falsity of

[1] Cf. Thomas Aquinas (*Summa Theologica*, i, qu. 79, art. 2): 'Intellectus autem humanus . . . est sicut tabula rasa in qua nihil est scriptum, ut Philosophus dicit in 3 de Anima, text. 14.' Also Gassendi in the passage cited above, p. 35.
[2] II. i. 24.

empiricism, that is to say, has nothing to do with the truth or falsity of representationalism. At one point in his argument Locke himself seems to be departing from his representationalism. It is in the discussion of sensitive knowledge in Book IV to which we have already referred. As we shall see, it is not wholly clear how far he is prepared to go. But he does seem to say that we know directly the existence of things in sensation and that we thus break out beyond ideas. In that case sense-experience is not merely having ideas, seeing colours, hearing sounds, and the like. It is also a knowledge of the *existence* of physical objects. That is to say, Locke is rejecting the view that we know through ideas only. Yet there is no reason to suppose that he wishes at the same time to reject his empiricism. He would still, no doubt, hold it to be true that all our knowledge of the external world begins with sense-experience, but that now the knowledge of the existence of a physical object is part of that sense-experience. In a similar manner, presumably, the intuition of the self which, on Locke's view, goes along with all reflection or introspection is part of the reflective experience. Now whether these theories are valid or not is not our present concern. The point is that empiricism on the above view need not entail representationalism; that the representationalism and 'idea-ism' of Book II also are but parts of the garb in which Locke tries to set out his empiricism.

To conclude, Locke's empiricism is the doctrine that for human beings sensory and reflective experience is essential if any knowledge is ever to be gained. It is not to be identified with narrow sensationalism, nor with the view that all ideas must be either simples or compounds of simples, nor again with the further view that we only know things mediately through ideas. It has to do with something more fundamental than any of these theories. It is the assertion of man's dependence upon sensation and reflection. Other beings more highly placed in the hierarchy of spiritual life may be independent of sensation and reflection. But for man the only possible foundation of the structure of knowledge is experience. Neither innately nor by 'high priori' methods alone can he hope to know. He depends upon experience and must always wait upon it.

III

One further distinction needs to be examined in order 'to discover the nature of our *ideas* the better, and to discourse of them intelligibly'.[1] This is the distinction between primary and secondary qualities. In considering this famous distinction it will be well, first, to expound the account given in the text; secondly, to link it up with previous thought; thirdly, to discuss the significance of what is indeed a very significant theory in Locke's *Essay*.

The main outlines of the theory are no doubt familiar to all who are acquainted even superficially with Locke's philosophy. The ideas we have of the qualities of things are divided by him into two classes. If we take as an example the ideas of qualities which go to make up our complex idea of an apple, we find that some of these are of qualities which belong to the apple in the sense that the apple cannot be conceived as lacking them, for instance, the apple is solid and extended. Others again are of qualities which may or may not belong to the apple, for instance, its taste, colour, smell, and so on. Now Locke calls the first type of qualities primary qualities and the second secondary qualities, and he holds that the ideas of the primary are exact representations of these qualities but those of the secondary are not so.[2] This is the general theory. It is when we consider the details and the implications of this theory that we meet with very serious difficulties.

For, to begin with, we are perplexed here again by ambiguities, most of which are the outcome of Locke's failure to distinguish sufficiently carefully between qualities and ideas of qualities—a fault which he himself confesses and for which he apologizes.[3] The consequence is that many interpretations of this theory become possible, for each of which some confirmation can be found in the text. We may best proceed by first setting out the alternatives clearly. (*a*) We know primary qualities of things directly. By primary qualities are meant solidity, extension, figure, motion or rest, and number.[4] We know the secondary qualities indirectly through our ideas of colours, sounds, smells, and so on. (*b*) We know the primary qualities of things directly as in (*a*), but secon-

---

[1] II. viii. 7.   [2] Cf. II. viii. 17–18.   [3] II. viii. 8.
[4] This is the list given in II. viii. 9. It is occasionally varied.

dary qualities are merely ideas in the mind. (c) We have ideas in experience which exactly resemble the primary qualities, that is, we do not know these qualities directly, but have an exact indirect knowledge of them. And we have ideas which are secondary qualities, as in (b). (d) We have ideas which exactly resemble the primary qualities, as in (c), and have other ideas which it is customary to call ideas of qualities, and which we may here call ideas of secondary qualities. Actually, however, these latter ideas are not copies of external qualities. They represent (though without copying) certain powers possessed by things which cause us to have these ideas on certain occasions. These powers probably depend 'upon the primary qualities of their minute and insensible parts, or, if not upon them, upon something yet more remote from our comprehension'.[1]

Now whilst the text does not rule out any of these four interpretations, the view which best accords with the rest of the *Essay* and which predominates in II. viii and elsewhere when Locke is discussing primary and secondary qualities is the fourth.[2] This will become clear if we summarize Locke's argument.

We must not too readily assume with the cruder kind of representationalist that every one of our ideas is an exact copy of what lies beyond it. We need to make a division of ideas into those which do exactly copy what is outside and those which do not. Now, first, we may consider the group of ideas which exactly resemble what is outside, namely, the ideas of primary qualities. In the past sufficient attention has not been given, I believe, to the very careful and deliberate language with which Locke describes the primary qualities and what we know of them. They are first said to be 'inseparable from the body in what estate soever it be'.[3] All corporeal objects possess the primary qualities whatever other qualities they may or may not possess. But how have we learnt this important truth? Firstly, 'sense constantly finds [them] in every

---

[1] IV. iii. 11.

[2] Fraser would prefer interpretation (a) or (b). I do not deny that there are passages which confirm Fraser's views, cf. II. viii. 22, but there are many more which support the fourth interpretation. For a discussion of Fraser's views cf. Mr. Reginald Jackson's article on this matter in *Mind* (January 1930).

[3] II. viii. 9.

particle of matter which has bulk enough to be perceived'.[1] This I take to mean that whenever we experience a physical object ideas of the primary qualities are part of the whole complex idea which we then have. Here is our first suggestion of the constant presence of these qualities in things. But Locke goes farther. Not only do we experience them in the ideas we have of those physical objects big enough to be seen and felt, but also 'the mind finds [them] inseparable from every particle of matter, though less than to make itself singly be perceived by our senses'. This is a very important addition. It means that our knowledge of the nature of corporeal objects is not confined to the information given in sensation. 'Take a grain of wheat,' Locke proceeds, 'divide it into two parts, each part has still *solidity, extension, figure, and mobility*; divide it again and it retains still the same qualities; and so divide it on till the parts become insensible, they must retain still each of them all those qualities'.[2] They *must* retain the primary qualities. Now it is not the senses which give Locke this information. What is the further faculty at work here, and how much does it reveal to us of the nature of the corporeal object? Before we seek to answer this question we must examine the rest of what Locke has to say about primary and secondary qualities.

Of primary qualities Locke remarks in II. viii. 15: 'Ideas of primary qualities are resemblances of them and their patterns do really exist in the bodies themselves.' Now the strange thing is that Locke nowhere offers proof of this all-important principle. Instead he devotes all his space to the attempt to show that there are no qualities in things resembling our ideas of secondary qualities. He apparently assumed that all his readers would agree with his theory about primary qualities so that there was no need for him to defend it. Consequently, there is no serious attempt to face the problem which, after the criticism initiated by Berkeley, became so real, namely, how we know that the ideas of primary qualities do resemble the qualities themselves.[3] This Locke accepts as part of the theory of representative perception and merely

---

[1] II. viii. 9.

[2] Ibid.

[3] He makes one or two incidental suggestions, for instance, in II. viii. 21, with which I shall deal later. Cf. p. 127 n.

states. He reserves his energies for the consideration of the other part of that theory which he could not accept.

Turning to secondary qualities, the ideas of these, we are told, do not resemble the qualities of things outside. Actually, the table is not brown, though I see brown when I look at it. This idea of brown which is mine does, however, 'represent' something. It represents those powers in the table, probably dependent on its primary qualities, which cause me to see brown. 'Such *qualities*, which in truth are nothing in the objects themselves but powers to produce various sensations in us by their *primary qualities*, i.e. by the bulk, figure, texture, and motion of their insensible parts, as colours, sounds, tastes, etc., these I call *secondary qualities*.'[1] To talk about ideas of secondary qualities is thus slightly misleading, for there are no secondary qualities in the sense in which there are primary qualities in things. This table has, Locke explains, a power to make me see brown. We are not sufficiently well acquainted with the thing to enable us to say precisely what that power is, though we may well suppose that it depends on the primary qualities of its insensible parts. Things also have a third sort of qualities, to which Locke refers, namely, the powers they have to affect other things and produce changes therein. Secondary qualities themselves are an instance of powers,[2] but of powers which affect our human bodies and particularly our sense-organs. We shall meet with Locke's conception of *power* later, and we need not examine it here. But these secondary qualities are a sufficiently singular group of powers to be considered alone.

To Locke's contemporaries the view that any ideas in the mind given by the senses were not resemblances of things or of their qualities was apparently somewhat novel and needed to be defended. Locke begins by reminding his readers of a group of ideas which though given in sensation are yet not usually considered to be resemblances, namely, ideas of pleasure and pain. The pain felt by the wounded man, it would be generally granted, does not at all resemble the actual wounding of the flesh. Why not extend

---

[1] II. viii. 10.
[2] Primary qualities are also powers, since all qualities are so. 'The power to produce any *idea* in our mind I call *quality*', II. viii. 8.

this to all ideas of secondary qualities? Why should they be supposed to resemble those motions in physical objects which bring
them about? 'It being no more impossible', Locke adds in words
curiously reminiscent of Occasionalism, 'to conceive that God
should annex such *ideas* to such motions with which they have no
similitude, than that he should annex the *idea* of pain to the
motion of a piece of steel dividing our flesh, with which that *idea*
hath no resemblance'.[1] Thus it may be possible that the ideas of
secondary qualities do not resemble them. Locke now proceeds to
prove this. He appeals to the mutability of the evidence of the
senses. This table looks brown in one light and grey in another.
This same water is warm to one hand and cold to another. Facts
of this sort suggest that the ideas we have are not always exact
copies. For if the table is brown then, when we see it to be grey,
the idea we have on that occasion is no exact copy of the quality
in the table itself. In the same manner if the water is warm it cannot also at the same time be cold. On the basis of instances of this
sort Locke proceeds (somewhat dogmatically) to assert that *none*
of the ideas of secondary qualities in our mind does copy the
qualities exactly.[2] This evidence also overthrows, in Locke's
opinion, the crude view that things themselves are brown, grey,
warm, and the like. The latter are merely ideas in our minds, and
they are ideas which do not even copy the qualities of things outside. What corresponds to such ideas in the things are so many
powers to make me see brown or grey in the appropriate circumstances. A physical object, then, possesses the primary qualities,
extension, figure, solidity, motion or rest, and number; it also
possesses, probably as the result of its possession of the primary
qualities, certain powers which influence the mind through the
sense-organs and give it the ideas it has of secondary qualities.

Such is Locke's account of the distinction between primary and
secondary qualities. What now of the historical background of
this theory? The terms of the distinction are not original to Locke,
for they are to be found in medieval speculation, at least so far

[1] II. viii. 13.
[2] II. viii. 15–22. The most he could say on this argument would be that not all
of them do.

back as Albertus Magnus.[1] But they are there used with a different meaning. The original distinction is one between those touch-qualities which, according to scholastic interpretation, Aristotle had regarded as fundamental[2] and the other qualities which depend upon these primary ones. The qualities both primary and secondary are, of course, wholly objective; there is no suggestion of any dependence upon mind. To understand Locke's distinction we need to pass to modern thought, and to the re-emergence of a species of atomism in the physical science which then arose. Another doctrine of Aristotle's has become important, that of the common sensibles, which now provide the new science with its basic concepts. Galileo, Gassendi, Descartes, and Hobbes all co-operate to work out the new distinction between two sorts of qualities, those which are essential to physical things and those which are subjective, and not in the physical things themselves.

It is Robert Boyle, however, who first expresses the new distinction in the old scholastic terminology. In 1666 Boyle published *The Origin of Forms and Qualities, according to the Corpuscular Philosophy.* In this work he regards matter as one in nature throughout, 'a substance extended, divisible, and impenetrable'. Within matter, however, changes occur as a consequence of motion, and the one matter becomes many different bodies. But however much these material bodies differ from each other they lose none of their essential properties. 'And since experience shows us that this division of matter is frequently made into insensible corpuscles or particles, we may conclude, that the minutest fragments as well as the biggest masses of the universal matter are likewise endowed each with its peculiar bulk or shape. For being a finite body its dimensions must be terminated and measurable

[1] Cf. Clemens Baeumker, 'Zur Vorgeschichte zweier Lockescher Begriffe', *Arch. Gesch. Phil.*, vol. xxi (1907–8), pp. 296–8 (a discussion of the phrase *tabula rasa*) and pp. 492–517. In vol. xxii (1908–9), p. 380 there is a further note with an apt quotation from Albertus Magnus (ed. Borgnet, v. 473 b). 'Dicuntur autem istae quatuor *qualitates primae*, quia non fluunt ab aliis, sed omnes aliae qualitates sive contrarietates proveniunt ex ipsis. . . . Et sic patet quod una contrarietas non dependit a reliqua; quare, ut dictum est, *qualitates primae* dicuntur. *Secundariae* autem sunt quae causantur ab istis, scilicet durum, molle, dulce et amarum, album et nigrum et similia.' St. Thomas also talks of *qualitates primae* in the same sense.

[2] *De Anima*, ii. and iii. Certain touch-qualities are 'primary differences', particularly hot and cold, wet and dry.

and though it may change its figure yet for the same reason it must necessarily have some figure or other.' In the same manner it must be in motion or at rest. But there is another group of qualities which for Boyle are subjective. These qualities only exist as the consequence of the existence of 'certain sensible and rational beings that we call men'. 'The figure, shape, motion, and texture of bodies without them' influence the sense-organs of men and produce what we know as sensible qualities. Such qualities we wrongly attribute to the corporeal objects themselves. 'We have been from our infancy apt to imagine that these sensible qualities are real beings in the objects they denominate, and have the faculty or power to work such and such things . . . whereas indeed there is in the body, to which these sensible qualities are attributed, nothing of real and physical, but the size, shape, and motion or rest of its component particles, together with that texture of the whole, which results from them being so contrived as they are',[1] that is to say, nothing but, as Boyle here calls them, the 'primary accidents' or qualities. The other qualities do not belong to the body itself; the primary alone belong to the body. 'I say not that there are no other accidents in bodies than colours, odours and the like, for I have already taught that there are simpler and more primitive affections of matter, from which these secondary qualities, if I may so call them, do depend: and that the operations of bodies upon one another spring from the same we shall see by and by.'[2]

It is unnecessary to follow Boyle further in his analysis of qualities. The distinction between primary and secondary qualities and again the terms themselves are already present. And Boyle's 'if I may so call them' in the last-quoted sentence reveals that he is conscious of using the words 'secondary qualities' in a new sense. Locke borrowed the terms from him—although since Boyle published this work when the co-operation between him and Locke was at its height, they might very well have been suggested by Locke himself or have been already in use in the scientific circles at Oxford to which both Locke and Boyle belonged. The whole theory might have been worked out in conjunction by

---

[1] Boyle, *Works*, vol. ii, p. 466. [2] Ibid.

Boyle, Locke, and the others. When, twenty-four years later, the theory re-emerges in the *Essay*, we find it developed in one respect. Boyle makes the secondary qualities subjective and they are equivalent to what Locke later called *ideas* of secondary qualities. Locke, however, set out the whole theory in representationalist terms, and, as we have seen, the *ideas* of secondary qualities do represent (though not copy) qualities in real things, namely, Locke's secondary qualities. Thus while secondary qualities for Boyle are wholly subjective (being identical with Locke's *ideas* of secondary qualities), they are objective for Locke, being powers in things and represented in the mind by ideas. However, the difference is largely one of terminology. Boyle, in my opinion, means the same thing as Locke, but the latter has used his terms more carefully. On this point there is no fundamental difference in the position of the two.[1]

Before concluding this chapter I propose to say a word or two about the significance of the division of ideas into those of primary and those of secondary qualities in Locke's philosophy.[2] The main purpose of this division in Locke's mind is obvious. He wishes to examine the ideas of the secondary qualities and it is to these that he gives most attention. But the more interesting and the more difficult questions arise when we try to understand his theory of primary qualities and our knowledge of them. With respect to secondary qualities, Locke's examination of them resulted in a serious modification of the theory of representative perception. That theory, if my interpretation is correct, still dominates the passages in which the distinction between primary and secondary qualities is set forth. Even the ideas of secondary qualities still 'represent'. But in respect to them he wholly denies the cruder copying theory. The ideas of secondary qualities are in a practical sense of very great value, so great that life would become impossible without them. None the less, colours, tastes, and sounds do not resemble those powers in things which produce them. The deeper significance of this side of his teaching lies perhaps here.

[1] I believe that Baeumker in the aforementioned article tends to exaggerate the difference between Locke and Boyle.

[2] Cf. also William Kneale, 'Sensation and the Physical World', *Phil. Quarterly*, vol. i (1950–1), pp. 109 ff.

It justifies and makes necessary an appeal beyond the senses. It shows why Locke could not possibly have been a mere sensationalist. For sense-experience of itself cannot provide us with the full truth about physical things. If it could, reasoning and theorizing would be superfluous and wisdom would lie in the passive acceptance of all that the senses give. But it cannot do so. Further inquiry becomes both possible and necessary. In other words, the real as it is is not just given in sense-experience, and so when the mind proceeds further by way of reasoning it is not of necessity leaving the real behind. It may very well be the case that it approaches nearer it. The scientist may have a truer conception of the physical world than has the unreflective man who contents himself with the evidence of the senses, and Locke believes that this is so.

But if we do not expect the senses to enlighten us about the qualities real things possess in the case of secondary qualities, why do we expect them to do so in the case of the primary? What is the explanation of the exception which Locke makes? I do not think one can find a definite answer in Locke. It is most regrettable that he should have given so little attention to the primary qualities and to our knowledge of them. He seems, however, to be saying two things. First, we do have ideas of these qualities in sensation and we also know certain things in connexion with them by reason. What we know by reason is that all corporeal objects possess the primary qualities, even including those objects which are too small to be sensible. Secondly, the ideas of the primary qualities resemble those qualities, although it is not, presumably, by the senses that we know this, for the most that sensation could do would be to provide the ideas.

I may deal with the first point first. If we know by reason or intuition or in any non-sensuous way that the things in the physical world are extended, solid, and so on, surely here is information and 'material' for thought not given in sensation and reflection. Is this inconsistent with Locke's empiricism? It may be so. On the other hand, the theory Locke has in mind might be of this kind: We begin with sensory experience, without which there could be no beginning. Now everything which I have ever experienced by means of the senses of sight and touch, the table, the chair, and all other objects, have been extended—to take this quality only. The idea of extension is always part of my complex ideas of things. Having observed and reflected on this, there flashes upon my mind an intuition for which experience has prepared me, the intuition that all external objects, which cause me to have the ideas I do have, are themselves extended. The intellect itself now perceives that extension is an essential property of corporeal objects, so that we can say that any corporeal object, even though it be so small as to be invisible, is extended. This intuition would be identical with Descartes's as he expounds it in the wax illustration in the *Meditations*. But Locke might still seek to safeguard his empiricism by arguing (*a*) that what we experienced prepared us for the intuition of the truth, (*b*)—a more important point—that our first idea of extension was given in sense-experience and that without it the intuition could not occur. The 'material' of this knowledge also, like all other 'material', is first presented empirically.

It is questionable whether these considerations would save Locke from inconsistency. But the point need not be pressed, for I am not sure that the above is what Locke really means. Does he mean that we have an intuition of this sort? He does not say so explicitly. The fact that he had not yet given his account of intuition may have hindered him from developing this side of the argument.[1] Nevertheless he does seem in II. viii to imply an intuition of the sort described above. And if it is an intuition, what precisely is intuited? Are we supposed to intuit an analytic proposition to the effect that matter, as it is defined by the scientist, is necessarily extended? II. viii. 9 does not seem to mean much more than this. Yet it does, I think, mean something more. He wants to say that *things* in the real world are material in the sense that they are extended. But is this further step justified? Do we intuit the essential nature of existent things? After all, these primary qualities are just the concepts which the scientist of the seventeenth century found it necessary to presuppose if his science was to be possible. He theorized in terms of extension, mass, motion, and number. And he theorized in these terms because

---

[1] We have met with the same difficulty in examining his account of our knowledge of the principles in Book I.

they were essential to any quantitative approach to reality, the sole approach of which he was capable. 'What is real is measurable.' The scientist claimed to discover (by measuring) the real dimensional properties, the sizes, shapes, and positions of things. But he could not discover the real colours and tastes which things have, if indeed they themselves have colours and tastes. Accordingly, the question arises naturally: Are we not to attribute the exception made by Locke in the case of the primary qualities to the exigencies of the physical science of Boyle, Newton, and the rest, rather than to any intuition of the nature of the reality lying outside? For Locke himself says later that the real essence of things is hidden from us. But surely, if I know that this piece of gold must be extended, solid, and so on, I know something about its real essence? What then of the theory that the real essence is unknown? Locke might reply that in knowing the primary qualities I know the nature of matter in general and not the real essence of this piece of gold. I only know that it must have some size and some shape. But can I, then, intuit the primary qualities of matter in general? Or are these qualities those which must be conceived to belong to matter as defined by the scientist? Are they necessary for science? Is Locke feeling his way towards the Critical position of Kant?

This point is linked with the other problem to be considered here, namely, the relation which exists between the ideas of the primary qualities and those qualities themselves. The idea 'resembles' the quality. This would seem to mean that, when I now see this table as a rectangular object, the table itself is rectangular. But, of course, if this is what Locke is saying, he is open to the criticism Berkeley makes, that we are as frequently misled about the precise shape of a thing as we are about its precise colour. Sometimes he certainly seems to be saying this and I do not know how else to interpret the words: 'The *ideas* of the *primary qualities* resemble them.' Yet when he first introduces primary qualities in II. viii. 9 he seems to be thinking of them not as *determinates*, if I may use W. E. Johnson's terminology, but as *determinables*, not as particular shapes, for instance, but as shape in general. The object so small as to be insensible must have *some* shape or other without definitely determining which particular shape it has. Now if it be asked: Are Locke's primary qualities determinates or determinables? I am afraid it is not possible to give a definite answer. If it is a case of having an idea through the senses and knowing that this idea is a true copy of what exists outside in respect to, let us say, figure, then presumably the idea would be of a determined figure, and the primary quality so known a determinate. On the other hand, if we are dealing with the abstract working concepts assumed by the scientists, or if with intuitions of the general nature of reality—if this latter is possible—then the primary quality is a determinable. Sometimes in II. viii Locke seems to have the former in mind and sometimes the latter, and no clear answer can be given.[1]

Locke's distinction between primary and secondary qualities then gives rise to many vexatious problems. He had certainly not thought out the distinction with sufficient care. Its meaning is never entirely clear and we are left in much doubt as to whether his empiricism still remains unimpaired. Nevertheless, three conclusions do emerge from this argument, vague and indefinite as it is, and these are conclusions which are surely of the first importance in epistemology: (1) that secondary qualities are not what we first think them to be; (2) that the primary are essential to material existence (leaving it an open question whether 'material existence', as the scientists of the seventeenth century conceived it, was real—as I believe Locke thought it to be—or a mere working hypothesis); (3) that these essential qualities are already given us as ideas in sense-experience.

---

[1] The attempts to defend the view that the primary qualities resemble the ideas we have of them are hardly serious. In II. viii. 18 he remarks: 'A circle or square are the same, whether in *idea* or existence, in the mind or in the manna.' But this hardly helps us when we want to know whether the object which I now see to be circular is actually circular and this is the point that needs defending. Again, in II. viii. 21, Locke remarks, after explaining how the same water may appear warm to one hand and cold to another: 'which yet figure never does, that never producing the *idea* of a square by one hand which has produced the *idea* of a globe by another'. But surely this is hardly a sufficient defence. The apparent shape of an object varies with the conditions of perception, just as the apparent temperature of the water does. None the less these ideas of primary qualities, though first suggested in experience, play the role of defining properties of physical existents, so making possible necessary and universal statements.

THE BEGINNINGS OF MODERN
PSYCHOLOGY

JOHN LOCKE is rightly regarded as the father of English psychology. He was not the first Englishman to interest himself in psychological topics. But what he wrote in the *Essay* was far more fruitful and influential than were the writings of his predecessors, and his approach to psychological problems was the one which dominated subsequent thought. And yet the *Essay* is not primarily a psychological dissertation. Locke's purpose in it is the examination of the nature and extent of human knowledge. Now consideration of human knowledge may, of course, be psychological. But if the greater stress is put on the objective side, on *what* we know rather than on the act of knowing, such an inquiry ceases to be psychology. This, for the most part, is the case with the *Essay*. The great problems of Book IV might have been handled in a psychological manner: actually the treatment is more logical and metaphysical, although psychological considerations are not wholly absent. It is in Book II that we find what can properly be called psychological discussions. But they are present here, it is interesting to note, as part of the general analysis of ideas. There is, as we have seen, one group of ideas, the ideas of reflection, which are the product of the mind's power to turn upon itself and to be aware of itself and of its 'operations' (a question-begging word which needed more careful notice than Locke gave it. But cf. Draft C, p. 60 above). To complete his account of ideas Locke had to say something about this group; hence the more psychological chapters of Book II. I use the words 'had to say something' advisedly, because, in spite of the fact that these chapters are of the utmost importance in the history of English psychology, they were not part of the original scheme of the *Essay*. Locke's main concern was with the ideas of sensation and our knowledge of the external world. The most significant omission from the Drafts in those parts of them which correspond to Book II of the *Essay* is the discussion of ideas of reflection. The chapters on perception and on the modes of thinking[1]—the two chief sources of psychological information in Book II—have nothing corresponding to them in the Drafts,[2] and there is little enough to correspond to the other psychological discussions which that book contains. Thus the psychology of the *Essay* is something of an afterthought. Locke realized that his description of ideas would not be complete without some account of ideas of reflection, and so he finds it necessary to say something about them. None the less, as he proceeds, these strictly psychological problems begin to interest him in themselves, and there can be no two opinions as to the value of what he has to say. His psychological pages, few as they are in a comparative sense, are rich in content and very deserving of serious study. In what follows I propose first to examine Locke's account of the operations of the mind, and then to discuss his description of mind in relation to matter and his theory of the self.

I

Most of our information about the mind comes through reflection, that is, introspection.[3] But Locke does not rule out the study of behaviour. On the contrary, he makes use of this method in observing the behaviour of children and animals, and deducing certain psychological information from what he has observed. He notices how the child shows signs of wonder at the world around it, how it seems most concerned with that world, rather than with the inward world of reflection, or how animals seem to be able to perceive, or how a bird will strive to remember a tune. 'For to pass by other instances, birds learning of tunes, and the endeavours one may observe in them to hit the notes right, put it past doubt with me that they have perception, and retain *ideas* in their memories, and use them for patterns.'[4] All such psychological information is gained by the observation of behaviour.

---

[1] II. ix and xix respectively.
[2] Unless § 21 of Draft B be said to correspond to II. ix.
[3] The word *reflection* does not, in this context, mean cogitation or even meditation. It is reflection in the sense of a bending or turning back upon oneself. The corresponding modern term is clearly introspection.
[4] II. X. 10.

None the less, the chief source of information in Locke's opinion was reflection. Reflection he defines in the following terms: 'By *reflection*, then, . . . I would be understood to mean that notice which the mind takes of its own operations, and the manner of them, by reason whereof there come to be *ideas* of these operations in the understanding.'[1] The definition, it will be noted, is representationalist. The mind takes notice of its own operations, but does not, apparently, know them directly, but has ideas of these operations as a consequence of the notice it has taken. And this representationalism is confirmed by the rest of the paragraph in which reflection is likened to sensation. 'This source of *ideas* every man has wholly in himself; and though it be not sense as having nothing to do with external objects, yet it is very like it, and might properly enough be called internal sense.'[2] But as we follow Locke in his account of these operations of the mind, perception, memory, comparison, and so on, the representationalism is not at all apparent. Indeed, these accounts would have been the same if Locke had never adopted the representationalist position. There is no hesitation about accepting the evidence of reflection on its face value. The modern psychologist has far more doubts about the validity of his introspective method than Locke had about reflection. Thus, though nominally Locke remains representationalist in his explanation of the knowledge we have of our minds, actually he proceeds as if we know ourselves and our operations directly in reflection and as if this knowledge was in all cases exact. Indeed, at the close of the *Essay* the mind alone of all existing things is said to be known directly without the mediation of an idea. We need ideas, he there says, because 'the things the mind contemplates are none of them, *besides itself*, present to the understanding'.[3] In Book II he prefers to retain at least the semblance of representationalism in dealing with our knowledge of the various operations of the mind, though little more than the semblance is retained.

Now reflection comes late. The child's first experiences are sensory; reflection and inward-looking are the marks of adult life. 'The first years are usually employed and diverted in looking

[1] II. i. 4.   [2] Ibid.   [3] IV. xxi. 4. (The italics are mine.)

abroad. Men's business in them is to acquaint themselves with what is to be found without; and so, growing up in a constant attention to outward sensations, seldom make any considerable reflection on what passes within them till they come to be of riper years, and some scarce ever at all.'[1] An important consequence of this is that the knowledge we have through introspection is knowledge of the human mind in maturity; and this incidentally helps to explain why in English psychology (a psychology in the past mainly introspective in method) the study of the adult human mind came first before child and animal psychology. As we have seen, Locke is not wholly silent about children and animals; in II. ix he has gathered together a good deal of psychological information of a sort about them. Also he has occasionally something to say about low states of consciousness, both permanent in certain animals and temporary in human beings.[2] But clearly his main interest lies in the adult human mind and in the information which reflection gives him about it.

Within that mind Locke recognizes two powers or 'faculties', those of 'perception or thinking and volition or willing'.[3] These he calls the simple ideas of reflection, since, as will later become clear, we can talk of other operations of the mind as so many modifications of these. For instance, all the cognitive powers we have, sense-perception, imagining, reasoning, inferring, and so on, may be grouped under the first head of perception or thinking. (The simple–complex division is here, however, used in a loose sense; we can hardly say that the complex ideas in this case are composed of so many simple ideas. And so far as the argument goes, the whole division can be completely disregarded.) Together with thinking and willing Locke also recognizes as present in the mind a capacity to feel pleasure and pain.[4] He thus sets down roughly the three main elements of subsequent psychological investigation, cognition, conation, and emotional feeling-tone. He calls the first two 'faculties', but it must not be supposed that he

[1] II. i. 8.
[2] Cf. II. ix, especially II. ix. 7, also his account of attention in II. x, and of the association of ideas in II. xxxiii.   [3] II. vi. 2.
[4] II. vii, though the capacity, as such, is not examined here. The paragraph is instead a discussion of the usefulness of the capacity. On pleasure and pain cf. Journal for 16 July, 1676 see von Leyden, *Law of Nature*, pp. 263 ff.

advocates a 'faculty theory', or asserts that different faculties exist as distinct entities in the mind. On the contrary, he expressly warns his readers against this view. 'The ordinary way of speaking', he says, 'is that the *understanding* and *will* are two *faculties* of the mind, a word proper enough if it be used, as all words should be, so as not to breed any confusion in men's thoughts by being supposed (as I suspect it has been) to stand for some real beings in the soul, that performed those actions of understanding and volition, . . . so many distinct agents in us which had their provinces and authorities and did command, obey, and perform several actions, as so many distinct beings.'[1] Thus Locke foresaw the misuse of the term *faculty*; and he is in no sense to be held responsible for the unfortunate 'faculty theory'.

Perception. The word *perception* is used, as Locke himself admits, in a very wide and even loose sense when it is identified, as in the above case, with *thinking*. We may continue to use it in this way, Locke holds, but if we do so we need to distinguish within it, for instance, between sense-perception and that perception which occurs in knowledge and which is identical with Descartes's intuition. In II. xxi. 5 Locke gives the term three meanings: 'Perception, which we make the act of understanding, is of three sorts: (1) the perception of *ideas* in our minds [that is, sense-perception and perception of ideas of reflection]. (2) The perception of the signification of signs. (3) The perception of the connexion or repugnancy, agreement or disagreement, that there is between any of our *ideas*.' He proceeds to point out that the last two senses of the word cover what we usually mean by the term *understanding*. It is regrettable, however, that Locke did not proceed further with this analysis. Does he mean, for instance, that there is a common element in sense-perception, in the apprehension of what a sign signifies, and in the perception of an agreement between ideas? This is an important point in itself, especially in connexion with the problem as to the relations between sense-experience and reason.[2] But it is also important in connexion with Locke's empiri-

[1] II. xxi. 6.
[2] Cf. further the fourth essay on the Law of Nature in the (1663-4) Latin essays in the Lovelace Collection (Bodl. MS. Locke, f. 31). Sensation and reason together illuminate the human mind and there is no other illumination.

cism. In II. i he confines the term *experience* to sensation and reflection. Did he sometimes vaguely feel that experience is as wide as perception in this triple sense? Why, after all, should experience be confined to sense-experience and reflection? Locke did, of course, so confine it; and yet one feels sometimes that he was the happier in his empiricism because for him experience was linked with perception, and because he could be vague and ambiguous about the connotation of the latter term, which certainly carried with it a wider meaning than mere sensation.

In the chapter in which he discusses perception,[1] however, Locke practically identifies perception with sense-perception, even with sensation in the narrowest sense, a state in which the mind passively receives what is given it, which he now contrasts with 'thinking'. 'Thinking in the propriety of the *English* tongue signifies that sort of operation of the mind about its *ideas* wherein the mind is active, where it, with some degree of voluntary attention, considers any thing. For in bare, naked *perception*, the mind is, for the most part, only passive, and what it perceives it cannot avoid perceiving.'[2] The characteristic mark of sensation is its involuntariness; the mind is, in that sense, passive. Of course, the mind must receive, it must 'take notice'. Sense-perception like other forms of perception is an act,[3] it does not proceed mechanically. As Locke says: 'Whatever impressions are made on the outward parts, if they are not taken notice of within, there is no perception.'[4] In other words, sense-perception for Locke is not merely a corporeal process, though it has a physical side. It is also mental, and the mind even in sensation is active. If the word 'impression' is used it is important to remember that in respect of mind this term is metaphorical only. The mind is not a piece of wax to take an impression. Something of the sort may be true of the brain. But the mind is an active entity possessing this power of being aware of things, although in sensation it must take what is given it and cannot at all choose, nor in sensation does it change the given in any way.[5]

The general question as to the relation between sensation and

[1] II. ix. [2] II. ix. I.
[3] II. vi. 2, xxi. 5, and elsewhere. [4] II. ix. 3. [5] Cf. II. xxix. 3.

knowledge need not now be considered by us. We may postpone
it until we come to a discussion of IV. ii. 14. But there remains one
further matter in connexion with Locke's account of perception
which should be noted here. A distinction is sometimes made today between sensation and perception. In sensation the mind
receives the given, but in perception it makes this significant to
itself. I *see* a rectangular patch of brown before me, but I *perceive*
a table, having legs (which I cannot now see), being made of wood
of a certain thickness, and so on. Now it is interesting to note that
Locke in this chapter on perception makes a like distinction,
though he does not use precisely the same terminology. He does
not use the term perception here in contra-distinction to sensation, as it is frequently used today. But he does say that the mind
immediately it receives its sensations 'judges' upon them and
thinks of what it judges rather than sees. 'The *ideas we receive
by sensation are often* in grown people *altered by the judgement*
without our taking notice of it.'[1] Locke gives an instance. A globe
of uniform colour is before me. I see 'a flat circle variously
shadowed'. But I immediately say that I see a globe of uniform
colour. 'We having by use been accustomed to perceive what kind
of appearance convex bodies are wont to make in us, what alterations are made in the reflections of light by the difference of the
sensible figures of bodies, the judgement presently, by an habitual
custom, alters the appearances into their causes.'[2] Locke is assuming that the ideas we receive in sensation are caused by things, but
when we do receive these ideas we have learnt to connect them
with the things and so immediately and almost without knowing
to ourselves we 'alter the appearances into the causes'. Locke does
not, however, describe farther how it is we know this thing or
cause. Is it also experienced? He does say that most often, if not
always, this farther judgement takes place in the case of what we
see, and the reason he gives for this is interesting. 'But this is not,
I think, usual in any of our *ideas* but those received by *sight*;
because sight, the most comprehensive of all our senses, conveying
to our minds the *ideas* of light and colours, which are peculiar
only to that sense, and also the far different *ideas* of space, figure,

[1] II. ix. 8.   [2] Ibid.

and motion, the several varieties whereof change the appearances of its proper objects, viz. light and colours; we bring ourselves by use to judge of the one by the other.'[1]

Now Locke has pointed out elsewhere[2] that space, figure, and motion are amongst those ideas given by more than one sense. Actually they are given by touch as well as by sight. Accordingly, Locke's theory here would seem to amount to the following: I learn to interpret the visible in terms of the tangible, and in doing so I am guided, first, by what (in Locke's opinion) is common to the two, namely, shape, size, and motion, and again by my past experience. Having experienced such and such a visible object I have then had such and such a tangible experience. In this latter respect Locke's theory is an approximation to Berkeley's in the *New Theory of Vision*, though Berkeley's is much more carefully conceived, and Berkeley would never admit the first point. He categorically denied the existence of any common sensibles in our sensory experience. None the less, he learnt a good deal from this passage.

It suggested a problem also to another Irishman, William Molyneux, which he forwarded to Locke, who included it in subsequent editions of the *Essay*.[3] A man born blind has learnt to distinguish by touch between a cube and a sphere. Suppose now he gains his sight and is shown the cube and the sphere without being permitted to touch them, would he be able to say which is the sphere and which the cube? Molyneux and Locke answered in the negative. So did Berkeley. We interpret one sensation or group of sensations in terms of the other only as the result of the constant experience gained by us in the past in which the visible and tangible experiences have come together and are attributed by us to the same source. In the case of the blind man such experience would be lacking and so he would not be able to judge what tangible experience would follow the new visible experience.[4]

[1] II. ix. 9.   [2] II. v.   [3] II. ix. 8.

[4] Leibniz (in his comment on this passage in the *Nouveaux Essais*) disagrees, answering with a modified affirmative. 'I think that supposing the blind man knows that these two figures which he sees are those of the cube and the globe, he could distinguish them.' At the very first moment of sight, no doubt, he would be too dazzled to distinguish anything. But if he were told that a globe and a cube lay before him, he could distinguish them. 'The basis of my view is that

This celebrated problem is not easily tested and, until recently, there was little reliable evidence one way or another. A. C. Fraser in his editions of the *Essay* and of Berkeley's *Works* has collected some empirical evidence of a very indefinite sort.[1] But the phenomenon has been studied more carefully recently by physiologists and the evidence is all in favour of Molyneux and Locke.[2] Certainly, the confusion and bewilderment of blind men on first coming to see is sufficiently attested, and this confirms Locke's main point, that in the course of our experience we have learnt to interpret what is seen. Were this lesson not learnt by us vision would not be the useful accomplishment it is.

Memory. The account which the *Essay* gives of memory is hardly satisfactory. This much perhaps may be said in its favour that subsequent accounts have been equally unsuccessful, for the problem of memory remains one of the most baffling in modern psychology. But Locke's treatment is slight and superficial, hardly ever coming to grips with the real difficulties. A criticism put forward by Norris, when the *Essay* first appeared, caused Locke to reconsider the matter and to alter the wording of the text for

in the globe there are no points distinguished by the side of the globe itself, all there being level, and without angles, while in the cube there are eight points distinguished from all the others.' Fundamentally, Leibniz would say, space is the same to a blind person who cannot see and to a paralytic who cannot touch, and geometry is the same, for though the images are different, the geometrical principles (apprehended by reason, according to Leibniz) are the same. Locke might agree with Leibniz on this latter point, but would urge that this does not justify the affirmative answer Leibniz gives. Berkeley, of course, would disagree, although when he says in the *New Theory of Vision* that the visible square is better fitted to be a sign of the tangible square than is the visible circle, he is perhaps admitting Leibniz's point.

[1] Mr. Michael Foster has referred me also to Voltaire's *Éléments de la philosophie de Newton*, iii. vi, where Voltaire reports an actual case in which a man born blind on coming to see failed to distinguish by sight between the round and the angular.

[2] Professor J. Z. Young sums up the evidence in his Reith Lectures, *Doubt and Certainty in Science*, Oxford, 1951, pp. 61 ff. 'One man when shown an orange a week after beginning to see said that it was gold. When asked "What shape is it?" he said "Let me touch it and I will tell you". After doing so he said that it was an orange. Then he looked at it and said, "Yes, I can see that it is round." Shown next a blue square, he said it was blue and round. A triangle he also described as round. When the angles were pointed out to him, he said, "Ah, yes, I understand now, one can *see* how they feel." For many weeks and months after beginning to see, the person can only with great difficulty distinguish between the simplest shapes, such as a triangle and a square.' p. 62. Cf. further 'But Now I See' by Richard Gregory, *The Listener*, 24 May 1962, pp. 908 ff.

subsequent editions, but his new position, it will be found, begs the question as completely as did the old.

Memory for Locke is one of the two forms of retention. The first is contemplation, whereby the mind retains the idea by 'keeping it for some time actually in view'. Memory is the second, which he defines as 'the power to revive again in our minds those *ideas* which after imprinting have disappeared, or have been as it were laid aside out of sight'.[1] To remember is, as he explains elsewhere, to perceive something 'with a consciousness that it was known or perceived before'.[2] Memory may be of two kinds: it may be a voluntary recalling, involving the mind in a conscious effort, as when we search for a forgotten word and find it, or it may be involuntary, the memories arising spontaneously. 'Sometimes, too, they start up in our minds of their own accord and offer themselves to the understanding; and very often are roused and tumbled out of their dark cells into open daylight by some turbulent and tempestuous passion.'[3]

But the acutest problem in connexion with memorizing, whether it be voluntary or involuntary, arises when the question is asked: How do we retain what is retained in memory? Or, in Locke's language, where is the idea when I have once experienced it, then forgotten it, but will in a few minutes recall it? At first Locke was content with the usual answer, that it was 'in the memory', and the memory he then described as 'the storehouse of our *ideas* . . . a repository to lay up those *ideas*, which at another time it [the mind] might have use of'.[4] But John Norris[5] neatly criticized Locke. If there are ideas in the mind of which we are at present unaware, 'latent ideas', as Locke calls them in Draft B, why should there not also be innate ideas in the mind of which we are not at first aware? What of Locke's earlier principle that there are no ideas in the mind 'which it perceives not'? Locke saw the point of the criticism, and in the second edition the following words were added: 'But our *ideas* being nothing but actual

---

[1] II. x. 2.
[2] I. iv. 20; cf. Hobbes, *Human Nature*, iii. 6: 'we take notice that it is again.'
[3] II. x. 7.
[4] II. x. 2.
[5] *Reflections upon an Essay concerning Human Understanding*, § 4.

perceptions in the mind, which cease to be any thing when there is no perception of them, this laying up of our *ideas* in the repository of the memory signifies no more but this—that the mind has a power, in many cases, to revive perceptions which it once had, with this additional perception annexed to them—that it has had them before. And in this sense it is that our *ideas* are said to be in our memories, when indeed they are actually nowhere, but only there is an ability in the mind when it will to revive them again, and, as it were, paint them anew on itself, though some with more, some with less, difficulty; some more lively, and others more obscurely.' The meaning of this passage is not wholly clear. Has he now given up the 'repository' theory so completely that he regards each instance of memory as a new fresh perceptual intuition, like the original perception in every respect, except that we remember that we have had this perception before? Such a theory might possibly do away with the difficulty as to the whereabouts of ideas we later recall when we are not actually recalling them. But a greater difficulty would then remain, that of distinguishing between perceiving and remembering. The distinction Locke makes between the two is based on the fact that we remember that we have had this experience before. But this ground is insufficient for the distinction, since we frequently perceive something we have perceived before, and remember to have perceived before, and yet this particular perception is not itself an instance of memory. Memory, if it is perception, is a peculiar kind which carries with it not merely the feeling that we have seen this before, but also that we are not now perceiving in the ordinary sense but remembering. As Locke himself says in this passage, it is a 'reviving' of the perception, and it is this reviving which needs to be explained. Locke leaves it unexplained, and as long as he does so his analysis of memory is inadequate.

In various passages Locke also discusses the relations between memory and certain other operations of the mind.

In the journal for 1678 an interesting note is to be found on memory and imagination. 'Memory is always the picture of something, the idea whereof has existed before in our thoughts, as near the life as we can draw it: but imagination is a picture drawn in our minds without reference to a pattern.'[1] What is interesting about the passage is the connexion which Locke proceeds to show between imagination and madness. Madness consists not in the lack of powers of reasoning, for madmen reason very well, but in a failure to distinguish between imagining and remembering. The madman thinks that he is remembering when he is only imagining. If he could be brought to see that his imaginations are imaginations only and not remembered realities he would be healed. 'Madness seems to be nothing but a disorder in the imagination, and not in the discursive faculty.'[2] With respect to the relations between memory and attention Locke tells us that ideas to which no attention is paid 'quickly fade and often vanish quite out of the understanding, leaving no more footsteps or remaining characters of themselves, than shadows do flying over fields of corn'.[3] No doubt, Locke adds, physical and physiological occurrences help or hinder memory, 'since we oftentimes find a disease quite strip the mind of all its *ideas*'.[4] Indeed, in the *Education*[5] he goes so far as to say: 'Strength of memory is owing to a happy constitution and not to any habitual improvement got by exercise.' None the less in the *Essay* he holds that our memories can be improved by attention, on the one hand, and by repetition, on the other. In the same manner, if our ideas are accompanied by pleasure or pain the attention we pay to them is greater and so we remember them the more easily. Finally, without memory knowledge would be impossible, for we should be confined to present objects.[6] A retentive memory means a mind well stocked with information; and a quick memory, which enables us speedily to recall what we need, makes for intelligence. God has no need of memory, for he sees all things instantaneously; but for man memory is a valuable gift without which his world would be narrow and limited beyond all present imagining.

Of the other operations of the mind Locke's analysis is still more meagre than it is in the case of perception and memory. Of *discerning* or distinguishing between ideas he remarks that, like memory, it is indispensable for knowledge. For were we not able

---

[1] Aaron and Gibb, p. 103.   [2] King, ii. 173, and cf. *Essay*, ii. xi. 13.
[3] ii. x. 4.   [4] ii. x. 5.   [5] § 176.   [6] ii. x. 8.

to distinguish between our ideas we could never perceive any agreements or disagreements between them. If pressed Locke must also have admitted that discerning is itself an instance of knowing, even in his limited sense of that term. If the reader compares the account given of intuition in IV. ii. I with that of discerning in II. xi. I, he will see that discerning is one instance of intuition. To perceive that white is not black, a circle not a triangle, is discerning in Book II and intuiting in Book IV. Even in Book II Locke describes discerning as perceiving that two ideas are the same or different and finds in it an instance of that knowledge of a truth which men have wrongly called innate.[1] The importance of discerning lies in the fact that it is a power which leads to exactness of judgement and clearness of reason. This enables Locke to make an interesting distinction between judgement and wit. 'For *wit* lying most in the assemblage of *ideas*, and putting those together with quickness and variety wherein can be found any resemblance or congruity, thereby to make up pleasant pictures and agreeable visions in the fancy; *judgement*, on the contrary, lies quite on the other side, in separating carefully one from another *ideas* wherein can be found the least difference, thereby to avoid being misled by similitude and by affinity to take one thing for another.'[2] Wit is something superficial, the quick perception of a congruity; judgement and estimation of truth by reason depend more upon discerning.

With discerning goes *comparing*. Upon it depends 'all that large tribe of *ideas* comprehended under *relations*'.[3] One would have thought that this was so important an operation that it demanded very close attention. Locke, however, merely mentions it here and adds that beasts compare but little. The fact is that the term *comparing* covers so vast a field that it could not possibly have been completely analysed in this chapter. Every act of knowing, and every judgement, as Locke interprets them, involve comparison. In the same way, *compounding* also, the putting together of several simple ideas, is merely mentioned, and Locke passes at

[1] II. xi. I.
[2] II. xi. 2. Laird (*Hobbes*, p. 267) points out that the same distinction is to be found in Hobbes. But cf. Thorpe, *Aesthetic Theory of Hobbes*, p. 97, n. 55.
[3] II. xi. 4.

once to instance one special kind of compounding, namely *enlarging*, where the same idea is repeated, the instance Locke gives being that of a dozen, where the unit is repeated a dozen times.[1]

There are other psychological chapters in Book II,[2] but they need not detain us at this point. For the first (II. xix) is little more than a catalogue of those operations which are cognitive, or, in Locke's language, modifications of thinking in its widest sense.[3] Locke realizes that even as a catalogue this is incomplete, as is, he admits, his whole account of the ideas of reflection. 'I do not pretend to enumerate them all nor to treat at large of this set of *ideas* which are got from *reflection*: that would be to make a volume.'[4] Again the material covered in the second and third of these chapters, dealing with the modes of pleasure and pain and with power, can best be dealt with in the section on Locke's moral philosophy.

A word should be added here, however, about Locke's theory of the association of ideas. The chapter dealing with this theory[5] only appeared in the fourth edition of the *Essay*, and this of itself suggests that it is not central to Locke's thinking. In Hume's philosophy a theory of association of ideas is central, for he explains the normal process of reasoning about all matters of fact in terms of this theory. Locke, on the other hand, only uses it to account for aberrations from the normal. It is 'a sort of madness'. In Book IV he assumes that we have knowledge (although it may be only probable) of the real connexions in things. But opposed to the 'natural connexions' of ideas thus gained Locke in this chapter admits certain other connexions of ideas 'wholly owing to chance or custom'.[6] These connexions are simply 'habits of thinking in the understanding'. For instance, hearing the first line of a poem we know, we tend to think of the remaining lines. Many connexions of this second sort are erroneous and misleading. 'This wrong connexion in our minds of *ideas*, in themselves loose and independent one of another, has such an influence and is of

---

[1] The two remaining operations considered in II. xi are *naming* and *abstracting*. I postpone discussion of these to Chapter VI below.

[2] II. xix, xx, and xxi.

[3] It is interesting to note how the differences between many of these can in Locke's opinion be interpreted in terms of degrees of attention. Cf. II. xix. 3–4. On attention cf. also II. xiv. 9–15.

[4] II. xix. 2.   [5] II. xxxiii.   [6] II. xxxiii. 5.

so great force to set us awry in our actions, as well moral as natural, passions, reasonings, and notions themselves, that perhaps there is not any one thing that deserves more to be looked after.'[1] Locke gives many instances: children dislike the dark because their nurses have told them stories of goblins and sprites that infest it; they dislike a book because they were once forced under threat of punishment to read it. A man will avoid a building or a town where something unpleasant to him once occurred. There are foolish beliefs and prejudices upon which frequently parties and sects are established, the beliefs being solely the outcome of this unfortunate association of ideas in our minds. Locke adopts the role of the practical psychologist and warns his readers against the errors that might arise from this source.[2]

II

Having considered Locke's account of the operations of the mind we now turn to consider his account of the mind itself, although in doing so we may be said to be leaving psychology in the narrow sense for metaphysics. Following traditional ways of thinking Locke regards the mind as a substance, but a substance which is immaterial. He accepts the usual dualism, the 'two parts of nature',[3] active immaterial substance and passive material substance. At the same time, he is, as we shall see later, most uneasy in his mind about the conception of substance itself, both material and immaterial. He finds it difficult to justify his use of the concept, and yet he cannot proceed without it. He feels himself to be on surer ground in making a distinction between the two sorts of substances. It is a fundamental point with him that the universe cannot be explained in terms either of matter alone or of mind alone. The one cannot be reduced to the other. Of the two, perhaps, mind is the more indispensable, for mind is the active, productive principle. Matter produces nothing. In

[1] II. xxxiii. 9.
[2] Locke thought his discussion here to be original: cf. Molyneux Correspondence, especially *Works*, iii. 554. On the history of this theory, cf. an interesting account in Laird's *Hume's Philosophy of Human Nature*, pp. 38–41.
[3] II. xxiii. 15.

particular, to think of it as producing thought, Locke agrees with Cudworth, is to think an absurdity.[1]

Locke's views were, thus far, the traditional ones, accepted by the Church and upheld by Cartesianism. He came into conflict with the latter, however, on the question of the mind's essence. Descartes had held that mind was essentially thinking, and Locke denied this on the ground that if thinking were the essence of mind it would be a permanent characteristic of it, and there would be no break in thought. But no proof can be offered that the soul is always thinking. Indeed, the evidence points the other way. Thinking is certainly one of the operations of mind, but hardly its essence.[2] It may be a fact that we do not cease to think in our sleep, and that we think the long night through, but forget our thoughts when we wake. Yet this, Locke thinks, is 'very hard to be conceived'.[3] The further doctrine that in sleep the mind, no longer affected by the senses, withdraws itself from the world of sensible things and gives itself over to contemplation upon pure, intelligible objects, Locke found somewhat absurd. When we wake up we remember no such contemplation. Moreover, if this thinking proceeds in sleep then the waking self is only one of two selves, and each man has a dual personality. This, Locke admits, may be the case; but on the whole it seems more sensible to suppose that in sound sleep thinking has ceased entirely. Dreaming is a state of thought which is vague and loose, when the mind does not concentrate on its thinking. But when a man sleeps soundly, moving neither hand nor foot, it is difficult to believe that his mind continues to think its thoughts. And it is a curious doctrine, he adds, referring to the Cartesians, that men fast asleep are still actively thinking, whilst animals in their waking moments and behaving in all respects as if they were thinking are said to be incapable of thought.[4]

---

[1] Cf. IV. x. 9–10. That he is here following Cudworth is clear from the journal of 1682. Cf. Aaron and Gibb, p. 118.

[2] II. i. 10.   [3] II. i. 14.

[4] II. i. 19. This latter is a shrewd scoring point. But it is to be doubted whether Locke had considered all the psychological evidence in favour of the view that the mind continues to be active in sleep. First, as Fraser points out, somnambulism shows mental (and bodily) activity in sleep not remembered by the sufferer on waking. Secondly, is Locke correct in supposing that we are ever wholly

His disagreement with the Cartesians on this point, however, does not seem to have disturbed his contemporaries. On the other hand, the strange and apparently heretical doctrine, that matter in some cases may itself have power of thought superadded to it, which he casually threw out at the beginning of Book IV, shocked the orthodox, once its implications were realized. Stillingfleet reserved his severest criticism for it. He regarded it as a serious blow against established belief, and ranked it amongst materialist doctrines of the human mind. His criticism, it must be admitted, was not wholly unjustified. Even in Book II Locke had talked of the human mind as if it were a thing in space. It is where the body is, and like it in that it moves. 'Finding that spirits as well as bodies cannot operate but where they are, and that spirits do operate at several times in several places, I cannot but attribute change of place to all finite spirits.'[1] Locke's thought here is evidently influenced by his consciousness of the close bond which exists between mind and body in the case of human beings. Even though the human mind be wholly other than the human body it is where that body is and moves with it.

It is consciousness of the same fact, doubtless, which prompted him to put forward the suggestion of iv. iii. 6. In that chapter Locke is considering the extent of human knowledge, and, after pointing out that our knowledge cannot possible extend further than our ideas, he adds that it does not extend even so far. For we may and do have ideas between which we can perceive no relations and so though we have ideas we have no knowledge. He takes as an example of this our inability to relate the ideas of *matter* and *thinking*. For we cannot determine whether matter has anywhere been given the power of thought; 'it being, in respect of our notions, not much more remote from our comprehension to conceive that God can, if he pleases, superadd to matter a faculty of thinking, than that he should superadd to it another substance with a faculty of thinking'. Matter and thinking are two ideas,

uninfluenced by the senses in sleep, even the deepest sleep? Lastly, it is a fact that we forget many dreams. Sometimes, a chance meeting recalls a dream which we should not have otherwise recalled. Locke did not examine all the evidence against him.

[1] II. xxiii. 19.

but in their case no relating with absolute certainty is possible, either positively or negatively. For while Locke's usual belief is that matter cannot think, he also sees the possibility that Omnipotency may have superadded the power of thought to matter.

Now although Locke introduces the doctrine in this casual way it is clear that it is no haphazard statement. It is the fruit of careful thought, and when his suggestion is later attacked he does not at all withdraw it but seeks to defend it.[1] It is possible, he contends, that thinking in human beings is superadded by an omnipotent cogitative Being to what is otherwise material. Locke himself continues to believe that the probability is that we are both material and immaterial substance. But this cannot be demonstrated from the evidence at our disposal. There is indeed evidence in support of the opposite view that substantially we are material but with power of thinking superadded. In his replies to Stillingfleet Locke adduces the materialistic accounts that accredited authors, such as Virgil and Cicero, give of the human spirit. It is air or fire or breath, and we find terminology of the same sort even in the Scriptures. So that to regard the mind of man as substantially material is no new doctrine. (Locke's appeal here seems a little unfair. Such writers hardly used those terms to defend the materiality of mind. All their terminology was material and they obviously chose the least solidly material, air and fire and the like, to describe mind.) Secondly, he argues that to deny this possibility, that material beings might be made to think, would be to deny the omnipotency of God. If we assume that the essential qualities of matter are extension and solidity, then, surely, no one would deny that God can and does add other qualities to it. Not even Descartes denied that God could add life and power of organization to matter in the case of vegetables, and sense and spontaneous motion to matter in animals. How then is it so impossible that God should have

[1] In later editions he modifies his earlier statements. These modifications are partly the consequence of the correspondence with Molyneux (cf. *Works*, iii. 523 and 526) and are designed to safeguard himself against the charge that on his supposition God himself might be a thinking material. But this is never Locke's position. Matter itself cannot originate thinking. The ultimate explanation of thought must itself be cogitative. None the less an omnipotent cogitative Being might very well have superadded power of thinking to material existence, and this might be the explanation of the human being.

added the power of thinking to matter in the case of man?[1] Of course, we cannot understand how matter could possibly think. But we also do not understand how immaterial substance thinks. On any view thinking and knowing are mysteries. Why should not God have added to matter this mysterious power of thinking and knowing? If life can be superadded to matter why not thought? It must be at least possible, Locke concluded, and our substance may be entirely material.

Stillingfleet was justified in seizing upon this crucial point. He argued that Locke had here broken with tradition and that his position was dangerous both to religion and morality. In reply Locke submitted that the break was with Descartes only. 'For, as far as I have seen, or heard, the fathers of the Christian Church never pretended to demonstrate that matter was incapable to receive a power of sensation, perception, and thinking from the hand of the omnipotent Creator.'[2] So far Locke is correct. No one doubted the omnipotency of God. At the same time, he is avoiding the real point at issue. The Church had taught that man is as essentially immaterial as he is material. Scholastic philosophy had worked out a system for which the human being was both matter and spirit. At death the body decomposed, but the soul being substantially different from it did not suffer decomposition.[3] Indeed, the soul could not suffer decomposition; its immortality could be deduced rationally from its nature. But if Locke's new position were accepted this could no longer be possible, as Locke admits. Until we prove that man is immaterial as well as material substance, we cannot *prove* that he is immortal. And since God is omnipotent it may be the case that we are not both material and immaterial. Not that, Locke thinks, belief in the immortality of the soul is at all shaken by this possibility, for that is already sufficiently established by revelation and does not need the support of reason. As God is able to cause material being to think so he can give immortality to that being, if he so chooses. None the less, the

---

[1] Cf. Second Reply to Stillingfleet, *Works*, i. 589, and with respect to the whole matter cf. First Reply, i. 374 ff., and Second, i. 587 ff.

[2] *Works*, i. 593 (1801 ed., iv. 469).

[3] Cf. Thomas Aquinas's discussion of the soul in Book II of *Contra Gentiles*, especially chapters 63 and 65.

criticism is fair as against Locke that, by merely suggesting the possibility that substantially we are wholly material, he had thereby denied the doctrine that the human soul is necessarily immaterial, and so had aimed a blow at Christian doctrine, if not at Christian faith.

There is another reason why Locke's new suggestion was opposed and feared. It savoured of the materialism of Hobbes. Though Locke would never admit that his thoughts were influenced by Hobbes, his position here certainly approaches the latter's. For Hobbes had taught that thinking as such is an abstraction, and so also is mind. The concrete is the 'thinking-body'.[1] Upon this basis he built what was in effect a materialist philosophy. Now Locke admitted the possibility of a 'thinking-body', but he could not accept the materialism, for he believed that 'thinking-body' does not explain itself nor is it explained by body. In other words, mere matter can never be the source of thought even though material beings think. He would admit the possibility that *we* are substantially material, but he could not deny the necessary existence of some pure cogitative Being to explain the presence of thought even in beings substantially material. Thus Locke was divided between two tendencies. He found it difficult to think of man consistently as composed of two distinct substances, material and immaterial. This violated for him the unity of human personality. And yet a mere materialism was equally impossible. For want of a better solution he accepted the traditional and Cartesian dualism. It was better than the one monism with which he was acquainted, namely, materialism. But IV. iii. 6 and the relevant passages in the Stillingfleet controversy mark his dissatisfaction with that dualist solution and his tentative, although perhaps not very convincing, effort at another.

Thus we are not in a position to say outright that man is a complex of material and immaterial substances. The problem of the mind–body relation is one which, in Locke's opinion, is at present beyond our powers, since the inner nature of mind itself as well as of body is so completely hidden from us. But though we cannot understand the ultimate nature of our own constitution as human

[1] *Elements of Philosophy*, I. iii. 4.

beings we continue to regard ourselves as so many *selves*,[1] and the problem which remains to be considered is how we come by this idea of a self. Locke's examination of this matter, in a chapter added in the second edition, contains some of the closest thinking in the *Essay*. The problem is neglected in the first edition. There, as we have seen, it is not wholly clear how much reflection or introspection reveals. It does reveal the operations of the mind, but does it reveal the mind itself? Book IV asserts that we have an intuitive knowledge of our own existence,[2] but this seems to be a knowledge that we exist merely, without knowing what we are. ''Tis past controversy that we have in us something that thinks; our very doubts about what it is confirm the certainty of its being, though we must content ourselves in the ignorance of what kind of *being* it is.'[3] And yet we constantly talk of our self. The word has obviously some meaning for us. Locke realized that he had not attended to the problem properly in the first edition and so adds a chapter in the second. He identifies *self* with *person*; to myself I am a self, to another a person. And the problem becomes one as to the meaning of personal identity, and is linked to the general problem of identity. The self is an identity, but what sort of an identity?

Now Locke distinguishes between four sorts of identities: (1) logical identity, *a* is *a*, (2) the identity of an object continuing through time, (3) the identity of an organization, (4) personal identity. In the first edition when he used the word *identity* he usually meant logical identity, as when he says that we know of every idea that it is identical with itself. He opens the present chapter on identity by reminding us of this first type of identity. 'When we see anything . . . we are sure (be it what it will) that it is that very thing and not another.'[4] He immediately passes to consider another sort of identity, that of identity in time. Identity here consists in the fact that apart from change in time there is no other change. The complex idea I have now of this table is

---

[1] The language is Locke's. Cf. i. xxvii. 9, 'every one is to himself that which he calls "self"', and the following sentences.   [2] iv. ix.

[3] iv. iii. 6. Later, in his *Examination of Malebranche*, § 46, he categorically asserts that reflection does not give us knowledge of the mind itself but only of its operations.   [4] ii. xxvii. 1.

the same in every respect as the idea of it that I had yesterday and so I say it is the identical idea. Or, as Locke puts it: 'In this consists *identity*, when the *ideas* it is attributed to vary not at all from what they were at that moment wherein we consider their former existence, and to which we compare the present.'[1] That which is thus identical in time has, of course, but one beginning, and from its beginning to the present moment it has been and is identical with itself.

This concept of identity through time Locke now proceeds to analyse further in an interesting way. A thing may be identical in this sense of being substantially and materially the same in spite of the passage of time. A heap of stones can be identical through time in this sense. If I add a stone or take one away it is not the same heap. Or if again I remove many or all of the stones and replace them by an equal number of exactly similar stones in an exactly similar arrangement it is yet not the same heap. But another kind of identity in time is possible. For some objects remain the same, and are thought of by us as identical, in spite of the fact that in the sense in which the heap of stones remains the same they do not remain the same. These are identical in a third sense, that is, in so far as a certain organization of parts is maintained, and in their case 'the variation of great parcels of matter alters not the identity'.[2] This is frequently true of certain inanimate bodies, for instance, machines. But a better instance is an organic body. Locke thus describes the identity of a plant: 'That being then one plant which has such an organization of parts in one coherent body, partaking of one common life, it continues to be the same plant as long as it partakes of the same life, though that life be communicated to new particles of matter vitally united to the living plant in a like continued organization conformable to that sort of plants.'[3] The point which Locke makes here is a very sound one and a very important one. The identity of the heap is not the only identity that can be conceived. There is a fundamental difference between a chance 'cohesion' of parts and an organization of parts. In its anxiety to reduce all things to simples Locke's generation frequently missed this difference, but

---

[1] II. xxvii. 1.   [2] II. xxvii. 3.   [3] II. xxvii. 4.

Locke asserts it explicitly, and his assertion is one more instance of his ability to pass beyond the conceptions of his day and to free himself from them. Identity of organization is as real as identity of a heap.

Now when we turn from plants and animals to ourselves we too are identities, first in the sense that we also are organisms. The human body is an organism. And when we talk of a man's identity we most often mean the identity of his body. If the soul of a man were ever to pass into a hog, we should not think the hog then a man. Again, a man who becomes another person (in the case of dual personality) would usually be held by us to be the identical man, simply because it is the same body.

There is, however, still another kind of identity of which we are aware. It is that peculiar sort which is linked with self-consciousness. 'When we see, hear, smell, taste, feel, meditate, or will anything, we know that we do so.'[1] And this means, in this context, not merely that we are aware of the passing perceptions, but of an abiding, identical I. Perceptions come and go, 'each perishing the moment it begins',[2] and in discussing personal identity we cannot be discussing the series of psychical events, the congeries of perceptions. Over and above these we are aware of an I continuing through time, an I which now enjoys such and such experiences and yesterday had others. And the identity of this I is not identical with the identity of an organism. For we are not sure that it may not cease to be for a time, for example, in sleep. Yet even if I as a person temporarily ceased to exist last night I know that I am now the same person that I was yesterday. The identity depends entirely on this consciousness I have of myself. Each person is conscious of himself at present and remembers himself in the past and he is conscious that he is now the same person as he was then.

Now our difficulties in connexion with this fourth type of identity all arise from the fact that we wish to reduce it to one or another of the other three types although, since it is an identity of a different sort, the attempt is doomed to failure from the start. We are living bodies, and as such we possess the kind of identity that an organism possesses. But our identity as persons is wholly

---

[1] II. xxvii. 9.　　　[2] II. xxvii. 2.

different, since it is not disturbed by breaks in the conscious life of the person. We are also substance—Locke, as we have seen, is not sure that we can say outright both material and immaterial substances. If we are merely material substances with the power of thinking superadded, then, obviously, the identity of person is not that of the corporeal substance. Supposing, however, that mind is immaterial substance, what would be the relation between the self or the person and this immaterial substance, and would the identity of the one be that of the other? Locke puts the problem in the following terms: 'Whether, if the same substance which thinks be changed, it can be the same person, or remaining the same it can be different persons?'[1] He answers both parts of this question in the affirmative. The substance may be changed and yet the person remain the same. If there are two immaterial substances A and B, and if A had an experience yesterday and B recalls this very same experience today as his own, then A and B would be two substances, but one and the same person. It *may* be the case that I am not now the same immaterial substance I was ten years ago, but I am certainly the same person because I can remember myself ten years ago. Of course, it is exceedingly probable if I am an immaterial substance at all that I am the same immaterial substance now that I was ten years ago. But we must at the same time admit the possibility 'that two thinking substances may make but one person'.[2] Similarly, the substance may remain the same and yet there may be two persons. If a man claimed to be the same immaterial substance as Socrates was, but could not recall Socrates's experiences as his own, then supposing his claim true, Socrates and he would share one substance but be two persons. And this again is possible, so far as our knowledge goes, though we usually regard it as impossible.

The conclusion to be drawn from this is that when I think of my own existence I may think of it in three ways, each way of existing being fundamentally different from the other so far as I know. I exist as a living body, I exist as a person, I may also exist as an immaterial substance. We cannot be sure that the identical person inhabits the identical body, or again that the identical

[1] II. xxvii. 12.   [2] II. xxvii. 13.

person is allied to the identical immaterial substance. Each of these three has its own identity. And though it is easier to think of one man as being one body, one immaterial substance, and one person knit together into a man, we cannot at all prove this to be the case. So far as personal identity goes the only test is consciousness. I am aware now that it was I who yesterday acted thus and thus and I realize that those actions were *mine*. It is this consciousness, in Locke's opinion, which provides us with our concept of an identical person. Without it there could be for him no morality and no responsibility. Person is 'a forensic term appropriating actions and their merit; and so belongs only to intelligent agents capable of a law and happiness and misery'.[1]

By way of criticism it is hardly necessary to point out that this analysis is not satisfactory. To begin with, we find here no adequate analysis of the concept of identity. Locke merely shows that the term is vague and carries with it more than one meaning. But the term remains vague even after II. xxvii. Again, no one would say that Locke has made clear the nature of the term 'person'. He claims to have shown how we come by the notion of personal identity, namely, by our consciousness of being a person now having these present experiences and being the same person to whom such-and-such happened yesterday. This claim itself can be questioned. The very fact that we say 'He has now forgotten that he did so-and-so, yet he *was* the person who did it,' or again 'He thinks that it was he who did so-and-so, but in fact it was another person' points to the conclusion that we have other criteria for determining personal identity than the one Locke mentions. Even if his theory were acceptable, however, it would still not tell us what a person is, what it is which now exists and abides through time. If it be said that a person merely *is* the consciousness of present and past experiences this is an interesting theory, but I do not think that it is Locke's either in this chapter or elsewhere. It is not possible to say what Locke thinks a person to be. He offers us a criterion for testing whether *A* is one and the same person yesterday and today, yet he does not at all enlighten us on what it is to be a person. Accordingly, the chapter is inadequate both as

[1] II. xxvii. 26.

an analysis of identity, and as an analysis of the self. Its worth and importance however lie, first, in a recognition of kinds of identity, and, secondly, in its emphasis upon the fact that there is this consciousness of an abiding self in our experience. I am not merely a series of perceptions, for I am conscious of a permanent self, an I who experiences these perceptions and who is now identical with the I who experienced perceptions yesterday.[1]

[1] On Locke's theory of personal identity cf. further H. P. Grice 'Personal Identity', *Mind* (200), October 1941, and Antony Flew 'Locke and the Problem of Personal Identity', *Philosophy* (96), January 1951.

V

MODES, SUBSTANCES, AND RELATIONS

WE have seen that Locke's division of ideas into simple and complex was not entirely successful, but it provided him with a basis for classification. In this chapter I propose to study the three sorts of complex ideas which he recognized. These are modes, substances, and relations. '*Modes* I call such complex *ideas* which, however compounded, contain not in them the supposition of subsisting by themselves, but are considered as dependences on or affections of substances.'[1] Locke gives three examples, gratitude, triangle, and murder. Secondly, 'the *ideas* of *substances* are such combinations of simple *ideas* as are taken to represent distinct particular things subsisting by themselves, in which the supposed or confused *idea* of substance, such as it is, is always the first and chief'.[2] Examples are the ideas of lead or of man. Lastly, cause and effect, or again identity, are instances of ideas of relations, though from the first Locke is a little vague about our ideas of relation. They 'consist in the consideration and comparing one *idea* with another'.[3] But comparing is hardly compounding, and in the fourth edition, as we have seen, he dropped even the pretence that these were complex ideas.

I

We may begin with modes. We should first note that the conception of mode itself is not wholly clear. It is not wholly clear, for instance, how mode is related to attribute. But as one reads the chapters on modes one gains the impression that Locke is less concerned with the clarification of this concept than with the verification of the empiricism set out in the opening chapters of Book II. Thus if he can more easily prove that an idea is ultimately

---

[1] II. xii. 4.   [2] II. xii. 6.   [3] II. xii. 7.

derived from sensation or reflection by grouping it with modes he will do so, even though it would be more natural to group it with relations.

And herein, doubtless, lies the explanation of the somewhat artificial classification of the ideas of space, time, number, and infinity in the *Essay*. In the two early Drafts he usually discusses these under relations, on the whole the more satisfactory classification. Why then in the *Essay* does their consideration form part of a theory of modes? The Drafts reveal the answer, and explain at the same time Locke's curious division of modes into simple and mixed. Draft A consists of an exposition of empiricism together with a defence against possible objections. One of these is that we have an idea of infinity which is neither given in sensation nor derived from it. In answer Locke seeks to show that even the idea of infinity is really a complex idea, made up of simples originally given in sensation or reflection. In order to prove this he argues, first, that our only clear conception of infinity is quantitative infinity, that is, infinite number. Secondly, any finite number may be regarded as a complex idea, gained by 'enlarging' a unit given in sensation, that is, repeating the same simple idea over and over again. For instance, a dozen is gained by repeating the unit twelve times; it is a complex idea formed of twelve simples. Locke terms this the simple mode[1] to distinguish it from those modes which are compounded of simple ideas of different kinds and are called mixed. But infinity is also a quantity though not a fixed one. It can also, in Locke's opinion, be regarded as a complex idea gained by enlarging, only the process of enlarging in this case is endless. Thus finite numbers and infinity itself are simple modes, and when so regarded it is easy to show their ultimate dependence upon the sensed unit. Moreover, in addition to number, space and time may be analysed in terms of simple modes. Any definite length is so many units of length set together; any period of time is so many seconds or minutes or hours. Even infinite space is a mode of space, and infinite time a mode of time. Consequently, when Locke writes his *Essay* he no longer talks of ideas of space, time, number, and infinity as relations but as

[1] Not to be confused with the simple *idea*, for the simple mode is a complex idea.

modes. His purpose in doing so is plain. In classing them as simple modes he can more easily and more effectively maintain and confirm the empiricism of Book II.

Space. One of the most striking facts about the chapters on space in the *Essay* is the absence of any definite statement in them as to the nature of space itself. From the *Essay* alone it is not possible to understand Locke's real position in connexion with this important matter, and it is difficult enough even when his other writings are taken into account. It is frequently said that Locke's theory of space is Newtonian, and no doubt one or two of his remarks might be held to imply a Newtonian view of space—though even here the influence of Gassendi, whose theory of space differs in certain details from that of Newton, is the more marked. But implicit in the *Essay* also is a profound criticism of Newton's view, whilst Locke's remarks outside the *Essay* are almost the direct opposite of the Newtonian theory.

For Newton space is an absolute continuum stretching infinitely in all directions. It is a positive entity within which things exist and move, but it itself does not move nor does it alter its nature in any manner. 'Absolute space', says Newton in his *Principia*, 'by its very nature without reference to anything external always remains similar and immobile.' For Locke in the journals space is either merely relative or it is 'a possibility for extended beings or bodies to be, or exist'. The former view is set forward in the brief entry of 27 February 1676.[1] He discusses 'imaginary space', that is, 'space separated in our thoughts from matter or body' and holds that it is nothing 'real or positive'. Real space is space filled by a body and exists only relatively to that body, or it is the space between two bodies and again exists relative to them. In the notes on space written in the journals of 1677 and 1678 he repeats this position. Any particular space is still a bare relation. But he does now admit the possibility of our conceiving space where there is no body. However, we do not then conceive absolute, positive, infinite space. All he means, he explains, is that we can always 'imagine a bare possibility that body may exist where now there is none'. 'Space, in itself, seems to be nothing but a capacity or

[1] See further the note in the Journal for 9 July, 1676 in *Law of Nature* (von Leyden), pp. 258-9.

possibility for extended beings or bodies to be or exist.'[1] Or, as the
1678 journal puts it: If we think of particular bodies, space is
'nothing but the relation of the distance of the extremities. But
when we speak of space in general, abstract and separate from all
consideration of any body at all or any other being, it seems not
then to be any real thing but the consideration of a bare possibility
of body to exist.'[2] This latter modification might very well be the
outcome of Locke's converse with the Gassendists, for, as Bernier
explains it, one of the main points of Gassendi's theory is that
space is no substance and no mode, but 'a capacity to receive entities'. Locke's account in the journals seems to be working towards
some such position though it never quite reaches it.

The publication of Newton's *Principia* in 1687, however, seems
to have left Locke in a quandary. He was as convinced as ever that
we have no positive idea of absolute space, and yet his reading of
Newton made him conscious of the difficulties in a merely rela-
tivist position. The crucial passage in the *Essay* is II. xiii. 27, where
for a moment he faces the issue squarely. Here he puts forward no
solution of his own. On the contrary, he is obviously anxious not
to commit himself. But the most significant fact in connexion
with this passage is that Newton's theory of space is not considered
in it even as one possible alternative. Apparently Locke is so convinced that it is wrong as it stands that he cannot regard it as
worthy of consideration.

The passage runs: 'But whether any one will take space to be
only a relation resulting from the existence of other beings at a
distance or whether they will think the words of the most knowing King Solomon, "The heaven and heaven of heavens cannot
contain thee", or those more emphatical ones of the inspired
philosopher, St. Paul, "In him, we live, move, and have our being"
are to be understood in a literal sense, I leave every one to consider.' In stating the alternatives in this passage there is no reference to Newton's theory—so little is the *Essay* Newtonian in its
conception of space! Locke recognizes two alternatives only. The
first is relativism in the sense explained above.[3] If, however, this

---

[1] Aaron and Gibb, p. 94.   [2] Ibid., p. 100.
[3] The sense afterwards maintained by Berkeley; cf. *Principles*, § 116.

alternative be rejected as inadequate, then we cannot merely assert with Newton that a positive, absolute, and infinite space exists. Our idea of infinite space is essentially negative, as Locke will later prove. The only way in which it could be made positive would be by identifying it in some way with the one positive infinity we can possibly conceive, namely, the Deity. Henry More had argued that infinite extension is divine and Locke had himself reflected on this possibility, as is clear from the journal of 1677.[1] Supposing God's being were positively conceived by us, and supposing he were extension, we might then have a positive idea of infinite extension. But Locke, although he plays with this alternative, does not accept it outright. For, first, he was not sure that we had a clear positive conception of God's infinity. Secondly, to assert that the Deity was an extended being might savour in 1690 of materialism or Spinozism. Yet this is the only form in which Locke will at all consider this second alternative, that absolute space exists as a positive entity. The words of St. Paul may be literally true. God may be the space in which all things exist. Then we should have a positive idea of absolute space, but on no other view is this possible.

The sequel to Locke's criticism is highly interesting. In 1713 Newton published the second edition of his *Principia* and in it he added a scholium in which he recognizes that God constitutes, although he is not identical with, duration and space. 'He endures for ever and is everywhere present; and by existing always and everywhere, he constitutes duration and space. . . . In him are all things contained and moved.'[2] It is not Locke's criticism alone, of course, that had influenced Newton, for others were as definite as Locke in their rejection of his position. But Locke's refusal to admit Newton's theory even as an alternative must have counted with the latter.

As to Locke's own view of space, it is clear that he first favoured a relativism which would accord best with his empiricism, and that he then seems to have felt some doubt about the adequacy of

[1] Aaron and Gibb, p. 96.

[2] *Principia*, the General Scholium to Book III; cf. Florian Cajori's edition (Cambridge, 1934), p. 545. In a note on the passage Cajori refers to Berkeley and Leibniz, but not to Locke.

this position as a basis for scientific procedure, in view of Newton's demand for a more positive conception of space. But he could not accept Newton's theory as presented in the first edition of the *Principia*, since he could not conceive a positive, absolute space. The one possibility was the linking of space with the Deity. But here again Locke hesitated. He would not openly accept the view that God is the space in which all things exist and move. At the same time, it is certainly true that some of his language in the rest of the *Essay* implies an absolute rather than a relative view of space.

Locke, then, avoids a discussion of the nature of space as such. Instead he sets before himself three distinct problems: (1) Can space be identified with body? (2) How may place be defined? (3) In what sense are all ideas of space derived from sensation?

Discussion of the first point takes up the whole of the second half of ii. xiii. The point at issue was an important one. If extension were the essence of body then Descartes's mathematical physics could rightly become the prototype of the physical science of the new age. On the other hand, if it were not no physics could succeed which did not take into account such other conceptions as force, gravity, and impenetrability. Now Locke begins by pointing out that body is usually regarded as both extended and solid, and these words are not usually supposed to be synonyms. It is true that we cannot think of solid body without thinking of it as extended. But this does not permit us to identify the two terms. Nor is space identifiable with body. Space offers no resistance to body, but one body resists another. The parts of space are inseparable and immovable, while the parts of bodies are separable and movable: 'Thus the determined *idea* of simple *space* distinguishes it plainly and sufficiently from *body*, since its parts are inseparable, immovable, and without resistance to the motion of body.'[1] To the argument that all entities are either substances or accidents, so that space, which is obviously not substance, must be an accident or a property, and so may very well be the essential property of body, Locke replies that it is a very great assumption to assume that substances and accidents are the sole existents

[1] ii. xiii. 14.

whilst we are so uncertain as to the nature of substance. Finally, Locke believes that a vacuum is possible, and if it is, then there exists space where there is no body, so that the two cannot possibly be identified. The existence or non-existence of a vacuum was another point in hot dispute on the Continent, and Locke brings forward the following arguments in favour of its existence. Since body is finite, a man 'at the extremity of corporeal beings' could yet stretch forth his hand beyond his body. In that case 'he would put his arm where there was before space without body'. Secondly, if God annihilated an object (as we must suppose he can), this would create a vacuum. Thirdly, the motion of objects ultimately necessitates a vacuum. Lastly, we have the idea of a vacuum, since we talk and argue about it, and this shows that our idea of body is not the same as that of space, for we can think of a space where there is no body. From all these arguments Locke concludes that there is a vacuum[1] and that body is not essentially extension. Impenetrability is as essential a characteristic of corporeal existence as is extension.[2]

The consideration of *place* need not long detain us. Locke rejects both the Aristotelian and the Gassendist (and again Newtonian) conception of place. For Aristotle the place of a thing is definable in terms of the vessel or body which contained it. If, for instance, a bottle is completely filled with water and closed, the place of the water can then be defined in terms of the inner sides of that vessel. For Gassendi and Newton place is a determined part of space, occupied by a body. In Newton's language: 'Place is a part of space which a body takes up.' In Locke's view, however, this latter description of place is 'confused'. He defines place in terms of 'two or more points', the place of an object O is the same today as it was yesterday if it remains at the same distance from two or more fixed points.[3] Thus place is a relative conception,

[1] Thinking in terms of a vacuum, it should be added, does not apparently necessitate acceptance of the Newtonian absolute continuum stretching infinitely in all directions. Observe the carefully qualified manner in which Locke speaks in II. xiii. 24 and 27.
[2] Nowhere is Gassendi's influence on Locke more obvious than in the argument summarized in the above paragraph.
[3] II. xiii. 10. Locke's argument here is obviously defective even of a plane. In

'nothing but', as he explains in Draft B, 'extension with relation to some other bodies or imaginary points that are at a certain determinate distance from it'.[1] Because this is so Locke thinks we cannot speak of the place of the universe, for there are no fixed points outside it to which we can relate it.

The third problem is the most important of the three. Unfortunately, it is also the one which Locke faces with least success. It is really the problem of the relation between the space perceived and the space conceived, between the *given* of sensation and the *conceived* of thought. Locke feels confident that all thoughts about space find their starting-point in sensation. My first idea of space is given in sensation. For instance, I see this patch of brown which I call a table and another patch of brown which I call a chair. I also see the shape of the two patches and I see the distance between the two. This is all part of the immediately given. Of course, that the table is two yards broad and that it is six yards from the chair is not immediately given. Sensation of itself would not enable us to understand these terms. Yet we do gain an idea of space in sensation. Locke, therefore, terms space a simple idea. And he continues to describe it as such even though he recognizes that it is divisible.[2] It is a simple idea as being the *given* of sensation and not as being indivisible. The real difficulty in connexion with the simple idea of space, however, arises when the question is asked: What precisely is given? Is it space as such? Hardly! Then is it the *minimum sensibile*, 'the least portion whereof we have clear and distinct *ideas*'?[3] He occasionally appears to be holding this view. But as the argument proceeds, the simple idea is almost identified with a stated length agreed upon as the unit of measure, for instance, an inch, a foot, a yard. Then any other determinate length is a mode of one of these, and the idea of it is gained by 'enlarging' the unit. But why should one inch be *given* rather than six or ten? Locke's argument is certainly weak here. He tries to deal with geometrical figures in the same way, to make them all

the diagram below, the points marked O and O′ are both the same distance from the points A and B, but they are not in the same place.   .O

A.   .B

.O′

[1] § 141.   [2] II. xv. 9.   [3] Ibid.

modes of a simple idea, namely, the line. Vary the manner in which lines are joined and you get the various figures. But, as Leibniz pointed out, this presupposes that every figure consists of more than one line, and this is certainly not the case, as the circle and the oval sufficiently prove. It is necessary to conclude, therefore, that Locke's attempt in the *Essay* to systematize his thoughts on space, particularly in terms of simple ideas and modes, was not very successful.

The failure of Locke's efforts, however, ought not to blind us to the real point of his argument. It is not whether we can talk of all spatial phenomena in terms of simple ideas and modes, but whether it is true that sensation does provide us with a minimum without which our further thinking about space could not occur. Locke, himself, would protest most emphatically against the view that sensation gives us all we know about space. He was quite clear that the mind could discover much rationally which was not revealed in sensation. But he did not believe that our knowledge of space was independent of sensation. If I understand Locke rightly what he wished to assert is a position frequently asserted today. I may quote Dr. Broad: 'All that I am maintaining is that these crude objects of sense-awareness do have properties that are evidently spatial, and that we can see in them the germs of the refined notions of points, straight lines, etc.'[1] I do not think that Locke claims more when he holds that spatial conceptions are ultimately derived from simple ideas of sensation. Yet it has to be admitted also that he never shows how we are to relate the *given* of sensation with the truths discovered in geometry, and with the intellectual conceptions upon which that study is based.

Time. Locke's account of time manages to avoid the major issues even more completely than does his account of space. Problems as to the reality or non-reality of time, as to its absoluteness or relativity, are never once considered. On the whole he seems to assume the Newtonian view as the basis of his discussion. Time flows on 'in one constant, equal, uniform course',[2] and its 'utmost bounds' are 'beyond the reach of thought'. Yet he never examines this position nor even states it explicitly or claims it as his own.

[1] C. D. Broad, *Scientific Thought*, p. 35.   [2] II. xiv. 21.

The consequence is that the chapter on time is somewhat un-distinguished. Locke contents himself with making two points. First, he distinguishes between duration and time. Descartes had also made this distinction and had made it in terms of modes. Time was a mode of duration.[1] This accorded very well with the view Locke wished to assert. For him also each interval of time is a mode of duration in general. Time is 'duration, as set out by certain periods and marked by certain measures or *epochs*'.[2] Our standard of measurement is fixed conventionally. The revolutions of the sun and moon, the flight of migratory birds, the coming of the seasons, the swing of the pendulum, or any other isochronous movements may be used. But Locke points out possible errors here against which it is necessary to guard oneself. Time must not be identified with the motion of the sun or the pendulum: nor must we say with Descartes and the Cartesians that it is 'the measure of motion'. Time is not motion, nor is it the measure of motion, since in measuring motion space and mass must also be taken into account.[3] The fact that all our standards of time are motions of various sorts misleads us into supposing that there is a closer relation between time and motion than actually exists. Yet it is not the motion in itself which is important, but motion in 'constantly repeated periods'. 'Nor indeed does motion any otherwise conduce to the measuring of duration than as it con-stantly brings about the return of certain sensible ideas in seem-ing equidistant periods.'[4] It is a mistake therefore either to identify time with motion or to suppose that time is simply the measure of motion.[5]

The second and more important point concerns the origin of the idea of duration in general. Our awareness of duration in the first instance is, Locke thinks, bound up with our consciousness of succession, which is 'suggested by our senses, yet is more con-stantly offered by what passes in our own minds'.[6] Succession,

---

[1] *Philosophiae Principia*, i. 57.
[2] II. xiv. 17.   [3] II. xiv. 22.   [4] Ibid.
[5] Once we have agreed upon a standard, for instance, the apparent revolutions of the sun, we may, of course, use it in measuring the passage of time even before these revolutions occurred or after they have ceased. We may talk of a million years before the sun came into being or after it has ceased to exist.
[6] II. vii. 9.

therefore, is experienced both in sensation and reflection, but best in reflection, when we consider the train of ideas which constantly succeed one another in the mind. Now duration is 'the distance between any parts of that succession, or between the appearance of any two *ideas* in our minds'.[1] Our idea of duration is thus bound up with and, apparently, consequent upon, our idea of 'the fleeting and perpetually perishing parts of succession'.[2] As against Locke it might be argued that the succession of which we are aware in this case must in the very first instance be recognized as temporal and known to be different in that respect from, for instance, a numerical succession. Consciousness of time is either simultaneous with, or prior to, consciousness of the sort of succession which Locke has here in mind. But in discussing the origin of the idea of duration Locke seems to be thinking not merely of our consciousness of time but of our first consciousness of a finite duration or length of time. The idea of duration is not the same, apparently, as the idea of succession (even temporal succession). We gain the former when we come to note how things endure throughout succession, so that we are led to think of a fixed length of duration. When we first observe 'a distance between any parts of that succession' we first become aware of measurable duration.[3]

But again the same difficulty arises in the case of time as arose in our treatment of space. What precisely is given? It is not time or duration as such in the wider sense. What is given us ceases to be when we are not attending to it; whereas time as such proceeds on its 'constant, equal, uniform course'. Yet we should, it appears, never become aware of time in this objective sense were not something given us from our earlier sensory and reflective experiences. This something given is, first, a succession of perishing parts, the succession being neither too rapid nor too slow to be discerned by us, and, secondly, a certain distance between parts of this succession. Thus we gain our first idea of a definite length of time. Is this then the simple idea of time out of which the modes are framed?

---

[1] II. xiv. 3.   [2] II. xiv. 1.

[3] II. xiv. 3 has sometimes been taken to mean that we must be aware of a permanent—the self or an object—before we can be aware of duration. I think this is reading too much into the passage. These are rather illustrations of durations, as is clearer from the corresponding passage in Draft B (§ 103).

Locke's answer is uncertain. In II. xv. 9 he suggests that we may regard the *minima sensibilia* as the simple ideas both in the case of the ideas of space and time. 'But the least portions of either of them', he there remarks, 'whereof we have clear and distinct *ideas*, may perhaps be fittest to be considered by us as the *simple ideas* of that kind, out of which our complex modes of *space, extension,* and *duration* are made up and into which they can again be distinctively resolved.' Now presumably this simple idea, the *minimum sensibile*, which, as Locke admits, varies from person to person, cannot be our unit in measurement. In that case, the unit itself would be a complex idea, whereas Locke assumes that it is a simple idea (largely because the number one, or unity, is in his opinion a simple idea). However, as is clear from the above passage, he is not wholly certain that the *minimum sensibile* is the simple idea, so that the unit may still be the simple idea. Locke, it is clear, has no definite theory to offer us as to the character of the *given* in our first awareness of time through sensation or reflection.

The discussion of space and time concludes with a comparison between them.[1] Both are infinite (in the negative sense which Locke later makes clear), both are capable of greater and less, both are divisible, and divisible into parts which are themselves extensions and durations respectively, and in both such parts are inseparable. All finite beings are in space and in time. And lastly, time is to duration as place is to space. So much they have in common. As to the differences: first, duration is in one dimension only, space in three, or, as Locke puts it, 'duration is as a line, expansion as a solid'. (He might also have added that duration is as a line pointing in one direction only.) Secondly, the parts of duration are never together but follow each other in a succession, whilst those of space are all together.

Number.[2] Judged even by the standards of his own day Locke's description of number is defective. To begin with he falls into the strange fault of considering integers alone. The reason for this is not difficult to find. He thinks he has found in number the neatest instance of the relation of simple mode to simple idea. The simple

---

[1] II. xv.   [2] See Appendix III, p. 321 below.

idea is the unit, having no 'shadow of variety nor composition in it',[1] and any other number is a mode of it, made by putting so many units together and giving the compound a name. The modes are completely distinct from each other and therein lies the explanation of that clarity which pertains to arithmetic. Locke, however, is oversimplifying his problems by neglecting fractions. The unit, after all, is a composite. There are fractions, not to mention incommensurables such as $\sqrt{2}$.

But even if we confine our attention to integers, Locke's account must still be written down as unsatisfactory. 'By the repeating of the idea of an unit and joining it to another unit, we make thereof one collective idea, marked by the name two.' Surely this is no adequate account of 2 and of its relation to 1. Is the idea of 200 gained by repeating to ourselves the unit two hundred times? And why does the number 2 reappear in 200? What is there common in 2, 20, 200, 2,000, and so on? Obviously, 2 is a member of a series of integers, built up according to a certain order, beginning not with 1 but with 0. Locke mentions the need for an order in II. xvi. 7, but he does not see that it is essential to number and that there is no description of number without taking it into account. Leibniz in discussing this chapter in the *Nouveaux Essais* is well aware of its defects, and he puts his finger on the explanation. 'You see then, sir, that your idea or your application of simple or mixed modes is greatly in need of correction.'[2]

Infinity. Some of the most interesting pages that Locke wrote about infinity are to be found in Draft A. As has already been pointed out, the whole purpose of the discussion of infinity and indeed of simple modes is here revealed. It is meant to answer the objection that might be made against Locke's empiricism, the objection that the idea of infinity is a positive idea gained independently of all sense-experience. Locke admits that we have this idea, but he claims that it is negative, not positive, and that it originates in sensation and reflection. In the Draft he seeks to prove this in two ways. First, he seeks to overthrow the argument

---

[1] II. xvi. 1.
[2] II. xvi. 5. It is good to think that we have been saved from the cumbersome arithmetical notation suggested by Locke in II. xvi. 6.

of the schools, that since the finite is negation and the infinite is the negation of the finite the latter is a double negative, and in that way most positive. He argues against this subtlety by claiming that the finite is not a negative. It is a positive, determined quantity, determined both as to its beginning and end, and though this does involve negation of what is not within the bounds of the finite, the idea of the finite is itself a positive idea. In the *Essay*, in which he has promised to follow the 'historical, plain method', he drops this argument altogether and bases his case on the second argument of Draft A. This consists in analysing the idea of infinity and showing that it is an idea of an endlessly growing progression, which idea is not positive but negative. We shall see how he develops this argument in the *Essay*. He makes another interesting point at the end of the discussion of the infinite in Draft A. Even if some people claim a positive idea of infinity, it still at most can only be a '*modus* of Number or Extension',[1] and therefore is ultimately derived from the given in sensation and reflection. Later, Locke drops this point also, maintaining that such people from the nature of the case cannot but be deceived.

Turning now to the discussion of the *Essay* we perceive its motive more plainly in the light of the foregoing. II. xvii is no inquiry into infinity in general. It is solely an attempt to demonstrate that the concept of infinity contains in it nothing not ultimately derived from sensation and reflection. To prove this Locke first endeavours to show that the only conception of infinity which can seriously be considered by us is the quantitative. Once this is admitted he then feels fairly certain that there can be no further hindrance in the way of his argument. The quantitative is not our only conception of infinity. But, Locke argues, it is the only one that is clear. We do conceive God as infinite and we know by revelation, if by no other means, that he is no mere quantity. But his infinity is on the whole beyond our comprehension. Our one clear conception of it is in quantitative terms. 'When we apply to that first and supreme Being our *idea* of infinite in our weak and narrow thoughts, we do it primarily in respect of his duration and ubiquity.'[1] If we would further seek to understand the infinity of

---

[1] § 45. Aaron and Gibb, p. 72.   [2] II. xvii. 1.

God's power, wisdom, and goodness, we can only do so with any measure of success in terms of quantity. God has the power of the most powerful human being and infinitely more; he has the wisdom of a Solomon and infinitely more; the goodness of the saint and infinitely more. It is clear we are thinking in quantitative terms. The only conception of infinity which is at all clear to us is the quantitative.

In so arguing Locke is challenging the thought of his day. He denies that we have a clear idea of the infinite as quality. He denies that we have a clear notion of the Absolute, the *Ens Perfectissimum*. If he is right Descartes's transcendent metaphysics and the whole of Spinoza's philosophy rest upon a conception which lacks clarity and is ambiguous. 'The true infinite', said Leibniz when he read this passage, 'exists, strictly speaking, only in *the absolute*, which is anterior to all composition, and is not formed by the addition of parts.'[1] This Locke denies. The only infinite we clearly conceive is endless progression in quantity. It is the infinitely great in quantity, whether in number, in space, in time, in wisdom, or in power. Infinite number is a series beginning (so Locke thought) with 1 but ending never. Infinite space is space stretching out endlessly in all directions from a given point. Infinite time is endlessness whether backwards from the present or forwards to the future. It is precisely the sempiternity of which Spinoza was so contemptuous. But for Locke no other idea of eternity and no other of infinity is clear. This chapter on infinity is a bold challenge to the rationalists to justify their position.

Now if it be once admitted that our only clear idea of infinity is quantitative Locke can then easily show that it is no positive idea and that it is ultimately derived, like all other ideas, from the simple ideas of sensation and reflection. We cannot gain a positive, determined idea of endless progression. A positive idea of an infinite number is, from the nature of the case, an absurdity. 'For our *idea of infinity* being, as I think, *an endless growing idea*, but the *idea* of any quantity the mind has being at that time terminated in that *idea* (for be it as great as it will, it can be no greater than it is), to join infinity to it is to adjust a standing measure to

[1] *Nouveaux Essais*, ii. xvii. 1.

a growing bulk.'[1] Thus absolute space and absolute time in so far as they are infinite are essentially negative conceptions. Even if we identify absolute space and time with the Deity it is still doubtful whether we have any positive concept of infinity.[2] Our thinking that we have leads us to antinomies of various sorts which can only be resolved by realizing that the idea of infinity is for us essentially negative.

This negative idea has originated in the following way. Experience gives us a finite length, a finite period of time, or a finite number of objects. We can think of these as doubled, as trebled, quadrupled, and so on 'without ever coming to an end'. Here already is the conception of infinity. We may begin with any positive number and pass on to higher and higher numbers proceeding forward endlessly. Infinity for Locke is this endless progression. It is, therefore, an idea ultimately derived from sense-experience; it rests upon what is given in sensation. Of course, sensation only provides the basis. We can never verify in experience the endlessness of the series. Locke would be prepared to admit that the mind itself works upon an assumption not gained in experience, namely, that if x be any number, there exists some number y of which we can say it is greater than x. But what Locke wants to argue is that the whole conception of number was first suggested to us by sensory experience, and that even this conception of infinite number derives from the same source. Infinity is a negative idea ultimately derived from simple ideas of sensation and reflection.

Thus even the idea of infinity, remote as it is from the first objects of sensation and reflection, ultimately rests upon sense-experience. Infinity is not itself *given* in sensation or reflection. Yet it is no positive idea known (for instance, innately) in complete independence of sense-experience. On the contrary, it is the consequence of the mind's enlarging of the *given* together with the mind's assuming that enlarging can go on for ever. In other words, to put it in Locke's terminology, infinity is essentially a mode of a simple idea. And when Locke has proved this he is content. Ideas of space, of time, of number, and even of infinity,

<hr>

[1] II. xvii. 7.   [2] II. xvii. 20.

are simple modes of simple ideas; and Locke does not desire to
prove more in connexion with them. 'I pretend not', he says,[1] 'to
treat of them in their full latitude; it suffices to my design to show
how the mind receives them, such as they are, from *sensation* and
reflection; and how even the *idea* we have of *infinity*, how remote
so ever it may seem to be from any object of sense or operation of
our mind, has nevertheless, as all our other *ideas*, its original there.
Some mathematicians, perhaps, of advanced speculations, may
have other ways to introduce into their minds *ideas* of infinity;
but this hinders not but that they themselves as well as all other
men got the first *ideas* which they had of infinity from sensation
and reflection in the method we have here set down.'

Other Simple Modes. 'For method's sake' Locke proceeds to
mention briefly a few more simple modes before passing to mixed
modes. Simple modes, he repeats, are the consequence of 'the
faculty the mind has to repeat its own *ideas*'.[2] There are modes of
motion, for instance, sliding, rolling, walking, and so on, and
modes of sound. 'Every articulate word is a different *modification
of sound*.'[3] There are modes of colour, that is, 'shades' of the same
colour. (Here again we see how artificial is the system of classification. For instance, I see an object coloured royal blue. Apparently
I am then, in so far as I see the colour, seeing a simple mode, i.e. a
complex idea, it being a mode of 'blue', which is the simple idea.
So the simple idea is blue in general, whilst the particular shades
are complex ideas.) Finally, there are modes of taste and smell,
although we hardly ever refer to these since we have few names
for them.

Proceeding, Locke considers 'the modes of thinking', to which
we have already referred, together with the modes of pleasure and
pain. The long chapter which follows on power can hardly be
held to be a discussion of a mode at all, whether simple or mixed.
The idea of power is said to be a simple idea, though Locke has to
confess that it *'includes in it some kind of relation'*.[4] The relation
between it and the simple mode is not at all clear. Are we to suppose that each of the mind's faculties is a mode of power? But in
that case thinking, which has its own modes, would itself be a

[1] II. xvii. 22.   [2] II. xviii. 1.   [3] II. xviii. 3.   [4] II. xxi. 3.

mode. In the chapter on power Locke's scheme seems to break down altogether.[1]

Mixed Modes. Locke completes his account of modes with a chapter on mixed modes, that is, modes made up of simple ideas which are not the same. II. xxii, however, is slight and in a sense merely introductory to the subject. He has much more to say of mixed modes in Book III, and we cannot fully discuss this highly important group of ideas until we come to consider that book. Some interesting points, however, emerge from the present chapter, which we may here note.

In the first place Locke tries to explain once again what he means by a mode. These mixed modes are 'such combinations of simple *ideas* as are not looked upon to be characteristical marks of any real beings that have a steady existence, but scattered and independent *ideas* put together by the mind'.[2] The underlying conception is of something dependent, not having an existence of its own. But to this is added, in the case of mixed modes, the further conception that we are here usually dealing with a creation of the mind. This latter fact is stressed by Locke. He never considers the objectivity or subjectivity of simple modes: he seems even to be avoiding the issue. But in the case of mixed modes he is quite explicit. The mind chooses what ideas it shall put together without considering whether there is anything in reality corresponding to the complex idea it has created; 'though I do not deny', Locke adds, 'but several of them might be taken from observation and the existence of several simple *ideas* so combined

---

[1] There is also the very curious fact that in the final section of this chapter Locke talks of having now brought to an end his discussion of 'original ideas', i.e. presumably certain simple ideas, rather than simple modes, as if the chapter were a discussion of simple ideas. 'Original ideas', however, are now confined to a few only of the simple ideas, all the rest being derived from them. 'I believe they all might be reduced to these very few primary and original ones, viz., *extension, solidity, mobility* or the power of being moved; which by our senses we receive from body; *perceptivity*, or the power of perception, or thinking; *motivity* or the power of moving; which by reflection we receive from our minds' (II. xxi. 73). To which we must also add, Locke thinks, existence, duration, and number, given in both sensation and reflection. We have here a division between original and derivative ideas which cuts across the earlier division into simple and complex, since many simple ideas, e.g. ideas of the secondary qualities, are obviously no longer original.

[2] II. xxii. I.

as they are put together in the understanding.'[1] The mind might be following the order of nature, but most usually it is creating without reference to that order. We simply put ideas together and give a name to the combination. Locke, perhaps, over-emphasizes the part the adoption of a name plays, for he seems to think there would be no idea had we no single name for it. To kill one's father is parricide, and here is one complex idea. On the other hand, the killing of an old man has no distinct name and therefore, Locke argues, there is no complex idea of that sort. But surely the killing of an old man is as distinct a notion as parricide, even though it is not symbolized by one word.

Locke notes three ways in which the mind is furnished with the complex ideas of mixed modes. '(1) By experience and *observation* of things themselves; thus by seeing two men wrestle or fence, we get the *idea* of wrestling or fencing. (2) By *invention*, or voluntary putting together of several simple *ideas* in our own minds: so he that first invented printing, or etching, had an *idea* of it in his mind before it ever existed. (3) Which is the most usual way, by *explaining the names* of actions we never saw, or notions we cannot see.'[2]

In concluding this section on modes we may point out that the conception grows and develops in Locke's hands, but never becomes really explicit. He is obviously borrowing his terminology from traditional sources, but refusing to be tied down to it. The one thing he is anxious to prove in this whole discussion is his own empiricist position. We might also add that he is so anxious to show that all our modes are ultimately derived by the mind from simple ideas of sensation and reflection that he tends to neglect the part which the mind itself contributes to the making of these complex ideas. He consequently neglects many very grave problems, but consideration of some of them at least is merely postponed, for he returns to them later in the *Essay*.

II

Having considered modes we must now consider *substances*. At the outset a distinction must be drawn between complex ideas

---

[1] II. xxii. 2.   [2] II. xxii. 9.

of particular substances and the conception of substance in general. Locke's concern is with the former and in the Drafts he examined these only, but when he came to write the *Essay* he had realized that a word must first be added about substance in general before the nature of our complex ideas of substances could rightly be understood. He accordingly adds an important paragraph at the opening of II. xxiii.

By substance the schools had meant two things, and one of the difficulties in the whole conception, as is clear from Stillingfleet's use of the term in his controversy with Locke, is that these two meanings were not distinguished with sufficient care. In the first place, substance is *ens*, real existence (or, sometimes, the essence, the 'true nature' of a real existence). In the second, it is that which supports accidents, *per se subsistens et substans accidentibus*. The second was regarded as the more philosophical usage of the term. From Aristotle's day onward the conception of substance had never been examined with the attention it merited. It is true that some doubts had been expressed in the schools, particularly amongst the nominalists. Can we, it had been asked, divide a thing into substance and accidents? If we take away all the accidents what then is left? Can substance so isolated mean anything positive?[1] But if a few of the schoolmen turned these questions over in their minds, without reaching any very definite results, philosophers generally were ready to accept the Aristotelian division into substances and accidents without further examination.

Now there was a special reason why Locke could not follow the fashion and acquiesce in the current terminology and conception. He had made it his business to examine all the ideas in the mind, particularly those which appeared at first sight to originate in a source other than sensation or reflection. The idea of substance appeared to be such an idea. Locke himself admits that we neither have nor can have this idea directly by sensation or reflection.[2] No one experiences substance, as such, directly. Nor is it gained by

---

[1] Cf. Tellkamp, *Das Verhältnis John Locke's zur Scholastik*, p. 72. He mentions Nicholas of Autrecourt as one who had questioned the validity of the conception.   [2] I. iv. 18.

enlarging or combining the ideas experienced. We experience size, colour, shape, and so on, but however much we enlarge these ideas we never get the positive idea of substance as such. Nor again does it come by combining. How then do we come by this idea of substance? This is the problem which Locke set himself.

It is important to note, before we proceed further, that Locke is dealing with ideas here. This means that any solution offered, from the nature of the case, applies only to ideas and does not apply, directly at least, to reality. It tells us what the nature of our idea is, and not what the nature of the real is. The most this method can do is to show how an idea is gained and what precisely it means. The idea of a substance, Locke discovers, is an idea of something supporting accidents. This involves no knowledge of the real existence of the something. For to have an idea or concept even of a thing's being is not to know that this thing exists. Locke analyses the *idea* only.

Now the problem is to show how this idea of substance in general is derived. Locke thinks that though it is not immediately experienced it can none the less be shown to be derived from what is experienced. This is only possible because we do not have a positive idea of substance but merely 'an obscure and relative idea'. How is it derived? It is derived, Locke thinks, from our experience of qualities and accidents. Our idea of substance in general, he asserts at the beginning of II. xxiii, is the idea of a support of qualities. 'If anyone will examine himself concerning his *notion of pure substance in general*, he will find he has no other *idea* of it at all, but only a supposition of he knows not what support of such qualities which are capable of producing simple *ideas* in us; which qualities are commonly called *accidents*. . . . The *idea*, then, we have, to which we give the general name substance, being nothing but the supposed, but unknown, support of those qualities we find existing, which we imagine cannot subsist *sine re substante*, without something to support them, we call that support *substantia*; which, according to the true import of the word is, in plain English, *standing under* or *upholding*.'[1] Our efforts to speak positively of substance are like those of children

[1] II. xxiii. 2.

when they seek to explain what they do not understand. Or we are like Locke's celebrated Indian 'who, saying that the world was supported by a great elephant, was asked what the elephant rested on? to which his answer was "A great tortoise"; but being again pressed to know what gave support to the broad-backed tortoise, replied—something, he knew not what'. So substance is a some-thing-I-know-not-what. That is to say, while the concept of a sup-port to accidents is clear, the concept of the support itself, of the something there common to all substances, is not clear. The idea of substance in general is, as he explains to Stillingfleet, 'a com-plex idea made up of the general idea of something or being, with the relation of a support to accidents'.[1]

This conception needs to be analysed further. It is a conception of substance in general and, therefore, abstract.[2] It is gained by abstracting from ideas of particular substances the element com-mon to all. Thus the idea of substance is already present in the idea of a particular substance or of a thing. How, then, is it derived in the case of the idea of a particular substance? Should we say that it is something known rationally, so that the substance–attribute relation is apprehended logically? But this is what Locke denies. The substance is a something-I-know-not-what, hence it is not possible to discern rationally the relation between the qualities observed and the substance, which is unknowable. How, then, can we speak of substance at all in this case? Locke does not provide a clear answer, yet it is most important to attempt an answer to this question. For here, surely, is the true source of the idea of substance in general. But though no explicit answer is to be found, an answer is given implicitly, and Locke throughout is assuming it in his argument. We may take an idea of a particular substance, for instance, the idea of this table. It is a complex idea consisting of the simple ideas of brown, hard, smooth, rectangular, and so on. But in addition there is an extra element. These ideas are experienced by me in this case as one group or family belonging together. As Locke himself tells us, they are observed 'to go

---

[1] *Works*, i. 367 (1801 ed., iv. 19).

[2] Locke is quite explicit about this. Cf. *Works*, i. 371 (First Letter): 'I must take the liberty to deny there is any such thing *in rerum natura* as a general substance that exists itself or makes any thing.'

together'. Moreover, they go constantly together. 'The mind being, as I have declared, furnished with a great number of simple *ideas* conveyed in by the *senses*, as they are found in exterior things, or by *reflection* on its own operations, takes notice also, that a certain number of these simple *ideas* go constantly together.'[1] There is an awareness of ideas as going together. The mind has not ideas of isolated qualities, but of qualities together in one unity. Now here, surely, is the empirical basis of the idea of substance. The 'togetherness' of these simple ideas is as real a part of the experience as are the ideas themselves. (It might also be said that one thing which I experience, namely, my own body, is still more definitely a whole as experienced. I certainly experience my own body as one thing having such and such qualities.)

Here then is that empirical basis for the particular, and so also the general, idea of substance. The general idea of substance as a something-I-know-not-what holding together accidents is an idea derived from the experience of qualities going together. Locke, however, does not explicitly derive the conception of *thinghood* or substantiality from experience in this way, for it would amount to saying that we know the *thing* or substance in experience, and this is what Locke cannot say. There are two reasons for this. First, the idea of the thing is a complex idea, and according to Locke's original position only the simple is given. Secondly, and this is more important for Locke, to say we experience *things* would suggest that in sensation we know through ideas things as they are. But sensation can never reveal the inner nature of existent things. On this Locke insists.

We must distinguish carefully, then, between our complex ideas of substances and the substances themselves. The complex idea is not the substance, it is not even a true representation of it. But whenever a thing affects me a certain number of ideas 'come together'. They suggest to me one thing, and I combine these ideas and give the whole combination a name, regarding it as the name of a substance, that is to say, of an entity in which qualities are held together. But this does not give me knowledge either of this underlying structure and support of qualities, or indeed of

[1] II. xxiii. 1.

all those qualities themselves, as they actually are. We call such complex ideas, ideas of substances or things, without having any clear positive conception of substance. Our ideas go together in groups or families. We become accustomed to this grouping, and it is this which suggests to us things or substances. But experience does not at all reveal the true nature of these substances. Indeed, the true nature of any substance is, Locke thinks, hidden for ever from us. He concludes, therefore, that our complex ideas of particular substances are ideas in the mind only, framed according to the suggestions of experience, it is true, but not providing us with exact knowledge of things or substances in nature.

Two further points of interest should be noticed in this discussion of our complex ideas of substances. For the most part the preceding discussion has been in terms of corporeal things, such as tables and chairs. Locke now turns to spiritual substances. All that we have said above applies here also. We have as clear a notion of spiritual substances as we have of corporeal; we know the one as well as the other—that is to say, fundamentally we know neither. In reflection we experience thinking, reasoning, fearing, and so on, 'which we concluding not to subsist of themselves, nor apprehending how they can belong to body, or be produced by it, we are apt to think these the actions of some other *substance*, which we call *spirit*'.[1] Locke here, however, neglects one important difference. The simple ideas come together in groups in the case of corporeal objects. But thinking, reasoning, and fearing, are not experienced together in precisely the same way. The only sense in which I can perceive the oneness of my thinking, reasoning, and fearing is by realizing that they are *mine*. Behind the conception of substance in this case is, apparently, a consciousness of self. And we may appropriately ask: Is this consciousness a consciousness of something-I-know-not-what which holds accidents together? In so far as we conceive self as a substance in the traditional sense, we must no doubt think of it as that which supports its qualities. But are we justified in so conceiving it? Locke in his discussion of personal identity shows that we cannot without further proof identify the self of which we are conscious in

[1] II. xxiii. 5.

experience with an immaterial substance. II. xxiii throws no additional light on this problem.

One wonders whether reflection upon spiritual substance might not be responsible for the second point to which we now refer. We find in Locke (not merely in the *Essay* but elsewhere, for instance, in the Drafts) what might be regarded as a tentative effort to describe substance more adequately. When he does try to get behind the veil of ideas what he finds are 'active and passive powers' or 'active powers and passive capacities'. In his corpuscular physics most qualities are really powers, and powers play an important part in his conception of corporeal objects. When we turn to reflect upon the mind it becomes still more obvious that spiritual substance consists of powers or faculties. Locke says himself that powers 'make a great part of our complex *ideas* of substances'.[1] There is here a germ of a new conception of substance to be developed by his successors, Berkeley and Leibniz, although in different ways. Nevertheless, it would be wrong to ascribe to Locke any doctrine identifying substance with power. Thus when he studied John Sergeant's *Solid Philosophy Asserted*, in which the view is expressed that the essential nature of material substance is potentiality, Locke writes in the margin 'Matter is a solid substance and not a power'.[2] What this solid substance which is not a power is we cannot say, for we do not know the inner and substantial nature of things, whether material or mental. And this 'we are not at all to wonder at, since we, having but some superficial *ideas* of things, discovered to us only by the senses from without, or by the mind reflecting on what it experiments in itself within, have no knowledge beyond that, much less of the internal constitution and true nature of things, being destitute of faculties to attain it'.[3] And it is in this agnosticism that Locke ultimately rests.

To conclude: Locke certainly 'bantered the idea of substance', to use Berkeley's phrase. He showed that the traditional view could not stand examination. He did not deny the being of substance,

---

[1] II. xxiii. 7–10.
[2] Cf. J. W. Yolton, 'Locke's Unpublished Marginal Replies to John Sergeant', *Journal of the History of Ideas* (October 1951), p. 558.   [3] II. xxiii. 32.

and he did not deny the need of a support to qualities. But he denied that we have knowledge of this substance. Experience itself suggests its existence, but it does not reveal its nature. It is hidden from us and will remain hidden from us, until we gain faculties, which we do not now possess, whereby the inner nature of the being of things will be revealed. Our idea of substance in general is an idea of a something-we-know-not-what supporting accidents, whilst our idea of a particular substance is a complex idea consisting of many simple ideas observed to go together, to which is superadded this idea of substance in general, the something supporting accidents.[1]

III

The third group of complex ideas considered by Locke consists of ideas of *relation*. These are the product of the mind's power of comparing. 'The comparing them one with another in respect of extent, degrees, time, place, or any other circumstances, is another operation of the mind about its *ideas*, and is that upon which depends all that large tribe of *ideas* comprehended under *relation*.'[2] Locke gives serious attention to this group and he is to be praised for realizing its importance. After the appearance of the *Essay* no philosopher could neglect relations. None the less, the analysis that we find here is crude and uncertain. The demands of his classification in this case become a positive hindrance. They help to muddle both Locke's thought and that of his reader.

It is interesting to compare the two Drafts in connexion with the idea of relation. One of the surprises provided by Draft A is that we find relations being discussed already in the third section, that is to say almost at its opening. So that when Locke first sat down to think out the nature and extent of human knowledge he lost no time in coming to this subject. In Draft B the account of relations comes at the end. He is there clearly trying to fix it into his scheme but failing to do so. He does not seem to know where exactly to introduce relations, and once he has dragged them in

[1] On Locke's theory of substance cf. further D. J. O'Connor, *John Locke*, pp. 73–88.
[2] II. xi. 4.

he does not know how further to develop his argument. But in the first draft his thoughts are on his main problem—the nature, limits, and extent of human knowledge—and realizing that a discussion of knowledge involves also a discussion of relations he loses no time in introducing them. At first he discusses them as a group of ideas wholly distinct from both simple and complex ideas, but very shortly[1] he is suggesting that they had best be considered as 'collected ideas' (the early name for complex ideas), of which substances are also instances. The purpose of this change we have already understood. It is easier then to talk of them as 'terminating in simple ideas' and so to justify his empiricism. The subsequent discussions of relations both in Draft B and the *Essay* seem to be dominated by this purpose, so much so that, as we have seen, two of what are termed in Draft B, 'the three grand relations of time, place, and causality'[2] are in the *Essay* no longer considered as relations but as simple modes. Their empirical origin can then be more easily demonstrated.

It thus happens that the difficulties inevitable in any discussion of relations are heightened by Locke's concern for his classification and by his anxiety to prove his empiricist presuppositions. The issue is further complicated by the fact that, in the language of the *Essay*, we ought to be dealing with ideas of relations and never with relations themselves. Strictly speaking, the immediate objects are never relations, even relations between ideas, but ideas of such relations, which ideas presumably might differ from the relations as much as our idea of a table differs from the table. But Locke could not possibly maintain his representationalism and continue to talk sensibly about relations. When on his guard he does speak of *ideas* of relation; but quite as often he talks of relations only, and he certainly assumes that we know relations between ideas directly. Relations themselves become ideas, rather than objects of which we have ideas.[3] At the same time they are not, apparently, mere ideas, mere phantasies or creations of the mind. Locke does not openly discuss the problem of the objec-

---

[1] § 6.   [2] § 145.

[3] In II. xi. 7, the idea is even said to be the comparing. 'The last sort of complex *idea* is that we call *relation*, which consists in the consideration and comparing one *idea* with another.' Locke's language here is obviously very loose.

tivity or subjectivity of relations. His position on that question is
vague. But what he seems to hold is that while relations do not
exist in the sense in which substances and their qualities exist,
while they are not as independent of the mind as such substances
are, for they are 'extraneous and super-induced'[1] upon the substances (being the products of the mind's activity in comparing),
none the less there is a foundation for the relation in reality. Ideas
of things can be compared because there is that in them which
admits of comparison, and this ultimately means that there is
something in that which they represent, the real existences, which
makes the relation possible. When Locke gives us illustrations he
obviously assumes that the relations being considered exist between real things, and though they only exist when we are explicitly and openly comparing, they are none the less objective as,
at least, referring ultimately to an objective fact. 'Having the
notion that one laid the egg out of which the other was hatched,
I have a clear *idea* of the relation of *dam* and *chick* between the
two cassiowaries in St. James's Park.'[2] Here, obviously, Locke has
in mind an objective foundation for the relation he discusses.

But no very explicit answer to the question as to whether relations are objective or subjective can be found in the *Essay*. Locke
is explicitly concerned with other problems which we can now
examine. He devotes a chapter to the discussion of 'relation in
general'.[3] He opens by showing how 'the understanding in the
consideration of any thing, is not confined to that precise object',
but can 'look beyond it' and compare it with some other thing.
Now the things so brought together are said to be 'related'. Each
thing of this sort can be described in two ways, first, as it is positive, secondly, as it is relative. For instance, if of Caius I say he is a
man, this is describing him positively, but if I say he is a *husband*,
this latter is a relative term, and I signify more than Caius here, I
signify another person. The relation between Caius and this other
person is that of one married person to another. There is for every
relation a 'foundation', here 'the contract and ceremony of marriage', and as a consequence of his entering into this contract I
am able to describe Caius by the relative term *husband*. The

---

[1] II. xxv. 8.   [2] Ibid.   [3] II. xxv, and cf. II. xxviii.

number of such terms is very great indeed. There is hardly a limit to the number of relations into which an individual may enter.[1] The two terms related are called co-relative terms, for instance husband–wife, father–son. Sometimes, however, a term may be relative and yet not possess a co-relative, for example, *concubine*, though there is, of course, something to which the object denoted by the term is related. And there are still further terms which 'conceal a tacit, though less observable, relation',[2] for example, *old, great, imperfect*, all relative terms though seemingly positive. Locke, however, does not discuss the further point whether there really exists a positive term which is in no sense relative. He assumes that there are such terms without discussion.

Now it is not necessary to know all there is to know about an individual before one can know how he, or it, is related to another individual. I may not know what a man essentially is, but if I know that he has entered into a contract of marriage with a woman, then he is a husband, and I know fully what this relation is. Similarly, there may be a change of relation without any change in the individual. 'E.g. *Caius*, whom I consider to-day as a father, ceases to be so to-morrow, only by the death of his son, without any alteration made in himself.'[3] (In this sense, some relations at least must be said to be external, although the problem of the externality or internality of relations is never really considered by Locke.) But he is sure we need not know the whole nature of *X* before we can know that it is related to *Y* in a certain way. Indeed, he thinks, 'the *ideas* which relative words stand for are often clearer and more distinct than of those substances to which they do belong'.[4]

The final point Locke wishes to establish is that 'relations all terminate in simple *ideas*', that is, that 'all the *ideas* we have of *relation* are made up, as the others are, only of simple *ideas*, and that they all, how refined or remote from sense soever they seem, terminate at last in simple *ideas*'.[5] He proposes to demonstrate this in particular instances of relations, to which we can now turn.

Cause and Effect. In his treatment of cause and effect Locke

---

[1] Cf. the long list in II. xxv. 7.   [2] II. xxv. 3.
[3] II. xxv. 5.   [4] II. xxv. 8.   [5] II. xxv. 11.

considers efficient causes only. The efficient was only one of the four causes recognized by Aristotle and the schools. 'As for the other three sorts of causes', Locke remarks in Draft A,[1] 'I do not at present so well understand their efficacy or causality.' The material, formal, and, especially, final causes were too 'metaphysical' for his 'historical, plain method'. Moreover, the only one of the four causes that mattered to the new science of Locke's day was the efficient cause so called. Accordingly Locke confines himself to its consideration.

The account that he gives of it, however, is far from satisfactory. Causality is 'the most comprehensive relation, wherein all things that do or can exist are concerned'.[2] Since this is so one might have expected a very full treatment of it. In II. xxvi, however (a chapter which is entitled 'Of Cause and Effect and other Relations'), only two meagre paragraphs are devoted to its examination. It is true that other passages are also relevant, for instance, the discussions of *power* in Book II, and of our knowledge of causes and effects in Book IV. But Locke's teaching on causation would have been easier to understand if he had discussed all these together (as was in fact his first intention, if we are to judge from the early Drafts). In the *Essay*, however, Locke has ever in mind the demands of his scheme. Power is a simple idea; cause and effect a relation; consequently, the two must be considered apart. (Oddly enough, as we have seen, he says most about power when dealing with modes, but it is first introduced as a simple idea.) Consideration of the knowledge of causes and effects, being part of the main epistemological problem, has to be postponed to Book IV. Consequently, there is nowhere in the *Essay* a satisfactory and adequate treatment of the problem of causation as a whole.

When, moreover, we do piece the scattered fragments together, the theory of causation that emerges is vague and incomplete. Locke does not write in ignorance of the difficulties. Sometimes his position is made to look much more naïve than it really is, and he is charged with taking more for granted than he actually does. People occasionally talk as if there was no problem of causation prior to Hume. This is certainly not the case. The difficulty about

[1] § 15.   [2] II. XXV. 11.

our knowledge of causal relations had troubled philosophers for a generation or more before Hume's *Treatise* appeared. One of the clearest statements of the regular sequence view ever put forward is already to be found in the pages of Berkeley's *Principles*.[1] What we know is a regular sequence of phenomena; we only assume causal relations. Moreover, the fact that in any single observation of a causal relation between bodies I see no causal activity as such had also been made perfectly plain. Géraud de Cordemoy in 1666 published his *Discernement du Corps et de l'Âme*, a work of genius. It is written in six discourses and deals with the mind–body problem in a highly original manner. We are concerned here with the fourth discourse, *De la première cause du mouvement*, where Cordemoy seeks to prove that movement is spiritually caused. It is true we usually think that bodies cause each other to move. But here we go beyond the evidence given us in experience. 'When we say, for example, that the body *B* has caused the body *C* to move from its place, if we examine carefully what we know with certainty here, all we see is that *B* moves, that it meets *C* which was at rest, and that after this meeting the first ceases to move and the second commences to move. But to say we know that *B* gives movement to *C*, is in truth, mere assumption.' Thus Cordemoy had understood quite clearly that we never *see* *B*'s causal activity —if such activity exists. (He himself wished to deny it altogether.) We see certain movements of patches of colour only.

Now Locke, also, understood this point. He may be indebted here to Cordemoy, whom he mentions twice in his journals. (Once, in 1678, he refers directly to this very book.)[2] There is no conclusive proof of such indebtedness, however, and it is well to remember that Locke puts forward his own doubts about our knowledge of the causal relation already in the Drafts of 1671. But whether his views are original or not, he certainly foresaw some parts of Hume's criticism. In sensation we do not directly perceive causality in the sense of perceiving the causal activity itself, the giving of movement to *C* in Cordemoy's example. This

---

[1] §§ 30–31. The same point is made, though not perhaps in so clear a manner, by Joseph Glanvill, *Vanity of Dogmatising*, pp. 189–90. Cf. Gibson, *Locke's Theory of Knowledge*, p. 259.   [2] Aaron and Gibb, p. 110.

Locke fully understood. He differs from Hume, however, in the explicit assertion of the general principle of causality, that all things which have a beginning must also have a cause. When Hume questions this he is going beyond Locke's position; but when he denies that we observe causal activity directly in sensation, he merely reasserts a point already made by Locke and his contemporaries.

One need only read the opening paragraphs of Locke's chapter on power to see that this is so. 'Power' is Locke's word for that which is 'able to make or able to receive any change'. Active power is able to make and passive power to receive. That which makes is also the cause, and the power as acting is the causal activity. Now in describing how we come by the idea of power Locke carefully avoids any language that might suggest we observe this causal activity directly in sensation. 'The mind, being every day informed, by the senses, of the alteration of those simple *ideas* it observes in things without, and taking notice how one comes to an end and ceases to be, and another begins to exist which was not before, ... and concluding, from what it has so constantly observed to have been, that the like changes will for the future be made in the same things by like agents, and by the like ways, considers in one thing the possibility of having any of its simple *ideas* changed, and in another the possibility of making that change; and so comes by that *idea* which we call *power*.'[1] This is of course the regular-sequence theory of causation, and the circuitous language that Locke uses in this passage is the outcome of his anxiety to avoid saying that we observe causal activity directly in sensation.

At the same time Locke does not accept the regular-sequence theory outright. He could see its weakness. The causal relation is not a relation of mere succession. He would not give up the further conception, namely, that the effect follows *from* the cause and does not merely follow it; it is *propter hoc* and not merely *post hoc*. If one studies Locke's words carefully one becomes conscious of a struggle in his mind between two views, first, that all we observe is mere succession, and, secondly, that we observe also some elusive, additional element, even though we never observe

[1] II. xxi. 1 and cf. II. xxi. 4.

the causal activity as such. Yet he never makes up his mind as between these two views, and it is this fact which accounts for the vagueness and indefiniteness of his theory.

We might illustrate this by referring to the difficulties Locke finds in deciding whether power is indeed a simple or a complex idea. If it were a simple idea we should perceive it directly. Sometimes Locke seems to be saying this, and yet, at other times, he is clearly denying it. He might have spoken consistently had he definitely accepted or rejected the regular-sequence view, but whilst he plays with it and also wants to say that we do perceive something more than mere succession he can never give a straightforward account of power. The same point is made manifest also in the opening paragraph of II. xxvi. Here Locke seeks in carefully chosen language to explain the origin of our ideas of cause and effect, but however careful he is he cannot free himself from his fundamental difficulty. 'In the notice that our senses take of the constant vicissitude of things, we cannot but observe that several particulars, both qualities and substances, begin to exist; and that they receive this their existence from the due application and operation of some other being. From this observation we get our *ideas* of *cause* and *effect*. . . . Thus finding that in that substance which we call wax, fluidity, which is a simple *idea*, that was not in it before, is constantly produced by the application of a certain degree of heat, we call the simple *idea* of heat, in relation to fluidity in wax, the cause of it, and fluidity the effect.' The key-phrase here is obviously 'produced by the application of'. If Locke had adhered strictly to the succession theory—which does rule his thoughts here up to a point—'produced by' would be a synonym for 'preceded by' and 'application' would be a neutral word like the 'meeting' of B and C in the passage quoted above from Cordemoy. But it is clear that Locke wants these words to mean more than this. Hence the difficulty. He will not say outright that we observe a mere sequence, but he also finds it impossible to say what more we do observe. The consequence is the laborious and unsatisfactory language of II. xxvi. I.[1]

---

[1] Cf. further the changes made between 1685 (Draft C) and the 1690 text, cf. pp. 61–62 above.

•

So far we have confined our attention to the observation which
is sensation. What has been said above, however, does not apply in
exactly the same way to the other sort of observation possible to
us, namely, reflection. For in reflection we gain, it seems, a deeper
insight into causal activity. When Locke first introduces the idea
of power—and that as a simple idea—it is obviously our experience of our own power that he has directly in mind. 'Power also
is another of those simple *ideas* which we receive from *sensation*
and *reflection*. For, observing in ourselves, that we do and can
think, and that we can at pleasure move several parts of our
bodies which were at rest, the effects also that natural bodies are
able to produce in one another occurring every moment to our
senses, we both these ways get the *idea* of *power*.'[1] We observe
that we can move our bodies, but in things perceived by the senses
it is the effects that are said to be perceived and not the power in
the causes. Thus we gain a clearer idea of power in reflection than
in sensation. That this is Locke's view is abundantly confirmed in
the later chapter on power. 'Bodies by our senses do not afford us
so clear and distinct an *idea* of *active power*, as we have from
reflection upon the operation of our minds. . . . The *idea* of the
beginning of motion we have only from reflection on what passes
in ourselves, where we find by experience that, barely by willing
it, barely by a thought of the mind, we can move the parts of our
bodies which were before at rest.'[2] Thus the idea of power is most
distinct when we reflect upon our own power, and strictly speaking it is a simple idea only as an idea of reflection, though there
is always some additional element in our observation of a causal
sequence by the senses which Locke, as we have seen, never satisfactorily explains. Even as an idea of reflection, however, Locke
does not claim that power is fully clear and distinct. All that he
will permit himself to say is that power and causal activity itself
are better understood by looking inwards than outwards. Indeed,
he leaves bodily 'impulse' (which is the name he gives to the passage of motion from one body to another, or as he describes it
'the continuation of the passion') largely unexplained. He does
not even say, as many of his contemporaries did, that all motion,

---

[1] ii. vii. 8.   [2] ii. xxi. 4.

even physical, is spiritual in origin, though he sometimes seems to be inclining to this view. On the whole he lapses into his accustomed agnosticism about the external world. We cannot properly know whether there are in it causal activities of exactly the same sort as the causal activity I experience when I will to move my arm. We do not know the true nature of physical causal relations, any more than we know the universal essence of the substances between which they occur.

And Locke does not hesitate to draw the only possible conclusion. Natural science cannot be certain, for it does not provide knowledge of the necessary causal connexions between things. It is a system built up of inductively established generalizations which at best are only probable. Locke never wavers on this point. We know causes and effects in the natural world only to the extent that they are revealed to us by the senses. I now observe heat applied to wax and see it turn fluid. 'I can have', Locke remarks in Draft A,[1] 'no other certain undoubted knowledge of the constant connexion of assigned causes and effects than what I have by my senses, which too is but a gross kind of knowledge, is no more but this, that I see when I apply fire to gold it melts it, a load stone near iron it moves it, that snow and salt put into a vessel of water in the inside hardens the water that touches it on the outside.' Precisely the same point is made in Draft B,[2] and again in the Essay.[3] No universal propositions stating causal relations can have greater certainty than the particular observations have upon which they are based. Obviously their certainty is much less since they go beyond experience in the universality of their application. And since we do not know in the particular case in which we observe A produce B precisely how the cause brings about the effect, we cannot say that A must produce B universally. We are merely guided by the regularity with which this particular sequence has occurred in the past. All natural science, therefore, is ultimately uncertain, even though some of its generalizations are such that we can hardly bring ourselves to doubt them. 'Certainty and demonstration are things we must not, in these matters,

[1] § 15.   [2] 135-7.
[3] Cf. IV. iii. 13, 16, 26, 29, and elsewhere.

pretend to.'[1] This is the logical consequence of Locke's position and he does not shirk it.

But while in this respect Locke carries out the full logical implications of his empiricism, there is another in which he does not at first view appear to do so, and with the consideration of this further point we may bring this discussion of causality to a close. For in the causal realm we can, according to Locke, affirm one generalization with apodeictic certainty, namely, that whatever has a beginning has a cause. This is asserted positively in the two Drafts,[2] negatively in the *Essay* in the proof of God's existence,[3] and again positively in the correspondence with Stillingfleet.[4] It is, perhaps, in the latter passage that we find Locke's best and most mature thinking on this subject. He first explains what statements he is and what he is not prepared to set down as apodictically certain. We cannot say that 'Everything must have a cause' is necessarily true, and we cannot suppose that anything just because it now exists must have had a cause. For we may certainly conceive a present existence as existing from and through eternity. 'But "Everything that has a beginning must have a cause" is a true principle of reason or a proposition certainly true; which we come to know by the same way, that is, by contemplating our ideas, and perceiving that the idea of beginning to be is necessarily connected with the idea of some operation; and the idea of operation with the idea of something operating which we call a cause; and so the beginning to be is perceived to agree with the idea of a cause, as is expressed in the proposition; and thus it comes to be a certain proposition; and so may be called a principle of reason as every true proposition is to him that perceives the certainty of it.' In contemplating its ideas the mind perceives that 'the idea of beginning to be is necessarily connected with the idea of something operating which we call a cause'. If reason does perceive this then, of course, whatever we think of as beginning to be must also be thought of as having a cause.

But now, does reason perceive that the idea of beginning to be is necessarily connected with the idea of a cause? They are two

[1] iv. iii. 26.   [2] Draft A, § 16; B, § 140.   [3] iv. x. 3.
[4] *Works*, i. 388 (1801 ed., iv. 61–62).

different ideas, and Locke has not shown why we are compelled to admit that the one inevitably involves the other. There may be a beginning which has no cause. Locke here, however, would no doubt make his appeal to experience, to our experienced idea of a beginning. As experienced it is invariably connected with an operating. We have never experienced anything beginning to be without at the same time experiencing 'something operating'. The 'instructive' or synthetic kernel in the general proposition is thus the knowledge in experience of a something operating and a consequent beginning to be, and this is the relation we call causal. The difficulty is, however, that Locke has not made this relation clear, and the weakness in his theory of causality lies here. His analysis of what we experience when we say, for instance, that we have experienced A causing B is inadequate and vague. And until this becomes clear we cannot know whether the assumption that anything which has a beginning must also have a cause is valid. It may be the case that when we experience a beginning, part of our actual experience then is of something operating. And it may be true that this latter experience is the idea of a cause. So much may be given in experience and thus the generalization which reason makes—'Everything that has a beginning must have a cause'—may rightly be said to be deducible from our ideas. But Locke can only show that this is the case after an adequate analysis of our ideas of beginning, of operating, and of causing, and it is here that he fails. Locke's theory of causality fails because his analysis of our experience of the causal relation fails. He may be on the right lines. It may be possible to put forward a theory of causation which is consistently empiricist. But one thing is certain. The analysis of our experience of the causal relation must first be made adequate.

Other Relations. Locke considers certain other relations in addition to the causal. He has something to say about the relations of time and place, but since in the *Essay* he gives detailed attention to time and place under simple modes, what he says here is not important. He also thinks this the most suitable place to insert the chapter on identity (added in the second edition), and for this purpose regards identity as a relation, namely, a relation between the thing and itself. But the language is strained and the chapter itself throws little light on the nature of relations. We have already dealt with this chapter elsewhere.

The twenty-eighth chapter concludes the discussion of relations. Of all the chapters in the *Essay* this one most faithfully follows the discussion of the early Drafts. Some of Locke's earliest thinking on these questions is contained in it. Four further groups of relations are now noted. First, there exist relations between simple ideas, for instance, hotter, sweeter, equal. 'These relations depending on the equality and excess of the same simple *idea* in several subjects, may be called, if one will, *proportional*.'[1] An interesting question arises here. Are these proportional relations simple or complex ideas? They should be complex being relations. And yet do we not directly observe that *A* is whiter than *B*? If we do, is not the idea simple? But Locke would argue that the idea is the result of comparing, and therefore not simple. In that case this conception of comparing needs more careful analysis and its relation to direct perceiving needs to be ascertained. For it is certainly difficult not to admit that I perceive directly that *A* is whiter than *B*, and yet, of course, there is a fundamental difference between perceiving white and perceiving that *A* is whiter than *B*. But Locke has not made this difference clear. The second sort of relations is the natural, for instance, that between father and son.[2] The third is the institutional, for instance, a general exists in a certain instituted relation to his army, a citizen to the township, a king to his subjects. 'All this sort depending upon men's wills, or agreement in society, I call *instituted*.'[3] Unlike the second sort of relations, these latter are alterable; a general, for instance, may be deprived of his rank. The fourth and last type of relations are the moral, 'the conformity or disagreement men's voluntary actions have to a rule'. We may postpone consideration of this last relation to a later chapter.[4]

Locke concludes his account by again seeking to show that in all these cases the relations terminate in simple ideas. But by this

[1] II. xxviii. 1.
[2] Locke speaks loosely here, speaking of the relative, e.g. father, brother, as if it were itself the relation.
[3] II. xxviii. 3.   [4] Part III, chapter 1.

time the reader is a little bewildered as to what relation is, and is not in a position to decide whether relations do or do not terminate in simple ideas. And if he searches beyond Book II for an explanation of the term his confusion is increased rather than decreased. In Book III relations are grouped (and, to all intents and purposes, identified) with mixed modes.[1] In Book IV again the relation is the object in knowing, for of the four sorts of agreements between ideas which may be known, three are 'truly nothing but relations'. Locke admits in Book II that his account of relations is incomplete. ''Twould make a volume to go over all sorts of relations.'[2] This incompleteness, however, might very well have been excused him if he had made the main conception of relation itself clear—but this he never does.

Locke's examination of modes, substances, and relations in Book II, we must conclude, is far from being an adequate treatment of the matters under consideration. Its primary purpose is to demonstrate the empiricist thesis, but even here it fails, because its analyses are always inadequate and incomplete. In Locke one only finds the crude beginnings of analysis, and to establish empiricism finally analysis would have to be complete. Yet it *is* a beginning. Locke did 'banter' the traditional idea of substance, and that at a time when European thinkers, Spinoza in particular, were basing their whole systems upon it, although the conception was not wholly clear to them. He 'bantered' as well ideas of space, of time, of infinity, of identity, and of relation. It would be foolish to say that this criticism of traditional conceptions was without value. It was exceedingly valuable, since it challenged contemporary thought to clarify its central conceptions. But it would be equally foolish to argue that Locke's analyses were final. The merit of Book II lies in the new method of criticism which is suggested in its pages rather than in the completeness and exhaustiveness with which this method is applied.

[1] Cf. III. v. 16, x. 33, &c.   [2] II. xxviii. 17.

VI

THE NATURE AND USE OF WORDS, PARTICULARLY OF GENERAL WORDS

W E have followed Locke in his classification of ideas, a classification which, as we have seen, was never intended to be complete. It was meant to show primarily that all ideas terminate in simple ones, so that the empiricist position set forth at the opening of Book II might be consolidated.[1] This task once completed Locke's original plan was to proceed at once to the discussion of knowledge in general; 'but upon a nearer approach I find that there is so close a connexion between *ideas* and words, and our abstract *ideas* and general words have so constant a relation one to another that it is impossible to speak clearly and distinctly of our knowledge, which all consists in propositions, without considering, first, the nature, use, and signification of langauge.'[2] Accordingly, Locke changes his plans and adds a new book, the third, an examination of the nature of words and language.

Opinions are divided as to the value of Book III. Some assert openly that it is valueless; others ignore it almost completely; a

---

[1] At the end of Book II will be found four chapters which form a sort of appendix to that book and do not develop the main theme. The evidence of Draft C shows that they were late writings, cf. p. 73 above, and probably Locke wrote them after sketching Book IV. He then seems to have realized that he should have said something in Book II about a matter much emphasized at the time, namely, the clarity, distinctness, and adequacy of ideas. It is unnecessary to consider these chapters in any great detail. Their most noteworthy feature is that Locke tends to define these characteristics in terms of sense-perception. Simple ideas are clear 'when they are such as the objects themselves, from whence they were taken, did or might, in a well-ordered sensation or perception, present them'. Complex are clear 'when the *ideas* that go to their composition are clear' (II. xxix. 2). The distinct idea is 'that wherein the mind perceives a difference from all other' (II. xxix. 4). 'Adequate *ideas* are such as perfectly represent their archetypes' (II. xxxi. 1). In addition there are two chapters on real and fantastical, true and false ideas respectively. But, as Locke himself admits, we cannot rightly talk of a true *idea* but only of a true proposition. As might be expected, what is important in these chapters is repeated again in Book IV, and consideration of it need not now delay us.   [2] II. xxxiii. 19.

few praise it. Locke himself was aware of its defects, for he apologizes more than once for its verbosity; none the less he considered it a most important part of the whole. He worked at it diligently. 'Some parts of that third book concerning words,' he wrote to Molyneux,[1] 'though the thoughts were easy and clear enough, yet cost me more pains to express than all the rest of my essay.' He certainly thought the book worthy of attention. And in this belief he was surely justified. It would be foolish for us today to disparage one of the earliest efforts in the English language at a close analysis of words and their meanings.[2] Nor can we, when we recall how frequently the misuse of language leads us into error, condemn so serious an effort to remedy the imperfections and abuses of language. In both respects Book III is valuable even if it does little more than point the way. The study of language and of words was also directly helpful to Locke in his preparations for Book IV. Knowledge is expressed in propositions and propositions consist of words. We must then understand the nature of words if we would understand knowledge. Furthermore, as Locke meditated upon this problem, he came to realize that the question which he faced was one as to the character of general words. For, with the exception of the proper name in the strictest and purest sense, all words are general rather than particular in their application. Thus it comes about that the essential problem in attempting to understand words is the understanding of how we generalize. Locke touches on generalization and abstraction in Book II, but his fullest thoughts on this matter and his most mature are to be found in Book III. The latter, consequently, contains in addition to a theory of language an even more important theory of universals which involves also an examination of the nature of species and of essence. Now there is no more important distinction in the *Essay* than that between real and nominal essences. And whatever be said about the worth of the rest of Book III, it is certain that there is no understanding of Book IV without first understanding the distinction which Locke here makes. In this sense, at least, Book III is an indispensable propaedeutic for Book

---

[1] *Works*, iii. 527–8, 20 January 1693 (1801 ed., ix. 306).
[2] Cf., for instance, the analysis of the word *but* in III. vii. 5.

IV. The present chapter, accordingly, is concerned with two matters: first, Locke's theory of universals, and, secondly, his theory of language. I propose to deal with them in that order.

I

In dealing with Locke's theory of universals it is first necessary to show the falsity of one interpretation which is still prevalent. Many interpret Locke's theory entirely in terms of his statement about triangles in IV. vii. 9, a statement which comes as an aside when Locke is discussing a matter quite different from that of general ideas. Moreover, the interpretation put even upon this statement is, in my opinion, unfair and the theory of universals which emerges is an absurdity that ought not to be attributed to Locke.

In IV. vii of the *Essay* Locke attacks the view that at the base of all knowledge lie certain innate, self-evident, highly abstract 'maxims'. These we are supposed to know first; but their very generality, Locke thinks, is sufficient to overthrow this view. For nothing is clearer to Locke than that we begin with particulars and that general ideas come later. General ideas are not formed easily, they 'carry difficulty with them'. To illustrate the point he proceeds: 'For example, does it not require some pains and skill to form the general *Idea* of a Triangle (which is yet none of the most abstract, comprehensive and difficult) for it must be neither Oblique, nor Rectangle, neither Equilateral, Equicrural, nor Scalenon; but all and none of these at once. In effect, it is something imperfect, that cannot exist; an Idea wherein some parts of several different and inconsistent *Ideas* are put together.'[1] These words are commonly interpreted to mean that the general idea of a triangle is a complex idea containing within itself contradictory simple ideas, an idea, therefore, which is both absurd and impossible. And on the strength of this interpretation Locke's theory of general ideas as a whole is rejected.

Now, in the first place, it is obviously unfair to consider this

---

[1] The passage appears thus in the first edition of the *Essay*, IV. vii. 9, and is unchanged in the three other editions which appeared during Locke's life, except that the words 'general Idea of a Triangle' at the opening are italicized in the fourth.

passage alone and to neglect those others in which Locke explicitly expounds his theory of general ideas. But, secondly, even if we confine ourselves to this passage it is more natural to interpret the words Locke uses in another way. For he does *not* say that we put inconsistent ideas together, but 'some parts of them' (which parts may very well be consistent). And he surely does not mean that we ever have in mind an idea of a triangle which is at one and the same time, let us say, both right-angled and not right-angled. Why should we attribute so absurd a view to a great thinker? Surely all Locke wishes to say is that the general idea of triangle —whatever it be—stands for the oblique, the rectangle, the equilateral, the equicrural, and the scalenon triangles, without being any one of them in particular. Locke was anxious here to make the framing of general ideas appear as difficult as possible and the consequence is that the passage is particularly open to misinterpretation. Yet if we consider these words fairly and impartially, there is nothing in them to *necessitate* the usual interpretation. Another is quite possible which is less absurd, and more in accord with the theory of general ideas found elsewhere in Locke.

The chief responsibility for the misinterpretation must lie with the young enthusiast Berkeley. For reasons which we need not consider he was particularly anxious to reject Locke's theory of abstraction and of general ideas. But he appears to have found some difficulty in arguing against Locke, until he came across this chance passage in the chapter on maxims. Here he found what he required. Abstract ideas, he writes in the *Commonplace Book*, 'include a contradiction in their nature. v. Locke, lib. 4, § 9, c. 7'.[1] It will be seen that he has already interpreted the passage in what I hold to be the false way, and it is on this interpretation that he bases his criticism in the *Introduction* to his *Principles*. For, though it is not quoted until near the end,[2] the passage is in his mind from the start of his polemic and colours all his argument. This is made abundantly clear from a quaint jotting in the *Commonplace Book*:[3] 'Mem. To bring the killing blow at the last e.g. in the matter of abstraction to bring Locke's general triangle at the last.' And in order to help his reader to interpret Locke's

[1] *Works* (Luce and Jessop), i. 70. No. 561.   [2] § 13.   [3] *Works*, i. 84. No. 687.

theory in his own way Berkeley, in quoting the passage (both in the 1710 and 1734 editions), sets the words 'all and none' and 'inconsistent' in italics, though in none of the four editions of the *Essay* which appeared in Locke's lifetime are they italicized. Consequently, in the phrase 'an idea wherein some parts of several different and *inconsistent ideas* are put together', the hasty reader seizes the word 'inconsistent' and interprets the passage in Berkeley's manner. (If any words of the phrase need to be stressed, however, in view of centuries of misinterpretation they are the words 'some parts of'.) Berkeley attacked a theory of abstract ideas which, I believe, Locke never held; but he attacked it so vigorously and so brilliantly that Locke was much discredited, and a prejudice against abstraction was created, not only in England but throughout Europe. Recent writers have found it necessary to remind us that abstraction is valid, useful, and fruitful in its consequences, and have sought to dispel the prejudice against it. If we wish to find one, at least, of the sources of that prejudice we need only turn to the *Introduction* to Berkeley's *Principles*.

My point is that Berkeley attacks a theory of general ideas, which is certainly absurd, but not Locke's in any sense. In what follows I shall try to set forward a more acccurate account of Locke's theory. It is possible to distinguish at least three strands in Locke's argument, which he himself never explicitly distinguishes and never wholly disentangles. This fact accounts for the ambiguity of his theory, and makes it open to criticism from more sides than one. Sometimes, however, the critics in criticizing one strand are blind to the presence of others—while Berkeley criticizes a theory of abstraction not to be found, as I believe, in Locke.

The first interpretation is the one which Locke seems to have held before he devoted serious attention to the problem. A universal is a particular idea which 'represents' many other particulars.[1] In the *Essay* Locke is never wholly satisfied with this view and so it is not easy to find an explicit statement of it. But there are constant traces of it when he deals with general ideas. Perhaps the nearest approach to an explicit statement is found in Book II

[1] Cf. Draft C (pp. 64–65 above) and observe the changes between C and 1690.

of the *Essay* in the paragraph on abstraction. '*Ideas* taken from particular beings become general representatives of all of the same kind.'[1] But if the whole paragraph be read, it will be seen that it would hardly be correct to describe the theory of universals there set forth merely in these terms. The other strands I propose to mention are already present in the paragraph. Indeed, one finds a much more explicit statement of this first position in Berkeley. For instance, in the *Introduction* to his *Principles* he remarks: 'An idea, which considered in itself is particular, becomes general by being made to represent or stand for all other particular ideas of the same sort.'[2] That is a more precise expression of the position than anything to be found in Locke's *Essay*. But I take Locke's ambiguity in this connexion to be a sign of his dissatisfaction with the theory. It is his first crude thought on the subject and he never sufficiently outgrows it to deny it openly, so that it remains a permanent element in his account of universals although he is never wholly satisfied with it.

There was ample ground for Locke's dissatisfaction. To say that we make a particular stand for many particulars and so achieve a universal or general idea is no explanation of the universal as such. It is no explanation because it misses the crucial point entirely. It does not explain how we determine what particulars are represented by the one particular—admitting for the moment that the universal is a particular standing for many other particulars of the same sort. In other words, the account presupposes that we already know the 'sort' of which the particular ideas are instances. But it is just this knowledge that we need to explain, and no satisfactory account of the universal is given until this is explained. For the universal according to this view is not the mere particular idea as such, it is the particular idea in its 'representative' capacity. To content oneself, therefore, with the explanation that a universal is a particular idea standing for many of the same sort, even if this be so far true, is to miss the real problem connected with universals in its entirety. Again, in the second place, is it correct to argue that the universal is a particular idea which has this specific representative function of standing for all particulars

[1] II. xi. 9.   [2] § 12.

of the same sort? Berkeley, at one stage of his philosophical career, would have held that it must be correct, since any idea in the mind is a particular concrete image, given in sensation or recalled in memory, and therefore the general idea, if it exists, is of necessity some such particular image, though it stands for many other images. But for Locke 'idea' is not identified with the concrete image. His definition of 'idea' permits him to include the image within it, but it is also wider. It is 'the object of the understanding when a man thinks'. Consequently, there is nothing in the term as he used it to compel him to think of the universal as a particular image; and though he began, no doubt, by identifying the universal which stood for the many particulars with a particular image, or 'appearance', as he sometimes called it,[1] he also found it possible later to think of the universal in other terms without contradicting his definition of 'idea'. Thus his second position to which we now turn does not involve the view that the general idea is a particular image as such. At most, it is something abstracted from that particular image, though its real importance does not lie in the fact that it is an abstraction of this sort, but elsewhere.

The second and third strands are seen most clearly in Book III, when general terms are being discussed. A general term is the symbol in language for a general idea. Locke never does away with the idea, so that it is wholly incorrect to describe him as a nominalist. The fact that Locke teaches that we only know nominal essences of things has misled some to class him with nominalists, but this is a mistake. The view that the universal is the *name* which can be ascribed to more than one particular, and that the concept or general idea is unnecessary, is not to be found in the *Essay*. The general name stands for the general idea.[2]

The second strand consists in the view that the universal is the resultant of a certain process of elimination carried out according to the guidance of experience. We eliminate all qualities except

---

[1] Cf. ii. xi. 9, particularly the last sentence.

[2] Cf. the following emphatic statements: (1) First Reply to Stillingfleet (*Works*, i. 369; 1801 ed., iv. 25). 'For he must think very oddly, who takes the general name of any idea to be the general idea itself: it is a mere mark or sign of it, without doubt, and nothing else.' (2) Second Reply to Stillingfleet (*Works*, i. 574; 1801 ed., iv. 430–1). 'You again accuse the way of ideas, to make a common nature no more than a common name. That, my Lord, is not my way, by ideas.'

only those which are common. Thus the general term 'man' stands for what remains when we have eliminated every quality possessed by James or John or Peter or any other individual man but not by all men, every quality that is peculiar. The universal in this case is not a particular 'appearance' in its concreteness, chosen to stand for many; it is a particular 'appearance' from which many qualities have been abstracted. In other words, it is no longer the particular 'appearance' as such. It is an idea made by abstraction; but made wholly, it should be added, by omission. As Locke explains, in framing such universals, we 'make nothing new, but only leave out'.[1] 'Words become general by being made the signs of general *ideas*; and *ideas* become general by separating from them the circumstances of time, and place, and any other *ideas* that may determine them to this or that particular existence. By this way of abstraction they are made capable of representing more individuals than one; each of which, having in it a conformity to that abstract *idea*, is (as we call it) of that sort.'[2]

The second element in Locke's theory cuts deeper than the first. Even so, it fails to satisfy. For, in the first place, it does not make clear the precise character of what remains after the process of elimination has taken place; the universal, as such, is still left unconsidered. In the second place, as has often been pointed out, doubts must arise, on reflection, as to whether we can possibly discover the universal by means of an elimination on purely empirical lines and be certain that we have discovered it. For though all the instances of X observed by us heretofore possess a quality Y, the very next instance may lack it; and so, if we include Y in our universal X, we shall have acted wrongly. In other words, the empirical method would compel us to examine every instance of X before we could be sure that Y was common; and since we cannot possibly examine every instance subsumed under most of the general terms which we need to use, there will always be uncertainty as to whether we have discovered the true common qualities which frame our universal, or whether some impurities in the shape of qualities not shared by all may not have entered into it. In the third place, as against both the first and second strands in

[1] III. iii. 7.   [2] III. iii. 6.

Locke's thought, there is room for this further criticism. On the first account the universal is identified with a particular idea, an 'appearance', synonymous with Berkeley's 'idea' as meaning sensation or image; on the second, it is identified with what is still part of a particular idea. In both cases, therefore, the universal is a particular idea, either as whole or as part. And yet, surely, a universal is nothing of the sort. A universal is no 'idea' as equivalent to image or appearance, or picture, and no part of such an 'idea'.

But now there remains still a third strand in Locke's *Essay*, which marks yet a further effort on his part to find a satisfactory theory of universals. The universal, in this third sense, is neither a particular idea nor a part of a particular idea. It is a meaning. It is a character or group of characters shared by particulars of the same sort. This character (or these characters) frames (or frame) the 'essence' of the sort, although the 'essence' in question may not be the 'real essence' of a species, as we shall see. The universal, therefore, is the 'essence' of a sort or species, and in its light we recognize to what species any particular belongs. Locke never really faces the difficult question as to whether the characters in the various particulars are merely alike, or whether they are truly identical. He talks of the 'sort' as being based on 'the similitude of things',[1] but this should not be interpreted to mean that the 'common agreements' in particulars of the same sort are mere likenesses. What is meant is that it is their presence which finally makes the particular objects alike. His position, however, seems rather to involve the view that the *characters* are identical in the various particulars and not merely alike. It is one and the same character (or group of characters) in the various particulars that enables us to class them as members of a species. For this view, accordingly, the universal is not at all what is left over after the empirical process of eliminating the peculiar. It is the essence meant when the general term is used, an essence whose nature is wholly clear to us. In Spinoza's language, it is no *idea summo gradu confusa*, resulting from the imagination's failure to form a determinate and concrete image of, for instance, man, in its attempt to get one image that shall stand for many men.[2] It is no

---

[1] Cf. iii. iii. 13 and elsewhere.   [2] *Ethics*, ii. xl, schol. i.

composite, 'generic image' that cannot possibly portray all the particulars. It is an *idea adequata*, a concept whose meaning we understand precisely. This meaning is fixed. It is, as Locke explicitly points out, an essence 'ingenerable and incorruptible'. '*Essences* being taken for *ideas* established in the mind, with names annexed to them, they are supposed to remain steadily the same, whatever mutations the particular substances are liable to. For whatever becomes of *Alexander* and *Bucephalus*, the *ideas* to which *man* and *horse* are annexed are supposed nevertheless to remain the same, and so the *essences* of those species are preserved whole and undestroyed, whatever changes happen to any or all of the individuals of those *species*. By this means the *essence* of a *species* rests safe and entire, without the existence of so much as one individual of that kind.'[1] The universal is the essence, fixed and immutable, that without which true science would be impossible. For Locke (in this phase) the universal is an unchangeable, permanent, and eternal meaning.

Now at least these three strands—there may be more—are present in Locke's thought concerning universals. They are never wholly disentangled and there is no consistent theory of universals in the *Essay*. As one reads Book III and compares it with the drafts one cannot but feel that the theory is being developed in the very act of writing the book. In this sense the thought of Book III is fresh and alive to a marked degree. Perhaps, if he had delayed the *Essay*'s publication still further, he would have developed in time a perfectly consistent theory, possibly putting all the emphasis on the third strand. And yet one may seriously doubt whether this could ever have happened. In his three later editions of the *Essay* Locke does not change his theory of universals substantially. To the end he prefers to present it in a hesitant and ambiguous form. He comes nearest to the position most consistent with the third view of the universal in his account of mathematics, but even here there is room for doubting whether he adopted the extreme rationalist standpoint sometimes ascribed to him. For an element is present in his thoughts which constantly clashes with rationalism. This will become clear if we now bring forward certain

[1] III. iii. 19.

further considerations in connexion with his theory, particularly those having to do with the kind of existence and of objectivity that Locke's universals possess.

We may deal, first, with the universals of the natural sciences. There are, Locke assumes, real individual things or substances in nature. We have complex ideas of these which more or less accurately represent them. The complex ideas are made by us under the guidance of our experience and observation. 'Men, observing certain qualities always joined and existing together, therein copied nature.'[1] Having gained these complex ideas, we now notice that several of them are alike, that is, they share some qualities in common. And as a result of this further observation we select, of our own free will, certain qualities, and frame therewith an essence. Thus I find the qualities *abc* in *X*, in *Y*, in *Z*, and in many other complex ideas. I accordingly decide to form a class of all those ideas which possess the essential features *abc*. My universal or general idea possesses a fixed content, namely, *abc*, and whatever complex idea possesses *abc* is an instance of my universal.

Now this view of the way in which a universal is framed leads to certain novel consequences. In the first place the fixity of the universal is determined from within rather than from without. Whereas for the orthodox Aristotelian standpoint we apprehend *abc* to be essential features of real objects external to and independent of us, so that our universal depends entirely on the nature of the objects outside us and is *discovered* by us, for Locke the universal is 'a creature of our own making'. It is we who decide that *abc* together frame what *we* mean by the general term (which we may call *M*). So much is this so that Locke expressly (in the case of universals of the natural sciences) holds *abc* to be the 'nominal' rather than the 'real' essence.[2] The essence *abc* is what we decide the name *M* to mean. It is not the real constitution of certain things in nature. From the commencement Locke has held that we have access to physical objects only through sensation, and

<hr/>

[1] III. vi. 28.
[2] Cf. III. iii. 15–18, vi. 3, and elsewhere. Cf. the interesting discussions in the Stillingfleet controversy, *Works*, i. 398–403, 575–7. I have no space here to discuss the historical origins of this distinction between real and nominal essences, but it seems to be present implicitly in the works both of Gassendi and of Boyle.

sensation, he has also held consistently throughout, does not give us the inner constitution, the essence, of anything in nature. While, therefore, the occurrence of certain uniformities in our sensory experiences leads us to frame the conception of a 'sort' or species having a certain essence, and so enables us to provide ourselves with the type of fixed and permanent object indispensable for the gaining of knowledge and for the communication of thought, that sensory experience does not reveal to us the essence of real things in nature, so that we cannot argue to the necessary existence of any 'sort' in nature. Nature may have its 'sorts', and this seems likely in view of our experience, though the existence of monsters and changelings and 'border-cases' between the various species suggests that nature is not quite so regularly ordered as might at first appear.[1] But the fixed set of characters in things pertaining to their inner constitution, and composing their real essence, is not revealed to us; and Locke, accordingly, rejects the Aristotelian view of the universal.[2]

In other words, Locke could not subscribe to the opinion that to know the universal in natural science is to know a natural species existing externally; for he could not identify the universal which we conceive with anything in the world of nature. But neither did he find it possible to adopt the other, more Platonic, view that the universal is 'a form or mould' never wholly embodied in any thing in nature (though natural things may more or less conform to it) but remaining apart in a pure ideal world of its own. This view Locke explicitly rejects.[3] If we do not know the real essence of things, we certainly do not know such ideal patterns or forms. Now both these interpretations of the universal are defective in Locke's opinion because they give the universal a kind of objectivity which, if his view of the universal is sound, it cannot possibly possess. If the term *objectivity* connotes fixity and permanency in meaning, then Locke has room for such objectivity—

---

[1] Cf. iv. iv. 14, and elsewhere. Cf. also Molyneux Correspondence, *Works*, iii. 523, 527.

[2] Ordinarily Locke talks as if knowledge of the real essence of a thing would be wholly adequate knowledge of that thing, but we should note the curious relativism of iv. vi. 11–12.

[3] Cf. iii. iii. 17; vi. 10, 24, &c.

at least when the third strand of his theory is uppermost in his mind. But in dealing with universals, he never has room for objectivity in the further sense, as meaning what is not created by the mind but is merely apprehended and discovered, and pertains to a world of realities wholly independent of the mind. The universal cannot possess such objectivity, because, in Locke's view, it is I myself who frame the universal. It is I who select *abc* and refuse to include *d* in my universal *M*. This was proved conclusively for Locke by the fact that the term *M* may mean something different to you from what it means to me. Your experiences may have been different from mine and they may have led you to include *d* with *abc* in framing the universal. What *M* signifies is as fixed for you as it is for me. In that sense it is a permanent, 'objective' (i.e. fixed) meaning. But we do not mean the same essence by it, and you would refuse to subsume certain complex ideas under *M* even though they possessed *abc*, because they did not also possess *d*, which, of course, I should never do. Thus the universal for Locke is neither the real essence of the Aristotelians as forming 'the very being of anything whereby it is what it is',[1] and as shared by all things of the same sort or pertaining to the same species, nor again is it the 'ideal' object of those who adhere to the doctrine of moulds or patterns. For Locke the universal is simply what we decide the term *M* to mean, using experience as a guide.

While, therefore, the *universals of natural philosophy* are objective, in Locke's opinion, as permanent, fixed identities, whatever variations may occur in experience, they do not exist 'without the mind', neither in the world of nature nor in an intellectual world of 'substantial forms' independent of the mind. In other words, they are not apprehended as independent existences. They are framed by the mind. The sensory experience does not *give* them: intellect does not apprehend them. At the same time they rest upon experience; they are framed by abstraction from the *given* of experience, and according to the relations and similitudes observed in the *given*. But they are none the less 'creatures of our understanding'. In one sense of the term they are objective, but

[1] III. iii. 15.

their objectivity is not the sort that rules out mind-dependency. And in the light of this we may understand why Locke hesitates to set forward his theory of universals wholly in terms of its third strand. He cannot admit that we ever apprehend an objective, independent universal, for a universal is a creation existing only 'within the mind', that is, within the individual mind of the person who frames it, and it has no further objectivity than that it is fixed and permanent in meaning. It is no mere image, but yet its source is one with the image. As the mind frames its images, so also does it frame its universals.

If we now turn from the realm of natural science to that of mathematics we find that here again the universal is what we decide it should be. Again we select the qualities, for instance, *abc*, and mean by *M* whatever possesses *abc*. But in the case of mathematical objects Locke notices a still greater freedom and arbitrariness in our choice. Whereas, when dealing with substances, we have always to keep one eye, as it were, on the experience given, we may in the mathematical realm, once we have gained our fundamental conceptions, close our eyes on experience and proceed merely according to the demand made upon us by a certain inner necessity of consistency in thought. From the point of view of following experience, therefore, we now proceed still more arbitrarily than before. Here 'the mind takes a liberty not to follow the existence of things exactly. It unites and retains certain collections as so many distinct specific *ideas*, whilst others, that as often occur in nature and are as plainly suggested by outward things, pass neglected without particular names or specifications.'[1] Thus we are still freer with regard to these ideas than with universals of substances. We need no longer try to think what the real actually is; we may forget it entirely and proceed to inspect our general ideas, intuiting relations between them and putting them out in such an order that the intuitions are more easily made. The universal here, the object of the mathematician, is certainly no actual thing in nature. Figures in the real world may help, but he is not dealing with them. He deals with abstract ideas. His object is not a real entity in the sense in which this table is a real entity.

[1] III. v. 3.

But neither is it for Locke some sort of intellectual entity independent of the mind. It is the mind's own creation as all other abstract ideas are. In a sense it is more completely 'in the mind' than is the abstract idea of a species of things, for it is not intended to represent anything beyond itself; it is its own archetype. Thus it cannot possibly be objective as being independent of the mind. Mathematical objects are not, for Locke, entities existing in an intellectual world of their own, and discovered there by the mind. It is true that they are not completely independent of experience—for the fundamental conceptions of space and number rest, in his opinion, on experience. Yet the mathematical object itself is an abstraction and a universal which is the mind's own creation. It is objective, like all other universals, but not as being mind-independent, but as being a meaning fixed by definition.

Thus we are able to conclude that Locke's theory of universals never involves that type of rationalism for which there exists a pure intellectual world with its own objects, objects that are independent of the mind and discovered (or not discovered) by it. This sort of rationalism is foreign to Locke, for the only reality that he recognizes is the reality revealed, so far as it is revealed at all, through experience. In other words, his theory is consonant with his empiricism. None the less, it must also be admitted that it is never clearly thought out, and that there are elements in it which might, by others, be developed in non-empiricist ways. His vagueness makes it at least easier for him to maintain his empiricist standpoint.

II

We have now to consider (a) Locke's theory of language, including his account of definition, (b) his examination of the imperfections and abuses in the use of language, and his suggestions for remedying these where remedy is possible.[1]

[1] Others in seventeenth-century England had concerned themselves with the philosophy of language, particularly Burthogge, *Organum Vetus et Novum* (1678), and John Wilkins, *Essay towards a Real Character and a Philosophical Language* (1668). I thank Mr. J .W. Yolton for these references. It is interesting that Wilkins uses the word 'particles' in the same way as Locke does. On Wilkins's use of the term cf. J. Cohen, 'On the Project of a Universal Character', *Mind*, 249 (January 1954), p. 58.

Man, Locke holds, is by nature a social being, and the first purpose of language is a social one. It facilitates communication of
thought. 'God having designed man for a sociable creature, made
him not only with an inclination and under a necessity to have
fellowship with those of his own kind, but furnished him also with
language, which was to be the great instrument and common tie
of society.'[1] Now Locke recognizes another possible use of language, namely, in the recording of our thoughts for our private
use. In this case, as Locke points out, we may choose whatever
word or whatever sign pleases us best.[2] The mathematician, for
instance, in his calculations, may choose any language and any
system of signs. As long as they are intelligible to him no one
else needs to be consulted. But if he wishes to communicate his
thoughts he must make his language intelligible to others as well.
In actual practice, both in mathematics and in daily intercourse,
he uses a language long since agreed upon, which he has learnt
rather than made. In conversation, for instance, he accepts and
uses the language of the society around him, and he must speak it
if he is to be understood.[3]

All languages are, however, conventional. The fact that they
may be handed down from generation to generation makes no
difference in this respect. They are all arbitrary in this sense, that
there is no natural connexion between the sign and that which it
signifies. The word, for instance, does not resemble what it signifies. It is simply accepted as the sign arbitrarily chosen by 'a voluntary imposition'. In support of this important principle Locke
only brings forward one argument. Were there a natural connexion between words and what they signify 'then there would be
but one language amongst all men'.[4] The fact that languages are
many proves their arbitrary character. Unfortunately, Locke does
not here examine those words which are obviously onomatopoeic,

---

[1] III. i. I.   [2] III. ix. 2.
[3] Locke does not include here a third use of language, the expressing of
emotion. But that such a use is possible is implicit in much that he says. No
more explicit statement of the emotive use of language can be found than in
Berkeley's *Introduction* to his *Principles* (§ 20), which shows the influence of
Locke. The fact that Locke deals with individual words and ideas rather than
with sentences and propositions limits his discussion considerably.
[4] III. ii. I.

nor again words derived from an onomatopoeic source (as Leibniz did in discussing this passage). Indeed, he makes no attempt to examine the historical origins of language, though this would have been in accordance with his own expressed method of procedure. It is true that etymology was in its infancy at the time, but Locke does not make use even of the limited information then available.

A word is an arbitrarily chosen, conventional sign. Words are not the only signs—certainly spoken words, which Locke seems here to have most in mind, are not.[1] There are also mathematical signs, pictures, gestures, and so forth. Locke does not attempt to make a complete inventory of the kinds of signs in use. But he does face the more important question: What does the sign signify? To this question he puts forward an answer which he knew to be unusual, but to which none the less he consistently adheres. The word *table* is usually thought to be the sign of the physical object. Words it is usually supposed signify things, at least some words do. This Locke categorically denies. The word, he thinks, signifies the idea. It is true that the idea has frequently a reference to something beyond itself, and in this way, no doubt, the word may signify a thing, but directly it signifies the idea. Moreover, *my* word signifies directly *my* idea and my idea only. Here again we usually think of the word which I now use in conversation as signifying the idea in the mind of another person as well as that in my own mind. But to do so is to invite confusion. 'Words in their primary or immediate signification stand for nothing but

---

[1] The *Essay* does not perhaps sufficiently distinguish between spoken and written words. But Locke is quite explicit that words (being signs) are part of the study of philosophy. In iv. xxi σημειωτική is said to be that part of philosophy which is logic. With Gassendi and in accordance with the traditional division Locke divided knowledge into three parts: logic, physics, and ethics. Logic is the study of ideas (as they are signs for things) and of words (as they are signs for ideas). The use of the word σημειωτική by Locke in this connexion is strange. According to the new Liddell and Scott the word is a medical term meaning a diagnosis, an examination of symptoms. Did Locke come across it in his medical studies and convert it to his own uses? Or again is it linked with the Epicurean doctrine of *signification* and the Epicurean criticism of the Stoic logic? Did the Gassendists use it as a term for logic? I cannot find it used in the works of Gassendi. (On the Epicurean theory of signification, cf. J. L. Stocks, 'Epicurean Induction', *Mind*, April 1925, republished in *The Limits of Purpose* (1932), pp. 262 ff. Cf. further L. J. Russell's note in *Mind*, July 1939, pp. 405–6, who links it with musical notation. Also P. Romanell, 'Locke and Sydenham', *Bulletin History of Medicine*, July 1958.)

the *ideas* in the mind of him that uses them.'[1] Locke stresses this point in order to bring out another which he regards as most important. The word I use is clear in so far as *my* idea is clear. We may illustrate the point by referring to the word *table*. The table itself as a physical object is what it is. It has its own positive character. But I cannot, therefore, assume that the meaning of the word *table* is altogether clear to me when I use it. For the word's clarity depends not on the thing but on the idea. Likewise the idea may be wholly clear in another's mind and not clear in my mind. My word is as clear as my idea but never clearer. We must not, therefore, be misled by this 'secret reference' to things and to other men's ideas. Of course, Locke adds, it is also true that we may and do use words without any signification whatsoever, that is to say, without having in mind any idea which the word signifies. We can learn sounds parrot-wise and repeat them. In that case, however, we are not using language significantly. Words may be names of simple ideas, of simple modes, of mixed modes and relations (here significantly grouped together), and of substances respectively. The main distinction as between these is set forward explicitly enough by Locke himself in III. iv. 17. Names 'of mixed modes stand for *ideas* perfectly arbitrary: those of substances are not perfectly so, but refer to a pattern, though with some latitude: and those of simple *ideas* are perfectly taken from the existence of things'. That is to say, words vary according as their ideas do. Mixed modes refer to nothing beyond themselves and the names of mixed modes, therefore, signify the ideas solely. But ideas of substances and simple ideas refer to things and qualities of things and so their names, though they also refer directly to the ideas only, refer indirectly to things and qualities, and they are as correct as the ideas are correct representations. Now in the case of substances we know that our ideas are at best nominal essences only and cannot represent adequately the real essence. Thus the name *table* as used by me never adequately signifies the thing table, but it does adequately signify my idea of table, namely, its nominal essence, which is framed as far as possible in accordance with nature, but not entirely so, since we do not know

[1] III. ii. 2.

real essences. Locke's theory in this respect is open to criticism. For if the word *table* has any reference whatever to something beyond the idea, so also has the word *justice* or *beauty*. But this concerns the general distinction which Locke makes between ideas of mixed modes and ideas of substances rather than the words which signify such ideas. Of the names of simple modes Locke has little to say.[1]

Locke remarks further that some words do not stand for, or refer to, any idea but rather signify the mind's own activity or operation in grouping ideas or propositions together. 'Besides words, which are names of ideas in the mind, there are a great many others that are made use of to signify the connection that the mind gives to ideas or propositions one with another.'[2] Such words are 'is' and 'not' and 'particles' such as 'and', 'but', 'therefore', 'of'. These are not words that can be used to refer to ideas and through them to things as can common nouns. They signify rather linguistic and logical operations. 'To think well, it is not enough that a man has ideas clear and distinct in his thoughts, nor that he observes the agreement or disagreement of some of them; but he must think in train and observe the dependence of his thoughts and reasonings one upon another; and to express well such methodical and rational thoughts, he must have words to show what connection, restriction, distinctness, opposition, emphasis, etc. he gives to each respective part of his discourse.'[3] Locke has in mind here an important difference between words that are used to refer to things and words that signify connexions in the thinking, operational or logical words as they have sometimes been called. This distinction, he thinks, has scarcely been noticed, though such words are greatly in need of attention. As an illustration he analyses the use of the word 'but'. Had he proceeded with these analyses he might have come across much of great philosophical and logical interest, but he excuses himself. 'I intend not here a full explication of this sort of signs.'[4]

A noteworthy feature of the discussion of the names of simple ideas is the account of *definition* contained in it. Here Locke frees himself from the traditional standpoint and prepares the way for

---

[1] But cf. iii. ix. 19.   [2] iii. vii. 1.   [3] iii. vii. 2.   [4] iii. vii. 6.

a new view of definition which is only being made explicit in our own day. The importance and value of Locke's contribution to the theory of definition have not been sufficiently realized. To all intents and purposes he rejects the traditional theory and sets in its place a theory of his own, having a more general and comprehensive basis. It will be recalled that according to the traditional account definition is by genus and differentia. These two together make up the essence, so that definition and essence are synonymous terms. Apart from the essence there are also the properties and the accidental qualities. The properties are those qualities peculiar to the subject but yet not its essence, the accidents are those others which happen to belong to it in this case, although the subject can without contradiction be imagined as lacking such qualities. Now it will be seen that the distinction between essence and property is made with difficulty. In effect, it is only possible when certain metaphysical assumptions are made. The chief assumption is that natural substances form real species; that the universe of nature consists of so many real species each differing from the other absolutely. Instances of such species are man, horse, buttercup, and so on. If this be granted, it is then possible to distinguish between essence and property, for the essence is the fixed central core, as it were, which the species *is*. The essence of any species may be set out in terms of a genus (under which the species is subsumed) and a differentia (that which makes this species different from the other species subsumed under the same genus). A man is an animal, but he is a rational animal. Therefore, his essence is rational animal and that also is his definition. (A property would be his ability to learn grammar.) To define is to state the genus and differentia which is also to discover the essence, the real being of the fixed natural type or species under consideration.

Now Locke's view of definition is fundamentally different from the foregoing, for he will not admit that definition and real essence are one and the same. To begin with it will be recalled that Locke doubts the existence of fixed types. He believes that some division corresponding loosely to the specific divisions we have in mind is actually to be found in nature, and that we are guided by nature in framing our species. But he doubts whether there is anything in nature corresponding precisely to the absolute division which we set up in thought between the species. On the contrary, the existence of monsters, changelings, and the like 'border-cases', suggests that nature may not be ordered into such fixed types. But even if it is, Locke would still hold that definition cannot be identical with real essence in every case for the simple reason that the real essence, according to him, cannot be known in every case. It cannot be known, for instance, in the case we have here in mind, namely, the case of natural substances. We do not know the real essence of things. How then can we ever define it if definition means stating its real essence? And yet, of course, definition is possible and does take place, so that definition is not necessarily the statement of the real essence.

What, then, is Locke's own view of definition? In the first place he makes it perfectly clear that definition is of words. To define is 'to show the meaning of one word by several other not synonymous terms'; it is 'to declare the signification of a word'. To show the meaning or declare the signification of a word is, however, merely to state what idea the word signifies. Or, as Locke himself puts it: 'The meaning of words, being only the *ideas* they are made to stand for by him that uses them, the meaning of any term is then showed, or the word is defined, when by other words the *idea* it is made a sign of and annexed to in the mind of the speaker is, as it were, represented or set before the view of another; and thus its signification ascertained. This is the only use and end of definitions.'[1] It follows from this that one never defines a substantial thing or natural object. At most one states what idea is meant by a word, and in the case of natural objects the word stands for the general idea, that is, the nominal essence which is not identical with the real essence. Thus definition and real essence are not synonymous. Again, it also follows that definition *per genus et differentiam* is one sort of defining, but not the only sort. Any form of words whose meaning is exactly equivalent to the meaning of another word can be held to be a definition of that word. Now it may very well be the case—and Locke does not

[1] III. iv. 6.

doubt that it frequently is so—that the most commodious way of defining is *per genus et differentiam*. But we are not bound to define in this way. As Locke remarks: 'This may show us the reason *why, in the defining of words*, which is nothing but declaring their signification, *we make use of the genus*, or next general word that comprehends it. Which is not out of necessity, but only to save the labour of enumerating the several simple *ideas* which the next general word or *genus* stands for; or, perhaps, sometimes the shame of not being able to do it. But though defining by *genus* and *differentia* . . . be the shortest way, yet, I think, it may be doubted whether it be the best. This I am sure, it is not the only, and so not absolutely necessary. For definition being nothing but making another understand by words what *idea* the term defined stands for, a definition is best made by enumerating those simple *ideas* that are combined in the signification of the term defined: and if instead of such an enumeration men have accustomed themselves to use the next general term, it has not been out of necessity or for greater clearness, but for quickness and despatch sake.'[1] To say that man is 'a solid, extended substance, having life, sense, spontaneous motion, and the faculty of reasoning' is to say at least as much as that man is 'a rational animal', which is the traditional definition *per genus et differentiam*.

The latter is one sort of defining, not because it states the real essence, for that it does not do in the case of natural substances, but because the genus and differentia put together mean what the word means. But it is only one sort of defining, and many other sorts are possible. In this way Locke arrives at a far more general conception of definition than that prevailing traditionally.

It follows from Locke's view that not all words are definable, and Locke explains why this must be so. (He claims that the point has not been explained by any one before him.)[2] If in defining one is merely enumerating the simple ideas contained in the complex idea, the name of which is being defined, then the name of a simple idea itself cannot be defined. 'The names of simple *ideas* are not capable of any definitions; the names of all complex *ideas* are.'[3] And this because the simple idea cannot be further

[1] III. iii. 10.   [2] III. iv. 4.   [3] III. iv. 4.

analysed into parts. Thus, if the idea is in no sense compounded its name cannot be defined. We are able to define only because we begin with certain indefinables already given; these cannot themselves be defined because, in Locke's opinion, they are simple in the sense of being indivisible.[1]

Having now considered Locke's general theory of language we may turn to the highly interesting chapters which close Book III, wherein Locke attempts to show what imperfections in the use of language are almost inevitable, what abuses creep in because of the folly and carelessness of men, and, lastly, what remedies are possible.

Language, as we have seen, may be used for the private recording of one's own thoughts, in which case the individual is entirely free in the choice of his language symbols, the sole requisite being consistency in their use; and again for communicating them to another, where agreement as to symbols is necessary in addition to consistency. We communicate our thoughts in conversation, a communication which Locke calls 'civil' communication, or again in the statement of scientific fact, 'philosophical' communication. The latter demands the greater exactitude. To secure complete precision we should need to know (a) that the word signifies precisely the same idea whenever it is used, (b) that it signifies precisely the same idea to the speaker on the one side, and to the hearer or hearers on the other. This is the ideal which, for reasons which Locke now explains, is hardly ever attained. Locke suggests four reasons: (1) Where the idea symbolized by the word is very complex it is easy for the hearer to omit a part of its content which the speaker includes, or to include something which the speaker omits, and so they would not be using the word in the

---

[1] One finds an interesting corollary to the above in III. iv. 16. Since simple ideas are indivisible, and supposing that the general idea is made by the elimination of elements which are not common to the species brought under the genus, it ought to follow that no simple idea can be a species of a genus, for it has no elements. Yet we do talk of red, blue, pink as species of the genus colour. Locke has to explain this in a circuitous and novel way: 'Therefore when, to avoid unpleasant enumerations, man would comprehend both *white* and *red*, and several other such simple *ideas*, under one general name; they have been fain to do it by a word which denotes only the way they get into the mind.' Thus the common element, in this case, is extrinsic to the simple idea as such.

same way and would not be able to communicate their thoughts properly to each other. (2) The idea may have 'no certain connexion in nature' and, therefore, no 'settled standard' by which the hearer can test his idea to see if it is in conformity with the speaker's. For after all, in Locke's opinion, the complex idea of table, though framed by us, is not framed by us arbitrarily, and the external influences causing us to frame the idea in the way we do are, Locke assumes, alike for both speaker and hearer. But this, Locke thinks, is not true of certain other ideas, particularly of mixed modes, for instance, *grace, perspicuity, beauty*, and the like, which are created by us in a more arbitrary fashion and point to nothing concrete outside them. Accordingly, it is in connexion with ideas of mixed modes that confusion arises most easily as the result of the above two reasons. Some of these are very complex ideas, and there is no standard beyond them by which to test them. (3) The idea may refer to a standard, but the standard may be difficult to know. (4) The idea may be identical with the nominal and not with the real essence. It is these two points which help to explain errors of communication in connexion with the signification of names of substances. If the speaker means by the word *gold* merely the nominal essence which he himself has framed—and he cannot mean more on Locke's theory —what he means must be entirely clear to the hearer if he is to communicate his thoughts with exactitude. Very frequently, however, this is not the case. Of course, in 'civil' communication such exactness is not necessary and language, as it is, is well fitted for the purposes of everyday conversation. But in the communication of scientific information, where precision and exactness are indispensable, these defects in the use of language become very serious. In the communication of scientific facts the use of words signifying the ideas both of substances and mixed modes (including also relations) needs to be most carefully examined. The difficulty is not so acute in the case of names of simple ideas or again of simple modes. Indeed, of all names those of simple ideas are most free from the foregoing imperfections. For what they signify is simple and they refer immediately to a perception. Thus the word *blue* is immediately understood in its full significance by any one who has seen blue and who knows that the word refers to that colour. (The issue, however, is not so straightforward as Locke makes out. Is my sensation of blue exactly the same as yours? Moreover, the word *blue* needs to be more precisely defined if it is to stand for the simple idea in its bare simplicity, for instance, this blue here now.) The names of simple modes also are usually unambiguous, for the meaning of *seven* and *triangle*, for instance, is perfectly clear. These ideas are, of course, created by us, but they are carefully defined and are clear and distinct. In their case, Locke thinks, so long as we stand by the definition, there is little likelihood of mistakes. It might be objected that in the same way the names of mixed modes might be made clear and distinct by careful definition. Locke does not deny this. His point is that precise definition of them is not so easy as is the case with mathematical terms.

Certain imperfections, then, in the use of words, particularly those which signify ideas of mixed modes and substances, are almost inevitable. But there are other imperfections in the use of language which might easily have been avoided and are due to men's 'wilful faults and neglect'. Locke sets forward seven such imperfections: (1) We use words when we have no ideas corresponding to them, or, again, no clear ideas. We may learn to repeat sounds parrot-wise. (2) We use words 'inconstantly', making the same word stand now for one collection of simple ideas and now for another. (3) We affect a jargon. We make ourselves purposely obscure, in order to give our words an appearance of subtlety or, perhaps, to veil the ambiguities which our thoughts contain. Locke does not mince his words in attacking this abuse which he finds all too prevalent in the works of logicians, scientists, and lawyers. (4) We 'take words for things', that is to say, we fall into supposing that if there is a word there must be a thing (not merely an idea) corresponding to it. 'Who is there that has been bred up in the peripatetic philosophy . . . that is not persuaded that *substantial forms, vegetative souls, abhorrence of a vacuum, intentional species*, etc. are something real?'[1] Again, we tend to suppose that there is something real corresponding to the word *matter* as

---

[1] III. X. 14.

opposed to body and distinct from it.[1] (5) We make words stand
for things they cannot possibly signify, as, for instance, when we
make the word *gold* stand for the real essence. (6) We use words,
whose meaning is clear to us, without making their meaning clear
to others. (7) We use figurative speech. In conversation, or in
poetry, this is a venial fault, since it increases pleasure and delight.
But in the pursuit of 'dry truth and real knowledge' the use of
figurative speech is dangerous. Herein lie the chief defect and
error of eloquence and rhetoric, as Locke makes clear, although
he adds characteristically enough: 'I doubt not but it will be
thought great boldness, if not brutality in me, to have said thus
much against it. *Eloquence*, like the fair sex, has too prevailing
beauties in it to suffer itself ever to be spoken against. And 'tis in
vain to find fault with those arts of deceiving wherein men find
pleasure to be deceived.'[2]

Such being the defects of language, both those natural to it and
those for which the wilful folly and carelessness of men are responsible, Locke in a final chapter considers possible remedies. He
suggests: (1) That care should be taken to use no word 'without a
signification'. In using a word one should know what idea it signifies. (2) That this idea should be known precisely and distinctly.
If the word signifies a simple idea this latter should be clear; if a
complex idea it should be 'determinate', that is, we should know
what simple ideas it contains and each of these should be clear.
If the complex idea is one of substance it should also be 'conformable to things as they exist'.[3] (3) That we should respect the conventions in the use of language, and, whenever possible, use words
in strict conformity with the common usage. (4) That if we deviate
from the common usage we should show in what way we do so. So
also, where there is some doubt about the appropriate use of a
word we should make its use plain. In the case of names of simple
ideas this can be done by pointing to an instance, in that of mixed
modes by defining, while, finally, in that of substances we need to
combine both methods. (5) Thus, as far as possible, we should 'use
the same word constantly in the same sense'.[4] Unfortunately, we

---

[1] III. x. 15. Locke here foreshadows an important point in Berkeley's argument.
[2] III. x. 34.   [3] III. xi. 10.   [4] III. xi. 26.

are frequently forced to use the same word in slightly different senses, but as far as possible it is well not to vary the signification of any one word if we would avoid ambiguity. If we observe these rules of procedure, Locke thinks we may avoid many of the pitfalls in the use of language into which we too readily fall.

VII

KNOWLEDGE AND PROBABILITY

AFTER the long and laborious work of preparation in the first three books of the *Essay* Locke now finds himself at the opening of Book IV free to face the main problem, namely, the determination of the nature and extent of human knowledge, 'together with the grounds and degrees of belief, opinion, and assent'. I propose in this chapter to consider Locke's theory of knowledge, dealing, first, with the nature of knowledge as such; secondly, with its limitations; thirdly, with existential knowledge; and, lastly, with probability and error.

I

Locke's most explicit teaching on the nature of knowledge is to be found in the opening chapters of Book IV. Now it is a highly interesting point that these chapters have no counterpart in the Drafts of 1671 and were not, apparently, part of the original scheme. They are the product of Locke's reflections between 1671 and 1690. Locke, at first, seems to have taken knowledge itself for granted and merely inquired into its limitations. Gradually, however, he came to see that these could not be properly determined until a precise description of knowledge had been given. This accurate description of knowledge was no doubt one of the problems which concerned him during his stay in France and it was there that he found the solution he needed. He had been vaguely assuming the traditional position, that the mind possesses the power of distinguishing truth from falsehood, is an *intellectus agens* able to know. But on the Continent in Cartesian circles he found a more explicit form of this same doctrine, set out in the language of his day. It was the intuitionism of Descartes, made most explicit in his *Regulae ad Directionem Ingenii*. This work was not published until 1701, but copies of it circulated amongst the Cartesians long before this. There is no evidence to show that Locke had actually seen a copy of the *Regulae*, though this is not at all impossible. But whether he was directly acquainted with it or not, he had certainly learnt its contents fully from the Cartesians, and had made the theory set forth in its pages his own. The resemblance between IV. ii of the *Essay* and some sections of the *Regulae* is remarkable.

For the source of IV. ii, then, it is not necessary to look further than to Descartes's *Regulae*. Locke's intuitionism on the subjective side is identical with that of Descartes. With him Locke holds that the best instance of knowing is intuiting and that non-intuitive knowledge, for instance, demonstration or indirect knowing, in so far as it is certain, contains also of necessity an intuitive element. By *intuition* is meant here a power which the mind possesses of apprehending truth. Though itself non-sensory, this power is analogous in many ways to seeing. It is direct and immediate. 'In this the mind is at no pains of proving or examining, but perceives the truth, as the eye doth light, only by being directed towards it.'[1] Intuition is the mind's immediate insight into the truth. Furthermore, it is infallible. Just as I cannot doubt that I now see brown, so my intuition is 'irresistible' and 'leaves no room for hesitation, doubt, or examination'. 'This kind of knowledge is the clearest and most certain that human frailty is capable of. . . . Certainty depends so wholly on this intuition that in the next degree of *knowledge*, which I call *demonstrative*, this intuition is necessary in all the connexions of the intermediate *ideas*, without which we cannot attain knowledge and certainty.'[2]

Here is as explicit a statement of intuitionism in the theory of knowledge as is to be found anywhere. The mind has the power to know truth with absolute certainty. This thesis Locke set in the forefront of his theory. To put anything else there, he would urge, would be entirely to misrepresent the nature of knowing. For instance, he resolutely opposes the view that in any account of human knowledge the chief stress should be put on syllogism or again on argument from 'maxims', *ex praecognitis et praeconcessis*. These are, of course, genuine methods of procedure and Locke does not deny their worth, although he thinks that logicians in the past and the school logicians in his own day had put

[1] IV. ii. I.   [2] Ibid.

too great a value upon them. He does, of course, hold that it is a very grave fault in logicians to seek to confine the knowing mind to the use of these methods and of these methods alone. Any method which helps the mind in its effort to know is valid, any method which succeeds in freeing our intuitive powers and enables them to function is of equal value with syllogism and argument from 'maxims'. Nevertheless, none of these methods deserves the central place in our account of knowledge. That place must be reserved for the intuition itself. And, accordingly, in the opening chapters of Book IV Locke gives chief attention to intuition.

One fundamental difficulty, however, faces any theorist who adopts the position Locke is now adopting. Intuition (or perception, for Locke uses the two terms synonymously) carries with it conviction. We know that we know. 'For what a man sees, he cannot but see; and what he perceives, he cannot but know that he perceives.'[1] But a difficulty arises when we recall the fact of error in human experience. For men also feel convinced when they err. As Locke himself points out in discussing the claims of 'enthusiasts' to indubitable knowledge: 'The strength of our persuasions is no evidence at all of their own rectitude: crooked things may be as stiff and unflexible as straight; and men may be as positive and peremptory in error as in truth.'[2] But in that case what guarantee have we of our conviction in intuition? Locke sometimes plays with the idea that the guarantee lies in the object. It is self-evident. But he is speedily driven from this position; for after all what we mean by a self-evident object is an object about whose truth we feel convinced, and it is this conviction which guarantees. Locke falls back on the only possible view, namely, that the conviction of intuition is unique in being wholly trustworthy. Although we fail frequently, and although we are constantly reminded of our fallibility, none the less there are occasions when doubt is entirely out of the question. Over and over again, in the controversy with Stillingfleet, Locke insists that there is no appeal to anything beyond intuition. Stillingfleet wishes to fall back on syllogism, on argument from known and indubitable principles, on reason. Locke replies that, in so far as these give us knowledge, that know-

---

[1] IV. xiii. 2.   [2] IV. xix. 11.

ledge is intuitive. Reason itself, as meaning the act of knowing, *is* intuition;[1] and the cognitive core of reasoning as inferring is also intuition. We cannot, therefore, appeal from intuition to reason. We must either grant that the intuitive faculty is, indeed, infallible, or be for ever sceptical of all knowledge. Locke himself puts his trust in intuition.

A word should be added about demonstration. Having shown that the knowing present in demonstration is itself intuitive, it is necessary to ask what differentiates it from intuition. Demonstration, also, may give absolute certainty. But it is not always so reliable as intuition. The intuition in it is, of course, completely certain. But there is more in demonstration than merely intuition. The additional factor which Locke finds present (again following Descartes) is memory. Intuition is a flash of illumination; demonstration is a process involving 'pains and attention' and frequently 'a long train of proof'. And in this long process memory is essential in order that the mind can recall the steps which enable it to pass to the desired conclusion. Now, where intuition is infallible, memory is notoriously fallible. Consequently, demonstration is not as reliable as intuition. So long as we remember the series of steps properly there can be no doubt about our conclusion. But our memories are frequently defective and so we err. Locke seems to trace every error in reasoning to a defect of memory. It is necessary to add that as an account of reasoning in general IV. ii is very inadequate. The importance of system, for instance, in reasoning and of logical relations within the system is here entirely neglected. Locke, however, in this chapter offers no final analysis of reasoning. What he really desires to show is that throughout demonstration an intuitive element is present, and he is content to make this one point clear.

The ideal of knowledge, then, has been shown to be intuition. And before we proceed to discover the extent of knowledge (in this strict sense) of which human beings are capable, we must first refer to the objective side of the knowing experience in order particularly to meet a difficulty of which the reader must by this time be conscious, namely, that of the relations between Locke's intuition-

[1] Locke himself avoids speaking of intuition as reason; reason for him is reasoning and is different from intuition and sense-perception. Cf. IV. xvii. 2.

ism and his empiricism. Is Locke inconsistent? Has he thrown his empiricism overboard and become a Cartesian rationalist? I do not think so. For while Locke's teaching is identical with Descartes's as to the subjective side of the experience, it is not so with regard to the objective. Here he is, I believe, in conscious opposition to Descartes. For Descartes the object of intuition is a pure non-sensuous object; for Locke it is a relation between certain *givens* of sensation or reflection or between complex ideas derived from the *given*. Intuition consists for Locke in the perception of a relation between ideas ultimately derived without exception from sensation or reflection. The object of intuition is never wholly intellectual and purely non-sensuous. In this sense Locke's position differs fundamentally from that of Descartes. Those early readers who like Leibniz classed Locke with the Gassendists must have been surprised at the remarkable likeness between IV. ii and the Cartesian teaching. But Locke no doubt felt that he was still a good Gassendist and was in no way deserting that school. He was merely completing its teaching and making it more explicit.[1] He accepts intuitionism but only as part of his empiricism. Locke himself does not seem to have felt that there was any inconsistency between the standpoint of Books II and IV of his *Essay*.[2] We must return to this point later.

The object of intuition, then, is no purely intellectual non-sensuous object. Locke defines knowledge as *'the perception of the connexion and agreement, or disagreement and repugnancy, of any of our ideas'*.[3] These ideas are ultimately derived from sensation or reflection, so that the definition of knowledge is still perfectly consistent with the empiricist theory of the origin of ideas. While this point is clear, however, the definition as a whole is ambiguous, for the meaning of the phrase *connexion and agreement* is never made completely clear. The examples of agreements given in IV. i are all propositions. And if we assume that he has the proposition in mind his analysis of the sorts of agreement is an

[1] For intuitionism is alien neither to Gassendi nor to English philosophy. Cf. pp. 10–11 above.

[2] Nor between Book IV and that account of the relation between sensation and reason which he gave as early as 1664. Cf. the fourth Essay in the *Law of Nature* (ed. von Leyden) and J. W. Gough, *Locke's Political Philosophy*, pp. 13–14.

[3] IV. i. 2.

analysis of propositions. Unfortunately, in Locke's day the theory of propositions was not well developed, as a glance at the contemporary logics will show. So that Locke could not turn to the logicians for the types of propositions. Moreover, the proposition is not the only 'agreement' between ideas which Locke actually does recognize. For he also uses the phrase 'perceiving an agreement between ideas', where he obviously means apprehending an implication. In other words, to perceive an agreement may mean perceiving a relation *within* propositions or, again, it may mean perceiving a relation, namely, implication, *between* propositions. Demonstration or inference is as much perception of agreement as is judgement. So that the vague term *agreement* covers the relation perceived between the terms of a proposition and also the implication apprehended in inference.

In spite of this ambiguity iv. i provides the most complete analysis of the forms of propositions to be found in Locke's works. Here Locke sets forward four ways in which ideas may agree or disagree, where ideas now obviously mean constituents of propositions: (1) Identity and diversity. The mind perceives the agreement between an idea and itself, and a disagreement in this respect between it and all others: e.g. White is white and not black. To perceive this is genuine knowledge but it is, of course, tautologous or, as Locke prefers to call it, 'trifling'. (2) Relation. The mind perceives a relation between its ideas: e.g. Two triangles upon equal bases between two parallels are equal. (3) Co-existence. The mind perceives a 'co-existence or non-co-existence in the same subject': e.g. Gold is fixed. (4) Real existence. The mind perceives 'actual real existence agreeing to any idea': e.g. God is.

In connexion with this analysis the following remarks must be made: (1) In one sense all the agreements are relations, for an agreement *is* a relation. Thus, it is only in a special sense that one sort of agreement can be called relation and the others not. 'Though identity and co-existence are truly nothing but relations, yet they are so peculiar ways of agreement or disagreement of our *ideas* that they deserve well to be considered as distinct heads and not under relation in general.'[1] But what this special sense is in

[1] iv. i. 7.

which we are to talk of relation in this context is not wholly clear from the text. The example given is mathematical and presumably most mathematical propositions would be included in this class. (2) The agreement which Locke calls *co-existence* is of great importance. Locke remarks of it in IV. i. 6: 'This belongs particularly to substances. Thus when we pronounce concerning *gold* that it is fixed, our knowledge of this truth amounts to no more but this, that fixedness or a power to remain in the fire unconsumed is an *idea* that always accompanies and is joined with that particular sort of yellowness, weight, fusibility, malleableness, and solubility in *aqua regia*, which make our complex *idea*, signified by the word *gold*.' Thus, to perceive this agreement is to perceive that the quality *d* always goes along with the qualities *abc* in the substance *X*. It is a knowledge of the co-existence of qualities. From the two examples which Locke here gives, 'Gold is fixed' and 'Iron is susceptible of magnetical impressions', one might think he had in mind propositions expressing predication, where a quality is predicated of a subject. And this might have been the case. But the agreement which is co-existence is clearly not the substance–attribute relation. Locke's emphasis is on the co-existence of this further quality *d* with the qualities *abc*, and not on the attribution of *d* to the substance *X*. (3) Locke does not confine propositions to the subject–predicate type, but recognizes three other types: the relational, the identical, and the existential. In this respect his theory of propositions accords better with the modern theory than with the traditional. (4) The fourth agreement presents special difficulties of its own. Can an existential proposition be analysed into two related ideas? On the whole, Locke would seem to be analysing it in this way. We perceive the agreement between our idea of God and our idea of existence. But this analysis of the proposition *God is*, it will be agreed, is highly artificial. And Locke actually *means* more than this, as we shall later see in considering his general account of existential knowledge. But it is already obvious that if all knowledge is the perception of the agreement between ideas, then the problem of existential knowledge is likely to present very grave difficulties. (5) We may add two points of a more general character. First,

Locke's account of knowledge implies that the object of know-ledge is always a proposition or an inference. This means that we never know an idea in isolation. Locke teaches this quite explicitly in Book IV, and it is only those who confine their reading to Book II who misinterpret him on this point. (6) Secondly, we should note that while Locke considers that the above fourfold division exhausts the sorts of agreements or disagreements which we can possibly perceive, he does not mean to assert that we actually do have certain, intuitive knowledge of all such agreements. On this point, again, his language is not unambiguous, but since he has not yet determined the limitations of human knowledge, it seems obvious that we cannot assume that there are instances of actual intuitions in each of the four cases mentioned. And in the sequel it becomes clear that our certain knowledge of co-existence, for instance, is very slight.

But if we know at all with absolute certainty our knowledge is perception or intuition. This is the central theme of Locke's epistemology. His solution of the epistemological problem is an intuitionism, set forward in Cartesian language, though differing fundamentally from Cartesianism in its teaching as to the nature of the object. Locke's intuitionism is one which accords, in its author's intention, with his own empiricism, and in no way con-tradicts it.[1]

II

The question with which we are concerned in this section is the very question which gave rise to the *Essay*. After the famous meeting of friends mentioned in the *Epistle* Locke had set him-self the task of determining the extent and limitations of human

---

[1] Some paragraphs at the end of IV. i on 'habitual knowledge' if developed in certain ways might have led Locke to a radical revision of his theory of knowledge. For they might have led him to consider the dispositional elements in our knowledge. The pressure of our physical and social environment upon us creates certain habits of behaviour, and the knowledge involved is very dif-ferent in character from the intuitive knowledge which Locke has been describ-ing. But the extent to which the intuitive theory rules Locke's thought at this point is made clear by these paragraphs themselves, for he deals in them only with the retention in memory of items of intuited truths, for instance, the storing up of the conclusions of complicated mathematical proofs even when the details of the proofs are forgotten.

knowledge. At first he seems to have thought that an adequate solution could be found speedily, and he apparently attempted to set it out in a short paper. He must have been dissatisfied with this paper, however, for a little later in the summer of 1671 we find him at work on Draft A. In this draft it is possible to see how what seemed at first sight to be a fairly straightforward problem developed into one of the most intricate, and how Locke was driven to give up his first conception of knowledge and to search for a new one. This new conception was not formulated explicitly until 1690, but the early drafts prepare us for the new position.

It is illuminating to follow the development of Locke's thought as it is revealed in Draft A. He begins by assuming that knowledge must be, first, absolutely certain, and secondly, of the real, that is to say, of real physical or mental existences. The conclusion to which he is then driven is that, in this sense of the term, very little knowledge is possible for the human mind. The source of his scepticism is revealed in the opening sections of the draft. The immediate object of mind is idea. If, then, we know the real physical object we know it mediately through idea. But our idea is complex, and to know the external object fully, even in this mediate manner, we should have to know that the complex idea in the mind represents it completely and adequately. But this we can never know. As Locke himself says: 'He that frames an idea that consists of a collection of all those simple ideas which are in any thing hath a perfect knowledge of that thing, but of this I must forbear an instance till I can find one.'[1] He might have gone further. From the nature of the case it is only too evident that no such instance could ever be found. For to know that the idea is adequate we should have to go beyond the idea, we should need to know the external object directly, and this *ex hypothesi* is impossible.

Scepticism is thus inevitable on this first view of knowledge. But even in Draft A a new view gradually emerges and in it Locke finds relief. Knowledge is still certain and to be distinguished from belief or opinion, but it is no longer of real objects but of relations between ideas.[2] The first instances of such knowledge which came

[1] § 7.   [2] Cf. § 27, 20 and also § 9.

to his mind were identical propositions. 'White is not black.' 'The whole is greater than the part.' These and the like are obvious instances of knowledge and no propositions could be more certain. Unfortunately, they are merely 'trifling'. To assert them is to trifle with words; 'or at best [it] is but like the monkey's shifting his oyster from one hand to the other and had he but words might no doubt have said, oyster in right hand is subject and oyster in left hand is predicate, and so might have made a self-evident proposition of oyster, i.e. oyster is oyster, and yet with all this not have been one whit the wiser or more knowing.'[1] Such propositions as these, though they are certain, can hardly be put forward as *the* instances of knowing. Is there anywhere a set of propositions as certain as the above, but also instructive? From the first it is clear that Locke looked to mathematics for an answer. But in 1671 his treatment of mathematical propositions was crude and the test of their validity was correspondence. 'Mathematical universal propositions are both true and instructive because as those ideas are in our minds so are the things without us.'[2] Nor is there advance in Draft B. But between 1671 and 1690, inspired no doubt by his frequent contacts with Cartesians, Locke re-examined mathematics (as various passages in his journals go to show)[3] and evolved a new theory which he found more satisfying. The emergence of this theory at the same time marks the completion of the change from one view of knowing to another. Thus, when we turn to the *Essay*, the opening chapters of Book IV are essentially an exposition of the kind of knowledge which Locke now thought mathematics to be.

It is a noteworthy fact, however, that the older theory was not wholly discarded. It suddenly reappears in the chapters dealing with our existential knowledge.[4] The explanation of this reappearance is bound up with the account which the *Essay* gives of the extent of human knowledge. If we now examine that account we

---

[1] § 28, cf. *Essay*, IV. viii. 3.

[2] § 30, cf. §§ 11 and 12. These latter sections reveal Locke in the very effort of finding empirical bases for geometry and arithmetic. In § 30, however, Locke argues (in spite of the passage quoted above) that mathematical propositions are analytic. Yet they are also instructive.

[3] Cf. 3 July 1679, 26 June, and 19 August 1681.

[4] IV. ix, x, xi.

may hope to discover why Locke was compelled to retain the old alongside the new, and why these two apparently contradictory theories of knowledge are both to be found in his final exposition.

Book IV begins with the new view, that knowledge is the perception of relations *between ideas*. The first limitation of human knowledge is then obvious. 'We can have *knowledge* no farther than we have *ideas*.'[1] And since ideas are either given directly in sensation or reflection, or are derived from one of these two sources, the above statement means that we cannot know what lies completely beyond our sensory and reflective experience. Now we have grounds for believing that sensory and reflective experience is, as a matter of fact, most decidedly limited. The very experiences we do gain make us conscious of our ignorance. For instance, we have some faint notions of God and infinity, notions derived ultimately from the senses; but we are well aware that our idea of God is not a clear one nor have we a positive conception of infinity. Again, from what we do experience we cannot doubt that numerous objects whose nature may very well be identical with those with which we are acquainted, on account of their remoteness or minuteness, are never revealed to us. Thus, there are doubtless worlds around us in this vast universe which are too remote to be perceived; while, on the other hand, extreme minuteness veils, and will apparently for ever veil, the inner corpuscular nature of those bodies which are nearest us, and which we do experience in the mass. This of itself explains why an exact and complete physical science will never be possible for the human mind. We can never experience the minute motions of the corpuscles which, in Locke's opinion, explain the movements of bodies and their operations on other bodies. 'I am apt to doubt', he remarks, 'that how far soever human industry may advance useful and *experimental* philosophy *in physical things, scientifical*, will still be out of our reach; because we want perfect and adequate *ideas* of those very bodies which are nearest to us and most under our command'.[2] Moreover, just as we are confined in our sensory experiences, so are we also in reflection. The full and complete nature of our minds is certainly not revealed to us in

---

[1] IV. iii. I.   [2] IV. iii. 26.

introspective experience. Thus, the narrow scope of both our sensory and our reflective experience seriously limits our knowledge from the outset. For where experience fails to provide us with ideas, knowledge cannot possibly occur.

But, secondly, we may have ideas and still lack knowledge. 'Our knowledge is narrower than our *ideas*.'[1] To have an idea is not to know. To know is to perceive agreements or disagreements between ideas. And we may have ideas before us between which we can perceive no agreements and no disagreements. We have seen that Locke recognizes four kinds of such agreement. Can we now make any general statement with regard to the extent and limits of knowledge in terms of this fourfold distinction? Locke thinks we can.

First, in the case of identity or diversity, 'our intuitive knowledge, is as far extended as our *ideas* themselves'.[2] Of every idea we may say that it is itself and not another. But such statements are trifling. Now Locke distinguishes between two sorts of trifling propositions. In the first place, trifling propositions may be verbal. 'White is not black' may mean that the word white is not the word black, and if this is all it does mean it is merely verbal. Verbal also, in Locke's opinion, is the proposition in which we predicate of a subject the whole or part of its nominal essence. That is to say, if there is a set of words which together are equivalent to the word *gold*, and if *metal* is one of this set, then 'Gold is a metal' is a verbal proposition.[3] But if there are trifling propositions of this sort which are purely verbal, there is another kind in which we assert the identity of an idea with itself (rather than of a word with itself). 'White is white and not black' may mean that the idea of white is that idea and no other. The proposition would not then

[1] IV. iii. 6.   [2] IV. iii. 8.
[3] Locke also thinks that if we affirm one abstract word of another our proposition is verbal. 'All propositions wherein two abstract terms are affirmed one of another are barely about the signification of sounds. For, since no abstract *idea* can be the same with any other but itself, when its abstract name is affirmed of any other term, it can signify no more but this, that it may or ought to be called by that name; or that these two names signify the same *idea*' (IV. viii. 12). To say that 'parsimony is frugality', merely makes clear the use of the word parsimony by asserting that it is used in language in precisely the same way as the word 'frugality'. This seems to be Locke's meaning, though the words *signification* and *signify* in the passage are not without ambiguity.

be verbal (for Locke, it will be remembered, does not identify idea and name), but it is still trifling.

All propositions stating identities of ideas are certain but trifling. And the only limit to knowledge in this case is the number of ideas we experience. But identity is not the only sort of necessary relation which we can intuit. Indeed, it appears to be but one instance of a group, which Locke terms by the general name, relations. In iv. iii, again, as throughout the *Essay*, the term 'relation' is used ambiguously. The one clear instance which Locke sets before us is that expressed in the mathematical proposition. But he is also anxious to show that absolutely certain knowledge of relations is not confined to mathematics, but can be found in at least one other sphere, namely, in morality. At the same time it is significant that Locke never works out this apodictically necessary system of morals, though he was pressed to do so by certain of his friends, as the Molyneux correspondence shows. None the less he believed that such a system could be worked out, and that the objects of moral knowledge were analogous to those of mathematics. It is clearly mathematics, however, which he has primarily in mind, and it is his account of this science which deserves our serious attention.

A mathematical proposition, in Locke's view, is in one respect like the identical proposition already considered, but unlike it in another. It is like the identical proposition in so far as it states a relation arising necessarily from the nature of the ideas expressed in the proposition. In mathematics we do intuit necessary relations between ideas. But it is unlike it as being 'instructive' rather than 'trifling'. There is no doubt that Locke taught this. He makes the point explicitly on many occasions. We may quote iv. viii. 8, where he is expressly distinguishing between trifling and instructive knowledge: 'We can know the truth and so may be certain in propositions which affirm something of another, which is a necessary consequence of its precise complex idea, but not contained in it; as that the external angle of all triangles is bigger than either of the opposite interior angles, which relation of the outward angle to either of the opposite internal angles, making no part of the complex idea signified by the name *triangle*, this is the real truth, and conveys with it instructive real knowledge.' According to Locke, we do more here than affirm of a triangle what pertains to it through definition. Our knowledge is not trifling. Yet it is certain as arising from a perception of a necessary relation involved in the ideas themselves.

For Locke mathematics is instructive yet wholly necessary. So much is clear. But if we think in terms of subsequent theorizing and ask whether in Locke's view mathematics is analytic or synthetic, it is not possible to give an unambiguous answer. There are passages, including the one quoted above, in which he might be held to argue that mathematics is *a priori* synthesis. We intuit relations which could not be deduced from the definitions of the terms related. But then Locke also seems to mean that these relations are the outcome of the nature of the mathematical objects themselves. They are already involved in the objects as such. Mathematics is a deduction, even though its propositions are not trifling and are not deduced from the definitions of the terms related. From this point of view, Locke seems to hold that mathematics is a purely analytic science but yet also instructive. His account of mathematics certainly does not make the ultimate nature of that science clear.[1]

He does, however, make four points about the inquiry, each one of which is important and worthy of notice: (1) Mathematics is wholly certain. It is demonstration in which every step is perceived intuitively. But it is demonstration of such a sort that it is as certain as a single intuition, and nothing can be more certain. This complete certainty is the outcome of the mathematician's method. The mathematician proceeds by easy stages, which he is able to record precisely (since he possesses a system of precise symbols), and which he can check repeatedly. He is thus safeguarded against any failure of memory, which, in Locke's opinion, is the

---

[1] There is, in fact, a deeper ambiguity which would first have to be removed before he could make his theory explicit, namely, the ambiguity in his general account of universals and of abstraction. For mathematical objects are, in Locke's view, essentially the fruit of abstraction, even though some of them are first suggested to us in experience. And no final theory of mathematics could be offered by him until the nature of universals and abstraction had been made clear. But, as we have seen, Locke's account of universals remains ambiguous to the end.

cause of error in demonstration. (2) Mathematical objects, if representative at all, are so only in a secondary sense. In their case the criterion of truth is not correspondence. The mathematical object is the shadow of nothing other than itself; it represents nothing beyond it. In Locke's language, 'it is its own archetype'. It is both real and nominal essence in one. In this respect it differs fundamentally from the object in the natural sciences, for in the latter case the idea is primarily representative, and the mind dealing with it can never free itself from bondage to the external. But in mathematics there is no need to ask: Do these ideas correspond to reality? Here intuition is able to play freely amongst ideas, the mind is not constrained by external fact. The only constraint upon it comes from the system of ideas itself. (3) There is apparently no limit to the knowledge which is possible within this field. For, in the first place, the mind, as we have just seen, is free to proceed without referring to anything beyond the mathematical system itself. Secondly, within this system there are apparently endless possibilities in accordance with the general laws of mathematics. (4) Mathematics is non-empirical. 'Mathematical demonstration depends not upon sense.'[1] It is a pure deductive inquiry and contains within it no inductive elements. It has achieved the ideal towards which the natural sciences also strive, but which they never attain.

A further word must be added, however, on this difficult matter of the relations between the mathematical object and sense-perception in Locke's philosophy. As an empiricist Locke holds that the ideas in mathematical propositions (as in all others) must be derived ultimately from experience, that is, from sensation or reflection. But how can this be if mathematics is non-empirical? The answer seems to be that though these ideas are derived from experience, they are now such that the knowledge of their nature and of the relations between them no longer depends upon experience. But then the phrase 'derived from' needs explanation. To begin with, it points at least to a pyschological fact. Experience is first necessary before men come to conceive mathematical objects. The first suggestions and intimations of mathematical

[1] IV. xi. 6.

concepts come through empirical channels, and had these suggestions not been given, the human mind would never have conceived mathematical objects. Experience provides the first suggestions of equality, unity, duality, multiplicity, greater, less, space, triangle, circle, and so on. And without such experience mathematical knowledge would have been impossible. Whether more gifted intelligences begin in any other way we do not know. But human beings certainly begin in this way. So much is psychologically true. Difficulties arise, however, when we seek the implications of this position. For the derivation in this case is obviously not a matter of mere chronological succession, first the experience and then the concept wholly independent of it as regards content. The concept derives some part, at least, of its content from the experience. Locke does not deny this. He expressly holds that unity, space, and the like are simple ideas. They are given in experience, and apparently given as universals. It may be that the content is refined and purified through abstraction. But there can be no doubt that something essential is given from the outset. What precisely is given, however, is not made clear. On this point Locke could not be explicit until he had set forward an adequate theory of universals. In the meantime, however, he continues to hold that mathematics is non-empirical, whilst yet asserting that its objects are ultimately derived from sensory experience, although no longer immediate objects of such experience.[1]

But though a considerable amount of ambiguity thus remains with regard to the exact relationship between sensory experience and mathematical thinking, Locke is quite sure that mathematical ideas are such that the mind on contemplating them can intuit necessary relations between them, and that there is no limit to the number of relations which may thus be known. On the other hand, if we now turn from relations to co-existences, the third sort of agreements considered by Locke, we shall find that our certain knowledge in this realm does not extend very far. Indeed, it is

---

[1] Locke recognizes that the mathematician continues to make use of sensible symbols (cf. iv. iii. 19, xi. 6, &c.). But in the *Essay*, at least, he never makes the mistake of supposing that the sensible symbol is itself the mathematical object. He might appear to be doing so in iv. iv. 13. But if the passage is read in connexion with the previous paragraph, it will be seen that this is not the case.

with difficulty that we find any single instance of certain knowledge of co-existences, in spite of the fact that herein 'consists the greatest and most material part of our knowledge concerning substances'.

The reason for our ignorance in this respect is not hard to find. To know the co-existence of the qualities of a thing with certainty we should have to know the inner corpuscular structure of that thing. But the details of this structure are so minute, as we have seen, that we can never hope to know them. Consequently, it is not possible to affirm that such and such qualities must co-exist in this thing. We can only wait on experience. Thus we observe that gold is yellow and malleable. But we do not know that these qualities must always co-exist in gold. Having always observed yellow and malleableness to go together in my experience of gold I assume that I shall always experience their co-existence. But I have no intuition of a necessary relation, and so no absolutely certain knowledge. Tomorrow I may experience gold which is yellow but not malleable. In other words, there is nothing in the simple idea of yellow to necessitate its co-existence with malleableness in gold. Our simple ideas 'carry with them in their own nature no visible necessary connexion or inconsistency with any other simple *ideas,* whose *co-existence* with them we would inform ourselves about'.[1] Moreover, to complicate things farther, yellow and malleable are secondary qualities and we do not know the primary qualities and the powers upon which they depend. But Locke does believe that an adequate explanation of our experience of co-existences is to be found in the nature of bodies, although this explanation, he perceives, is never likely to be known by us. He makes an interesting effort to find a few instances of certain knowledge in this sphere. 'Figure necessarily supposes extension' and 'receiving or communicating motion by impulse supposes solidity'.[2] These co-existences we know with certainty. But, on examination, the first seems to be tautologous, and the second so vague, the terms (for instance, solidity) so ill-defined, that the propositions do not carry conviction as instances. Even so, these are the only two instances of absolutely certain knowledge of co-existences as

---

[1] IV. iii. 10.   [2] IV. iii. 14.

universal and necessary relations which Locke can find. He adds that one 'in-co-existence' may be known, namely, that no opposite qualities will co-exist in a thing at one and the same time and in respect to the same part of it. But of particular concrete 'in-co-existences' we have, apparently, no certain and necessary knowledge. Thus, to all intents and purposes, we have no necessary knowledge of the co-existences of qualities in material substances. We are wholly dependent on experience. And the case is precisely the same in our knowledge of spiritual existences. We experience ourselves in reflection, but we do not intuit within ourselves co-existences which are necessary.[1] Thus there is little, if any, universal and necessary knowledge of co-existences.

Locke has now arrived at the following position in his attempt to determine the extent of human knowledge: we are limited, in the first place, by experience itself; where we have no ideas we cannot have knowledge. But even when experience provides us with ideas, we cannot always intuit necessary relations between them. We can always know that an idea is itself, and that it is not another. We can also know certain necessary relations between ideas, when through abstraction we free them from their reference outwards and deal with them as ideas which are their own archetypes. There is then no limit to the knowledge obtainable, particularly in mathematics. But when we consider ideas as representing the external world the mind can know few, if any, necessary relations between them. No science (in the strict sense) of the natural world, nor again of human nature, is possible for us. In these spheres the human mind must perforce wait upon experience, and here no exact system of necessary knowledge will ever be gained by us.

III

Having come to this position it is impossible to avoid a question which Locke found most difficult to answer. Admitting that a science of natural objects in the above sense is impossible, can we then *know* (in Locke's sense of the term) that these natural objects exist? Indeed, can we know with certainty that anything exists?

---

[1] iv. iii. 17.

According to his theory, knowledge is 'the perception of the connexion and agreement, or disagreement and repugnancy, of our ideas'. How then can we know that things (which are neither ideas nor relations between ideas) exist? Now in iv. i. 7 it might appear that Locke wished to argue that even the knowledge expressed in existential propositions is a perception of a relation between ideas. To say 'The table exists' is to affirm a relation between two ideas, namely, the idea of table and the idea of existence. But Locke himself very quickly realized that an answer of this sort was completely unsatisfactory. It is obvious that when I say 'God exists' or 'The table exists' I do not mean to assert a relation between two ideas in my mind. My reference is not at all to ideas but to entities whose existence I assert. I go beyond ideas. Yet if knowledge be invariably the perception of relations between ideas, how is such a reference beyond the ideal realm possible? Locke himself faces the difficulty squarely in the dramatic opening paragraph of iv. iv: 'Of what use is all this fine knowledge of men's own imaginations to a man that inquires after the reality of things?' If we are confined within our ideas, how can we ever know (what we obviously need and desire to know) that which transcends our ideas, that which is real rather than ideal?

The first interesting and significant point about Locke's reply to this objection is that he makes no attempt to save himself by adopting any sort of idealism, that is to say, by denying the reality of the distinction between idea and thing. On the contrary, he reasserts this distinction in the most explicit manner. The rest of iv. iv is a desperate, but unsuccessful, effort to bridge the gulf between idea and thing. Our knowledge is real if ideas conform to the real, which we know mediately through ideas. But in what way can we test their conformity? Or as Locke himself asks: 'How shall the mind, when it perceives nothing but its own ideas, know that they agree with things themselves?' He admits that the application of the correspondence test in these conditions 'wants not difficulty'. The plain truth is that it can never be applied, as Locke himself recognized in another passage,[1] and his attempt to apply it in iv. iv was doomed to failure from the start.

[1] *Examination of Malebranche*, § 51.

For this reason it is not necessary to devote much space to the consideration of IV. iv. Locke tries to show that there is a sense in which we can say that both simple and complex ideas may be real. Simple ideas are real in the peculiar and unusual sense that, though for practical purposes we may think of them as if they were real, actually they are real only as being products of the real. They 'are not fictions of our fancies but the natural and regular productions of things without us really operating upon us; and so carry with them all the conformity which is intended or which our state requires'.[1] As for complex ideas, they are of two sorts; those which are, and those which are not, their own archetypes. The former need not correspond to anything outside them. None the less there is a sense in which they also can claim to be real. If amongst real things there happen to be circular or square objects then all we say of circles and squares in geometry applies with equal force to such objects. So that in this sense geometry (and mathematics) is a knowledge of the real. With regard to ideas of substances, they are not their own archetypes, and these ideas are real only if they conform in every respect with the real facts in the external world. But here again Locke does not reveal how we are to know whether they do or do not conform. Hence IV. iv provides us with no true answer to the objection that human knowledge on his showing is confined to ideas and so can never be of the real.

Locke's real answer, however, is to be found in those later chapters of Book IV in which he discusses our knowledge of self, of God, and of things. Now if we examine these chapters we shall see that in them Locke breaks away completely from the theory set forward in the earlier chapters. Within the terms of the definition of knowledge set out in IV. i he could not explain existential knowledge. He tried to do so in IV. iv but failed. To explain it he finds himself compelled to assert that knowledge, on occasion at least, is a direct apprehension of the real without the intervention of ideas.

This new view of knowledge is essentially different from that first set forth in the *Essay*. It even goes further than the first crude thoughts of Draft A, for although in the draft Locke had once

[1] IV. iv. 4.

thought that knowledge was of real objects and not of relations
between ideas, he still vaguely supposed that such knowledge
would be gained somehow through ideas. Now, however, our
knowledge of the self, at least, is direct intuition without the intervention of ideas, and there seems to be some element of direct
intuition also in our knowledge of physical objects. Locke understood well enough that he was introducing new views which did
not accord with his definition of knowledge in iv. i. But he sought
to save himself from the charge of inconsistency in this respect
by pointing out[1] that in the first eight chapters of Book IV he had
been dealing with universals and relations between universals,
whereas from the beginning of the ninth he proposes to deal with
particulars. The definition of iv. i, he appears now to be saying,
applies only to knowledge of universal propositions. We may note
in passing that no such reservation as this was made in iv. i when
the definition was first put before the reader. But it is now set forward as the justification of the sudden change of theory which
had become necessary if existential knowledge was to be explained.

Locke had been considering this distinction between general
and particular knowledge for some time. In his journal for 26 June
1681 there is an entry beginning: 'There are two sorts of knowledge in the world, general and particular, founded upon two
different principles, i.e. true ideas and matter of fact or history.'[2]
In this entry he limits certain knowledge to the knowledge of
generals while knowledge of particulars is held to be probable
only. But in the *Essay*, in the chapters now to be considered by
us, he has realized that some certainties are possible even in our
knowledge of particulars and that such knowledge cannot be
defined as the perception of the agreements or disagreements
between ideas. When he grasped this point he ought no doubt to
have retraced his steps and rewritten the earlier chapters of Book
IV so as to bring them into line with the later chapters, which
would not have been an impossible task. But he lacked either the
energy or the time or possibly the interest. When he returned to
England from Holland there were other more exciting things to

[1] iv. ix. i.   [2] Aaron and Gibb, p. 116.

do in the realm of practical affairs, and Locke was ever ready to sacrifice speculation to practice.

Hence Locke left the two theories of knowledge standing side by side with little effort to make them consistent. Knowledge is the perception of relations between ideas: but we also know particular existences directly, and in this case knowledge is not the perception of relations between ideas. What now do we know with certainty of particulars? 'We have the knowledge of *our own existence* by intuition; of the *existence* of God by demonstration; and of other things by sensation.'[1] In the first place I know with certainty that I myself exist. Locke concerns himself here merely with the existence of the self; the reader who expects an analysis of the concept of self will be disappointed. All Locke does is to point to the fact that whenever I experience anything I am aware of myself at the time as experiencing it. All consciousness is also self-consciousness. He terms this consciousness of self an intuition. It is not reflective knowledge (in Locke's sense) of a state of the mind or of operations of the mind. It is intuitive knowledge of a single concrete existent, an 'internal infallible perception'. Any experience, whatever it be that I experience, is at the same time an experience of myself. Descartes's *Cogito ergo sum* is used by Locke as an illustration of the general point. 'If I doubt of all other things, that very doubt makes me perceive my own *existence*, and will not suffer me to doubt of that.'[2] Throughout my waking experience I constantly intuit my own existence.[3]

I thus know that I exist intuitively. From this knowledge I can prove God's existence demonstratively. The proof is to be found

---

[1] IV. ix. 2.

[2] Incidentally, it is very wrong to suppose that Locke borrowed the argument from Descartes to *prove* the existence of the self. For Locke says explicitly that our own existence 'neither needs nor is capable of any proof' (IV. ix. 3). He does not use the *Cogito* in the way in which Descartes uses it. For him it is merely one further illustration of the general principle that we intuit our own selves when we are conscious of anything.

[3] We thus know our own selves immediately. Our knowledge of other minds, on Locke's showing, seems to be mediate. In IV. iii. 27 he remarks: 'That there are minds and thinking beings in other men, as well as himself, every man has a reason from their words and actions to be satisfied.' Angels and higher spirits may have a more immediate knowledge of each other. Cf. II. xxiii. 36, III. vi. 11, IV. ix. 9, 12.

in the famous tenth chapter of Book IV. The argument of that
chapter is not very original; the influence of Cicero, Cudworth,
and Nicole, to mention these only, is very apparent.[1] Nor, as we
shall try to show, is it wholly cogent. But Locke had thought the
matter out for himself, and even though the argument was defi-
cient, it had a certain strength of its own and was not without its
influence on subsequent English thought.

Locke's proof of the being of God is a form of the cosmological
argument. He rejects the ontological. In the *Essay* he does not
disprove the latter, but holds it to be too slight a foundation for
a philosophical theology.[2] But he explicitly rejects it as false in a
paper entitled *Deus*, which he wrote six years after the appearance
of the *Essay*, and which was published by King.[3] In this paper he
forestalls the central criticism of Kant. The idea we have of a
perfect being may carry with it the idea of necessary existence.
But this does not prove that the perfect being exists. 'Any idea,
simple or complex, barely by being in our minds, is no evidence of
the real existence of any thing out of our minds answering that
idea. Real existence can be proved only by real existence; and
therefore the real existence of a God can only be proved by the
real existence of other things.'[4] 'Our ideas alter nothing in the
reality of things.' Consequently the ontological argument, on
Locke's view, rests on no solid foundation.[5]

He himself begins his argument with real existence, namely, his
own existence. I myself exist, that is to say, something exists. Now
nothing cannot produce being. 'If therefore we know there is some
real being, and that non-entity cannot produce any real being, it is
an evident demonstration that from eternity there has been something; since what was not from eternity had a beginning; and

[1] In IV. x. 6 Locke refers explicitly to Cicero's *De Legibus*, but the argument
is also reminiscent of the *De Natura Deórum*. He repeats in substance some
parts of IV. x in IV. xx. 15, and here he is fairly certainly borrowing from the
De Natura Deorum, II. 37. His journal for 18 February 1682 reveals the extent
of his debt to Ralph Cudworth's *The True Intellectual System of the Universe*.
Cf. also 'Locke and Nicole: Their proofs of the existence of God and their
attitude towards Descartes', by Wolfgang von Leyden in *Sophia*, January 1948,
pp. 41–55.   [2] IV. x. 7 and cf. the First Letter to Stillingfleet on this point.
[3] *Life of Locke*, ii. 133–9.   [4] Ibid. ii. 138.
[5] For further arguments for God's existence in Lovelace MSS. cf. von
Leyden's introduction (p. 65) to *Law of Nature* and the fourth essay.

what had a beginning must be produced by something else.'[1] This is the first step in the argument by means of which he attempts to prove the existence of God.

A criticism which has been urged against the cosmological argument cannot be urged against it in the above form. It cannot be argued that Locke is assuming that an infinite series of causes is impossible and that, therefore, the series must end in a First Cause. For the above argument permits of the possibility that what exists at present is the effect of an infinite series of causes. Nor does it rule out the other possibility that what exists at present has existed from eternity. It merely argues from the existence of anything at the present moment to the existence of something from eternity. But the criticism can be made, if we are prepared to make it, that Locke is assuming that anything which had a beginning must have had a cause. Locke, as we have seen, sets this down as a fundamental principle which could not be doubted, even though he admitted that the concept of causality itself was not entirely free from ambiguity. Again, it must also be admitted that Locke uses the term 'from eternity' loosely. Eternity was no positive concept in Locke's mind, and, since this was so, could he say anything truly significant about it in a positive sense? In particular, had he a right to say that something must exist from eternity? On the other hand, it might be held that the real point of Locke's argument is that real being cannot be conceived by us as coming into being from nothing, the present existence of real being necessarily presupposes the existence of real being in the past from eternity. But what does this mean? Nothing other, it would seem, than that the idea of real being carries with it the conception of its necessary existence. In other words, the cosmological argument, by a sudden twist, has become the ontological. Kant argued that this was inevitable.[2] Locke might have answered that he began not with the *idea* of real existence but with real existence iself. This is true, but the question remains: Is the step from present existence to necessary existence from eternity anything more than ideal? And if it is merely ideal, has not the cosmological argument revealed itself to be in essence the onto-logical, an argument which Locke himself rejected?

Thus even the first step in Locke's argument is not above sus-picion. The next, however, makes still bigger assumptions. These are (1) that what exists at present has not always existed, but is the effect of a limited series of causes. In other words, a First Cause exists. (2) The First Cause contains all that the effect contains either *formaliter* or (as is actually the case here) *eminenter*. These assumptions can be justified neither by reason nor by experience, although they satisfy reason's demand for an ordered universe. But Locke assumes both points. And once they are granted Locke then shows that the Eternal Being, whose existence has now been proved, cannot be material. A world in which we find intelligence cannot possibly be explained by a materialistic naturalism, for this would be putting more into the effect than the cause contains, that is to say, contradicting the second of Locke's assumptions. Hence the Eternal Being is of necessity a thinking person: 'in-cogitative being cannot produce a cogitative'. The Eternal Being must also be the source of wisdom, of power, and of strength, and so he is omniscient and omnipotent. In this way Locke claims to have proved the existence of the God of Christian theology.

But the self and God are not the only existents which Locke claims we may know with certainty. There are also the 'other things' of iv. xi, that is to say, natural physical objects in the ex-ternal world. The existence of these we know by sensation. Now the claim that we know in sensing seems at first sight to contradict two principles set down earlier in the *Essay*. For, first, sensation, according to Book II, merely provides materials *for* knowledge but is never itself knowledge. Secondly, knowing according to Book IV is intuiting, and this is a purely intellectual activity, wholly independent of sensation on the subjective side.[1] None the less we now find Locke asserting that sensation is itself knowledge, for we know in it the existence of things.

One may well understand why Locke felt it necessary to make this claim, even though it contradicted his principles. Through-out he was a realist. He was as convinced of the existence of tables

---

[1] Although not on the objective side, cf. p. 224 above.

and chairs as he was of his own self, and he was convinced that their existence was no merely ideal existence. Certainly, my complex idea of a table is in my mind, but there also exists the table itself which is no construct of mine. And in seeing I know that this real table exists.

Now this might be an inconvenient fact for Locke's general theory of knowledge, but it had to be faced, and Locke faces it boldly. He considers the matter in iv. xi, but he had introduced it earlier in the opening chapters of Book IV. For at the end of the second chapter which deals with the degrees of knowledge, he adds an important section entitled 'Sensitive Knowledge'. In addition to intuitive and demonstrative we must also recognize the existence of sensitive knowledge. The manner in which he introduces this third kind of knowledge reveals his uncertainty as to its precise nature. 'There is, indeed, another *perception* of the mind employed about *the particular existence of finite beings* without us; which going beyond bare probability, and yet not reaching perfectly to either of the foregoing degrees of certainty, passes under the name of knowledge.'[1] He explains that in our knowledge of general truths we can say outright that the only certainty comes by way of intuition and demonstration. But in the knowledge of particulars we must also reckon with a third sort of knowledge, which is more than probable, and yet has not that transparent assurance which belongs to intuition and demonstration. When Locke attempts to give further details of sensitive knowledge both in iv. ii. 14 and in iv. xi he speaks in the most uncertain tones. It is a conviction, a feeling, which cannot be further explained. 'I ask any one whether he be not invincibly conscious to himself of a different perception when he looks on the sun by day and thinks on it by night.'[2] Sensation carries with it a tang of reality in a way in which imagination does not. However many doubts may arise from reflection on illusion, hallucination, and the like, I still feel convinced that the sun I now see exists and that the table I see and touch exists, and that they both exist not as ideas in my mind but as real physical entities. This is sensitive knowledge. It is to be noted that Locke does not say that seeing a

[1] iv. ii. 14.   [2] Ibid.

colour or hearing a sound is knowing. In that sense it is still correct to say that sensation merely provides materials for knowledge. But whenever we sense we also know the existence of a physical world independent of us which contains many objects. Locke cannot bring himself to deny this additional element in all sensory experience. In iv. xi he seeks for confirmation of the conviction that things exist in such facts as that we cannot choose what we would see but appear to be dependent on something outside us, and that the view that things do exist externally is a satisfactory explanation of our sensory experience. But the existence of objects independent of us is no inference for Locke, nor is it a hypothesis. Whenever we sense we are directly assured that things exist independently of us.

We thus know that particular physical objects exist in addition to the self and God. Do we know more of these objects in sensation than the mere fact of their existence? The answer Locke makes is important. We do know more, and on this extra knowledge is based the whole of our natural philosophy. We know particular co-existences, that is to say, we know the co-existence of certain powers which produce in us the sensations we enjoy. We do not know those powers directly, but we enjoy sensory experiences of secondary qualities which come together in regular patterns, and these experiences enable us to gain such insight as we possess into the structure of things themselves. Thus we not merely know that things exist in sensation, but we also know particular co-existences in things.[1]

We may conclude then that the fact of existential knowledge has caused Locke to introduce thoroughgoing alterations into his account of knowledge. He opens Book IV of the *Essay* with a theory of knowledge applicable, as it proves, merely to knowledge of relations between abstract ideas, a universal, hypothetical, and highly abstract knowledge, best typified in mathematics. Another theory becomes necessary for knowledge of particular existences. Consequently, Locke's whole account of knowledge is far from consistent, for he does not even try to remove this dualism or to relate the two theories. The knowledge of God is attempted

[1] Cf. iv. iv. 12.

demonstration and it is not different in its nature from demonstration elsewhere, for instance, in mathematics. But the knowledge of the self and again of the existence of things could never be defined as 'the perception of the agreement or disagreement between ideas'. Precisely how much importance is to be attributed to the fact that Locke terms both the perception of relations and the knowledge of self *intuition* is not clear. Apparently, they possess certain likenesses in their nature, but Locke never discusses their relationship. At the same time he is obviously not at all clear in his own mind as to the exact description he should offer of sensitive knowledge. By way of explanation of the dualism in his theory he does suggest that we ought not to expect knowledge of universals to be the same as knowledge of particulars. But this is little more than a hint, and is never developed adequately. Thus we must conclude that Locke's theory of knowledge is defective in being both incomplete and incoherent. But it would be wrong to assume that it is without value. On the contrary, his views on the extent and limitations of human knowledge are extremely valuable and have been confirmed by subsequent speculation, while his very failure to present a finished theory is clearly the consequence of his strong desire to do justice to all the facts.

IV

The remaining chapters of the *Essay* are chiefly concerned with the examination of probable knowledge. Locke recognized the importance of probability, and it is to his credit that he did so. Perhaps the main lesson he has to teach us is that human life is ruled for the most part by probability rather than by certainty. The extent of our certain knowledge is slight and we cannot live by it alone. 'He that in the ordinary affairs of life would admit of nothing but direct plain demonstration would be sure of nothing in this world but of perishing quickly.'[1] It is so also in the systematic pursuit of knowledge. Certainty may be found in highly abstract realms, such as mathematics, but elsewhere one must be content with probability. In view of these assertions one might

[1] IV. xi. 10.

have expected to find the examination of probability given a very prominent place, indeed the central place, in the theory of knowledge of Book IV, but in this expectation we are disappointed. Locke's treatment, it must be admitted, is superficial; his analysis of probability is far too slight; he offers us no logic of induction and no examination of the presuppositions of induction. It is not at all to be wondered at that Leibniz, in discussing these chapters in the *Nouveaux Essais*, was led to remark that a precise logic of probability was much to be desired. The want of it in Locke is so plain. The fact seems to be that the struggle to think out the opening chapters of Book IV, and to explain the certainty which pertains to mathematics, had exhausted Locke's mental energies. If the *Essay* and Draft A be compared on this point it will be seen that in writing up his final account of probability he simply returned to the first Draft and restated the theory he found there, with little attempt at development or elaboration. He thus missed a golden opportunity, that of being the founder of the modern logic of probability. But he seems to have been more anxious to finish the *Essay* as quickly as he could, than to make fresh fame for himself in its final chapters.

Actually, he sets before himself two problems in connexion with probability, namely, (*a*) how to distinguish it from certainty, and (*b*) how to measure the degree of probability which pertains to a proposition.

With respect to the first point, Locke contents himself for the most part with stressing the subjective difference. Each man experiences knowing and opining in himself as fundamentally different states of mind. In opining I am aware that I may be mistaken, but in knowing I have certainty. The difference is not one of degree but of kind. Knowing is an infallible intuition; opining is coming to a conclusion after weighing the evidence, but without having attained certainty. It is, to use Locke's own word, judgement. Judgement or belief, he says, is given us 'to supply the want of clear and certain knowledge, in cases where that cannot be had'.[1] Knowledge intuits relations; belief or judgement presumes them; they are thus wholly different faculties. To

---

[1] IV. xiv. 3.

confirm this distinction Locke points to certain objective considerations. Some ideas, we know, are such that our intellects can never perceive a necessary relation between them. In such a case probability alone is possible. On the other hand, we are not to assume that the mind actually does gain intuitive knowledge on every occasion upon which the object is such that intuitive knowledge might have occurred. For instance, I am capable of having intuitive knowledge of such and such a geometrical truth, but I may instead accept the geometrician's word for it, and believe rather than know. Thus the distinction we have in mind cannot be set out wholly in objective terms. Locke himself makes this point clear in contrasting knowledge and probability from the objective side: 'As demonstration is the showing the agreement or disagreement of two ideas by the intervention of one or more proofs, which have a constant, immutable, and visible connexion one with another; so probability is nothing but the appearance of such an agreement or disagreement by the intervention of proofs, whose connexion is not constant and immutable, *or at least is not perceived to be so*; but is, or appears for the most part to be so, and is enough to induce the mind to judge the proposition to be true or false, rather than the contrary.'[1] When I intuit I perceive a necessary connexion; when I believe I presume a connexion, not because I perceive it to be necessary, but because of some extraneous reason, for instance, that so and so, whom I think reliable, affirms the connexion.[2]

The next question concerns the degree of probability. Some propositions are more probable than others. How are we to measure this probability? Locke suggests two criteria: (*a*) the measure of agreement between what the proposition suggests and the rest of one's experience, (*b*) the character of the evidence adduced in its favour. The first test is a sort of coherence test; although as the argument develops it becomes clear that Locke

----

[1] IV. xv. I. (The italics are mine; I have omitted Locke's italics in this passage. He italicizes *ideas*, *probability*, and *judge*.)

[2] Cf. IV. xv. 3. 'That which makes me believe is something extraneous to the thing I believe; something not evidently joined on both sides to, and so not manifestly showing the agreement or disagreement of those *ideas* that are under consideration.'

has not in mind coherence in the sense of self-consistency or non-contradiction. (He does make use of this test in connexion with the examination of evidence, when he demands that every report of an occurrence should be consistent with itself.) But the coherence of the first test is an 'agreeableness' with the rest of our experience, and the principle on which it rests is not non-contradiction but uniformity of nature. Now implicit in Locke's teaching about natural philosophy is the view that the principle of the uniformity of nature is established empirically. We believe that nature is orderly, that the universe is one piece, and so we demand that our experience should be throughout consistent. Our ground for making this demand, however, is that we have always observed things happening 'after the same manner', and we find that the reported experience of others confirms our own observation. That iron sinks in water is 'agreeable to our constant experience' and never once controverted.[1] If any one were to say that he saw iron float in water we should find the statement difficult to believe, because it would be inconsistent with our own experience. But our belief that nature is uniform in this and in every other case is merely an empirically established expectation. Hence it could never be a test of certain knowledge if we ever needed such a test. (Locke himself would say that a test of certain knowledge would be unnecessary.) But it remains an exceedingly useful test of probability. Thus consistency with the rest of what we opine is one test whereby to measure the probability of any proposition.

The other test consists in the careful examination of the evidence in favour of the proposition. Locke suggests that we should carry out this examination bearing in mind the following six points: (1) the number of witnesses who attest to it, (2) their integrity, (3) their skill, (4) the design of the author (if the evidence is furnished in a book), (5) the consistency of the parts and circumstances of the relation, (6) contrary testimonies.

Now the highest degree of probability is attained when a belief accords with the rest of one's experience and with the testimony 'of all men in all ages'. We accept such beliefs as, for instance, that iron sinks in water, with complete assurance, although we realize

[1] IV. xvi. 6 and cf. IV. xvii. 17.

that theoretically they may be doubted. Where a belief accords with part only of our experience and not with the whole of it, or again when it is only partially confirmed by the testimony of others, our doubt is greater. In matters of which we ourselves can have no direct experience, for instance, matters occurring before our birth, we can only be guided by the evidence of witnesses. Wherever possible we try to get the evidence of the intelligent onlooker. We are more ready to doubt the evidence of a man reporting at second hand, and the greater the distance in time between his report and the event the more ready we are to doubt it. Incidentally, for this reason, if for no other, the pronouncements of historians cannot be held to be either completely certain or even as certain as are the statements of natural philosophers, for instance, that iron sinks in water. But this, Locke adds, in no way lessens 'the credit and use of *history*'.[1]

Thus far we have dealt with probable knowledge of the observable. Where we seek to know what cannot be observed, analogy is said to be our guide.[2] By this means alone can we say anything at all about angels, or about those material things which are wholly beyond our ken. It is analogy also that helps us to conceive 'the manner of operation in most parts of the works of nature; wherein, though we see the sensible effects, yet their causes are unknown and we perceive not the ways and manner how they are produced.... Thus, observing that the bare rubbing of two bodies violently one upon another produces heat, and very often fire itself, we have reason to think that what we call "heat" and "fire" consists in a violent agitation of the imperceptible minute parts of the burning matter.' Unfortunately, beyond adding that 'a wary reasoning from analogy' is likely to be helpful, Locke does not further examine the nature of argument from analogy. Judging by the remarks he does make about this form of reasoning he might indeed be thought to be setting forward an unusual theory. Argument from analogy, in the usual sense, is an argument from the observation of like characteristics in *a* and *b*, let us say, to the presence in *b* of certain further characteristics which have already been observed in *a*. But Locke's language in this passage seems at

[1] IV. xvi. 10–11. [2] IV. xvi. 12.

first sight to suggest that *b* is completely unobserved and unknown. In that case it is hard to see how analogy in the ordinary
sense could be possible. A more careful examination of Locke's
words, however, and of the examples given, will show that though
he talks of *b* as being unobserved by sense (and unobservable) he
does not mean that we are completely ignorant of it when we
argue from analogy. We at least assume certain things; for instance, in the case of angels, we assume that they can think, communicate their thoughts, praise God, and so on. It is on the basis
of these assumed common characteristics that we proceed to
ascribe to them further characteristics which we know to belong
to men. Locke's actual words do not make this point plain, but it
is implied in what he says.[1]

To complete our account of knowledge one further instance of
it remains to be considered, a knowledge which is higher than
probability, which is indeed certain, although its certainty is not
demonstrative. This is revelation. A true revelation cannot, in
Locke's opinion, be doubted. Acceptance of such revealed truth is
faith, and Locke, like all his contemporaries, was greatly concerned about the relations between faith and reason. It is to this
problem that he devotes most of his attention in these closing
chapters of the *Essay*. He first makes clear what he means by
reason, identifying it with reasoning or mediate thinking whether
it lead to certainty or only to probability. The account he gives of
reason contains three noteworthy features. First, in defining it he
reasserts his empiricism. '*Reason*, therefore,' he remarks, 'I take
to be the discovery of the certainty or probability of such propositions or truths which the mind arrives at by deductions [a term
used here loosely] made from such *ideas* which it has got by the
use of its natural faculties, namely, by sensation or reflection.'[2]
Secondly, he launches a bitter attack on the logic of the schools,
on the grounds of its narrowness and pedantry and its blind faith

[1] Whether Locke had also realized that argument from analogy involves a
universal mediating concept so that it cannot proceed from mere particular to
mere particular is not clear. It might be argued that he had not, and IV. xvii. 8,
'we reason about particulars', might be adduced in defence of this view. But
IV. xvii. 8 needs to be used with the greatest caution, as I have tried to show
elsewhere (cf. *Proc. Aris. Soc.*, 1932-3, 'Locke's Theory of Universals', pp. 184-5).
[2] IV. xviii. 2.

in syllogism. 'Reason,' he argues, 'by its own penetration where it is strong and exercised, usually sees quicker and clearer without syllogism.'[1] Lastly, he suggests a neat fourfold analysis of inference. It is (1) the discovery of 'proofs', i.e. of premisses; (2) the 'laying them in a clear and fit order to make their connexion and force be plainly and easily perceived'; (3) perceiving the connexion or apprehending the implication; (4) 'making a right conclusion'.[2]

Locke thus identifies reason with inferring or demonstrating, whether the inference yields certainty or only probability. How is this reason related to faith? It is related, Locke thinks, in the following manner: Faith, as we have seen, is the acceptance of revelation. We can rest content in this acceptance if we feel sure that the revelation is genuine. But not all alleged revelation is genuine. Many who claim to have enjoyed this supreme privilege have not really enjoyed it. Now it is reason that tests the genuineness of revelation. It does so in two ways. It examines the external circumstances. Who is it who puts forward the alleged revelation, and under what circumstances? Secondly, it inquires into the content itself, testing it by its own laws. Revelation may go beyond reason, but we assume that it never contradicts it. If it did we could not accept it, we should immediately doubt its genuineness. Revelation is 'reason enlarged'.[3] The revolt against reason in religion is a sign not of true religion but of obscurantism and superstition. *Credo quia impossibile est* is 'a very ill rule for men to choose their opinions or religion by', however well it passes for a 'sally of zeal'.[4] '*Reason*', Locke holds, 'must be our last judge and guide in everything. . . . God, when he makes the prophet, does not unmake the man.'[5] Thus the relations between reason and faith are very close. It is not reason that gives the revelation; revelation itself is independent of reason. But faith none the less rests on reason, for we can only accept as revelation what accords with reason and what is rationally acceptable. Faith is 'an assent founded on the highest reason'.

Before concluding the present chapter it is necessary to add a word on Locke's theory of error. A discussion of this matter will

[1] IV. xvii. 4.   [2] IV. xvii. 3.   [3] IV. xix. 4.   [4] IV. xviii. 11.
[5] IV. xix. 14. 'Revelation must be judged of by reason.'

be found towards the end of the *Essay*,[1] but this discussion needs to be supplemented by many other passages elsewhere. Perhaps the most important point which Locke makes is one that Descartes had made before him, and one which every intuitionist must make, namely, that error cannot possibly be due to a defect of the knowing act. 'Knowledge being to be had only of visible certain truth, error is not a fault of our knowledge.'[2] This follows from the account given of knowledge. It is infallible intuition. It cannot, therefore, be the cause of error. Error, Locke thinks, is a failure not of knowing but of judging. We weigh the evidence and come to an opinion, and the opinion may be false. We 'give our assent to that which is not true'. Locke has explained elsewhere what he means by truth.[3] Truth and falsehood pertain to propositions, and truth is to be defined as 'the joining or separating of signs, as the things signified by them do agree or disagree one with another'. The signs are the terms of the propositions and the 'things signified' may mean ideas, or again things in the natural world. In other words, the signs may stand for ideas which are their own archetypes, or again for ideas which have an archetype outside them, and in the latter case the signs of the proposition, if it is true, are joined or separated not only as the ideas are joined or separated but as things in the natural world are joined or separated. If this correspondence is not present, then the judgement is false.

There are many kinds of error, and we may now enumerate those mentioned by Locke. (1) In IV. xx he is mostly concerned with the error which consists in taking as probable what is really improbable. Since there are degrees of probability, we may hold a proposition to be more probable than it actually is. Lack of leisure for reflection, 'the hot pursuit of pleasure', laziness, or, again, mere stupidity—one or the other of these may account for an error of this sort, and indeed for most sorts of error. Sometimes prejudice and passion make a man over-ready to accept favourable evidence, whilst they blind him to the evidence on the other side. As a consequence he may sincerely accept as probable what an unprejudiced observer would at once perceive to be most

[1] IV. XX.   [2] IV. XX. I.   [3] IV. V.

improbable. *Quod volumus facile credimus.* (2) But to accept the improbable as probable is not the only error into which we fall. Elsewhere in the *Essay* Locke mentions other kinds of error. There is the error which results from a defective memory. Even demonstration, as we saw, since it involves memory, does not possess the full measure of certainty which intuition possesses; although we may evolve a method in demonstration which frees us from dependence on memory. The mathematical seems to be such a method. (3) Again, we may easily confuse nominal with real essence. In that case we should be supposing that the object of our thought was a thing in the physical world when actually it was a mere idea. (4) The senses frequently deceive us. We certainly err if we suppose that the real is identical with what appears. 'We are quite out of the way when we think that things contain within themselves the qualities that appear to us in them.'[1] Too great a trust in the senses is a common cause of error. (5) Finally, there is the error which arises from the misuse of language. We have already dealt with this in discussing Book III.

These are the kinds of error into which we fall. Where we intuit we cannot err; and if we desire certainty it is wise to wait till intuition becomes possible. But in most cases intuition never is possible, and where it is impossible we must choose the most probable, weighing and testing the evidence with the greatest care, and suspending our judgement if the evidence before us is inadequate. Error is due to precipitancy, prejudice, and laziness; we ought not to regard it as inevitable. Locke believes that it is our duty to rid our minds of it. Much ignorance, however, would still remain, even though the ignorance which results from error had been removed. For man cannot hope to possess all knowledge; much is hidden from him. Yet, Locke thinks, he may, if he so chooses, know enough to live a happy and contented life, enough to fulfil his duties. All the knowledge his state requires is within his reach.

[1] IV. vi. II.

PART III

I

MORAL PHILOSOPHY

Locke's purposes were always practical. One of the aims of his philosophical work was to ascertain whether moral knowledge was within the reach of man. The *Essay*, it will be remembered, originated in a conversation between friends about 'the principles of morality and revealed religion'; and it is clear that one of its most important conclusions, in the eyes of its author, was that an exact science of morals was possible. In all his writings Locke assumes as a fundamental principle that man knows enough to live a good and righteous life if he chooses. His faculties are well suited for moral knowledge. But the moral knowledge of the ordinary man, although it is sufficient for his needs, is not exact. And the question which has to be faced is this: Is a science of morality possible which is comparable to the science of mathematics? Can one build a necessary, eternally true, system of morals? The *Essay* returns an affirmative answer. A *science* of morals is possible.

But though Locke thinks it possible and desirable, he does not himself furnish us with such a science.[1] To Molyneux he writes that the work would require a great deal of leisure and much careful concentration. Moreover, it could not be said to be an urgent task since Holy Scripture revealed an ethic entirely adequate for all practical purposes. But a deeper reason for Locke's failure to provide the system he visualized lies in an inner contradiction in his thoughts, a contradiction which becomes plain when we read the various statements he makes from time to time about morality. As was often the case elsewhere, so here in morals he could feel the force of more than one tendency. Two theories compete with each other in his mind. Both are retained; yet their

[1] Some of the Lovelace MSS. appear to be the first drafts for a projected work on a necessary system of morals, cf. Bodl. MS. Locke, c. 28, foll. 142–3, entitled 'Ethica B', and Bodl. MS. Locke, c. 28, foll. 140–1, entitled 'Morality'.

retention means that a consistent moral theory becomes difficult
to find. The first is hedonism, which, in Locke's writings, assumes
the form that the good is whatever produces pleasure, so that our
judgement about good and evil ultimately rests on our feeling of
pleasure and pain. The second is rationalism, the view that reason
alone can determine what is truly good. Writers in the past have
attributed the hedonism in Locke's writings to Hobbes and the
rationalism to Ralph Cudworth, and have held that Locke was in
the main influenced by these two writers. This view, however, can
hardly be true. Cudworth's influence cannot be denied, although
he was certainly not the sole rationalist influence;[1] but it is doubtful whether Locke's hedonism was ever derived from Hobbes.
Gassendi and Bernier are undoubtedly the chief influences in
this connexion. Locke's hedonism (and indeed his whole ethical
theory) has much in common with that of Gassendi. Gassendi, as
we have seen, was the main partisan of epicureanism in his
day, but he reinterpreted it in terms of Christian theology, much
as Locke did after him. Surely Locke's debt is to the Christian
hedonism of the Gassendists rather than to the materialistic
hedonism of Hobbes. But whatever be their source, hedonism and
rationalism are both present in Locke's ethical teaching, and this
fact makes it difficult for him to produce a science of morals. It is
significant that Clarke, a decade later, first emphatically rejected
hedonism, before attempting to formulate his science of morals.
Locke tries to retain it, and yet plays with the idea of a purely
rationalist system of ethics. The ensuing vagueness in his teaching
is almost inevitable.[2]

We may first examine Locke's hedonism. Hedonism for Locke
does not consist in a simple identification of 'good' with 'pleasant'
and 'evil' with 'painful'.[3] But it asserts that 'good' can only be
understood in terms of what we feel to be pleasant; for that is good
which produces pleasure and that evil which produces pain. 'That

---

[1] Nor was his influence entirely rationalist in character, to judge by his manuscript remains in the B.M. Cf. J. A. Passmore, *Ralph Cudworth*, C.U.P., 1951.
Cudworth's influence on Locke's moral psychology would repay study.
[2] On the development of Locke's thought on ethics from 1663 to 1690 cf. von
Leyden, *Law of Nature*, pp. 69–73.
[3] He appears to identify them in II. xxviii. 5, but immediately corrects himself.

we call *good* which is apt to cause or increase pleasure, or diminish pain in us; or else to procure or preserve us the possession of any other good, or absence of any evil.'[1] By stating the hedonistic theory in this manner he is able to find room within the class 'good acts' for those which are pleasant, not in themselves, but only in their consequences. When the pleasure is enjoyed immediately at the moment of action then the act is good, but the pleasure may not be enjoyed till later and still the act, since it procures pleasure, is to be classed with good acts. 'Pleasure' in this context is used widely to signify 'whatsoever delights us'. 'For whether we call it satisfaction, delight, pleasure, happiness . . . they are still but different degrees of the same thing.'[2] It need not be confined to bodily pleasure. Locke also expressly mentions pleasures of the mind. Some pleasures, both of the body and of the mind, are more lasting than others. Locke in an early paper[3] mentions five lasting pleasures, namely, health, a good name, knowledge, 'doing good', and eternal bliss. These are pursued because they are pleasant and we judge that act good which helps to bring them about. Even 'doing good' is here regarded as a source of pleasure and interpreted selfishly. 'I find', Locke explains in this passage, 'the well-cooked meat I eat today does now no more delight me . . . the perfumes I smelt yesterday now no more affect me with any pleasure; but the good turn I did yesterday, a year, seven years since, continues still to please and delight me as often as I reflect on it.' It is in this sense that 'doing good' is a lasting pleasure. Locke talks almost entirely in terms of the individual's rather than of the community's pleasure. But he does hold that a sin against society is greater than one against an individual: 'that being always the greatest vice whose consequences draw after it the greatest harm, and therefore the injury and mischiefs done to society are much more culpable than those done to private men, though with greater personal aggravations.'[4] On the same principle, presumably, we might argue that an act which secures the happiness of one is not so good as that which secures the happiness of many. Thus the lastingness and the distribution of the pleasure must be taken into account in estimating the degree of goodness

---

[1] II. xx. 2. [2] II. vii. 2. [3] Cf. King, ii. 120. [4] King, ii. 95.

pertaining to an act. But an act is good always in so far as it pro-
motes pleasure or happiness, whether individual or social.

So far the hedonism is plain, and it shares in the defects which
usually belong to this type of thinking. Supposing it be admitted
that the good is that which procures pleasure, who is to judge of
the pleasant? Apparently the decision rests with each individual
—'according to every one's relish'. And since individuals vary in
their opinion as to what is and is not pleasant, 'good' will be
relative to each individual judgement. Furthermore, although the
individual may be perfectly clear in his own mind as to what is
pleasant and what unpleasant, he still cannot be sure that such
and such an act is good. For his only test of the goodness of an act,
on this theory, is the amount of pleasure it produces; and he can
never say outright that an act is good, because he can never know
all the consequences. Although the known consequences of an act
may on the whole appear to increase pleasure, further consequences may yet come to light of an opposite nature.[1] It therefore
follows that all moral judgement is probable only. A science of
morals in the strict sense becomes wholly impossible on this basis.
The universality and necessity essential for such a science are absent.

It becomes essential here, however, to note a very important
modification which Locke makes in his hedonism. Not all good,
he holds, is moral good. We need to distinguish between natural
and moral good. Eating food when the body needs food is good
naturally but not morally. Putting one's finger in the fire is naturally evil, because its consequence is pain, but it is not morally evil.
For moral good, he now explains, is that which produces pleasure
of a particular kind, namely, the pleasure with which God rewards
certain acts which he considers desirable. In order to secure
obedience to his laws God has attached pleasures to them, so that
whoever obeys them enjoys these pleasures. Moral good is still to
be recognized by the pleasure it produces, but the pleasure in the
case of moral goodness is not the natural consequence of the act. It
is intelligently appointed. 'The difference between moral and
natural good and evil is only this: that we call that naturally good

---

[1] There is the additional difficulty of measuring and computing pleasures and
pains.

and evil, which, by the natural efficiency of the thing, produces pleasure or pain in us; and that is morally good or evil which, by the intervention of the will of an intelligent free agent, draws pleasure or pain after it, not by any natural consequence but by the intervention of that power.'[1] A related position is to be found in the *Essay*: 'Moral good and evil, then, is only the conformity or disagreement of our voluntary actions to some law, whereby good or evil is drawn on us, from the will and power of the law-maker.'[2] Now God's laws are immutable like himself. To discover them is to know what must promote man's happiness in the most lasting manner. Here then, to some measure, is an objective good, independent of variations in our human judgements as to what is pleasant. Nevertheless, an element of contingency may still remain; for the good is that which God takes to be good, and if his choice of the good be held to be arbitrary and his will free, then a contingent, irrational element still remains in morality.

If, however, we connect this modified hedonism with Locke's rationalism, certain other possibilities emerge. If God acts rationally and not arbitrarily, if he chooses those laws which reason perceives to be good in themselves, and good from the nature of the case, then Locke's modified hedonism may also be a rationalism. For the rationalist may enter into God's thoughts and himself see why these laws are the laws human beings should obey. But they who perceive the rational grounds of morality in this way will be few, and none can expect to perceive the whole explanation. Most men do not bother to inquire into the reason of things. They are hedonists, their end is happiness. And God, who understands man, joins happiness with virtue. Men do what is good because it brings happiness and, moreover, reckon it as good for this very reason that happiness follows in its train. The rationalist, however, also perceives that it is good in itself. Such is the view which seems to be behind Locke's thought, synthesizing hedonism and rationalism. Yet it must be added that nowhere in Locke's works is this view affirmed explicitly and nowhere are its implications worked out. Locke never says that the dependence of goodness upon pleasure is an illusion of the finite mind, resultant upon the fact that

God has so ordained things that good is always followed by pleasure. But this does seem to be the final outcome of his teaching.

If again we approach the problem from the rationalist side, we
shall find ourselves coming to the same conclusion. In discussing
the rationalist elements in Locke's teaching we begin naturally
with the celebrated and interesting suggestion set forward in the
Essay. This suggestion was the consequence of applying to the
moral sphere the most important epistemological discovery which
Locke had made. As we have seen, Locke demonstrated that
mathematics was distinct from natural science and that, whereas
in the first case certainty was possible, certainty was not possible
in the second. Mathematics can be certain because its object (unlike the object of natural science) is 'the idea which is its own
archetype', a mode whose real essence is one with its nominal
essence. In mathematics we discover necessary connexions between abstract ideas whose precise definition we know. Now in the
same sense, Locke argued, a science of morals is also possible. For
such abstract ideas as justice, fortitude, temperance, and the like
are also 'ideas which are their own archetypes', modes whose real
essences are one with their nominal essences. We may therefore
search in just the same way for necessary agreements and disagreements between these abstract ideas, and if we find any we
shall have gained certain knowledge. Furthermore, as in mathematics, so in morals any such knowledge will be gained independently of our experience of the real world. If the real corresponds
to the ideal, then connexions in the ideal will have corresponding
connexions in the real. 'If it be true in speculation, that is, in *idea*,
that *murder deserves death*, it will also be true in reality of any
action that exists conformable to that *idea* of *murder*.'[1] But our
knowledge is true independently of any reference to real events.
Thus a necessary, certain system of morals is possible, in which
knowledge is gained intuitively or demonstratively as in mathematics.[2] In one respect only is the science of morals likely to be

---

[1] IV. iv. 8.

[2] This system, however, is not known innately, nor does it rest on principles
which are known innately. 'Moral principles require reasoning and discourse
and some exercise of the mind to discover the certainty of their truth. They lie
not open as natural characters engraven on the mind' (I. iii. I). Nor is conscience

more difficult than the science of mathematics. The abstract ideas of morality are mixed (rather than simple) modes, and are frequently highly complex. Moreover, their only symbol is the word. They possess no further sensible symbols. On the other hand, geometrical concepts, for instance, are symbolized both by words and by figures on paper. This helps to make the precise meaning of a geometrical term clearer. Moral concepts are signified by words only, and so it is easier to fall into error and confusion in the use of them. Locke has referred previously to this difficulty in connexion with mixed modes, and he can only re-emphasize at this point the need for care in the use of language. But the difficulty is not fundamental; if the necessary care be taken, as exact a science of morals can be achieved as of mathematics.[1]

Critics of the formalistic and rationalist ethics outlined above have been very many from Berkeley's time onward. Berkeley affirms quite bluntly that such a science would be wholly trifling: 'To demonstrate morality it seems one need only make a dictionary of words and see which included which.'[2] And this criticism has been frequently repeated since. Locke, it is said, reduced ethics to a game using as counters unreal and artificial abstractions of his own creation. To show the force of the criticism we may take one of the two examples which Locke himself gives us of the kind of knowledge he has in mind.[3] 'Where there is no property there is no injustice.' This proposition, Locke holds, must be true because 'the idea of property being a right to any thing, and the idea to which the name "injustice" is given being the invasion or violation of that right', it follows that there can be no injustice as defined where there is no property as defined. Now obviously, if we define our terms in this way, the proposition cannot be denied. But clearly its truth depends on the truth of the definitions. It only refers hypothetically to the real world. And in this passage Locke is, in fact, merely informing us as to the way in which he uses terms, and the proposition is truly tautologous. The critics of

a unique kind of knowing, present only in morality. It is 'nothing else but our own opinion or judgement of the moral rectitude or pravity of our own actions' (I. iii. 8).

[1] Cf. III. xi. 15, IV. iii. 18–20. This was a point he had seen at least as early as 1681; cf. Aaron and Gibb, p. 117.   [2] *Commonplace Book*, J. 702.   [3] IV. iii. 18.

Locke seem justified. Locke himself in a paper entitled *Of Ethick in General* deprecates an ethical theory that concerns itself wholly with the analysis of terms. Ethics ought to consider 'species of action in the world, as justice, temperance, and fortitude, drunkenness and theft'; yet frequently it has become merely a dispute about words. 'But all the knowledge of virtues and vices which a man attained to this way would amount to no more than taking the definitions or the significations of the words of any language, either from the men skilled in that language or the common usage of the country, to know how to apply them and call particular actions in that country by their right names, and so in effect would be no more but the skill how to speak properly. . . . The end and use of morality being to direct our lives and by showing us what actions are good, and what bad, prepare us to do the one and avoid the other; those that pretend to teach morals mistake their business and become only language masters.'[1] This passage was probably written after the *Essay*, and we cannot rule out the possibility that Locke had in mind in writing it his own suggestion of a science of morals. Yet this is unlikely. It is more probable that Locke would have defended his theory against this kind of criticism. He would not have agreed that the science of morals, as he conceived it, concerned itself with terms only. For it had to do primarily with ideas and not with the terms which signify them. He might even have gone a step farther. These ideas, although abstract, and although they are their own archetypes, are empirically derived and so are connected with real existences, even though in our perception of relations between them we are wholly independent of such reference.

But it is exceedingly doubtful whether Locke could have saved himself from criticism in this way. If there is a reference beyond the ideas to real things, this reference is clearly irrelevant to moral science as he expounds it. In the same way, the stressing of a supposed difference between idea and term will hardly help him, for this difference also is not truly relevant. The science of morals, as explained by Locke, is possible because each term or idea is adequately defined, and the work of the moralist is to discover the

[1] King, ii. 125–7 and cf. p. 129, § 9.

further implications involved in a system of concepts defined in this way. Surely what Locke proposes is an elaborate analysis of terms in order that all their implications may be made clear. He could not defend himself against the view that the task he imposes upon moralists is one of analysis. But why should he try to do so? The analysis of ethical concepts is highly desirable. The discovery of new implications by analysis is well worth while. Can we not, therefore, say that Locke's demand for a science of morals is a demand for a close analysis of moral concepts? And will not this suffice to silence the critics?

But the critics are not so easily silenced. In the first place, it does not seem to be true that Locke meant his science to be *merely* analysis. Secondly, even regarded as analysis his proposed inquiry is exceedingly defective. It completely neglects to analyse the most important conception in morality, namely, obligation. Moreover, it is only because it neglects the analysis of this conception that the close comparison between mathematics and morals becomes possible. Locke assumes moral obligation throughout; he uses the terms 'should' and 'ought' constantly. Yet he treats morals as if its propositions were of precisely the same sort as those of mathematics. He does not ask how a science whose propositions express obligation can be like another whose propositions express logical relation. The resultant error is a serious one. There may certainly be likenesses between moral theory and mathematics, but any comparison of them which neglects the fundamental difference between moral obligation and logical relation is surely far too superficial. And Locke's comparison, on which his whole suggestion of a science of morals rests, does neglect this difference completely. For this reason alone, we must conclude, Locke's suggestion is defective.

But the formalistic rationalism of the *Essay* is not the only rationalist element in Locke's philosophy. He was well acquainted with, and accepted from his contemporaries, the concept of a law of nature. A law holds upon men independently of all institution whether human or divine. It is knowable by reason[1] and universal

---

[1] Though its material content is ultimately derived from sensation and reflection. Cf. the Latin essays on the Law of Nature in the Lovelace Collection.

in its application. We may consider this historic conception in greater detail in the next chapter, for it is in his political writings that Locke makes greatest use of it. It is sufficient here to notice that the law of nature might well have served as a basis for a rationalist system of ethics and that Locke on occasion, as we shall see, does seek to derive from it various ethical truths. But on the whole he seems to have found it too abstract a conception to serve as a ground for a science of morals. He prefers to rest morality upon a more concrete basis, namely, upon the being of God. The difficulty then, however, is to find an adequate place for the law of nature within this divinely ordained system.

God's will is 'the true ground of morality'.[1] This is the position to which Locke most constantly adheres. God sets his law before man and the moral life is obedience to that law. But why should man obey, and why should he feel obliged to live the moral life? Should he obey out of a sense of duty, because he knows that this action is good and that he ought to do the good? Or should he obey because God commands obedience, and because God has powers to reward the obedient and punish the disobedient?[2] Locke does not give any satisfactory answer to these questions. Nor does he face the greater difficulty which had bothered medieval theologians. Do the moral laws hold in human life simply because they are ordained by God, or does God see them to be good and so ordain them? Did God arbitrarily choose the laws we are to obey, or was he himself constrained by his knowledge of what was good in choosing them? From the rationalist point of view the second alternative is the better. The good is not God's capricious choice, but is determinable by reason. Yet to adopt this alternative and to suppose that God is constrained, is to limit his power of action and choice, and to deny his omnipotency. The point at issue can be put in another way. If God acts arbitrarily, then all moral law is his positive command, and its assertion a fiat of his will. There is no such thing as a law of nature. Our moral obligations cannot possibly rest on 'the eternal law and nature of

---

[1] I. iii. 12.

[2] For Locke's views on the morality of punishment cf. II. xxviii. 5. Cf. also *Works*, i. 229–30, and more generally *Treatise on Government*, ii. 7–12, and *Works*, iii. 539–41.

things'.[1] All law is positive; natural law, determinable by reason independently of God and holding necessarily for man, is a figment of the philosopher's thinking. This issue aroused considerable controversy in late medieval speculation, the nominalists on the whole tending to the view that law was positive, the realists affirming a law of nature. Locke finds it impossible to accept either view outright. He does not wish to deny the law of nature. He accepts it. When in Book I of the *Essay* he rejects innate moral knowledge, he expressly adds a warning that he is not to be taken as affirming positively revealed law to be the sole law and as denying 'a law knowable by the light of nature'.[2] He rejects innate law but affirms natural law. But he also cannot allow that God is determined. On the whole, it would seem, Locke would prefer to give up the concept of a law of nature rather than to deny the omnipotency of God. God is the final source of law. As Locke explains, there is no law without a law-giver, a being who has the power to punish those who disobey.[3] And the sole universal law-giver is an omnipotent Deity. How then can we reconcile the two views? In a letter to Tyrell[4] Locke suggests a possible compromise. The law of nature he there describes as 'a branch of the divine law'. Reason can perceive that it is good for man to obey the natural law, yet it *is* law, it is obligatory upon man, because it, like all other law, is divinely ordained. In this sense of being imposed upon us by God, we may say that the law of nature is also a positive law. This is the sort of compromise which Locke appears to favour.[5]

Thus we once more reach the conclusion, although now from an examination of the rationalist side of Locke's teaching, that moral law, whilst it is divinely ordained, is none the less consonant with human reason, so far as human reason goes. God acts not capriciously but according to reason, and yet he is free.[6] Locke never solves the difficulties involved in this position, indeed, he never begins to examine them. It is in vain that we search in his

---

[1] II. xxi. 56.   [2] I. iii. 13.   [3] II. xxviii. 6.   [4] Cf. King, i. 368.
[5] It is in no way original to Locke. For instance W. A. Dunning in his *History of Political Theories from Luther to Montesquieu*, pp. 137–8, shows how Suarez sought a like compromise and refers to the latter's *Tractatus de Legibus* (1613), II. vi. Cf. also Hobbes's *Leviathan*, i, ch. xv.   [6] Cf. II. xxi. 49.

pages for a consistent ethical theory. We ought to obey moral laws, he teaches, because it is God's will that we should obey them. To enforce his will upon us God gives rewards for obedience and punishes disobedience. And yet, Locke also feels, the law we thus obey at the bidding of God is the one best suited to our nature, and the one to which our reason itself would ultimately guide us.

To complete this account of Locke's ethical theory we need to touch on two further points. Though God's law alone is universal, he is not the only law-giver. In a secondary sense the state enacts laws and compels its citizens to obey them. But also society or public opinion has its law, the 'law of fashion' as Locke terms it.[1] This law varies from age to age and it is not always consonant either with reason or with the divine law, and yet its power over men is very great. Its sanctions, loss of reputation and good name, unpopularity and social disgrace, are very effective—much more effective actually than the divine sanctions, since they are more immediate in their operation. But fashion, 'this common measure of virtue and vice', is no true guide in the affairs of life, and the truly good man finds his standard elsewhere.

The second point to which we must refer is Locke's theory of liberty as expounded in II. xxi of the *Essay*. Locke begins by correcting certain errors into which people fall. First, a man may act voluntarily and yet not be free. A lazy person in the stocks may enjoy sitting there. A student locked in a room may enjoy his study and not desire to leave. But neither is free. 'Voluntary, then, is not opposed to necessary, but to involuntary.'[2] Secondly, the question as to man's freedom is not rightly described as one concerning the freedom of the will. It is not the will which acts or does not act but the man. To say the will acts is to adopt the unfortunate faculty theory at its worst. '*Liberty*, which is but a power, belongs only to agents and cannot be an attribute or modification of the *will*, which is also but a power.'[3] Willing is a power of an agent. It is not itself an agent, and so there is no sense in asking whether the will is free. The problem before us in discussing liberty is whether man is free.

When, then, is a man free? The first step in the answer, Locke

[1] Cf. II. xxviii. 10.					[2] II. xxi. 11.					[3] II. xxi. 14.

thinks, is fairly straightforward. 'So far as anyone can, by the direction or choice of his mind preferring the existence of any action to the non-existence of that action and *vice versa*, make it to exist or not to exist, so far he is *free*.'[1] This is the *libertas a co-actione* of the schools, freedom from external compulsion. I choose a certain line of action and there is nothing in the conditions in which I attempt to perform the act which restrains me in any way. In that sense I am free. But why do I choose this action rather than another, or rather than inactivity? Am I free in choosing? Am I free to will? This question is not so easy to answer. On the whole Locke feels that we are not free to will, that we are determined as to what we do will. In the first edition of the *Essay* he argued that we are determined by what we conceive to be the greatest positive good, so that in the second sense of liberty, *libertas a necessitate*, Locke is here a determinist.

In the second edition, however, he holds that this account of the matter is contrary to the facts and puts forward another theory, which, while still determinist in the main, does leave a loophole for freedom *a necessitate* and so makes moral responsibility a fact. We are determined, he now holds, not by the greatest good in view, but by 'the most pressing uneasiness'. We lack something and are uneasy, and it is this uneasiness which determines our will. This must be so, for we may know the good and yet not do it. But how could this be if we were always determined by the greatest good in view? Clearly, we are not so determined. We are determined by the desire to remove an uneasiness, by a pain, by the absence of a good, and until this uneasiness is removed we do not attempt to attain the greatest good even though we realize that it is the greatest good. Until our desire for the greatest good becomes stronger than all other desires, and the felt uneasiness consequent upon its absence becomes more powerful than all the other uneasinesses which influence us, the greatest good will be an ideal which we recognize but for which we do not strive. The mind is determined to will by the greatest uneasiness at any time. This new theory is still determinist, but Locke now adds one further consideration which somewhat modifies the position in

---

[1] II. xxi. 21.

respect to determinism and indeterminism. Generally it is true
that we are determined by the greatest uneasiness, but it is not
always true. There is an exceptional case of the highest importance for the moralist. The mind can 'suspend the execution and
satisfaction of any of its desires'.[1] If it acts at all it will act to
remove an uneasiness, to satisfy a desire. But it is not bound to act.
It is determined still in not acting, but determined by its own
judgement. And, Locke thinks, 'to be determined by our own
judgement is no restraint to liberty'.[2] It is in this sense, it now
appears, that God and the angels are free. However strong our
desire, however great our uneasiness, we may yet suspend action.
'Nor let any one say, he cannot govern his passions, nor hinder
them from breaking out and carrying them into action; for what
he can do before a prince or a great man, he can do alone, or in the
presence of God, if he will.'[3] It is in this sense only that man may
be free a necessitate. He is not bound to be ruled by mere desire;
desire can be guided and controlled by judgement. And thus
Locke shows how man may be free not only from external con-
straining forces but also from inner compulsion. But the argument establishing man's liberty and moral responsibility is not
without its difficulties, as Locke himself acknowledges at the end
of this chapter.[4]

[1] II. xxi. 47. [2] II. xxi. 48. [3] II. xxi. 53.
[4] II. xxi. 72. The Molyneux Correspondence is particularly interesting in connexion with this chapter. Cf. the 1692-3 letters. Apropos of this chapter it is
also worth observing that Tellkamp has pointed out some interesting parallelisms between Locke's views on freedom in the Second Edition and those of the
medieval thinker, Buridan. Cf. Tellkamp, *Das Verhältnis John Locke's zur
Scholastik*, p. 107.

II

POLITICAL THEORY

LOCKE's political theory is to be found in his *Two Treatises of Civil Government*, particularly in the second of these. The immediate aim of that treatise is apparent: to justify the Revolution of 1688 and to help 'establish the throne of our great restorer, our present King William'.[1] But this aim is achieved by securing in turn a great and fundamental political principle, true for the English nation in 1688 and true, in Locke's opinion, for all well regulated communities everywhere and at all times, that government must be with the consent of the governed, that a ruler who has lost the confidence of his people no longer has the right to govern them.

The principle involves a particular view of government and of political community. Locke set himself to refute two theories which were used to justify privilege, oppression, and political slavery. The first was the theory of the divine right of kings as put forward by Robert Filmer,[2] that the king is the divinely ordained father of his people, and that the relation between king and subject is precisely the same as that between father and child. Locke ridicules the comparison. In the modern state, a large, highly complex organization, parental or patriarchal government is no longer possible, and the claim that it is divinely ordained cannot be substantiated. The second theory, implicit no doubt in Filmer, is to be found in its most explicit form in the works of Hobbes, although Locke does not refer to Hobbes by name, at least in the *Treatise*. Government, in this theory, necessarily involves the complete subjection of the governed to the absolute will of the governor, for without such subjection no civil society is possible. Locke denies this theory categorically. The facts of human experience are against it and reason is against it. A political community is possible in which the power of the governor is limited,

[1] The Preface.
[2] On Filmer cf. the introductions to Peter Laslett's editions of *Patriarcha*, Basil Blackwell, Oxford, 1949 and *Two Treatises of Government*, Cambridge, 1960.

in which sovereignty ultimately pertains not to the monarch, as opposed to those whom he governs, but to the people as a whole. Government becomes an instrument for securing the lives, property, and well-being of the governed, and this without enslaving the governed in any way. Government is not their master; it is created by the people voluntarily and maintained by them to secure their own good. Those who, because of their superior talent, have been set to rule by the community, rule not as masters over slaves, or even as fathers over children. They are officers elected by the people to carry out certain tasks. Their powers are to be used in accordance with 'that trust which is put into their hands by their brethren'.[1] For Locke government is a 'trust' and a political community is an organization of equals, of 'brothers', into which men enter voluntarily in order to achieve together what they cannot achieve apart.

Such was the view of government which Locke adopted, and the second treatise is an effort to discover a rational justification of this view. Locke might have appealed to experience and to history, or again he might have contented himself with showing the public utility of the theory he advocated. But the late seventeenth century was rationalist and would listen to no arguments other than rationalist ones, and so Locke analysed the notion of political society in order to prove rationally that it was from the first a community of free individuals and that it remained so throughout. He spoke in the language of his day and he made use of the theories of his day. In particular, he borrowed two concepts from earlier political theorists, the law of nature and the social contract, and it would be as well to give a brief account of these before proceeding to the details of Locke's argument.

The law of nature, as we have seen, provided a basis for the rationalist strand in Locke's ethics, and it reappears in a still more prominent form in his political writings. This fact need not surprise us, for the seventeenth century was the golden age of the Natural Law School. The concept of a law of nature is, however, much older than the seventeenth century. It can be traced back to Aristotle, and was put forward very explicitly by the Stoics. They

[1] ii, § 231.

held that men were citizens of a divine city, that one universal, immutable law held for all men, whatever other laws they might also be called upon to obey. This was the law of nature, discovered to man by his reason. The Romans, influenced profoundly by Stoic teaching, recognized a *jus naturale* as opposed to the *jus civile*, and Christianity also found the Stoic doctrine not incompatible with its own insistence on the brotherhood of man. In medieval literature the theory is present, and there was considerable dispute as to the relations between the law of nature, rational and universal, on the one hand, and the more positive laws, both secular and divine, on the other. Thus the concept was already old in the seventeenth century, but at no period was its use so extensive. In the writings of Grotius, Pufendorf, Hobbes, Spinoza, and of many lesser writers, it played a highly important part.[1] These authors were not all agreed as to the content of the law. It meant, for most, the equality of all men by nature: *omnes homines natura aequales sunt.* But as to its further content, or even as to the definition of equality, there was little agreement. Each author chose that which he himself regarded as most worthy of obedience and held this to be part of the law. As described by Locke the law of nature demands just such conduct as would be expected of any educated Christian gentleman. It was obviously a vague conception awaiting more careful analysis.[2]

The social contract theory was closely linked with that of the law of nature. In one sense, the former is the corollary of the latter. In nature all men are equal, but in political society some are rulers and others ruled. This difference needs to be explained and is explained by the theory of the social contract. According to this theory the difference is due to the fact that men entered into a pact whereby, in order to gain certain ends, some men allowed themselves to be ruled by others. At first there was a state of complete equality in which every individual was free, but then men came

---

[1] For an excellent study cf. Otto Gierke, *Natural Law and the Theory of Society 1500–1800*, trans. by Ernest Barker. Cambridge, 1934.

[2] The Latin essays on the law of nature in the Lovelace Collection, edited by von Leyden, show Locke's deep interest in the subject. They are not, however, primarily an account of the content of the law (though the seventh essay has something to say on this head) but rather of how we come to know the law, how we are bound by the law and how the law is related to self-interest.

to an agreement and the outcome of this agreement was the political state. In making the contract the people would naturally safeguard themselves as much as possible, so that the powers of the ruler were likely to be limited from the first.[1] Thus on the whole the social contract theory proved most useful to radical and liberal theorists. It was part of the subtlety of Hobbes that he should have used a radical argument as a basis for his own absolutist theory, but such a usage was unusual.

The main points of criticism which can be directed against the social contract theory are familiar. As it stands, it is bad history. It is not true that political societies began in this way. History and sociology lend but little support to this theory of free men entering into a compact and so creating a political group. Usually, so far as can be seen, the more primitive the society the less free the individual, and the free individual of the pre-political state seems to be a mythical creation of the political theorist. It is also bad psychology. The free individual tends to be depicted as largely isolated, a *mere* individual with no social ties. But man is by nature social. The 'unsocial' individual of the pre-political stage is an unreal abstraction. Thus historically and psychologically the theory of the social contract is defective. Otto Gierke has criticized it in another way. A contract of necessity entails duality, whereas the true political society is one. 'The contractual relation must always involve a duality of persons; a personality of the Ruler must always emerge by the side of the personality of the People, equally essential to the existence of the State.'[2] Gierke, perhaps, overstressed the need for unity in the modern state. Even so the social contract theory can perhaps be interpreted in such a way as to meet his objection, and it is doubtful whether the criticism applies, for instance, to Locke's account of the social contract. For Locke does not conceive it as a contract between ruler and ruled. On his view the contract is between all the members of the society, as a consequence of which a trust is imposed upon one or more individuals. The ruler does not stand opposite to the people; he is

---

[1] Although the limitation of the monarch's power is not *necessarily* involved, since the people might think their best security to lie in an absolute government.
[2] *Natural Law and the Theory of Society*, p. 53.

one of them, but entrusted with exceptional duties. The contract theory modified in this way does not seem to be open to the criticism which Gierke makes.

We may now turn to the *Treatises*. Their full title adequately reveals their purpose: *Two Treatises of Government. In the former the False Principles and Foundation of Sir Robert Filmer and his Followers are Detected and Overthrown. The Latter is an Essay concerning the Original, Extent and End of Civil Government.* The work was published in 1690. It was probably begun shortly after the appearance of Filmer's *Patriarcha* in 1680, and Locke no doubt carried the manuscript into exile with him in 1683. The book was completed with a second part in which the right of the English people to rebellion was demonstrated. In the meantime, however, a good deal of the manuscript of Part I had been lost, but since this was part of the refutation of Filmer, and since that refutation as it stands is adequate enough, Locke did not bother to rewrite the missing pages. The book is thus incomplete, although one can rest satisfied that nothing vital is omitted. Part II is complete, and this is by far the more important part.[1]

The refutation of Filmer in Part I need not long detain us. Filmer had argued that Adam was divinely ordained master of Eve, of their children, and of the whole created world, and that all kingly power was inherited from Adam and was as absolute as Adam's was. Locke replied that, in the first place, Filmer had not proved that Adam ever was sovereign in any absolute sense. He had absolute rights neither over Eve nor over his children. It is true that children should honour their parents (although honour is due not to the father alone, but to both parents). But we cannot deduce from this that parents have complete authority over them.

[1] That the missing section was part of the reply to Filmer is clear from Locke's preface to the book. 'If these papers have that evidence I flatter myself is to be found in them, there will be no great miss of those which are lost and my reader may be satisfied without them. For I imagine I shall have neither the time, nor inclination, to repeat my pains and fill up the wanting part of my answer, by tracing Sir Robert again, through all the windings and obscurities which are to be met with in the several branches of this wonderful system.' The missing sections, no doubt, followed § 169, that is, the end of Part I.

It is also true that for a long period a child is unable to reason for itself, and then it is the right and duty of the parents to fend for it and to think for it, and the child must learn obedience. But when it comes to years of discretion this parental authority ceases. Parental authority, Locke insists, is fundamentally different in character from the authority of a ruler in a state and it is thoroughly misleading to confuse the two. But even if Filmer could show that Adam had received absolute powers over others, to complete his argument it would still be necessary for him to prove that the English kings had inherited these powers. It would still be necessary for him to trace the succession from Adam to Charles II, a task which, as Locke easily shows, is completely impossible.

Having dismissed Filmer's false principles of civil government Locke turns in Part II to the consideration of true principles, and I now propose to expound the main lines of Locke's argument— although without following his order. Civil government invariably begins with a contract, and this brings to an end a pre-political state known to Locke and his contemporaries as the state of nature. Now to understand the civil state it is necessary to understand why men left the state of nature. By nature all men are free, 'equal and independent'.[1] Within certain limits each individual has a right to anything he may desire; the sole restraining force within these limits is his own reason. But so far as he is restrained rationally his conduct will conform to the law of nature known by reason.[2] Thus he will not kill another; he will not destroy himself. He keeps his promises, and he deals honourably with those who come into contact with him. He respects other men, and does not regard them as so many instruments whereby he might secure his own ends. We are not made 'for one another's uses'. Consequently, though the individual in the state of nature is free, he is not unaware of his duties to others. And he cannot rightly, on Locke's view, be described as 'unsocial'. He enters into relations with other men from the first, and it is in these relations that the law of nature regulates his activity. Thus the state of nature

[1] ii, § 6.
[2] Locke does not say here how the law is known; his best account of this, inadequate as it is, is in the Latin essays, cf. p. 272, n. 2, above.

(as it ought to be) is a state in which men live together in peace, each one is free, and each one enjoys the fruits of his own labour.

Unfortunately, it is difficult to maintain such a state. Men are never wholly rational. And a man's rapacity and greed might lead him to action which is contrary to the law of nature and contrary to reason. He might covet his neighbour's property, and if he attempts to seize it forcibly his neighbour has a right to meet force with force and war ensues. Now the state of nature does not inevitably develop on these lines. Hobbes is wrong in holding that it *must* be a state of war. If it becomes a state of war it ceases to be the state of nature, that is, a state in which all men are obedient to the law of nature. But Locke has to admit that it may become a state of war, simply because men do not always obey the law of nature. The state of nature would be perfect if men conducted their lives in a perfectly rational manner. But they do not, and the consequence is that while it *is* a state of peace, it is (to use Pollock's language) a state of 'precarious peace'. Here is one reason why men leave the state of nature. Conflict and war are always possible and men cannot be secure in the enjoyment of their lives and property.[1]

It is necessary here to deviate for a moment from the main argument in order to show how private property may belong to a man in the state of nature. Locke had accepted the traditional communism of medieval thought—in the modified and diluted form in which it was handed on to the seventeenth century. It was no longer held that men actually possess all things in common in a positive way and Locke did not teach this. But God had given all things 'to mankind in common', the earth, the air, the sunshine, and the rain, and man was to use them for his own convenience. Yet to use, one must possess, and possess absolutely and not communally. 'God gave the world to men in common,' says Locke, 'but since he gave it for their benefit and the greatest

---

[1] It is in this connexion that Locke attempts a half-hearted defence of slavery. The individual in the state of nature who acts contrary to the law of nature puts himself outside the law. If he fights and is conquered, his life is no longer his own. And if the conqueror so chooses, the conquered may become his slave and no injustice is done. At the same time, the children of slaves, it appears, should not be regarded as slaves, for they have not committed the sin against reason. Cf. ii, §§ 21–23, 85, 116, 182.

conveniences of life they were capable to draw from it, it cannot be supposed he meant it should always remain common and uncultivated.'[1] Thus so long as a thing is possessed in common no one is using it. Land which is common is uncultivated. A piece of land taken and cultivated is the private property of the individual who has cultivated it. In this way, although starting with communism of a sort, Locke can none the less justify property.

Locke's theory of property runs as follows. In the first place, each man possesses himself, his own person, absolutely.[2] But in addition he also possesses anything 'with which he has mixed his labour'. 'Whatsoever', Locke explains, 'he removes out of the state that Nature hath provided and left it in, he hath mixed his labour with, and joined to it something that is his own and thereby makes it his property.'[3] 'Though the water running in the fountain is every one's, yet who can doubt but that in the pitcher is his only who drew it out.'[4] Thus it is labour which creates property. It is labour also which gives value to most things. 'It is labour indeed that puts the difference of value on everything. . . . Of the products of the earth useful to the life of man, nine-tenths are the effects of labour.'[5] Locke here suggested a labour theory of value which was to be extensively developed by later thinkers, particularly by socialist writers.[6] But neither his theory of property nor of labour is fully worked out. There are, it seems, certain limitations to the amount of property one may possess. One may only possess 'as much as any one can make use of, to any advantage of life, before it spoils'.[7] Moreover, one may only take from the common stock when 'there is enough and as good left' in common for others.[8] But Locke unfortunately does not develop these theories, nor does he face the very real difficulties which arise in connexion with them.[9] He is content to show that the possession of private

---

[1] ii, § 34.

[2] A very doubtful principle, incidentally, according to the legal codes of most countries.   [3] ii, § 26.   [4] ii, § 28.   [5] ii, § 40.

[6] Cf. Max Beer, *History of British Socialism*: the theory 'was destined to be made into the main weapon of socialism', i. 57 (1929 edition).   [7] ii, § 31.

[8] ii, § 33. What if there is *not* enough to go round? Who is to arbitrate between the various claims and what are the principles upon which the arbitrator proceeds?

[9] For instance, what precisely is the produce of *my* labour? It obviously

property is fundamental in human life and belongs to man in the state of nature.

Now, to return to the main argument, one of the inconveniences of the state of nature is that an individual who has gained his property honestly may lose it through the covetousness and greed of another, who has ceased to live the rational life. This possibility, as we have seen, produces a feeling of insecurity, which is one of the reasons why men leave the state of nature. But there is another reason. Even when men seek to behave in accordance with the law of nature, their judgement is not wholly reliable. In the state of nature each man is his brother's judge, and has a right to punish him if he break the law of nature. But he may frequently judge wrongly. The state of nature lacks 'an established, settled, known law, received and allowed by common consent to be the standard of right and wrong, and the common measure to decide all controversies between them'.[1] In this respect the law of nature is not definite enough. Moreover, in things which concern us closely it is most difficult to be impartial and unprejudiced. 'In the state of nature there wants a known and indifferent judge, with authority to determine all differences according to the established law.'[2] And even if our judgements are correct we frequently lack the power to enforce them. For all these reasons men decide to leave the state of nature. They make a solemn compact with each other whereby they found a new state. The terms of this compact are simple. Each individual gives up that power which was rightly his in the state of nature, of judging and punishing, and allows these functions to be performed by the state. 'Whenever, therefore, any number of men are so united into one society as to quit every one his executive power of the law of nature, and to resign it to the public, there and there only is a political or civil society.'[3]

includes what I produce by the labour of my own hands. But what of the wealth produced by my beasts of burden and by my machines? Even more, what of the wealth produced by my servants and my employees? In § 27 Locke writes: 'Thus, the grass my horse has bit, *the turfs my servant has cut*, and the ore I have digged in any place where I have a right to them in common with others, become my property without the assignation or consent of anybody.' (My italics.) How seriously should we take this sentence? Is it meant to be a justification of capitalism? Cf. C. B. Macpherson, *The Political Theory of Possessive Individualism* and Appendix v.

[1] ii, § 124.   [2] ii, § 125.   [3] ii, § 89.

In return the individual gains security in the enjoyment of his remaining rights.

The new state is a state which wields political power, and Locke has defined political power carefully at the outset of his book. 'Political power, then, I take to be a right of making laws with penalties of death, and consequently all less penalties, for the regulating and preserving of property, and of employing the force of the community in the execution of such laws, and in the defence of the commonwealth from foreign injury, and all this only for the public good.'[1] Thus when the individual departs from the state of nature it is this right of judging and punishing his fellow man, the right of enforcing the law of nature, which he gives up. He does not relinquish all his rights. There is no suggestion that he is henceforward the puppet of the new state, deprived of all his rights. Only in this one respect, for his own better security, he allows the state to act and promises faithfully his obedience and support.[2]

The compact thus made needs to be renewed in the case of each individual in the subsequent history of the state. Pufendorf had argued that the compact made by one generation would henceforward hold for all subsequent generations and need not be renewed. But in such a case, Locke thought, the individual might feel that the compact no longer held for him. Thus it must be renewed with each individual. At the same time, it was so obvious that individuals do not in fact enter into such a contract that Locke found it necessary to admit a distinction between open and tacit consent. The individual tacitly acquiesces in the social contract if, having reached years of discretion, he still remains in that community and does not depart from it. He is free to depart if he chooses. 'A child is born a subject of no country or government.'[3] If, when he has grown to manhood, he remains in the state, this can be taken as a sign that he has entered into the compact which binds the community into one.

So much for the origin of civil society. But in making its origin

[1] ii, § 3.   [2] This signifies too a readiness to fall in with the majority view. Cf. ii. §§ 95-9 and *see* W. Kendall, *John Locke and the Doctrine of Majority Rule*, chapter vii.
[3] ii, § 118. Pollock comments: 'Another opinion which no modern lawyer will accept.' *Locke's Theory of the State*, p. 24.

clear we have also revealed its purpose. Civil society exists to free individuals from the insecurity of the state of nature. Men unite voluntarily 'for the mutual preservation of their lives, liberties, and estates, which I call by the general name, property'.[1] This sounds true Whig doctrine, as no doubt it was meant to be. But there is no need to interpret it in too narrow a fashion. There is nothing to show that Locke regarded government as necessarily evil. Within its limits it can work beneficially for the human race, and much that Locke says about its functions would accord ill with any narrow *laissez-faire* doctrine. Yet the individual's rights must be jealously preserved. Locke would not tolerate the subjection of the individual to the government except only in the bare minimum described above which he conceives to be necessary. And even in respect to this minimum the individual himself agrees to relinquish his natural rights. It is not subjection; it is contract. The individual enters into the political society, and as a member he recognizes his responsibility and his duty. And the whole force and power of this community of free individuals are derived directly from that recognition.

What constitution is best fitted for a free people? Of the three forms, democracy, oligarchy, and monarchy, Locke felt that none was wholly satisfactory in itself, and he favoured a mixed constitution, namely, the constitutional or limited monarchy, which the Whigs were then establishing. In accordance with this constitution, the people elect the legislative assembly and grant it the 'legislative power', that is, 'the power . . . to direct how the force of the commonwealth shall be employed for preserving the community and the members of it'.[2] In the main, this direction will take the form of legislation, although apparently it need not always do so. Next, there is the 'executive', 'to see to the execution of the laws that are made'.[3] As Locke explains the functions of this office it becomes clear that it contains both the judiciary and the executive in the modern sense, and it would have been well if he had distinguished between these offices. But he does not do so. The 'executive power', in Locke's sense, is usually placed in the hands of a single person, that is, the monarch. Finally, Locke

[1] ii, § 123.   [2] ii, § 143.   [3] ii, § 144.

introduces the 'federative', the name he gives to the office which concerns itself with foreign affairs. Locke finds that the federative and executive offices are usually united in the same person, that of the monarch, and he thinks this to be the wiser course. But on the whole he prefers to see the legislative and executive powers in separate hands. He is not perhaps as zealous for this separation as some have made out. But he does bring forward two arguments in favour of the separation of powers. First, as long as government continues in being the executive must be in being, but the legislative need sit only whilst it legislates and this is unlikely to take up the whole time of the members of the assembly. Secondly, a more important argument: 'it may be too great temptation to human frailty, apt to grasp at power, for the same persons who have the power of making laws to have also in their hands the power to execute them.'[1] For these reasons Locke thinks that 'in all moderated monarchies and well-framed governments . . . the legislative and executive power are in distinct hands'.[2]

A question of considerable difficulty which now arises is that as to sovereignty. Who is sovereign in Locke's state? The monarch, having executive and federative powers, is none the less responsible to the legislative. Accordingly he is not supreme, except in a secondary sense. But the legislative again is responsible to the people and can be dismissed by the people. No doubt, the proper answer to the question is that the people are sovereign—although this answer would be clearer if we knew more precisely whom we are to understand by the term 'the people'. Once the legislative is appointed, however, and a government comes into being the sovereignty passes from the hands of the people into those of the legislative. The supremacy of the legislative while in session is a point which Locke stresses. Moreover, the monarch, the chief executive officer, also shares in the sovereignty. He has the right to dissolve the legislative assembly and possesses other prerogative powers which make him, on occasion at least, truly sovereign. Consequently, Locke's political theory is devoid of any clear-cut theory of sovereignty. In this respect it compares unfavourably with Hobbes's. In the *Leviathan* there is no doubting the identity

[1] ii, § 143.   [2] ii, § 159.

of the sovereign; it is the absolute ruler. All the power of the state resides in him. Hobbes's theory is the more definite and logical and in that sense the more satisfying to the intellect. Yet it is logical at a price. It involves absolutism. Locke's problem is to find a constitution for a community which is determined to remain free, determined to avoid tyranny in any form. And he puts forward this system of check and countercheck wherein those who possess authority are limited in their powers and are throughout responsible for their actions.

As long as it sits 'the legislative is the supreme power . . . and all other powers in any members or parts of the society derived from and subordinate to it'.[1] 'In a very tolerable sense' the monarch also may be called supreme. He is the supreme executive and supreme federative officer of the state. But in both respects he is answerable to the legislative body. Other minor officers, of whom of course there must be many, 'are all of them accountable to some other power in the commonwealth'.[2] If, however, the government ceases to exist and is dissolved this does not mean the dissolution of the political society. It means that the sovereignty has returned to its original source, the people, who have the right and the power to set up a new legislative and executive. It is in this sense that 'the community perpetually retains a supreme power'.[3]

In this way Locke secures what he most strongly desires. If either the legislative body or, as Locke thinks more likely, the monarch, usurps its or his power in any way, then the people have a right to withdraw their support and to dissolve the government. Locke recognizes that the monarch has certain privileges. In a constitution of the kind sketched by him it will be necessary to leave many matters to the discretion of the chief executive officer. 'This power to act according to discretion for the public good, without the prescription of the law and sometimes even against it, is that which is called prerogative.'[4] Locke admits prerogative as necessary for the proper functioning of the governmental system. It is part of the king's prerogative also to dissolve the legislative and to assemble it when he thinks this will best serve the interest of the public. But if a monarch seeks to rule without the legislative

[1] ii, § 150.   [2] ii, § 149.   [3] Ibid.   [4] ii, § 160.

body, if he interferes with its work and liberty, if he changes the
method of electing the legislative without the consent of the
people, if he 'delivers the people into the subjection of a foreign
power', or, lastly, if he so neglects his executive duties as to cause
the country to fall into a state of anarchy, then the people have a
right to dismiss him. A monarch (or any other person) who seeks
to become tyrant and to take absolute powers upon himself
threatens the inner harmony of the society. He has put himself
into a state of war with the people, and the people have a right to
use force against him in order to rid themselves of him. Locke was
not blind to the horrors of war. He particularly disliked the adula-
tion paid to military men. 'We are apt to make butchery and
rapine the chief marks and very essence of human greatness.'[1]
And yet he could not bring himself to renounce war. Force must
be met by force, lest the innocent should suffer for ever. And a
people have a right to use force if necessary against their ruler.
Locke admits the right of rebellion. He here touches on what had
been for some time a thorny problem. Even the more radical
thinkers had hesitated before ascribing this right to the people.
But Locke does not hesitate. The people, being always the
supreme authority in any state, have a right to depose; it is their
sacred duty to overthrow any individual who seeks to make his
power over them absolute and despotic. To the objection that this
will make for unsettled government Locke answers that the
people are usually very loath to rebel, that they will suffer much
before they resort to force. But there are limits to their patience.
What is of vital importance is that they should always retain their
supremacy and sovereignty in the state. To retain this, rebellion is
justified.[2]

Such is the political doctrine which Locke sets forward in his
second treatise. It is not free from defects. Locke is not thorough
and does not exhaust his topic. He is too ready to set down general
principles without considering all their implications. He neglects
the details and brushes aside without sufficient consideration, or

[1] *Of Study*: King, i. 178–9; cf. *Education*, pp. 53–54.
[2] Locke does not consider the possible effectiveness of constitutional amend-
ment without rebellion.

wholly neglects, many difficulties. Moreover, it cannot be denied that he deals too frequently in artificialities. His individual is artificial. He has no family ties. He tends to be conceived as a somewhat isolated being even when he enters into social relations with others. So also Locke's state is artificial. It is a community of free and independent individuals bound together by a compact into which they have entered freely for the better security of their lives, liberties, and estates—and it is nothing more. But surely a political or civil society is much more. For instance, Locke omits all reference to family and race. Racial or tribal sentiment, he thinks, may be neglected in discussing the origin of civil society. And yet to neglect race in this way is to commit as serious an error as is committed by those who see in a political society merely a racial group and who hold that race alone matters. Both views are artificial and over-simplified.

I may mention one further, and still more radical, defect. Locke is an individualist; yet his individualism is left undefined, for no definite solution is to be found in his works of the vexed problem of the relations between individual and community. There is one brand of individualism which can hardly be attributed to him, namely, that which would permit the individual complete licence. Locke's individual is never free without limitations. Even in the state of nature he is a rational being and so knows, even though he may disobey, the law of nature. And if he does disobey, other men punish him, so that an element of compulsion enters. In civil society he is bound by a positive legal code. Thus he is not free to do whatever he desires to do. None the less, we are not to suppose that his freedom is necessarily curtailed because he obeys the law. At least from the point of view of the more rationalist side of Locke's moral and political teaching, obedience to law is not bondage. Reason knows the law and delights in obeying it. This point is not altogether explicit in Locke, but in a tentative way it is present. To be rational is to know law, and to live under the law is to live the free life. 'Freedom of men under government is to have a standing rule to live by, common to everyone of that society and made by the legislative power erected in it, a liberty to follow my own will in all things where that rule prescribes not; and not to be

POLITICAL THEORY   285

subject to the inconstant, uncertain, unknown, arbitrary will of
another man: as freedom of nature is to be under no other restraint
but the law of nature.'[1] The individual is free in spite of certain
restraints upon him.

This point is clear. But the defect in Locke's position is that he
does not discuss the case of the individual who, for one reason or
another, finds the restraints imposed upon him by the community
unjust, a violation of what he conceives to be his individual rights.
What if the dictates of a man's conscience and the civil law conflict? Is the individual free when he then obeys the civil law?
Moreover, what if the civil law is enacted by a legislative body in
whose election the individual has had no say? (Locke apparently
would not grant universal suffrage.) Is the individual then free
when he obeys, perhaps contrary to his own choice? Locke might
still hold him to be free, since he has entered into the contract
which is the basis of the society. But in that case the artificiality
of Locke's theory would be hiding the real problem from him.
No doubt a contract would be implicit in the democratic society
which Locke had in mind. It is implicit in the individual's recognition of his duty to the community, the recognition which gives
strength to a democracy. But a civil society as described by Locke,
this group of free individuals, who have explicitly entered into
a compact, is very different from civil society in its concrete
actuality. The latter rests on much more than contract, and to
say that each individual who finds himself in the state is there
wholly by contract is to misrepresent the truth.

It must be concluded that the problem of the relations between
individual and community is one which Locke does not finally
solve. Nevertheless, Locke's individualism is a fact and needs to be
stressed. He is first an individualist in so far as he sets as narrow
limits as are possible to the state's power. Government can demand the individual's obedience only in limited spheres. Within
these spheres its authority is final. But outside them it has no
authority. The individual is wholly free, for instance, in his
family, or again in his religious life, as long as he does not

[1] ii, § 21.

interfere with the liberty of others. In the same way he can use his leisure in whatever way he desires, and choose whatever profession he desires. But, in the second place, Locke is also individualist in the further sense that he views government as itself an instrument to promote the individual's good. It is true that it seeks the greatest good of the greatest number, 'the public good', and so an occasional individual may find his own good sacrificed. But civil society does not exist to further any other purpose than that of the public good. Locke's individualism is largely a question of emphasis. He puts all his stress on the rights of the individual which should never be sacrificed except in the extreme case in which the freedom of one individual must be curtailed to give freedom to others. There is a sense in which Locke could accept the principle, *Gemeinnutz vor Eigennutz*. He is not afraid of governmental interference in the life of the individual. After all, he was mercantilist in his economic theories and admitted the need for governmental control in trade. And there are other spheres where Locke would consider government could profitably intervene. But if it does so, it intervenes to better the prospects of the greatest number of individuals. In a word, government is an instrument to be used for the good of individuals. The state is made for the individual and not the individual for the state. It is in this sense, more than in any other, that Locke is the champion of individualism.[1]

[1] There have been many recent studies of Locke's political philosophy. For an account of, and comment on, these studies cf. Appendix V.

III

EDUCATION AND RELIGION

THERE still remain to be considered Locke's thoughts on education and on religion. In both fields his thinking was widely influential, and what he wrote on education, in particular, remains fresh and valuable.

I

Locke realized the supreme importance of education. 'Of all the men we meet with, nine parts of ten are what they are, good or evil, useful or not, by their education.'[1] He himself had been led to inquire into the subject as the consequence of his interest in Edward Clarke's family. When in exile in Holland he wrote long letters to Clarke instructing him how best to educate his son. Later, in 1693, he gathered the drafts of these letters together and after modifying them in certain particulars published them as *Some Thoughts concerning Education*.[2] In reading the book it is well to remember that he is dealing with a limited problem: How best to educate the son of the squire who will one day be squire himself. He has before his mind young Edward Clarke, who showed little promise of great scholarship, or of greatness of any kind, but was plainly destined to live the life of the average English gentleman of good birth. Locke believed in the individual method in education, as he himself informs us. The details of educational procedure should vary with the idiosyncrasies of each pupil. And here he is outlining a system of education for Edward Clarke in particular, with the hope that its general principles will hold for the education of the normal boy of the squire class.

First, Locke deals with the health of the body. Children when

---

[1] *Education*, § 1.   [2] The first draft of the *Thoughts* has been published privately (1933) and differs considerably from the first edition. Cf. 'John Locke. Directions concerning Education, Being the First Draft of his *Thoughts Concerning Education* now printed from Add. MS. 38771 in the Brit. Mus. With an introduction by F. G. Kenyon.' Oxford. Printed for presentation to the members of the Roxburghe Club, 1933. On *Some Thoughts* see further James L. Axtell's edition, *The Educational Writings of John Locke*, 1968, with its useful introduction.

young are not to be coddled and spoilt, but their bodies are to be gradually hardened to withstand external changes. Their clothes should be light and loose-fitting. They should spend much of their time in the open and be given sufficient exercise. Locke recommends cold baths and leaky shoes as aids in the process of hardening. Sleep, 'the great cordial of nature', should not be neglected. Children should be given little meat and no strong drinks, and regular habits should be established. They should be permitted to romp and play to their heart's content. The theory that children should be seen, but not heard, finds little support in Locke's pages. Their 'gamesome humour, which is wisely adapted by nature to their age and temper, should rather be encouraged, to keep up their spirits, and improve their strength and health, than curbed or restrained: and the chief art is to make all that they have to do sport and play too'.[1] In this way, by obedience to rules of health, the body may be made strong and active.

In respect to the education of the mind, the first thing to emphasize, in Locke's opinion, is that a sound mind does not mean merely a well informed mind. A pupil may know all the scholastic philosophy, may write perfect Greek and Latin exercises, and yet be badly educated. Character, Locke thinks, is indeed more important than learning. Virtue, wisdom, good breeding—these are the marks of the sound mind. Learning is secondary. First comes the good life, based, as Locke thinks, on a knowledge of God. Then comes wisdom, not crafty cunning, but sagacity and prudence in the conduct of one's affairs. Thirdly, good breeding, which Locke neatly defines as 'not thinking meanly of ourselves nor of others', not being 'sheepishly bashful' on the one hand, nor 'negligent and disrespectful in one's carriage' on the other.[2]

Now virtue, wisdom, and good breeding cannot be taught directly as one teaches the multiplication table. And certainly they cannot be enforced. Nothing is more dangerous and nothing in the long run more ineffective than an attempt to compel a child against its will to a certain mode of life. Compulsion at best can only succeed in breaking the child, and so unfitting it for life. 'Dejected minds,' says Locke, 'timorous and tame and low spirits

[1] § 63.   [2] § 141 and cf. 142–6.

are hardly ever to be raised and very seldom attain to any thing'.[1] The successful teacher does not need to compel; and the use of force, for instance, in corporal punishment is a sign of failure on the teacher's part. A good teacher will teach much by example and by suggestion. Children, of course, with their readiness to emulate others, learn quickly from the example of others. For this reason, they should be reared in the company of virtuous, wise, and well-mannered men and women. Speaking generally, children should be as frequently as possible in the company of their parents, and although occasionally a maid may have greater virtue than her mistress—and then it is best to leave the child to the maid—in general a mother should rear her own offspring. On the difficult question of whether a child should be sent away to school or not, Locke thinks that in the majority of cases it is best for the child to remain at home in the care of its parents for as long as possible. It is foolish 'to hazard one's son's innocence and virtue for a little Greek and Latin'.[2] It is true that the child away from home will learn manliness and self-reliance more quickly, although this may develop into 'a forward pertness' not consonant with good manners. But these virtues can be learnt at home in a well regulated household, and it is easier there to learn the further lesson which boys find difficult to learn, that, whilst courage is good, cruelty is always evil. Accordingly, Locke would recommend for most gentlemen's sons an education at home carried forward under the watchful eye of the parent, but with a tutor from outside to help in the work.

The tutor will have to be carefully chosen, for much depends on the right choice. By precept, and even more by example, he will teach the child to control and discipline itself. He will discourage the desire for pleasure, never restraining forcibly, but carefully refraining from encouraging the natural desire for pleasure present in every child. For instance, he will not reward a good act with the gift of a sugar plum, lest the pleasure of winning the reward fill the child's mind. Wherever possible, and as soon as possible, he will appeal to the rational element. He will treat his pupil as a rational creature and encourage him to reason for

[1] § 46.   [2] § 70.

himself and to see the rationality and wisdom of the conduct suggested to him. Rules should be as few as possible, although it is
well that these few should be obeyed.

In this way will virtue, wisdom, and good breeding best be taught.
In addition, the child needs a stock of useful knowledge. And here
the method of teaching is all-important. For the young child, at
least, learning must be made another form of playing. Children
cannot learn under compulsion; restraint paralyses them. The
skilful teacher knows how to impart his information in so interesting a fashion that the children learn with the same zest as they
play. He finds an ally in the natural curiosity of childhood. Children are very curious; they are full of questions about the things
they see and hear. 'They are travellers newly arrived in a strange
country, of which they know nothing: we should, therefore, make
conscience not to mislead them.'[1]

The child should first be instructed in its own tongue so that it
speaks, reads, and writes that tongue correctly. Then as soon as
possible it should begin to learn another language, for instance,
the English child might learn French. In a year or two Latin also
should be taught, and taught by the conversational or direct
method. (Children should not begin with exercises in Latin grammar. Let the teacher talk to them in Latin and let them learn to
read the language fluently, and then it will be time enough to turn
to grammar.) When they have gained some mastery over these
languages, Locke cannot recommend the practice of his age that
pupils should then spend the rest of their time learning other
ancient languages, Greek, Hebrew, and Arabic, together with
rhetoric and logic. He recommends instead geography, history,
and anatomy, subjects which require little reasoning powers but
some memorizing. At the same time a beginning should also be
made with the study of more abstract inquiries, arithmetic, geometry, and astronomy. Later, the growing youth should learn a
little civil law and a little ethics. And his education might be
completed with an introduction into the various hypotheses in
natural philosophy, both physical and metaphysical. He will not,
of course, be a specialist in any of these subjects. His knowledge

[1] § 120.

will be general and not very deep. But it will be enough for his needs.

For recreation, after more serious study, Locke will turn his pupil's mind to the arts and the crafts. The young gentleman, however, is not to take these too seriously. The enjoyment of poetry, for instance, is pleasant and so is its writing, but it is an art not to be encouraged in a young man. No father is anxious to see his son a poet: 'For it is very seldom seen that any one discovers mines of gold or silver in Parnassus. 'Tis a pleasant air, but a barren soil.'[1] Towards music Locke is somewhat more sympathetic, although he thinks proficiency at a musical instrument hardly worth the time taken to acquire it. Moreover, it engages a young man 'in such odd company'. 'Men of parts and business' do not commend it.[2] Nevertheless, some recreation is certainly necessary. Locke thinks sport rather a waste of time. His own recommendation is that young men, even young gentlemen, should learn a trade, such as gardening or carpentry, in their leisure hours. Finally, he thinks travel good, although not at the usual age, that is between sixteen and twenty-one. A youth travels for one of two purposes: to learn a foreign tongue, or to make acquaintance with men of note abroad and to understand the political and social conditions in which they live. For the first purpose the usual age for travel is much too late, and for the second it is too early.

No book of Locke's is more readable than his *Some Thoughts concerning Education*. Most of its teaching has long since become part of the generally accepted educational theory of this country, although in many places practice still lags behind theory. In his own day, however, to judge from the evidence to hand, it must have been regarded as highly heretical. His contemporaries must have been surprised by his assertion that the teacher's first task was to create character; while his suggestions that logic and rhetoric could be neglected, and geography, history, and anatomy substituted in their place, that English should be studied as thoroughly as Latin and that Greek could be entirely omitted from the curriculum, must have been regarded as revolutionary

[1] § 174.   [2] § 197.

in the extreme. But the pleasant, fresh style of the work, its force-fulness, and, at the same time, its general good sense, captured the imagination of men and also appealed to their intellect. *Some Thoughts concerning Education* is a very definite step forward in educational theory and few other English books have influenced educational thought so deeply.[1]

II

Religion was Locke's dominating interest in the closing years of his life. The works he wrote on religious topics in that last decade, the *Reasonableness of Christianity* and its *Vindications*, together with the commentaries on the *Epistles*, make up a volume larger than the *Essay* itself. Earlier, he had been com-pelled to devote most of his attention to secular matters, but thoughts of God and immortality and of the religious life of man were never far from his mind. One of his first tasks had been to make his choice between Anglicanism and Dissent. He had chosen membership within the Church of England, first, because he disliked the wild rantings and the fanaticism of many noncon-formists, and, secondly, because he regretted and feared narrow sectarianism. At the same time his Anglicanism was always very broad. He shared his views on church government and on the priesthood with many dissenters. A church is a voluntary institution of believers; if a church appoints one from amongst its members to minister in a special way to its spiritual needs, his authority is as great as the members of the church choose to make it. The opposite view that a priest, whether pope, bishop, or pres-byter, has absolute authority over his flock in matters spiritual was as abhorrent to Locke as that other view that monarchs have absolute rights over their subjects. In the religious sphere, more than in any other, the individual must enjoy perfect freedom.

---

[1] It has been held that Locke was indebted for many of his educational theories to two earlier writers on education, namely, Rabelais and Montaigne. Cf. further (1) Arnstädt, F. A., *François Rabelais und sein Traité d'Éducation mit besonderer Berücksichtigung der pädagogischen Grundsätze Montaigne's, Locke's und Rousseau's,* Leipzig, 1872; (2) Villey, P., *L'Influence de Montaigne sur les idées pédagogiques de Locke et de Rousseau,* Paris, 1911; (3) Thiele, A. E., *Montaigne und Locke, ihre Stellung zur Erziehung und zur Selbsttätigkeit,* Leipzig, 1920. Locke's own influence on Rousseau's *Émile* is obvious enough.

Religion begins with communion between God and the individual in the solitariness of the inner life. And it is a communion into which the individual enters freely.

Holding such views as these it is not surprising that Locke advocated toleration.[1] He was not, of course, the first to argue for toleration. On paper at least the battle was wellnigh won before Locke wrote. The plea for freedom in religion was a plea with which Englishmen had long been acquainted, and by Locke's time it was obvious to the discerning that religious toleration was not only a primary necessity for the spiritual health of the individual, but that it also increased the national strength. It made for understanding and for an inner unity, even at the cost of sacrificing uniformity in worship. Moreover, the economic advantages to be gained from toleration, as the instance of Holland made abundantly clear, were many. But it was not upon arguments such as these that Locke based his case, although they were doubtless in his mind. He tried rather to prove his point by arguing from the essential nature of a religious community on the one hand, and from the inevitable limitation of man's knowledge on the other.

Locke's main arguments are three in number. In the first place, from its very nature no church has a right to persecute, nor has it a right to use the civil power for this purpose. A church is a 'voluntary society of men'. To that extent it is, in Locke's view, analogous to a state, but it differs from the state in one important respect. When a state comes into being the individuals composing it give up their own power of executing punishment, and entrust

[1] In 1660, influenced no doubt by the political situation at the time, Locke's tone had been more reactionary than usual, to judge from the paper on the magistrate's right of interference in 'indifferent things'. (Yet see page 366 below.) But after 1667 his point of view in all his private papers when discussing toleration is identical with that in his *Letter*. The *Epistola de Tolerantia* was written in 1685/6 in Holland and addressed to Limborch. It is he who seems to have been responsible for its publication in 1689. In the same year an English edition appeared, translated from the Latin by William Popple. In 1690 Proast 'considered and answered' Locke, and in the same year Locke replied. His *Third Letter*, again in reply to Proast, appeared in 1692. For further information *see Epistola de Tolerantia*, an edition of the Latin text by Raymond Klibansky and translated by J. W. Gough (Oxford, 1968).

this power to the state. Now when individuals join a church they do not give it any powers of this sort. A church has no power to use force; whereas a state has. But the state has no right to use its force in religious matters. The purely religious sphere is not political. The care of the citizen's body and of his property is the proper concern of the civil magistrate, but no one, neither God nor man, has entrusted the care of the citizen's soul to him. Accordingly, a church has no right to persecute through its own agents, nor again has it a right to persecute through the civil power.

In the second place, it is most unlikely that any church or any individual man possesses the full truth about human life and destiny. And this very limitation makes intolerance at once unjustifiable. For when two men genuinely disagree after a sincere search for truth, what possible justification can there be for intolerance and persecution on the part of one of these men? Surely no man has a right to persecute another because this other fails to see eye to eye with him. The persecuted party may be nearer the truth than the persecuting. All over Europe in Locke's day the differing sects persecuted each other. Not more than one of them could possess the full truth, and the extreme probability was that none of them possessed it fully. And yet one had the incongruous spectacle of men 'punished in Denmark for not being Lutherans, in Geneva for not being Calvinists, and in Vienna for not being Papists'. It will be time enough to be intolerant when the full truth is known.

But, thirdly, even though we did know the truth, little could be gained by intolerance. The use of force may certainly secure an empty outward conformity, but such conformity does not carry with it inward conviction. It breeds hypocrisy and false religion. Persuasion and example are the true weapons of a church. Persecution is not one of them. Intolerance is not merely evil; it is also ineffective.

These are the arguments upon which Locke bases his plea for toleration. He demands complete freedom for the individual in religious matters, and makes but one exception. If an individual as the result of his religion does positive harm either to another individual or to the state, then he cannot be permitted to practise his religion. For instance, a religion having human sacrifice as part of its ritual could not be tolerated in any modern community. Locke includes as instances of this exceptional case two groups to whom he would not grant toleration. Atheists cannot be trusted, not having the proper basis for morality, namely, a belief in God. They are, consequently, very likely to do harm to their fellow citizens, and so should not be tolerated. Again, some religions demand from their believers allegiance to a foreign potentate. Locke instances the case of the Mahometans, although it is clear that he has Roman Catholics most in mind. The state can only permit such religions at considerable risk to itself. In all cases, however, where the state intervenes and suppresses, it does so not on religious grounds (for in this purely religious sphere it has no rights whatsoever) but on political and social grounds only.[1]

But while Locke advocated toleration in the religious life, he could not but regret the disunion and schism which he saw around him. His ideal was a broad, comprehensive church which could contain within itself men of different opinions. He was convinced that the Latitudinarian position was sound, that belief in one or two essential tenets of the Christian religion should be sufficient for membership. Locke had been brought up a Calvinist, but under the influence of Latitudinarians, Cambridge Platonists, and Remonstrants in Holland he adopted a position in theology more consonant with the liberalism and rationalism of his politics. This becomes apparent in his *Reasonableness of Christianity*.

This book is the outcome of a critical study of the Gospels. Locke approached Holy Scripture with the reverence of a believing Christian, but this did not prevent him from studying it in an intelligent manner. In his historical and critical approach to the Scriptures Locke is a worthy forerunner of Schleiermacher; he is a pioneer of modern Biblical criticism, as is shown both by the *Reasonableness of Christianity* and even more by his commentaries on the Epistles of St. Paul. The introductory essay to the commentaries, *An Essay for the Understanding of St. Paul's*

---

[1] It is most doubtful whether Locke could successfully justify any exception to universal toleration on these grounds.

Epistles by consulting St. Paul Himself, is an able plea for the critical method in the study of the Epistles.

Locke bases his thesis in the *Reasonableness of Christianity* upon an appeal to Scriptures, studied in the same careful and intelligent manner. He argues that if we read the Bible carefully we shall find that the theologians with their endless creeds and dogmas, their innumerable mysteries, and their tiresome articles, confuse the issue. Christianity in its essentials is a rational creed, natural and simple. It demands of the believer, first, that he should believe in Christ the Messiah, one sent from God to reveal his true nature; secondly, that he should live in accordance with the Christian morality, the morality based on this new revelation of God. These are the essentials, and any one who fulfils these is a Christian. The theologian's creeds, the priest's elaborate ritual, do not make a Christian. Christianity is something simpler, although it may very well be more difficult. 'Lustrations and processions are much easier than a clean conscience and a steady course of virtue; and an expiatory sacrifice, that atoned for the want of it, is much more convenient than a strict and holy life.'[1]

Christianity is reasonable. It will be recalled that for Locke revelation must be tested by reason. This does not mean that we believe only that which reason gives us. Revelation may well go beyond reason; but it never contradicts it. Now, if we understand the core of the Christian religion properly we shall see that it also is no exception to this general rule. We may admit that the central doctrine of Christianity is that of Justification by Faith. If this were interpreted in the way in which many interpret it, for instance, the Calvinists, it might be difficult to make it rational. Justification by Faith does not, however, in Locke's opinion, involve Original Sin, and so it does not involve Atonement in the usual sense. Adam was immortal, but his disobedience deprived him of this immortal life. In due course he died. (The theologians say he descended into hell, but Locke thinks this non-scriptural and refuses to accept the belief in hell.) Adam's children also died, not because they were Adam's children, but because they could not live in complete accordance with the Law. Like Adam they

[1] *Works*, ii. 575 (1801 ed. vii. 139).

sinned and so lost immortality. Thus, the Jews believed that death awaited all who had fallen from the high standards of the Law and since no man could attain to those standards death awaited all. In the face of this despairing doctrine God in due course sent a messenger, the Messiah, Son of God, born of a virgin, to reveal a deeper truth. God is merciful; he does not demand complete fulfilment of the Law. It is enough if a man accepts Christ, that is, accepts his view of God, and repents of his sin, striving to live in accordance with Christ's teaching. Even though he then fails to attain the full perfection of righteousness he will be justified by his faith in Christ, and through God's grace will enjoy immortal life.[1]

Now, if this is the true interpretation of Justification by Faith, the one essential doctrine of Christianity—and Locke thinks that it is—it is not difficult to show that Christianity is reasonable through and through. In the first place, the Law of Moses is the law of nature, the law of reason. Secondly, reason teaches us plainly that God must be one and supreme. Moreover, his mercy and grace are qualities which our reason also would have revealed to us in time. There is nothing irrational in the belief that God is merciful. Mercy in a human being is so clearly a virtue, that it is very rational to suppose the Source of all perfections to possess it as well. Thirdly, the morality of the New Testament is strictly in accordance with human reason. The Gospel is a revelation, but it is reasonable throughout. Its delineation of the Godhead as one Supreme Being, its description of him as merciful, its interpretation of man's duties and of the Law, and its doctrine of Justification by Faith (rightly understood), are all wholly rational. Nothing in Christianity contradicts our human reason.

This interpretation of Christian doctrine is clearly very radical. It is not altogether surprising that Edwards should have held the

[1] The immortality of the human soul is *revealed*, according to Locke, and not known by reason. He had examined the attempts at a rational proof of immortality, but was never satisfied with any of them. Cf. the important passage in his journal (Aaron and Gibb, pp. 121–3). A proof that the immaterial soul is indestructible is no proof of eternal *life*. For often the immaterial soul is insensible, for instance, in sleep, and if the immortality which pertained to it was that of eternal sleep this would not be the immortality of Scripture. Moreover, he points out in his correspondence with Stillingfleet (*Works*, i. 597) that the immortality of Scripture is not the eternal existence of the soul. The soul did not pre-exist its present state. It is an eternity as to the future only.

Reasonableness of Christianity to be 'all over Socinianized'. Its account of Justification by Faith could not but give offence to a large section of Protestant theologians. It was accepted gladly by most Arminians, and by Unitarians, then increasing in number. The Unitarian leader, the philanthropic merchant Thomas Firmin, was an old friend of Locke's, and undoubtedly influenced his theology. The *Reasonableness* does not deny the doctrine of the Trinity, but it does stress the unity of the Godhead, and it omits the Doctrine of the Trinity from the list of reasonable doctrines. The Atonement is also whittled away, and the Cross ceases to be central in Christian theology. The first Unitarians must have derived considerable satisfaction from reading Locke's works. None the less, he cannot be classed with them. In the *Vindications*, which he wrote in answer to Edwards's attacks upon him, he definitely states on more than one occasion that he is no Socinian, that he does not deny Christ's divinity, nor any of the main Mysteries of the Christian religion. If he was in agreement with Unitarians on some points he could not agree with them on others.[1]

What of his relations with Deism? On more than one occasion he has been called the father of Deism. But this is a title to which he clearly has no right, since it belongs to Lord Herbert of Cherbury. Deism began with Lord Herbert, although half a century was to go by before it came to play a large part in the religious and intellectual life of the country. Toland, Collins, Blount, Tindal, Wollaston, Morgan, and Chubb are some of the more famous names in Deist literature. They ignored professed revelation and tended to reject entirely the mysterious and supernatural elements in the Christian religion. To all intents and purposes they identified the religious life with the moral. Their chief stress was on Natural Religion and on reason. Now Locke had much in common with theorists of this sort. He emphasized as much as they did the place of reason in the religious life, and the supreme importance of the moral life. He would not make the acceptance of the Thirty-Nine Articles, or of any like body of creeds, essential to the religious life. He recommended a critical approach to

[1] On this matter cf. also the interesting correspondence between Locke and Limborch during these later years.

the Scriptures. Moreover, one of the Deists, Toland, openly boasted that Locke was his inspiration, whilst another, Collins, was an intimate of Locke in his last years, and, as we have seen, Locke thought most highly of him. And yet Locke can no more be classed with Deists than with Unitarians. It is significant that though he was charged with Socinianism, none of his opponents ever charged him in his own day with being a Deist.[1] In the Molyneux correspondence when writing of Toland, and again in the Stillingfleet controversy, Locke emphatically denied that he was one of this school. And it is important to bear in mind that the most orthodox of Christians in Locke's time was quite as anxious as any Deist to make his religion appear rational and 'in accordance with nature'. Locke admittedly was not orthodox, but yet he was no Deist. He differed from the Deists in one most important respect. He held that whilst religion never contradicted reason, reason itself cannot take us the whole way. Since we are finite and limited beings, reason cannot reveal to us all we need to know in order to live the religious life. We do know how to live that life, but only because God has spoken his Word to man through Christ. That event was not merely rational and not merely natural. The supernatural remains in Locke's theology; the Mysteries remain. Locke believes in the Virgin Birth and the Resurrection from the Dead. The miracles remain; they are the sure testimony of the supernatural power and authority of Christ.[2] For reasons such as these Locke cannot be classed with the Deists.[3]

[1] Mr. J. W. Yolton informs me of one exception, John Edwards, *A Free Discourse Concerning Truth and Error* (1701), pp. 80–87. The charge was frequently made in the decade after Locke's death.

[2] On miracles cf. Locke's interesting *Discourse on Miracles*. They are the marks of the 'over-ruling power' of Christ. Locke meets with a difficulty in trying to define a miracle. We cannot hold that to be a miracle in which a law of nature is broken, for this assumes that natural laws are known to us as ultimates, laws which can never be broken. But Locke does not believe that any inductively established laws are ultimate in this sense. He, accordingly, defines a miracle cautiously as 'a sensible operation, which being above the comprehension of the spectator and in his opinion contrary to the established cause of nature, is taken by him to be divine'.

[3] On this whole question of Locke's relations to Deism cf. further: Ernst Crous, *Die religionsphilosophische Lehre Lockes und ihre Stellung zu dem Deismus seiner Zeit.* (Phil. u. ihre Gesch., 1910, Abt. 3). Also Hefelbower, *The Relation of John Locke to English Deism*, Chicago, 1918.

Locke is radical and yet conservative; he is a rationalist and yet he finally puts his faith on what is not reason. That is why he differs from both Unitarians and Deists. This apparently paradoxical attitude of his is the outcome of a prudent realization of human limitations. Reason alone is inadequate. It is inadequate in the sphere of religion, just as it is inadequate in the sphere of natural science. There we have to wait on sense-experience. And it seems as if Locke recognizes in religion also a religious experience, a feeling and an intuition of God, Pascal's knowledge of 'the heart', which supplements reason. In the *Essay* Locke distinguishes between the revelation which comes from God through reason and that which comes through His Spirit.[1] For beings constituted as we are, children of the twilight, the former is not enough. And it is dangerous to erect a faith on it alone—as dangerous as it is to deduce a science of nature *a priori*. Locke does not analyse this second kind of knowledge, this consciousness of the presence of God in our life. He hardly ever talks of it. But he makes it none the less clear that it is an essential element in religion. Locke differs from Deists and Unitarians not because his faith in reason is less than theirs, but because he does not put his faith in reason alone.[2]

And when we pass from the particular problems of Christian theology to the final problem of theology itself, that of the being and nature of God, it is clear that Locke does not expect reason to provide the full solution in this case either. He thinks we can prove God's *existence* by reason, and offers a proof in IV. x of the *Essay*. That proof, we have seen, is not beyond suspicion. But it is obvious in reading it that it is an attempted rationalization of what is already believed. Locke believes first, and then seeks rational justification for his belief in the cosmological argument. Why does Locke believe? His education and the custom of the age clearly account in some part for this fact. But the belief plays too great a part in his philosophy to be attributed entirely to these sources. Locke, no doubt, did feel that a First Cause was essential, and he also felt that we ourselves needed explaining. Surely the

---

[1] IV. vii. II.   [2] Richard Ashcraft in 'Faith and Knowledge in Locke's Philosophy' in *John Locke, Problems and Perspectives*, pp. 194 ff., holds that it is only in the light of Locke's commitment to the Christian *faith* that it is possible to understand the motivation of his work and, particularly, of his *Essay*.

cause of 'cogitative beings' must itself be 'cogitative'. The First
Cause must be Spirit. Again, the order in the universe—however
we account for its disorder and its evil—is too great to allow us to
suppose that it is the result of an accidental 'concourse of atoms';[1]
it must surely be the work of an intelligent Creator. Moreover,
man is not merely cogitative, he is also moral; and although Locke
never presents us with an adequate analysis of the moral consciousness, he does vaguely feel something of what Kant made
clear later, that morality (if we interpret it in the Kantian way)
necessitates the being of God. Of all this and more Locke was
aware. Yet one cannot but feel that his real ground for believing
was no rational argument of any kind. It was the knowledge of
God 'through His Spirit', this deep intuition of his presence. The
piety and deep religious feeling of Locke's works forcibly suggest
such a view.

/ As to the nature of God Locke has little to say. We cannot hope
to know him fully as he is. We frame an idea of him as best we
may, a complex idea, framed, as all complex ideas are framed,
from ideas of sensation and reflection. We think of all the qualities that are worth possessing and attribute these to God—not,
however, as they are to be found amongst us, but as they are in
their perfection. God is one, enduring from eternity to eternity;
in him is all true pleasure and happiness; he is omniscient, wholly
good, and omnipotent. But ours is no positive idea of God. When
we say that God is good what we mean is that he is better than
anyone else, that his goodness is greater than the greatest goodness we have yet known. When we say that he is wise we mean
that his wisdom surpasses all the wisdom we know positively. It is
no positive conception. Our complex idea of God must fall far
short of the reality; in his true nature he must be very different
from our best conception of him. That this is so is not to be wondered at if we recall our ignorance even of finite things, even of
our own selves. It is not strange if the infinite is almost wholly
hidden from us. God is incomprehensible. And yet, Locke thinks,
we are aware of him as a powerful presence in our life, and in this
knowledge find strength and peace.

[1] Cf. *Essay*, IV. xx. 15.

CONCLUSION

LOCKE's contributions to his age were many and varied. In the first place, he led men to think more deeply over problems which had previously been handled superficially. He showed the inadequacy of much traditional teaching. He questioned where men had been apt to take for granted. In this connexion much of the credit which has gone to Hume really belongs to Locke. Secondly, certain sections of the *Essay* stand out as very valuable contributions to philosophy. Valuable in this respect are the account of primary and secondary qualities, the analysis of the idea of substance, the discussion of personal identity, the examination of words, the treatment of definition, the division of the sciences, the theory of knowledge, and the empiricism. The philosophical treasures which the *Essay* contains are still far from being exhausted. In the third place, Locke contributed to the political life of his day. In his political writings he supported the Whig cause and provided it with a rational justification for its epoch-making revolution. He also furnished that party with principles upon which to base its future programme. In the religious sphere he advocated far-reaching reforms and strengthened the hands of those pioneers who attempted an intelligent and critical interpretation of the Scriptures. Finally, his writings on subjects connected with finance and economics, and again his practical activities as Commissioner of Trade and Plantations, were of considerable importance. He certainly helped to prepare the way for the industrial and colonial expansion of this country in the century which followed.

If, however, we are asked for Locke's main contribution to his age and to subsequent ages we may perhaps best answer in this way: His writings secured for posterity the advances which had been made by the most radical and progressive elements of society in the seventeenth century. He consolidated the advanced positions. He did not accept everything which his radical predecessors had taught. Some of their teaching he considered impracticable. But what he saw to be living and important he retained, and in his statement of these matters captured the public ear so completely that it was impossible for his contemporaries and for many subsequent generations to ignore him. Locke's works dominated the English mind in the first half of the eighteenth century, and his influence was almost as great in America and in France.

Locke was fortunate in his period. He came at the end of a century of intense intellectual activity and real advance. In politics there had been many significant and, sometimes, strange movements culminating (in this country) in the decisive struggle between monarch and parliament. As the century wore on the demand for a democracy and for political equality became definite. (Winstanley and his followers had gone even farther; they had demanded economic equality as well as political. But seventeenth-century England was not ripe for communism.) In the religious sphere a fierce battle had been fought. A new note of bold criticism had been struck. Radicals demanded complete liberty in religion and complete toleration. In the sciences also substantial progress had been made, and the main hopes of the century centred upon it. Here it was felt a new weapon of incalculable worth was being forged for man's use. The closer control of nature which was promised would increase wealth and prosperity, bring greater comforts, improve health, and so ensure a longer life. The Cartesian dream of a 'universal mathematics' which would provide man with a complete and certain knowledge of nature had captured the imagination of the century. How much might be achieved for the amelioration of the human lot through the complete conquest of nature!

Locke's sympathies were wholly with these progressives. In politics and religion he shared their dreams and hopes, and he was as eager a supporter of the 'new philosophy' as any. But he was also their critic. He had his standards. He would reform prudently.[1] He would accept all that could be accepted, but reject the imprudent. In this way he could best safeguard the real advance made by his predecessors. This clearly is his aim in politics. His observations in this sphere had led him to conclude that a

---

[1] Prudence in his case was a blend of experience and reason, the combination of long observation of human life with long reflection upon it.

monarchy was essential for seventeenth- and eighteenth-century Britain. Accordingly he dismissed republicanism. In the same way he had also concluded that the rights of individuals to private property had to be maintained in an age when British industrialists and British merchants needed to be encouraged to capture their full share of the world's expanding trade and increasing wealth. But once these reservations were made, the theory which then emerged in his political works was entirely radical. The true sovereign of his state was the people, which, however, delegated its authority to a legislative assembly. This assembly was itself elected by the people, and controlled by general elections. The power of the monarchy was hedged around in every possible manner. It was a constitutional monarchy deriving its authority explicitly from the consent of the people. The state, as conceived by Locke, was democratic in the most important sense that its unity and strength lay in the willing acceptance of law by a free people, whose legislative had itself framed the law it was to obey. Locke's *Civil Government* was the last word of the seventeenth century on the radical side and it made the issues clear to the eighteenth.

In respect to religion also Locke applied his standards rigidly. He accepted the views of Latitudinarians and other progressives that the essential beliefs which should be demanded for membership in a church ought to be as few as possible, that the blind acceptance of dogma was not to be recommended, that religion was first a way of life and then a creed. He was foremost in his demand for toleration. If he advocated certain limitations to complete toleration he advocated them, as we have seen, on political rather than on religious grounds. There should be, he argued, no interference in the private religious life of each individual. In this realm, more than in any other, the individual should be given complete freedom. No outside authority should be permitted to impose its will upon him. Reason and conscience alone should guide him. But although Locke accepted and himself advocated these liberal proposals, there was one extreme position which he would not accept. He would not accept the view that revelation was worthless, and that the only true religion was natural religion.

Reason in man was too narrow a foundation for the religious life. It must be helped out by revelation; although the final judge and arbiter as to the genuineness of a particular revelation must in each case be the individual's reason. But reason of itself is not enough. The extreme radical position which would reject revelation must itself be rejected lest true advance in religion be impeded.

In this way Locke attempted to consolidate the advances already made in the seventeenth century. And it is not overfanciful to regard the *Essay* also as consolidation in the field of knowledge and of philosophy. In philosophy the progressive party was the Cartesian. The pioneers were either confessed Cartesians or men linked closely to that school. (The Gassendists were exceedingly few, and counted for little.) And the main advance which the Cartesians claimed to have made was in physics. They had discovered afresh the certainty and fecundity of mathematical reasoning. With the aid of mathematics much greater advance had already been shown to be possible by the scientists of the Renaissance, particularly by Galileo, than the medievalists had ever conceived. The schools still confined themselves to their syllogisms. But the Cartesians argued that the mathematical procedure could be yet more extensively applied. They applied it to physics and intended to apply it to every branch of human inquiry. They aimed at a universal mathematics, a final philosophy in which all the problems which then vexed the human mind could be solved.

Now Locke realized that the Cartesians had set before themselves an ideal which they could never attain. He accordingly opposed them. But he did not oppose them in any reactionary spirit. He certainly did not defend the schools. He was as impatient of the restrictions they would have set upon reason, their syllogisms, their arguments from maxims, as was Descartes—perhaps even more impatient. But he opposed the Cartesians because, so he thought, they were too optimistic and their optimism endangered sound advance. They thought reason, working in the void, by proceeding in accordance with those 'high priori' methods which admittedly had succeeded so well in mathematics, could gain complete knowledge of the physical world of nature.

They had not realized that physics and all the other natural sciences were essentially different from the mathematical sciences, different because their objects were completely different. The object in the case of mathematics is an abstraction; in the case of physics, Locke held, it is the concrete physical thing. Descartes and his followers had neglected this distinction. They were not entirely unaware of it. They knew that the physical object as experienced was such that it could not be dealt with wholly in mathematical terms, but they neglected all its qualities except extension; they framed a new abstraction and a new object which could be handled by pure mathematics, and so erected a system which they called physics, but which was in reality a fanciful creation of their own imagination. But a true physics, Locke urged, must proceed and can only proceed through reasoning upon material provided in experience. And that material is not such that it can be handled entirely in mathematical terms. Nor again can it be handled deductively, for we do not know the inner and necessary connexions holding between qualities in a thing, so that we cannot deduce with certainty what qualities must pertain to the thing and how it will behave in relation to other things. We can only conclude, from frequent recurrences of a relation in our experience, and from our failure to discover a negative instance, that this relation probably holds universally. Never does physics and never do the other natural sciences become purely deductive like the mathematical sciences. They rest finally on induction. In the mathematical sciences reason, once it has gained its fundamental ideas, for instance, number and space,[1] can proceed independently of all reference to experience. But in the natural sciences reason must wait upon experience and be guided by it throughout, and this in turn means that it cannot gain complete certainty. (If we define 'science' in the narrow sense in which Locke defined it, as meaning certain knowledge, then the natural sciences are not truly sciences.)

Now Locke's criticism of the Cartesians is that they neglected this all-important division of the sciences and as a consequence

---

[1] How these fundamental ideas are gained is never satisfactorily cleared up in the *Essay*, as we have seen. Locke seeks for an empirical source.

sought to turn sciences which, from their very nature, had to be inductive into deductive ones having a full measure of certainty. They were bound to fail. As far as the natural sciences are concerned the only possible advance is by the careful observation of nature, by experimentation, and by following the guidance of experience. The main lesson of the *Essay*, although it is not its only lesson, is that the *historical, plain* method is the one method which can be used in our inquiries into nature. If we would advance in these inquiries, therefore, it must be by this method. Descartes and the Cartesians misled men; the true lines of advance are those laid down by Boyle, Newton, and the empiricists.

It is thus possible to conceive the whole of Locke's work as consolidation through criticism, and preparation for future advance. His aim was clear: to forward man's progress in material prosperity, in his social relationships, and in his religion. Locke, like most of his contemporaries, was severely practical and severely utilitarian. The real business of life and its true end was the increase of human pleasure and well-being. 'The business of men', he wrote in his journals, 'being to be happy in this world by the enjoyment of the things of nature subservient to life, health, ease, and pleasure, and by the comfortable hopes of another life when this is ended; and in the other world by an accumulation of higher degrees of bliss in an everlasting security; we need no other knowledge for the attainment of those ends but of the history and observation of the effects and operations of natural bodies within our power, and of our duties in the management of our own actions as far as they depend upon our will.'[1] Locke knew the value of recreations—games, good conversation, friendship, poetry, eloquence, the arts, even knowledge for knowledge's sake. But these were 'entertainments'. The true business of man was the improvement of his lot. There is no denying the thorough-going utilitarianism of Locke's philosophy and no denying also that occasionally its utilitarianism is both narrow and harsh. Yet it was in accord with the spirit of his day. It was the austere philosophy of an age inspired wholly by one great hope, that of progress. Locke viewed man as a child of twilight, the lowest intelligence

---

[1] Journal, 8 February 1677 (Aaron and Gibb, p. 88).

in that spiritual chain of being descending from the highest, God, to man. Man's ignorance is inevitably great. Yet his present ignorance is greater than it need be, and so also is his present unhappiness. He must bestir himself. He has faculties which properly used can advance knowledge and increase happiness. But this end will not be secured through wild experimentation in the political and religious life nor through wild speculation in philosophy. The end can only be gained by a cautious and diligent reflection upon experience. Man must learn the hard lesson, to wait humbly and patiently upon experience, and frequently to be content with probability.

APPENDIX I

THE LOVELACE COLLECTION

It has been suggested to me that I might give some account of the rediscovery of Locke's papers in 1935.

The seventh Lord King in *The Life and Letters of John Locke* (1829) published many of the papers and letters which Locke had bequeathed to Peter King, but very little use was made of this collection in the nineteenth century. Benjamin Rand knew of it at the beginning of the present century, and in 1927 published 91 letters from it to Locke from Edward Clarke. In 1931 he published the early draft of Locke's *Essay* which we now know as Draft B, speaking of it as the 'original' draft.

It was not Rand's references to the collection, however, which aroused my curiosity, but rather what King had said a century earlier. In the Preface to his book King had described what was obviously a large collection, most of which was unpublished, consisting of letters, journals, common-place books, manuscripts, and printed books. He explained, too, that he was publishing part of the papers only. Most tantalizing was a reference (second edition, 1830, i. 10) to 'the original copy' of the *Essay*, the beginning of which was quoted. It was dated 1671, and the few lines quoted were enough to show that this was not the early draft of the *Essay* which Rand had printed.

I believe I assumed that the papers to which King referred were no longer in existence since Rand did not appear to know of them, but I wrote to the Earl of Lovelace, on the off chance, declaring my interest and asking if he still possessed any of Locke's manuscript remains and whether I could consult them. Some time elapsed before a reply came and when it did, it came not from the Earl of Lovelace but from Jocelyn Gibb, whose brother was married to the Earl's sister. The Earl was abroad in Africa at the time and Mr. Gibb, who held his power-of-attorney, invited me to stay at his family home in Hampshire to show me the Locke material which he was then putting in order.

He and his father, Sir Alexander Gibb, were most kind. I found there thousands of letters (most of them to Locke) and a great number of manuscripts. I spent some days working through the papers and well remember the most exciting moment when in turning over the leaves of a common-place book I came across that early draft of the *Essay* of which King had quoted the first paragraph. Such moments as these are the deepest and most satisfying rewards of scholarship. Later that day I discussed the draft with Jocelyn Gibb and we decided, if we could, to publish the work together, Mr. Gibb to be responsible for preparing the text, which I was to check, edit, and annotate. I wrote at once to Sir David Ross of Oxford asking, first, whether the University Press there might be interested in the publication and, secondly, describing the collection, pointing out its value and suggesting that its permanent home should be the Bodleian. (Mr. Gibb has informed me since that, on the suggestion of Sir George Clarke and Dr. R. W. Chapman, the Librarian of the Bodleian, Dr. (later Sir) Edmund Craster, was already in correspondence with him about the collection, but I knew nothing of this at the time.) In his reply Sir David told me that the Press was interested and that he had spoken to Dr. Craster. The latter agreed that the collection was most valuable; both he and Sir David would indeed be very happy to see it in the Bodleian.

These events occurred towards the end of 1935. Draft A was published by Oxford University Press in 1936, and Mr. Gibb deposited the collection in the Bodleian at the beginning of the war, giving the Library a form of option on its purchase, which eventually took place in 1947. A full and scholarly report was written on the collection for the Bodleian by Dr. von Leyden, and a brief account of the history and contents of the collection will be found in his *Essays on the Law of Nature*, pp. 1–7. I should add that the common-place book containing Draft A was not deposited with the other papers in the Bodleian but is now (1962) in America.

MANUSCRIPTS IN THE LOVELACE COLLECTION IN THE
BODLEIAN DEALING WITH PHILOSOPHICAL SUBJECTS

1. Notebook on Logic. 1652(?).
2. Notebook entitled 'Lemata: ne'. *c.* 1660.
3. Treatise on the Civil Magistrate, in reply to a treatise by Edward Bagshaw. 1660.
4. 'An Magistratus civilis . . .' (essay in Latin on the right of the civil magistrate to interfere in things relating to religious worship). 1660.
5. Essays on the Law of Nature, in Latin. 1663.
6. 'An Essay Concerning Toleracōn 1667'.
   [This is the final version of the essay. Three other manuscript copies are known:
   (*a*) the earliest draft, in the Huntington Library;

(*b*) the version in the Shaftesbury Papers, Public Record Office, printed by Fox Bourne, *Life of John Locke*, 1876, i. 174–94;

(*c*) the copy in Locke's Commonplace book 1661, of which Lord King printed the end (*Life*, 1858, p. 156).]

7. 'Intellectus 1671 JL'.

[This is 'Draft B' of the *Essay Concerning Human Understanding* published by B. Rand (Harvard U.P., 1931). Two other manuscript versions written in 1671 are

(*a*) 'Draft A', written in Locke's Commonplace book 1661 (now in America, privately owned) and published by R. I. Aaron and J. Gibb (O.U.P., 1936).

(*b*) 'A(i)', a copy of part of Draft A in the Public Record Office.

A further manuscript, 'Draft C', in the Pierpont Morgan Library, New York, is a draft of the first two books of the *Essay*, dated 1685.]

8. 'Sapientia' (map of knowledge). 1672.

9. 'Essay de morale. 77' (notes on Locke's translation of three of Nicole's Essays). Partly printed by King, *Life*, 1858, pp. 130–1. 1677.

10. 'Adversaria 19 Aug. 77' 1677.

11. 'Adversaria 12 Nov. 77' 1677.

12. Notes on Stillingfleet's sermon 'The Mischief of Separation' (1680) and his treatise 'The Unreasonableness of Separation' (1681). Partly printed by King, *Life*, 1858, pp. 346–58. *c*. 1681–3.

13. Summary of the *Essay*. 1687(?). Printed by King, *Life*, 1858, pp. 365–98.

14. (*a*) 'Thus I thinke' and 'of Ethick in General'. 1689–90(?).

(*b*) 'Physica. . . .' 1689(?) (notes for *Essay*, iv. xx, in Latin and Greek).

15. 'Case of allegiance due to Sovereigne Powers.' 1691 (notes on a pamphlet by William Sherlock).

16. Criticisms of the *Essay* by William King, Bishop of Derry. 1692.

17. 'JL to Mr Norris' 1692 (unpublished reply).

18. Commonplace sheet. 1693.

19. 'JL Of Seeing all things in God 1693' (*Examination of Malebranche*).

20. 'Some other loose thoughts . . . in a perusal of Mr Norris's writeings.' 1693.

21. Single sheet 'Recherche'. 1693(?).

22. 'Understanding A' (Additions to *Essay*, Book II). 1694. Printed by King, *Life*, 1858, pp. 323–5, 327–8, 359–60.

23. Additions to *Essay*, iii. x. 11. 1694. Printed by King, *Life*, 1858, pp. 361–4.

24. Draft of *Conduct of the Understanding*: Additions to the *Essay*. 1695; 1697.

25. '*Deus* Des Cartes's proof of a god from the Idea of necessary existence examined 1696'. Printed by King, *Life*, 1858, pp. 313–16.

26. Three copies of Leibniz's Remarks on Locke's *Essay*. 1696–7 (first published as an appendix to Locke's letter to Molyneux, 10 April 1697, in *Familiar Letters*).

27. Fair copy of part of the draft of *Conduct of the Understanding*.
    1697(?).
28. 'Ethica B' (notes on ethics). 1690's(?).
29. 'Morality' 1690's(?).
30. Table of knowledge. 1690's (?).
31. Draft of part of the *Fourth Letter for Toleration*. 1704. (This, the last
    of Locke's writings, was written on the blank sides of old letters,
    one of which is endorsed 'P. King 8 Aug. 04'.)

(Cf. 'Notes concerning Papers of John Locke in the Lovelace Collection',
by W. von Leyden. *Phil. Quart.*, January 1952, pp. 63–69.)

For a full catalogue of the Lovelace Collection, cf. P. Long: *A Summary Catalogue of the Lovelace Collection of the Papers of John Locke in the Bodleian Library*. Oxford Bibliographical Society Publications, New Series, Vol. 8 (1959). The above list of the philosophical manuscripts in the Collection I owe to Mrs. C. S. Johnston.

APPENDIX II

THE PRINTING HISTORY OF THE FIRST
FOUR EDITIONS OF THE
ESSAY CONCERNING HUMAN UNDERSTANDING

By CHARLOTTE S. JOHNSTON

I

Of the first edition of the *Essay* there are two issues. The one, which may be termed issue A, has the imprint 'Printed by *Eliz. Holt*, for **Thomas Basset**, at the *George* in *Fleetstreet*, near St. *Dunstan's* Church. MDCXC.'

The other, issue B, has 'Printed for *Tho. Basset*, and sold by *Edw. Mory* at the Sign of the *Three Bibles* in St. *Paul's* Church-Yard. MDCXC.'

There has been some controversy about the priority of these two issues, but from bibliographical and collateral evidence, it is clear that the A issue is properly to be regarded as the first.

From an examination of the two issues, the following facts emerge:

(*a*) The title-leaf of the A issue is an integral part of the first gathering, whereas the title-leaf of the B issue is a reset can-cellans, with a different arrangement of type-ornaments, and the ss of *Essay* inverted.

(*b*) The sheets used are the same in both issues. Most of the errors or peculiarities in pagination and Running Titles throughout the book are common to the eleven copies examined (8 of the A and 3 of the B issue); of the remaining peculiarities, cor-rected and uncorrected states occur indiscriminately in both A and B issues.

(*c*) All examined copies of the A issue have corrections, in ink. These are: 'certainly' on the last page of the Epistle Dedicatory is corrected to 'extremely', and the word 'some' is inserted before 'Discovery' on the first page of the Epistle to the Reader.

Since the sheets used in the edition have text from the same setting up of type, and the paper throughout has uniform water-marks, the evidence of the cancellans and cancellandum title-pages alone must decide whether precedence is to be given to either of the issues.

If it were a case of simple planned cancellation, no priority for the
A issue could be established; Basset the undertaker or publisher
hand-corrected his preliminaries, the subsidiary Mory did not. Contemporaneous issue is as much suggested on this hypothesis as
priority for either.[1]

But the cancellans title-page has been completely reset, and is
clearly no part of the original sheets. If, before public sale had begun,
Basset and Mory had come to an agreement about the distribution
of the edition, then the imprint could have been altered in press.
The type of a title-page was often left undistributed for some considerable time, so why was the whole title-page reset? It seems clear
that a change occurred in the printing arrangements some time after
all the sheets with their Holt-Basset title pages had been run off. As
Bowers says: 'The fact that the cancellans title is reset and cannot
be established as part of continuous printing is in itself sufficient
evidence of reissue of some variety under changed circumstances
from those originally intended.'[2]

From the bibliographical evidence alone, then, it is just to call that
issue the first in which the title-page is an integral part of the sheets
as originally printed, i.e. the so-called A issue. This inference is
supported by data concerning the *Essay* which show that Basset—
and Basset alone—was the original publisher and that therefore
Edward Mory was a subsidiary and a later figure.

To begin with, the agreement drawn up between Locke and his
publisher is extant,[3] and names only Basset. The contract was
endorsed by Locke 'Bassets Articles 24 May 89', and sets out the
terms and manner of printing and publishing: '. . . the Printing
thereof shall be begun immediately and continued after the rate of
at least fower sheets a weeke untill the whole booke be Printed . . .
the said Thomas Basset doth promise and agree to and wth the said
John Locke to Print or cause the same to be Printed, in the time & in
ye forme and manner above said. . . .'

From the document we should expect the published book to bear
in its imprint only the names of Basset himself and the printer whom,
by the terms of the articles, he was entitled to engage. The imprint
of the A issue exactly fulfils these expectations: 'Printed by Eliz.

[1] See *Bibliographical Notes and Queries*, vol. ii, nos. 6, July 1936 (J. M.
Keynes); 9, January 1938 (J. Carter); 12, May 1939 (J. Carter).
[2] *Principles of Bibliographical Description*, Princeton U.P., 1949, p. 81.
[3] MS. Locke, b. 1, f. 109.

Holt, for Thomas Basset, at the George in Fleetstreet near St. Dunstan's Church.'

This is the issue which was entered in the Term Catalogue for Hilary Term February 1689/90,[1] an indication that this was the originally planned imprint, and that it was Basset who saw to it that the book was advertised in this way. Furthermore, it was from Basset that Locke received his first copies of the book. No mention is made of Mory, so that Basset was acting as distributor and book-seller. From entries in one of his notebooks we know that between 3 December 1689 and 26 September 1690 Locke received altogether 45 copies of his book, sent to him by Mrs. Holt or by Thomas Basset. In none of these entries[2] is Mory mentioned. It is probable that Mory acquired his rights in the book only shortly before the advertisement in the *London Gazette* of 29 May 1690 which gives his name as publisher.

It is clear then that early in December 1689 presentation copies of the *Essay*—from the printer Elizabeth Holt—were in Locke's hands. They were not unbound sheets, the name of Graves the bookbinder occurs in the notebook and journal entries, and amongst Locke's accounts is a bill from Graves dated 'January ye 9 89' for binding:

1 Human Understanding Turkey	0	6	0
9 Idem Gilt Back		18	0
1 Idem in Parchment		1	2[3]

Had printing begun immediately and proceeded at the rate set out in the Articles, one might have expected the 58 agreed sheets to have been finished in fourteen and a half weeks, by the beginning of September, and not the beginning of December.

As to the date on the title-page, it was common practice for a book published at the end of the year to be imprinted with the date of the year following, so that it is not surprising that the 1690 *Essay* should have been on sale in December 1689. It reached the book-shops in Oxford about the middle of the month, Tyrrell tells Locke in his letter of 20 December—'It came down to Oxford last week and many copyes are sold of it.'[4] By March, the month Campbell Fraser

---

[1] *Term Catalogues*, ii. 302.

[2] MS. Locke, f. 29, p. 36: 'Basset copys recd 3 Dec. of Mrs. Holt by Graves [a bookbinder] 12/6 Ditto 13/18 of Mr. Basset by Graves 3.' A duplicate list occurs in his Journal 1689–1704. MS. Locke, f. 10, pp. 29, 32.

[3] MS. Locke, b. 1, f. 122.   [4] MS. Locke, c. 22, f. 71.

assigns to its appearance, the *Essay* was being read with such attention that Tyrrell was busy defending Locke against his adversaries in Oxford.[1]

2

There are two issues of the second edition also, and of the first issue there are two states. The imprint of the first state of the first issue reads: 'London, Printed for **Thomas Dring**, at the *Harrow*, over=against the *Inner-Temple Gate* in *Fleet-street*; and **Samuel Manship,** at the *Black Bull* in *Cornhill*, near the *Royal Exchange*, MDCXIV.'

A variant state of this first issue title-page has Manship's later address in its imprint: 'London. . . . **Samuel Manship,** at the *Ship* in *Cornhill*. . . .'

[Neither is listed in S.T.C. (Wing) 2740.]

Another and later issue contains in its imprint the names of Awnsham and John Churchill, to whom Dring sold his half share of the *Essay*. This imprint reads: 'Printed for **Awnsham** and **John Churchil,** at the *Black Swan* in *Pater-Noster-Row*, and **Samuel Manship,** at the *Ship* in *Cornhill*, near the *Royal Exchange*, MDCXCIV.'[2]

Locke was thinking of a second, more concise edition midway through 1692,[3] and on the 28 February 1692/3, Basset wrote to him:

I were lately at yor Lodgings to speake wth you about Reprinting yor Book . . . . . ye Impression of yor Books are so neare sold y^t I am ready to Reprint it but thought it necessary to acquaint y^u first with it because y^u shewed me some alterations & Additions y^t y^u had made, and if y^u have finished what y^u intended, I desire y^u would be pleased to send it by ye first oppertunity.

yor obliged servt to comand
Tho Bassett

28 ffeb 1692.
ffrom ye George in[4]
ffleetstreet

---

[1] MS. Locke, c. 22, f. 86, Tyrrell to Locke, 18 March.

[2] This is the imprint which appears in the tardy Term Catalogue advertisement for February 1965, *Term Catalogues*, ii. 541.

[3] See Leclerc's letter to Locke, 15 July 1692: 'vous êtes, monsieur, le premier Auteur, à qui j'ai oui parler de publier une seconde Edition *corrigée & abrigée*. On met toujours *augmentée*.' MS. Locke, c. 13, f. 56.

[4] MS. Locke, c. 3, f. 160.

At the end of May a transaction was recorded between them which shows that Basset had undertaken the second edition. It is dated 30 May 1693, and ends:

> I recd of Mr. Basset the fower pounds ten shillings & nine pence wch he was to repay me upon reprinting of my booke, for wch I gave him a rec[t]
>
> John Locke.[1]

In June an agreement[2] was drawn up specifying the payment of ten shillings for each sheet 'that shall be added to this second edition whether in the text or Table'.

However, when the second edition was published in the spring of 1694, Basset's name did not appear on the title-page of either of the two issues. He had sold the copy to Manship 'and one more' (presumably Dring), as Manship explains in a letter to Locke dated 10 March 1693/4:

> Sr
>
> I have sent you what papers yt are printed this weake and shall continu sending tel it tis finished. Mr. Basset has disposed of ye Copy to me and one more we shall take care to satisfye you as if he had it himselfe, he having left your agrement with us. Mr. Basset sence is removed to ye fryers & his shop is shut up and has caried all his goods awaye . . . . . your Effigie his worked of.[3]

A postscript to this letter gives Manship's address as the 'Black Bull in Cornhil', which appears in the imprint of the first issue of the second edition.

Thomas Dring, the other to whom Basset sold his copy must have sold out his share not long after acquiring it, as the following entry on behalf of Awnsham and John Churchill in the Stationers' Register shows:

> Entred . . . . . booke or coppy by virtue of an assignem[t] beareing date the 5th day of March Anno Dom 1693, [i.e. 1693/4] under the hand and seale of Thomas Dring and by virtue of the above mencened order entituled the moiety or one halfe parte of *An Essay concerning humane* ~~learninge~~ (sic) *understanding* by John Locke, Gent[l]., with large addicons now a reprinting in folio.[4]

---

[1] MS. Locke, b. 2, f. 115: 'Account with Thomas Bassett'.

[2] MS. Locke, b. 1, f. 168, London, 13 June 1693.   [3] MS. Locke, c. 15, f. 204.

[4] Eyre and Rivington, *Transcript of Stationers' Register 1640–1708*, iii. 462. The entry is under 29 April 1695, and the order mentioned is an order in court of that date. The Churchills with Manship were printing the third edition of the *Essay*; but the 'assignement' shows that although they were not enrolled in the Stationers Register, they had taken over from Dring during the printing of the second edition.

Some account of the progress of the printing of the edition is given in two of William Popple's letters to Locke. On 25 January 1693/4 he mentioned the 'end of the second book of your Essay' as being in the printers' hands, and on 3 February he reported 'your Printer has now the last leaves of the 3rd Book in his hands'.[1] Tyrrell wrote on 15 March rejoicing that the new edition was 'so near comeing out'.[2] The Term Catalogue advertisement came a year later, Hilary Term 1694/5.

In the second edition Locke's name appears on the title-page, and there is a portrait by Brownover, the 'Effigie' mentioned in Manship's letter. Also added were an Index, numerous additional sentences, and an entirely new chapter (II. xxvii. Of Identity and Diversity).

In the first edition the Contents pages, found after the text, were preceded by a Contents leaf summarizing the arguments of all four books; in the second edition these brief summaries were transferred to the margins of the appropriate pages in the text. The main Contents list was retained and preceded the text.

The additions were printed separately and sent to Locke's friends to bring their first editions up to date. The printing had been slow, and made more lengthy by the printing of this additional material. The type was kept standing when the rest of the gathering was distributed, and then printed in continuous pages for the individual owners to cut into strips and insert according to the directions before each interpolation. The additions to the fourth edition were also printed in this way.

But slow as it had been, the printing of this second edition was far from satisfactory. Locke wrote to Clarke that he had corrected only the large errata, 'for the small ones are infinite'. Since the copy was so imperfect, but both booksellers 'very respectful' and ready to do whatever he was pleased to direct, Locke suggested that the edition should be sold very cheap, to make way speedily for a new and more correct edition.[3]

At the end of October Locke mentioned to Limborch that 'the second edition of my book on the human understanding is being sold more quickly than I thought possible.[4] By March of the follow-

---

[1] MS. Locke, c. 17, ff. 209v, 211v.

[2] MS. Locke, c. 22, f. 126.

[3] Locke to Clarke, 30 March 1694. Rand, *Correspondence of Locke and Clarke*, O.U.P. 1927, p. 394.

[4] 26 October 1694. *Fam. Lett. Works* 1727, iii. 612.

ing year he was able to report to Molyneux that the third edition was forthcoming, probably that summer.[1]

3

Exactly when the edition appeared is not certain. Fox Bourne gives the date as end of June 1695,[2] but it was not published before July at the earliest. On 2 July Locke mentions to Molyneux John Wynne's abridgement of the *Essay* which is 'in Mr. Churchill's hands and will be printed as soon as the third edition of my Essay, which is now in the press, is printed off'.[3]

But the third edition was simply a reprint of the second. As far as p. 134 it was a page for page reprint, differing only in being more carelessly done, with many more misprints.

The edition was not exhausted until the end of January 1698/9.

4

In June 1699 an agreement[4] was signed by Manship and Churchill respecting the copies of the fourth edition of the *Essay*. Locke was to receive 6 copies of the book 'well bound in calves skin and guilt at ye back as soon as ye next edition of ye Essay shall be reprinted', and 6 copies for every impression 'that shall hereafter be made of the Essay' during Locke's lifetime.

Manship, for his half share in the copy, promised to pay Locke ten shillings a sheet for all the additions to be made. This part of the document was superscribed 'June ye 8th 1699', and was followed by a similar undertaking for their half share, signed by the Churchill brothers and dated June 14. Churchill wrote on 24 August 1700[5] of owing Locke for the additions, but payment from Manship was not to be forthcoming till January 1701. 'Mr. Manship yesterday left 3.15.0 his part for the seven shts & additions to yo[r] Last Edition of the Essay.'[6]

As with the second edition, the additions were printed separately. They were more extensive in this fourth edition, and lagged well

---

[1] 28 March 1694/5. *Fam. Lett. Works*, iii. 531.
[2] *Life*, ii. 273.
[3] *Fam. Lett. Works*, iii. 537.
[4] MS. Locke, b. 1, f. 218.
[5] MS. Locke, c. 5, f. 107.
[6] Ibid., f. 126.

behind the text in coming out. As late as the end of April Churchill was promising Locke the completion of the additions 'this weeke'.[1]

The book itself was published before the end of 1699, although, as with the first edition of the *Essay*, it bore the date of the following year. Locke wrote from Oates to Sir Hans Sloane on 2 December saying that before leaving town Locke had sent him a copy of the edition with its new chapters on Enthusiasm and Association of Ideas.[2]

It was advertised in Hilary Term, February 1700.[3] For the fourth edition Locke worked over the text of the previous editions, and it appeared, as advertised on the title-page, 'with large additions', which included the two new chapters (II. xxxiii, IV. xix).

The quotation from Ecclesiastes xi. 5. first appears on the title-page, and the Epistle Dedicatory bears the place and date of composition 'Dorset Court, 24th May, 1689'.

The edition was divided between the two booksellers, each having his own printer. The last two books are more carelessly printed than the first two.

This was the last English edition published in Locke's lifetime. In 1700 appeared the French translation of the *Essay* which Pierre Coste had made under Locke's supervision. He had given Coste some additions, notably to the chapter on Power (II. xxi), which were to appear in the fifth English edition (1706). The Latin translation, by Richard Burridge, a friend of Molyneux, was published in 1701.

In Locke's own lifetime the *Essay* had gone into four editions; it had been made a text-book in one university,[4] and had narrowly escaped being banned in another.[5] By 1894, when it appeared as no. 72 in *Sir John Lubbock's Hundred Books* series, there had been over forty editions. In the same year Campbell Fraser brought out his edition, where the first four editions are collated.

---

[1] MS. Locke, c. 5, f. 100.
[2] *Original Letters*, 1847, p. 67.
[3] *Term Catalogues*, iii. 176.
[4] Molyneux to Locke, 22 December 1692. *Fam. Lett. Works* 1727, iii. 506.
[5] Tyrrell to Locke, 28 February 1703/4. MS. Locke, c. 22, f. 165.

APPENDIX III

LOCKE AND MODERN THEORIES OF NUMBER[1]

1. The exposition of Locke's theory of number on pp. 165–6 above is brief and has no reference to its historical significance. As we shall see Frege commented on the theory but rejected it. The suggestion has been made by Mr. Edward E. Dawson that Locke's theory is closely related to some of our contemporary theories, particularly the intuitionist theory of number. Mr. Dawson holds that Locke's account of number was not merely 'a good effort in his own day' but that 'what Locke had to say really was quite fundamental, and a good deal of modern mathematics assumes his position, either explicitly or implicitly'.[2] This is a valuable suggestion and a discussion of it may throw further light on Locke's theory.

2. We may begin by recalling Locke's position. The chapter on number is part of the execution of the general strategy of Book II of the *Essay*. Its task was to show that all our ideas of the external world were derived from sense-perception. From the first Locke foresaw considerable difficulty with the idea of infinity, and it is clear that the account of number in II. xvi is preparatory to the empiricist theory of infinity to be offered in the next chapter. Now it was essential for this theory to ground all ideas of number in something given in sensory experience. Locke finds this ground in the number 1 which he takes to be a simple idea of sensation. 'Amongst all the ideas we have . . . there is none more simple than that of unity or one.'[3] It is given; 'every object our senses are employed about . . . brings this idea along with it'. He places the idea of 1 squarely in the category of simple ideas of sensation. The idea of 2, on the other hand, is a complex idea. It will be recalled that Locke divided complex ideas into modes, substances and relations, and the modes again into simple and complex. Now the number 2 and all natural

---

[1] Mr. Philip Walters and I were interested in a suggestion of Mr. Edward E. Dawson that Locke in II. xvi of the *Essay* had anticipated modern theories of number. The outcome of our discussions on this matter was a paper in *Philosophy*, July 1965 which we wrote together. The opening sections of that paper have been omitted, but the rest is published here as it appeared in *Philosophy*, with the consent of Professor Acton, the editor of *Philosophy*.

[2] *Philosophical Quarterly*, 1959, p. 302.

[3] II. xvi. 1.

numbers other than 1 is for Locke a simple mode, made by repetition of the same given idea. 'By repeating this idea in our minds, and adding the repetitions together, we come by the complex ideas of the modes of it. Thus by adding one to one we have the complex idea of a couple.'[1]

Thus Locke sees a fundamental distinction between the ideas of 1 and 2; the idea of the former is given, the latter is constructed. With this in mind we find it difficult to accept Dawson's statement, 'Locke was primarily concerned with indicating what is given to us in experience, and in saying that we are presented with the natural numbers only, he was anticipating the later famous remark of Kronecker's "God made the integers, all the rest is the work of man"'.[2] But this will not do, for obviously Locke thinks the ideas of 2, of 3 and of all natural numbers other than 1 are the work of man. The point is made clear in II. xv. 1–2, and of course it is essential as a basis for the empiricist theory of infinity which he is about to put forward.

This at once greatly limits the likeness between Locke's theory and that of modern mathematicians. The latter disagree fundamentally between themselves on many points, but we know of no one who would distinguish between the idea of 1 and the idea of 2 in the way in which Locke does. Further, Locke ignores much in this chapter that any modern theory of mathematics must take into account. He speaks of the natural numbers only and says nothing of zero, of negative, fractional, irrational, and imaginary numbers, so it is not possible to compare his position with the moderns on such points. But he does give an account of natural numbers. Yet his distinction between the simple idea of 1 and the complex idea of 2 seems to have little in common with modern thought. From this point of view, therefore, it would appear erroneous to say that modern mathematics assumes his position.

3. Dawson quotes the opening paragraph of Heyting's discussion of natural numbers in *Intuitionism*[1] which he claims to be 'particularly Lockian in tone'. Heyting (who refers his readers to Brouwer for corroborative support) remarks: 'In the perception of an object we conceive the notion of an entity by a process of abstracting from the particular qualities of the object. We also recognize the possibility

[1] II. xvi. 2.
[2] Ibid., p. 304.
[3] A. Heyting, *Intuitionism, An Introduction*, Amsterdam, 1965, p. 13.

of an indefinite repetition of the conception of entities. In these notions lies the source of the concept of natural numbers.' We agree that this passage is 'Lockian in tone' but there is no suggestion here that Heyting would accept the view that the idea of 1 is simple and that of 2 is complex in Locke's sense. Heyting thinks of the notion of natural numbers as simple. He begins this paragraph: 'We start with the notion of the natural numbers 1, 2, 3, etc. They are so familiar to us, that it is difficult to reduce this notion to simpler ones.' But Heyting is not using 'simple' as a synonym for 'given' in Locke's sense. It is necessary to quote not only Heyting's first paragraph but also his second, where he is asking whether these considerations are metaphysical. 'They become so', he replies, 'if one tries to build up a theory about them, e.g. to answer the question whether we form the notion of an entity by abstraction from actual perception of objects, or if, on the contrary, the notion of an entity must be present in our mind in order to enable us to perceive an object apart from the rest of the world.' These words are certainly not Lockian in tone and not empiricist; Locke in Book II would emphatically reject the second alternative which is left an open question by Heyting.

4. The point of likeness, however, which Dawson would most want to stress presumably is that between Locke's account of the generation of 2, 3, 4 . . . and Heyting's statement: 'We also recognise the possibility of an indefinite repetition of the conception of entities.' The reference is to the inductive definition of numbers greater than 1. This definition is basic not only for Heyting and the intuitionists but for most modern mathematicians. Dawson makes the claim that Locke gives a description which to a certain extent anticipates this definition and that he sets it out in the *Essay*. He does not claim that Locke proposes a definition of numbers or that he was interested in the problem of definition, but he thinks that the underlying notion is present. Any attempt at defining number on the basis (a) that 1 is a number and (b) that $a+1$ is a number, if a is a number, rests on the notions of repetition and addition to which Locke refers.

We agree with Dawson that this suggestion is present in II. xvi of the *Essay* and that pp. 165–6 above should have drawn attention to this point. Let us see what exactly Locke says. We have already quoted II. xvi. 2; equally relevant is II. xvi. 5: 'By the repeating . . . of the idea of an unit, and joining it to another unit, we make thereof one collective idea, marked by the name "two". And whosoever can do this and proceed on, still adding one more to the last collective idea which he had of any number, and give a name to it, may count. ... So that he that can add one to one, and so to two, and go on with his tale, taking still with him the distinct names belonging to every progression, and so again by subtracting an unit from each collection retreat and lessen them, is capable of all the ideas of numbers within the compass of his language, or for which he hath names, though not perhaps of more.'

It can, we think, be fairly argued that the principle of mathematical induction is at least suggested in this passage and in II. xvi. 2. Numbering is a progression beginning with 1 and adding 1 to make in the first instance 2, then 3 and so on. The principle of mathematical induction is never formally stated by Locke,[1] but its gist is stated here. In this view we agree with Dawson. He seems to be implying, however, that Locke is making an original contribution in this chapter anticipating modern mathematical thought, but the originality seems to us questionable. There is a quite explicit use of the principle of mathematical induction in Pascal: *Treatise on the Arithmetic Triangle*, which was written in 1653.[2] H. Eves, the historian of mathematics, claims this to be one of the first statements of the principle.[3] It seems evident, however, that Fermat was also aware of this principle. In his *Works*[4] will be found a letter setting forward his Method of Infinite or Indefinite Descent. In the course of his letter the theory of the generation of numbers, later found in Locke, is throughout implicit and, though he is not using the principle of mathematical induction itself, that principle is also implicit in what he says. Now Locke was not a leading mathematician, but he was mathematician enough to read, say, Pascal's *Treatise* and to discuss the work with his mathematical friends. We may find here another instance of his ability to pick up emergent ideas and use them for his own purposes. What is new in Locke's account is the description of natural numbers greater than 1 as 'simple modes': but this is a theory, it will be generally agreed, in which he does not anticipate modern mathematicians.

But whether Locke's account is original or not, it is certainly not free from ambiguity. He has to do with 1, with repetition, with

---

[1] It may be written formally thus: $[[P(o)\&(n)[P(n) \supset P(n+1)]] \supset (n)P(n)]$.

[2] cf. D. E. Smith, *Source Book in Mathematics*, p. 73 (Proof of Corollary 12).

[3] H. Eves, *An Introduction to the History of Mathematics*, p. 261.

[4] *Œuvres* (ed. Tannery et Henry), vol. ii, p. 431, Fermat to Carcari, 1659. W. Kneale (*Probability and Induction*, p. 37) thinks the principle was formulated by Fermat, and no doubt has this passage in mind.

adding, counting, and collections. Now 1, according to Locke, is
given in experience. (Locke speaks of 'the idea of one'; to avoid
complication let us here speak of one.) But what Locke says in xvi, 1
is that 'unity or one' is given, and this identification of unity and one
at once reveals ambiguity. 'Every object our senses are employed
about' is one and so provides us with knowledge of 1. That is to say,
the object is unique and isolated. But this would seem to imply that
our perception of the object (if it is one amongst others) provides us
with 2 also, with *this* object and at least one other different from it.
Yet on Locke's scheme only 1 is given. Now this unity is repeated.
But, if mere unity were repeated, all we should get would be unity.
There is thus ambiguity in the notion of repetition, for Locke is
thinking of the repetition which results in our having the numbers
2, 3, 4, etc. Moreover, it is a repetition which is an adding, and
adding is not mere repeating; yet the difference is not made clear in
II. xvi. Further, is the adding a counting, as the passage suggests?
It need not be so necessarily. For instance, Locke speaks of the adding as providing us with 'collections', but the collection may not have
been counted. II, xvi is certainly full of ambiguities, and this is
another reason why it is dangerous to claim that it anticipates
modern mathematical thought.

It is interesting that Frege considered the above passage and commented upon it. He rejects Locke's theory that the number 1 is
suggested to us by every object,[1] and examines Locke's position that
definition of number is possible in terms of the unit or one.[2] The
identification of unit and one, he thinks, causes us to be blind to the
difficulty 'of reconciling identity of units with distinguishability'. It
would be better if, instead of speaking of 'unit', we spoke of 'object'
or 'thing'. 'We start by calling the things to be numbered "units",
without detracting from their diversity; then subsequently the
concept of putting together (or collecting or uniting or annexing,
or whatever we choose to call it) transforms itself into that of
arithmetical addition, while the concept word "unit" changes un-
perceived into the proper name "one". And there we have our
identity.'[3] Frege sees in Locke's position a paradox which Locke
does nothing to remove, it being hidden from him by the ambiguity
of his account of the number 1 and of what it is to add 1. Adding
different objects will not give us a number, for the objects still have

[1] *The Foundations of Arithmetic* (tr. by J. L. Austin), § 31.
[2] Ibid., §§ 37-9.   [3] Ibid., § 39.

those properties which distinguish them; on the other hand if we add one and one, where one is undifferentiated, all we have is one. Or, as Frege puts it,[1] 'If we try to produce the number by putting together different distinct objects, the result is an agglomeration in which the objects contained remain still in possession of precisely those properties which serve to distinguish them from one another; and that is not the number. But if we try to do it in the other way, by putting together identicals, the result runs perpetually together into one and we never reach a plurality.'

5. Locke thinks the idea of one is given us in all our experience. He does not say that the idea of two is also given, as he might on the ground that to be given the oneness of the thing is to be given its difference from another, assuming that there is another. His strategy as we have seen leads him to explain two as a complex idea, made or constructed by the mind by repeating precisely the same simple idea of one; it is a simple mode. But this is inadequate as an account of the generation of two, for, as Frege points out, on this method we never reach a plurality. Many modern mathematical theorists do distinguish between mental entities which can and those which cannot be constructed, but they would not wish to base this distinction on the difference between 1 and the other natural numbers. Nor does Dawson, if we understand him rightly, wish to rest his comparison between Locke and the modern mathematician on this particular distinction between simple idea and simple mode. But he does wish to argue that Locke's account of number generation in terms of a constructing by repetition and addition and a naming has its counterpart in modern mathematics, particularly in intuitionism. 'In stressing the *process* of number generation, Locke insures that he will be able to *construct* any number which he can *name*, and in this he clearly anticipates the modern Intuitionist mathematicians.'[2] Let us examine this further claim.

Dawson has in mind the passage (already quoted) at the beginning of the discussion of natural numbers in Heyting's *Intuitionism* (p. 13). Heyting holds that we gain 'the notion of an entity by a process of abstracting from the particular qualities of an object', further he asserts 'the possibility of an indefinite repetition of the conception of entities'. Locke, Dawson argues, has set forward the same doctrine, and it insures that he can construct any number that he can name.

[1] Ibid., § 39.   [2] Ibid., 304.

Does he not therefore anticipate the intuitionists? Now in so far as Locke can be said to have suggested a notion of constructivity he might be said to anticipate many of the moderns, and not merely the intuitionists. Yet there are big differences between him and the latter. To begin with, as Heyting's second paragraph, which we have quoted, shows, Heyting would not necessarily agree that the idea of 1 is given in the way in which Locke describes. More important, Heyting holds too in this second paragraph that the questions we are now considering 'have nothing to do with mathematics'. 'We simply state the fact that the concepts of an abstract entity and of a sequence of such entities are clear to every normal human being, even to young children.'[1] In other words he sets up a distinction between the mathematical and the pre-mathematical. 'Mathematics begins after the concepts of natural numbers and of equality between natural numbers have been formed. Of course the dichotomy between mathematics and pre-mathematics is artificial, just as is every splitting of human thought, but this dichotomy corresponds to an important difference in methods.'[2] So that the generation of natural numbers from experience and by repetitions which interests Locke is pre-mathematical in Heyting's account of the matter. It follows too that when Heyting speaks of construction he does not mean the constructions of Locke's chapter, which he would link, it appears, with the pre-mathematical. He is concerned with mathematical and not pre-mathematical construction. This surely puts a great difference between his account and Locke's.

Now Locke does not use the terms 'construction' and 'construct' in II. xvi. 1. 2 & 5, but it is not unfair to speak of his account of the generation of the natural numbers other than 1 as an account of a construction of a sort. Up till 1690, though his additions in later editions of the Essay suggest a change of mind, every complex idea is a construction; it is the mind's 'workmanship'; and this applies to the ideas of 2, 3, 4 and of all natural numbers other than 1. Moreover, he does refer in II. xvi. 5 to the 'progression' of numbers which is also part of the constructing involved. What is implicit in this passage, however, is not clear. To admit that consciousness of progression is part of the idea would be to cast doubt upon the simplicity of a simple mode; the complex idea in this case is made by repeating precisely the same simple idea. If there is more in the mode than the repetition of the same idea, and this viewing of the generation of

[1] *Intuitionism*, p. 13.   [2] Ibid., p. 15.

numbers as involving the notion of progression suggests as much, then the mode becomes complex. This, as we have seen, would defeat Locke's general purpose in Book II. But the distinction between simple *modes* and complex modes seems to be breaking down even in II. xii and later the more general distinction between simple *ideas* and complex ideas is itself considerably toned down. Yet, in whatever way we interpret the mind's workmanship, Dawson is not wholly unjustified in speaking of Locke's constructionalism in this chapter. Now the modern intuitionists too speak of constructionalism. Can we assume they are speaking of the same thing? Our view in this paper is that we cannot, if the constructionalism of the Lockian theory of the generation of numbers is pre-mathematical and that of Heyting is mathematical.

6. The constructionalism of the intuitionist theory is not easy to understand and no attempt will be made here to expound it fully. But we should like to refer to a central point in intuitionist constructionalism which would appear to make it a very different theory from Locke's. To avoid complication we shall confine our comment to the intuitionist whom Dawson has in mind, namely, Heyting.

Locke's theory allows him, says Dawson, 'to construct any number which he can name'. That is, presumably, to construct it in principle. Take the number $87342^{281} \times 4375^{7561}$. We have named it, but it would not in fact be possible for us to construct it in accordance with the Lockian theory of repetition. Still it would be possible to do this in principle. But Heyting is thinking of a constructionalism in which a natural number could be entertained that we could not, given the present state of our knowledge, possibly construct. He says: 'Let us compare two definitions of natural numbers, say k and l. (1) k is the greatest prime such that $k-1$ is also a prime, or $k=1$ if such a number does not exist. (2) l is the greatest prime such that $l-2$ is also a prime, or $l=1$ if such a number does not exist. Classical mathematics neglects altogether the obvious difference in character between these definitions. k can actually be calculated $(k=3)$ whereas we possess no method for calculating l, as it is not known whether the sequence of pairs of twin primes p, $p+2$ is finite or not.'[1] In this case the number l is defined, but we cannot calculate (i.e. for Heyting construct) it. On this point then there is considerable difference between the position of Locke and that of Heyting.

[1] *Intuitionism*, p. 2.

Heyting proceeds in the same paragraph: 'Therefore intuitionists reject (2) as a definition of an integer; they consider an integer to be well defined only if a method for calculating it is given. Now this line of thought leads to the rejection of the principle of excluded middle, for if the sequence of twin primes were either finite or not finite, (2) would define an integer.' On the classical theory l is defined but the intuitionists narrow the connotation of the term 'definition' for their own purposes. Yet to establish that l is not well defined they are led to reject a logical principle. They have to reject the principle of the excluded middle. Needless to say, there is nothing of this in *Essay*, II. xvi.

The sort of constructionalism we can attribute to Locke—and it should be repeated that in II. xvi he does not speak of construction or constructionalism—is the repetition and progression in number generation. The intuitionists would regard this as pre-mathematical. They think of construction in terms of the subsequent mathematical calculation. Moreover their constructionalism involves fundamental restrictions on the methods of proof. It would be more plausible to suggest that if a notion of mathematical constructivity can be said to be found in Locke, then it is best thought of as anticipating the constructivist trend sometimes called 'finitism' rather than intuitionism. For while the intuitionist conception of constructivity imposes restrictions on methods of proof by requiring a non-standard logic, finitism is independent of such considerations.

7. To conclude, Dawson is entirely justified in drawing our attention to the likeness between Locke's account of the generation of numbers and the later inductive definition of natural numbers. He is right in saying that the account of number given on page 166 could well have included a discussion of this matter. In fact the text approached Locke's theory from a different angle, that of Leibniz, Frege, and Russell. Whilst recognizing this, we none the less feel that Dawson overstates his case. A commentator less sympathetic to Leibniz and to logicism generally, even an intuitionist or finitist in his mathematical theories, might still doubt whether Locke does anticipate the moderns to the extent that Dawson suggests. There is much in Locke's thought that would at once be rejected by any modern theorist. There is much that is ambiguous. The claim to originality— if Dawson makes that claim—is doubtful. Is Locke saying anything more about number than the seventeenth-century mathematicians

were already saying? If there is something additional, is it not the trimming of the theory to make it fit into the defence he was building up for his empiricist philosophy? Still the suggestion—the ambiguous suggestion—of the inductive definition of numbers is there, and commentators must note it. But the verdict of pp. 165–6 remains true that Locke's account of numbers is inadequate and defective.

APPENDIX IV

THE LIMITS OF LOCKE'S RATIONALISM[1]

I

As is well known, historians of philosophy were slow to acknowledge that the writings of John Locke contain rationalist elements. They were misled by an over-facile division of seventeenth-century philosophy into two schools, the rationalist, of which Descartes was the founder, and the empiricist. It was assumed, quite wrongly, that these two schools were entirely distinct from each other, and that consequently since Locke, for instance, was an empiricist he could not also be a rationalist. But from the middle of the last century onwards a saner view, based on a better understanding of Locke's works, has prevailed, and it has become clear that rationalism is as essential an element of Locke's philosophy as it is of Descartes's.

The present article deals with the limits of Locke's rationalism and takes the rationalism itself for granted. Surely only a rationalist could have written *The Reasonableness of Christianity*, a book which aims at proving that the tenets of the Christian faith are in accordance with reason, and which assumes as something not open to question that such tenets become more worthy of our acceptance once their rationality has been demonstrated. Only a rationalist again could have chosen the method Locke adopts in his *Two Treatises on Civil Government*. In that book his final purpose was to show that a democratic constitutional monarchy was the form of government best suited to a free people. He uses the argument of the book, as he himself explains, 'to establish the throne of our great restorer, our present King William . . . and to justify to the world the people of England'. But the *Civil Government* is more than a piece of special pleading for the Revolution of 1688. It is more also than a Whig tract. That Locke was the prophet of the Whigs is true, and that his somewhat ingenious defence of property, and even his plea for the liberty of the individual, helped the Whigs to establish their supremacy in the eighteenth century is beyond all doubt. Nevertheless, it is surely wrong to regard the *Civil Government* as a mere

[1] This paper was first published in *Seventeenth Century Studies, Presented to Sir Herbert Grierson*, Oxford, 1938. I have amended it, particularly to take into account the manuscripts in the Lovelace Collection.

party document. It is Locke's political testament, the fruit of a life-time's observation and reflection. He was well placed for observing the political life of his country. His experience of political affairs was extensive, and he had learnt also from the experience of others. He had come to the conclusion that the only form of constitution which could secure the people's freedom and yet provide strong government was a democracy of the type which he sketched in the *Civil Government.* Whether this conclusion was sound or not need not here be considered; the interesting point is that when he attempted to state his case he made very little appeal to experience, either to his own or to that of others, nor again to public utility. Instead he adopted the rationalist method. He attempted to prove his thesis rationally, just as one proves a theorem in geometry. Beginning with the premiss that society is such and such in its origin and nature, he attempted to prove apodictically that democracy is the eternally true form of government. For he knew that the appeal to experience and to utility, however successful, would convince neither himself nor his contemporaries. A rationalist apology for democracy was necessary and it was this which he offered his readers.

The rationalism of the *Essay Concerning Human Understanding* is still more obvious. That work consists of four books, the first three of which are preparatory to the fourth. Book IV deals with the nature and extent of human knowledge. Locke took almost twenty years to write the *Essay,* and during this period he considered many possible theories of knowledge. It is significant that the one which he finally adopted was the rationalist theory of Descartes. Knowledge which is certain is intuition or demonstration, the *intuitus* and *deductio* of Descartes, the very core of the Cartesian rationalism. Locke was opposed to the Cartesians on most other points, and it is all the more significant that on this essential and central point he openly accepted the rationalist position, and set it out almost in the Cartesian terminology. At the same time it is well to observe that the rationalism which he did accept was not the peculiar property of the Cartesians. For the identification of knowing with intuiting has been common to many rationalists. But Descartes had restated it and Locke was clearly influenced by this re-statement. Knowing is intuiting which is infallible. And each step in mediate knowing is intuited, for thus alone can certainty be gained. 'Certainty depends so wholly on this intuition, that in the next degree of knowledge, which I call demonstrative, this intuition is necessary in all the

connexions of the intermediate ideas, without which we cannot attain
knowledge and certainty.'[1] The theory of knowledge set forward in
the opening chapters of Book IV is entirely rationalist in tone.

One might discover many other illustrations of Locke's rationalism
in his works, but these will suffice to show that if Descartes had a
right to the title of rationalist so also had Locke. Indeed, from one
point of view Locke's rationalism is more thorough-going than that
of Descartes. Descartes stipulated that the free use of reason was to
be permitted only in the pursuit of scientific knowledge, and that
its use in politics and religion was to be carefully superintended.
There is no such stipulation in Locke. He would give reason free
play in the political and in the religious realm, as well as in the
scientific. This difference between the two philosophers may be
accounted for, in part at least, by a change in public opinion. Even
if Descartes had believed what Locke believed, he would have found
it dangerous to say so in the middle of the seventeenth century. But
at the end of that century Locke's rationalism was welcomed by all.
And by the beginning of the eighteenth century the triumph of
rationalism was complete. Reason had come into its own; its
authority was recognized everywhere and in every sphere. It is not
untrue to say that Locke belongs more closely to the Age of Reason
than Descartes—not only in time but also in spirit.

That this is so is confirmed by another important fact. The book
which most influenced the rationalist eighteenth century was not
the *Discourse* of Descartes, or any of his other works, but the *Essay*
of Locke. The eighteenth century treated Descartes with considerable respect, but was none the less suspicious of him. Voltaire, for
instance, in his *Lettres philosophiques*, holds that Descartes was too
speculative, and contrasts him in this respect with Locke. (Incidentally, Voltaire saw the differences between Locke and Descartes more
clearly than he saw the resemblances between them, and he, more
than any one else, perhaps, is responsible for the false tradition
according to which the two thinkers have nothing in common.
Professor Kemp Smith has pointed out that Locke gave back to the
France of the eighteenth century what he himself had received from
the France of the seventeenth. This is true, but what he gave back
differed in many important respects from what he himself received,
and it is not altogether strange that Voltaire should have failed to
realize the measure of Locke's debt to France.) Locke, it is clear, and

[1] IV. ii. I.

not Descartes is the supreme formative influence on the France of the eighteenth century, on Voltaire, Buffier, Montesquieu, Condillac, and Rousseau. Locke also influenced eighteenth-century rationalist England in its literature, as the works of Pope, Addison, and Sterne in particular show, and in its philosophy.

That Locke should have influenced the rationalist eighteenth century so deeply has always been something of a paradox to those historians of philosophy who rank him with the empiricists. But once the true position is understood there is no paradox. It is not at all strange that the *Essay*, the *Civil Government*, *The Reasonableness of Christianity*, and *Some Thoughts Concerning Education* should have led men to put their trust in reason. For they were written by a rationalist whose aim was to increase men's faith in reason.

But this was not Locke's only aim. For the most significant fact about Locke is that he found it necessary to modify his rationalism. He was a rationalist, but he was the critic of rationalism as well. He restricted it, and in this very restriction is to be found his most important contribution to philosophy. Locke was the executor of the seventeenth century in a philosophical sense. He gathered together all that was living and vital in the thought of that brilliant age and handed it forward as a heritage to the eighteenth century. The chief bequest was rationalism, and it is not surprising that the new age was the Age of Reason. Yet the rationalism which Locke thus passed on to the next generation was tempered by non-rationalist elements. Locke had faith in reason, but it was never a blind faith. He knew its limitations. And the eighteenth century, however much it extolled reason, never entirely forgot the criticism latent in Locke's works. The scepticism which flowered in Hume and which destroyed the Age of Reason's faith in itself is already present in Locke. The rationalist spirit of a classical age pervades his writings, but the seeds of revolt against rationalism are present as well.

In what follows I propose to examine the limits of Locke's rationalism, and to show that rationalism is restricted by him in two important respects. In the first place, the materials upon which reason works are provided, according to Locke's view, not in a rational intuition, which penetrates into real being, but in sensation and introspection. Man is a rational animal, but he is also sensitive, and his sensitive experiences are basic both in life and in knowledge. Secondly, certain truths which, in Locke's opinion, are the proper and urgent concern of mankind none the less lie beyond the scope of man's reason, and in this respect also his reason is limited. In dealing with these limitations upon reason it will be necessary to touch upon two problems, first, that of the relations between experience and reason, and, secondly, that of the relations between revelation and reason.

II

To understand properly the nature of this first restriction upon reason it is necessary to consider the character of Locke's rationalism in greater detail, beginning with the *Essay*. From Descartes Locke has borrowed the conception of knowledge as essentially intuitive, an intuition which pervades mediate knowledge also. This doctrine that man is capable of infallible *intuitus* is the very centre and core of Descartes's rationalist epistemology, and once Locke accepts it, though he did not do so till late in his preparation for writing the *Essay*, it becomes the centre of his epistemology too. But it then conflicts with other elements in that epistemology. It is significant that Locke does not speak of 'intuition' as 'reason', but tends to use the latter term as synonymous with 'reasoning'. In the chapter on 'Reason'[1] he is obviously thinking of reason as equivalent to reasoning, including inductive reasoning which does not give certainty; although even here he talks of reason as that which perceives the 'necessary and indubitable connexion of all ideas or proofs one to another in each step of any demonstration that produces knowledge'.[2] But it is not his theory of *reasoning* which makes him a cartesian rationalist, it is rather this insistence on the possibility of a knowledge which is necessary, infallible, and indubitable, and the further insistence that where demonstration is certain it is so only because it contains an intuitive element. 'In every step reason makes in demonstrative knowledge, there is an intuitive knowledge of that agreement or disagreement it seeks with the next intermediate idea.'[3]

In respect to this central point there is no difference then between the positions of Descartes and Locke. For both an infallible intuition is possible; man can know with complete certainty. But when we turn from the consideration of the knowing to that which it knows, from the subjective side to the objective, profound differences in theory emerge. In Descartes's view *intuitus* must have its own object,

[1] iv. xvii.
[2] iv. xvii. 2.
[3] iv. ii. 7.

and its certainty is as much due to the character of the object as it is to the purity of the faculty. The object of true knowledge is a 'simple nature', wholly clear and wholly distinct. It is clear in the sense that it is transparent through and through, so that nothing is hidden; and it is distinct in the sense that it is completely isolated, so that the mind can comprehend it in its full totality. Now of no objects revealed in sensation can we say that they are clear and distinct in this sense. It is part of Descartes's theory that the 'simple nature' must be a purely intellectual object.

But the object of Locke's intuition is neither simple in this sense nor purely intellectual. He would perhaps agree with Descartes that such an object would be the ideal for intuition if it were possible, and that knowledge would then be a sheer intuition of a sheer intellectual simple. But the sheer simple is not a possible object of knowledge. Descartes himself in the *Regulae* soon finds it necessary to introduce 'simple propositions'. And Locke defines knowledge as 'the perception of the connexion and agreement, or disagreement and repugnancy, of any of our ideas'.[1] Knowledge is of relations, not of simple entities. Gaining a simple idea, on Locke's theory, is not knowing. To know is to perceive a relation, although the relation may very well hold between simple ideas.

In the second place, the object cannot, in Locke's opinion, be purely intellectual. The relation apprehended must be between ideas, and every idea is empirically derived. It need not be immediately given in experience for it may be that which the mind makes of the immediately given. And it need not be an idea of sensation, for Locke also recognizes reflection (or introspection) as a source of material for knowledge. But all ideas are either themselves given in sensation or reflection, or they are in some way derived from the given of sensation or reflection. Consequently, any relation between ideas is a relation between empirically derived entities. The pure intellectual object of human knowledge is a figment of a false rationalism.

This, then, is the first restriction upon reason. It has to concern itself with materials not known by rational intuition, but given to the mind in sensory or reflective experience. And the extent and significance of this limitation will only be understood if Locke's theory of ideas is recalled. If the ideas were real physical objects, our knowledge, although not of pure intellectual objects, would at

[1] IV. i. 2.

least be of relations between real physical things. But Locke does not identify ideas with physical objects. He accepts the theory of representative perception. What we see immediately is a representation 'in the mind' which may or may not copy exactly the external physical object. Locke believes that for the most part the representation, or idea, is not an adequate and exact copy of the external, physical object. For instance, colours, sounds, tastes, and so an, are not in the things themselves. It thus happens that reason works on materials of which we cannot be sure that they do adequately represent the real. It is no certain and indubitable intuition of the real world; it does not even work with adequate representations of the real physical objects in that world. It works with ideas either given to the mind (although the fact that they are given is no guarantee that they truly represent the real) or created through the mind's activity on the ideas given.

The thesis that all ideas are empirically derived is defended energetically in Book II of the *Essay*. Locke shows what ideas we gain in sensation and reflection. Ideas of memory are clearly derived from these first experiences. So also are images, although in imagination we are free to change the order of the experience and can, for instance, imagine horses with wings. All abstract ideas, again, are abstracted from sense-data and ideas of reflection. However abstract our thought becomes it is never so abstract as to be underived from sensory and reflective experience. Locke gives much attention to the idea of infinity, which seems to be so remote from experience as to owe nothing to it. Yet this conception also, he thinks, is empirically derived. For our conception of infinity is clear only in so far as it means a never-ending progression, whether in space, in time, or in number. And Locke attempts to show that as much positive content as the idea contains is derived from the sensory experience of space, the reflective experience of time, and that experience of unity or oneness which is both sensory and reflective, and which lies at the base of our idea of number. Even our idea of God is derived empirically and can be analysed ultimately into experienced elements. Not that our idea of God is adequate, for God is incomprehensible to mortal minds, but we can only frame an idea of God in terms of sensory and reflective experience.

All those sublime thoughts which tower above the clouds, and reach as high as heaven itself, take their rise and footing here: in all that great extent wherein the mind wanders in those remote speculations it may seem to be elevated with, it stirs not one jot beyond those ideas which sense or reflection have offered for its contemplation.[1]

No one would claim for Locke that he has proved his empiricist thesis outright in Book II. There are stubborn facts such as the existence in our minds of ideas of substance, of causality, and the like, which he cannot explain entirely in empiricist terms. And it is doubtful whether he does truly answer the objection that the idea of infinity is non-empirical. Yet there is no doubt about Locke's purpose. Again and again he asserts that no idea can be wholly independent of experience. What is not given in, or derived from, experience is not significant. Book II puts forward a theory of meaning. That has meaning which is either immediately experienced in sensation or reflection, or is derived from such an experience.

Now reason, if it is to function at all, has to deal with ideas of this kind, for such ideas alone, in Locke's opinion, form the object of human thought and knowledge. It has been said that Locke forgets this theory in Book IV and reverts to a rationalism which is identical with the cartesian, not only on the subjective but also on the objective side. And, certainly, if Locke holds in Book IV that the object in knowing is purely intellectual, and is not derived from experience, then that book contradicts Book II. At the same time, the argument that Book IV is rationalist whereas Book II is empiricist, and that, therefore, Book IV contradicts Book II, cannot be admitted to be sound. It is one further illustration of the false view that there is nothing in common between rationalism and empiricism. Locke's rationalism contradicts his empiricism only if it follows Descartes on the objective as well as on the subjective side. But he can assert that knowing is intuiting, and yet also hold that the object of knowledge is a relation between empirically derived ideas. And this is what Locke does assert. He believes that knowing is intuition and demonstration, but he also thinks that all significant objective content is empirically derived. It may follow from this that we shall find few instances of knowing with certainty. And Locke's theory might then be criticized as leading to scepticism, but it cannot be said to be inconsistent.

'But is not his theory of mathematics', it will be asked, 'wholly inconsistent with the empiricism of Book II? Are not the objects of mathematics purely intellectual in his view? Does he not hold that here we are completely independent of experience, and so may have

[1] II. i. 24.

certain, necessary, and universal knowledge? Does he not base the
certainty of mathematics on the fact that this science is independent
of experience?'

Now it is clear that throughout the opening chapters of Book IV
Locke has mathematics in mind. Most of the instances of certain
knowledge which he gives are mathematical, and in one place he
expressly states: 'Mathematical demonstration depends not upon
sense'.[1] Certainty is possible in mathematics, because the ideas in
this case are, as Locke explains, 'ideas which are their own archetypes', that is to say, they have no reference to anything beyond
themselves, they are not representations of the external physical
objects. Here the mind is concerned solely with the ideas and it
intuits relations holding necessarily between them, which relations
follow from the nature of the ideas. Surely, it will be said, mathematical ideas are purely intellectual. They are universals, fixed
meanings, logical contents, i.e. wholly intellectual objects. To some
extent Locke would, of course, agree, but if the objection means that
we have in this instance an idea not derived from experience, he
would disagree. In Book II he is at great pains to show that mathematical ideas are empirically derived, and nowhere in Book IV does
he say that mathematical ideas are purely intellectual. He must have
meant that they are what he explains them to be in Book II. It
would be easier to understand his position if he had given a satisfactory account of universals, particularly of mathematical universals. But he does not do so. None the less, nothing that he says
necessitates the view that mathematical objects as conceived by
him are purely intellectual objects. For although mathematical
truths are not discovered in sensing, and although they hold true
whether the real world outside confirms their truth or not, yet here,
as everywhere else, the content of the idea is derived empirically.
The mathematical universal is an abstraction from the given of
experience. This, it seems to me, is what Locke wishes to say, and
Books II and IV may be quite consistent. It should be added, however, that Locke has not shown how the mathematical idea is related
to those experiences upon which it is ultimately based.

Thus, in spite of this first restriction upon reason, certainty is still
possible on Locke's theory, whenever we can know necessary relations between ideas, either directly in intuition or indirectly through
demonstration. But the spheres in which certainty is possible are

[1] iv. xi 6.

indeed very limited. In particular, certain knowledge becomes impossible, if Locke's empiricism is sound, where perhaps we most need it, namely, in our attempt to know the world of real entities around us, both physical and mental. A *science* of nature becomes impossible. The only object for intuition is the ideal. Therefore, we never intuit the real: it is forever hidden from us. We cannot know the internal constitution of real physical objects, for these are not represented adequately in our ideas. And as a consequence we cannot know (*a*) any necessary relations within things. We do not know *how* qualities cohere in a thing (if this is a proper description of what occurs) nor what qualities do necessarily cohere in a particular case. In Locke's language, the coexistences of qualities cannot be known by us. Nor (*b*) can we know necessary relations between things, for instance, the causal relation, if there be such. Our inquiries in these realms never reach certainty. We do not here rationally intuit the truth, but we follow (as best we may) the guidance of experience. In our experience certain ideas always come together and this guides us in our framing of complex ideas of substances. Again, particular groups of qualities are frequently repeated in our experience, and we are led to think of physical objects as divided according to fixed natural types. In the same way, as the consequence of our experience, we generalize on the probable interactions which occur between things, although we do not know the inner nature of these things to account for these interactions, nor do we clearly understand the nature of the interactions themselves. It has not been sufficiently noticed in the past how very guarded are Locke's statements in connexion with causality. But his language in the *Essay* when he discusses causality suggests that its nature was a complete mystery to him. When we say we know causal laws, all we mean is that we have 'constantly observed' some new substances or new qualities of substances to begin to exist after 'the due application' of some other being. But of the true relation here we know nothing. And our causal law is merely an empirical generalization.

In the same way we are ignorant of the true inner nature of that immaterial substance—if it is an immaterial substance—which we call our minds. Psychology can never be a science in the strict sense; all its laws will be empirical generalizations. Probability in this realm also is the most we can expect. Thus the knowledge which is intuition, the true knowledge of the rationalist, is possible only in a very limited sphere. We enjoy no certain knowledge of real existences whether material or mental. We are confined to probabilities.

One reservation, however, must be made, although it does not change our general conclusion. The discussion up to this point is based on the theory of knowledge set forward in the opening chapters of Book IV. But that book contains another theory (in chapters ix and xi), according to which we have an intuitive knowledge of the existence of various entities. Every man intuits—Locke actually uses this word—the existence of his own self. Whether this intuition is precisely of the same kind as the intuition, for instance, in mathematics is not clear. If it is, it is so on the subjective side only; for the object now is not an idea but a real entity existing in nature. Locke also holds that we know the existence of physical things in 'sensitive knowledge'. This type of knowledge, again, is not clearly described. We are sure that the sun exists now when we see it, but we do not possess this assurance when we only imagine it. Hume says that the difference is entirely in the ideas, the one coming with greater force and vivacity than the other. But Locke seems to think that here we break out beyond ideas and know the real existence of real things. It is the realist in him overcoming the representationalist. Yet even if we do enjoy in this case an intuition of the real, this intuitive (and so rational) knowledge of the *existence* of things is not an intuitive knowledge of the *nature* of these things. To make natural science and psychology possible we should need knowledge of the essential and universal nature of things. This the intuition of existence in chapters ix and xi would not provide. The main restriction upon rationalism remains.

Thus we conclude that Locke is both a rationalist and an empiricist at one and the same time, and it is possible to argue that he is both without being inconsistent. But his empiricism limits his rationalism radically. Man's reason can and does gain certain knowledge. Mathematics is an instance of this. But in our knowledge of the external world and of minds, reason is hampered by the fact that the materials of knowledge are ideas, and that no intuition into the nature of real existences is possible. We must wait upon experience and learn from it. It may be possible that Locke thought we intuited the *existence* of particular objects in the real world; even so the knowledge we have of the nature of these objects, of their inner relations and of their inter-relations is probable only, the outcome of careful and systematic observation. By no intuition and by no pure *a priori* demonstration can we determine with certainty the character of the real world. This is the first respect in which reason is restricted, and it cannot be denied that this restriction is most serious in its consequences.

III

The restrictions on Locke's rationalism in the *Essay* have now been discussed, and the discussion centres on his acceptance of cartesian intuitionism at the beginning of Book IV as the solution of his own epistemological problems. He had hesitated about accepting this solution, and the difficulty of fitting it into his theory is evident. But he feared, not without reason, that his theory of knowledge was leading him to scepticism, and to save himself he felt the need at some point of an infallible knowledge. He thought he could find this in the cartesian theory of intellectual intuition, and he thought too that he could introduce this rationalist theory into his own account of human knowledge, if only he limited intuition to the knowledge (i) of relations between ideas which were their own archetypes, and (ii) of implications in inference.

The nature of the change in Locke's epistemology in Book IV can best be understood if we compare it with the epistemology of his earlier writings. In particular a study of *Essays on the Law of Nature*, 1664, is valuable.[1] The first essay asks whether there is a rule of morals, or law of nature, and gives an affirmative answer. This, it is explained, is God's world and, as such, it is intelligently ordered. There is an objective rule for all intelligent life and this is the law of nature. Some hold that the law is known by 'right reason' (*recta ratio*), but about this there is much disagreement. The essay maintains that 'right reason' is to be distinguished from reason as a faculty 'which forms trains of thought and deduces proofs'; it is rather the set of principles of action on which the moral life rests. These two senses of 'reason' must not be confused. Again, some hold that the law of nature is a decree of the divine will; others that it is

---

[1] The two drafts A and B of the *Essay* are not so revealing. They bring out Locke's empiricism, and we also see emerging the notion of ideas which are their own archetypes and the beginnings of what was later to be known as the analytic-synthetic distinction, analytic knowledge being certain. Compare, for instance, Draft A §§ 7–12 and 31. But the information provided in these drafts as to Locke's view of reason is slight.

a dictate of human reason. The essay considers the latter interpretation dangerous; for reason 'does not so much establish and pronounce this law of nature as search for it and discover it'.[1] It is established and pronounced by a superior will, but it can be discovered by us by the light of nature.

The reference to the light of nature might suggest Augustinian illumination; the law is implanted in our hearts and we are illuminated; but Locke does not propose to interpret it in this way. For in his second essay he explains how the phrase 'light of nature' is to be used in this context. It is not to be understood 'in the sense that some inward light is by nature implanted in man'.[2] To know by the 'light of nature' as Locke interprets it, is to know by making a 'proper use of the faculties' with which a man is naturally endowed. Now the faculty in question here, it might be held, is reason; it is reason that sets down the fundamental principles. Locke denies this. Reason is not pure knowledge of first principles. 'Nothing indeed is achieved by reason, that powerful faculty of arguing, unless there is first something posited and taken for granted.'[3] Reason 'does not lay a foundation'. Given the foundation it will erect the building. But how, then, are the first principles known? Not, argues Locke, by inscription, they are not known innately. Nor again are they known by tradition. We hear others speak of them, but we cannot rest satisfied with a second-hand knowledge of so important a set of principles, and anyhow people contradict one another as to what they are. They are known, Locke somewhat surprisingly declares, by sense-perception, 'which we declare to be the basis of our knowledge of the law of nature.'[4] Not that we see, or hear, or touch, the principles of the law of nature, but that, having perceived through the senses objects, occurrences, and events, we then use our reasoning powers to infer the law of nature. This is what Locke means by 'knowing by the light of nature'. As he explains later in the fourth essay knowledge is gained by the co-operation of these two 'faculties' of sense-perception and reason, the former providing 'the subject-matter of discourse' and reason then ordering the material, relating it and seeing what can be inferred from it.[5] Reason is 'the discursive faculty of the mind which advances from things known to things

[1] *Essays on the Law of Nature*, p. 111.
[2] Ibid., p. 123.
[3] Ibid., p. 125.
[4] Ibid., p. 131.
[5] Ibid., p. 147.

unknown,'[1] but reason does not provide the starting-points. Even where its operation is most evident, for instance, in mathematics, it does not and cannot provide the starting-point of the inquiry.

Here, then, at the beginning of his reflection on human knowledge, Locke very severely limits the role of reason. It works upon the subject-matter once it be provided, but it does not itself provide it. This is true of both theoretical knowledge and of practical. The law of nature is not laid down by human reason. Like every other law it is a dictate, and the dictate of one who has the right to command. Only God can command the law of nature as a law which all men should obey. By his act of willing he creates an obligation on all mankind to obey the law. No human reason can dictate it, but human reason can reflect upon it and come to understand how obedience to the law is obligatory. Locke speaks of 'a rational apprehension of what is right'[2] and of a harmony, a *convenientia*, between the law of nature and human nature.[3] Thus a rational being knows what he ought to do, he understands that it follows from the fact that he is what he is that he must behave thus and thus. But if he understands it, he only understands it in so far as he recognizes that the promulgation of the law is God's will. The voluntarism in Locke's account of the basis of morality itself further limits the role of reason in that account.

The *Essays on the Law of Nature* thus reveal the limitations of Locke's rationalism from the outset. Man cannot know all things by reason; he cannot begin to know by reason. The 'faculty of reason' is the faculty of reasoning, of reflecting upon the given, of relating elements within it, of finding what premises are permitted, and what conclusions can be logically deduced from these premises. So far as our knowledge of our world goes, it is sense-perception which gives us our first information. Unfortunately, as has been seen, the information then given is not completely reliable, and this means that wholly certain knowledge of the structure of the world is not possible and we have to be content with probability. *Scientia* is not possible. This breeds scepticism, and Locke acknowledges that reason cannot dissipate scepticism about our knowledge of the real world. Is there then certainty in any field, or is man limited to probable knowledge? This is the problem upon which Locke reflected through the period 1664 to 1690. His answer, as we know, was to accept a very limited rationalism. Not only has man discursive powers, not only can he

---

[1] *Essays on the Law of Nature*, p. 149.   [2] Ibid., p. 185.   [3] Ibid., p. 199.

infer, but he can also intuit. He can intuit relations between ideas, and in deductive thinking itself he intuits that the premises imply (or do not imply) the conclusion. Thus Locke takes over part of the cartesian theory of intuition, and this enables him to open Book IV of the *Essay* with an account of wholly certain knowledge. Now in the *Regulae* intellectual intuitionism is the core of Descartes's rationalism. Locke, on the other hand, takes over the cartesian theory but never speaks of intuition as reason. Yet this element in his teaching is rationalist; in no sense, for instance, could it be called empiricist. Nevertheless, in his quest for certainty Locke has not given up the beliefs of 1664 and 1671. We can find complete certainty *only* in knowledge of relations between ideas which are their own archetypes, *only* when the question of correspondence between ideas and things or events in the external world does not arise. Any knowledge of the external world remains probable; but the mind can contemplate and analyse its ideas and there find certainties. It is rationalism—but always a strictly limited rationalism.

IV

It is the same restricted rationalism that we find in Locke's account of morality and religion. This has been seen already in the case of Locke's ethical teaching in *Essays on the Law of Nature*. Man by reasoning upon what is empirically gained can deduce certain consequences about how he ought to live; he deduces that he lives in a world divinely ordered, that he himself is part of the created world and his creator has endowed him with reason, that the morality which fits his nature is the morality enshrined in the natural law. Thus it is rational for him to live in accordance with that law. Yet this does not account for the obligation upon him to do so. In Locke's opinion this arises from the fact that God wills that men should obey the law. Here is a non-rationalist element implicit in human morality, so that no purely rationalist ethics is possible. Yet this is not to deny the rationalist element. It is possible to make rational deductions about human behaviour from what one knows of human nature and these deductions will be as certain, Locke tells us in the seventh essay, as that 'it follows from the nature of a triangle that, if it is a triangle, its three angles are equal to two right angles.' Locke, as we know,[1] was from this point onward

---

[1] Cf. Part III, Chapter I above, pp. 256–67.

intrigued with the possibility of a *science* of ethics, in which eternally true, universal statements could be put forward. An instance he gives in the *Essay concerning Human Understanding* is that we know by conceptual analysis alone that murder deserves death. But nowhere in the *Essay* do we find this science worked out, even in outline. Locke himself expresses doubt whether such a study of definitions and significations could ever be an adequate treatment of morals and his doubts may explain the absence of a full discussion of this matter in the *Essay*. Von Leyden suggests that the paper *Of Ethick in General* in the Lovelace Collection was meant to follow IV. xx, the patently incomplete final chapter of the *Essay*.[1] This may well be the case and it is highly significant that Locke withheld it, if he proposed at first to include it. He was presumably doubtful about the worth of a mere rationalist, analytic study of ethical terms. It is also clear from the paper that the hedonistic elements in Locke's thinking which we have discussed previously[2] could not easily be accommodated within his rationalistic, objective system of morals.

If now we turn to religion, we find that Locke does not think that a wholly rationalist account of knowledge is possible in this sphere either. Today the debate between natural and revealed religion is no longer of general concern to philosophers, but in Locke's age it was felt to be crucial. And the position which Locke adopted in this debate illustrates excellently his views on the limitations of human reason. For while in general he sided with the rationalists, he yet could not believe that reason of itself was an adequate mentor in the religious life. For just as the mind in its dealings with the world of material objects has to wait on sensory experience and cannot by reason alone know the truth, so in religion also reason must be supported and supplemented by a non-rational source of information, namely, revelation.

There are certain truths, essential for the religious life, which we should never know were they not revealed. The writings of Locke nowhere contain an explicit analysis of the concept of revelation. But his use of the term shows that he meant by it a direct imparting of information by God to man. It is only rarely that God chooses to reveal a truth to mankind in this way, and what he does then reveal is of the very greatest importance. 'It cannot be expected that God should send one into the world on purpose to inform men of things

[1] *Essays on the Law of Nature*, pp. 69 ff.
[2] Above, pp. 257 ff.

indifferent and of small moment, or that are knowable by the use of
their natural faculties'.[1] But Locke does not inform us as to the way
in which God imparts this information. The one point that is clear'
is that it does not come through the ordinary channels. Actually all
man's faculties are given to him by God, so that any knowledge
through them is, from this point of view, revealed knowledge, but
revelation itself is none the less a distinct and peculiar source of
information. As Locke explains in the *Essay*:[2] 'When we find out an
idea, by whose intervention we discover the connexion of two others,
this is a revelation from God to us by the voice of reason. For we
then come to know a truth that we did not know before. When God
declares any truth to us, this is a revelation to us by the voice of his
Spirit and we are advanced in our knowledge.' Both may be said to
be instances of divine revelation, but the second is revelation in a
very special sense, 'by the voice of his Spirit'. Locke himself claims
no special revelations in this sense, although he does claim in the
Second Vindication of the Reasonableness of Christianity to know
something of the guidance of the Spirit in his effort to discover the
true meaning of the Scriptures.[3] But revelation itself is a mystery to
Locke, which he cannot explain. His own experiences in the religious
life, and his conviction of the worth of the revelations which have
been made from time to time in history, make it impossible for him
to doubt that God does occasionally speak directly to man. None the
less he does not attempt to explain how this occurs. But he adds that
when knowledge is thus gained no more certain knowledge can be
conceived. It carries with it 'assurance beyond doubt, evidence beyond exception'. Thus Locke recognizes a source of full assurance
amounting to indubitable certainty in a non-natural faculty, the
power of receiving a message directly from God.

But this knowledge is vouchsafed to few men. The mass of men
learn from the few and accept the information which they give. This
acceptance of revelation on the word of another is what Locke calls
faith. He defines it as 'the assent to any proposition not made out by
the deductions of reason, but upon the credit of the proposer, as
coming from God in some extraordinary way of communication'.[4]
Now, while no knowledge can be more certain than revelation, if it is
truly revelation (for then it is the word of God), faith is not so
certain. It is believing that this is the word of God. And, as Locke

---

[1] *A Discourse on Miracles, Works* (1740), iii. 472.
[2] IV. vii. 11.   [3] *Works*, ii. 691.   [4] *Essay*, IV. xviii. 2.

explains to Stillingfleet: 'with what assurance soever of believing I assent to any article of faith, so that I steadfastly venture my all upon it, it is still but believing. Bring it to certainty and it ceases to be faith'.[1] Thus faith is never complete certainty.

In the religious realm we believe certain things, then, not because reason proves them to be true, but because they are either directly revealed to us or, more usually, to some other inspired person whose word we accept, perhaps because of a sense of the power displayed in his deeds and of the force of his personality. But this does not mean that reason has no place in the religious life. On the contrary, in no realm is reason more valuable, both as a source of information, and as the critic of information alleged to have been gained by means of revelation.

As has been explained, it is only rarely that truth is gained through revelation. For the rest, man depends upon reason. And Locke believed that reason could lead us to many truths even in the religious realm. Morality, which was, in Locke's opinion, closely bound up with religion, could possibly be demonstrated rationally, and demonstrated in such a way that all men would be compelled to admit its truth. Similarly, the central conceptions of theology, for instance, that God exists, that he is an omniscient and omnipotent Spirit, that he is just and yet merciful, can all be proved rationally. Where rational knowledge of this sort is possible it is to be preferred to revelation. Not that we can doubt true revelation if we are sure of its truth, but it is difficult to be sure; whereas if a thing is proved rationally there can be no room for doubt. For this reason Locke prefers natural religion to revealed—in so far as a natural religion is possible. The point is made plain in Locke's discussion in the *Essay* of the difficulty men have in interpreting the Scriptures because of the inevitable imperfections of words.

We ought to magnify his goodness [he remarks, in concluding the passage] that he hath spread before all the world, such legible characters of his works and providence, and given all mankind so sufficient a light of reason, that they to whom the written word never came, could not (whenever they set themselves to search) either doubt of the being of a God or of the obedience due to Him. Since, then, the precepts of natural religion are plain, and very intelligible to all mankind, and seldom seem to be controverted; and other revealed truths which are conveyed to us by books and languages, are liable to the common and natural obscurities and difficulties incident to words: methinks it would become us to be

[1] *Second Letter, Works,* i. 430.

more careful and diligent in observing the former, and less magisterial, positive, and imperious in imposing our own sense and interpretations on the latter.[1]

It is not at all strange, in view of such passages as these, that Toland, Collins, and those Deists who, after Locke's day, defended a natural religion as the only religion worthy of the respect of men, should have claimed an ally in Locke. His desire to establish a rational and natural religion was as great as theirs. He cannot, however, be classed with the Deists, for he did not believe that all the truths necessary for a religious life could be gained rationally. Yet he is sure that many such truths can be so gained, and where a rational knowledge is possible he prefers it to any other.

Reason is useful in the religious life, too, as the critic of revelation. In his youth Locke had come into contact with 'enthusiasts' who claimed a divine origin for any mad fancies that chanced to enter their heads. Reason can reject such claims outright. But it also tests the more serious claims to revelation. It is able to test these because all revelation must be conformable to reason. This is a fundamental principle on which Locke never wavers. Reason and revelation, since they both reveal the truth, cannot contradict each other. Consequently, if an alleged revelation is found to be inconsistent with reason, it can be denied. It is no true revelation. Locke will not accept the principle: *Credo quia impossibile est*. If reason teaches him that a thing is impossible, by no act of faith can he then believe it. If a tenet is rationally impossible then belief in it is equally impossible. In this sense, also, Locke is a thorough-going rationalist.

But Locke does not agree with those who hold that the tenets of religion, particularly of the Christian religion, are irrational, that is to say, opposed to reason. The whole aim of *The Reasonableness of Christianity*, as its title suggests, is to show that there is nothing in that religion contrary to reason. Of course, much therein is revealed. Some truths which reason could have discovered were as a matter of fact revealed, simply because men would have remained so long in ignorance had not God chosen to reveal these truths to them directly. The history of mankind shows

by the little that has hitherto been done in it, that 'tis too hard a task for unassisted reason to establish morality in all its parts upon its true foundation, with a clear and convincing light. And 'tis at least a surer and a shorter way to the apprehensions of the vulgar and mass of man-

---

[1] III. ix. 23.

kind, that one manifestly sent from God . . . should . . . tell them their duties and require their obedience, than leave it to the long and sometimes intricate deductions of reason to be made out to them.[1]

But there are also other truths which are 'above reason', and these can only be known by revelation. Reason unguided by 'some light from above'[2] would never know them. None the less, since they are true they do not contradict reason, and, so far as reason goes, it confirms them.

We may thus conclude that Locke is a rationalist even in the realm of religious experience. He trusts reason in this realm as in every other. Whenever possible he uses it (and it alone) to discover truths. He uses it again to test and check information which comes through revelation. Nothing that contradicts reason is true. Nevertheless, he also adds that reason of itself is not enough. Revelation is essential since some truths lie beyond the grasp of human reason. They do not contradict it. It would be best if they could be rationally known by us, as higher intelligences no doubt do know them. But this in our case is impossible. Here then is another restriction; some truths which must be known by us are 'above reason'.

V

In these respects, therefore, Locke's rationalism is limited. The external world is not known by reason alone, we depend first upon the information of the senses. Nor can reason alone guide us in our practical life. In Locke's opinion, the ultimate moral basis is God's will; the latter is known to us partly (but never wholly) by reason. In religion man has a source of information other than his own reason, namely, God's revelation of himself.

In spite of these limitations, however, Locke's rationalism remains. The epistemology of the opening chapters of Book IV of the *Essay* is rationalist, as rationalist as Descartes's in its confident assertion of intellectual intuition. Yet for Locke the intuitions are always intuitions of relations between empirically derived ideas. Now it may, as some hold, be impossible to relate consistently the rationalist with the empiricist elements in Locke's philosophy, but the former are not to be denied. Locke is attempting to modify rationalism, though perhaps not very successfully, but he is not rejecting it. Again the assertion that the deepest knowledge we gain comes by

[1] *Works*, ii. 575.
[2] *Works*, ii. 578.

way of revelation in no way contradicts a rationalism which affirms that we know (and know with certainty) by reason. Locke is merely denying that it is the only source of certainty. He believes that some truths are revealed, but he thinks that knowledge through revelation is exceptional and a somewhat rare occurrence in human experience.

Thus we must continue to regard Locke as a rationalist, in spite of the groupings of the historians of philosophy. Moreover, we must recognize that his rationalism is fundamental, empiricism being but a modification of it. To those who are acquainted only with the *Essay* (and, perhaps, only with Book II of the *Essay*) this fact is not obvious. But it will become wholly clear if the rest of his work is taken into account. Moreover, rationalism was more than an abstract theory for him; it was a way of life. His biographers tell us that he tried to live his life in accordance with the dictates of reason, and this in spite of the fact that his own emotional life was strong. But he distrusted the emotions, as did most of his contemporaries, and feared the appeal to the emotions in poetry, in rhetoric, or in religion. If it is true that the thought of the eighteenth century rests more on Locke's philosophy than on any other, then its foundation is most assuredly a rationalism. And yet one must always return to the point I wish to make here, namely, that it was a rationalism slowly becoming aware of its own limitations. I do not mean that Locke was the herald of the Romantic Movement. Such language in the circumstances would be far too strong. And certainly there is nothing of the romantic in Locke himself. But from the first Locke's rationalism goes hand in hand with a serious (although, no doubt, uncertain) criticism of rationalism. If he does not herald romanticism he certainly heralds the scepticism of Hume and the criticism of Kant.

APPENDIX V

SOME RECENT WRITINGS ON LOCKE'S POLITICAL PHILOSOPHY

As contrasted with the comparative fewness of studies on, for instance, the *Essay Concerning Understanding*, there has been quite a spate on Locke's political philosophy during the post-war period. These writings have, almost without exception, been lively and stimulating and worthy of the reader's careful attention. I append here a brief account of some of them.

I

It would be wise to begin by mentioning some new editions of Lockian texts. In the past Locke has not been too well served by his editors: Hans Aarsleff in the final essay of the collection edited by J. W. Yolton, entitled *John Locke, Problems and Perspectives* (Cambridge, 1969) complains of 'the deplorable state' of the Lockian texts in general.[1] Satisfactory texts of Berkeley and Dugald Stewart, and the beginnings of good texts of Bentham and John Stuart Mill, now exist, but on the whole, he thinks, the editing of the works of British philosophers has been poor and this has been particularly true of John Locke. 'For seventy years', says Aarsleff, 'the standard text of the *Essay* was Fraser's wretched and misleading edition.' These adjectives are strong but they are not wholly undeserved; a reliable and scholarly text of the *Essay* is much to be desired. Until recently the available texts of the political works were equally unsatisfactory, but in the last two decades the position has altered considerably. First and foremost we have Laslett's splendid edition of the *Two Treatises of Government* (Cambridge, 1960); then we have the scholarly edition by Klibansky and Gough of Locke's *Epistola de Tolerantia* (Oxford, 1968), with a translation and a clear account of the relation between the original Latin work and William Popple's famous translation.[2] We should mention too (although this is not a political text) James L. Axtell's useful edition of *Some Thoughts*

---

[1] p. 270.
[2] Reference should be made also to C. A. Viano's edition, *John Locke, Scritti Editi e Inediti Sulla Tolleranza* (Turin, 1960).

concerning Education in *The Educational Writings of John Locke* (Cambridge, 1968) with a valuable introduction.

Very important are editions of certain previously unpublished manuscripts in the Lovelace Collection. Philip Abrams has published two of these, one in English, the other in Latin, both dealing with the theme of the rights of the civil authority in determining 'the use of indifferent things' in religious worship. The book, entitled *Two Tracts on Government* (Cambridge, 1967) discusses a matter of wide concern at the time of the Restoration. It is a reply to Edward Bradshaw's *The Great Question Concerning Things Indifferent in Religious Worship* (1660), and argues that the civil authority should have permission to decide questions of religious ceremony, such as whether surplices are to be worn, whether prayers should be set prayers or spontaneous, whether and when it is permissible to make the sign of the cross in the service and so on. In view of Locke's later published work on toleration his reply in these 1660 manuscripts is unexpected: 'The supreme magistrate of every nation what way soever created must necessarily have an absolute and arbitrary power over all the indifferent actions of his people.'[1] Not everything in religion should be left to the individual's private judgement and conscience. Abrams provides a very helpful commentary on the tracts to which we must refer later. A further manuscript, concluded 'Sic Cogitavit J. Locke, 1664', and concerned with the law of nature, has been published by the leading authority on the Lovelace Collection, W. von Leyden of Durham, under the title *Essays on the Law of Nature* (Oxford, 1954), with an admirable introduction. These essays, composed in Latin and translated by von Leyden, are remarkable as revealing as early as 1664 some of the basic positions upon which both the *Essay* and the *Two Treatises on Government* rest. The rationalism in Locke's thought, which was later to create a tension in his mind when it conflicted with a growing hedonism, or with a more empirical approach to the problems of politics and sociology, is very obvious in these essays. The order in the world, and the moral character of this order, show the presence of God in the world. There is a law of nature or a rule of morals and this can be known by man. It is not, however, known directly by reason, for reason is just the 'powerful faculty of arguing',[2] and presupposes

[1] *Two Tracts*, ed Abrams, pp. 122–3.
[2] *Essays*, p. 125. Neither here nor in the *Essay* is reason identified with intuition. Reason is sagacity and illation, but not intuition. Cf. *Essay*, IV. xvii. 2.

some other source of information, namely sense-perception, 'which we declare to be the basis of our knowledge of the law of nature'.[1] The law of nature can be deduced rationally from our sensory experience of the world. It is not known innately, as something inscribed beforehand on the mind, for no human knowledge is so inscribed; it is known by inference from the experienced. The law is binding perpetually and universally and, though man's private interest and desire are not its basis, none the less action in accordance with the law of nature works in the true interest of all. Much of the actual material used in Drafts A and B (1671) of the *Essay Concerning Human Understanding* comes from the *Essays on the Law of Nature*.[2] It is remarkable, too, how many of the fundamental Lockian principles of epistemology, on the one hand, and of political philosophy on the other, are found here.

II

To turn, now from texts to books written recently on Locke's political philosophy; in 1941 Willmoore Kendall produced a fresh study of the *Two Treatises* from a new angle, entitled *John Locke and the Doctrine of Majority-rule*.[3] Kendall holds that Locke espoused the principle of rule by majority (and was one of the earliest political writers to do so). But the consequence is that, having set up a political system to safeguard the person, liberties, rights and property of the individuals in the society, he allows the society to be ruled by those who are the majority whenever a decision is made. This might well lead to the sacrifice of the individual rights of the minority, so that Locke's system involves an inner inconsistency. Kendall accordingly re-examines the *Second Treatise* and comes to the conclusion that the defence of the individual is not as central a point in Locke's philosophy as has been thought, and that what Kendall calls the 'collectivist' elements in his philosophy are many. Locke's system does not in fact guarantee the indefeasible rights of each and every citizen, but assuming that the majority are good and responsible men who will have a care for the well-being of the minority, then their decisions will be in 'the public good'. Rule by majority does enable all to participate in making the decisions and, if men are both just and rational, then their decisions are likely to result ultimately in the good of all. Kendall's arguments are con-

---

[1] *Essays*, p. 131.   [2] Cf. ibid., p. 65.   [3] Urbana, Illinois.

sidered in J. W. Gough's careful and balanced *John Locke's Political Philosophy*[1] which gives us eight studies of Locke's thought. The second of these is an examination of Kendall's position. Gough agrees that there are collectivist elements in Locke, but argues that Kendall over-stresses their significance, so much so that he presents the general decision, the public good and the public will, as the core of Locke's account of politics. Locke is presented as another Rousseau, if not another Hegel. But this, Gough holds, is not the Locke of the *Second Treatise*. Locke may fail to distinguish clearly between the public interest and the interest of the individual, between the general good (and the general will) and the particular good (and the individual will). But he *is* concerned about the individual's freedom and about his rights, the right of consent, the right of dissent if the government breaks trust, and the right to the preservation of his own person and property. It is misleading, therefore, to say that his system is collectivist. Gough's book contains seven other studies: on the law of nature, government by consent, property, the separation of powers and sovereignty, political trusteeship, toleration, and Locke and the Revolution of 1688.

Much more radical criticism of Locke than Kendall's was on the way. In 1953 Leo Strauss published *Natural Right and History*[2] with a chapter on Hobbes and Locke. Contrary to the usual view he regarded both these writers as teaching the same doctrine, namely, that men are motivated by the desire to preserve themselves and their property and in return for security are ready to submit themselves to completely authoritarian government and to give up their liberties. This is the stark foundation of political theory which, in Locke's case, is overlaid by talk of a divinely established egalitarian and just polity, and by judicious quotation from the Scriptures and from Hooker. The truth is 'that Locke cannot have recognized any law of nature in the proper sense of the term.'[3] This theme is developed by Richard H. Cox in his *Locke on War and Peace*.[4] Locke lived in dangerous days and was by nature cautious, evasive, even devious. If, therefore, he had become convinced of the essential truth of Hobbes's diagnosis of political society he would wish to hide this fact. He accordingly 'accommodated his philosophical argument to the prevailing political, philosophical and religious atmosphere in such a way as to partially conceal its radical character.'[5] So there are

---

[1] Oxford, 1950.   [2] Chicago University Press.
[3] Ibid., p. 220.   [4] Oxford, 1960.   [5] Ibid., p. 72.

always 'two levels of meaning' in Locke's political writings. The expert reader will penetrate beneath the surface to the hidden truth, namely, that men are by nature anarchical and survive only by subjecting themselves to absolute power. He will not be deceived by the somewhat idyllic opening sections of the *Second Treatise* but will wait for that revelation of man's true state that is made in the ninth chapter of the *Treatise* and in what follows. Man is a creature of primitive passions that can be temporarily appeased through labour within a society that provides security. To gain this end the society has its sovereign or supreme power that expresses the public will both domestically and in foreign affairs.

It was left to C. B. Macpherson to give a Marxist slant to this line of interpretation. In two papers in the *Western Political Quarterly*, 1951 and 1954, and again in his book *The Political Theory of Possessive Individualism*,[1] he put forward with considerable force and brilliance a thesis which viewed seventeenth century English political thought, and Locke's thought in particular, as essentially an assertion of a bourgeois possessive individualism. Locke seeks to provide a moral and rational justification for unlimited appropriation of property in a capitalist society. According to Locke the chief end of government is the preservation of property. By the law of nature every man has a natural right to a share of the property available, provided that he works for it (that is, 'mixes his labour with it'). But this 'same law of nature, that does by this means give us property does also bound that property too.'[2] A man can only appropriate 'as long as there is enough and as good left in common for others' and on the understanding that he can use whatever he takes. There is thus far no justification for unlimited appropriation. But now, according to MacPherson, Locke takes a step which enables him to justify to his own satisfaction even unlimited appropriation. Men for their greater convenience introduce the convention of money, and one of the consequences is that wealth can now accumulate without perishing, for gold and silver do not perish when hoarded. There is therefore no reason why the appropriation of property including land should in any way be limited, if, on the one hand, it can be marketed in money and if, on the other, it can be shown that such an appropriation works for the good of all in the community. The latter is the case since wealth begets greater wealth, increases opportunities for industry, and so generally raises the standard of

---

[1] Oxford, 1963.   [2] *Second Treatise*, § 31.

living. Furthermore, by this same law of nature a man's labour is his own property and he has a right to sell it to others. One man consequently can avail himself of the labour of another and pay an agreed wage for it, and the wage earner will be happy in the security of his earnings. 'Thus in saying that men, after the introduction of money, have a right to more land than leaves enough for others Locke is not contradicting his original assertion of the natural right of all men to the means of subsistence.'[1] It follows that differentiation should be made between the men of property who make the wealth, and the property-less labourers; the former show initiative and are able to lead, the latter are content with earning enough to live; the former will produce the leaders and rulers, the latter are not interested in politics and lack understanding. The workers lack the rationality of the property owners and are not fully members of the political society. So Locke has established both the morality and the rationality of a capitalist system, in which the poor are kept in sub-jection, given enough to subsist, but given no opportunities for education and self-improvement, except only that they are en-couraged to virtue and to religion, so that they be good and con-tented workers.

Very different in tone from this is the study by Raymond Polin, entitled *La Politique Morale de John Locke*.[2] According to Polin Locke's aim is to set down the principles of a society that is at once free and rational. These principles are put forth clearly and Locke is not the inconsistent, vague thinker that he is frequently supposed to be. Polin begins by studying Locke's account of man, and it is a very different account from that given by Hobbes. Man is a moral creature, in the sense that morality is the central feature of his life. Since each individual is a unique moral being it follows that men are 'not made for one another's uses'[3] or, to use the language of later philosophers, each is an end in himself. Yet Locke is not to be regarded as a prophet of absolute individualism, for to set up the individual over against the community is an abstraction. The individual is already, wherever we meet him, a social being, and society is a society of individuals. It cannot and should not be other-wise. Now a feature of all political society is political power, but its presence in the society is not justified patriarchally, nor by the fiat of a tyrant or a conqueror. It is justifiable finally only by the fact

---

[1] *The Political Theory of Possessive Individualism*, p. 214.
[2] Presses Universitaires de France, 1960.   [3] *Second Treatise*, § 7.

that the people consent, and consent on the grounds of rationality and morality. 'Tout pouvoir, pour être politique, doit d'abord être juste. Le problème de la formation des cités . . c'est un problème moral.'[1] In this light only can Locke's account of the supreme power as resting in the people be understood: and it is in this light too that we should consider his views on property. The reader will find the same point of view admirably expressed in Polin's recent contribution, 'John Locke's Conception of Freedom' in *John Locke: Problems and Perspectives.*[2]

A most erudite study of Locke's politics which in spirit and in its general conclusions is not far removed from Polin's is Dr. Seliger's *The Liberal Politics of John Locke.*[3] Seliger is interested in the character of modern liberalism as a political force, and discounts the assumption that it exists to fight authoritarianism. It is much more complex than this. Consequently, though he regards Locke as a founder of modern liberalism (in spite of possible youthful deviations) he is not surprised that his mature thought contains authoritarian elements. His book includes careful discussions of the knowability of the law of nature and its applicability when known, of the state of nature and of the origins of political society. In Seliger's opinion Locke uses the state of nature theory as a hypothesis to delineate man's condition: man begins with a knowledge of the ideal of what social life could be, but he is motivated too by disruptive tendencies. The true character of human society is seen not merely in its acceptance of government but also in its possible rejection of government and (something different) in the possible dissolution of the society itself. On property Seliger is not satisfied that Macpherson's statement of the position is accurate, for Macpherson neglects many of the points which Locke is assuming throughout the argument. On the other hand the patriarchal theory is also not Locke's. There are patriarchal elements in his philosophy, but they are not such as to make society non-contractual. A political society is an historical growth, but it also has a permanent moral basis. The four final chapters of Seliger's book deal with constitutional matters. The sense in which the individual consents is a difficult matter. If he holds property in a political society that no doubt is a sign of consent, yet even the property-less consents in so far as he abstains from specific acts of dissent. This, Seliger thinks,

[1] *La Politique Morale de John Locke*, p. 196.
[2] Ed. Yolton, pp. 1–18.
[3] Allen and Unwin, 1968.

is the only indication of an 'express' consent pertaining to all members of the society. He also takes the view that Locke never seriously entertained the notion of universal suffrage, though the individual, however humble his circumstances, had the right in Locke's society to express his dissent, and this meant the *right* to revolution. Seliger concludes a valuable study with a discussion of executive and legislative and the distribution of authority between them.

The historical approach, as contrasted with the philosophical, marks the work of a recent group of Cambridge writers. I have already mentioned the texts edited by Laslett and Abrams. In his commentary Laslett shows conclusively that Locke's *Second Treatise*, quite as much as the *First*, is aimed at Filmer and that Locke was more deeply influenced by Filmer's patriarchal approach than is sometimes supposed, even though he was also the critic of Filmer's more exaggerated claims. Locke's political thought is not an exercise in logical reasoning, it is the expression of a tradition resting on a theistic philosophy, and this fact about it is not to be ignored. Abrams too shows the strength of this conservatism in Locke's thought and believes it goes some way to account for the marked authoritarianism of the *Two Tracts*. That his mature thought is more liberal should not blind us to the presence throughout of traditional influences. The *Two Tracts* reveal the strength of these influences on the young Locke.

Finally John Dunn, a Cambridge historian, has given distinguished expression to this general point of view in his *Political Thought of John Locke*.[1] The book has the sub-title *An Historical Account of the Argument of the Two Treatises of Government*, and this shows the angle from which it is written. The book is divided into five parts, the first dealing with the Oxford period, in which the young Locke is seen as apprehensive in the fearful, disorderly world in which he finds himself; but yet as conscious, in his religious life, of an eternal order which is the basis of value and morality. At first in the *Two Tracts* his thoughts turn to what Dunn terms 'the assertion of a symmetrical order of repression'[2] in order to secure peace, but soon his views are modified as he reflects on the law of nature and on the merits of toleration. The second part deals with the period of co-operation with Shaftesbury and his anti-Filmer colleagues, and with the preparation of the *Two Treatises*. The third discusses, still from the historical point of view, the argument of

---

[1] Cambridge, 1969.   [2] Ibid., p. 18.

the *Two Treatises* and the chief points of contention in the work. These contentions are considered further in the fourth part in relation to the consistency and coherence of Locke's mind. The point is made that the alleged contradictions and the many varied accounts of the *Two Treatises* are due to a failure to understand its permanent underlying assumptions, which are expounded in the final pages of Dunn's study, namely, the Calvinist doctrine of the Calling that Locke had learnt of in his boyhood and that guided his thought and actions throughout his life.[1]

III

These books, which are all worthy of the reader's attention, show the many different opinions current today about Locke's political teaching. They are proof enough of the abiding vitality of his thought even in our own age, and they reflect the very real complexity of his political philosophy. I should like, in concluding, to comment very briefly on the different interpretations put forward.

If the claim that Locke's political philosophy is collectivist signifies that it is not wholly individualist it is a claim that finds ample justification in the *Two Treatises*.[2] If Locke tends to speak of men, as for instance in the state of nature, as mere individuals this is abstraction. In the concrete situation man is a social being. The people who are the supreme power are not so many isolated individuals, they are the society and the decisions that they make are collectivist. (The only supreme individualist is the tyrant or the wholly arbitrary absolute monarch.) Locke's polity is collectivist; but then the delicate problem arises of the relation between community and the

---

[1] To make the list of Lockian studies which have appeared since the war complete I should have to refer to other books, for instance, by C. A. Viano, Gabriel Bonno and others, also to chapters in books, for instance, ch. 6 of J. Plamenatz's *Man and Society* (Longman, 1963), vol. i. There are also many papers on Locke's political philosophy in journals and collections. I have already mentioned the collection of essays in *John Locke: Problems and Perspectives*, ed. J. W. Yolton (Cambridge, 1969), seven of the twelve essays bearing on politics. In *Locke and Berkeley* ed. by C. B. Martin and D. M. Armstrong (Macmillan, 1968) three papers (by Monson, Macpherson, and Alan Ryan) are on political issues. I may mention, too, papers by Sir Isaiah Berlin (*Pol. Quart.*, 1964), J. D. Day (*Phil. Quart.*, 1966), R. W. K. Hinton (*Pol. Studies*, 1967 and 1968), J. J. Jenkins (*Philosophy*, 1967), G. Parry (*Pol. Studies*, 1964), and there are many others of note, including papers by the authors whose books have been considered above.

[2] On Locke's individualism cf. above pp. 284–6.

individual, for, in Locke's opinion, the individual having moral responsibility is not lost in society, but is the source of its strength and power. Yet the good of one individual does not always coincide with the good of other individuals, or with the good of the majority. It is interesting that Locke does explicitly affirm the doctrine of majority-rule, though he nowhere thinks in terms of universal suffrage, and never faces the difficulties inherent in the doctrine—as, for instance, his disciple John Stuart Mill did.

In so far as the society is collectivist it is to a certain extent authoritarian. The individual retains the right to dissent, he may emigrate to another society, he may work to bring about the dissolution of the government of the society, but as long as he remains in the society he must abide by the contract on which the society rests and he must accept the decisions made by the supreme power. This is certainly an element in Locke's teaching. On the other hand, as has been seen, the suggestion has been made that this is all that Locke *really* has to say. The individual can only survive in a society that has political power, and it is a society which demands complete and full authority over its members. But since such a doctrine is unpalatable, and was particularly unpalatable in 1688, Locke, it is argued, is compelled to set up a smoke-screen; all the rest of what he says is aimed at veiling the true doctrine which only the few are meant to grasp. One may think that this is a pretty drastic account of Locke's political philosophy. The obvious way to refute it would be to bring forward those passages in the *Two Treatises* and elsewhere which set up limits to authoritorianism, particularly the individual's indefeasible rights. Those who support the Strauss-Cox view, however, would argue that all such passages are part of the smoke-screen set up by Locke and not to be taken seriously. Consequently, there is no means of arguing against them. Yet the case which Locke makes in setting bounds to authoritarianism rests on the view he puts forward about human nature, and this not merely in the *Two Treatises* but in his other works as well. But is it not then absurd to suggest that large portions of the *Essay Concerning Human Understanding*, the whole *Letter on Toleration*, the *Conduct of the Understanding*, and the *Reasonableness of Christianity*, not to mention the commentaries on books of the New Testament, are all part of a gigantic smoke-screen thrown up by Locke to veil the truth?

Macpherson's thesis, which has affinities with that of Strauss and Cox, is not so concerned to present Locke as an authoritarian (though this is part of his thesis) but rather as the father of bourgeois, capitalist philosophy. He views Locke as a complex thinker who is not always self-consistent, but who never deviates from the doctrine that the chief end of political society is the preservation of property. This is Locke's central and abiding concern in politics, and his aim, on Macpherson's view, is to justify the capitalist's unlimited appropriation of property, and to show that it is both rational and moral for the capitalist property-owner to behave in the way he does. Now Locke certainly believes that the chief end of bringing political society into being is the preservation of property (though 'property' is sometimes, and in key passages, taken by him to mean 'the lives, liberties and estates' of the citizens[1] and not merely their possessions in a narrow sense). By the law of nature man has the right to appropriate what he needs and by mixing his labour with it makes it his own; but, Locke holds, the same law which *gives* also *binds* and *limits*, and a man has the right, as has been seen, to take only what he will not waste and that only on the understanding that there is enough left for others. So appropriation is limited. Yet once money is instituted there is then no danger of wastage in accumulation; further, by enlarging his own wealth the rich man can heighten the general standard of living. Now Locke does say this, and what he says is open to considerable criticism, but Macpherson takes it to mean that Locke thereby intends to justify unlimited appropriation both morally and rationally. This I do not find in Locke. If unlimited appropriation were morally and rationally justifiable then it would, in principle, be just for one man in a particular society to appropriate the wealth of *all* others, subjecting them to slavery. But the end of political society in Locke's view is to provide every citizen with security in his person, his liberty and his possessions. The governments make laws to this end. Unlimited appropriation of property and the exploitation of the property-less would be held to be unjust.[2] Each individual is a person, a moral agent, and 'we are not made for one another's uses'. There will be laws to protect the property owner against the unscrupulous, and laws to protect the wage-earner in his dealings with his employer. Further, there is little in Locke's works to support the harsh doctrine, which Marxists very properly attack, that the working-classes are a class apart, that they

---

[1] *Second Treatise*, § 123.
[2] As early as 1664 Locke is very clear about this. Cf. *Essays on The Law of Nature*, Essay VIII, particularly p. 211.

lack the rationality, the intelligence and the virtue of the higher property class and that therefore their subjection is inevitable. At the end of the seventeenth century some of the poor were held to be idlers, and Locke and his age had little sympathy for them and very little understanding of their problems. But he praised the diligent wage-earners and was anxious that they should be given better opportunities. Moreover, he knew that virtue and wisdom were not the monopoly of the rich. He regarded each man, whether rich or poor, as an end in himself, as a moral agent and a son of God. Nor is there justification in the texts for supposing that Locke regarded religion as the opium wherewith the labouring classes could be doped and kept docile. Thus whilst certain paragraphs in the *Two Treatises* may be read as supporting some part of Macpherson's case, the book as a whole, and the rest of Locke's works, do nothing to justify it. Locke was a Whig and the Whigs tended to be heedless of the poor; but Locke would have condemned the ruthless, capitalist exploiter of the masses as readily and as heartedly as Macpherson himself does.

Locke cannot properly be regarded, then, as an apologist for a brutal, enslaving capitalism. But what of his authoritarianism? Does it make Locke a Hobbist? Locke emphatically denied that he was a Hobbist, but this might have been part of his alleged deviousness. On the Taylor-Warrender interpretation of Hobbes's account of the source of morality the gap between Hobbes and Locke is lessened and it would then be wrong to say, with John Dunn,[1] that Hobbes sets out to construct political society 'from an ethical vacuum'. But even on this interpretation, which is not accepted by everybody, the gap is still large. The best way to realize that this is so is to read again the description of the 'mortal God' at the end of ii. 17 of Hobbes's *Leviathan* and of the rights of the sovereign in ii. 18. The latter are such that there is no room for dissent amongst the citizens, the covenant on which the commonwealth rests is not between sovereign and citizen so that the sovereign cannot break it, nor can any of his sovereign acts be unjust. Consequently, the sovereign cannot be brought to trial and cannot be punished. Nor has the citizen the right to dissent whether in speech or writing. Further, the sovereignty is indivisable. If it be objected that the condition of the subject is 'very miserable' in such a society it is less so, Hobbes

---

[1] *The Political Thought of John Locke*, p. 79.

replies, than in a state of civil war. Now Locke's *Two Treatises* are
expressly aimed at Filmer; it may be the case (though I find it
impossible to believe this) that Locke never had Hobbes in mind in
writing the book. It none the less remains true that Locke's account
of political society involves, with or without intent, a rejection of
Hobbes's conception of the sovereign, and of the rights pertaining
to the sovereign, in *Leviathan*, ii. 17 and 18. Members of a political
society, on Locke's view, have a right to dissent and to organize
opposition; distinction is to be made between the executive and the
supreme power (that is to say, the people), and the executive has
power on trust only and can be deprived of it. In the sense in which
the executive and the legislative body have sovereign power
sovereignty is, and should be, divisible. Government should work for
the public good, but if it fails to do so—and the people are the final
judge—it can be changed. In all this Locke is plainly in opposition
to Hobbes, and it is totally misleading to describe him as 'Hobbist'.

The final question that needs to be asked is whether the conservative elements in Locke's thought have been neglected, as
recent Cambridge writers suggest? The term 'conservative' is vague.
Is there in Locke's political philosophy a greater consciousness of
political development and historical growth than we have sometimes
supposed, and is he more conservative in that sense than we think?
In the *Essays on the Law of Nature* his approach is rationalist, but
in the *Two Treatises*, it may be claimed, the method is somewhat
more 'historical' in the sense of empirical.

Or was Locke conservative in the sense that he was more deeply
influenced by scholasticism than we usually suppose? He was influenced by the remnants of scholasticism in the universities, but he
was no more influenced, and no more conservative in this sense, than
were other writers of his day; indeed he was consciously in revolt
against the scholastic methods. Possibly he was conservative in his
religious attitude. He was not a Catholic. (No one has yet suggested
as one further interpretation of Locke's thought that he was a
Catholic in disguise.) Dunn draws attention to his dogmatist Calvinist upbringing. Yet in his youth he chose Anglicanism and when
he found himself later in a Calvinist society in Holland it was the
Reformed Calvinists that he supported. None the less, it is true that
Locke's thought, particularly on social and political questions, was
deeply influenced by his religion, by his deep sense of being called,
and by the Protestant emphasis from Luther onwards on the importance of the individual.

Again, if one thinks of seventeenth century British history, a division between conservative and liberal might be made in terms of the royalist-parliamentarian conflict. In this sense of the term Locke's upbringing was clearly not conservative and his attitude in 1664 and through to his death was not conservative. He was the defender of parliament against the doctrine of the arbitrary power of the monarch. There still remains, however, the very awkward problem of the 1660 *Tracts*.

Locke and Hobbes had at least this in common, that they had lived through the Civil War and both longed for a stable system of government that would secure peace. When Locke came up to Oxford this was much in his mind. He ceased to be a party man, if he had ever been one, and he found his friends amongst royalists as well as parliamentarians. He welcomed the Restoration. This act did not of necessity mark him out as a conservative, for many 'liberals' welcomed the return of Charles II and had some reason to believe that his government would be liberal. In 1659, to judge from his letter to 'S.H.' (presumed to be Henry Stubbe, who had just published a vigorous defence of toleration), Locke was strongly pro-toleration, only qualifying his support in one respect namely that (for political and not religious reasons) Catholics should not be tolerated. Yet in the Lovelace Collection there are two tracts about the civil authority's rights in the determination of questions on religious worship written in 1660-1 which are strongly conservative (in the sense now being considered) in their opposition to toleration and in their advanced authoritarianism. What are we to make of these tracts?

I admit that when in 1935 I first read the manuscript of the English tract (without the Preface) I did not know what to make of it since it was so very different in spirit and tone from the rest of Locke's work. The manuscript was in Locke's hand, but the first thought that came to me was that it was not his authorship but a copy of someone else's work. Not everything in Locke's hand in the Lovelace Collection is his authorship. But the corrections and redraftings, also in Locke's hand, made this suggestion highly improbable. Yet if the tracts were composed by Locke how can we account for them? A possible answer is that Locke is here preparing a case at the request of someone or other, and the opening of the letter (to an unknown person) attached to the last page of the English manuscript is in this respect significant. There is a suggestion that his correspondent had asked for the tract, or at least hinted that Locke should write it, and his composing it shows 'that I can refuse you nothing within the reach of my power'.[1] Did Locke prepare a case for someone 'in obedience to your commands'—possibly the Dean of his College or his friend Towerson? If so, Locke need not necessarily have agreed with everything that was said in the tract. There is, however, some evidence for supposing that he intended to publish it anonymously, and it may be argued that he would not have wanted to publish even anonymously something with which he did not wholly agree. Yet the evidence that he intended to publish is not completely convincing. Considering the whole matter, it seems to me that there can be genuine doubt whether these tracts do give us Locke's own views in 1660 on the question at issue. It is *possible* that this is a piece of special pleading, and this very possibility of itself should make us hesitate lest we build too much upon these manuscripts in an account of the development of his thinking. In any case, whatever be said of the composition of the manuscripts of 1660–1, we may certainly accept Abrams's verdict on them that they belong to a 'pre-Lockian tradition of political thought'.[2]

---

[1] Abrams, *Two Tracts*, p. 174. I may quote the opening sentences of the letter: 'In obedience to your commands I here send you my thoughts of that treatise which we not long since discoursed of, which if they convince you of nothing else, yet I am confident will of this, that I can refuse you nothing that is within the reach of my power. I know not what entertainment they will deserve from you, yet I am sure that you have this reason to use them favourably, that they owe their original to you. . . . This candour I may with justice expect from you since I should never have gone out of my way had not you engaged me in the journey.'

[2] Ibid., p. 80.

BIBLIOGRAPHY

The appended bibliography is in no sense complete. I have only included those books and pamphlets which I have found useful. A fuller bibliography is that of Christophersen, H. O., *A Bibliographical Introduction to the Study of John Locke*, 1930 (*Skrifter utgitt av det Norske Videnskaps-Akademi*, Hist.-Filos. Klasse, 1930, no. 8), although this also is incomplete.

I. LOCKE'S PUBLISHED WORKS

1654 In a book of poems published by John Owen in honour of Cromwell are two poems, one in Latin, the other in English, by Locke.

1660–1 *Two Tracts on Government* edited by Philip Abrams, Cambridge, 1967 (text included in *Scritti editi e inediti sulla tolleranza* ed. C. A. Viano, Turin, 1961).

1662 *Domiduca Oxoniensis sive Musae Academicae*. Poem by Locke: 'On the Marriage of King Charles II with the Infanta of Portugal.'

1663–4 *Essays on the Law of Nature*. (The Latin text with a translation ed. by W. von Leyden, 1954.)

1668 In Sydenham's treatise (2nd edition) *Methodus curandi Febres*, 1668, there is a Latin poem signed by J. Locke: 'In Tractatum de Febribus D. D. Sydenham, praxin Medicam apud Londinenses mira solertia aeque ac felicitate exercentis.'

1671 Draft A. (*An Early Draft of Locke's Essay Together with Excerpts from his Journals*, ed. by Aaron and Gibb, Oxford, 1936.)
Draft B. (*An Essay concerning the Understanding, Knowledge, Opinion, and Assent*, ed. by Benjamin Rand, Harvard, 1931.)

1675–9 *Locke's Travels in France, As related in his Journals, Correspondence and other papers*. Ed. John Lough, C.U.P., 1953.

1686 (In Leclerc's *Bibliothèque Universelle et Historique*, July, p. 315): 'Méthode nouvelle de dresser des Recueils. Communiqué par l'Auteur.' (Reappeared in English in the *Posthumous Works*, 1706.)

1688 (In the same journal, January, pp. 49–142): 'Essai Philosophique concernant l'Etendement où l'on montre quelle est l'étendue de nos connaissances certaines, et la manière dont nous y parvenons.'

1689 *Epistola de Tolerantia ad Clarissimum Virum*. Gouda.

1689 *A Letter concerning Toleration* (translation of above by Wm. Popple). Printed for Awnsham Churchill, at the Black Swan at Amen Corner.

1690 *A Second Letter concerning Toleration*. Printed for Awnsham and John Churchill, at the Black Swan in Ave-Mary-Lane, near Pater-Noster-Row.

1692 *A Third Letter for Toleration*. Printed for Awnsham and John Churchill, at the Black Swan in Pater-Noster Row. ('Part of a

Fourth Letter for Toleration' appeared in *Posthumous Works*, 1706.)

1690 *Two Treatises of Government*. London. Printed for Awnsham Churchill at the Black Swan in Ave-Mary Lane by Amen Corner. 1694, Second edition. 1698, Third edition.

(Cf. *Two Treatises of Government: A Critical Edition*, ed. Peter Laslett, Cambridge, 1960.)

1690 *An Essay Concerning Humane Understanding: In Four Books*. [first issue] Printed by Eliz. Holt for Thomas Basset at the George in Fleet St., near St. Dunstan's Church; [second issue] Printed for Tho. Basset and sold by Edw. Mory at the Sign of the Three Bibles in St. Paul's Churchyard. See Appendix II.

1694 Second Edition, *'with large Additions'*. [first issue] Printed for T. Dring at the Harrow over-against the Inner Temple Gate in Fleet-street and S. Manship at the Black Bull in Cornhill, near the Royal Exchange; [second issue] Printed for Awnsham and John Churchill at the Black Swan in Paternoster Row and Samuel Manship at the Ship in Cornhill, near the Royal Exchange.

1695 Third Edition. A reprint of second edition.

1700 Fourth Edition, *'with large Additions'*. Printed for Awnsham and John Churchil and Samuel Manship.

1706 Fifth Edition, *'with many large Additions'*. Printed for Awnsham and John Churchill and Samuel Manship.

1692 *Some Considerations of the Consequences of the Lowering of Interest and the Raising of the Value of Money*.

1693 *Some Thoughts Concerning Education*. Printed for A. and J. Churchill.

1695 *Short Observations on a printed Paper, intituled For Encouraging the Coinage of Silver Money in England and after for keeping it here*.

1695 *Further Considerations Concerning Raising the Value of Money Etc*.

1695 *The Reasonableness of Christianity, as delivered in the Scriptures*. Printed by A. and J. Churchill.

1695 *A Vindication of the Reasonableness of Christianity Etc. From Mr. Edwards's Reflections*.

1697 *A Second Vindication of the Reasonableness of Christianity Etc. By the Author of the Reasonableness of Christianity*.

1697 *A Letter to the Right Rev. Edward Ld. Bishop of Worcester, concerning some Passages relating to Mr. Locke's Essay of Humane Understanding. In a late Discourse of his Lordship's in Vindication of the Trinity*. By John Locke, Gent. Printed by H. Clark, for A. and J. Churchill and Edw. Castle.

1697 *Mr. Locke's Reply to the Right Rev. The Lord Bishop of Worcester's Answer to his Letter*.

1699 *Mr. Locke's Reply to the Right Rev. The Lord Bishop of Worcester's Answer to his Second Letter*.

1705–7 Paraphrases of the Epistles of St. Paul. (For further information and full titles of paraphrases consult Christophersen.) With an introductory *Essay for the Understanding of St. Paul's Epistles by consulting St. Paul himself.*

1706 *Posthumous Works of Mr. John Locke: viz. I. Of the Conduct of the Understanding. II. An Examination of P. Malebranche's opinion of seeing all things in God. III. A Discourse on Miracles. IV. Part of a fourth Letter on Toleration. V. Memoirs relating to the Life of Anthony, first Earl of Shaftesbury. To which is added VI. His new Method of a Common-place-Book, written originally in French and now translated into English.* J. Churchill, London.

1714 *The Remains of John Locke.* E. Curll, London.

1714 *Works of John Locke,* 3 vols. Churchill & Manship, London. Second ed. 1722, third 1727, fourth 1740, tenth 1801 (in 10 vols.).

1720 *A Collection of Several pieces of Mr. John Locke, never before printed, or not extant in his Works.* [P. Des Maiseaux's Collection.]

1754 *Some Thoughts on the Conduct of the Understanding in the Search of Truth.* Glasgow. 1762, London.

(Many other works are attributed to Locke; cf. Christophersen.)

For Locke's letters cf. *Works,* 1740, vol. 3; T. Forster, *Original Letters of Locke, Algernon Sidney and Anthony, Lord Shaftesbury,* London, 1830; B. Rand, *The Correspondence of John Locke and Edward Clarke,* Oxford, 1927; *Lettres Inédites de Le Clerc à Locke,* ed. Gabriel Bonno, Univ. of California, 1959; H. Ollion, *Notes sur la Correspondence de John Locke.* The standard edition of Locke's letters is shortly to appear, ed. E. S. de Beer, Oxford.

II. CONTEMPORARY CRITICISM

BECCONSALL, T. *The Grounds and Foundation of Natural Religion.* 1698.

BOLD, S. *A Short Discourse of the True Knowledge of Christ Jesus.* 1697.

—— *A Reply to Mr. Edward's Brief Reflections.* 1697.

—— *Observations on the Animadversions (Lately printed at Oxford) on a late Book, entituled The Reasonableness Etc.* 1698.

—— *Some Considerations on the Principal Objections and Arguments which have been published against Mr. Locke's Essay Etc.* 1699.

—— *A Discourse Concerning the Immateriality of the Soul.* 1705.

—— *A Collection of Tracts publish'd in Vindication of Mr. Locke's Reasonableness of Christianity . . . and of his Essay Concerning Humane Understanding.* 1706.

BURNET, T. *Remarks upon an Essay concerning Humane Understanding, in a letter addressed to the Author.* 1697.

—— *Second Remarks upon an Essay Etc.* 1697.

—— *Third Remarks upon an Essay Etc.* 1699.

CARROLL, WM. *A Dissertation on the Tenth Chapter of the Fourth Book of Mr. Locke's Essay.* London, 1706.

COCKBURN, MRS. C. *A Defence of the Essay of Humane Understanding.* 1702.

EDWARDS, J. *Some Thoughts concerning the several Causes and Occasions of Atheism especially in the present Age. With some Brief Reflections on Socinianism: And on a late Book entituled The Reasonableness of Christianity as delivered in the Scriptures.* 1695.
—— *Socinianism Unmasked.* 1696.
—— *The Socinian Creed.* 1697.
—— *A Brief Vindication of the Fundamental articles of the Christian Faith, as also of the Clergy, Universities and Publick Schools from Mr. Locke's Reflections upon them in his book of Education.* 1697.

LEE, H. *Anti-Scepticism, or Notes upon each chapter of Mr. Locke's Essay Etc.* 1702.

LOWDE, J. *A Discourse Concerning the Nature of Man, both in his Natural and Political Capacity.* 1694.
—— *Moral Essays, wherein some of Mr. Locke's and Monsr. Malebranche's Opinions are briefly examined.* 1699.

NORRIS, J. *Cursory Reflections upon a Book called An Essay Concerning Human Understanding.* Appended to *Christian Blessedness: Or Discourses upon the Beatitudes of our Lord and Saviour Jesus Christ.* 1690.

SERGEANT, J. *Solid Philosophy, asserted against the Fancies of the Ideists: Or, the Method to Science farther illustrated with Reflections on Mr. Locke's Essay Etc.* 1697.

SHERLOCK, WM. *Discourse concerning the Happiness of good men, and punishment of the wicked in the next world.* 1704.

STILLINGFLEET, E. *Discourse in Vindication of the Trinity.* 1696.
—— *The Bishop of Worcester's Answer to Mr. Locke's Letter concerning some passages relating to his Essay Etc.* 1697.
—— *The Bishop of Worcester's Answer to Mr. Locke's Second Letter; wherein his Notion of Ideas is proved to be Inconsistent with it self, and with the Articles of the Christian Faith.* 1698.

III. BIOGRAPHY

1. BOURNE, H. R. Fox. *The Life of John Locke.* London, 1876. 2 vols.
2. CHRISTOPHERSEN, H. O. *John Locke, En filosofis forberedelse og grundleggelse (1632–1689)* (contains many useful references in English). Oslo, 1932.
3. COSTE, PIERRE. *The Character of Mr. Locke. Desmaizeaux's Collection, 1720.* (The original was published in French in Amsterdam, 1705.)
4. CRANSTON, MAURICE. *John Locke: A Biography.* Longmans, 1957.
5. DEWHURST, KENNETH. *John Locke, Physician and Philosopher,* Wellcome Hist. Medicine Lib., 1963.

6. HARRISON, J. and LASLETT, P. *The Library of John Locke*, Oxford Bibl. Soc., Oxford, 1965.
7. LASLETT, P. 'John Locke, the great recoinage, and the origins of the Board of Trade, 1695–1698', *John Locke, Problems and Perspectives*, ed. J. W. Yolton, Cambridge, 1969.
8. LECLERC. *The Life and Character of John Locke. Author of the Essay concerning Humane Understanding. Written in French by Mr. Leclerc. And done into English by J. F. P. Gent*, London *1706*. (The original was written in 1705.)
9. LORD KING. *The Life of John Locke, with Extracts from his Correspondence, Journals, and Common Place Books*, 1829, new and fuller edition, 1830. 2 vols. (All references in this book to second edition.)

IV. GENERAL

1. ALEXANDER, S. *Locke*. In 'Philosophies Ancient and Modern', London, 1908.
2. BROAD, C. D. 'John Locke.' *Hibbert Journal*, xxxi (1932–3).
3. COLLIE, ROSALIE. 'The essayist in his *Essay*', *John Locke, Problems and Perspectives*, ed. J. W. Yolton, Cambridge, 1969.
4. COUSIN, V. *La Philosophie de Locke*. 1819.
5. FECHTNER, E. *John Locke, ein Bild aus den geistigen Kämpfen Englands im 17. Jahrhundert*. Stuttgart, 1898.
6. FOWLER, T. *Locke*. In 'English Men of Letters', London, 1880.
7. FRASER, A. C. *Locke*. In 'Philosophical Classics', Blackwood, Edinburgh, 1890.
   Cf. also his edition of the *Essay*, Oxford, 1894.
8. GIBSON, J. *John Locke*. Brit. Acad. Henriette Hertz Lecture. 1933.
9. JAMES, D. G. *The Life of Reason. Hobbes, Locke and Bolingbroke*. London, 1949.
10. MACLEAN, K. *John Locke and English Literature of the Eighteenth Century*. Yale University Press, 1936.
11. MARTIN, C. B. and ARMSTRONG, D. M., editors, *Locke and Berkeley*, a collection of papers, Macmillan, 1968.
12. MORRIS, C. R. *Locke, Berkeley, Hume*. Oxford, 1931.
13. O'CONNOR, D. J. *John Locke*. Pelican, London, 1952.
14. OLLION, H. L. *La Philosophie générale de John Locke*. Paris, 1908.
15. ROMANELL, PATRICK. 'Locke and Sydenham.' *Bulletin History of Medicine*, July 1958.
16. SMITH, N. K. *John Locke*. Tercentenary Address. Manchester University Press, 1933.
17. SORLEY, W. R. '*John Locke*.' *Cambridge History of English Literature*, vol. viii, 1912, pp. 328–48. (A bibliography is added, pp. 471–6.)

18. TAGART, E. *Locke's Writings and Philosophy historically considered and vindicated from the Charge of contributing to the Scepticism of Hume.* London, 1855.
19. VIANO, CARLO AUGUSTO. *John Locke: Dal Razionalismo all' Illuminismo.* Einaudi, 1960.
20. WEBB, T. E. *The Intellectualism of Locke: An Essay.* 1857.
21. YOLTON, J. W. 'Locke's Unpublished Marginal Replies to John Sergeant.' *Journal of the History of Ideas,* October 1951.
22. —— *John Locke and the Way of Ideas.* London, 1956.

V. INFLUENCES UPON LOCKE

1. BERNIER, F. *Abrégé de la philosophie de Gassendi.* Lyon, 1678 and 1684.
2. ERDMANN, B. 'Locke und Descartes.' *Archiv f. d. Gesch. Phil.,* Bd. III, Heft 4, pp. 579 ff., 1890.
3. GEIL, G. *Über die Abhängigkeit Locke's von Descartes. Eine philosophiegeschichtliche Studie.* Strassburg, 1887.
4. HERTLING, G. VON. *John Locke und die Schule von Cambridge.* Freiburg, 1892.
5. KRAKOWSKI, É. *Les Sources médiévales de la philosophie de Locke.* Paris, 1915.
6. SCHRÖDER, W. *John Locke und die mechanische Naturauffassung. Eine kritisch-philosophische Untersuchung.* Erlangen, 1915.
7. SOMMER, R. *Locke's Verhältnis zu Descartes.* Berlin, 1887.
8. TELLKAMP, A. *Das Verhältnis John Locke's zur Scholastik.* Münster i. W., 1927.
9. WARE, C. S. 'The Influence of Descartes on John Locke.' *Rev. Int. de Phil.* (April 1950).

VI. THEORY OF KNOWLEDGE, LOGIC AND METAPHYSICS

1. AARON, R. I. (i) 'Locke's Theory of Universals.' *Proc. Arist. Soc.,* N.S. xxxiii (1932–3).
   (ii) *The Theory of Universals,* O.U.P., 1952, ch. 2, 'The Character of Locke's Conceptualism'.
2. ANDERSON, F. H. *The Influence of Contemporary Science on Locke's Method and Results.* University of Toronto Studies in Philosophy, vol. ii, 1923.
3. ARMSTRONG, R. L. 'John Locke's Doctrine of Signs'. *Journal Hist. Ideas,* July 1965.
4. BAEUMKER, C. (i) 'Locke's primäre und secundäre Qualitäten.' *Phil. Jahrbuch,* Bd. 21, 1898.
   (ii) 'Zur Vorgeschichte zweier Lockescher Begriffe.' *Arch. Gesch. Phil.,* Bd. 21, Leipzig, 1907–8, with additional note in Bd. 22.

5. EWING, A. C. 'Some Points in the Philosophy of Locke.' *Philosophy*, xii. 45.
6. FREYTAG, W. *Die Substanzen-Lehre Lockes*. Bonn, 1898. (Republished with second part. 1899.)
7. GIBSON, J. *Locke's Theory of Knowledge*. Cambridge, 1917.
8. HARTENSTEIN, G. 'Locke's Lehre von der menschlichen Erkenntnis in Vergleichung mit Leibniz's Kritik derselben.' *Abh. Phil. Hist. könig. sächs. Ges. der Wiss.*, Bd. 4, Leipzig, 1865.
9. HOFSTADTER, A. *Locke and Scepticism*. New York, 1935.
10. JACKSON, R. 'Locke's Distinction between Primary and Secondary Qualities', *Mind*, xxxviii, N.S. 149; and 'Locke's Version of the Doctrine of Representative Perception', *Mind*, xxxix, N.S. 153.
11. KLEMMT, ALFRED. *John Locke: Theoretische Philosophie*. Westkulturverlag Anton Hain. Meisenheim/Glan, 1952.
12. LEIBNIZ, G. W. VON. *Nouveaux Essais sur l'Entendement humain*. First published, 1765.
13. LEYDEN, W. VON. *Seventeenth Century Metaphysics, An Examination of Some Main Concepts and Theories*, Duckworth, 1968.
14. —— 'What is a nominal essence the essence of?' in *John Locke, Problems and Perspectives*, ed. J. W. Yolton, Cambridge, 1969.
15. LINNELL, J. S. 'Locke's Abstract Ideas.' *Phil. and Phen. Research*, March 1956.
16. LODGE, R. C. *The Meaning and Function of Simple Modes in the Philosophy of John Locke*. Minneapolis, 1918.
17. MANDELBAUM, M. 'Locke's Realism', *Philosophy, Science and Sense Perception*, Baltimore, 1964.
18. MARTINAK, E. *Zur Logik Lockes. John Lockes Lehre von den Vorstellungen, aus dem* Essay concerning Human Understanding *zusammengestellt und untersucht*. Graz, 1887. (Republished with a second part in 1894.)
19. REESE, W. L. 'The Experimentum Crucis in Locke's Doctrine of Abstraction.' *Phil. and Phen. Research*, June 1961.
20. ROSE, F. O. 'Die Lehre von den eingeborenen Ideen bei Descartes und Locke.' *Berner Studien zur Phil. u. ihre Gesch.* Bd. 31, 1901.
21. RYLE, G. *Locke on the Human Understanding*. Tercentenary Addresses. Oxford, 1933.
22. YOLTON, JOHN W. 'The science of nature', *John Locke, Problems and Perspectives*, ed. J. W. Yolton, Cambridge, 1969.

VII. MORAL AND POLITICAL PHILOSOPHY

1. AARSLEFF, H. 'The state of nature and the nature of man in Locke', *John Locke, Problems and Perspectives*, ed. J. W. Yolton, Cambridge, 1969.

2. BASTIDE, CH. *John Locke, ses théories politiques et leur influence en Angleterre. Les Libertés politiques. L'Église et l'état. La Tolérance.* Paris, 1906.

3. BERLIN, ISAIAH. 'Hobbes, Locke and Professor Macpherson', *Political Quarterly*, 1964.

4. BROGAN, A. P. 'John Locke and Utilitarianism.' *Ethics*, 1959.

5. COX, R. H. *Locke on War and Peace.* Oxford, 1960.

6. CURTIS, M. M. *An Outline of Locke's Ethical Philosophy.* Leipzig, 1890.

7. DAY, J. P. 'Locke on Property', *Phil. Quarterly*, 1966.

8. DE BEER, ESMOND S. 'Locke and English liberalism, the *Second Treatise of Government* in its contemporary setting', *John Locke, Problems and Perspectives*, ed. J. W. Yolton, Cambridge, 1969.

9. DUNN, JOHN. *The Political Thought of John Locke*, Cambridge, 1969.

10. FIGGIS, J. N. *The Divine Right of Kings.* 1914.

11. FILMER, R. *Patriarcha and other Political Works of Sir Robert Filmer*, ed. Peter Laslett, Oxford, 1949.

12. GIERKE, O. *Natural Law and the Theory of Society, 1500–1800.* Tr. by Ernest Barker, 2 vols., Cambridge, 1934.

13. GOUGH, J. W. *John Locke's Political Philosophy.* Oxford, 1950.

14. HUDSON, J. W. *The Treatment of Personality by Locke, Berkeley and Hume. A Study in the Interests of Ethical Theory, of an Aspect of the Dialectical of English Empiricism.* Missouri, Columbia, 1911.

15. KENDALL, WILLMORE. 'John Locke and the Doctrine of Majority Rule.' *Illinois Studies in the Social Sciences*, xxvi. 2.

16. LAMPRECHT, S. *The Moral and Political Philosophy of John Locke.* New York, 1918.

17. LARKIN, P. *Property in the Eighteenth Century, with special reference to England and Locke.* Cork, 1930.

18. LASKI, H. J. *The Rise of European Liberalism.* 1936.

19. LASLETT, PETER. *John Locke's Two Treatises of Government*, Cambridge, 1960.

20. MACLEAN, A. H. 'George Lawson and John Locke.' *Camb. Hist. Journal*, 1947, i. 69–77.

21. MACPHERSON, C. B. (i) 'Locke on Capitalist Appropriation.' *Western Political Quarterly*, Dec. 1951.
    (ii) 'The Social Bearing of Locke's Political Theory.' *Western Political Quarterly*, March 1954.
    (iii) *The Political Theory of Possessive Individualism: Hobbes to Locke.* Oxford, 1962.

22. MARTIN, KINGSLEY. *French Liberal Thought in the Eighteenth Century.* 1929.

23. MESSER, A. 'Die Behandlung des Freiheitsproblems bei Locke.' *Archiv f. Gesch. der Phil.*, Bd. xi, 1897.

24. MONSON, C. H. 'Locke and his Interpreters'. *Pol. Studies*, 1958.

25. PARRY, GERAINT. 'Individualism, Politics and the Critique of Paternalism in Locke', *Pol. Studies*, 1964.

26. PLAMENATZ, JOHN. *Man and Society*, 2 vols., Longmans, 1963.

27. POLIN, R. 'John Locke's conception of freedom', *John Locke, Problems and Perspectives*, ed. J. W. Yolton, Cambridge, 1969.

28. POLIN, RAYMOND. *La Politique morale de John Locke*. Presses Universitaires, Paris, 1960.

29. POLLOCK, F. *Locke's Theory of the State*. Proc. Brit. Acad. 1930–4. (Republished in *Essays in Law*, 1922.)

30. RYAN, ALAN. 'Locke and the Dictatorship of the Bourgeoisie', *Pol. Studies*, 1965.

31. SCHOCHET, GORDON J. 'The family and the origins of the state in Locke's political philosophy', *John Locke, Problems and Perspectives*, ed. J. W. Yolton, Cambridge, 1969.

32. SELIGER, M. (i) *The Liberal Politics of John Locke*, Allen and Unwin, 1968.
    (ii) 'Locke, liberalism and nationalism', *John Locke, Problems and Perspectives*, ed. J. W. Yolton, Cambridge, 1969.

33. STOCKS, J. L. *Locke's Contribution to Political Theory*. Tercentenary Addresses. Oxford, 1933.

34. STRAUSS, LEO. *Natural Right and History*, Chicago, 1953.

35. TAWNEY, R. H. *Religion and the Rise of Capitalism*. 1927.

36. VAUGHAN, C. E. *Studies in the History of Political Philosophy*, vol. i. Manchester, 1925.

(For books on Locke's economic theories, compare note to p. 38 above.)

VIII. RELIGION, TOLERATION, AND EDUCATION

1. ADAMSON, J. W. *The Educational Writings of John Locke*. 1912.

2. ASHCRAFT, R. 'Faith and Knowledge in Locke's philosophy', *John Locke, Problems and Perspectives*, ed. J. W. Yolton, Cambridge, 1969.

3. AXTELL, J. L. *The Educational Writings of John Locke*, Cambridge, 1968.

4. CRAGG, G. R. *From Puritanism to the Age of Reason*, Cambridge, 1950.

5. CROUS, ERNST. *Die Grundlagen der religionsphilosophischen Lehren Lockes*. Halle, 1909. (Republished with additional material in *Abh. z. Phil. u. ihre Geschichte*, Halle, 1910.)

6. HEFELBOWER, S. G. *The Relation of John Locke to English Deism*. Chicago, 1918.

7. JEFFREYS, M. V. C. *John Locke: Prophet of Common Sense*, Methuen, 1967.

8. JORDAN, W. K. *The Development of Religious Toleration in England from the beginning of the Reformation to the Death of Queen Elizabeth*. London, 1932.

9. KLIBANSKY, R. and GOUGH, J. W. *Locke's Epistola de Tolerantia*, Oxford, 1968.

10. McLACHLAN, H. *The Religious Opinions of Milton, Locke and Newton*. Manchester, 1941.

11. RAMSEY, I. T. Introduction to an edition of Locke's *Reasonableness of Christianity*, Black, London, 1958.

12. RUSSELL SMITH, H. F. *Theory of Religious Liberty in the Reigns of Charles II and James II*. 1911.

13. SEATON, A. A. *Theory of Toleration under the later Stuarts*. Cambridge, 1911.

(On education cf. also note to p. 292 above.)

INDEX

I. SUBJECTS

II. PROPER NAMES